Moriz Heyne, And others

Beówulf - An Anglo-Saxon poem - II The fight at Finnsburh - A

Fragment.

With Text and Glossary on the Basis of M. Heyne

Moriz Heyne, And others

Beówulf - An Anglo-Saxon poem - II The fight at Finnsburh - A Fragment.
With Text and Glossary on the Basis of M. Heyne

ISBN/EAN: 9783337079048

Printed in Europe, USA, Canada, Australia, Japan

Cover: Foto ©Andreas Hilbeck / pixelio.de

More available books at **www.hansebooks.com**

I. BEÓWULF:

AN ANGLO-SAXON POEM.

II. THE FIGHT AT FINNSBURH:

A FRAGMENT.

WITH TEXT AND GLOSSARY ON THE BASIS OF M. HEYNE.

EDITED, CORRECTED, AND ENLARGED, BY

JAMES A. HARRISON,

PROFESSOR OF ENGLISH AND MODERN LANGUAGES, WASHINGTON AND
LEE UNIVERSITY,

AND

ROBERT SHARP (Ph.D. Lips.),

PROFESSOR OF GREEK AND ENGLISH, UNIVERSITY
OF LOUISIANA.

BOSTON:
PUBLISHED BY GINN & COMPANY.
1885.

J. S. CUSHING & CO., PRINTERS, 115 HIGH STREET, BOSTON.

NOTE I.

———◦◦◦———

THE present work, carefully edited from Heyne's fourth edition, (Paderborn, 1879), is designed primarily for college classes in Anglo-Saxon, rather than for independent investigators or for seekers after a restored or ideal text. The need of an American edition of "Beówulf" has long been felt, as, hitherto, students have had either to send to Germany for a text, or secure, with great trouble, one of the scarce and expensive English editions. Heyne's first edition came out in 1863, and was followed in 1867 and 1873 by a second and a third edition, all three having essentially the same text.

So many important contributions to the "Beówulf" literature were, however, made between 1873 and 1879 that Heyne found it necessary to put forth a new edition (1879). In this new, last edition, the text was subjected to a careful revision, and was fortified by the views, contributions, and criticisms of other zealous scholars. In it the collation of the unique "Beówulf" Ms. (Vitellius A. 15 : Cottonian Mss. of the British Museum), as made by E. Kölbing in Herrig's *Archiv* (Bd. 56; 1876), was followed wherever the present condition of the Ms. had to be discussed; and the researches of Bugge, Rieger, and others, on single passages, were made use of. The discussion of the metrical structure of the poem, as occurring in the second and third editions, was omitted in the fourth, owing to the many controversies in which the subject is still involved. The present editor has thought it best to do the same, though, happily, the subject of Old English *Metrik* is undergoing a steady illumination through the labors of Schipper and others.

Some errors and misplaced accents in Heyne's text have been corrected in the present edition, in which, as in the general revision of the text, the editor has been most kindly aided by Prof. J. M. Garnett, late Principal of St. John's College, Maryland.

In the preparation of the present school edition it has been thought best to omit Heyne's notes, as they concern themselves principally with conjectural emendations, substitutions of one reading for another, and discussions of the condition of the Ms. Until Wülcker's text and the photographic fac-simile of the original Ms. are in the hands of all scholars, it will be better not to introduce such matters in the school room, where they would puzzle without instructing.

For convenience of reference, the editor has added a head-line to each "fit" of the poem, with a view to facilitate a knowledge of its episodes.

WASHINGTON AND LEE UNIVERSITY,
LEXINGTON, VA., June, 1882.

NOTE II.

———•◦•———

THE editors now have the pleasure of presenting to the public a complete text and a tolerably complete glossary of "Beówulf." The edition is the first published in America, and the first of its special kind presented to the English public, and it is the initial volume of a "Library of Anglo-Saxon Poetry," to be edited under the same auspices and with the coöperation of distinguished scholars in this country. Among these scholars may be mentioned Professors F. A. March of Lafayette College, T. R. Price of Columbia College, and W. M. Baskervill of Vanderbilt University.

In the preparation of the Glossary the editors found it necessary to abandon a literal and exact translation of Heyne for several reasons, and among others from the fact that Heyne seems to be wrong in the translation of some of his illustrative quotations, and even translates the same passage in two or three different ways under different headings. The orthography of his glossary differs considerably from the orthography of his text. He fails to discriminate with due nicety the meanings of many of the words in his vocabulary, while criticism more recent than his latest edition (1879) has illustrated or overthrown several of his renderings. The references were found to be incorrect in innumerable instances, and had to be verified in every individual case so far as this was possible, a few only, which resisted all efforts at verification, having to be indicated by an interrogation point (?). The references are exceedingly numerous, and the labor of verifying them was naturally great. To many passages in the Glossary, where Heyne's translation could not be trusted with entire certainty, the editors have added other translations of phrases and sentences or of special words; and in this they have been aided by a careful study of the text and a comparison and utilization of the views of Kemble and Professor J. M. Garnett (who takes Grein for his foundation). Many new references have been added;

and the various passages in which Heyne fails to indicate whether a given verb is weak or strong, or fails to point out the number, etc., of the illustrative form, have been corrected and made to harmonize with the general plan of the work. Numerous misprints in the glossary have also been corrected, and a brief glossary to the Finnsburh-fragment, prepared by Dr. Wm. Hand Browne, and supplemented and adapted by the editor-in-chief, has been added.

The editors think that they may without immodesty put forth for themselves something more than the claim of being re-translators of a translation : the present edition is, so far as they were able to make it so, an adaptation, correction, and extension of the work of the great German scholar to whose loving appreciation of the Anglo-Saxon epic all students of Old English owe a debt of gratitude. While following his usually sure and cautious guidance, and in the main appropriating his results, they have thought it best to deviate from him in the manner above indicated, whenever it seemed that he was wrong. The careful reader will notice at once the marks of interrogation which point out these deviations, or which introduce a point of view illustrative of, or supplementary to, the one given by the German editor. No doubt the editors are wrong themselves in many places, — " Beówulf " is a most difficult poem, — but their view may at least be defended by a reference to the original text, which they have faithfully and constantly consulted.

A good many cognate Modern English words have been introduced here and there in the Glossary with a view to illustration, and other addenda will be found between brackets and parenthetical marks.

It is hoped that the present edition of the most famous of Old English poems will do something to promote a valuable and interesting study.

JAMES A. HARRISON,
Washington and Lee University, Lexington, Va.

ROBERT SHARP,
University of Louisiana, New Orleans.

April, 1883.

The responsibility of the editors is as follows : H. is responsible for the Text, and for the Glossary from **hrinan** on ; S. for the List of Names, and for the Glossary as far as **hrinan.**

DEDICATED

TO

PROFESSOR F. A. MARCH,

OF LAFAYETTE COLLEGE, PA.,

AND

FREDERICK J. FURNIVALL, Esq.

FOUNDER OF THE "NEW SHAKSPERE SOCIETY,"
THE "CHAUCER SOCIETY," ETC., ETC.

NOTE TO THE SECOND REVISED EDITION.

THE editors feel so encouraged at the kind reception accorded their edition of Beówulf (1883), that, in spite of its many short-comings, they have determined to prepare a second revised edition of the book, and thus endeavor to extend its sphere of usefulness. About twenty errors had, notwithstanding a vigilant proof-reading, crept into the text, — errors in single letters, accents, and punctuation. These have been corrected, and it is hoped that the text has been rendered generally accurate and trustworthy. In the List of Words one or two corrections have been made, and in the Glossary numerous mistakes in gender, classification, and translation, apparently unavoidable in a first edition, have been rectified. Wherever these mistakes concern *single* letters, or occupy very small space, they have been corrected in the plates; where they are longer, and the expense of correcting them in the plates would have been very great, the editors have thought it best to include them in an Appendix of Corrections and Additions, which will be found at the back of the book. Students are accordingly referred to this Appendix for important longer corrections and additions. It is believed that the value of the book has been much enhanced by an Appendix of Recent Readings, based on late criticisms and essays from the pens of Sievers, Kluge, Cosijn, Holder, Wülker, and Sweet. A perplexed student, in turning to these suggested readings, will often find great help in unravelling obscure or corrupt passages.

The objectionable ä and æ, for the short and the long diphthong, have been retained in the revised edition, owing to the impossibility of removing them without entirely recasting the plates.

In conclusion, the editors would acknowledge their great indebtedness to the friends and critics whose remarks and criticisms have materially aided in the correction of the text, — particularly to Profs. C. P. G. Scott, Baskervill, Price, and J. M. Hart; to Prof. J. W. Bright, and to the authorities of Cornell University, for the loan of periodicals necessary to the completeness of the revision. While the second revised edition still contains much that might be improved, the editors cannot but hope that it is an advance on its predecessor, and that it will continue its work of extending the study of Old English throughout the land.

JUNE, 1885.

ARGUMENT.

—◆—

THE only national [Anglo-Saxon] epic which has been preserved entire is Beówulf. Its argument is briefly as follows:—The poem opens with a few verses in praise of the Danish Kings, especially Scild, the son of Sceaf. His death is related, and his descendants briefly traced down to Hroðgar. Hroðgar, elated with his prosperity and success in war, builds a magnificent hall, which he calls Heorot. In this hall Hroðgar and his retainers live in joy and festivity, until a malignant fiend, called Grendel, jealous of their happiness, carries off by night thirty of Hroðgar's men, and devours them in his moorland retreat. These ravages go on for twelve years. Beówulf, a thane of Hygelac, King of the Goths, hearing of Hroðgar's calamities, sails from Sweden with fourteen warriors to help him. They reach the Danish coast in safety; and, after an animated parley with Hroðgar's coast-guard, who at first takes them for pirates, they are allowed to proceed to the royal hall, where they are well received by Hroðgar. A banquet ensues, during which Beówulf is taunted by the envious Hunferhð about his swimming-match with Breca, King of the Brondings. Beówulf gives the true account of the contest, and silences Hunferhð. At night-fall the King departs, leaving Beówulf in charge of the hall. Grendel soon breaks in, seizes and devours one of Beówulf's companions; is attacked by Beówulf, and, after losing an arm, which is torn off by Beówulf, escapes to the fens. The joy of Hroðgar and the Danes, and their festivities, are described, various episodes are introduced, and Beówulf and his companions receive splendid gifts. The next night Grendel's mother revenges her son by carrying off Æschere, the friend and councillor of Hroðgar, during the absence of Beówulf. Hroðgar appeals to Beówulf for vengeance, and describes the haunts of Grendel and his mother. They all proceed thither; the scenery of the lake, and the monsters that dwell in it, are described. Beówulf plunges into the water, and attacks Grendel's mother in her dwelling at the bottom of the lake. He at length overcomes her, and cuts off her head, together with that of Grendel, and brings the heads to Hroðgar. He then takes leave of Hroðgar, sails back to Sweden, and relates his adventures to Hygelac.

Here the first half of the poem ends. The second begins with the accession of Beówulf to the throne, after the fall of Hygelac and his son Heardred. He rules prosperously for fifty years, till a dragon, brooding over a hidden treasure, begins to ravage the country, and destroys Beówulf's palace with fire. Beówulf sets out in quest of its hiding-place, with twelve men. Having a presentiment of his approaching end, he pauses and recals to mind his past life and exploits. He then takes leave of his followers, one by one, and advances alone to attack the dragon. Unable, from the heat, to enter the cavern, he shouts aloud, and the dragon comes forth. The dragon's scaly hide is proof against Beówulf's sword, and he is reduced to great straits. Then Wiglaf, one of his followers, advances to help him. Wiglaf's shield is consumed by the dragon's fiery breath, and he is compelled to seek shelter under Beówulf's shield of iron. Beówulf's sword snaps asunder, and he is seized by the dragon. Wiglaf stabs the dragon from underneath, and Beówulf cuts it in two with his dagger. Feeling that his end is near, he bids Wiglaf bring out the treasures from the cavern, that he may see them before he dies. Wiglaf enters the dragon's den, which is described, returns to Beówulf, and receives his last commands. Beówulf dies, and Wiglaf bitterly reproaches his companions for their cowardice. The disastrous consequences of Beówulf's death are then foretold, and the poem ends with his funeral. — H. Sweet, in Warton's *History of English Poetry*, Vol. II. (ed. 1871). Cf. also Ten Brink's *History of English Literature*.

BEÓWULF.

I. The Passing of Scyld.

HWÄT! we Gâr-Dena   in geâr-dagum
    þeód-cyninga   þrym gefrunon,
hû þâ äðelingas   ellen fremedon.
Oft Scyld Scêfing   sceaðena þreátum,
5 monegum maegðum   meodo-setla ofteáh.
Egsode eorl,   syððan ärest wearð
feá-sceaft funden :   he þäs frôfre gebâd,
weôx under wolcnum,   weorð-myndum ðâh,
ôð þät him äghwylc   þâra ymb-sittendra
10 ofer hron-râde   hŷran scolde,
gomban gyldan :   þät wäs gôd cyning!
þäm eafera wäs   äfter cenned
geong in geardum,   þone god sende
folce tô frôfre ;   fyren-þearfe ongeat,
15 þät hie är drugon   aldor-_leáse_
lange hwîle.   Him þäs lîf-freá,
wuldres wealdend,   worold-âre forgeaf ;
Beówulf wäs breme   (blæd wîde sprang),
Scyldes eafera   Scede-landum in.
20 Swâ sceal _geong guma_   gôde gewyrcean,
fromum feoh-giftum   on fäder _wine_,
þät hine on ylde   eft gewunigen
wil-gesîðas,   þonne wîg cume,
leóde gelæsten :   lof-dædum sceal
25 in mægða gehwære   man geþeón.
Him þâ Scyld gewât   tô gescäp-hwîle
fela-hrôr fêran   on freán wa·re ;
hi hyne þâ ätbæron   tô brimes faroðe,

swǽse gesíðas,　　　swá he selfa bäd,
30 þenden wordum weóld　　wine Scyldinga,
leóf land-fruma　　lange áhte.
Þær ät hýðe stôd　　hringed-stefna,
ísig and útfús,　　äðelinges fär;
á-lédon þá　　leófne þeóden,
35 beága bryttan　　on bearm scipes,
mærne be mäste.　　Þær wäs mádma fela,
of feor-wegum　　frätwa gelæded:
ne hýrde ic cymlícor　　ceól gegyrwan
hilde-wæpnum　　and heaðo-wædum,
40 billum and byrnum;　　him on bearme läg
mádma mänigo,　　þá him mid scoldon
on flôdes æht　　feor gewîtan.
Nalas hi hine lässan　　lácum teódan,
þeód-gestreónum,　　þonne þá dydon,
45 þe hine ät frumsceafte　　forð onsendon
ænne ofer ýðe　　umbor wesende:
þá gyt hie him ásetton　　segen gyldenne
heáh ofer heáfod,　　léton holm beran,
geáfon on gár-secg:　　him wäs geômor sefa,
50 murnende môd.　　Men ne cunnon
secgan tô sôðe　　sêle rædenne,
häleð under heofenum,　　hwá þäm hläste onfêng.

II. THE HALL HEOROT.

Þá wäs on burgum　　Beówulf Scyldinga,
leóf leód-cyning,　　longe þrage
55 folcum gefræge　　(fäder ellor hwearf,
aldor of earde),　　ôð þät him eft onwôc
heáh Healfdene;　　heóld þenden lifde,
gamol and gúð-reów,　　gläde Scyldingas.
Þäm feówer bearn　　forð-gerîmed

60 in worold wôcun, weoroda ræswan,
Heorogâr and Hrôðgâr and Hâlga til;
hŷrde ic, þät Elan cwên *Ongenþeówes wäs*
Heaðoscilfinges heals-gebedde.
þâ wäs Hrôðgâre here-spêd gyfen,
65 wiges weorð-mynd, þät him his wine-mâgas
georne hŷrdon, ôð þät seó geogoð geweôx,
mago-driht micel. Him on môd bearn,
þät heal-reced hâtan wolde,
medo-ärn micel men gewyrcean,
70 þone yldo bearn æfre gefrunon,
and þær on innan eall gedælan
geongum and caldum, swylc him god sealde,
bûton folc-scare and feorum gumena.
þâ ic wîde gefrägn weorc gebannan
75 manigre mægðe geond þisne middan-geard,
folc-stede frätwan. Him on fyrste gelomp
ädre mid yldum, þät hit wearð eal gearo,
heal-ärna mæst; scôp him Heort naman,
se þe his wordes geweald wîde häfde.
80 He beót ne âlêh, beágas dælde,
sinc ät symle. Sele hlifade
heáh and horn-geáp: heaðo-wylma bâd,
lâðan lîges; ne wäs hit lenge þâ gen
þät se ecg-hete âðum-swerian
85 äfter wäl-nîðe wäcnan scolde.
þâ se ellen-gæst earfoðlîce
þrage geþolode, se þe in þŷstrum bâd,
þät he dôgora gehwam dreám gehŷrde
hlûdne in healle; þær wäs hearpan swêg,
90 swutol sang scôpes. Sägde se þe cûðe
frum-sceaft fira feorran reccan,
cwäð þät se älmihtiga eorðan worhte,
wlite-beorhtne wang, swâ wäter bebûgeð,
gesette sige-hrêðig sunnan and mônan

95 leóman tô leóhte   land-bûendum,
   and gefrätwade   foldan sceátas
   leomum and leáfum ;   lîf eác gesceôp
   cynna gehwylcum,   þâra þe cwice hwyrfaþ.
   Swâ þâ driht-guman   dreámum lifdon
100 eádiglîce,   ôþ þät ân ongan
   fyrene fremman,   feónd on helle :
   wäs se grimma gäst   Grendel hâten,
   mære mearc-stapa,   se þe môras heóld,
   fen and fästen ;   fîfel-cynnes eard
105 won-sælig wer   weardode hwîle,
   siþþan him scyppend   forscrifen häfde.
   In Caines cynne   þone cwealm gewräc,
   êce drihten,   þäs þe he Abel slóg ;
   ne gefeah he þære fæhðe,   ac he hine feor forwräc,
110 metod for þŷ mâne   man-cynne fram.
   Þanon untydras   ealle onwôcon,
   eotenas and ylfe   and orcnêas,
   swylce gigantas,   þâ wið gode wunnon
   lange þrage ;   he him þäs leán forgeald.

III. GRENDEL'S VISITS.

115 GEWÂT þâ neósian,   syþþan niht becom,
   heán hûses,   hû hit Hring-Dene
   äfter beór-þege   gebûn häfdon.
   Fand þâ þær inne   äðelinga gedriht
   swefan äfter symble ;   sorge ne cûðon,
120 won-sceaft wera.   Wiht unhælo
   grim and grædig   gearo sôna wäs,
   reóc and rêðe,   and on räste genam
   þritig þegna :   þanon eft gewât
   hûðe hrêmig   tô hâm faran,
125 mid þære wäl-fylle   wîca neósan.

Þá wäs on uhtan   mid ær-däge
Grendles gûð-cräft   gumum undyrne:
þá wäs äfter wiste   wôp up áhafen,
micel morgen-swêg.   Mære þeóden,

130 äðeling ær-gôd,   unblíðe sät,
þolode þryð-swyð,   þegn-sorge dreáh,
syððan hie þäs láðan   lást sceáwedon,
wergan gástes;   wäs þät gewin tô strang,
láð and longsum.   Näs hit lengra fyrst,

135 ac ymb áne niht   eft gefremede
morð-beala máre   and nô mearn fore
fæhðe and fyrene;   wäs tô fäst on þám.
Þá wäs eáð-fynde,   þe him elles hwær
gerúmlícor   räste sôhte,

140 bed äfter búrum,   þá him gebeácnod wäs,
gesägd sôðlíce   sweotolan tácne
heal-þegnes hete;   heóld hine syððan
fyr and fästor,   se þám feónde ätwand.
Swá ríxode   and wið rihte wan

145 ána wið eallum.   Oð þät ídel stôd
húsa sélest.   Wäs seó hwíl micel:
twelf wintra tíd   torn geþolode
wine Scyldinga,   weána gehwelcne,
sídra sorga;   forþam syððan wearð

150 ylda bearnum   undyrne cúð,
gyddum geômore,   þätte Grendel wan
hwíle wið Hróðgár;—   hete-níðas wäg,
fyrene and fæhðe   fela missera,
singale säce,   sibbe ne wolde

155 wið manna hwone   mägenes Deniga
feorh-bealo feorran,   feó þingian,
ne þær nænig witena   wênan þorfte
beorhtre bôte   tô banan folmum;
atol äglæca   êhtende wäs.

160 deore deáð-scûa   duguðe and geogoðe

seomade and syrede.   Sin-nihte heóld
mistige móras;   men ne cunnon,
hwyder hel-rúnan   hwyrftum scríðað.
Swâ fela fyrena   feónd man-cynnes,
165 atol ân-gengea,   oft gefremede
heardra hýnða;   Heorot eardode,
sinc-fâge sel   sweartum nihtum
(nô he þone gif-stôl   grêtan môste,
mâððum for metode,   ne his myne wisse);
170 þät wäs wræc micel   wine Scyldinga,
môdes brecða.   Monig-oft gesät
rîce tô rûne;   ræd eahtedon,
hwät swîð-ferhðum   sêlest wære
wið fær-gryrum   tô gefremmanne.
175 Hwîlum hie gehêton   ät härg-trafum
wig-weorðunga,   wordum bædon,
þät him gâst-bona   geóce gefremede
wið þeód-þreáum.   Swyle wäs þeáw hyra,
hæðenra hyht;   helle gemundon
180 in môd-sefan,   metod hie ne cûðon,
dæda dêmend,   ne wiston hie drihten god,
ne 'hie hûru heofena helm   hêrian ne cûðon,
wuldres waldend.   Wâ bið þäm þe sceal
þurh slîðne nîð   sâwle bescûfan
185 in fýres fäðm,   frôfre ne wênan,
wihte gewendan;   wel bið þäm þe môt
äfter deáð-däge   drihten sêccan
and tô fäder fäðmum   freoðo wilnian.

IV. HYGELAC'S THANE.

Swâ þâ mæl-ceare   maga Healfdenes
190 singala seáð;   ne mihte snotor häleð
weán onwendan: wäs þät gewin tô swýð,
lâð and longsum,   þe on þâ leóde becom,

nýd-wracu níð-grim,   niht-bealwa mæst.
Þät fram hám gefrägn   Higeláces þegn,
195 gód mid Geátum.   Grendles dæda:
se wäs mon-cynnes   mägenes strengest
on þäm däge   þysses lífes.
äðele and eácen.   Hét him ýð-lidan
gódne gegyrwan;   cwäð he gúð-cyning
200 ofer swan-ráde   sécean wolde,
mærne þeóden,   þá him wäs manna þearf.
Þone síð-fät him   snotere ceorlas
lyt-hwon lógon,   þeáh he him leóf wære;
hwetton higerófne,   hæl sceáwedon.
205 Häfde se góda   Geáta leóda
cempan gecorone,   þára þe he cénoste
findan mihte;   fíftena sum
sund-wudu sóhte;   secg wísade,
lagu-cräftig mon.   land-gemyrcu.
210 Fyrst forð gewát: flota wäs on ýðum,
bát under beorge.   Beornas gearwe
on stefn stigon;   streámas wundon
sund wið sande;   secgas bæron
on bearm nacan   beorhte frätwe,
215 gúð-searo geatolíc;   guman út scufon,
weras on wil-síð   wudu bundenne.
Gewát þá ofer wæg-holm   winde gefýsed
flota fámig-heals   fugle gelícost,
óð þät ymb án-tíd   óðres dógores
220 wunden-stefna   gewaden häfde,
þät þá líðende   land gesáwon,
brim-clifu blícan.   beorgas steápe,
síde sæ-nässas: þá wäs sund liden,
eoletes ät ende.   Þanon up hraðe
225 Wedera leóde.   on wang stigon,
sæ-wudu säldon   (syrcan hrysedon,
gúð-gewædo);   gode þancedon,

þäs þe him ýð-láde　　eáðe wurdon.

Þá of wealle geseah　　weard Scildinga,

230　se þe holm-clifu　　healdan scolde,

beran ofer bolcan　　beorhte randas,

fyrd-searu fúslícu;　　hine fyrwyt bräc

môd-gehygdum,　　hwät þá men wæron.

Gewât him þá tô waroðe　　wicge rídan

235　þegn Hróðgâres,　　þrymmum cwehte

mägen-wudu mundum,　　meðel-wordum frägn:

"Hwät syndon ge　　searo-häbbendra

"byrnum werede,　　þe þus brontne ceól

"ofer lagu-stræte　　lædan cwômon,

240　"hider ofer holmas　　*helmas bæron?*

"Ic wäs ende-sæta,　　æg-wearde heóld,

"þät on land Dena　　láðra nænig

"mid scip-herge　　sceððan ne meahte.

"Nô her cûðlícor　　cuman ongunnon

245　"lind-häbbende;　　ne ge leáfnes-word

"gûð-fremmendra　　gearwe ne wisson,

"mâga gemêdu.　　Næfre ic mâran geseah

"eorla ofer eorðan,　　þonne is eówer sum,

"secg on searwum;　　nis þät seld-guma

250　"wæpnum geweorðad,　　näfne him his wlite leóge,

"ænlíc an-sýn.　　Nu ic eówer sceal

"frum-cyn witan,　　ær ge fyr heonan

"leáse sceáweras　　on land Dena

"furður fêran.　　Nu ge feor-bûend

255　"mere-líðende　　mínne gehýrað

"ân-fealdne geþôht:　　ôfest is sélest

"tô gecýðanne,　　hwanan eówre cyme syndon."

V. The Errand.

Him se yldesta   andswarode,
werodes wîsa   word-hord onleác:
260 " We synt gum-cynnes   Geáta leóde
" and Higeláces   heorð-geneátas.
" Wäs mîn fäder   folcum gecýðed,
" äðele ord-fruma   Ecgþeów hâten ;
" gebâd wintra worn,   ær he on weg hwurfe,
265 " gamol of geardum ;   hine gearwe geman
" witena wel-hwylc   wîde geond corðan. —
" We þurh holdne hige   hlâford þinne,
" sunu Healfdenes,   sêcean cwômon,
" leód-gebyrgean :   wes þu ûs lârena gôd !
270 " Habbað we tô þäm mæran   micel ærende
" Deniga freán ;   ne sceal þær dyrne sum
" wesan, þäs ic wêne.   Þu wâst, gif hit is,
" swâ we sôðlíce   secgan hýrdon,
" þät mid Scyldingum   sceaða ic nât hwylc,
275 " deógol dæd-bata,   deorcum nihtum
" eáweð þurh egsan   uncûðne nîð,
" hýnðu and hrâ-fyl.   Ic þäs Hrôðgâr mäg
" þurh rûmne sefan   ræd gelæran,
" hû he frôd and gôd   feónd oferswýðeð,
280 " gyf him ed-wendan   æfre scolde
" bealuwa bisigu,   bôt eft cuman,
" and þa cear-wylmas   côlran wurðað :
" oððe â syððan   earfoð-þrage,
" þreá-nýd þolað,   þenden þær wunað
285 " on heáh-stede   hûsa sêlest."
Weard maðelode,   þær on wicge süt,
ombeht unforht :   " Æghwäðres sceal
" scearp scyld-wiga   gescâd witan,
" worda and worca,   se þe wel þenceð.

290 " Ic þät gehȳre,   þät þis is hold weorod
" freán Scyldinga.   Gewítaδ forδ beran
" wæpen and gewædu,   ic eów wîsige:
" swylce ic magu-þegnas   mîne hâte
" wiδ feónda gehwone   flotan cówerne,
295 " niw-tyrwedne   nacan on sande
" ârum healdan,   ôδ þät eft byreδ
" ofer lagu-streámas   leófne mannan
" wudu wunden-hals   tô Weder-mearce.
" Gûδ-fremmendra   swylcum gifeδe biδ,
300 " þät þone hilde-ræs   hâl gedígeδ."
Gewiton him þâ féran   (flota stille bâd,
seomode on sâle   sîd-fäδmed scyp,
on ancre fäst);   eofor-líc sciónon
ofer hleór-beran   gehroden golde
305 fâh and fȳr-heard,   ferh wearde heóld.
Gûδmôde grummon,   guman onetton,
sigon ätsomne,   ôδ þät hy säl timbred
geatolíc and gold-fâh   ongytan mihton;
þät wäs fore-mærost   fold-bûendum
310 receda under roderum,   on þäm se ríca bâd;
lixte se leóma   ofer landa fela.
Him þâ hilde-deór   hof môdigra
torht getæhte,   þät hie him tô mihton
gegnum gangan;   gûδ-beorna sum
315 wicg gewende,   word äfter cwäδ:
" Mæl is me tô féran;   fäder alwalda
" mid âr-stafum   eówic gehealde
" sîδa gesunde!   ic tô sæ wille,
" wiδ wrâδ werod   wearde healdan."

VI. BEÓWULF'S SPEECH.

320 STRÆT wäs stán-fáh,　　 stíg wísode
    gumum ätgädere.　　Gúð-byrne seán
    heard hond-locen.　　hring-íren scír
    song in searwum.　　þá híe tó sele furðum
    in hyra gryre-geatwum　　gangan cwómon.

325 Setton sæ-méðe　　síde scyldas,
    rondas regn-hearde　　wið þäs recedes weal,
    bugon þá tó bence;　　byrnan hringdon,
    gúð-searo gumena;　　gáras stódon,
    sæ-manna searo,　　samod ätgädere,

330 äsc-holt ufan græg:　　wäs se íren-þreát
    wæpnum gewurðad.　　Þá þær wlonc häleð
    oret-mecgas　　äfter äðelum frägn:
    "Hwanon ferigeað ge　　fätte scyldas,
    "græge syrcan　　and grim-helmas,

335 "here-sceafta heáp?—　　Ic com Hróðgáres
    "ár and ombiht.　　Ne seah ic el-þeódige
    "þus manige men　　módiglicran.
    "Wén' ic þät ge for wlenco,　　nalles for wräc-síðum,
    "ac for hige-þrymmum　　Hróðgár sóhton."

340 Him þá ellen-róf　　andswarode,
    wlanc Wedera leód　　word äfter spräc,
    heard under helme:　　"We synt Higeláces
    "beód-geneátas;　　Beówulf is mín nama.
    "Wille ic äsecgan　　suna Healfdenes,

345 "mærum þeódne　　mín ärende,
    "aldre þínum,　　gif he ús geunnan wile,
    "þät we hine swá gódne　　grétan móton."
    Wulfgár maðelode　　(þät wäs Wendla leód,
    wäs his mód-sefa　　manegum gecýðed,

350 wíg and wís-dóm):　　"ic þäs wine Deniga,
    "freán Scildinga　　frínan wille,

"beága bryttan, swâ þu béna eart,
"þeóden maerne ymb þinne sîð;
"and þe þâ andsware ädre gecyðan,
355 "þe me se góda âgifan þenceð."
Hwearf þâ hrädlîce, þær Hróðgâr sät,
eald and unhâr mid his eorla gedriht;
eode ellen-rôf, þät he for eaxlum gestôd
Deniga freán, cûðe he dugnðe þeáw.
360 Wulfgâr maðelode tô his wine-drihtne:
"Her syndon geferede feorran cumene
"ofer geofenes begang Geáta leóde:
"þone yldestan oret-meegas
"Beówulf nemnað. Hy bénan synt,
365 "þät hie, þeóden mîn, wið þe môton
"wordum wrixlan; nô þu him wearne getcóh,
"þînra gegn-cwida glädnian, Hróðgâr!
"Hy on wîg-geatwum wyrðe þinceað
"eorla geæhtlan; hûru se aldor deáh,
370 "se þæm heaðo-rincum hider wîsade."

VII. HROTHGAR'S WELCOME.

HRÓÐGÂR maðelode, helm Scyldinga:
"Ic hine cûðe cniht-wesende.
"Wäs his eald-fäder Ecgþeó hâten,
"þäm tô hâm forgeaf Hrêðel Geáta
375 "ângan dôhtor; is his eafora nu
"heard her cumen, sôhte holdne wine.
"Þonne sägdon þät sæ-lîðende,
"þâ þe gif-sceattas Geáta fyredon
"þyder tô þance, þät he þrittiges
380 "manna mägen-cräft on his mund-gripe
"heaðo-rôf häbbe. Hine hâlig god
"for âr-stafum ûs onsende,

"tô West-Denum,   þäs ic wên häbbe,
"wið Grendles gryre: ic þäm gôdan sceal
385 "for his môd-þräce   mâdmas beôdan.
"Beó þu on ôfeste,   hât hig in gân,
"seón sibbe-gedriht   samod ätgädere;
"gesaga him eác wordum,   þät hie sint wil-cuman
"Deniga leôdum."   Þâ wið duru healle
390 *Wulfgâr eode.*   word inne âbeád:
"Eów hêt secgan   sige-drihten mîn,
"aldor Eâst-Dena,   þät he eôwer äðelu can
"and ge him syndon   ofer sæ-wylmas,
"heard-hicgende,   hider wil-cuman.
395 "Nu ge môton gangan   in eôwrum gûð-geatawum,
"under here-grîman.   Hrôðgâr geseón;
"lætað hilde-bord   her onbidian,
"wudu wäl-sceaftas,   worda geþinges."
Arâs þâ se rîca,   ymb hine rinc manig,
400 þryðlic þegna heáp;   sume þær bidon,
heaðo-reáf heóldon,   swâ him se hearda bebeád.
Snyredon ätsomne,   þâ secg wîsode
under Heorotes hrôf;   *hyge-rôf eode,*
heard under helme.   þät he on heoðe gestôd.
405 Beówulf maðelode   (on him byrne scân,
searo-net seówed   smiðes or-þancum):
"Wes þu Hrôðgâr hâl!   ic com Higelâces
"mæg and mago-þegn;   häbbe ic mærða fela
"ongunnen on geogoðe.   Me wearð Grendles þing
410 "on mînre êðel-tyrf   undyrne cûð:
"secgað sæ-lîðend,   þät þes sele stande,
"reced sêlesta,   rinca gehwylcum
"îdel and unnyt,   siððan æfen-leóht
"under heofenes hâdor   beholen weorðeð.
415 "Þâ me þät gelærdon   leóde mîne,
"þâ sêlestan,   snotere ceorlas,
"þeóden Hrôðgâr,   þät ic þe sôhte;

"forþan hie mägenes cräft minne cûðon:
"selfe ofersâwon, þâ ic of searwum cwom,
420 "fâh from feóndum, þær ic fîfe geband,
"ŷðde eotena cyn, and on ŷðum slôg
"niceras nihtes, nearo-þearfe dreáh,
"wräc Wedera nîð (weán âhsodon)
"forgrand gramum: and nu wið Grendel sceal,
425 "wið þam aglæcan, âna gehegan
"þing wið þyrse. Ic þe nu þâ,
"brego Beorht-Dena, biddan wille,
"eodor Scyldinga, ânre bêne;
"þät þu me ne forwyrne, wigendra hleó,
430 "freó-wine folca, nu ic þus feorran com,
"þät ic môte âna and mînra eorla gedryht,
"þes hearda heáp, Heorot fælsian.
"Häbbe ic eác geâhsod, þät se äglæca
"for his won-hŷdum wæpna ne rêceð:
435 "ic þät þonne forhicge, swâ me Higelâc sîe,
"mîn mon-drihten, môdes blîðe,
"þät ic sweord bere oððe sîdne scyld,
"geolo-rand tô gûðe; ac ic mid grâpe sceal
"fôn wið feónde and ymb feorh sacan,
440 "lâð wið lâðum; þær gelŷfan sceal
"dryhtnes dôme se þe hine deáð nimeð.
"Wên' ic þät he wille, gif he wealdan môt,
"in þäm gûð-sele Geátena leóde
"etan unforhte, swâ he oft dyde
445 "mägen Hrêðmanna. Nâ þu mînne þearft
"hafalan hŷdan, ac he me habban wile
"dreóre fâhne, gif mec deáð nimeð,
"byreð blôdig wäl, byrgean þenceð,
"eteð ân-genga unmurnlîce,
450 "mearcað môr-hôpu: nô þu ymb mînes ne þearft
"lîces feorme leng sorgian.
"Onsend Higelâce, gif mec hild nime,

" beadu-scrûda betst,   þät mine breóst wereð,
" hrägla sélest ;   þät is Hréðlan lâf,
455 " Wélandes geweorc.   Gæð â Wyrd swâ hió scel !"

VIII. Hrothgar tells of Grendel.

Hróðgâr maðelode,   helm Scyldinga :
" for *were*-fyhtum þu,   wine min Beówulf,
" and for âr-stafum   ûsic sôhtest.
" Geslôh þin fäder   fæhðe mæste,
460 " wearð he Heaðolâfe   tô hand-bonan
" mid Wilfingum ;   þâ hine Wedera cyn
" for here-brôgan   habban ne mihte.
" Þanon he gesôhte   Sûð-Dena folc
" ofer ýða gewealc,   Âr-Scyldinga ;
465 " þâ ic furðum weóld   folce Deninga,
" and on geogoðe heóld   gimme-rîce
" hord-burh häleða :   þâ wäs Heregâr deâd,
" min yldra mæg   unlifigende,
" bearn Healfdenes.   Se wäs betera þonne ic !
470 " Siððan þâ fæhðe   feó þingode ;
" sende ic Wylfingum   ofer wäteres hrycg
" ealde mâdmas :   he me âðas swôr.
" Sorh is me tô secganne   on sefan minum
" gumena ængum,   hwät me Grendel hafað
475 " hýnðo on Heorote   mid his hete-þancum,
" fær-niða gefremed.   Is min flet-werod,
" wig-heáp gewanod ;   hie Wyrd forsweóp
" on Grendles gryre.   God eáðe mäg
" þone dol-scaðan   dæda getwæfan !
480 " Ful oft gebeótedon   beóre druncne
" ofer ealo-wæge   oret-mecgas,
" þät hie in beór-sele   bîdan woldon
" Grendles gûðe   mid gryrum ecga.

" Þonne wäs þeós medo-heal   on morgen-tíd,
485 " driht-sele dreór-fáh,   þonne dæg lixte,
" eal benc-þelu   blóde bestýmed,
" heall heoru-dreóre :   áhte ic holdra þ $\hat{y}$ läs,
" deórre duguðe,   þe þá deáð fornam.
" Site nu tó symle   and onsæl meoto,
490 " sige-hréð secgum,   swá þín sefa hwette ! "
Þá wäs Geát-mäcgum   geador ätsomne
on beór-sele   benc gerýmed ;
þær swíð-ferhðe   sittan eodon
þryðum dealle.   Þegn nytte beheóld,
495 se þe on handa bär   hroden ealo-wæge,
scencte scîr wered.   Scóp hwílum sang
hádor on Heorote ;   þær wäs häleða dreám,
duguð unlytel   Dena and Wedera.

IX. Hunferth Objects to Beówulf.

Hûnferð maðelode,   Ecgláfes bearn,
500 þe ät fótum sät   freán Scyldinga ;
onband beadu-rûne   (wäs him Beówulfes síð,
módges mere-faran,   micel äf-þunca,
forþon þe he ne ûðe,   þät ænig óðer man
æfre mærða þon má   middan-geardes
505 geheðde under heofenum   þonne he sylfa) :
" Eart þu se Beówulf,   se þe wið Brecan wunne,
" on sídne sæ   ymb sund flite,
" þær git for wlence   wada cunnedon
" and for dol-gilpe   on deóp wäter
510 " aldrum nêðdon ?   Ne inc ænig mon,
" ne leóf ne láð,   beleán mihte
" sorh-fullne síð ;   þá git on sund reón,
" þær git eágor-streám   earmum þehton,
" mæton mere-stræta,   mundum brugdon,

515 " glidon ofer gár-secg ;   geofon ýðum weól,
" wintres wylme.   Git on wæteres æht
" seofon niht swuncon ;   he þe ät sunde oferflát,
" häfde máre mägen.   Þá hine on morgen-tíd
" on Heaðo-ræmas   holm up ätbär,
520 " þonon he gesóhte   swæsne éðel
" leóf his leódum   lond Brondinga,
" freoðo-burh fägere,   þær he folc áhte,
" burg and beágas.   Beót eal wið þe
" sunu Beánstánes   sóðe gelæste.
525 " Þonne wéne ic tó þe   wyrsan geþinges,
" þeáh þu heaðo-ræsa   gehwær dohte,
" grimre gúðe,   gif þu Grendles dearst
" niht-longne fyrst   neán bídan !"
Beówulf maðelode,   bearn Ecgþeówes :
530 " Hwät þu worn fela,   wine mín Húnferð,
" beóre druncen   ymb Brecan spræce,
" sägdest from his síðe !   Sóð ic talige,
" þät ic mere-strengo   máran áhte,
" eafeðo on ýðum,   þonne ænig óðer man.
535 " Wit þät geowædon   cniht-wesende
" and gebeótedon   (wæron begen þá git
" on geogoð-feore)   þät wit on gár-secg út
" aldrum néðdon ;   and þät geäfndon swá.
" Häfdon swurd nacod,   þá wit on sund reón,
540 " heard on handa,   wit unc wið hron-fixas
" werian þóhton.   Nó he wiht fram me
" flód-ýðum feor   fleótan meahte,
" hraðor on holme,   nó ic fram him wolde.
" Þá wit ätsomne   on sæ wæron
545 " fíf nihta fyrst,   óð þät unc flód tódráf,
" wado weallende,   wedera cealdost,
" nípende niht   and norðan wind
" heaðo-grim andhwearf :   hreó wæron ýða.
" Wäs mere-fixa   mód onhréred :

550 " þær me wið láðum   líc-syrce mín,
   " heard hond-locen,   helpe gefremede;
   " beado-hrägl broden   on breóstum läg,
   " golde gegyrwed.   Me tó grunde teáh
   " fáh feónd-scaða,   fäste häfde
555 " grim on grápe: hwäðre me gyfeðe wearð,
   " þät ic aglæcan   orde geræhte,
   " hilde-bille;   heaðo-ræs fornam
   " mihtig mere-deór   þurh míne hand.

X. BEÓWULF'S CONTEST WITH BRECA.—THE FEAST.

   " Swá mec gelóme   láð-geteónan
560 " þreátedon þearle.   Ic him þénode
   " deóran sweorde,   swá hit gedéfe wäs;
   " näs hie þære fylle   gefeán häfdon,
   " mán-fordædlan,   þät hie me þégon,
   " symbel ymb-sæton   sæ-grunde neáh,
565 " ac on mergenne   mécum wunde
   " be ýð-láfe   uppe lægon,
   " sweordum áswefede,   þät syððan ná
   " ymb brontne ford   brim-líðende
   " láde ne letton.   Leóht eástan com,
570 " beorht beácen godes;   brimu swaðredon,
   " þät ic sæ-nässas   gescón mihte,
   " windige weallas.   Wyrd oft nereð
   " unfægne eorl,   ðonne his ellen deáh!
   " Hwäðere me gesælde,   þät ic mid sweorde ofslóh
575 " niceras nigene.   Nó ic on niht gefrägn
   " under heofones hwealf   heardran feohtan,
   " ne on ég-streámum   earmran mannan;
   " hwäðere ic fára feng   feore gedígde,
   " síðes wérig.   Þá mec sæ óðbär,
580 " flód äfter faroðe,   on Finna land,

"wadu weallendu.   Nó ic wiht fram þe
"swylera searo-nîða   secgan hýrde,
"billa brôgan: Breca næfre git
"ät heaðo-lâce,   ne gehwäðer incer
585 "swâ deórlîce   dæd gefremede
"fâgum sweordum   . . . .
". . . . . . .   nô ic þäs gylpe;
"þeáh þu þínum brôðrum   tô banan wurde,
"heáfod-mægum;   þäs þu in helle scealt
590 "werhðo dreógan,   þeáh þîn wit duge.
"Secge ic þe tô sôðe,   sunu Ecglâfes,
"þät næfre Grendel swâ fela   gryra gefremede,
"atol äglæca   ealdre þînum,
"hýnðo on Heorote,   gif þîn hige wære,
595 "sefa swâ searo-grim,   swâ þu self talast.
"Ac he hafað onfunden,   þät he þâ sæhðe ne þearf,
"atole ecg-þräce   eówer leóde
"swîðe onsittan,   Sige-Scyldinga;
"nymeð nýd-bâde,   nænegum ârað
600 "leóde Deniga,   ac he on lust wîgeð,
"swefeð ond sendeð,   sæcce ne wêneð
"tô Gâr-Denum.   Ac him Geáta sceal
"eafoð and ellen   ungeâra nu
"gûðe gebeódan.   Gæð eft se þe môt
605 "tô medo môdig,   siððan morgen-leóht
"ofer ylda bearn   ôðres dôgores,
"sunne swegl-wered   sûðan scîneð!"
Þâ wäs on sâlum   sinces brytta
gamol-feax and gûð-rôf,   geôce gelýfde
610 brego Beorht-Dena;   gehýrde on Beówulfe
folces hyrde   fäst-rædne geþôht.
Þær wäs häleða hleahtor;   hlyn swynsode,
word wæron wynsume.   Eode Wealhþeów forð,
cwén Hrôðgâres.   cynna gemyndig.
615 grétte gold-hroden   guman on healle,

and þá freólíc wíf   ful gesealde
ærest Eást-Dena   éðel-wearde,
bäd hine blíðne   üt þære beór-þege,
leódum leófne;   he on lust geþeah
620 symbel and sele-ful,   sige-róf kyning.
Ymb-eode þá   ides Helminga
dugnðe and geogoðe   dæl æghwylene;
sinc-fato sealde,   ðð þät säl âlamp,
þät hió Beówulfe,   beág-hroden cwên,
625 móde geþungen,   medo-ful ätbär;
grêtte Geáta leód,   gode þancode
wís-fäst wordum,   þäs þe hire se willa gelamp,
þät heó on ænigne   eorl gelýfde
fyrena frófre.   He þät ful geþeah,
630 wäl-reów wîga   üt Wealhþeón,
and þá gyddode   gûðe gefýsed,
Beówulf maðelode,   bearn Ecgþeówes:
"Ic þät hogode,   þá ic on holm gestâh,
"sæ-bât gesät   mid mínra secga gedriht,
635 "þät ic ânunga   eówra leóda
"willan geworhte,   oððe on wäl crunge,
"feónd-grâpum fäst.   Ic gefremman sceal
"eorlíc ellen,   oððe ende-däg
"on þisse meodu-healle   mínne gebîdan."
640 Þam wîfe þá word   wel lícodon,
gilp-ewide Geátes;   eode gold-hroden
freólícu folc-cwên   tô hire freán sittan.
Þâ wäs eft swâ ær   inne on healle
þrýð-word sprecen,   þeód on sælum,
645 sige-folea swêg.   Oð þät semninga
sunu Healfdenes   sêcean wolde
æfen-räste;   wiste ät þäm ahlæcan
tô þäm heáh-sele   hilde geþinged,
siððan hie sunnan leóht   gescón ne meahton,
650 oððe nîpende   niht ofer ealle,

scadu-helma gesceapu   scríðan cwóman,
wan under wolcnum.   Werod eall árás.
Grétte þá *giddum*   guma óðerne,
Hróðgár Beówulf,   and him hæl ábeád,
655 win-ärnes geweald   and þät word ácwäð:
" Næfre'ic ænegum men   ær Alfíde,
" siððan ic hond and rond   hebban mihte,
" þryð-ärn Dena   búton þe nu þá.
" Hafa nu and geheald   húsa sélest;
660 " gemyne mærðo,   mägen-ellen cýð,
" waca wið wráðum!   Ne bið þe wilna gád,
" gif þu þät ellen-weorc   aldre gedígest."

XI. THE WATCH FOR GRENDEL.

þá him Hróðgár gewát   mid his häleða gedryht,
eodur Scyldinga   út of healle;
665 wolde wíg-fruma   Wealhþeó sécan,
cwén tó gebeddan.   Häfde kyninga wuldor
Grendle tó-geánes,   swá guman gefrungon,
sele-weard áseted: sundor-nytte beheóld
ymb aldor Dena,   eoton weard ábeád;
670 húru Geáta leód   georne trúwode
módgan mägnes,   metodes hyldo.
þá he him of dyde   ísern-byrnan,
helm of hafelan,   sealde his hyrsted sweord,
írena cyst   ombiht-þegne,
675 and gehealdan hét   hilde-geatwe.
Gespräc þá se góda   gylp-worda sum
Beówulf Geáta,   ær he on bed stige:
" Nó ic me an here-wæsmun   hnágran talige
" gúð-geweorca,   þonne Grendel hine;
680 " forþan ic hine sweorde   swebban nelle,
" aldre beneótan,   þeáh ic eal mæge.

" Nât he þâra gôda,   þät he me on-geán sleá,
" rand geheáwe,   þeáh þe he rôf sîe
" nîð-geweorca;   ac wit on niht sculon
685 " seege ofersittan,   gif he gesêcean dear
" wîg ofer wæpen,   and siððan witig god
" on swâ hwäðere hond   hâlig dryhten
" mærðo dême,   swâ him gemet þince."
Hylde hine þâ heaðo-deór,   hleór-bolster onfêng
690 eorles andwlitan;   and hine ymb monig
snellîc sæ-rinc   sele-reste gebeáh.
Nænig heora þôhte   þät he þanon scolde
eft eard-lufan   æfre gesêcean,
folc oððe freó-burh,   þær he âfêded wäs,
695 ac hie häfdon gefrunen,   þät hie ær tô fela micles
in þäm win-sele   wäl-deáð fornam,
Denigea leóde.   Ac him dryhten forgeaf
wîg-spêda gewiofu,   Wedera leódum
frôfor and fultum,   þät hie feónd heora
700 þurh ânes cräft   ealle ofercômon,
selfes mihtum: sôð is gecŷðed,
þät mihtig god   manna cynnes
weóld wîde-ferhð.   Com on wanre niht
scrîðan sceadu-genga.   Sceótend swæfon,
705 þâ þät horn-reced   healdan scoldon,
ealle buton ânum.   Þät wäs yldum cûð,
þät hie ne môste,   þâ metod nolde,
se syn-scaða   under sceadu bregdan;
ac he wäccende   wrâðum on andan
710 bâd bolgen-môd   beadwa geþinges.

XII. Grendel's Raid.

Þá com of móre   under mist-hleoðum
Grendel gongan,   godes yrre bär.
Mynte se mán-scaða   manna cynnes
sumne besyrwan   in sele þam heáu;
715 wód under wolcnum,   tó þäs þe he win-reced,
gold-sele gumena,   gearwost wisse
fättum fáhne.   Ne wäs þät forma sīð,
þät he Hróðgáres   hám gesóhte:
næfre he on aldor-dagum   ær ne siðða̱n
720 heardran häle,   heal-þegnas fand!
Com þá tó recede   rinc siðian
dreámum bedäled.   Duru sóna onarn
fýr-bendum fäst,   syððan he hire folmum hráu;
onbräd þá bealo-hydig,   þá he ábolgen wäs,
725 recedes múðan.   Raðe äfter þon
on fágne flór   feónd treddode,
eode yrre-mód;   him of eágum stód
līge gelícost   leóht unfäger.
Geseah he in recede   rinca manige,
730 swefan sibbe-gedriht   samod ätgädere,
mago-rinca heáp: þá his mód áhlóg.
mynte þät he gedälde,   ær þon däg cwóme,
atol aglæca.   ánra gehwylces
līf wið līce,   þá him álumpen wäs
735 wist-fylle wén.   Ne wäs þät wyrd þá gen,
þät he má móste   manna cynnes
þicgean ofer þá niht.   Þryð-swyð beheóld
mæg Higeláces,   hú se mán-scaða
under fær-gripum   gefaran wolde.
740 Ne þät se aglæca   yldan þóhte,
ac he gefëng hraðe   forman sīðe
slæpendne rinc,   slát unwearnum,

bât bân-locan, blôd êdrum dranc,
syn-snædum swealh : sôna häfde
745 unlyfigendes eal gefeormod
fêt and folma. Forð neár ätstôp,
nam þâ mid handa bige-þihtigne
rinc on räste ; ræhte ongeán
feónd mid folme, he onfêng hraðe
750 inwit-þancum and wið earm gesät.
Sôna þät onfunde fyrena hyrde,
þät he ne mêtte middan-geardes
eorðan sceáta on elran men
mund-gripe mâran : he on môde wearð
755 forht on ferhðe, nô þŷ ær fram meahte ;
hyge wäs him hin-fûs, wolde on heolster fleón,
sêcan deófla gedräg : ne wäs his drohtoð þær,
swylce he on ealder-dagum ær gemêtte.
Gemunde þâ se gôda mæg Higelâces
760 æfen-spræce, up-lang âstôd
and him fäste wiðfêng. Fingras burston ;
eoten wäs ût-weard, eorl furður stôp.
Mynte se mæra, þær he meahte swâ,
wîdre gewindan and on weg þanon
765 fleón on fen-hôpu ; wiste his fingra geweald
on grames grâpum. Þät wäs geócor sîð,
þät se hearm-scaða tô Heorute âteáh :
dryht-sele dynede, Denum eallum wearð,
ceaster-bûendum, cênra gehwylcum,
770 eorlum ealu-scerwen. Yrre wæron begen,
rêðe rên-weardas. Reced hlynsode ;
þâ wäs wundor micel, þät se win-sele
wiðhäfde heaðo-deórum, þät he on hrusan ne feól,
fäger fold-bold ; ac he þäs fäste wäs
775 innan and ûtan íren-bendum
searo-þoncum besmiðod. Þær fram sylle âbeág
medu-bene monig mîne gefræge,

golde geregnad,   þær | â graman wunnon;
þäs ne wéndon ær   witan Scyldinga,
780 þät hit â mid gemete   manna ænig
betlic and bân-fâg   tôbrecan meahte,
listum tôlûcan,   nymðe líges fäðm
swulge on swaðule.   Swég up âstâg
niwe geneahhe;   Norð-Denum stôd
785 atelíc egesa   ânra gehwylcum
þâra þe of wealle   wôp gehÿrdon,
gryre-leóð galan   godes andsacan,
sige-leásne sang,   sâr wânigean
helle häftan.   Heóld hine tô fäste
790 se þe manna wäs   mägene strengest
on þäm däge   þysses lîfes.

XIII. BEÓWULF TEARS OFF GRENDEL'S ARM.

NOLDE eorla hleó   ænige þinga
þone cwealm-cuman   cwicne forlætan,
ne his lîf-dagas   leóda ænigum
795 nytte tealde.   Þær genehost brägd
eorl Beówulfes   ealde lâfe,
wolde freá-drihtnes   feorh ealgian
mæres þeódnes,   þær hie meahton swâ;
hie þät ne wiston,   þâ hie gewin drugon,
800 heard-hicgende   hilde-mecgas,
and on healfa gehwone   heáwan þôhton,
sâwle sécan,   þät þone syn-scaðan
ænig ofer eorðan   îrenna cyst,
gûð-billa nân   grétan nolde;
805 ac he sige-wæpnum   forsworen häfde,
ecga gehwylcre.   Scolde his aldor-gedâl
on þäm däge   þysses lîfes
earmlíc wurðan   and se ellor-gâst

on feónda gewcald   feor síðian.

810 þá þät onfunde   se þe fela æror
módes myrðe   manna cynne
fyrene gefremede   (he *wäs* fág wið god)
þät him se líc-homa   læstan nolde,
ac hine se módega   mæg Hygeláces

815 häfde be honda;   wäs gehwäðer óðrum
lifigende láð.   Líc-sár gebád
atol äglæca,   him on eaxle wearð
syn-dolh sweotol,   seonowe onsprungon
burston bán-locan.   Beówulfe wearð

820 gúð-hréð gyfeðe;   scolde Grendel þonan
feorh-seóc fleón   under fen-hleoðu,
sécean wyn-leás wíc;   wiste þé geornor,
þät his aldres wäs   ende gegongen,
dógera däg-rím.   Denum eallum wearð

825 äfter þam wäl-ræse   willa gelumpen.
Häfde þá gefælsod,   se þe ær feorran com,
snotor and swýð-ferhð   sele Hróðgáres,
genered wið níðe.   Niht-weorce gefeh,
ellen-mærðum ;   häfde Eást-Denum

830 Geát-mecga leód   gilp gelæsted,
swylce oncýððe   ealle gebétte,
inwid-sorge,   þe hie ær drugon
and for þreá-nýdum   þolian scoldon,
torn unlytel.   Þät wäs tácen sweotol,

835 syððan hilde-deór   hond álegde,
earm and eaxle   (þær wäs eal geador
Grendles grápe)   under geápne hróf.

XIV. The Joy at Heorot.

Þá wäs on morgen   míne gefræge
ymb þá gif-healle   gúð-rinc monig:
840 férdon folc-togan   feorran and neáu
geond wíd-wegas   wundor sceáwian,
láðes lástas.   Nð his líf-gedál
sárlíc þúhte   secga ænegum,
þára þe tír-leáses   trode sceáwode,
845 hú he wérig-mód   on weg þanon,
níða ofercumen,   on nicera mere
fæge and geflýmed   feorh-lástas bär.
Þær wäs on blóde   brim weallende,
atol ýða geswing   eal gemenged
850 hátan heolfre,   heoro-dreóre weól;
deáð-fæge deóg,   siððan dreáma leás
in fen-freoðo   feorh álegde
hæðene sáwle,   þær him hel onféng.
Þanon eft gewiton   eald-gesíðas,
855 swylce geong manig   of gomen-wáðe,
fram mere módge,   mearum rídan,
beornas on blancum.   Þær wäs Beówulfes
mærðo mæned;   monig oft gecwäð,
þätte súð ne norð   be sæm tweonum
860 ofer eormen-grund   óðer nænig
under swegles begong   sélra nære
rond-häbbendra,   ríces wyrðra.
Ne hie húru wine-drihten   wiht ne lôgon,
glädne Hróðgár,   ac þät wäs gód cyning.
865 Hwílum heaðo-rófe   hleápan léton,
on gellit faran   fealwe mearas,
þær him fold-wegas   fägere þúhton,
cystum cúðe;   hwílum cyninges þegn,
guma gilp-hläden   gidda gemyndig,

870 se þe eal-fela   eald-gesegena
    worn gemunde,   word óðer fand
    sóðe gebunden :   secg eft ongan
    sið Beówulfes   snyttrum styrian
    and on spéd wrecan   spel geráde,
875 wordum wrixlan,   wel-hwylc geewäð,
    þät he fram Sigemunde   secgan hŷrde,
    ellen-dædum,   uncûðes fela.
    Wälsinges gewin,   wide síðas,
    þára þe gumena bearn   gearwe ne wiston,
880 fæhðe and fyrene,   buton Fitela mid hine,
    þonne he swylces hwät   secgan wolde
    eám his nefan,   swâ hie â wæron
    ät níða gehwam   nŷd-gesteallan :
    häfdon eal-fela   eotena cynnes
885 sweordum gesæged.   Sigemunde gesprong
    äfter deáð-däge   dóm unlŷtel,
    syððan wiges heard   wyrm âcwealde,
    hordes hyrde ;   he under hârne stân,
    äðelinges bearn,   âna genêðde
890 frécne dæde ;   ne wäs him Fitela mid.
    Hwäðre him gesälde,   þät þät swurd þurhwôd
    wrätlícne wyrm,   þät hit on wealle ätstôd,
    dryhtlíc íren ;   draca morðre swealt.
    Häfde aglæca   elne gegongen,
895 þät he beáh-hordes   brûcan môste
    selfes dôme :   sæ-bât gehlôd,
    bär on bearm scipes   beorhte frätwa,
    Wälses eafera ;   wyrm hât gemealt.
    Se wäs wreccena   wide mærost
900 ofer wer-þeóde,   wîgendra hleó
    ellen-dædum   (he þäs ær onþáh),
    siððan Heremôdes   hild sweðrode
    eafoð and ellen.   He mid eotenum wearð
    on feónda geweald   forð forlácen,

905   snûde forsended.   Hine sorh-wylmas
      lemede tô lange,   he his leódum wearð,
      eallum äðelingum   tô aldor-ceare ;
      swylce oft bemearn   ærran mælum
      swîð-ferhðes sîð   snotor ceorl monig,
910   se þe him bealwa tô   bôte gelýfde,
      þät þät þeódnes bearn   geþeón scolde,
      fäder-äðelum onfôn,   folc gehealdan,
      hord and hleó-burh,   häleða rîce,
      éðel Scyldinga.   He þær eallum wearð,
915   mæg Higelâces   manna cynne,
      freóndum gefägra ;   hine fyren onwôd.

      Hwîlum flîtende   fealwe stræte
      mearum mæton.   Þâ wäs morgen-leóht
      scofen and scynded.   Eode scealc monig
920   swîð-hicgende   tô sele þam heán,
      searo-wundor seón,   swylce self cyning,
      of brýd-bûre   beáh-horda weard,
      tryddode tîr-fäst   getrume micle,
      cystum gecýðed,   and his cwên mid him
925   medo-stîg gemät   mägða hôse.

XV. HROTHGAR'S GRATULATION.

      Hrôðgâr maðelode   (he tô healle geóng,
      stôd on stapole,   geseah steápne hrôf
      golde fâhne   and Grendles hond):
      "þisse ansýne   al-wealdan þanc
930   "lungre gelimpe !   Fela ic lâðes gebâd,
      "grynna ät Grendle :   â mäg god wyrcan
      "wunder äfter wundre,   wuldres hyrde !
      "þät wäs ungeâra,   þät ic ænigra me
      "weána ne wénde   tô wîdan feore

935 "bôte gebídan　　þonne blôde fâh
"hûsa sêlest　　heoro-dreórig stôd;
"weá wîd-scofen　witena gehwylcne
"þâra þe ne wêndon,　þät hie wîde-ferhð
"leóda land-gewcorc　lâðum beweredon
940 "scuccum and scinnum.　Nu scealc hafað
"þurh drihtnes miht　dæd gefremede,
"þe we ealle　ær ne meahton
"snyttrum besyrwan.　Hwät! þät secgan mäg
"efne swâ hwylc mägða,　swâ þone magan cende
945 "äfter gum-cynnum,　gyf heó gyt lyfað,
"þät hyre eald-metod　êste wære
"bearn-gebyrdo.　Nu ic Beówulf
"þec, secg betsta,　me for sunu wylle
"freógan on ferhðe;　heald forð tela
950 "niwe sibbe.　Ne bið þe nænigra gâd
"worolde wilna,　þe ic geweald häbbe.
"Ful-oft ic for lässan　leán teohhode
"hord-weorðunge　hnâhran rince,
"sæmran ät säcce.　Þu þe self hafast
955 "dædum gefremed,　þät þîn dôm lyfað
"âwâ tô aldre.　Alwalda þec
"gôde forgylde,　swâ he nu gyt dyde!"
Beówulf maðelode,　bearn Ecgþeówes:
"We þät ellen-weorc　êstum miclum,
960 "feohtan fremedon,　frêcne genêððou
"eafoð uncûðes;　ûðe ic swîðor,
"þät þu hine selfne　gescón môste,
"feónd on frätewum　fyl-wêrigne!
"Ic hine hrädlîce　heardan clammum
965 "on wäl-bedde　wrîðan þôhte,
"þät he for mund-gripe　mînum scolde
"licgean lîf-bysig,　bûtan his lîc swice;
"ic hine ne mihte,　þâ metod nolde,
"ganges getwæman,　nô ic him þäs georne ätfealh,

970 " feorh-geniðlan ;   wäs tó fore-mihtig
    " feónd on fèðe.   Hwäðere he his folme forlét
    " tó lif-wraðe   lást weardian,
    " earm and eaxle ;   nó þær ænige swá þeáh
    " feá-sceaft guma   frófre gebohte :
975 " nó þý leng leofað   láð-geteóna
    " synnum geswenced,   ac hyne sár hafað
    " in nýd-gripe   nearwe befongen,
    " balwon bendum :   þær ábídan sceal
    " maga máne fáh   miclan dómes,
980 " hú him scír metod   scrifan wille."
    þá wäs swígra secg,   sunu Ecgláfes,
    on gylp-spræce   gúð-geweorca,
    siððan äðelingas   eorles cräfte
    ofer heáhne hróf   hand sceáwedon,
985 feóndes fingras,   foran æghwylc ;
    wäs stéde nägla gehwylc,   stýle gelícost,
    hæðenes hand-spern   hilde-rinces
    egle unheóru ;   æg-hwylc gecwäð,
    þät him heardra nán   hrínan wolde
990 íren ær-gód,   þät þäs ahlæcan
    blódge beadu-folme   onberan wolde.

XVI. The Banquet and the Gifts.

    þá wäs háten hreðe   Heort innan-weard
    folmum gefrätwod :   fela þæra wäs
    wera and wífa,   þe þät win-reced,
995 gest-sele gyredon.   Gold-fág scinon
    web äfter wagum,   wundor-sióna fela
    secga gehwylcum   þára þe on swylc starað.
    Wäs þät beorhte bold   tóbrocen swíðe
    eal inne-weard   íren-bendum fäst,
1000 heorras tóhlidene ;   hróf ána genäs

ealles ansund,   þâ se aglæca,
fyren-dædum fâg   on fleám gewand,
aldres or-wêna.   Nô þät ȳðe byð
tô befleónne   (fremme se þe wille!)
1005 ac gesacan sceal   sâwl-berendra
nȳde genȳdde   niðða bearna
grund-bûendra   gearwe stôwe,
þær his lîc-homa   leger-bedde fäst
swefeð äfter symle.   Þâ wäs sæl and **mæl**,
1010 þät tô healle gang   Healfdenes sunu;
wolde self cyning   symbel þicgan.
Ne gefrägen ic þâ mægðe   **máran weorode**
ymb hyra sinc-gyfan   ˈsêl gebæran.
Bugon þâ tô bence   blæd-âgende, .
1015 fylle gefægon.   Fägere geþægon
medo-ful manig   mâgas † þâra ᴹ   ,
swîð-hicgende   on sele þam heán,
Hróðgâr and Hróðulf.   Heorot innan **wäs**
freóndum âfylled;   nalles fâcen-stafas
1020 Þeód-Scyldingas   þenden fremedon.
Forgeaf þâ Beówulfe   bearn Healfdenes
segen gyldenne   sigores tô leáne,
hroden hilte-cumbor,   helm and byrnan;
mære mâððum-sweord   manige gesâwon
1025 beforan beorn beran.   Beówulf geþah
ful on flette;   nô he þære feoh-gyfte
for sceótendum   scamigan þorfte,
ne gefrägn ic freóndlîcor   feówer mâdmas
golde gegyrede   gum-manna fela
1030 in ealo-bence   ôðrum gesellan.
Ymb þäs helmes hrôf   heáfod-beorge
wîrum bewunden   walan ûtan heóld,
þät him fêla lâfe   frêcne ne meahton
scûr-heard sceððan,   þonne scyld-freca
1035 ongeán gramum   gangan scolde.

Héht þá eorla hleó　　eahta mearas,
fäted-hleóre,　　on flet teón
in under eoderas ;　　þára ánum stód
sadol searwum fáh　　since gewurðad,
1040 þät wäs hilde-setl　　heáh-cyninges,
þonne sweorda geláe　　sunu Healfdenes
efnan wolde ;　　næfre on óre läg
wid-cúðes wig,　　þonne walu feóllon.
And þá Beówulfe　　bega gehwäðres
1045 eodor Ingwina　　onweald geteáh,
wicga and wæpna ;　　hét hine wel brúcan.
Swá manlice　　mære þeóden,
hord-weard häleða　　heaðo-ræsas geald
mearum and máðmum,　　swá hý næfre man lyhð,
1050 se þe secgan wile　　sóð äfter rihte.

XVII. Song of Hrothgar's Poet -- The Lay of Hnaef and Hengest.

Þá gyt æghwylcum　　eorla drihten
þára þe mid Beówulfe　　brim-láde teáh,
on þære medu-bence　　máððum gesealde,
yrfe-láfe,　　and þone ænne héht
1055 golde forgyldan,　　þone þe Grendel ær
máne áewealde,　　swá he hyra má wolde,
nefne him witig god　　wyrd forstóde
and þäs mannes mód :　　metod eallum weóld
gumena cynnes,　　swá he nu git déð ;
1060 forþan bið andgit　　æghwær sélest,
ferhðes fore-þanc !　　fela sceal gebídan
leófes and láðes,　　se þe longe her
on þyssum win-dagum　　worolde brúceð.
Þær wäs sang and swég　　samod ätgädere

1065 fore Healfdenes   hilde-wísan,
gomen-wudu grēted,   gid oft wrecen,
þonne heal-gamen   Hróðgáres scóp
äfter medo-bence   mænan scolde
Finnes eaferum,   þá hie se fær begeat:
1070 "Häleð Healfdenes,   Hnäf Scyldinga,
"in Fr..es wäle   feallan scolde.
"Ne húru Hildeburh   hérian þorfte
"eotena treówe: unsynnum wearð
"beloren leófum   ät þam lind-plegan
1075 "bearnum and bróðrum;   hie on gebyrd hruron
"gáre wunde;   þät wäs geómuru ides.
"Nalles hólinga   Hóces dóhtor
"meotod-sceaft bemearn,   syððan morgen com,
"þá heó under swegle   geseón meahte
1080 "morðor-bealo mága,   þær heó ær mæste heóld
"worolde wynne: wíg ealle fornam
"Finnes þegnas,   nemne feáum ánum,
"þät he ne mehte   on þäm meðel-stede
"wíg Hengeste   wiht gefeohtan,
1085 "ne þá weá-láfe   wíge forþringan
"þeódnes þegne;   ac hig him geþingo budon,
"þät hie him óðer flet   eal gerýmdon,
"healle and heáh-setl,   þät hie healfre geweald
"wið eotena bearn   ágan móston,
1090 "and ät feoh-gyftum   Folcwaldan sunu
"dógra gehwylce   Dene weorðode,
"Hengestes heáp   hringum wenede,
"efne swá swíðe   sinc-gestreónum
"fättan goldes,   swá he Fresena cyn
1095 "on beór-sele   byldan wolde.
"Þá hie getrúwedon   on twá healfa
"fäste friðu-wære;   Fin Hengeste
"elne unflitme   áðum benemde,
"þät he þá weá-láfe   weotena dóme

1100 " Ârum heolde,   þät þær ænig mon
      " wordum ne worcum   wære ne bræce,
      " ne þurh inwit-searo   æfre gemænden,
      " þeáh hie hira beág-gyfan   banan folgedon
      " þeóden-leáse,   þâ him swâ geþearfod wäs :
1105 " gyf þonne Frysna hwyle   frêcnan spræce
      " þäs morðor-betes   myndgiend wære,
      " þonne hit sweordes ecg   syððan scolde.
      " Âð wäs geäfned   and icge gold
      " âbäfen of horde.   Here-Scyldinga
1110 " betst beado-rinca   wäs on bæl gearu ;
      " ät þäm âde wäs   êð-gesŷne
      " swât-fâh syrce,   swŷn eal-gylden,
      " eofer íren-heard,   äðeling manig
      " wundum âwyrded ;   sume on wäle crungon.
1115 " Hêt þâ Hildeburh   ät Hnäfes âde
      " hire selfre sunu   sweoloðe befästan,
      " bân-fatu bärnan   and on bæl dôn.
      " Earme on eaxle   ides gnornode,
      " geômrode giddum ;   gûð-rinc âstâh.
1120 " Wand tô wolcnum   wäl-fŷra mæst,
      " hlynode for hlâwe ;   hafelan multon,
      " ben-geato burston,   þonne blôd ätspranc
      " lâð-bite lîces.   Lîg ealle forswealg,
      " gæsta gîfrost,   þâra þe þær gûð fornam
1125 " bega folces ;   wäs hira blæd scacen.

XVIII. The Gleeman's Tale is Ended.

      " Gewiton him þâ wîgend   wîca neósian,
      " freóndum befeallen   Frysland geseón,
      " hâmas and heá-burh.   Hengest þâ gyt
      " wäl-fâgne winter   wunode mid Finne
1130 " ealles unhlitme ;   eard gemunde,

"þeáh þe he *ne* mealte   on mere drífan
" hringed-stefnan ;   holm storme weól,
" won wið winde ;   winter ýðe beleác
" ís-gebinde   ôð þät ôðer com
1135 "geâr in geardas,   swâ nu gyt dêð,
" þâ þe syngales   sêle bewitiað,
" wuldor-torhtan weder.   þâ wäs winter scacen,
" fäger foldan bearm ;   fundode wrecca,
" gist of geardum ;   he tô gyrn-wräce
1140 " swíðor þôhte,   þonne tô sæ-lâde,
" gif he torn-gemôt   þurhteón mihte,
" þät he eotena bearn   inne gemunde.
" Swâ he ne forwyrnde   worold-rædenne,
" þonne him Hûnlâfing   hilde-leóman,
1145 " billa sêlest,   on bearm dyde :
" þäs wæron mid eotenum   ecge cûðe.
" Swylce ferhð-frecan   Fin eft begeat
" sweord-bealo slîðen   ät his selfes hâm,
" siððan grimne gripe   Gûðlâf ond Ôslâf
1150 " äfter sæ-sîðe   sorge mændon,
" ätwiton weâna dæl ;   ne mealte wäfre môd
" forhabban in hreðre.   þâ wäs heal hroden
" feónda feorum,   swilce Fin slägen,
" cyning on corðre,   and seó cwên numen.
1155 " Sceótend Scyldinga   tô scypum feredon
" eal in-gesteald   corð-cyninges,
" swylce hie ät Finnes hâm   findan meahton
" sigla searo-gimma.   Hie on sæ-lâde
" drihtlîce wîf   tô Denum feredon,
1160 " læddon tô leódum."   Leóð wäs âsungen,
gleó-mannes gyd.   Gamen eft âstâh,
beorhtode benc-swêg,   byrelas sealdon
wîn of wunder-fatum.   þâ cwom Wealhþeó forð
gân under gyldnum beáge,   þær þâ gôdan twegen
1165 sæton suhter-gefäderan ;   þâ gyt wäs hiera sib ätgädere

æghwylc ðörum trŷwe.   Swylce þær Húnferð þyle
ät fötum sät freán Scyldinga : gehwylc hiora his ferhðe
           treówde,
þät he häfde möd micel,   þeáh þe he his mágum nære
árfäst ät ecga gelácum.   Spräc þá ides Scyldinga:

1170 "Onföh þissum fulle,   freó-drihten mín,
"sinces brytta ;   þu on sælum wes,
"gold-wine gumena,   and tö Geátum sprec
"mildum wordum !   Swá sceal man dön.
"Beó wið Geátas gläd,   geofena gemyndig ;
1175 "neán and feorran   þu nu friðu hafast.
"Me man sägde,   þät þu þe for sunu wolde
"here-rinc habban.   Heorot is gefælsod,
"beáh-sele beorhta ;   brúc þenden þu möte
"manigra méda   and þinum mágum læf
1180 "folc and ríce,   þonne þu forð scyle
"metod-sceaft sceón.   Ic minne can
"glädne Hröðulf,   þät he þá geogoðe wile
"árum healdan,   gyf þu ær þonne he,
"wine Scildinga,   worold oflætest ;
1185 "wéne ic, þät he mid góde   gyldan wille
"uncran eaferan,   gif he þät eal gemon,
"hwät wit tö willan   and tö worð-myndum
"umbor wesendum ær   árna gefremedon."
Hwearf þá bí bence,   þær hyre byre wæron,
1190 Hröðríc and Hröðmund,   and häleða bearn,
giogoð ätgädere ;   þær se góda sät
Beówulf Geáta   be þæm gebröðrum twæm.

XIX.

BEÓWULF's JEWELLED COLLAR. THE HEROES REST.

Him wäs ful boren　　and freónd-laðu
wordum bewägned　　and wunden gold
1195 éstum geeáwed,　　earm-hreáde twâ,
hrägl and hringas,　　heals-beága mæst
þâra þe ic on foldan　　gefrägen häbbe.
Nænigne ic under swegle　　sélran hýrde
hord-mâððum häleða,　　syððan Hâma ätwäg
1200 tô þære byrhtan byrig　　Brosinga mene,
sigle and sinc-fät,　　searo-níðas fealh
Eormenríces,　　geceás éene ræd.
Þone hring häfde　　Higeláe Geáta,
nefa Swertinges,　　nýhstan síðe,
1205 siððan he under segne　　sinc ealgode,
wäl-reáf werede;　　hyne Wyrd fornam,
syððan he for wlenco　　weán âhsode,
faehðe tô Frysum;　　he þâ frätwe wäg,
corclan-stânas　　ofer ýða ful,
1210 ríee þeóden,　　he under rande gecrane;
gehwearf þâ in Francna fäðm　　feorh cyninges,
breóst-gewaedu　　and se beáh somod:
wyrsan wíg-frecan　　wäl reáfedon
äfter gúð-sceare.　　Geáta leóde
1215 hreá-wíc heóldon.　　Heal swége onféng.
Wealhþeó maðelode,　　heó fore þäm werede spräc:
"Brúe þisses beáges,　　Beówulf, leófa
"hyse, mid haele,　　and þisses hrägles neót
"þeód-gestreóna,　　and geþeóh tela,
1220 "een þec mid cräfte　　and þyssum cnyhtum wes
"lâra líðe!　　ic þe þäs leán geman.
"Hafast þu geféred,　　þät þe feor and neáh

"calne wíde-ferhð　weras ehtigað,
"efne swâ síde　swâ sæ bebûgeð
1225 "windige weallas.　Wes, þenden þu lifige,
"æðeling eádig!　ic þe an tela
"sinc-gestreóna.　Beó þu suna mínum
"dædum gedéfe　dreám healdende!
"Her is æghwylc eorl　ôðrum getrýwe,
1230 "módes milde,　man-drihtne hold,
"þegnas syndon geþwære,　þeód eal gearo:
"druncne dryht-guman,　dôð swâ ic bidde!"
Eode þâ tô setle.　þær wäs symbla cyst,
druncon wín weras :　wyrd ne cûðon,
1235 geó-sceaft grimme,　swâ hit âgangen wearð
eorla manegum,　syððan æfen cwom
and him Hróðgâr gewât　tô hofe sínum,
ríce tô räste.　Reced weardode
unrîm eorla,　swâ hie oft ær dydon :
1240 bene-þelu beredon,　hit geond-bræded wearð
beddum and bolstrum.　Beór-scealca sum
fûs and fæge　flet-räste gebeág.
Setton him tô heáfdum　hilde-randas,
bord-wudu beorhtan ;　þær on bence wäs
1245 ofer äðelinge　ýð-geséne
heaðo-steápa helm,　hringed byrne,
þrec-wudu þrymlíc.　Wäs þeáw hyra,
þät hie oft wæron　an wíg gearwe,
ge ät hâm ge on herge,　ge gehwäðer þâra
1250 efne swylce mæla,　swylce hira man-dryhtne
þearf gesælde ;　wäs seó þeód tilu.

XX.

GRENDEL'S MOTHER ATTACKS THE RING-DANES.

Sigon þâ tô slæpe.   Sum sâre angeald
æfen-ræste,   swâ him ful-oft gelamp,
siððan gold-sele   Grendel warode,
1255 unriht æfnde,   ôð þät ende becwom,
swylt æfter synnum.   Þät gesýne wearð,
wîd-cûð werum,   þätte wrecend þâ gyt
lifde æfter lâðum,   lange þrage
æfter gûð-ceare ;   Grendles môdor,
1260 ides aglæc-wîf   yrmðe gemunde,
se þe wäter-egesan   wunian scolde,
cealde streámas,   siððan Cain wearð
tô ecg-banan   ângan brêðer,
fäderen-mæge ;   he þâ fâg gewât,
1265 morðre gemearcod   man-dreám fleón,
wêsten warode.   Þanon wôc fela
geósceaft-gâsta ;   wäs þæra Grendel sum,
heoro-wearh hetelic,   se ät Heorote fand
wäccendne wer   wîges bîdan,
1270 þær him aglæca   ät-græpe wearð ;
hwäðre he gemunde   mägenes strenge,
gim-fäste gife,   þe him god sealde,
and him tô anwaldan   âre gelýfde,
frôfre and fultum :   þý he þone feónd ofercwom,
1275 gehnægde helle gâst :   þâ he heán gewât,
dreáme bedæled   deáð-wîc seón,
man-cynnes feónd.   And his môdor þâ gyt
gîfre and galg-môd   gegân wolde
sorh-fulne sîð,   suna deáð wrecan.
1280 Com þâ tô Heorote,   þær Hring-Dene
geond þät säld swæfun.   Þâ þær sôna wearð
ed-hwyrft eorlum,   siððan inne fealh

Grendles môdor;   wäs se gryre lässa
efne swâ micle,   swâ bið mägða cräft,
1285 wîg-gryre wîfes   be wæpned-men,
þonne heoru bunden,   hamere geþuren,
sweord swâte fâh   swîn ofer helme,
ecgum dyhtig   andweard scireð.
Þâ wäs on healle   heard-ecg togen,
1290 sweord ofer setlum,   sîd-rand manig
hafen handa fäst;   helm ne gemunde,
byrnan sîde,   þe hine se brôga angeat.
Heó wäs on ôfste,   wolde ût þanon
feore beorgan,   þâ heó onfunden wäs;
1295 hraðe heó äðelinga   ânne häfde
fäste befangen,   þâ heó tô fenne gang;
se wäs Hrôðgâre   häleða leófost
on gesîðes hâd   be sæm tweonum,
rîce rand-wiga.   þone þe heó on räste âbreât,
1300 blæd-fästne beorn.   Näs Beówulf þær,
ac wäs ôðer in   ær geteohhod
äfter mâððum-gife   mærum Geáte.
Hreám wearð on Heorote.   Heó under heolfre genam
cûðe folme; cearu wäs geniwod
1305 geworden in wîcum: ne wäs þät gewrixle til,
þät hie on bâ healfa   bicgan scoldon
freónda feorum.   Þâ wäs frôd cyning,
hâr hilde-rinc,   on hreón môde,
syððan he aldor-þegn   unlyfigendne,
1310 þone deórestan   deádne wisse.
Hraðe wäs tô bûre   Beówulf fetod,
sigor-eádig secg.   Samod ær-däge
eode eorla sum.   äðele cempa
self mid gesîðum,   þær se snottra bâd,
1315 hwäðre him al-walda   æfre wille
äfter weá-spelle   wyrpe gefremman.
Gang þâ äfter flôre   fyrd-wyrðe man

mid his hand-scale   (heal-wudu dynede)
þät he þone wîsan   wordum hnægde
1320 freán Ingwina;   frägn gif him wære
äfter neód-laðu   niht getæse.

XXI. Sorrow at Heorot: Æschere's Death.

Hróðgâr maðelode,   helm Scildinga:
"Ne frin þu äfter sælum!   Sorh is geniwod
"Denigea leódum.   Deád is Äsc-here,
1325 "Yrmenlâfes   yldra bróðor,
"mîn rûn-wita   and mîn ræd-bora,
"eaxl-gestealla,   þonne we on orlege
"hafelan weredon,   þonne hniton fêðan,
"eoferas cnysedan;   swylc scolde eorl wesan
1330 "*äðeling* ær-gôd,   swylc Äsc-here wäs.
"Wearð him on Heorote   tô hand-banan
"wäl-gæst wäfre;   ic ne wât hwäder
"atol æse wlanc   eft-sîðas teáh,
"fylle gefrægnod.   Heó þâ fæhðe wräc,
1335 "þe þu gystran niht   Grendel cwealdest
"þurh hæstne hâd   heardum clammum,
"forþan he tô lange   leóde mîne
"wanode and wyrde.   He ät wîge gecrang
"ealdres scyldig,   and nu ôðer cwom
1340 "mihtig mân-scaða,   wolde hyre mæg wrecan,
"ge feor hafað   fæhðe gestæled,
"þäs þe þincean mäg   þegne monegum,
"se þe äfter sinc-gyfan   on sefan greóteð,
"hreðer-bealo hearde;   nu seó hand ligeð,
1345 "se þe eów wel-hwylcra   wilna dohte.
"Ic þät lond-bûend   leóde mîne
"sele-rædende   secgan hŷrde,
"þät hie gesâwon   swylce twegen

"micle mearc-stapan   móras healdan,
1350 "ellor-gæstas: þæra óðer wæs,
"þäs þe hie gewislicost   gewitan meahton
"idese onlícnes.   Óðer earm-sceapen
"on weres wästmum   wräc-lástas träd,
"näfne he wäs mára   þonne ænig man óðer,
1355 "þone on geár-dagum   Grendel nemdon
"fold-búende: nó hie fäder cunnon,
"hwäðer him ænig wäs   ær ácenned.
"dyrnra gásta.   Hie dýgel þnd
"warigeað, wulf-hleoðu,   windige nässas,
1360 "frécne fen-geläd.   þær fyrgen-streám
"under nässa genipu   niðer gewíteð,
"flód under foldan;   nis þät feor heonon
"míl-gemearces.   þät se mere standeð,
"ofer þäm hongiað   hrínde bearwas,
1365 "wudu wyrtum fäst,   wäter oferhelmað.
"þær mäg nihta gehwäm   níð-wundor seón,
"fýr on flóde;   nó þäs fród leofað
"gumena bearna,   þät þone grund wite;
"þeáh þe hæð-stapa   hundum geswenced,
1370 "heorot hornum trum   holt-wudu séce,
"feorran geflýmed,   ær he feorh seleð,
"aldor on ófre,   ær he in wille,
"hafelan hýdan.   Nis þät heóru stǫw:
"þonon ýð-geblond   up ástígeð
1375 "wǫn tó wolcnum.   þonne wind styreð
"láð gewidru.   óð þät lyft drysmað,
"roderas reótað.   Nu is ræd gelang
"eft ät þe ánum!   Eard git ne const,
"frécne stówe.   þær þu findan miht
1380 "sinnigne secg: séc gif þu dyrre!
"Ic þe þá fæhðe   feó leánige,
"eald-gestreónum,   swá ic ær dyde,
"wundnum golde,   gyf þu on weg cymest."

XXII.

BEÓWULF SEEKS THE MONSTER IN THE HAUNTS OF THE NIXIES.

BEÓWULF maðelode, bearn Ecgþeówes:
1385 " Ne sorga, snotor guma! sêlre bið æghwäm,
 " þät he his freónd wrece, þonne he fela murne;
 " ûre æghwylc sceal ende gebîdan
 " worolde, lifes; ● wyrce se þe môte
 " dômes ær deáðe! þät bið driht-guman
1390 " unlifgendum äfter sêlest.
 " Âris, rîces weard; uton hraðe fêran,
 " Grendles mâgan gang sceáwigan!
 " Ic hit þe gehâtt: nô he on helm losað,
 " ne on foldan fäðm, ne on fyrgen-holt,
1395 " ne on gyfenes grund, gâ þær he wille.
 " Þys dôgor þu geþyld hafa
 " weána gehwylces, swâ ic þe wêne tô!"
 Âhleóp þâ se gomela, gode þancode,
 mihtigan drihtne, þäs se man gespräc.
1400 Þâ wäs Hrôðgâre hors gebæted,
 wicg wunden-feax. Wîsa fengel
 geatolic gengde; gum-fêða stôp
 lind-häbbendra. Lâstas wæron
 äfter wald-swaðum wîde gesŷne,
1405 gang ofer grundas; gegnum fôr þâ
 ofer myrcan môr, mago-þegna bär
 þone sêlestan sâwol-leásne,
 þâra þe mid Hrôðgâre hâm eahtode.
 Ofer-eode þâ äðelinga bearn
1410 steáp stân-hliðo, stîge nearwe,
 enge ân-paðas, un-cûð gelâd,
 neowle nässas, nicor-hûsa fela;
 he feára sum beforan gengde

wísra monna, wong sceáwian,
1415 ðð þät he færinga fyrgen-beámas
ofer hárne stán hleonian funde,
wyn-leásne wudu; wäter under stðd
dreórig and gedréfed. Denum eallum wäs,
winum Scyldinga, weorce on móde,
1420 tð geþolianne þegne monegum,
oncýð eorla gehwäm, syððan Äsc-heres
on þam holm-clife hafelan métton.
Flód blóde weól (fole tð sægon)
hátan heolfre. Horn stundum song
1425 fúslíc fyrd-leóð. Féða eal gesät;
gesáwon þá äfter wätere wyrm-cynnes fela,
sellíce sæ-dracan sund cunnian,
swylce on näs-hleoðum nicras liegean,
þá on undern-mæl oft bewitigað
1430 sorh-fulne síð on segl-ráde,
wyrmas and wil-deór; hie on weg hruron
bitere and gebolgne, bearhtm ongeáton,
gúð-horn galan. Sumne Geáta leód
of flán-bogan feores getwæfde,
1435 fð-gewinnes, þät him on aldre stðd
here-stræl hearda; he on holme wäs
sundes þe sænra, þe hyne swylt fornam.
Hräðe wearð on fðum mid cofer-spreótum
heoro-hócyhtum hearde genearwod,
1440 níða genæged and on näs togen
wunderlíc wæg-bora; weras sceáwedon
gryrelícne gist. Gyrede hine Beówulf
eorl-gewædum, nalles for ealdre mearn:
scolde here-byrne hondum gebroden,
1445 síd and searo-fáh, sund cunnian,
seó þe bán-cófan beorgan cúðe,
þät him hilde-gráp hreðre ne mihte,
eorres inwit-feng, aldre gesceððan;

ac se hwíta helm hafelan werede,
1450 se þe mere-grundas mengan scolde,
sécan sund-gebland since geweorðad,
befongen freá-wrásnum, swá hine fyrn-dagum
worhte wæpna smið, wundrum teóde,
besette swín-lícum, þät hine syððan nð
1455 brond ne beado-mécas bítan ne meahton.
Näs þät þonne mætost mägen-fultuma,
þät him on þearfe láh þyle Hróðgáres;
wäs þám häft-méce Hrunting nama,
þät wäs án foran eald-gestreóna;
1460 ecg wäs íren, áter-tánum fáh,
áhyrded heaðo-swáte; næfre hit ät hilde ne swác
manna ængum þára þe hit mid mundum bewand,
se þe gryre-síðas gegán dorste,
folc-stede fára; näs þät forma síð,
1465 þät hit ellen-weorc äfnan scolde.
Húru ne gemunde mago Ecgláfes
eafoðes cräftig, þät he ær gespräc
wíne druncen, þá he þäs wæpnes onláh
sélran sweord-frecan: selfa ne dorste
1470 under ýða gewin aldre genéðan,
driht-scype dreógan; þær he dóme forleás,
ellen-mærðum. Ne wäs þám öðrum swá,
syððan he hine tó gúðe gegyred häfde.

XXIII. The Battle with the Water-Drake.

Beówulf maðelode, bearn Ecgþeówes:
1475 "geþenc nu, se mæra maga Healfdenes,
"snottra fengel, nu ic eom síðes fús,
"gold-wine gumena, hwät wit geó spræcon,
"gif ic ät þearfe þínre scolde
"aldre linnan, þät þu me á wære

1480 " forð-gewitenum　　on fäder stäle;
　　" wes þu mund-bora mínum　　mago-þegnum,
　　" hond-gesellum,　　gif mec hild nime:
　　" swylce þu þá mádmas,　　þé þu me scaldest,
　　" Hróðgár leófa,　　Higeláce onsend.
1485 " Mäg þonne on þäm golde ongitan　　Geáta dryhten,
　　" geseón sunu Hréðles,　　þonne he on þät sinc starað,
　　" þät ic gum-cystum　　gódne funde
　　" beága bryttan,　　breác þonne móste.
　　" And þu Húnferð læt　　ealde láfe,
1490 " wrätlíc wæg-sweord　　wíd-cûðne man
　　" heard-ecg habban;　　ic me mid Hruntinge
　　" dóm gewyrce,　　oððe mec deáð nimeð."
　　Äfter þæm wordum　　Weder-Geáta leód
　　éfste mid elne,　　nalas andsware　　　-
1495 bídan wolde;　　brim-wylm onféng
　　hilde-rince.　　Þá wäs hwíl däges,
　　ær he þone grund-wong　　ongytan mehte.
　　Sóna þät onfunde,　　se þe flóda begong
　　heoro-gífre beheóld　　hund missera,
1500 grim and grædig.　　þät þær gumena sum
　　äl-wihta eard　　ufan cunnode.
　　Gráp þá tógeánes,　　gúð-rinc geféng
　　atolan clommum:　　nó þý ær in gescód
　　hálan líce:　　hring útan ymb-bearh,
1505 þät heó þone fyrd-hom　　þurh-fón ne mihte,
　　locene leoðo-syrcan　　láðan fingrum.
　　Bär þá seó brim-wylf,　　þá heó tó botme com,
　　hringa þengel　　tó hofe sínum,
　　swá he ne mihte nó　　(he þäs módig wäs)
1510 wæpna gewealdan,　　ac hine wundra þäs fela
　　swencte on sunde,　　sæ-deór monig
　　hilde-tuxum　　here-syrcan bräc.
　　éhton aglæcan.　　Þá se eorl ongeat,
　　þät he in nið-sele　　nát-hwylcum wäs,

1515 þær him nænig wäter   wihte ne sceðede,
ne him for hróf-sele   hrînan ne mehte
fær-gripe flôdes :   fŷr-leóht geseah,
blâcne leóman   beorhte scînan.
Ongeat þâ se gôda   grund-wyrgenne,
1520 mere-wîf mihtig ;   mägen-ræs forgeaf
hilde-bille,   hond swenge ne ofteáh,
þät hire on hafelan   hring-mæl âgôl
grædig gûð-leóð.   Þâ se gist onfand,
þät se beado-leóma   bîtan nolde,
1525 aldre sceððan,   ac seó ecg geswâc
þeódne ät þearfe :   þolode ær fela
hond-gemôta,   helm oft gescär,
fæges fyrd-hrägl :   þät wäs forma sîð
deórum mâðme,   þät his dôm âläg.
1530 Eft wäs án-ræd,   nalas elnes lät,
mærða gemyndig   mæg Hygelâces ;
wearp þâ wunden-mæl   wrättum gebunden
yrre oretta,   þät hit on eorðan läg,
stîð and stŷl-ecg ;   strenge getrûwode,
1535 mund-gripe mägenes.   Swâ sceal man dôn,
þonne he ät gûðe   gegân þenceð
longsumne lof,   nâ ymb his lîf cearað.
Geféng þâ be eaxle   (nalas for fæhðe mearn)
Gûð-Geáta leód   Grendles môdor ;
1540 brägd þâ beadwe heard,   þâ he gebolgen wäs,
feorh-genîðlan,   þät heó on flet gebeáh.
Heó him eft hraðe   and-leán forgeald
grimman grâpum   and him tôgeánes fêng ;
oferwearp þâ wêrig-môd   wîgena strengest,
1545 fêðe-cempa.   þät he on fylle wearð.
Ofsät þâ þone sele-gyst   and hyre seaxe geteáh,
brâd and brûn-ecg   wolde hire bearn wrecan,
ângan eaferan.   Him on eaxle läg
breóst-net broden ;   þät gebearh feore,

1550 wið ord and wið ecge   ingang forstód.
Häfde þá forstód   sunu Ecgþeówes
under gynne grund,   Geáta cempa,
nemne him heaðo-byrne   helpe gefremede,
here-net hearde,   and hálig god
1555 geweóld wíg-sigor.   witig drihten;
rodera rædend   hit on ryht gescéd,
ýðelice   syððan he eft ástód.

XXIV. BEÓWULF SLAYS THE SPRITE.

GESEAH þá on searwum   sige-eádig bil,
eald sweord eotenisc   ecgum þyhtig,
1560 wígena weorð-mynd: þät wäs wæpna cyst,
búton hit wäs máre   þonne ænig mon óðer
tó beadu-láce   ätberan meahte
gód and geatolic   giganta geweorc.
He geféng þá fetel-hilt,   freca Scildinga,
1565 breóh and heoro-grim   hring-mæl gebrägd,
aldres orwéna,   yrringa slóh,
þät hire wið halse   heard grápode,
bán-hringas bräc,   bil eal þurh-wód
fægne flæsc-homan,   heó on flet gecrong;
1570 sweord wäs swátig,   secg weorce gefeh.
Lixte se leóma,   leóht inne stód,
efne swá of hefene   hádre scíneð
rodores candel.   He äfter recede wlát,
hwearf þá be wealle,   wæpen hafenade
1575 heard be hiltum   Higeláces þegn,
yrre and án-ræd.   Näs seó ecg fracod
hilde-rince,   ac he braðe wolde
Grendle forgyldan   gúð-ræsa fela
þára þe he geworhte   tó West-Denum

1580 oftor micle ꝥonne on ænne sîð,
ꝥonne he Hróðgáres heorð-geneátas
slôh on sweofote, slæpende frät
folces Denigea fŷf-tyne men
and ôðer swyle ût of-ferede,
1585 lâðlîcu lâc. He him ꝥäs leán forgeald,
rêðe cempa, tô ꝥäs ꝥe he on räste geseah
gûð-wêrigne Grendel liegan,
aldor-leásne, swâ him ær gescôd
hild ät Heorote; hrâ wîde sprong,
1590 syððan he äfter deáðe drepe ꝥrowade,
heoro-sweng heardne, and hine ꝥâ heáfde becearf.
Sôna ꝥät gesâwon snottre ceorlas,
ꝥá ꝥe mid Hróðgâre on holm wliton,
ꝥät wäs ŷð-geblond eal gemenged,
1595 brim blôde fâh: blonden-feaxe
gomele ymb gôdne ongeador spræcon,
ꝥät hig ꝥäs äðelinges eft ne wêndon,
ꝥät he sige-hrêðig sêcean côme
mærne ꝥeóden; ꝥâ ꝥäs monige gewearð,
1600 ꝥät hine seó brim-wylf âbroten häfde.
ꝥâ com nôn däges. Näs ofgeâfon
hwate Scyldingas; gewât him hâm ꝥonon
gold-wine gumena. Gistas sêtan,
môdes seóce, and on mere staredon,
1605 wiston and ne wêndon, ꝥät hie heora wine-drihten
selfne gesâwon. ꝥâ ꝥät sweord ongan
äfter heaðo-swâte hilde-gicelum
wig-bil wanian; ꝥät wäs wundra sum,
ꝥät hit eal gemealt îse gelîcost,
1610 ꝥonne forstes bend fäder onlæteð,
onwindeð wäl-râpas, se ꝥe geweald hafað
säla and mæla; ꝥät is sôð metod.
Ne nom he in ꝥæm wîcum, Weder-Geáta leód,
mâðm-æhta mâ, ꝥêh he ꝥær monige geseah,

1615 búton þone hafelan and þá hilt somod,
since fáge; sweord ær gemealt,
forbarn broden mæl: wäs þät blód tó þäs hát,
ættren ellor-gæst. se þær inne swealt.
Sóna wäs on sunde, se þe ær ät sæcce gebád
1620 wíg-hryre wráðra, wäter up þurh-deáf;
wæron fð-gebland eal gefælsod,
eácne eardas. þá se ellor-gást
oflét líf-dagas and þás lænan gesceaft.
Com þá tó lande lid-manna helm
1625 swíð-móð swymman, sæ-láce gefeah,
mägen-byrðenne þára þe he him mid häfde.
Eodon him þá tógeánes, gode þancodon,
þrýðlic þegna heáp. þeódnes gefégon,
þäs þe hi hyne gesundne gescón móston.
1630 þá wäs of þäm hróran helm and byrne
lungre álýsed: lagu drusade,
wäter under wolcnum, wäl-dreóre fág.
Férdon forð þonon féðe-lástum
ferhðum fägne, fold-weg mæton,
1635 cúðe stræte; cyning-balde men
from þäm holm-clife hafelan bæron
earfoðlíce heora æghwäðrum
fela-módigra: feówer scoldon
on ðäm wäl-stenge weorcum geferian
1640 tó þäm gold-sele Grendles heáfod,
óð þät semninga tó sele cómon
frome fyrd-hwate feówer-tyne
Geáta gongan; gum-dryhten mid
módig on gemonge meodo-wongas träd.
1645 þá com in gán ealdor þegna,
dæd-céne mon dóme gewurðad,
häle hilde-deór, Hróðgár grétan:
þá wäs be feaxe on flet boren
Grendles heáfod, þær guman druncon,

1650 egeslíc for eorlum   and þære idese mid:
     wlite-seón wrätlíc   weras onsâwon.

XXV. Hroþgar's Gratitude: He Discourses.

Beówulf maðelode,   bearn Ecgþeówes:
"Hwät! we þe þás sæ-lác,   sunu Healfdenes,
"leód Scyldinga,   lustum bróhton,
1655 "tíres tó tâcne,   þe þu her tó lócast.
"Ic þät unsôfte   ealdre gedígde:
"wíge under wätere   weorc geneðde
"earfoðlíce,   ät-rihte wäs
"gúð getwæfed,   nymðe mec god scylde.
1660 "Ne meahte ic ät hilde   mid Hruntinge
"wiht gewyrcan,   þeáh þät wæpen duge,
"ac me geúðe   ylda waldend,
"þät ic on wage geseah   wlitig hangian
"eald sweord eácen   (oftost wísode
1665 "winigea leásum)   þät ic þý wæpne gebräd.
"Ofslôh þá ät þære sæcce   (þâ me sæl âgeald)
"húses hyrdas.   Þá þät hilde-bil
"forbarn, brogden mæl,   swâ þät blôd gesprang,
"hâtost heaðo-swâta: ic þät hilt þanan
1670 "feóndum ätferede;   fyren-dæda wräc,
"deáð-cwealm Denigea,   swâ hit gedêfe wäs.
"Ic hit þe þonne gehâte,   þät þu on Heorote môst
"sorh-leás swefan   mid þínra secga gedryht,
"and þegna gehwylc   þínra leóda,
1675 "duguðe and iogoðe,   þät þu him ondrædan ne þearft,
"þeóden Scyldinga,   on þá healfe,
"aldor-bealu eorlum,   swâ þu ær dydest."
     Þâ wäs gylden hilt   gamelum rince,
     hârum hild-froman,   on hand gyfen,
1680 enta ær-geweorc,   hit on æht gehwearf

æfter deófla hryre   Denigea freán,
wundor-smiða geweore,   and þá þás worold ofgeaf
grom-heort guma,   godes andsaca.
morðres scyldig.   and his módor eác;
1685 on geweald gehwearf   worold-cyninga
þám sélestan   be sæm tweónum
þára þe on Sceden-igge   sceattas dælde.
Hróðgár maðelode.   hylt sceáwode,
ealde láfe.   on þám wäs ór writen
1690 fyrn-gewinnes :   syððan flód ofslóh,
gifen geótende,   giganta cyn,
frécne geférdon :   þät wäs fremde þeód
écean dryhtne,   him þäs ende-leán
þurh wäteres wylm   waldend scalde.
1695 Swá wäs on þæm scennum   scíran goldes
þurh rún-stafas   rihte gemearcod,
geseted and gesæd.   hwam þät sweord geworht,
írena cyst   ærest wære.
wreoðen-hilt and wyrm-fáh.   þá se wísa spräc
1700 sunu Healfdenes   (swigedon ealle) :
" þät lá mäg secgan,   se þe sóð and riht
" fremeð on folce.   (feor eal gemon
" eald éðel-weard),   þät þes eorl wære
" geboren betera !   Blæd is áræred
1705 " geond wíd-wegas,   wine mín Beówulf.
" þín ofer þeóda gehwylce.   Eal þu hit geþyldum healdest,
" mägen mid módes snyttrum.   Ic þe sceal mine gelæstan
" freóde, swá wit furðum spræcon ;   þu scealt tó frófre
weorðan
" eal lang-twidig   leódum þínum,
1710 " häleðum tó helpe.   Ne wearð Heremód swá
" eaforum Ecgwelan.   Ár-Scyldingum :
" ne geweóx he him tó willan.   ac tó wäl-fealle
" and tó deáð-cwalum   Deniga leódum ;
" breát bolgen-mód   beód-geneátas,

1715 " eaxl-gesteallan,   Ôð þät he âna hwearf,
 " mære þeóden.   mon-dreámum from :
 " þeáh þe hine mihtig god   mägenes wynnum,
 " eafeðum stépte,   ofer ealle men
 " forð gefremede,   hwäðere him on ferhðe greów
1720 " breóst-hord blôd-reów :   nallas beágas geaf
 " Denum äfter dôme ;   dreám-leás gebâd,
 " þät he þäs gewinnes   weorc þrowade,
 " leód-bealo longsum.   Þu þe lær be þon,
 " gum-cyste ongit !   ic þis gid be þe
1725 " âwräc wintrum frôd.   Wundor is tô secganne,
 " hû mihtig god   manna cynne
 " þurh sîdne sefan   snyttru bryttað,
 " eard and eorl-scipe,   he âh ealra geweald.
 " Hwîlum he on lufan   læteð hworfan
1730 " monnes môd-geþonc   mæran cynnes,
 " seleð him on êðle   eorðan wynne,
 " tô healdanne   hleó-burh wera,
 " gedêð him swâ gewealdene   worolde dælas,
 " sîde rîce,   þät he his selfa ne mäg
1735 " for his un-snyttrum   ende geþencean ;
 " wunað he on wiste,   nô hine wiht dweleð,
 " âdl ne yldo,   ne him inwit-sorh
 " on sefan sweorceð,   ne gesacu ôhwær,
 " ecg-hete eóweð,   ac him eal worold
1740 " wendeð on willan ;   he þät wyrse ne con,
 " ôð þät him on innan   ofer-hygda dæl
 " weaxeð and wridað,   þonne se weard swefeð,
 " sâwele hyrde :   bið se slæp tô fäst,
 " bisgum gebunden,   bona swîðe neáh,
1745 " se þe of flân-bogan   fyrenum sceóteð.

XXVI.

The Discourse is Ended. — Beówulf Prepares to Leave.

"Þonne biÐ on hreÐre　　under helm drepen
"biteran sträle :　　him bebeorgan ne con
"wom wundor-bebodum　　wergan gástes ;
"þinceÐ him tó lytel,　　þät he tó lange heóld,
1750 "gýtsaÐ grom-hydig,　　nallas on gylp seleÐ
"fätte beágas　　and he þá forÐ-gesceaft
"forgyteÐ and forgýmeÐ,　　þäs þe him ær god sealde,
"wuldres waldend,　　weorÐ-mynda däl.
"Hit on ende-stäf　　eft gelimpeÐ,
1755 "þät se líc-homa　　læne gedreóseÐ,
"fæge gefealleÐ ;　　fëhÐ óÐer tó,
"se þe unmurnlíce　　máÐmas däleÐ,
"eorles ær-gestreón,　　egesan ne gýmeÐ.
"Bebeorh þe þone bealo-niÐ,　　Beówulf leófa,
1760 "secg se betsta,　　and þe þät sélre geceós,
"éce rædas ;　　oferhyda ne gým.
"mære cempa !　　Nu is þines mägnes blæd
"áne hwíle ;　　eft sóna biÐ,
"þät þec ádl óÐÐe ecg　　eafoÐes getwæfeÐ,
1765 "óÐÐe fýres feng　　óÐÐe flódes wylm,
"óÐÐe gripe méces　　óÐÐe gáres fliht,
"óÐÐe atol yldo,　　óÐÐe eágena bearhtm
"forsiteÐ and forsworceÐ　　semninga biÐ,
"þät þec, dryht-guma,　　deáÐ oferswýÐeÐ.
1770 "Swá ic Hring-Dena　　hund missera
"weóld under wolcnum,　　and hig wíge beleác
"manigum mægÐa　　geond þysne middan-geard,
"äscum and ecgum,　　þät ic me ænigne
"under swegles begong　　gesacan ne tealde.

1775 "Hwät! me þäs on éðle edwenden cwom,
"gyrn äfter gomene, sceoððan Grendel wearð,
"eald-gewinna, in-genga mîn :
"ic þære sôcne singales wäg
"môd-ceare micle. Þäs sig metode þanc,
1780 "écean drihtne, þäs þe ic on aldre gebâd,
"þät ic on þone hafelan heoro-dreórigne
"ofer eald gewin eágum starige!
"Gâ nu tô setle, symbel-wynne dreóh
"wîg-geweorðad : unc sceal worn fela
1785 "máðma gemænra, siððan morgen bið."
Geát wäs gläd-môd, geóng sôna tô,
setles neósan, swâ se snottra hêht.
Þâ wäs eft swâ ær ellen-rôfum,
flet-sittendum fägere gereorded
1790 niówan stefne. Niht-helm gesweare
deorc ofer dryht-gumum. Duguð eal ârâs ;
wolde blonden-feax beddes neósan,
gamela Scylding. Geát ungemetes wel,
rôfne rand-wîgan restan lyste :
1795 sôna him sele-þegn sîðes wérgum,
feorran-cundum forð wîsade,
se for andrysnum ealle beweotede
þegnes þearfe, swylce þý dôgore
heáðo-liðende habban scoldon.
1800 Reste hine þâ rûm-heort ; reced hlifade
geáp and gold-fâh, gäst inne swäf,
ôð þät hräfn blaca heofones wynne
blîð-heort bodode. Þâ com beorht *sunne*
scacan *ofer grundas;* scaðan onetton,
1805 wæron äðelingas eft tô leódum
fûse tô farenne, wolde feor þanon
cuma collen-ferhð ceóles neósan.
Hêht þâ se hearda Hrunting beran,
sunu Ecglâfes, hêht his sweord niman,

1810 leóflic íren;   sägde him þäs leánes þanc,
cwäð he þone gúð-wine   gódne tealde,
wíg-cräftigne,   nales wordum lóg
méces ecge: þät wäs módig secg.
And þá síð-frome   searwum gearwe
1815 wígend wæron,   eode weorð Denum
äðeling tó yppan,   þær se óðer wäs
häle hilde-deór,   Hróðgár grétte.

XXVII. The Parting Words.

Beówulf maðelode,   bearn Ecgþeówes:
" Nu we sæ-líðend   secgan wyllað
1820 " feorran cumene,   þät we fundiað
" Higeláce sécan.   Wæron her tela
" willum bewenede;   þu ús wel dohtest.
" Gif ic þonne on eorðan   ówihte mäg
" þínre mód-lufan   máran tilian,
1825 " gumena dryhten,   þonne ic gyt dyde,
" gúð-geweorca   ic beó gearo sóna.
" Gif ic þät gefricge   ofer flóda begang,
" þät þec ymbe-sittend   egesan þywað,
" swá þec hetende   hwílum dydon.
1830 " ic þe þúsenda   þegna bringe.
" häleða tó helpe.   Ic on Higeláce wát,
" Geáta dryhten,   þeáh þe he geong sý,
" folces hyrde,   þät he mec fremman wile
" wordum and worcum,   þät ic þe wel herige,
1835 " and þe tó geóce   gár-holt bere
" mägenes fultum,   þær þe bið manna þearf;
" gif him þonne Hréðríc   tó hofum Geáta
" geþingeð, þeódnes bearn,   he mäg þær fela
" freónda findan: feor eýðe beóð
1840 " <u>sélran</u> gesóhte   þám þe him selfa deáh."

Hróðgár maðelode   him on andsware:

"Þe þá word-cwydas   wittig drihten

"on sefan sende!   ne hýrde ic snotorlícor

"on swá geongum feore   guman þingian:

1845 "þu eart mägenes strang   and on móde fród,

"wís word-cwida.   Wén ic talige,

"gif þät gegangeð,   þät þe gár nymeð,

"hild heoru-grimme   Hréðles eaferan,

"ádl oððe íren   ealdor þínne,

1850 "folces hyrde,   and þu þín feorh hafast,

"þät þe Sæ-Geátas   sélran näbben

"tó geceósenne   cyning ænigne,

"hord-weard häleða,   gif þu healdan wylt

"mága ríce.   Me þín mód-sefa

1855 "lícað leng swá wel,   leófa Beówulf:

"hafast þu gefered,   þät þám folcum sceal,

"Geáta leódum   and Gár-Denum

"sib gemænum   and sacu restan,

"inwit-níðas,   þe hie ær drugon;

1860 "wesan, þenden ic wealde   wídan ríces,

"máðmas gemæne,   manig óðerne

"gódum gegrétan   ofer ganotes bäð;

"sceal hring-naca   ofer heáðu bringan

"lác and luf-tácen.   Ic þá leóde wát

1865 "ge wið feónd ge wið freónd   fäste geworhte,

"æghwäs untæle   ealde wísan."

Þá git him eorla hleó   inne gesealde,

mago Healfdenes   máðmas twelfe,

hét hine mid þæm lácum   leóde swæse

1870 sécean on gesyntum,   snúde eft cuman.

Gecyste þá   cyning äðelum gód,

þeóden Scildinga   þegen betstan

and be healse genam;   hruron him teáras,

blonden-feaxum: him wäs bega wén,

1875 ealdum infródum,   óðres swíðor,

þät hí sceóððan   gescón móston
módige on meðle.   Wäs him se man tó þon leóf,
þät he þone breóst-wylm   forberan ne mehte,
ac him on hreðre   hyge-bendum fäst
1880 äfter deórum men   dyrne langað
beorn wið blóde.   Him Beówulf þanan,
gúð-rinc gold-wlanc   gräs-moldan träd,
since hrémig: sæ-genga bád
ágend-freán,   se þe on ancre rád.
1885 þá wäs on gange   gifu Hróðgáres
oft geæhted: þät wäs án cyning
æghwäs orleahtre,   óð þät hine yldo benam
mägenes wynnum,   se þe oft manegum scód.

XXVIII.

BEÓWULF RETURNS TO GEATLAND.—THE QUEENS HYGD AND THRYTHO.

Cwom þá tó flóde   fela-módigra
1890 häg-stealdra heáp;   hring-net bæron,
locene leoðo-syrcan.   Land-weard onfand
eft-síð eorla,   swá he ær dyde;
nó he mid hearme   of hlíðes nosan
gästas grétte,   ac him tógeánes rád;
1895 cwäð þät wilcuman   Wedera leódum
scawan scír-hame   tó scipe fóron.
þá wäs on sande   sæ-geáp naca
bladen here-wædum,   hringed-stefna
mearum and máðmum: mäst hlifade
1900 ofer Hróðgáres   hord-gestreónum.
He þäm bát-wearde   bunden golde
swurd gescealde,   þät he syððan wäs
on meodu-bence   máðme þý weorðra,

yrfe-láfe   Gewât him on ýð-nacan,
1905 dréfan deóp wäter,   Dena land ofgeaf.
Þâ wäs be mäste   mere hrägla sum,
segl sâle fäst.   Sund-wudu þunede,
nó þær wêg-flotan   wind ofer ýðum
sîðes getwæfde ;   sæ-genga fôr,
1910 fleát fámig-heals   forð ofer ýðe,
bunden-stefna   ofer brim-streámas,
þät hie Geáta clifu   ongitan meahton,
cûðe nässas.   Ceól up geþrang,
lyft-geswenced   on lande stôd.
1915 Hraðe wäs ät holme   hýð-weard gearo,
se þe ær lange tîd,   leófra manna
fûs, ät faroðe   feor wlâtode ;
sælde tô sande   sîd-fäðme scip
oncer bendum fäst,   þý läs hym ýða þrym
1920 wudu wynsuman   forwrecan meahte.
Hêt þâ up beran   äðelinga gestreón,
frätwe and fät-gold ;   näs him feor þanon
tô gesêcanne   sinces bryttan :
Higelác Hrêðling   þær ät hâm wunað,
1925 selfa mid gesîðum   sæ-wealle neáh ;
bold wäs betlic,   brego-rôf cyning,
heá on healle,   Hygd swîðe geong,
wîs, wel-þungen,   þeáh þe wintra lyt
under burh-locan   gebiden häbbe
1930 Häreðes dôhtor :   näs hió hnâh swâ þeáh,
ne tô gneáð gifa   Geáta leódum,
mâðm-gestreóna.   Môd Þryðo wäg,
fremu folces cwên,   firen ondrysne :
nænig þät dorste   deór genêðan
1935 swæsra gesîða,   nefne sin-freá,
þät hire an däges   eágum starede ;
ac him wäl-bende   weotode tealde,
hand-gewriðene :   hraðe seoððan wäs

äfter mund-gripe méce geþinged,
1940 þät hit sceaðen-mæl scyran móste,
cwealm-bealu cýðan. Ne bið swylc cwénlíc þeáw
idese tó efnanne, þeáh þe hió ænlícu sý,
þätte freoðu-webbe feores onsäce
äfter lige-torne leófne mannan.
1945 Hůru þät onhóhsnode Heminges mæg;
ealo drincende óðer sædan,
þät hió leód-bealewa läs gefremede,
inwit-níða, syððan ærest wearð
gyfen gold-hroden geongum cempan,
1950 äðelum dióre. syððan hió Offan flet
ofer fealone flód be fäder láre
stóc gesóhte, þær hió syððan wel
in gum-stóle, góde mære,
líf-gesceafta lifigende breác,
1955 hióld heáh-lufan wið häleða brego,
ealles mon-cynnes míne gefræge
þone sélestan bí sæm tweónum
eormen-cynnes; forþam Offa wäs
geofum and gúðum gár-céne man,
1960 wíde geweorðod; wísdóme heóld
éðel sínne, þonon Eómær wóc
häleðum tó helpe, Heminges mæg,
nefa Gármundes, níða cräftig.

XXIX. His Arrival. Hygelac's Reception.

Gewát him þá se hearda mid his hond-scole
1965 sylf äfter sande sæ-wong tredan,
wíde waroðas. Woruld-candel scán,
sigel súðan fús: hí síð drugon,
elne gecodon, tó þäs þe eorla hleó,

      bonan Ongenþeówes   burgum on innan,
1970 geongne gûð-cyning   gôdne gefrunon
      hringas dœlan.   Higelâce wäs
      sîð Beówulfes   snûde gecŷðed,
      þät þær on worðig   wîgendra hleó,
      lind-gestealla   lifigende cwom,
1975 heaðo-lâces hâl   tô hofe gongan.
      Hraðe wäs gerŷmed,   swâ se rîca bebeád,
      fêðe-gestum   flet innan-weard.
      Gesät þâ wið sylfne,   se þâ säcce genäs,
      mæg wið mæge,   syððan man-dryhten
1980 þurh hleóðor-cwyde   holdne gegrêtte
      meaglum wordum.   Meodu-scencum
      hwearf geond þät reced   Häreðes dôhtor:
      lufode þâ leóde,   lið-wæge bär
      hælum tô handa.   Higelâc ongan
1985 sînne geseldan   in sele þam heán
      fägre friegean,   hyne fyrwet bräc,
      hwylce Sæ-Geáta   sîðas wæron:
      "Hû lomp eów on lâde,   leófa Biówulf,
      "þâ þu færinga   feorr gehogodest,
1990 "säcce sêcean   ofer sealt wäter,
      "hilde tô Hiorote?   Ac þu Hrôðgâre
      "wîd-cûðne weán   wihte gebêttest,
      "mærum þeódne?   Ic þäs môd-ceare
      "sorh-wylmum seáð,   sîðe ne trûwode
1995 "leófes mannes;   ic þe lange bäd,
      "þät þu þone wäl-gæst   wihte ne grêtte,
      "lête Sûð-Dene   sylfe geweorðan
      "gûðe wið Grendel.   Gode ic þanc secge,
      "þäs þe ic þe gesundne   geseón môste."
2000 Biówulf maðelode,   bearn Ecgþiówes:
      "Þät is undyrne,   dryhten Higelâc,
      "*mære* gemêting   monegum fira,
      "hwylc *orleg*-hwîl   uncer Grendles

"wearð on þam wange,　　þær he worna fela
2005 "Sige-Scildingum　　sorge gefremede,
"yrmðe tó aldre;　　ic þät eal gewräc,
"swá ne gylpan þearf　　Grendeles maga
"ænig ofer corðan　　uht-hlem þone,
"se þe lengest leofað　　láðan cynnes,
2010 "fenne bifongen.　　Ic þær furðum cwom,
"tó þam hring-sele　　Hróðgár grétan:
"sóna me se mæra　　mago Healfdenes,
"syððan he mód-sefan　　mínne cúðe,
"wið his sylfes sunu　　setl getæhte.
2015 "Weorod wäs on wynne;　　ne seah ic wídan feorh
"under heofenes hwealf　　heal-sittendra
"medu-dreám máran.　　Hwílum mæru cwén.
"friðu-sibb folca　　flet eall geond-hwearf,
"bædde byre geonge;　　oft hió beáh-wriðan
2020 "secge sealde.　　ær hió tó setle geóng.
"Hwílum for duguðe　　dóhtor Hróðgáres
"eorlum on ende　　ealu-wæge bär,
"þá ic Freáware　　flet-sittende
"nemnan hýrde,　　þær hió nägled sinc
2025 "häleðum sealde:　　sió geháten wäs,
"geong gold-hroden,　　gladum suna Fródan;
"hafað þäs geworden　　wine Scyldinga
"ríces hyrde　　and þät ræd talað,
"þät he mid þý wífe　　wäl-fæhða dæl,
2030 "säcca gesette.　　Oft nó seldan hwær
"äfter leód-hryre　　lytle hwíle
"bon-gár búgeð,　　þeáh seó brýd duge!

XXX. Beówulf's Story of the Slayings.

"Mæg þäs þonne ofþyncan   þeóden Headobeardna
"and þegna gehwam   þâra leóda,
2035 "þonne he mid fæmnan   on flett gæð,
"dryht-bearn Dena   duguða biwenede:
"on him gladiað   gomelra lâfe
"heard and hring-mæl,   Headobeardna gestreón,
"þenden hie þâm wæpnum   wealdan môston,
2040 "ð þät hie forlæddan   tô þam lind-plegan
"swæse gesîðas   ond hyra sylfra feorh.
"Þonne cwið ät beóre,   se þe beáh gesyhð,
"eald äsc-wiga,   se þe eall geman
"gâr-cwealm gumena   (him bið grim sefa),
2045 "onginneð geómor-môd   geongne cempan
"þurh hreðra gehygd   higes cunnian,
"wîg-bealu weccean   and þät word âcwyð:
"'Meaht þu, mîn wine,   mêce gecnâwan,
"'þone þin fäder   tô gefeohte bär
2050 "'under here-grîman   hindeman sîðe,
"'dŷre îren.   þær hyne Dene slôgon,
"'weóldon wäl-stôwe   (syððan wiðer-gyld läg
"'äfter häleða hryre)   hwate Scyldungas?
"'Nu her þâra banena   byre nât-hwylces,
2055 "'frätwum hrêmig   on flet gæð,
"'morðres gylpeð   and þone mâððum byreð,
"'þone þe þu mid rihte   rædan sceoldest!'"
"Manað swâ and myndgað   mæla gehwylce
"sârum wordum,   ð þät sæl cymeð,
2060 "þät se fæmnan þegn   fore fäder dædum
"äfter billes bite   blôd-fâg swefeð,
"ealdres scyldig;   him se ôðer þonan
"losað lifigende,   con him land geare.

" Þonne biðð brocene   on bá healfe
2065 " Að-sweord eorla ;   syððan Ingelde
" weallað wäl-nîðas   and him wíf-lufan
" äfter cear-wälmum   côlran weorðað.
" Þý ic Heaðobeardna   hyldo ne telge,
" dryht-sibbe dæl   Denum unfæcne,
2070 " freónd-scipe fästne.   Ic sceal forð sprecan
" gen ymbe Grendel.   þät þu geare cunne,
" sinces brytta.   tô hwan syððan wearð
" hond-ræs häleða.   Syððan heofones gim
" glâd ofer grundas,   gäst yrre cwom,
2075 " eatol æfen-grom.   ûser neósan,
" þær we gesunde   säl weardodon ;
" þær wäs Hondsció   hild onsæge,
" feorh-bealu fægum,   he fyrmest läg,
" gyrded cempa ;   him Grendel wearð,
2080 " mærum magu-þegne   tô mûð-bonan,
" leófes mannes   líc eall forswealg.
" Nô þý ær ût þá gen   ídel-hende
" bona blôdig-tôð   bealewa gemyndig,
" of þam gold-sele   gongan wolde,
2085 " ac he mägnes rôf   mín costode,
" grâpode gearo-folm.   Glôf hangode
" síd and syllíc   searo-bendum fäst,
" sió wäs orþoncum   eall gegyrwed
" deófles cräftum   and dracan fellum :
2090 " he mec þær on innan   unsynnigne,
" diór dæd-fruma,   gedôn wolde,
,   " manigra sumne :   hyt ne mihte swâ,
" syððan ic on yrre   upp-riht âstôd.
" Tô lang ys tô reccenne.   hû ic þam leód-sceaðan
2095 " yfla gehwylces   ond-leán forgeald ;
" þær ic. þeóden mín,   þíne leóde
" weorðode weorcum.   He on weg losade,
" lytle hwíle   líf-wynna breác ;

" hwäðre him sió swîðre swaðe weardade
2100 " hand on Hiorte and he heán þonan.
" môdes geômor mere-grund gefeóll.
" Me þone wäl-ræs wine Scildunga
" fättan golde fela leánode,
" manegum máðmum. syððan mergen com
2105 " and we tô symble geseten häfdon.
" þær wäs gidd and gleó; gomela Scilding
" fela friegende feorran rehte;
" hwilum hilde-deór hearpan wynne,
" gomen-wudu grêite; hwilum gyd âwräc
2110 " sôð and sârlic; hwilum syllîc spell
" rehte äfter rihte rûm-heort cyning.
" Hwilum eft ongan eldo gebunden,
" gomel gûð-wîga gioguðe cwîðan
" hilde-strengo; hreðer inne weóll,
2115 " þonne he wintrum frôd worn gemunde.
" Swâ we þær inne andlangne däg
" nióde nâman, ôð þät niht becwom
" ôðer tô yldum. þâ wäs eft hraðe
" gearo gyrn-wräce Grendeles môdor,
2120 " sîðode sorh-full; sunu deáð fornam,
" wîg-hete Wedra. Wif unhŷre
" hyre bearn gewräc, beorn âcwealde
" ellenlîce; þær wäs Äsc-here,
" frôdan fyrn-witan, feorh ûðgenge;
2125 " nôðer hy hine ne môston. syððan mergen cwom,
" deáð-wérigne Denia leóde
" bronde forbärnan, ne on bäl hladan
" leófne mannan: hió þät lîc ätbär
" feóndes fäðmum under firgen-streám.
2130 " þät wäs Hrôðgâre hreówa tornost
" þâra þe leód-fruman lange begeâte;
" þâ se þeóden mec þîne lŷfe
" healsode hreóh-môd, þät ic on holma geþring

       " eorl-scipe efnde,   ealdre genéðde,
2135 " mærðo fremede :   he me méde gehét.
       " Ic já þäs wälmes,   je is wíde cúð,
       " grimne gryrelícne   grund-hyrde fond,
       " þær unc hwíle wäs   hand gemæne :
       " holm heolfre weóll   and ic heáfde becearf
2140 " in þam grund-sele   Grendeles módor
       " eácnum ecgum,   unsófte þonan
       " feorh ððferede ;   näs ic fæge þá gyt,
       " ac me eorla hleó   eft gesealde
       " máðma menigeo,   maga Healfdenes.

                    XXXI.

   HE GIVES PRESENTS TO HYGELAC. HYGELAC
   REWARDS HIM. HYGELAC'S DEATH.
              BEÓWULF REIGNS.

2145 " Swá se þeód-kyning   þeáwum lyfde ;
       " nealles ic þám leánum   forloren häfde,
       " mägnes méde, ac he me máðmas geaf,
       " sunu Healfdenes,   on sínne sylfes dóm ;
       " þá ic þe, beorn-cyning,   bringan wylle,
2150 " éstum geýwan.   Gen is eall ät þe
       " lissa gelong :   ic lyt hafo
       " heáfod-mága,   nefne Hygelác þec !"
       Hét já in beran   eafor, heáfod-segn,
       heaðo-steápne helm,   háre byrnan,
2155 gúð-sweord geatolíc,   gyd äfter wräc :
       " Me þis hilde-sceorp   Hróðgár sealde,
       " snotra fengel,   sume worde hét,
       " þät ic his ærest   þe eft gesägde,
       " cwäð þät hyt häfde   Hiorogár cyning,
2160 " leód Scyldunga   lange hwíle :

"nô] ꝥ ær suna sínum   syllan wolde,
"hwatum Heorowearde.   þeáh he him hold wære,
"breóst-gewædu.   Brûc ealles well!"
Hŷrde ic ꝥät þâm frätwum   feówer mearas
2165 lungre gelíce   lâst weardode,
äppel-fealuwe;   he him ôst geteáh
meara and mâðma.   Swâ sceal mæg dôn,
nealles inwit-net   ôðrum bregdan,
dyrnum cräfte   deáð rénian
2170 hond-gesteallan.   Hygelâce wäs,
níða heardum,   nefa swŷðe hold
and gehwäðer ôðrum   hróðra gemyndig.
Hŷrde ic ꝥät he þone heals-beáh   Hygde gesealde,
wrätlícne wundur-mâððum,   þone þe him Wealhþeó geaf,
2175 þeódnes dôhtor,   þrió wicg somod
swancor and sadol-beorht;   hyre syððan wäs
äfter beáh-þege   breóst geweorðod.
Swâ bealdode   bearn Ecgþeówes,
guma gûðum cûð,   gôdum dædum,
2180 dreáh äfter dôme,   nealles drunene slôg
heorð-geneátas;   näs him hreóh sefa,
ac he man-cynnes   mæste cräfte
gin-fästan gife,   þe him god sealde,
heóld hilde-deór.   Heán wäs lange,
2185 swâ hyne Geáta bearn   gôdne ne tealdon,
ne hyne on medo-bence   micles wyrðne
drihten wereda   gedôn wolde;
swŷðe oft sägdon,   ꝥät he sleac wære,
äðeling unfrom: edwenden cwom
2190 tîr-eádigum menn   torna gehwylces.
Hêt þâ eorla hleó   in gefetian,
heaðo-rôf cyning,   Hrêðles láfe,
golde gegyrede;   näs mid Geátum þâ
sine-mâððum sêlra   on sweordes hâd;
2195 þät he on Biówulfes   bearn âlegde,

and him geſealde　　ſeofan þúſendo,
bold and brego-ſtôl.　　Him wäs bâm ſamod
on þam leód-ſcipe　　lond gecynde,
eard éðel-riht.　　Ôðrum ſwíðor
2200 ſíde ríce.　　þam þær ſélra wäs.
Eft þät geiode　　ufaran dôgrum
hilde-hlämmum,　　ſyððan Hygelâc läg
and Heardréde　　hilde-méeeas
under bord-hreóðan　　tô bonan wurdon,
2205 þâ hyne geſôhtan　　on ſige-þeóde
hearde hilde-frecan,　　Heaðo-Scilfingas,
níða genægdan　　nefan Hereríces.
Syððan Beówulfe　　bráde ríce
on hand gehwearf:　　he geheóld tela
2210 fíftig wintru　　(wäs þâ frôd cyning,
eald éðel-weard).　　Ôð þät ân ongan
deorcum nihtum　　draca ríesian,
ſe þe on heáre hæðe　　hord beweotode,
ſtân-beorh ſteápne:　　ſtíg under läg,
2215 eldum uncûð.　　þær on innan gióng
níða nât-hwylces　　neódu geſêng
hæðnum horde　　hond . d . . geþ . . hwylc
ſince fâhne,　　he þät ſyððan . . . . .
. . . þ . . . lð . þ . . l . g
2220 ſlæpende be fýre,　　fyrena hyrde
þeófes cräfte,　　þät ſie . . . . ðioð . . . . .
. idh . folc-beorn,　　þät he gebolgen wäs.

XXXII. The Fire-Drake. The Hoard.

Nealles mid geweoldum　　wyrm-horda . . . cräft
ſôhte ſylfes willan,　　ſe þe him ſâre geſceód,
2225 ac for þreá-nédlan　　þeów nât-hwylces
häleða bearna　　hete-ſwengeas fleáh,

*for ofer-*þearfe and þær inne fealh
secg syn-bysig. Sóna in þá tíde
þät . . . . . þam gyste . . . . br . g . stód,
2230 hwäðre earm-sceapen . . . .
. . ð . . . sceapen o . . . . i r . . e se fæs begeat,
sinc-fät *geseah:* þær wäs swylcra fela
in þam corð-*scräfe* ær-gestreóna,
swá hy on geár-dagum gumena nát-hwylc
2235 cormen-láfe äðelan cynnes
þanc-hycgende þær gehýdde,
deóre máðmas. Ealle hie deáð fornam
ærran mælum, and se án þá gen
leóda dugúðe, se þær lengest hwearf,
2240 weard wine-geómor wíscte þäs yldan,
þät he lytel fäc long-gestreóna
brúcan móste. Beorh eal gearo
wunode on wonge wäter-ýðum neáh,
niwe be nässe nearo-cräftum fäst:
2245 þær on innan bär eorl-gestreóna
hringa hyrde hard-fyrdne dæl
fättan goldes, feá worda cwäð:
"Heald þu nu hruse, nu häleð ne móston,
"eorla æhte. Hwät! hit ær on þe
2250 "góde begeáton; gúð-deáð fornam,
"feorh-bealo frécne fyra gehwylene,
"leóda mínra, þára þe þis *líf* ofgeaf,
"gesáwon sele-dreám. Náh hwá sweord wege
"oððe *fetige* fäted wæge,
2255 "drync-fät deóre: dugúð ellor scóc.
"Sceal se hearda helm *hyrsted* golde
"fätum befeallen: feormiend swefað,
"þá þe beado-gríman býwan sceoldon,
"ge swylce seó here-pád, sió ät hilde gebád
2260 "ofer borda gebräc bite írena,
"brosnað äfter beorne. Ne mäg byrnan hring

" äfter wíg-fruman   wíde féran
" háleðum be healfe ;   näs hearpan wyn,
" gomen gleó-beámes.   ne gód hafoc
2265 " geond säl swinged,   ne se swifta mearh
" burh-stede beáteð.   Bealo-cwealm hafað
" fela feorh-cynna   feorr onsended !"
Swá giómor-mód   giohðo mænde.
án äfter eallum   unbliðe hweóp.
2270 däges and nihtes,   oð þät deáðes wylm
hrán ät heortan.   Hord-wynne fond
eald uht-sceaða   opene standan,
se þe byrnende   biorgas séceð
nacod nið-draca,   nihtes fleógeð
2275 fýre befangen ;   hyne fold-búend
wíde gesáwon.   He gewunian sceall
hláw *under* brusan,   þær he hæðen gold
waráð wintrum fród ;   ne byð him wihte þé sél.
Swá se þeód-sceaða   preó hund wintra
2280 heóld on hrusan   hord-ärna sum
eácen-cräftig,   oð þät hyne án ábealh
mon on móde :   man-dryhtne bär
fäted wæge,   frioðo-wære bäd
hláford sinne.   þá wäs hord rásod.
2285 onboren beága hord.   béne gettðad
feá-sceaftum men.   Freá sceáwode
fira fyrn-geweorc   forman síðe.
þá se wyrm onwóc,   wróht wäs geniwad ;
stonc þá äfter stáne,   stearc-heort onfand
2290 feóndes fót-lást :   he tó forð gestóp,
dyrnan cräfte,   dracan heáfde neáh.
Swá mäg unfæge   eáðe gedigan
weán and wräc-síð,   se þe waldendes
hyldo gehealdeð.   Hord-weard sóhte
2295 georne äftr grunde.   wolde guman findan,
þone þe him on sweofote   sáre geteóde :

hât and hreóh-môd   hlæw oft ymbe hwearf,
calne ûtan-weardne ;   ne þær ænig mon
wäs on þære wêstenne.   Hwäðre hilde gefeh,
2300 beado-weorces :   hwîlum on beorh äthwearf,
sinc-fät sôhte ;   he þät sôna onfand,
þät häfde gumena sum   goldes gefandod
heáh-gestreóna.   Hord-weard onbâd
earfoðlíce,   ôð þät æfen cwom ;
2305 wäs þâ gebolgen   beorges hyrde,
wolde se láða   lîge forgyldan
drinc-fät dýre.   Þâ wäs däg sceacen
wyrme on willan,   nô on wealle leng
bídan wolde,   ac mid bæle fôr,
2310 fýre gefýsed.   Wäs se fruma egeslíc
leódum on lande,   swâ hyt lungre wearð
on hyra sinc-gifan   sâre geendod.

XXXIII.

BEÓWULF RESOLVES TO KILL THE FIRE-DRAKE.

Þâ se gäst ongan   glêdum spîwan,
beorht hofu bärnan ;   bryne-leóma stôd
2315 eldum on andan ;   nô þær áht cwices
láð lyft-floga   læfan wolde.
Wäs þäs wyrmes wîg   wîde gesŷne,
nearo-fâges nîð   neán and feorran,
hû se gûð-sceaða   Geáta leóde
2320 hatode and hŷnde :   hord eft gesceát,
dryht-sele dyrnne   ær däges hwíle.
Häfde land-wara   lîge befangen,
bæle and bronde ;   beorges getrûwode,
wîges and wealles :   him seó wên geleáh.
2325 Þâ wäs Biówulfe   brôga gecŷðed
snûde tô sôðe,   þät his sylfes him

bolda sélest   bryne-wylmum mealt,
gif-stól Geáta.   Þät þam gódan wäs
hreów on hreðre,   hyge-sorga mæst :
2330 wénde se wisa,   þät he wealdende,
ofer calde riht,   écean dryhtne
bitre gebulge :   breóst innan weóll
þeóstrum geþoncum,   swá him geþýwe ne wäs.
Häfde líg-draca   leóda fästen,
2335 eá-lond útan,   eorð-weard þone
glédum forgrunden.   Him þäs gúð-cyning,
Wedera þióden,   wräce leornode.
Hcht him þá gewyrcean   wígendra hleó
eall-írenne,   eorla dryhten
2340 wíg-bord wrätlíc ;   wisse he gearwe,
þät him holt-wudu   helpan ne meahte,
lind wið líge.   Sceolde læn-daga
äðeling ær-gód   ende gebídan
worulde lífes   and se wyrm somod,
2345 þeáh þe hord-welan   heólde lange.
Oferhogode þá   hringa fengel,
þät he þone wíd-flogan   weorode gesóhte,
sídan herge ;   nó he him þá säcce ondréd,
ne him þäs wyrmes wíg   for wiht dyde,
2350 eafoð and ellen ;   forþon he ær fela
nearo néðende   níða gedígde,
bilde-hlemma,   syððan he Hróðgáres,
sigor-eádig secg,   sele fälsode
and ät gúðe forgráp   Grendeles mægum,
2355 láðan cynnes.   Nó þät läsest wäs
hond-gemota,   þær mon Hygelác slóh,
syððan Geáta cyning   gúðe ræsum,
freá-wine folces   Freslondum on,
Hréðles eafora   hioro-dryncum swealt,
2360 bille gebeáten ;   þonan Biówulf com
sylfes cräfte,   sund-nytte dreáh ;

† hǣfde him on earme . . . XXX
hilde-geatwa, þā he tō holme stāg.

Nealles Hetware hrēmge þorfton
2365 fēðe-wīges, þe him foran ongeán
linde bǣron : lyt eft becwom
fram þam hild-frecan hāmes niósan.
Oferswam þā sióleða bigong suna Ecgþeówes,
earm ān-haga eft tō leódum,
2370 þǣr him Hygd gebeád hord and rīce,
beágas and brego-stól : bearne ne trūwode,
þät he wið äl-fylcum ēðel-stólas
healdan cūðe, þā wäs Hygelāc deád.
Nō þȳ ǣr feá-sceafte findan meahton
2375 ät þam äðelinge ǣnige þinga,
þät he Heardrēde hlāford wǣre,
oððe þone cyne-dóm ciósan wolde ;
hwäðre he him on folce freónd-lārum heóld,
ēstum mid āre, ōð þät he yldra wearð,
2380 Weder-Geátum weóld. Hyne wräc-mǣcgas
ofer sǣ sōhtan, suna Ôhteres :
häfdon hy forhealden helm Scylfinga,
þone sēlestan sæ-cyninga,
þāra þe in Swió-rīce sinc brytnade,
2385 mǣrne þeóden. Him þät tō mearce wearð ;
he þǣr on feorme feorh-wunde hleát
sweordes swengum, sunu Hygelāces ;
and him eft gewāt Ongenþiówes bearn
hāmes niósan, syððan Heardrēd läg ;
2390 lēt þone brego-stól Biówulf healdan,
Geátum wealdan : þät wäs gōd cyning.

XXXIV.

Retrospect of Beówulf. — Strife between Sweonas and Geatas.

Se þäs leód-hryres　　leán gemunde
uferan dôgrum,　　Eádgilse wearð
feá-sceaftum feónd.　　Folce gestepte
2395 ofer sæ síde　　sunu Ôhteres
wígum and wæpnum :　　he gewräc syððan
cealdum cear-síðum,　　cyning ealdre bineát.
Swâ he níða gehwane　　genesen häfde,
slíðra geslyhta,　　sunu Ecgþiówes,
2400 ellen-weorca,　　ôð þone ânne däg,
þe he wið þam wyrme　　gewegan sceolde.
Gewât þâ twelfa sum　　torne gebolgen
dryhten Geáta　　dracan sceáwian :
häfde þâ gefrunen,　　hwanan sió fähð ârâs,
2405 bealo-níð biorna ;　　him tô bearme cwom
mâððum-fät mære　　þurh þäs meldan hond.
Se wäs on þam þreáte　　þreotteoða secg,
se þäs orleges　　ôr onstealde,
häft hyge-giômor,　　sceolde heán þonon
2410 wong wísian :　　he ofer willan gióng
tô þäs þe he corð-sele　　ânne wisse,
hlæw under hrusan　　holm-wylme nêh,
ýð-gewinne,　　se wäs innan full
wrätta and wîra :　　weard unhióre,
2415 gearo gûð-freca,　　gold-mâðmas heóld,
eald under corðan ;　　näs þät ýðe ceáp,
tô gegangenne　　gumena ænigum.
Gesät þâ on nässe　　níð-heard cyning,
þenden hælo âbeád　　heorð-geneátum
2420 gold-wine Geáta :　　him wäs geômor sefa,
wäfre and wäl-fûs,　　Wyrd ungemete neáh,

se þone gomelan grétan sceolde,
sécean sáwle hord, sundur gedǽlan
lif wið lîce: nô þon lange wäs
2425 feorh äðelinges flǽsce bewunden.
Biówulf maðelade, bearn Ecgþeówes:
"Fela ic on giogoðe gûð-ræsa genäs,
"orleg-hwîla: ic þät eall gemon.
"Ic wäs syfan-wintre, þâ mec sinca baldor,
2430 "freá-wine folca ät mînum fäder genam,
"heóld mec and häfde Hrêðel cyning,
"geaf me sinc and symbel, sibbe gemunde;
"näs ic him tô lîfe lâðra ôwihte
"beorn in burgum, þonne his bearna hwylc,
2435 "Herebeald and Hæðcyn, oððe Hygelâc mîn.
"Wäs þam yldestan ungedéfelîce
"mæges dǽdum morðor-bed strêd,
"syððan hyne Hæðcyn of horn-bogan,
"his freá-wine flâne geswencte,
2440 "miste mercelses and his mæg ofscêt,
"brôðor ôðerne, blôdigan gâre:
"þät wäs feoh-leás gefeoht, fyrenum gesyngad,
"hreðre hyge-mêðe; sceolde hwäðre swâ þeáh
"äðeling unwrecen ealdres linnan.
2445 "Swâ bið geômorlîc gomelum ceorle
"tô gebîdanne, þät his byre rîde
"giong on galgan, þonne he gyd wrece,
"sârigne sang, þonne his sunu hangað
"hrefne tô hrôðre and he him helpan ne mäg,
2450 "eald and in-frôd, ænige gefremman.
"Symble bið gemyndgad morna gehwylce
"eaforan ellor-sîð; ôðres ne gýmeð
"to gebîdanne burgum on innan
"yrfe-weardes, þonne se ân hafað
2455 "þurh deáðes nýd dǽda gefondad.
"Gesyhð sorh-cearig on his suna bûre

" win-sele wêstne,   wind-gereste,
" reote berofene ;   rídend swefað.
" häleð in hoðman ;   nis þær hearpan swêg,
2460 " gomen in geardum,   swylce þær iú wæron.

XXXV.

Memories of Past Time. — The Feud with the Fire-Drake.

" Gewîteð þonne on sealman,   sorh-leóð gäleð
" ân äfter ânum :   þûhte him eall tô rûm,
" wongas and wîc-stede.   Swâ Wedra helm
" äfter Herebealde   heortan sorge
2465 " weallende wäg,   wihte ne meahte
" on þam feorh-bonan   fæhðe gebêtau :
" nô þŷ ær he þone heaðo-rinc   hatian ne meahte
" láðum dædum,   þeáh him leóf ne wäs.
" He þâ mid þære sorge,   þe him sió sâr belamp,
2470 " gum-dreám ofgeaf,   godes leóht geceás ;
" caferum læfde,   swâ dêð eádig mon,
" lond and leód-byrig,   þâ he of life gewât.
" Þâ wäs synn and sacu   Sweona and Geáta,
" ofer wîd wäter   wrôht gemæne,
2475 " here-nîð hearda,   syððan Hrêðel swealt,
" oððe him Ongenþeówes   caferan wæran
" frome fyrd-hwate,   freóde ne woldon
" ofer heafo healdan,   ac ymb Hreosna-beorh
" eatolne inwit-scear   oft gefremedon.
2480 " Þät mäg-wine   mîne gewræcan,
" fæhðe and fyrene,   swâ hyt gefræge wäs,
" þeáh þe ôðer hit   caldre gebohte,
" heardan ceápe :   Hæðcynne wearð,
" Geáta dryhtne,   gûð onsæge.

2485 " Þâ ic on morgne gefrägn　　mæg ôðerne
" billes ecgum　　on bonan stælan,
" þær Ongenþeów　　Eofores niósade:
" gûð-helm tôglâd,　　gomela Scylfing
" hreás *heoro*-blác ;　　hond gemunde
2490 " fæhðo genôge,　　feorh-sweng ne ofteáh.
" Ic him þâ mâðmas,　　þe he me scalde,
" geald ät gûðe,　　swâ me gifeðe wäs,
" leóhtan sweorde :　　he me lond forgeaf,
" eard êðel-wyn.　　Näs him ænig þearf,
2495 " þät he tô Gifðum　　oððe tô Gâr-Denum
" oððe in Swió-rîce　　sêcean þurfe
" wyrsan wîg-frecan,　　weorðe gecŷpan ;
" symle ic him on fêðan　　beforan wolde,
" âna on orde,　　and swâ tô aldre sceall
2500 " säcce fremman,　　þenden þis sweord þolað,
" þät mec ær and sîð　　oft gelæste,
" syððan ic for dugeðum　　Däghrefne wearð
" tô hand-bonan,　　Huga cempan :
" nalles he þâ frätwe　　Fres-cyninge,
2505 " breóst-weorðunge　　bringan môste,
" ac in campe gecrong　　cumbles hyrde,
" äðeling on elne.　　Ne wäs ecg bona,
" ac him hilde-grâp　　heortan wylmas,
" bân-hûs gebräc.　　Nu sceall billes ecg,
2510 " hond and heard sweord　　ymb hord wîgan."
Beówulf maðelode,　　beót-wordum spräc
niéhstan sîðe :　　" Ic genêðde fela
" gûða on geogoðe ;　　gyt ic wylle,
" frôd folces weard,　　fæhðe sêcan,
2515 " mærðum fremman,　　gif mec se mân-sceaða
" of eorð-sele　　ût gesêceð !"
Gegrêtte þâ　　gumena gehwylcne,
hwate helm-berend　　hindeman sîðe,
swæse gesîðas :　　" Nolde ic sweord beran,

2520 " wæpen tô wyrme,   gif ic wiste hû
     " wið þam aglæcean   elles meahte
     " gylpe wiðgrîpan,   swâ ic giô wið Gren lle dyde;
     " ac ic þær heaðu-fŷres   hâtes wêne,
     " rêðes and-hâttres :   forþon ic me on hafu
2525 " bord and byrnan.   Nelle ic beorges weard
     " oferfleôn fôtes trem,   feónd unhŷre,
     " ac unc sceal weorðan ät wealle,   swâ unc Wyrd geteôð,
     " metod manna gehwäs.   Ic eom on môde from,
     " þät ic wið þone gûð-flogan   gylp ofersitte.
2530 " Gebîde ge on beorge   byrnum werede,
     " secgas on searwum,   hwäðer sêl mæge
     " äfter wäl-ræse   wunde gedŷgan
     " uncer twega.   Nis þät eôwer sîð,
     " ne gemet mannes,   nefne mîn ânes,
2535 " þät he wið aglæcean   eofoðo dæle,
     " eorl-scype efne.   Ic mid elne sceall
     " gold gegangan   oððe gûð nimeð,
     " feorh-bealu frêcne,   freán eôwerne ! "
     Ârâs þâ bî ronde   rôf oretta,
2540 heard under helm,   hioro-sercean bär
     under stân-cleofu,   strengo getrûwode
     ânes mannes :   ne bið swylc earges sîð.
     Geseah þâ be wealle,   se þe worna fela,
     gum-cystum gôd,   gûða gedîgde,
2545 hilde-hlemma,   þonne huitan fêðan,
     (stôd on stân-bogan)   streám ût þonan
     brecan of beorge ;   wäs þære burnan wälm
     heaðo-fŷrum hât :   ne meahte horde neáh
     unbyrnende   ænige hwîle
2550 deôp gedŷgan   for dracan lôge.
     Lét þâ of breôstum,   þâ he gebolgen wäs,
     Weder-Geáta leôd   word ût faran,
     stearc-heort styrmde ;   stefn in becom
     heaðo-torht hlynnan   under hârne stân.

2555 Hete wäs onhrêred,　　hord-weard oncniów
　　　mannes reorde;　　näs þær mâra fyrst,
　　　freóde tô friclan.　　From ærest cwom
　　　oruð aglæcean　　ût of stâne,
　　　hât hilde-swât;　　hruse dynede.
2560 Biorn under beorge　　bord-rand onswâf
　　　wið þam gryre-gieste,　　Geáta dryhten:
　　　þâ wäs hring-bogan　　heorte gefýsed
　　　säcce tô sêceanne.　　Sweord ær gebräd
　　　gôd gûð-cyning　　gomele lâfe,
2565 ecgum ungleáw,　　æghwäðrum wäs
　　　bealo-hycgendra　　brôga fram ôðrum.
　　　Stîð-môd gestôd　　wið steápne rond
　　　winia bealdor,　　þâ se wyrm gebeáh
　　　snûde tôsomne:　　he on searwum bâd.
2570 Gewât þâ byrnende　　gebogen scrîðan tô,
　　　gescîfe scyndan.　　Scyld wel gebearg
　　　lîfe and lîce　　lässan hwîle
　　　mærum þeódne,　　þonne his myne sôhte,
　　　þær he þý fyrste　　forman dôgore
2575 wealdan môste,　　swâ him Wyrd ne gescrâf
　　　hrêð ät hilde.　　Hond up âbräd
　　　Geáta dryhten,　　gryre-fâhne slôh
　　　incge lâfe,　　þät sió ecg gewâc
　　　brûn on bâne,　　bât unswîðor,
2580 þonne his þiód-cyning　　þearfe häfde,
　　　bysigum gebæded.　　þâ wäs beorges weard
　　　äfter heaðu-swenge　　on hreóum môde,
　　　wearp wäl-fýre,　　wîde sprungon
　　　hilde-leóman:　　hrêð-sigora ne gealp
2585 gold-wine Geáta,　　gûð-bill geswâc
　　　nacod ät niðe,　　swâ hyt nô sceolde,
　　　îren ær-gôd.　　Ne wäs þät êðe sið,
　　　þät se mæra　　maga Ecgþeówes
　　　grund-wong þone　　ofgyfan wolde;

2590 sceolde *wyrmes* willan   wíc eardian
elles hwergen,   swá sceal æghwylc mon
álætan læn-dagas.   Näs þá long tó þon,
þät þá aglæcean   hy eft gemétton.
Hyrte hyne hord-weard,   breðer æðme weóll,
2595 niwan stefne   nearo þrowode
fýre befongen   se þe ær folce weóld.
Nealles him on heápe   hand-gesteallan,
äðelinga bearn   ymbe gestódon
hilde-cystum,   ac hy on holt bugon,
2600 ealdre burgan.   Hiora in ánum weóll
sefa wið sorgum: sibb æfre ne mäg
wiht onwendan,   þam þe wel þenceð.

XXXVI. WIGLAF HELPS BEÓWULF IN THE FEUD.

WÍGLÁF wäs háten   Weoxstánes sunu,
leóflic lind-wiga,   leód Scylfinga,
2605 mæg Ælfheres: geseah his mon-dryhten
under here-gríman   hát þrowian.
Gemunde þá þá áre,   þe he him ær forgeaf
wíc-stede weligne   Wægmundinga,
folc-rihta gehwylc,   swá his fäder áhte:
2610 ne mihte þá forhabban,   hond rond geféng,
geolwe linde,   gomel swyrd getcáh,
þät wäs mid eldum   Eánmundes láf,
suna Óhteres,   þam ät säcce wearð
wracu wine-leásum   Weohstánes bana
2615 méces ecgum,   and his mágum ütbär
brún-fágne helm,   hringde byrnan,
eald sweord eotonisc,   þät him Onela forgeaf,
his gädelinges   gúð-gewædu,
fyrd-searo fúslíc: nó ymbe þá fæhðe spräc,
2620 þeáh þe he his bróðor   bearn ábredwade.

He frätwe geheóld   fela missera,
bill and byrnan,   ôð þät his byre mihte
eorl-scipe efnan.   swá his ær-fäder;
geaf him þå mid Geátum   gûð-gewæda
2625 æghwäs unrîm;   þå he of ealdre gewât,
frôd on forð-weg.   Þå wäs forma sîð
geongan eempan,   þät he gûðe ræs
mid his freó-dryhtne   fremman sceolde;
ne gemealt him se môd-sefa,   ne his mæges lâf
2630 gewâc ät wîge: þät se wyrm onfand,
syððan hie tôgädre   gegân häfdon.
Wîglâf maðelode   word-rihta fela,
sägde gesîðum,   him wäs sefa geômor:
" Ic þät mæl geman,   þær we medu þégun,
2635 " þonne we gehéton   ûssum hlâforde
" in biór-sele,   þe ûs þâs beágas geaf,
" þät we him þå gûð-geatwa   gyldan woldon,
" gif him þyslîcu   þearf gelumpe,
" helmas and heard sweord: þe he ûsic on herge geceás
2640 " tô þyssum sîð-fate   sylfes willum,
" onmunde ûsic mærða   and me þâs mâðmas geaf,
" þe he ûsic gâr-wîgend   gôde tealde,
" hwate helm-berend,   þeáh þe hlâford ûs
" þis ellen-weorc   âna âþôhte
2645 " tô gefremmanne,   folces hyrde,
" forþam he manna mæst   mærða gefremede,
" dæda dollîcra.   Nu is se däg cumen,
" þät ûre man-dryhten   mägenes behôfað
" gôdra gûð-rinca: wutun gangan tô,
2650 " helpan hild-fruman,   þenden hyt sŷ,
" glêd-egesa grim!   God wât on mec,
" þät me is micle leófre,   þät mînne lîc-haman
" mid mînne gold-gyfan   glêd fäðmie.
" Ne þynceð me gerysne,   þät we rondas beren
2655 " eft tô earde,   nemne we æror mägen

" fâne gefyllan, feorh ealgian
" Wedra þiódnes. Ic wât geare,
" þät mæron eald-gewyrht, þät he âna scyle
" Geáta duguðe gnorn þrowian,
2660 " gesîgan ät säcce : sceal ûrum þät sweord and helm,
" byrne and byrdu-serûd bâm gemæne."
Wôd þâ þurh þone wäl-réc, wîg-heafolan bär
freán on fultum, feá worda cwäð :
" Leófa Biówulf, læst eall tela,
2665 " swâ þu on geoguð-feore geâra gecwæde,
" þät þu ne âlæte be þe lifigendum
" dôm gedreósan : scealt nu dædum rôf,
" äðeling ân-hydig, ealle mügene
" feorh ealgian ; ic þe fullæstu ! "
2670 Äfter þâm wordum wyrm yrre cwom,
atol inwit-gäst ôðre sîðe,
fýr-wylmum fäh fiónda niósan,
lâðra manna ; lîg-ýðum forborn
bord wið ronde : byrne ne meahte
2675 geongum gâr-wigan geóce gefremman :
ac se maga geonga under his mæges scyld
elne geeode, þâ his âgen wäs
glêdum forgrunden. þâ gen gûð-cyning
mærða gemunde, mägen-strengo,
2680 slôh hilde-bille, þät hyt on heafolan stôd
nîðe genýded : Nägling forbärst,
geswâc ät säcce sweord Biówulfes
gomol and græg-mæl. Him þät gifeðe ne wäs,
þät him irenna ecge milhton
2685 helpan ät hilde ; wäs sió hond tô strong,
se þe méca gehwane mîne gefræge
swenge ofersôhte, þonne he tô säcce bär
wæpen wundrum heard, näs him wihte þê sêl.
þâ wäs þeód-sceaða þriddan sîðe,
2690 frécne fýr-draca fæhða gemyndig,

ræsde on þone rófan,   þâ him rûm âgeald,
hât and heaðo-grim,   heals ealne ymbefêng
biteran bânnm;   he geblôdegod wearð
sâwul-drióre;   swât ŷðum weóll.

XXXVII. Beówulf Wounded to Death.

2695 Þâ ic ät þearfe *gefrägn* þeód-cyninges
    and-longne eorl   ellen cŷðan,
    cräft and cênðu,   swâ him gecynde wäs;
    ne hêdde he þäs heafolan,   ac sió hand gebarn
    môdiges mannes,   þær he his mæges healp,
2700 þät he þone nîð-gäst   nioðor hwêne slôh,
    secg on searwum,   þät þät sweord gedeáf
    fâh and fäted,   þät þät fŷr ongon
    sweðrian syððan.   Þâ gen sylf cyning
    geweóld his gewitte,   wäll-seaxe gebräd,
2705 biter and beadu-scearp,   þät he on byrnan wäg:
    forwrât Wedra helm   wyrm on middan.
    Feónd gefyldan   (ferh ellen wräc),
    and hi hyne þâ begen   âbroten häfdon,
    sib-äðelingas: swylc scoolde secg wesan,
2710 þegn ät þearfe.   Þät þam þeódne wäs
    sîðast sige-hwîle   sylfes dædum,
    worlde geweorces.   Þâ sió wund ongon,
    þe him se corð-draca   ær geworhte,
    swêlan and swellan.   He þät sôna onfand,
2715 þät him on breóstum   bealo-nîð weóll,
    âttor on innan.   Þâ se äðeling gióng,
    þät he bî wealle,   wîs-hycgende,
    gesät on sesse;   seah on enta geweorc,
    hû þâ stân-bogan   stapulum fäste
2720 êce corð-reced   innan heóldon.
    Hyne þâ mid handa   heoro-dreórigne

þeóden mærne   þegn ungemete till,
wine-dryhten his   wätere gelafede,
hilde-sädne   and his helm onspeón.

2725 Biówulf maðelode,   he ofer benne spräc,
wunde wäl-bleáte   (wisse he gearwe,
þät he däg-hwila   gedrogen häfde
corðan wynne ;   þá wäs eall sceacen
dógor-gerímes,   deáð ungemete neáh) :

2730 " Nu ic suna minum   syllan wolde
" gúð-gewædu,   þær me gifeðe swá
" ænig yrfe-weard   äfter wurde,
" líce gelenge.   Ic þás leóde heóld
" fíftig wintra :   näs se folc-cyning

2735 " ymbe-sittendra   ænig þára,
" þe mec gúð-winum   grétan dorste,
" egesan þeón.   Ic on earde bád
" mæl-gesceafta,   heóld min tela,
" ne sóhte searo-nîðas,   ne me swór fela

2740 " áða on unriht.   Ic þäs ealles mäg,
" feorh-bennum seóc,   gefeán habban :
" forþam me witan ne þearf   waldend fira
" morðor-bealo mága,   þonne min sceaceð
" líf of líce.   Nu þu lungre

2745 " geong, hord sceáwian   under hárne stán,
" Wíglaf leófa,   nu se wyrm ligeð,
" swefeð sáre wund,   since bereáfod.
" Bió nu on ófoste,   þät ic ær-welan,
" gold-æht ongite,   gearo sceáwige

2750 " swegle searo-gimmas,   þät ic þý séft mæge
" äfter máððum-welan   min álætan
" líf and leód-scipe,   þone ic longe heóld."

XXXVIII.

The Jewel–Hoard. The Passing of Beówulf.

Þá ic snúde gefrägn   snnu Wihstánes
äfter word-cwydum   wundum dryhtne
2755 hýran heaðo-siócum,   -hring-net beran.
brogdne beadu-sercean   under beorges hróf.
Geseah þá sige-hréðig,   þá he bí sesse geóng,
mago-þegn módig   máððum-sigla fela,
gold glitinian   grunde getenge,
2760 wundur on wealle   and þäs wyrmes denn,
ealdes uht-flogan,   orcas stondan,
fyrn-manna fatu   feormend-leáse,
hyrstum behrorene: þær wäs helm monig,
eald and ómig,   earm-beága fela,
2765 searwum gesæled.   Sinc eáðe mäg,
gold on grunde,   gumena cynnes
gehwone ofer-higian,   hýde se þe wylle!
Swylce he siomian geseah   segn eall-gylden
heáh ofer horde,   hond-wundra mæst,
2770 gelocen leoðo-cräftum: of þam leóma stód,
þät he þone grund-wong   ongitan mealte,
wräte giond-wlítan.   Näs þäs wyrmes þær
onsýn ænig,   ac hyne ecg fornam.
Þá ic on hläwe   gefrägn hord reáfian,
2775 eald enta geweorc   ánne mannan,
him on bearm hladan   bunan and discas
sylfes dóme,   segn eác genom,
beácna beorhtost;   bill ær-gescód
(ecg wäs íren)   eald-hláfordes
2780 þam þára máðma   mund-bora wäs
longe hwíle.   líg-egesan wäg
hátne for horde,   hioro-weallende,

middel-nihtum. Óð þät he morðre swealt.
Âr wäs on ófoste eft-siðes georn.
2785 frätwum gefyrðred : hyne fyrwet bräc,
hwäðer collen-ferð cwicne gemétte
in þam wong-stede Wedra þeóden,
ellen-siócne, þær he hine ær forlét.
He þá mid þám máðmum mærne þióden,
2790 dryhten sinne driórigne fand
ealdres ät ende : he hine eft ongon
wätere weorpan, óð þät wordes ord
breóst-hord þurhbräc. *Beówulf maðelode,*
gomel on giohðe (gold sceáwode) :
2795 "Ic þára frätwa freán ealles þanc
" wuldur-cyninge wordum secge,
" écum dryhtne, þe ic her on starie,
" þäs þe ic móste mínum leódum
" ær swylt-däge swylc gestrýnan.
2800 " Nu ic on máðma hord mine behohte
" fróde feorh-lege, fremmað ge nu
" leóda þarfe ; ne mäg ic her leng wesan.
" Hátað heaðo-mære hlæw gewyrcean,
" beorhtne äfter bæle ät brimes nosan ;
2805 " se scel tó gemyndum mínum leódum
" heáh hlifian on Hrones nässe,
" þät hit sä líðend syððan hátan
" Biówulfes biorh, þá þe brentingas
" ofer flóda genipu feorran drífað."
2810 Dyde him of healse hring gyldenne
þióden þrist-hydig, þegne gesealde,
geongum gár-wigan, gold-fáhne helm,
beáh and byrnan, hét hyne brúcan well :
" Þu eart ende láf ûsses cynnes.
2815 " Wægmundinga ; ealle Wyrd forsweóf,
" mine mágas tó metod-sceafte,
" eorlas on elne : ic him äfter sceal."

þät wäs þam gomelan   gingeste word
breóst-gehygdum,   ær he bæl cure,
2820 háte heaðo-wylmas: him of hreðre gewât
sáwol sécean,   sóð-fästra dóm.

XXXIX. The Coward–Thanes.

þâ wäs gegongen   guman unfrôdum
earfoðlîce,   þät he on corðan geseah
þone leófestan   lîfes ät ende
2825 bleáte gebærran.   Bona swylce läg,
egeslîc corð-draca,   ealdre bereáfod,
bealwe gebæded: beáh-hordum leng
wyrm woh-bogen   wealdan ne môste,
ac him îrenna   ecga fornâmon,
2830 hearde heaðo-scearpe   homera láfe,
þät se wîd-floga   wundum stille
hreás on hrusan   hord-ärne neáh,
nalles äfter lyfte   lâcende hwearf
middel-nihtum,   mâðm-æhta wlonc
2835 ansŷn ŷwde: ac he corðan gefeóll
for þäs hild-fruman   hond-geweorce.
Hûru þät on lande   lyt manna þâh
mägen-âgendra   mîne gefræge,
þeáh þe he dæda gehwäs   dyrstig wære,
2840 þät he wið âttor-sceaðan   oreðe geræsde,
oððe hring-sele   hondum styrede,
gif he wäccende   weard onfunde
bûan on beorge.   Biówulfe wearð
dryht-mâðma dæl   deáðe forgolden;
2845 häfde æghwäðer   ende gefêred
lænan lîfes.   Näs þâ lang tô þon,
þät þâ hild-latan   holt ofgêfan,
tydre treów-logan   tyne ätsomne,

þâ ne dorston ær   dareðum lâcan
2850 on hyra man-dryhtnes   miclan þearfe;
ac hy scamiende   scyldas bæran,
gûð-gewædu,   þær se gomela läg:
wlitan on Wîglâf.   He gewêrgad sät,
fêðe-cempa   freán eaxlum neáh,
2855 wehte hyne wätre;   him wiht ne speôw;
ne mealhte he on corðan,   þeáh he ûðe wel,
on þam frum-gâre   feorh gehealdan.
ne þäs wealdendes *willan*   wiht oncirran;
wolde dôm godes   dædum rædan
2860 gumena gehwylcum,   swâ he nu gen deð.
þâ wäs ät þam geongum   grim andswaru
êð-begête þâm þe ær   his elne forleás.
Wîglâf maðelode,   Weohstânes sunu,
secg sârig-ferð   seah on unleófe:
2865 " þät lâ mäg secgan,   se þe wyle sôð sprecan,
" þät se mon-dryhten,   se eôw þâ mâðmas geaf,
" eôred-geatwe,   þe ge þær on standað,
" þonne he on ealu-bence   oft gesealde
" heal-sittendum   helm and byrnan,
2870 " þeóden his þegnum,   swylce he þryðlîcost
" ôhwær feor oððe neáh   findan mealhte,
" þät he genunga   gûð-gewædu
" wrâðe forwurpe.   þâ hyne wîg beget,
" nealles folc-cyning   fyrd-gesteallum
2875 " gylpan þorfte;   hwäðre him god ûðe,
" sigora waldend,   þät he hyne sylfne gewräc
" âna mid ecge.   þâ him wäs elnes þearf,
" Ic him lîf-wraðe   lytle mealhte
" ätgifan ät gûðe   and ongan swâ þeáh
2880 " ofer mîn gemet   mæges helpan:
" symle wäs þŷ sæmra.   þonne ic sweorde drep
" ferhð-genîðlan.   fŷr unswîðor
" weóll of gewitte.   Wergendra tô lyt

"þrong ymbe þeóden.   þâ hyne sió þrag becwom.
2885 "Nu sceal sinc-þego   and swyrd-gifu
"eall êðel-wyn   eówrum cynne,
"lufen âlicgean: lond-rihtes môt
"þære mæg-burge   monna æghwylc
"idel hweorfan,   syððan äðelingas
2890 "feorran gefricgean   fleám eówerne,
"dôm-leásan dæd.   Deáð bið sêlla
"eorla gehwylcum   þonne edwît-lîf!"

XL. THE SOLDIER'S DIRGE AND PROPHECY.

HÉHT þâ þät heaðo-weorc   tô hagan biódan
up ofer êg-clif,   þær þät eorl-weorod
2895 morgen-longne däg   môd-giômor sät,
bord-häbbende,   bega on wênum
ende-dôgores   and eft-cymes
leófes monnes.   Lyt swîgode
niwra spella,   se þe näs gerâd,
2900 ac he sôðlîce   sägde ofer ealle;
"Nu is wil-geofa   Wedra leóda,
"dryhten Geáta   deáð-bedde fäst,
"wunað wäl-reste   wyrmes dædum;
"him on efn ligeð   ealdor-gewinna,
2905 "siex-beannum seóc: sweorde ne meahte
"on þam aglæcean   ænige þinga
"wunde gewyrcean.   Wîglâf siteð
"ofer Biówulfe,   byre Wihstânes,
"eorl ofer ôðrum   unlifigendum,
2910 "healdeð hige-mêðum   heáfod-wearde,
"leófes and lâðes.   Nu ys leódum wên
"orleg-hwîle,   syððan underne
"Froncum and Frysum   fyll cyninges
"wîde weorðeð.   Wäs sió wrôht scepen

2915 " heard wið Hugas, syððan Higelác ewom
" faran flot-herge on Fresna land,
" þær hyne Hetware hilde gehnægdon,
" elne geeodon mid ofer-mägene,
" þät se byrn-wîga• bûgan seeolde,
2920 " feóll on fêðan : nalles frätwe geaf
" ealdor dugoðe ; ûs wäs â syððan
" Merewioinga milts ungyfeðe.
" Ne ie tô Sweó-þeóde sibbe oððe treówe
" wihte ne wêne ; ae wäs wîde cûð,
2925 " þätte Ongenþió ealdre besnyðede
" Hæðeyn Hrêðling wið Hrefna-wudu,
" þâ for on-mêdlan ärest gesôhton
" Geáta leóde Gûð-seilfingas.
" Sôna him se frôda fäder Ôhtheres,
2930 " eald and eges-full ond-slyht âgeaf,
" âbreót brim-wîsan, brŷd âheórde,
" gomela ió-meowlan golde berofene,
" Onelan môdor and Ôhtheres,
" and þâ folgode feorh-genîðlan
2935 " ôð þät hî ôðeodon earfoðlice
" in Hrefnes-holt hlâford-leáse.
" Besät þâ sin-herge sweorda lâfe
" wundum wêrge, weán oft gehêt
" earmre teohhe andlonge niht :
2940 " ewäð he on mergenne môces ecgum
" getan wolde, sume on galg-treówum
" fuglum tô gamene. Frôfor eft gelamp
" sârig-môdum somod ær-däge,
" syððan hie Hygeláces horn and bŷman
2945 " gealdor ongeáton. þâ se gôda com
" leóda dugoðe on lâst faran.

XLI. He Tells of the Swedes and the Geatas.

"Wäs sió swât-swaðu   Sweona and Geáta,
" wäl-ræs wera   wîde gesŷne,
" hû]á folc mid him   fæhðe tôwehton.
2950 " Gewât him]á se gôda   mid his gädelingum,
" frôd fela geômor   fästen sêcean,
" eorl Ongen]ió   ufor oncirde ;
" häfde Higeláces   hilde gefrunen,
" wlonces wig-cräft,   wiðres ne trûwode,
2955 "]ät he sæ-mannum   onsacan mihte,
" heáðo-liðendum   hord forstandan,
" bearn and brŷde ;   beáh eft]onan
" eald under eorð-weall.   ]â wäs æht boden
" Sweona leódum,   segn Higeláce.
2960 " Freoðo-wong]one   forð ofereodon,
" syððan Hrêðlingas   tô hagan]rungon.
"]ær wearð Ongen]ió   eegum sweorda,
" blonden-fexa   on bîd wrecen,
"]ät se þeód-cyning   ]afian sceolde
2965 " Eofores ânne dôm :   hyne yrringa
" Wulf Wonrêding   wæpne geræhte,
"]ät him for swenge   swât ædrûm sprong
" forð under fexe.   Näs he forht swâ þêh,
" gomela Scilfing,   ac forgeald hraðe
2970 " wyrsan wrixle   wäl-hlem]one,
" syððan þeód-cyning   ]yder oncirde :
" ne meahte se snella   sunu Wonrêdes
" ealdum ceorle   ond-slyht giofan,
" ac he him on heáfde   helm ær gescer,
2975 "]ät he blôde fâh   bûgan sceolde,
" feóll on foldan ;   näs he fæge]â git,
" ac he hyne gewyrpte,   þeáh þe him wund hrine.
" Lét se hearda   Higeláces þegn

" brádne méce,   þá his bróðor lǽg,

2980 " eald sweord eotonisc,   entiscne helm,

" brecan ofer bord-weal :   þá gebeáh cyning,

" folces hyrde,   wäs in feorh dropen.

" þá wǽron monige,   þe his mǽg wriðon,

" ricone árærdon,   þá him gerýmed wearð,

2985 " þät hie wäl-stówe   wealdan móston.

" Þenden reáfode   rinc óðerne,

" nam on Ongenþió   íren-byrnan,

" heard swyrd hilted   and his helm somod;

" háres hyrste   Higeláce bär.

2990 " He þám frätwum féng   and him fägre gehét

" leána fore leódum   and geläste swá :

" geald þone gúð-ræs   Geáta dryhten,

" Hréðles eafora,   þá he tó hám becom,

" Jofore and Wulfe   mid ofer-máðmum,

2995 " sealde hiora gehwäðrum   hund þúsenda

" landes and locenra beága ;   ne þorfte him þá leán

óðwítan

" mon on middan-gearde, syððan hie þá mærða geslógon ;

" and þá Jofore forgeaf   ángan dóhtor,

" hám-weorðunge,   hyldo tó wedde.

3000 " Þät ys sió fæhðo   and se feónd-scipe,

" wäl-nið wera,   þäs þe ic wén hafo,

" þe ús séceað tó   Sweona leóde,

" syððan hie gefriegeað   freán úserne

" ealdor-leásne,   þone þe ær geheóld

3005 " wið hettendum   hord and rīce,

" äfter häleða hryre   hwate Scylfingas,

" folc-ræd fremede   oððe furður gen

" eorl-scipe efnde.   Nu is ófost betost,

" þät we þeód-cyning   þær sceáwian

3010 " and þone gebringan,   þe ús beágas geaf,

" on ád-färe.   Ne sceel ánes hwät

" meltan mid þam módigan,   ac þær is máðma hord,

"gold unrîme   grimme geceápod
"and nu ät sîðestan   sylfes feore
3015 "beágas *gebohte*;   þâ sceal brond fretan,
"äled þeccean,   nalles eorl wegan
"mâððum tô gemyndum,   ne mägð scŷne
"habban on healse   hring-weorðunge,
"ac sceall geômor-môd   golde bereáfod
3020 "oft nalles æne   el-land tredan,
"nu se here-wîsa   hleahtor âlegde,
"gamen and gleó-dreám.   Forþon sceall gâr wesan
"monig morgen-ceald   mundum bewunden,
"häfen on handa,   nalles hearpan swêg
3025 "wîgend weccean,   ac se wonna hrefn
"fûs ofer fægum,   fela reordian,
"earne secgan,   hû him ät æte speów,
"þenden he wið wulf   wäl reáfode."
Swâ se secg hwata   secgende wäs
3030 lâðra spella;   he ne leág fela
wyrda ne worda.   Weorod eall ârâs,
eodon unblîðe   under Earna näs
wollen-teáre   wundur sceáwian.
Fundon þâ on sande   sâwul-leásne
3035 hlim-bed healdan,   þone þe hiin hringas geaf
ärran mælum: þâ wâs ende-däg
gôdum gegongen,   þät se gûð-cyning,
Wedra þeóden,   wundor-deáðe swealt.
Ær hî gesêgan   syllîcran wiht,
3040 wyrm on wonge   wiðer-rähtes þær
lâðne licgean: wäs se lêg-draca,
grimlîc gry*re-gäst*,   glêdum beswæled,
se wäs fîftiges   fôt-gemearces
lang on legere,   lyft-wynne heóld
3045 nihtes hwîlum,   nyðer eft gewât
dennes niósian;   wäs þâ deáðe fäst,
häfde eorð-scrafa   ende genyttod.

Him big stódan   bunan and orcas,
discas lágon   and dýre swyrd,
3050 ómige þurh-etone.   swá hie wið corðan fäðm
þúsend wintra   þær eardodon:
þonne wäs þät yrfe   eácen-cräftig,
iú-monna gold   galdre bewunden,
þät þam hring-sele   hrínan ne móste
3055 gumena ænig,   nefne god sylfa,
sigora sóð-cyning,   sealde þam þe he wolde
(he is manna gehyld)   hord openian,
efne swá hwylcum manna,   swá him gemet þúhte.

XLII.

WÍGLAF SPEAKS. THE BUILDING OF THE BALE-FIRE.

Þá wäs gesýne,   þät se sið ne þáh
3060 þam þe unrihte   inne gehýdde
wräte under wealle.   Weard ær ofslóh
feára sumne; þá sió fæhð gewearð
gewrecen wráðlíce.   Wundur hwár, þonne
eorl ellen-róf   ende gefére
3065 líf-gesceafta,   þonne leng ne mäg
mon mid his mágum   medu-seld búan?
Swá wäs Bíówulfe,   þá he biorges weard
sóhte, searo-níðas: seolfa ne cúðe,
þurh hwät his worulde gedál   weorðan sceolde;
3070 swá hit óð dómes däg   dióþe benemdon
þeódnas mære,   þá þät þær dydon,
þät se secg wære   synnum scildig,
hergum gebeaðerod,   hell-bendum fäst,
wommum gewitnad,   se þone wong stráde.
3075 Näs he gold-hwät: gearwor häfde

âgendes êst   ær gesceáwod.

Wîglâf maðelode,   Wihstânes sunu:

"Oft sceall eorl monig   ânes willan

"wræc âdreógan,   swâ ûs geworden is.

3080 "Ne meahton we gelæran   leófne þeóden,

"ríces hyrde   ræd ænigne,

"þät he ne grétte   gold-weard þone,

"léte hyne licgean,   þær he longe wäs,

"wîcum wunian   óð woruld-ende.

3085 "Heóldon heáh gesceap: hord ys gesceáwod,

"grimme gegongen;   wäs þät gifeðe tó swîð,

"þe þone þeóden   þyder ontyhte.

"Ic wäs þær inne   and þät eall geond-seh,

"recedes geatwa,   þá me gerýmed wäs,

3090 "nealles swæslîce   sîð âlýfed

"inn under corð-weall.   Ic on ófoste gefêng

"micle mid mundum   mägen-byrðenne

"hord-gestreóna,   hider ût ätbär

"cyninge mînum: cwico wäs þá gena,

3095 "wîs and gewittig;   worn eall gespräc

"gomol on gehðo   and eówic grêtan hêt,

"bäd þät ge geworhton   äfter wines dædum

"in bæl-stede   beorh þone heán

"micelne and mærne,   swâ he manna wäs

3100 "wîgend weorð-fullost   wîde geond eorðan,

"þenden he burh-welan   brûcan móste.

"Uton nu êfstan   óðre sîðe

"seón and sêcean   searo-geþräc,

"wundur under wealle!   ic eów wîsige,

3105 "þät ge genóge   neán sceáwiað

"beágas and brâd gold.   Sîe sió bær gearo

"ädre geäfned,   þonne we ût cymen,

"and þonne geferian   freán ûserne,

"leófne mannan,   þær he longe sceal

3110 "on þäs waldendes   wære geþolian."

Hét þá gebeódan   byre Wihstânes,
hæle hilde-diór,   hæleða monegum
bold-âgendra,   þät hie bæl-wudu
feorran feredon,   folc-âgende
3115 gódum tógénes :   '' Nu sceal glêd fretan
'' (weaxan wonna lêg)   wîgena strengel,
'' þone þe oft gebâd   ísern-scûre,
'' þonne stræla storm,   strengum gebæded,
'' scôc ofer scild-weall,   sceft nytte heóld,
3120 '' feðer-gearwum fûs   flâne full-eode.''
Hûru se snotra   sunu Wihstânes
âcígde of corðre   cyninges þegnas
syfone tósomne   þâ sélestan,
eode eahta sum   under inwit-hróf;
3125 hilde-rinc sum   on handa bär
äled-leóman,   se þe on orde geóng.
Näs þâ on hlytme,   hwâ þät hord strude,
syððan or-wearde   ænigne dæl
secgas gesêgon   on sele wunian,
3130 læne licgan :   lyt ænig mearn,
þät hi ófostlice   ût geferedon
dýre mâðmas ;   dracan êc scufun,
wyrm ofer weall-clif,   léton wæg niman,
flôd fäðmian   frätwa hyrde.
3135 Þær wäs wunden gold   on wæn hladen,
æghwäs unrîm,   äðeling boren,
hâr hilde-rinc   tó Hrónes nässe.

XLIII. Beówulf's Funeral Pyre.

Him þá gegiredan   Geáta leóde
Âd on eorðan   un-wâclícne,
3140 helmum behongen,   hilde-bordum,
beorhtum byrnum,   swâ he bêna wäs;
Âlegdon þâ tô-middes   mærne þeóden
hüleð hiófende,   hlâford leófne.
Ongunnon þâ on beorge   bæl-fŷra mæst
3145 wîgend weccan :   wudu-rêc âstâh
sweart ofer swioðole,   swôgende lêg,
wôpe bewunden   (wind-blond geläg)
Oð þät he þâ bân-hûs   gebrocen häfde,
hât on hreðre.   Higum unrôte
3150 môd-ceare mændon   mon-dryhtnes cwealm;
swylce giðmor-gyd   † lat . ^{con.} meowle
. . . . . wunden heorde . . .
serg (?) cearig sælde   geneahhe
þät hio hyre . . . . gas hearde
3155 . . . . . ede   wälfylla wonn . .
hildes egesan   hyðo
haf mid   heofon rêce swealh (?)
Geworhton þâ   Wedra leóde
hlæw on hliðe,   se wäs heáh and brâd,
3160 wæg-lîðendum   wîde gesŷne,
and betimbredon   on tyn dagum
beadu-rôfes bêen :   bronda betost
wealle beworhton,   swâ hyt weorðlîcost
fore-snotre men   findan mihton.
3165 Hî on beorg dydon   bêg and siglu,
eall swylce hyrsta,   swylce on horde ær
nîð-hydige men   genumen häfdon;
forlêton eorla gestreón   eorðan healdan,
gold on greóte,   þær hit nu gen lifað

3170 eldum swá unnyt,   swá hit *æror* wäs.
    Þá ymbe hlæw riodan   hilde-deóre,
    äðelinga bearn   ealra twelfa,
    woldon *ceare* cwíðan,   kyning mænan,
    word-gyd wrecan   and ymb wer sprecan,
3175 eahtodan eorl-scipe   and his ellen-weorc
    duguðum démdon,   swá hit ge-*défe* bið,
    þät mon his wine-dryhten   wordum hêrge,
    ferhðum freóge,   þonne he forð scile
    of lic-haman   *læne* weorðan.
3180 Swá begnornodon   Geáta leóde
    hláfordes *hryre*,   heorð-geneátas,
    cwædon þät he wære   woruld-cyning
    mannum mildust   and mon-þwærust,
    leódum liðost   and lof-geornost.

APPENDIX.

The Attack in Finnsburg.*

". . . . . näs byrnað næfre."
Hleoðrode þā heaðo-geong cyning:
" Ne þis ne dagað eástan, ne her draca ne fleógeð,
" ne her þisse healle hornas ne byrnað,
5 " ac fēr forð berað, fugelas singað,
" gylleð græg-hama, gūð-wudu hlynneð,
" scyld scefte oncwyð. Nu scýneð þes mōna
" waðol under wolcnum; nu ārísað weá-dæda,
" þe þisne folces nīð fremman willað.
10 " Ac onwacnigeað nu, wígend míne,
" hebbað eówre handa, hicgeað on ellen,
" winnað on orde, wesað on mōde!"
Þā ārās monig gold-hladen þegn, gyrde hine his
swurde ;
þā tō dura eodon drihtlíce cempan,
15 Sigeferð and Eaha, hyra sweord getugon,
and ät ōðrum durum Ordláf and Gūðláf,
and Hengest sylf; hwearf him on lāste.
Þā git Gārulf Gūðere styrode,
þät hie swā freólíc feorh forman síðe
20 tō þære healle durum hyrsta ne bæran,
nu hyt nīða heard ānyman wolde:
ac he frägn ofer eal undearninga,
deór-mōd häleð, hwā þā duru heólde.
" Sigeferð is mín nama (cwäð he), ic eom Secgena
leód,

* See v. 1069 *seqq.*

25 " wrecca wîde cûð.　Fela ic weána gebâd,
" heardra hilda ;　þe is gyt her witod,
" swäðer þu sylf tô me　sêcean wylle."
þâ wäs on wealle　wäl-slihta gehlyn,
sceolde cêlod bord　cênum on handa
30 bân-helm berstan.　Buruh-þelu dynede,
ðð þät ät þære gûðe　Gârulf gecrang,
ealra ærest　eorð-bûendra,
Gûðlâfes snnu ;　ymbe hine gôdra fela
hwearf lacra hræw.　Hräfn wandrode
35 sweart and sealo-brûn ;　swurd-leóma stôd
swylce eal Finns-buruh　fŷrenu wære.
Ne gefrägn ic næfre wurðlîcor　ät wera hilde
sixtig sige-beorna　sêl gebæran,
ne næfre swânas swêtne　medo sêl forgyldan,
40 þonne Hnäfe guldon　his häg-stealdas.
Hig fuhton fîf dagas,　swâ hyra nân ne feól
driht-gesîða,　ac hig þâ duru heóldon.
þâ gewât him wund häleð　on wäg gangan,
sæde þät his byrne　âbrocen wære,
45 here-sceorpum hrôr,　and eác wäs his helm þyrl.
þâ hine sôna frägn　folces hyrde,
hû þâ wîgend　hyra wunda genæson
oððe hwäðer þæra hyssa . . . .

LIST OF NAMES

AND

GLOSSARY.

ABBREVIATIONS.

— ◦◦◦ —

m.: masculine.

f.: feminine.

n.: neuter.

nom., gen., etc.: nominative, genitive, etc.

w.: weak.

w. v.: weak verb.

st.: strong.

st. v.: strong verb.

I., II., III.: first, second, third pers.

comp.: compound.

imper.: imperative.

w.: with.

instr.: instrumental.

G. and Goth.: Gothic.

O.N.: Old Norse.

O.S.: Old Saxon.

O.H.G.: Old High German.

M.H.G.: Middle High German.

The vowel ä = a in *glad* }
The diphthong æ = a in *hair* } approximately.

The names **Leo, Bugge, Rieger**, etc., refer to authors of emendations.

Words beginning with **ge-** will be found under their root-word.

Obvious abbreviations, like **subj.**, etc., are not included in this list.

LIST OF NAMES.

bel, Cain's brother, 108.

Ælf-here (gen. Älf-heres, 2605), a kinsman of Wiglâf's, 2605.

Äsc-here, confidential adviser of King Hrôðgâr (1326), older brother of Yrmenlâf (1325), killed by Grendel's mother, 1295, 1324, 2123.

Beán-stân, father of Breca, 524.

Beó-wulf, son of Scyld, king of the Danes, 18, 19. After the death of his father, he succeeds to the throne of the Scyldings, 53. His son is Healfdene, 57.

Beó-wulf (Biówulf, 1988, 2390; gen. Beówulfes, 857, etc., Biówulfes, 2195, 2808, etc.; dat. Beówulfe, 610, etc., Biówulfe, 2325, 2843), of the race of the Geátas. His father is the Wægmunding Ecgþeów (263, etc.); his mother a daughter of Hrêðel, king of the Geátas (374), at whose court he is brought up after his seventh year with Hreðel's sons, Herebeald, Hæðcyn, and Hygelâc, 2429 ff. In his youth lazy and unapt (2184 f., 2188 f.); as man he attains in the gripe of his hand the strength of thirty men, 379. Hence his victories in his combats with bare hands (711 ff., 2502 ff.), while fate denies him the victory in the battle with swords, 2683 f. His swimming-match with Breca in his youth, 506 ff. Goes with fourteen Geátas to the assist-ance of the Danish king, Hrôðgâr, against Grendel, 198 ff. His combat with Grendel, and his victory, 711 ff., 819 ff. He is, in consequence, pre-sented with rich gifts by Hrôðgâr, 1021 ff. His combat with Grendel's mother, 1442 ff. Having again re-ceived gifts, he leaves Hrôðgâr (1818–1888), and returns to Hyge-lâc, 1964 ff. — After Hygelâc's last battle and death, he flees alone across the sea, 2360 f. In this bat-tle he crushes Däghrefn, one of the Hûgas, to death, 2502 f. He re-jects at the same time Hygelâc's kingdom and the hand of his widow (2370 ff.), but carries on the gov-ernment as guardian of the young Heardrêd, son of Hygelâc, 2378 ff. After Heardrêd's death, the king-dom falls to Beówulf, 2208, 2390. — Afterwards, on an expedition to avenge the murdered Heardrêd, he kills the Scylfing, Eádgils (2397), and probably conquers his country. — His fight with the drake, 2539 ff. His death, 2818. His burial, 3135 ff.

Breca (acc. Brecan, 506, 531), son of Beánstân, 524. Chief of the Brondings, 521. His swimming-match with Beówulf, 506 ff.

Brondingas (gen. Brondinga, 521). Breca, their chief, 521.

Brosinga mene, corrupted from, or according to Müllenhoff, written by mistake for, Breosinga mene (O.N., Brisinga men, cf. Haupts Zeitschr. XII. 304), collar, which the Brisingas once possessed.

Cain (gen. Caines, 107): descended from him are Grendel and his kin, 107, 1262 ff.

Däg-hrefn (dat. Däghrefne, 2502), a warrior of the Hûgas, who, according to 2504-5, compared with 1203, and with 1208, seems to have been the slayer of King Hygelâc, in his battle against the allied Franks, Frisians, and Hûgas. Is crushed to death by Beówulf in a hand-to-hand combat, 2502 ff.

Dene (gen. Dena, 242, etc., Denia, 2126, Deniga, 271, etc.; dat. Denum, 768, etc.), as subjects of Scyld and his descendants, they are also called Scyldings; and after the first king of the East Danes, Ing (Runenlied, 22), Ing-wine, 1045, 1320. They are also once calledHrêðmen, 445. On account of their renowned warlike character, they bare the names Gâr-Dene, 1, 1857, Hring-Dene (Armor-Danes), 116, 1280, Beorht-Dene, 427, 610. The great extent of this people is indicated by their names from the four quarters of the heavens: Eást-Dene, 392, 617, etc., West-Dene, 383, 1579, Sûð-Dene, 463, Norð-Dene, 784.— Their dwelling-place " in Scedelandum," 19, " on Scedenîgge," 1687, " be sæm tweónum," 1686.

Ecg-lâf (gen. Ecglâfes, 499), Hûnferð's father, 499.

Ecg-þeów (nom. Ecgþeów, 263, Ecgþeó, 373; gen. Ecgþeówes, 529, etc., Ecgþiówes, 2000), a far-famed hero of the Geátas, of the house of the Wægmundings. Beówulf is the son of Ecgþeów, by the only daugh-

ter of Hrêðel, king of the Geátas, 262, etc. Among the Wylings, he hasslain Heaðolâf(460), and in consequence he goes over the sea to the Danes(463), whose king, Hrô Ngâr, by means of gold, arranges the strife for him, 470.

Ecg-wela (gen. Ecg-welan, 1711). The Scyldings are called his descendants, 1711. Grein considers him the founder of the older dynasty of Danish kings, which closes with Heremôd. See **Heremôd**.

Elan, daughter of Healfdene, king of the Danes, (?) 62. According to the restored text, she is the wife of Ongenþeów, the Scylling, 62, 63.

Earna-näs, the Eagle Cape in the land of the Geátas, where occurred Beówulf's fight with the drake, 3032.

Eádgils (dat. Eádgilse, 2393), son of Ohthere, and grandson of Ongenþeów, the Scylling, 2393. His older brother is

Eánmund (gen. Eánmundes, 2612). What is said about both in our poem (2201-2207, 2380-2397, 2612-2620) is obscure, but the following may be conjectured: —

The sons of Ohthere, Eánmund and Eádgils, have rebelled against their father (2382), and must, in consequence, depart with their followers from Swiórice, 2205-6, 2380. They come into the country of the Geátas to Heardrêd (2380), but whether with friendly or hostile intent is not stated; but, according to 2203 f., we are to presume that they came against Heardrêd with designs of conquest. At a banquet (on feorme; or feorine, MS.) Heardrêd falls, probably through treachery, by the hand of one of the brothers, 2386, 2207. The murderer must have been Eánmund, to whom, according to 2613, "in battle the revenge of Weohstân brings death." Weohstân takes revenge for his murdered king, and exercises upon Eánmund's body the booty-right, and robs it of helm, breastplate, and sword (2616–17), which the slain man had received as gifts from his uncle, Onela, 2617-18. But Weohstân does not speak willingly of this fight, although he has slain Onela's brother's son, 2619–20. — After Heardrêd's and Eánmund's death, the descendant of Ongentheów, Eádgils, returns to his home, 2388. He must give way before Beówulf, who has, since Heardrêd's death, ascended the throne of the Geátas, 2390. But Beówulf remembers it against him in after days, and the old feud breaks out anew, 2392–94. Eádgils makes an invasion into the land of the Geátas (2394–95), during which he falls at the hands of Beówulf, 2397. The latter must have then obtained the sovereignty over the Sweonas (3005-6, where only the versi n, Scylfingas, can give a satisfactory sense).

Eofor (gen. Eofores, 2487, 2965; dat. Jofore, 2994, 2998), one of the Geátas, son of Wonrêd and brother of Wulf (2965, 2979), kills the Swedish king, Ongenþeów (2487 ff., 2978–82), for which he receives from King Hygelâc, along with other gifts, his only daughter in marriage, 2994–99.

Eormen-rîc (gen. Eormenrîces, 1202`, king of the Goths (cf. about him, W. Grimm, Deutsche Heldensage, p. 2, ff.). Hâma has wrested the Brosinga mene from him, 1202.

Eómær, son of Offa and þrýðc (cf. þrýðo), 1961.

Finn (gen. Finnes, 1069, etc.; dat. Finne, 1129), son of Folcwalda (1090), king of the North Frisians and of the Eotenas, husband of Hildeburg, a daughter of Hôce, 1072, 1077. He is the hero of the inserted poem on the Attack in Finnsburg, the obscure incidents of which are, perhaps, as follows: In Finn's castle, Finnsburg, situated in Jutland (1126–28), the Hôcing, Hnäf, a relative — perhaps a brother — of Hildeburg is spending some time as guest. Hnäf, who is a liegeman of the Danish king, Healfdene, has sixty men with him (Finnsburg, 38). These are treacherously attacked one night by Finn's men, 1073. For five days they hold the doors of their lodging-place without losing one of their number (Finnsburg, 41, 42). Then, however, Hnäf is slain (1071), and the Dane, Hengest, who was among Hnäf's followers, assumes the command of the beleaguered band. But on the attacking side the fight has brought terrible losses to Finn's men. Their numbers are diminished (1081 f.), and Hildeburg bemoans a son and a brother among the fallen (1074 f., cf. 1116, 1119). Therefore the Frisians offer the Danes peace (1086) under the conditions mentioned (1087–1095), and it is confirmed with oaths (1097), and money is given by Finn in propitiation (1108). Now all who have survived the battle go together to Friesland, the home proper of Finn, and here Hengest remains during the winter, prevented by ice and storms from returning home (Grein). But in spring the feud breaks out anew. Gûðláf and Osláf avenge Hnäf's fall, probably after they have brought help from home (1150). In the battle, the hall is filled with the corpses of the enemy. Finn himself is killed, and the queen is captured and carried away, along with the booty, to the land of the Danes, 1147–1160.

Finna land. Beówulf reaches it in his swimming-race with Breca, 580.

Fitela, the son and nephew of the Wälsing, Sigemund, and his companion in arms, 876–890. (Sigemund had begotten Fitela by his sister, Signŷ. Cf. more at length Leo on Beówulf, p. 38 ff., where an extract from the legend of the Walsungs is given.)

Folc-walda (gen. Folc-waldan, 1090), Finn's father, 1090.

Francan (gen. Francna, 1211; dat. Froncum, 2913). King Hygelác fell on an expedition against the allied Franks, Frisians, and Hûgas, 1211, 2917.

Fresan, Frisan, Frysan (gen. Fresena, 1094, Frysna, 1105, Fresna, 2916; dat. Frysum, 1208, 2913). To be distinguished, are : 1) North Frisians, whose king is Finn, 1069 ff.; 2) West Frisians, in alliance with the Franks and Hûgas, in the war against whom Hygelác falls, 1208, 2916. The country of the former is called Frysland, 1127; that of the latter, Fresna land, 2916.

Fr..es wäl (in Fr..es wäle, 1071), mutilated proper name.

Freawaru, daughter of the Danish king, Hróðgár; given in marriage to Ingeld, the son of the Heaðo-

beard king, Fróda, in order to end a war between the Danes and the Heaðobeardnas, 2023 ff., 2065.

Fróda (gen. Fródan), father of Ingeld, the husband of Freáware, 2026.

Gârmund (gen. Gârmundes, 1963), father of Offa. His grandson is Eómœr, 1961–63.

Geátas (gen. Geáta, 205, etc.; dat. Geátum, 195, etc.), a tribe in Southern Scandinavia, to which the hero of this poem belongs; also called Wedergeátas, 1493, 2552; or, Wederas, 225, 423, etc.; Gûðgeátas, 1539; Sægeátas, 1851, 1987. Their kings named in this poem are: Hréðel; Hæðcyn, second son of Hréðel; Hygelác, the brother of Hæðcyn; Heardréd, son of Hygelác; then Beówulf.

Gifðas (dat. Gifðum, 2495), Gepidœ, mentioned in connection with Danes and Swedes, 2495.

Grendel, a fen-spirit (102–3) of Cain's race, 107, 111, 1262, 1267. He breaks every night into Hróðgár's hall and carries off thirty warriors, 115 ff., 1583 ff. He continues this for twelve years, till Beówulf fights with him (147, 711 ff.), and gives him a mortal wound, in that he tears out one of his arms (817), which is hung up as a trophy in the roof of Heorot, 837. Grendel's mother wishes to avenge her son, and the following night breaks into the hall and carries off Äschere, 1295. Beówulf seeks for and finds her home in the fen-lake (1493 ff.), fights with her (1498 ff.), and kills her (1567); and cuts off the head of Grendel, who lay there dead (1589), and brings it to Hróðgár, 1648.

Gūð-lāf and Oslāf, Danish warriors under Hnäf, whose death they avenge on Finn, 1149.

Hālga, with the surname, *til,* the younger brother of the Danish king, Hrōðgār, 61. His son is Hrōðulf, 1018, 1165, 1182.

Hāma wrests the *Brosinga mene* from Eormenrîc, 1199.

Hāreð (gen. Hāreðes, 1982), father of Hygd, the wife of Hygelâc, 1930, 1982.

Hæðcyn (dat. Hæðcynne, 2483), second son of Hrêðel, king of the Geátas, 2435. Kills his oldest brother, Herebeald, accidentally, with an arrow, 2438 ff. After Hrê-ðel's death, he obtains the kingdom, 2475, 2483. He falls at Ravenswood, in the battle against the Swedish king, Ongenþeów, 2925. His successor is his younger brother, Hygelâc, 2944 ff., 2992.

Helmingas (gen. Helminga, 621). From them comes Wealhþeów, Hrōðgâr's wife, 621.

Heming (gen. Heminges, 1945, 1962). Offa is called Heminges mæg, 1945; Eómær, 1962. According to Bachlechner (Pfeiffer's Germania, I., p. 458), Heming is the son of the sister of Gârmund, Offa's father.

Hengest (gen. Hengestes, 1092; dat. Hengeste, 1084): about him and his relations to Hnäf and Finn, see **Finn.**

Here-beald(dat. Herebealde,2464), the oldest son of Hrêðel, king of the Geátas (2435), accidentally killed with an arrow by his younger brother, Hæðcyn, 2440.

Here-mōd (gen. Heremōdes, 902), king of the Danes, not belonging to the Scylding dynasty, but, ac-cording to Grein, immediately preceding it; is, on account of his unprecedented cruelty, driven out, 902 ff., 1710.

Here-rîc (gen. Hererîces, 2207). Heardrêd is called Hererîces nefa, 2207. Nothing further is known of him.

Het-ware or Franks, in alliance with the Frisians and the Hûgas, conquer Hygelâc, king of the Geátas, 2355, 2364 ff., 2917.

Healf-dene (gen. Healfdenes, 189, etc.), son of Beówulf, the Scylding (57); rules the Danes long and gloriously (57 f.); has three sons, Heorogâr, Hrōðgâr, and Hâlga (61), and a daughter, Elan, who, according to the renewed text of the passage, was married to the Scylfing, Ongenþeów, 62, 63.

Heard-rêd (dat. Heardrêde, 2203, 2376), son of Hygelâc, king of the Geátas, and Hygd. After his father's death, while still under age, he obtains the throne (2371, 2376, 2379); wherefore Beówulf, as nephew of Heardrêd's father, acts as guardian to the youth till he becomes older, 2378. He is slain by Ohthere's sons, 2386. This murder Beówulf avenges on Eádgils, 2396–97.

Heaðo-beardnas (gen. -beardna, 2033, 2038, 2068), the tribe of the Lombards. Their king, Frôda, has fallen in a war with the Danes, 2029, 2051. In order to end the feud, King Hrōðgâr has given his daughter, Freáware, as wife to the young Ingeld, the son of Frôda, a marriage that does not result happily; for Ingeld, though he long defers it on account of his love for his wife, nevertheless takes revenge for his father, 2021–2070 (Widsíð, 45–49).

Heaðo-láf (dat. Heaðo-láfe, 460), a Wylfingish warrior. Ecgþeów, Beówulf's father, kills him, 460.

Heaðo-ræmas reaches Breca in the swimming-race with Beówulf, 519.

Heoro-gár (nom. 61; Heregár, 467; Hiorogár, 2159), son of Healfdene, and older brother of Hróðgár, 61. His death is mentioned, 467. He has a son, Heoroweard, 2162. His coat of mail Beówulf has received from Hróðgár (2156), and presents it to Hygelâc, 2158.

Heoro-weard (dat. Heorowearde, 2162), Heorogár's son, 2161–62.

Heort, 78. Heorot, 166 (gen. Heorotes, 403; dat. Heorote, 475, Heorute, 767, Hiorte, 2100). Hróðgár's throne-room and banqueting hall and assembly-room for his liegemen, built by him with unusual splendor, 69, 78. In it occurs Beówulf's fight with Grendel, 720 ff. The hall receives its name from the stag's antlers, of which the one-half crowns the eastern gable, the other half the western.

Hildeburh, daughter of Hóce, relative of the Danish leader, Hnäf, consort of the Frisian king, Finn. After the fall of the latter, she becomes a captive of the Danes, 1072, 1077, 1159. See also under **Finn**.

Hnäf (gen. Hnäfes, 1115), a Hócing (Widsíð, 29), the Danish King Healfdene's general, 1070 ff. For his fight with Finn, his death and burial, see under **Finn**.

Hond-sció, warrior of the Geátas: dat. 2077.

Hóc (gen. Hóces, 1077), father of Hildeburh, 1077; probably also of Hnäf (Widsíð, 29).

Hreðel (gen. Hreðles, 1486), son of Swerting, 1204. King of the Geátas, 374. He has, besides, a daughter, who is married to Ecgþeów, and has born him Beówulf, (374), three sons, Herebeald, Hæðcyn, and Hygelâc, 2435. The eldest of these is accidentally killed by the second, 2440. On account of this inexpiable deed, Hreðel becomes melancholy (2443), and dies, 2475.

Hreðla (gen. Hreðlan, MS. Hrædlan, 454), the same as Hreðel (cf. Müllenhoff in Haupts Zeitschrift, 12, 260), the former owner of Beówulf's coat of mail, 454.

Hreð-men (gen. Hreð-manna, 445), the Danes are so called, 445.

Hreð-ríc, son of Hróðgár, 1190, 1837.

Hrefna-wudu, 2926, or Hrefnes-halt, 2936, the thicket near which the Swedish king, Ongenþeów, slew Hæðcyn, king of the Geátas, in battle.

Hreosna-beorh, promontory in the land of the Geátas, near which Ongenþeów's sons, Óhthere and Onela, had made repeated robbing incursions into the country after Hreðel's death. These were the immediate cause of the war in which Hreðel's son, King Hæðcyn, fell, 2478 ff.

Hróð-gár (gen. Hróðgáres, 235, etc.; dat. Hróð-gáre, 64, etc.), of the dynasty of the Scyldings; the second of the three sons of King Healfdene, 61. After the death of his elder brother, Heorogár, he assumes the government of the Danes, 465, 467 (yet it is not certain whether Heorogár was king of the Danes before Hróðgár, or whether his death occurred while his father, Healfdene, was still alive). His consort is Wealhþeów (613), of the stock of the Helmings (621), who has born him two sons, Hréðric and Hróðmund (1190), and a daughter, Freáware (2023), who has been given in marriage to the king of the Heaðobeardnas, Ingeld. His throneroom (78 ff.), which has been built at great cost (74 ff.), is visited every night by Grendel (102, 115), who, along with his mother, is slain by Beówulf (711 ff., 1493 ff). Hróðgâr's rich gifts to Beówulf, in consequence, 1021, 1818; he is praised as being generous, 71 ff., 80, 1028 ff., 1868 ff.; as being brave, 1041 ff., 1771 ff.; and wise, 1699, 1725. — Other information about Hróðgâr's reign for the most part only suggested: his expiation of the murder which Ecgþeów, Beówulf's father, committed upon Heaðoláf, 460, 470; his war with the Heaðobeardnas; his adjustment of it by giving his daughter, Freáware, in marriage to their king, Ingeld; evil results of this marriage, 2021–2070. — Treachery of his brother's son, Hróðulf, intimated, 1165–1166.

Hróð-mund, Hróðgâr's son, 1190.

Hróð-ulf, probably a son of Hâlga, the younger brother of King Hróðgâr, 1018, 1182. Wealhþeów expresses the hope (1182) that, in case of the early death of Hróðgâr, Hróð-ulf would prove a good guardian to Hróðgâr's young son, who would succeed to the government; a hope which seems not to have been accomplished, since it appears from 1165, 1166 that Hróð-ulf has abused his trust towards Hróðgâr.

Hrones-nâs (dat. -nässe, 2806, 3137), a promontory on the coast of the country of the Geátas, visible from afar. Here is Beówulf's grave-mound, 2806, 3137.

Hrunting (dat. Hruntinge, 1660), Hûnferð's sword, is so called, 1458, 1660.

Hûgas (gen. Hûga, 2503), Hygelâc wars against them allied with the Franks and Frisians, and falls, 2195 ff. One of their heroes is called Däghrefn, whom Beówulf slays, 2503.

Hûn-ferð, the son of Ecgláf, þyle of King Hróðgâr. As such, he has his place near the throne of the king, 499, 500, 1167. He lends his sword, Hrunting, to Beówulf for his battle with Grendel's mother, 1456 f. According to 588, 1168, he slew his brothers. Since his name is always alliterated with vowels, it is probable that the original form was, as Rieger (Zachers Ztschr., 3,414) conjectures, Unferð.

Hûn-lâfing, name of a costly sword, which Finn presents to Hengest, 1144.

Hygd (dat. Hygde, 2173), daughter of Häreð, 1930; consort of Hygelâc, king of the Geátas, 1927; her son, Heardrêd, 2203, etc. — Her noble, womanly character is emphasized, 1927 ff.

Hyge-lâc (gen. Hige-lâces, 194, etc., Hygelâces, 2387; dat. Higelâce, 452, Hygelâce, 2170), king of the Geátas, 1203, etc. His grandfather is Swerting, 1204; his father, Hrêðel, 1486, 1848; his older brothers, Herebeald and Hæðcyn, 2435; his sister's son, Beówulf, 374, 375. After his brother, Hæðcyn, is killed by Ongenþeów, he undertakes the

9

government (2992 in connection with the preceding from 2937 on). To Eofor he gives, as reward for slaying Ongenþeów, his only daughter in marriage, 2998. But much later, at the time of the return of Beówulf from his expedition to Hróðgâr, we see him married to the very young Hygd, the daughter of Hæreð, 1930. The latter seems, then, to have been his second wife. Their son is Heardrêd, 2203, 2376, 2387. — Hygelâc falls during an expedition against the Franks, Frisians, and Hûgas, 1206, 1211, 2356–59, 2916–17.

Ingeld (dat. Ingelde, 2065), son of Fróda, the Heaðobeard chief, who fell in a battle with the Danes, 2051 ff. In order to end the war, Ingeld is married to Freáware, daughter of the Danish king, Hróðgâr, 2025–30. Yet his love for his young wife can make him forget only for a short while his desire to avenge his father. He finally carries it out, excited thereto by the repeated admonitions of an old warrior, 2042–70 (Widsið, 45–59).

Ing-wine (gen. Ingwina, 1045, 1320), friends of Ing, the first king of the East Danes. The Danes are so called, 1045, 1320.

Mere-wioingas (gen. Mere-wioinga, 2922), a name of the Franks, 2922.

Nägling, the name of Beówulf's sword, 2681.

Offa (gen. Offan, 1950), king of the Angles (Widsið, 35), the son of Gârmund, 1963; married (1950) to Þryðo (1932), a beautiful but cruel woman, of unfeminine spirit (1932 ff.), by whom he has a son, Eómær, 1961.

Ôht-here (gen. Ôhtheres, 2929, 2933; Ôhteres, 2381, 2393, 2395, 2613), son of Ongenþeów, king of the Swedes, 2929. His sons are Eánmund (2612) and Eádgils, 2393.

Onela (gen. Onelan, 2933), Ôhthere's brother, 2617, 2933.

Ongen-þeów (nom. -þeów, 2487, -þió, 2952; gen. þeówes, 2476, -þiówes, 2388; dat. -þió, 2987), of the dynasty of the Scylfings; king of the Swedes, 2384. His wife is, perhaps, Elan, daughter of the Danish king, Healfdene (62), and mother of two sons, Onela and Ôhthere, 2933. She is taken prisoner by Hæðcyn, king of the Geátas, on an expedition into Sweden, which he undertakes on account of her sons' plundering raids into his country, 2480 ff. She is set free by Ongenþeów (2931), who kills Hæðcyn, 2925, and encloses the Geátas, now deprived of their leader, in the Ravenswood (2937 ff.), till they are freed by Hygelâc, 2944. A battle then follows, which is unfavorable to Ongenþeów's army. Ongenþeów himself, attacked by the brothers, Wulf and Eofor, is slain by the latter, 2487 ff., 2962 ff.

Ôs-lâf, a warrior of Hnäf's, who avenges on Finn his leader's death, 1149 f.

Scede-land, 19. **Sceden-ig** (dat. Sceden-igge, 1687), O.N., Scân-ey, the most southern portion of the Scandinavian peninsula, belonging to the Danish kingdom, and, in the above-mentioned passages of our poem, a designation of the whole Danish kingdom.

Scêf or **Sceáf,** the father of Scyld, 4.

Scyld (gen. Scyldes, 19), a Scêfing, 4. His son is Beówulf, 18, 53;

his grandson, Healfdene, 57; his great-grandson, Hrôðgâr, who had two brothers and a sister, 59 ff. — Scyld dies, 26; his body, upon a decorated ship, is given over to the sea (32 ff.), just as he, when a child, drifted alone, upon a ship, to the land of the Danes, 43 ff. After him his descendants bear his name.
Scyldingas (Scyldungas, 2053; gen. Scyldinga, 53, etc., Scyldunga, 2102, 2160; dat. Scyldingum, 274, etc.), a name which is extended also to the Danes, who are ruled by the Scyldings, 53, etc. They are also called Ar-Scyldingas, 464; Sige-Scyldingas, 598, 2005; Þeód-Scyldingas, 1020; Here-Scyldingas, 1109.
Scylfingas, a Swedish royal family, whose relationship seems to extend to the Geátas, since Wiglâf, the son of Wihstân, who in another place, as a kinsman of Beówulf, is called a Wægmunding (2815), is also called leód Scylfinga, 2604. The family connections are perhaps as follows: —

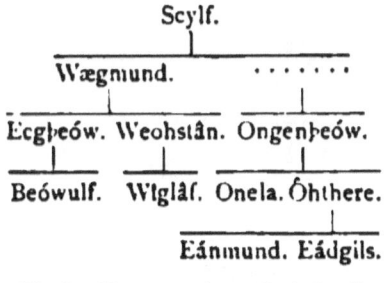

Scylf.

Wægmund.   . . . .

Ecgþeów. Weohstân. Ongenþeów.

Beówulf. Wîglâf. Onela. Ôhthere.

Eánmund. Eádgils.

The Scylfings are also called Heaðo-Scilfingas, 63, Gûð-Scylfingas, 2928.
Sige-mund (dat. -munde, 876, 885), the son of Wäls, 878, 898. His (son and) nephew is Fitela, 880, 882. His fight with the drake, 887 ff.

Swerting (gen. Swertinges, 1204), Hygelâc's grandfather, and Hrê-ðel's father, 1204.
Sweon (gen. Sweona, 2473, 2947, 3002), also Sweó-þeód, 2923. The dynasty of the Scylfings rules over them, 2382, 2925. Their realm is called Swiórîce, 2384, 2496.
Þryðo, consort of the Angle king, Offa, 1932, 1950. Mother of Eómær, 1961, notorious on account of her cruel, unfeminine character, 1932 ff. She is mentioned as the opposite to the mild, dignified Hygd, the queen of the Geátas.
Wäls (gen. Wälses, 898), father of Sigemund, 878, 898.
Wæg-mundingas (gen. Wægmundinga, 2608, 2815). The Wægmundings are on one side, Wihstân and his son Wiglâf; on the other side, Ecgþeów and his son Beówulf (2608, 2815). See under Scylfingas.
Wederas (gen. Wedera, 225, 423, 498, etc.), or Weder-geátas. See Geátas.
Wêland (gen. Wêlandes, 455), the maker of Beówulf's coat of mail, 455.
Wendlas (gen. Wendla, 348) : their chief is Wulfgâr. See Wulfgâr. The Wendlas are, according to Grundtvig and Bugge, the inhabitants of Vendill, the most northern part of Jutland, between Limfjord and the sea.
Wealh-þeów (613, Wealh-þeó, 665, 1163), the consort of King Hrôð-gâr, of the stock of the Helmings, 621. Her sons are Hrêðric and Hrôðmund, 1190; her daughter, Freáware, 2023.
Weoh-stân (gen. Weox-stânes, 2603, Weoh-stânes, 2863, Wih-stânes,

2753, 2908, etc.), a Wægmunding (2608), father of Wiglâf, 2603. In what relationship to him Ælfhere, mentioned 2605, stands, is not clear. — Weohstân is the slayer of Eánmund (2612), in that, as it seems, he takes revenge for his murdered king, Heardrêd. See **Eánmund.**

Wîg-lâf, Weohstân's son, 2603, etc., a Wægmunding, 2815, and so also a Scylfing, 2604; a kinsman of Ælfhere, 2605. For his relationship to Beówulf, see the genealogical table under **Scylfingas.** — He supports Beówulf in his fight with the drake, 2605 ff., 2662 ff. The hero gives him, before his death, his ring, his helm, and his coat of mail, 2810 ff.

Won-rêd (gen. Wonrêdes, 2972), father of Wulf and Eofor, 2966, 2979.

Wulf (dat. Wulfe, 2994), one of the Geátas, Wonrêd's son. He fights in the battle between the armies of Hygelâc and Ongenþeów with Ongenþeów himself, and gives him a wound (2966), whereupon Ongenþeów, by a stroke of his sword, disables him, 2975. Eofor avenges his brother's fall by dealing Ongenþeów a mortal blow, 2978 ff.

Wulf-gâr, chief of the Wendlas, 348, lives at Hrôðgâr's court, and is his "âr and ombiht," 335.

Wylfingas (dat. Wylfingum, 461). Ecgþeów has slain Heaðolâf, a warrior of this tribe, 460.

Yrmen-lâf, younger brother of Æschere, 1325.

GLOSSARY.

A

ac, conj. denoting contrariety: hence 1) *but* (like N.II.G. sondern), 109, 135, 339, etc. — 2) *but* (N.II.G. aber), *nevertheless,* 602, 697, etc. — 3) in direct questions: nonne, numquid, 1991.

aglæca, ahlæca, äglæca, -cea, w. m. (Goth. aglô, *trouble;* agl-s, Ags. egle, *troublesome;* O.II.G. egilcihhi, *trouble*); original meaning, *bringer of trouble:* hence 1) *evil spirit, demon, a demon-like being;* of Grendel, 159, 433, 593, etc.; of the drake, 2535, 2906, etc. — 2) *great hero, mighty warrior;* of Sigemund, 894; of Beówulf: gen. sg. aglæcan(?), 1513; of Beówulf and the drake: nom. pl. þâ aglæcean, 2593.

aglæc-wif, st. n., *demoniacal, in the form of a woman;* of Grendel's mother, 1260.

aldor. See ealdor.

al-wealda. See eal-w.

am-biht (from and-b., Goth. and-baht-s), st. m., *servant, man-servant:* nom. sg. ombeht, of the coast-guard, 287; ombiht, of Wulfgâr, 336.

ambiht-þegn (from ambiht n. officium and þegn, which see), *servant, man-servant:* dat. sg. ombihtþegne, of Beówulf's servant, 674.

an, prep. with the dat., *on, in, with respect to,* 678; *with, among, at, upon* (position after the governed word), 1936; with the acc., 1248. Elsewhere on, which see.

ancor, st. m., *anchor:* dat. sg. ancre, 303, 1884.

ancor-bend, m. (?) f. (?), *anchor-cable:* dat. pl. oncer-bendum, 1919.

and, conj. (the form ond is rare; for example, 601, 1149, 2041), and, 33, 39, 40, etc.

anda, w. m., *excitement, vexation, horror:* dat. wrâðum on andan, 709, 2315.

and-git, st. n., *insight, understanding:* nom. sg., 1060. See gitan.

and-hâtor, st. m. n., *heat coming against one:* gen. sg. rêðes and-hâttres, 2524.

and-lang, -long, adj., *very long:* hence 1) *at whole length, raised up high:* acc. andlongne eorl, 2696 (cf. Bugge upon this point, Zachers Ztschr., 4, 217). — 2) *continual, entire;* andlangne däg, 2116, *the whole day;* andlonge niht, 2939.

and-leán, st. n., *reward, payment in full:* acc. sg., 1542, 2095 (hand-, hond-lean, MS.).

and-risno, st. f. (von rîsan surgere, decere), *that which is to be observed, that which is proper, etiquette:* dat. pl. for andrysnum, *according to etiquette,* 1797.

and-saca, w. m., *adversary :* godes andsaca (Grendel), 787, 1683.

and-slyht, st. m., *blow in return :* acc. sg., 2930, 2973 (MS. both times hond-slyht).

and-swarn, st. f., *act of accosting :* 1) to persons coming up, *an address*, 2861. — 2) in reply to something said, *an answer*, 354, 1494, 1841.

and-weard, adj., *present, existing :* acc. sg. n. swin ofer helme and-weard (*the image of the boar, which stands on his helm*), 1288.

and-wlita, w. m., *countenance :* acc. sg. -an, 690.

an-sund, adj., *entirely unharmed :* nom. sg. m., 1001.

an-sýn, f., *the state of being seen :* hence 1) *the exterior, the form*, 251 : ansýn ýwde, *showed his form*, i.e. appeared, 2835. — 2) *aspect, appearance*, 929; on-sýn, 2773.

an-walda, w. m., *He who rules over all, God*, 1273.

atol, adj. (also eatol, 2075, etc.), *hostile, frightful, cruel :* of Grendel, 159, 165, 593, 2075, etc.; of Grendel's mother's hands (dat. pl. atolan), 1503 ; of the undulation of the waves, 849 ; of battle, 597, 2479. — cf. O.N. atall, fortis, strenuus.

atelîc, adj., *terrible, dreadful :* atelîc egesa, 785.

Â

â, adv. (Goth. áiv, acc. from aiv-s aevum), *ever, always*, 455, 882, 931, 1479: â sýððan, *ever afterwards, ever, ever after*, 283, 2921. — *ever*, 780. — Comp. nâ.

âd, st. m. *funeral pile :* acc. sg. âd, 3139; dat. sg. âde, 1111, 1115.

âd-faru, st. f., *way to the funeral pile :* dat. sg. on âd-fâre, 3011.

âdl, st. f., *sickness*, 1737, 1764, 1849.

âð, st. m., *oath in general, =740 : oath of allegiance*, 472 (?); *oath of reconciliation of two warring peoples*, 1098, 1108.

âð-sweord, st. n., *the solemn taking of an oath, the swearing of an oath :* nom. pl., 2065. See sweord.

âðum-swerian, m. pl., *son-in-law and father-in-law :* dat. pl., 84.

âgan, verb, pret. and pres., *to have, to possess*, w. acc.: III. prs. sg. âh, 1728 ; inf. âgan, 1089 ; prt. âhte, 487, 522, 533; with object, geweald, to be supplied, 31. Form contracted with the negative: prs. sg. 1. nâh hwâ sweord wege (*I have no one to wield the sword*), 2253.

âgen, adj., *own, peculiar*, 2677.

âgend (prs. part. of âgan), *possessor, owner, lord :* gen. sg. âgendes, *of God*, 3076. — Compounds : blæd-, bold-, folc-, mägen-âgend.

âgend-freá, w. m., *owner, lord :* gen. sg. âgend-freán, 1884.

âhsjan, ge-âhsjan, w. v.: 1) *to examine, to find out by inquiring :* pret. part. ge-âhsod, 433. — 2) *to experience, to endure :* pret. âhsode, 1207; pl. âhsodon, 423.

âht, st. n. (contracted from â-wiht, which see), *something, anything :* âht ewices, 2315.

ân, num. The meaning of this word betrays its original demonstrative character : 1) *this, that*, 2411, of the hall in the earth mentioned before ; similarly, 100 (of Grendel, already mentioned), cf. also 2775. — 2) *one*, a particular one among many, a single one, in numerical sense : ymb âne niht (*the next night*), 135; þurh ânes cräft, 700;

þára ânum, 1038; ân æfter ânum,
one for the other (Ilreðel for
Herebeald), 2462: similarly, ân
æfter eallum, 2269; ânes hwät, *some
single thing, a part*, 3011; se ân
leóda duguðe, *the one of the heroes of
the people*, 2238; ânes willan, *for the
sake of a single one*, 3078, etc. —
Hence, again, 3) *alone, distinguished*, 1459, 1886. — 4) *a*, in the
sense of an indefinite article : ân . . .
feónd, 100; gen. sg. ânre bêne (or to
No. 2[?]), 428; ân...draca, 2211 —
5) gen. pl. ânra, in connection with
a pronoun, *single;* ânra gehwilces,
every single one, 733; ânra gehwylcum, 785. Similarly, the dat. pl.
in this sense : nemne feáum ânum,
except a few single ones, 1082. —
6) solus, *alone:* in the strong form,
1378, 2965; in the weak form, 145,
425, 431, 889, etc.; with the gen.,
âna Geáta duguðe, *alone of the
warriors of the Gedtas*, 2658. — 7)
solitarius, *alone, lonely*, see æn. —
Comp. nân.

ân-feald, adj., *simple, plain, without
reserve:* acc. sg. ânfealdne geþôht,
simple opinion, 256.

ân-genga, -gengea, w. m., *he who
goes alone*, of Grendel, 165, 449.

ân-haga, w. m., *he who stands alone*,
solitarius, 2369.

ân-hydig, adj. (like the O.N. ein-
râd-r, *of one resolve*, i.e. of firm resolve), *of one opinion*, i.e. firm,
brave, decided, 2668.

ânga, adj. (only in the weak form),
single, only : acc. sg. ângan dôhtor,
375, 2998; ângan eaferan, 1548;
dat. sg. ângan brêðer, 1263.

ân-pað, st. m., *lonely way, path:* acc.
pl. ânpaðas, 1411.

ân-ræd, adj. (cf. under ân-hydig),

of firm resolution, resolved, 1530,
1576.

ân-tîd, st. f., *one time*, i.e. the same
time : ymb ân-tîd ôðres dôgores,
about the same time the second day
(they sailed twenty-four hours), 219.
— ân stands as in ân-môd, O.H.G.
ein-muoti, *harmonious, of the same
disposition*.

ânunga, adv., *throughout, entirely,
wholly*, 635.

âr, st. m., *ambassador, messenger*,
336, 2784.

âr, st. f., 1) *honor, dignity:* ârum healdan, *to hold in honor*, 296; similarly, 1100, 1183. — 2) *favor, grace,
support:* acc. sg. âre, 1273, 2607;
dat. sg. âre, 2379; gen. pl. hwât...
ârna, 1188. — Comp. worold-âr;
also written ær.

âr-fäst, adj., *honorable, upright*,
1169; of Hûnferð (with reference
to 588). See fâst.

ârian, w. v., (*to be gracious*), *to spare:*
III. sg. prs. w. dat. nænegum âraÞ;
of Grendel, 599.

âr-staf, st. m., (elementum honoris),
grace, favor: dat. pl. mid ârstafum,
317. — *Help, support:* dat. pl. for
âr-stafum, *to the assistance*, 382,
458. See stäf.

âter-tân, m., *poisonous branch:* dat.
pl. îren âter-tânum fâh (steel which
is damasceened by the sap of
branches used in sorcery), 1460.

âttor, st. n., *poison*, here of the poison
of the dragon's bite: nom., 2716,

âttor-sceaða, w. m., *poisonous
enemy, of the poisonous dragon :*
gen. sg. -sceaðan, 2840.

âwâ, adv. (certainly not the dative,
but a reduplicated form of â, which
see), *ever :* âwâ tô aldre, *for ever
and ever*, 956.

Ā

ädre, adv., *hastily, directly, immediately,* 77, 354, 3107.

äðele, adj., *noble :* nom. sg., of Beówulf, 198, 1313; of Beowulf's father, 263, where it can be understood as well in a moral as in a genealogical sense; the latter prevails decidedly in the gen. sg. äðelan cynnes, 2235.

äðeling, st. m., *nobleman, man of noble descent,* especially the appellation of a man of royal birth; so of the kings of the Danes, 3; of Scyld, 33; of Hrôðgâr, 130; of Sigemund, 889; of Beówulf, 1226, 1245, 1597, 1816, 2189, 2343, 2375, 2425, 2716, 3136; perhaps also of Däghrefn, 2507; — then, in a broader sense, also denoting other noble-born men : Äschere, 1295; Hrôðgâr's courtiers, 118, 983; Heremôd's courtiers, 907; Hengest's warriors, 1113; Beówulf's retinue, 1805, 1921, 3172; noble-born in general, 2889. — Comp. sib-äðeling.

äðelu, st. n., only in the pl., *noble descen', nobility,* in the sense of noble lineage : acc. pl. äðelu, 392; dat. pl. cyning äðelum gôd, *the king, of noble birth,* 1871; äðelum diôre, *worthy on account of noble lineage,* 1950; äðelum (hæleþum, MS.), 332. — Comp. fäderäðelu.

äfnan, w. v. w. acc., *to perform, to carry out, to accomplish :* inf. ellenweorc äfnan, *to do a heroic deed,* 1465; pret. unriht äfnde, *perpetrated wrong,* 1255.

ge-äfnan, 1) *to carry out, to do, to accomplish :* pret. pl. þät geäfndon swâ, *so carried that out,* 538; pret. part. âð wäs geäfned, *the oath was*

sworn, 1108. — 2) *get ready, prepare :* pret. part. geäfned, 3107. See **efnan.**

äfter (comparative of a f, Ags. of, which see; hence it expresses the idea of *forth, away, from, back*), a) adv., *thereupon, afterwards,* 12, 341, 1390, 2155. — ic him äfter sceal, *I shall go after them,* 2817; in word äfter cwäð, 315, the sense seems to be, *spoke back, having turned :* b) prep. w. dat., 1) (temporal) *after,* 119, 128, 187, 825, 1939, etc.; äfter beorne, *after the* (death of) *the hero,* 2261, so 2262; äfter mâððum-welan, *after* (obtaining) *the treasure,* 2751.— 2) (causal) as proceeding from something, denoting result and purpose, hence, *in consequence of, conformably to :* äfter rihte, *in accordance with right,* 1050, 2111; äfter faroðe, *with the current,* 580; so 1321, 1721, 1944, 2180, etc., äfter heaðo-swâte, *in consequence of the blood of battle,* 1607; äfter wälnîðe, *in consequence of mortal enmity,* 85; *in accordance with, on account of, after, about :* äfter äðelum (hæleþum, MS.) frägn, *asked about the descent,* 332; ne frin þu äfter sælum, *ask not after my welfare,* 1323; äfter sincgyfan greóteð, *weeps for the giver of treasure,* 1343; him äfter deórum men dyrne langað, *longs in secret for the dear man,* 1880; ân äfter ânum, *one for the other,* 2462, etc. — 3) (local), *along :* äfter gumcynnum, *throughout the races of men, among men,* 945; sôhte bed äfter bûrum, *sought a bed among the rooms of the castle* (the castle was fortified, the hall was not), 140; äfter recede wlât, *looked along the hall,* 1573; stone äfter stâne, *smelt along the* *rocks*, 2289; äfter lyfte, *along the air, through the air*, 2833; similarly, 996, 1008, 1317, etc.

äf-þunea, w. m., *anger, chagrin, vexations affair:* nom., 502.

äglæcea. See **nglæcea.**

äled (Old Sax. eld, O.N. eld-r), st. m., *fire*, 3016.

äled-leóma, w. m., (*fire-light*), *torch:* acc. sg. leóman, 3126. See **leóma.**

äl-fylce from äl-, Goth. ali-s, ἄλλος, and fylce, O.N. fylki, collective form from fulc), st. n., *other folk, hostile army:* dat. pl. wiδ älfylcum, 2372.

äl-mihtlg (for eal-m.), adj., *almighty:* nom. sg. m., of the weak form, se äl-mihtiga, 92.

äl-wiht, st. m., *being of another species, monster:* gen. pl. äl-wihta eard, of the dwelling-place of Grendel's kindred, 1501.

äppel-fealu, adj., *dappled sorrel,* or *dappled yellow:* nom. pl. äppelfealuwe mearas, *dappled yellow steeds,* 2166.

ärn, st. n., *house,* in the compounds heai-, hord-, medo-, þryδ-, win-ärn.

äsc, st. m., *ash* (does not occur in Beówulf in this sense), *lance, spear,* because the shaft consists of ash wood: dat. pl. (quâ instr.) äscum and ecgum, *with spears and swords,* 1773.

äsc-holt, st. n., *ash wood, ashen shaft:* nom. pl. äsc-holt ufan græg, *the ashen shafts gray above* (spears with iron points), 330.

äsc-wiga, w. m., *spear-fighter, warrior armed with the spear:* nom. sg., 2043.

ät, prep. w. dat., with the fundamental meaning of nearness to something, hence 1) local, a) *with, near,* *at, on, in* (rest): ät hýδe, *in harbor,* 32; ät symle, *at the meal,* 81; ät åde, *on the funeral-pile,* 1111, 1115; ät þe ânum, *with thee alone,* 1378; ät wige, *in the fight,* 1338; ät hilde, 1660, 2082; ät æte, *in eating,* 3027, etc. b) *to, towards, at, on* (motion to): deáδes wylm hrân ät heortan, *seized upon the heart,* 2271; gehêton ät härgtrafum, *vowed at* (or *to*) *the temples of the gods,* 175. c) with verbs of taking away, *away from* (as starting from near an object): ge: eah þät ful ät Wealhþeón, *took the cup from W.,* 630; fela ic gebâd grynna ät Grendle, *from Grendel,* 931; ät minum fäder genam, *took me from my father to himself,* 2430.−2) temporal, *at, in, at the time of:* ät frumsceafte, *in the beginning,* 45; ät ende, *at an end,* 224; fand sinne dryhten ealdres ät ende, *at the end of life, dying,* 2791; similarly, 2823; ät feohgyftum, *in giving gifts,* 1090; ät siδestan, *finally,* 3014.

ät-græpe, adj., *laying hold of,* prehendens, 1270.

ät-rihte, adv., *almost,* 1658.

Æ

ædre, êdre, st. f., *aqueduct, canal* (not in Beów.), *vein* (not in Beów.), *stream, violent pouring forth:* dat. pl. swât ædrum sprong, *the blood sprang in streams,* 2967; blôd êdrum dranc, *drank the blood in streams*(?), 743.

eδm, st. m., *breath, gasp, snort:* instr. sg. hreδer æδme weóll, *the breast* (of the drake) *heaved with snorting,* 2594.

æfen, st. m., *evening,* 1236.

æfen-gram, adj., *hostile at evening, night-enemy:* nom. sg. m. æfengrom, of Grendel, 2075.

æfen-leóht, st. n., *evening-light:* nom. sg., 413.

æfen-ræst, st. f., *evening-rest:* acc. sg. -ræste, 647, 1253.

æfen-spræc, st. f., *evening-talk:* acc. sg. gemunde ... æfen-spræce, *thought about what he had spoken in the evening,* 760.

æfre, adv., *ever, at any time,* 70, 280, 504, 693, etc.: in negative sentences, æfre ne, *never,* 2601.— Comp. næfre.

æg-hwâ (O.H.G. êo-ga-hwër), pron., *every, each:* dat. sg. æghwäm, 1385. The gen. sg. in adverbial sense, *in all, throughout, thoroughly:* æghwäs untæle, *thoroughly blameless,* 1866; ægh-wäs unrîm, *entirely innumerable quantity,* i.e. an enormous multitude, 2625, 3136.

æg-hwäðer (O.H.G. êo-ga-hwëdar): 1) *each* (of two): nom. sg. häfde æghwäðer ende gefëred, *each of the two* (Beówulf and the drake) *had reached the end,* 2845; dat. sg. æghwäðrum wäsbrôga framôðrum, *to each of the two* (Beówulf and the drake) *was fear of the other,* 2565; gen. sg. æghwäðres ... worda and worca, 287.— 2) *each* (of several): dat. sg. heora æghwäðrum, 1637.

æg-hwär, adv., *everywhere,* 1060.

æg-hwile (O.H.G. êo-gi-hwëlih), pron., unusquisque, *every* (one): 1) used as an adj.: acc. sg. m. dæl æghwylcne, 622.— 2) as substantive, a) with the partitive genitive: nom. sg. æg-hwyle, 9, 2888; dat. sg. æghwylcum, 1051. b) without gen.: nom. sg. æghwyle, 985, 988; (wäs) æghwyle ôðrum trýwe, *each one* (of two) *true to the other,* 1166.

æg-weard, st. f., *watch on the sea-shore:* acc. sg. æg-wearde, 241.

æht (abstract form from âgan, denoting the state of possessing), st. f.: 1) *possession, power:* acc. sg. on flôdes æht, 42; on wäteres æht, *into the power of the water,* 516; on æht gehwearf Denigea freán, *passed over into the possession of a Danish master,* 1680.— 2) *property, possessions, goods:* acc. pl. æhte, 2249.— Comp. mâðm-, goldæht.

æht (O.H.G. âhta), st. f., *pursuit:* nom. Þâ wäs æht boden Sweona leódum, segn Higelâce, *then was pursuit offered to the people of the Sweonas,* (*their*) *banner to Hygelâc* (i.e. the banner of the Swedes, taken during their flight, fell into the hands of Hygelâc), 2958.

ge-æhtan, w. v., *to prize, to speak in praise of:* pret. part. geæhted, 1886.

ge-æhtla, w. m., or **ge-æhtle,** w. f., *a speaking of with praise, high esteem:* gen. sg. hy ... wyrðe Þinceað eorla geæhtlan, *seem worthy of the high esteem of the noble-born,* 369.

æn (parallel form of ân), num., *one:* acc. sg. m. Þone ænne Þone ..., *the one whom* ..., 1054; oftor micle Þonne on ænne sið, *much oftener than one time,* 1580; forð onsendon ænne, *sent him forth alone,* 46.

æne, adv., *once:* oft nalles æne, 3020.

ænig, pron., *one, any one,* 474, 503, 510, 534, etc.: instr. sg. nolde ... ænige Þinga, *would in no way, not at all,* 792; lyt ænig mearn, *little did any one sorrow* (i.e. no one), 3130.— With the article: näs se folccyning ... ænig, *no people's king,* 2735.— Comp. nænig.

æn-lîc, adj., *alone, excellent, distinguished:* ænlîc ansŷn, *distinguished appearance*, 251; þeáh þe hió ænlîcu sŷ, *though she be beautiful*, 1942.

ær (comparative form, from â): 1) adv., *sooner, before, beforehand*, 15, 656, 695, 758, 901, etc., *for a long time*, 2596: eft swâ ær, *again as formerly*, 643; ær ne siððan, *neither sooner nor later*, 719; ær and sið, *sooner and later* (all times), 2501; nô þŷ ær (*not so much the sooner*), *yet not*, 755, 1503, 2082, 2161, 2467. — 2) conjunct., *before, ere:* a) with the ind.: ær hió tô setle geóng, 2020. b) w. subjunc.: ær ge f.r fêran, *before you travel farther*, 252; ær he on weg hwurfe, 264, so 677, 2819; ær þon däg cwôme, *ere the day break*, 732; ær correlative to ær adv.: ær he feorh seleð, aldor an ôfre, ær he wille ..., *he will sooner* (rather) *leave his life upon the shore, before* (than) *he will* . . ., 1372. — 3) prepos. with dat., *before:* ær deáðe, *before death*, 1389; ær däges hwile, *before daybreak*, 2321; ær swyltdäge, *before the day of death*, 2799.

æror, comp. adv., *sooner, beforehand*, 810; *formerly*, 2655.

ærra, comp. adj., *earlier:* instr. pl., ærran mælum, *in former times*, 908, 2238, 3036.

ærest, superl.: 1) adv., *first of all, foremost*, 6, 617, 1698, etc. — 2) as subst. n., *relation in the beginning:* acc. þät ic his ærest þe eft gesägde (*told thee, in what relation it stood at first to the coat of mail that has been presented*), 2158.

ær-däg, st. m. (*before-day*), *morning-twilight, gray of morning:* dat. sg. mid ærdäge, 126; samod ærdäge, 1312, 2943.

ærende, st. n., *errand, trust:* acc. sg., 270, 345.

ær-fäder, st. m., *late father, deceased father:* nom. sg. swâ his ærfäder, 2623.

ær-gestreón, st. n., *old treasure, possessions dating from old times:* acc. sg., 1758; gen. sg. swylcra fela ærgestreóna, *much of such old treasure*, 2233. See **gestreón**.

ær-geweorc, st. n., *work dating from old times:* nom. sg. enta ærgeweorc, *the old work of the giants* (of the golden sword-hilt from Grendel's water-hall), 1680. See **geweorc**.

ær-gôd, adj., *good since old times, long invested with dignity* or *advantages:* äðeling ærgôd, 130; (eorl) ærgôd, 1330; iren ærgôd (*excellent sword*), 990, 2587.

ær-wela, w. m., *old possessions, riches dating from old times:* acc. sg. ærwelan, 2748. See **wela**.

æs, st. n., *carcass, carrion:* dat. (instr.) sg. æse, of Aschere's corpse, 1333.

ät, st. m., *food, meat:* dat. sg., hû him ät æte speów, *how he fared well at meat*, 3027.

ættren (see **âttor**), adj., *poisonous:* wäs þät blôd tô þäs hât, ættren ellorgâst, se þær inne swealt, *so hot was the blood,* (*and*) *poisonous the demon* (Grendel's mother) *who died therein*, 1618

B

bana, bona, w. m., *murderer*, 158, 588, 1103, etc.: acc. sg. bonan Ongenþeówes, of Hygelâc, although

in reality his men slew Ongenþeów
(2905 ff.), 1969. Figuratively of
inanimate objects: ne wäs ecg
bona, 2507; wearð wracu Weoh-
stânes bana, 2614. — Comp.: ecg-,
feorh-, gâst-, hand-, mûð-bana.
bon-gâr, st. m. *murdering spear*,
2032.
ge-bannan, st. v. w. acc. of the
thing and dat. of the person, *to
command, to bid:* inf., 74.
bâd, st. f., *pledge*, only in comp.: nýd-
bâd.
bân, st. n., *bone:* dat. sg. on bâne
(on the bony skin of the drake),
2579; dat. pl. heals ealne ymbe-
feng biteran bânum (here of the
teeth of the drake), 2693.
bân-côfa, w. m., "cubile ossium"
(Grimm) of the body: dat. sg.
-côfan, 1446.
bân-fâg, adj., *variegated with
bones*, either with ornaments made
of bone-work, or adorned with
bone, perhaps deer-antlers; of
Hrôðgâr's hall, 781. The last
meaning seems the more probable.
bân-fät, st. n., *bone-vessel*, i.e. the
body: acc. pl. bân-fatu, 1117.
bân-hring, st. m., *the bone-struc-
ture, joint, bone-joint:* acc. pl.
hire wið halse . . . bânhringas bräc
(*broke her neck-joint*), 1568.
bân-hûs, st. n., *bone-house*, i.e. the
body: acc. sg. bânhûs gebräc,
2509; similarly, 3148.
bân-locа, w. m., *the enclosure of the
bones*, i.e. the body: acc. sg. bât
bânlocan, *bit the body*, 743; nom.
pl. burston bânlocan, *the body burst*
(of Grendel, because his arm was
torn out), 819.
bât, st. m., *boat, craft, ship*, 211. —
Comp. sæ-bât.
bât-weard, st. m., *boat-watcher, he*

who keeps watch over the craft:
dat. sg. -wearde, 1901.
bäð, st. n., *bath:* acc. sg. ofer ganotes bäð, *over the diver's bath* (i.e.
the sea), 1862.
bärnan, w. v., *to cause to burn, to
burn:* inf. hêt . . . bânfatu bärnan, *bade that the bodies be burned*,
1117; ongan . . . beorht hofu bärnan, *began to consume the splendid
country-seats* (the dragon), 2314.
for-bärnan, w. v., *consume with
fire:* inf. hy hine ne môston . . .
brondefor-bärnan, *they* (the Danes)
could not burn him (the dead
Äschere) *upon the funeral-pile*,
2127.
bädan (Goth. baidjan, O.H.G. bei-
ða), *to incite, to encourage:* pret.
bädde byre geonge, *encouraged
the youths* (at the banquet), 2019.
ge-bädan, w. v., *to press hard:* pret.
part. bysigum gebäded, *distressed
by trouble, difficulty, danger* (of
battle), 2581; *to drive, to send
forth:* stræla storm strengum gebäded, *the storm of arrows sent
from the strings*, 3118; *overcome:*
draca . . . bealwe gebäded, *the
dragon . . . overcome by the ills of
battle*, 2827.
bäl (O.N. bâl), st. n., *fire, flames:*
(wyrm) mid läcle fûr, *passed*
(*through the air*) *with fire*, 2309;
häfde landwara lige befangen, bäle
and bronde, *with fire and burning*, 2323. — Especially, *the fire of
the funeral-pile, the funeral-pile*,
1110, 1117, 2127; ær he bäl cure,
ere he sought the burning (i.e.
died), 2819; hâtað . . . hläw ge-
wyrcean . . . äfte bäle, *after I am
burned, let a burial mound be
thrown up* (Beówulf's words),
2804.

bæl-fȳr, st. n., *bale-fire, fire of the funeral-pile:* gen. pl. bælfȳra mæst, 3144.

bæl-stede, st. m., *place for the funeral pile:* dat. sg. in bæl-stede, 3098.

bæl-wudu, st. m., *wood for the funeral-pile*, 3113.

bær, st. f., *bier*, 3106.

ge-bæran, w.v.. *to conduct one's self, behave:* inf. w. adv., ne gefrägn ic þâ mægðe ... sêl gebæran, *I did not hear that a troop bore itself better, maintained a nobler deportment*, 1013; he on eorðan geseah þone leófestan lîfes ät ende bleáte gebæran, *saw the best-beloved upon the earth, at the end of his life, struggling miserably* (i.e. in a helpless situation), 2825.

ge-bætan (denominative from bæte, *the bit*), w. v., *to place the bit in the mouth of an animal, to bridle:* pret. part. þâ wäs Hrôðgâre hors gebæted, 1400.

be, prep. w. dat. (with the fundamental meaning *near*, "but not of one direction, as ät, but more general"): 1) local, *near by, near, at, on* (rest): be ȳdlâfe uppe lægon, *lay above, upon the deposit of the waves* (upon the strand, of the slain nixies), 566; häfde be honda, *held by the hand* (Beówulf held Grendel), 815; be sæm tweonum, *in the circuit of both the seas*, 859, 1686; be mäste, *on the mast*, 1906; be fȳre, *by the fire*, 2220; be nässe, *at the promontory*, 2244; sät be þæm gebrôðrum twæm, *sat by the two brothers*, 1192; wäs se gryre lässa efne swâ micle swâ bið mägða cräft be wäpnedmen, *the terror was just so much less, as is the strength of woman to the*

warrior (i.e. is valued by), 1285, etc. — 2) also local, but of motion from the subject in the direction of the object, *on, upon, by:* gefêng he eaxle, *seized by the shoulder*, 1538; âlêdon leófne þeóden be mäste, *laid the dear lord near the mast*, 36; be healse genam, *took him by the neck, fell upon his neck*, 1873; wæpen hafenade be hiltum, *grasped the weapon by the hilt*, 1575, etc. — 3) with this is connected the causal force, *on account of, for, according to:* ic þis gid be þe âwräc, *I spake this solemn speech for thee, for thy sake*, 1724; þû þe lær be þon, *learn according to this, from this*, 1723; be fäder lâre, *according to her father's direction*, 1951. — 4) temporal, *while, during:* be þe lifigendum, *while thou livest, during thy life*, 2666. See bî.

bed, st. n., *bed, couch:* acc. sg. bed, 140, 677; gen. sg. beddes, 1792; dat. pl. beddum, 1241. — Comp.: deað-, hlin-, läger-, morðor-, wäl-bed.

ge-bedde, w. f., *bed-fellow:* dat. sg. wolde sêcan cwên tô gebeddan, *wished to seek the queen as bed-fellow, to go to bed with her*, 666. — Comp. heals-gebedde.

begen, fem. bû, *both:* nom. m., 536, 770, 2708; acc. fem. on bâ healfa, *on two sides* (i.e. Grendel and his mother), 1306; dat. m. bâm, 2197; and in connection with the possessive instead of the personal pronoun, ûrum bâm, 2661; gen. n. bega, 1874, 2896; bega gehwäðres, *each one of the two*, 1044; bega folces, *of both peoples*, 1125.

ge-belgan, st. v. (properly, *to cause to swell, to swell*), *to irritate:* w.

dat. (pret. subj.) þät he êcean dryhtne bitre gebulge, *that he had bitterly angered the eternal Lord,* 2332; pret. part. gebolgen, 1540; (gebolge, MS.), 2222; pl. gebolgne, 1432; more according to the original meaning in turne gebolgen, 2402.

â-belgan, *to anger:* pret. sg. w. acc. ôð þät hyne ân âbealh mon on môde, *till a man angered him in his heart,* 2281; pret. part. âbolgen, 724.

ben, st. f., *wound:* acc. sg. benne, 2725. — Comp.: feorh-, seax-ben.

bene, st. f., *bench:* nom. sg. benc, 492; dat. sg. bence, 327, 1014, 1189, 1244. — Comp.: ealu-, medu-benc.

bene-swêg, st. m., (*bench-rejoicing*), *rejoicing which resounds from the benches,* 1162.

bene-þel, st. n., *bench-board, the wainscotted space where the benches stand:* nom. pl. benc-þelu, 486; acc. pl. bencþelu beredon, *cleared the bench-boards* (i.e. by taking away the benches, so as to prepare couches), 1240.

bend, st. m. f., *bond, fetter:* acc. sg. forstes bend, *frost's bond,* 1610; dat. pl. bendum, 978. — Comp.: fyr-, hell-, hyge-, îren-, oncer-, searo-, wäl-bend.

ben-geat, st. n., (*wound-gate*), *wound-opening:* nom. pl. ben-geato, 1122.

bera (O.N. beri), w. m., *bearer:* in comp. hleor-bera.

beran, st. v. w. acc., *to carry:* III. sg. pres. byreð, 296, 448; þone mâððum byreð, *carries the treasure* (upon his person), 2056; pres. subj. bere, 437; pl. beren, 2654; inf. beran, 48, 231, 291, etc.; hêht

þâ se hearda Hrunting beran, *to bring Hrunting,* 1808; up beran, 1921; in beran, 2153; pret. bär, 495, 712, 847, etc.; mandryhtne bär fäted wæge, *brought the lord the costly vessel,* 2282; pl. bæron, 213, 1636, etc.; bæran, 2851; pret. part. boren, 1193, 1648, 3136. — The following expressions are poetic paraphrases of the forms *go, come:* þät we rondas beren eft tô earde, 2654; gewltað forð beran wæpen and gewædu, 291; ic gefrägn sunu Wihstânes hringnet beran, 2755; wígheafolan bär, 2662; helmas bæron, 240 (conjecture); scyldas bæran, 2851: they lay stress upon the connection of the man with his weapons.

ät-beran, *to carry to:* inf. tô beadolâce (*battle*) ätberan, 1562; pret. þâ hine on morgentîd on Heaðoræmas holm up ätbär, *the sea bore him up to the Heaðoræmas,* 519; hiô Beówulfe medoful ätbär, *brought Beowulf the mead-cup,* 625; mägenbyrðenne ... hider ût ätbär cyninge mînum, *bore the great burden hither to my king,* 3093; pl. hî hyne ätbæron tô brimes faroðe, 28.

for-beran, *to hold, to suppress:* inf. þät he þone breóstwylm forberan ne mehte, *that he could not suppress the emotions of his breast,* 1878.

ge-beran, *to bring forth, to bear:* pret. part. þät lâ mäg secgan se þe sôð and riht fremeð on folce ... þät þes eorl wære geboren betera (*that may every just man of the people say, that this nobleman is better born*), 1704.

ôð-beran, *to bring hither:* pret. þâ mec sæ ôðbär on Finna land, 579.

on-beran (O.H.G. in bĕran, intpĕ-
ran, but in the sense of carerc), auferre, *to carry off, to take away:*
inf. Iren ærgôd þät þäs ahkœan
blôdge beadufolme onberan wolde,
*excellent sword which would sweep
off the bloody hand of the demon,*
991; pret. part. (wäs) onboren
beága hord, *the treasure of the
rings had been carried off,* 2285.
— Compounds with the pres. part.:
helm-, sâwl-berend.

berian (denominative from bär,
naked), w. v., *to make bare, to
clear:* pret. pl. bencl-elu beredon,
cleared the bench-place (by removing the benches), 1240.

berstan, st. v., *to break, to burst:*
pret. pl. burston bânlocan, 819;
bengeato burston, 1122. — *to crack,
to make the noise of breaking:* fingras burston, *the fingers cracked*
(from Beówulf's gripe), 761.

for-berstan, *break, to fly asunder:*
pret. Nägling forbärst, *Nägling*
(Beówulf's sword) *broke in two,*
2681.

betera, adj. (comp.), *better:* nom.
sg. m. betera, 469, 1704.

bet-lîc, adj., *excellent, splendid:*
nom. sg. n., of Hrôðgâr's hall,
781; of Hygelâc's residence, 1926.

betst, betost (superl.), *best, the
best:* nom. sg. m. betst beadurinca,
1110; neut. nu is ôfost betost, þät
we ..., *now is haste the best, that
we* ..., 3008; voc. m. secg betsta,
948; neut. acc. beaduscrûda betst,
453; acc. sg. m. þegn betstan,
1872.

bên, st. n., (*beacon*), *token, mark,
sign:* acc. sg. betimbredon beadu-
rôfes bêcn (of Beówulf's grave-
mound), 3162. See **beacen**.

bêg. See **beág.**

bên, st. f., *entreaty:* gen. sg. bêne,
428, 2285.

bêna, w. m., *suppliant,* supplex:
nom. sg. swâ Ju bêna eart (*as thou
entreatest*), 352; swâ he bêna wäs
(*as he had asked*), 3141; nom. pl.
hy bênan synt, 364.

ge-bêtan: 1) *to make good, to remove:* pret. ac Ju Hrôðgâre wîdcûð-
ne weán wihte gebêttest, *hast thou
in any way relieved Hrôðgâr of the
evil known afar,* 1992; pret. part.
acc. sg. swylce oncyððe ealle ge-
bêtte, *removed all trouble,* 831. —
2) *to avenge:* inf. wihte ne meahte
on þam feorhbonan fæhðe gebêtan,
*could in no way avenge the death
upon the slayer,* 2466.

beadu, st. f., *battle, strife, combat:*
dat. sg. (as instr.) beadwe, *in combat,* 1540; gen. sg. bâd beadwa
ge-þinges, *waited for the combats*
(with Grendel) *that were in store
for him,* 710.

beadu-folm, st. f., *battle-hand:* acc.
sg. -folme, of Grendel's hand, 991.

beado-grîma, w. m., (*battle-mask*),
helmet: acc. pl. -grîman, 2258.

beado-hrägl, st. n., (*battle-garment*), *corselet, shirt of mail,* 552.

beado-lâc, st. n., (*exercise in arms,
tilting*), *combat, battle:* dat. sg. tô
beado-lâce, 1562.

beado-leôma, w. m., (*battle-light*),
sword: nom. sg., 1524.

beado-mêce, st. m., *battle-sword.*
nom. pl. beado-mêcas, 1455.

beado-rlnc, st. m., *battle-hero, warrior:* gen. pl. betst beadorinca, 1110.

beadu-rôf, adj., *strong in battle:*
gen. sg. -rôfes, of Beówulf, 3162.

beadu-rûn, st. f., *mystery of battle:*
acc. sg. onband beadu-rûne, *solved
the mystery of the combat,* i.e. gave
battle, commenced the fight, 501.

beadu-scearp, adj., *battle-sharp, sharp for the battle*, 2705.

beadu-scrûd, st. n., (*battle-dress*), *corselet, shirt of mail :* gen. pl. beaduscrûda betst, 453.

beadu-serce, w. f.,(*battle-garment*), *corselet, shirt of mail :* acc. sg. brogdne beadu-sercean (because it consists of interlaced metal rings), 2756.

beado-weorc, st. n., (*battle-work*), *battle :* gen. sg. gefeh beado-weorces, *rejoiced at the battle*, 2300.

beald, adj., *bold, brave :* in comp. cyne-beald.

bealdian, w. v., *to show one's self brave :* pret. bealdode gôdum dædum (*through brave deeds*), 2178.

bealdor, st. m., *lord, prince :* nom. sg. sinca baldor, 2429; winia bealdor, 2568.

bealu, st. n., *evil, ruin, destruction :* instr. sg. bealwe, 2827 ; gen. pl. bealuwa, 281 ; bealewa, 2083 ; bealwa, 910. — Comp.: cwealm-, ealdor-, hreðer-, leód-, morðor-, niht-, sweord-, wîg-bealu.

bealu, adj., *deadly, dangerous, bad :* instr. sg. hyne sâr hafað befongen balwon bendum, *pain has entwined him in deadly bands*, 978.

bealo-cwealm, st. m., *violent death, death by the sword* (?), 2266.

bealo-hycgende, pres. part., *thinking of death, meditating destruction :* gen. pl. æghwäðrum bealo-hycgendra, 2566.

bealo-hydig, adj., *thinking of death, meditating destruction :* of Grendel, 724.

bealo-nîð, st. m., (*zeal for destruction*), *deadly enmity :* nom. sg., 2405 ; *destructive struggle :* acc. sg. bebeorh þe þone bealonîð, *be-*

ware of destructive striving, 1759; *death-bringing rage :* nom. sg. him on breóstum bealo-nîð weóll, *in his breast raged deadly fury* (of the dragon's poison), 2715.

bearhtm (see beorht): 1) st. m., *splendor, brightness, clearness :* nom. sg. eágena bearhtm, 1767. — 2) *sound, tone :* acc. sg. bearhtm ongeâton, gûðhorn galan, *they heard the sound,* (*heard*) *the battle-horn sound*, 1432.

bearm, m., *gremium, sinus, lap, bosom :* nom. sg. foldan bearm, 1138; acc. sg. on bearm scipes, 35, 897; on bearm nacan, 214; him on bearm hladan bunan and discas, 2776. — 2) figuratively, *possession, property*, because things bestowed were placed in the lap of the receiver (so 40 and 2195, on bearm licgan, âlecgan); dat. sg. him tô bearme cwom mâððumfät mære, *came into his possession*, 2405.

bearn,st. n.,1) *child, son :* nom. sg. bearn Healfdenes, 469, etc.; Ecgláfes bearn, 499, etc.; dat. sg. bearne, 2371; nom. pl. bearn, 59; dat. pl. bearnum, 1075. — 2) in a broader sense, *scion, offspring, descendant :* nom. sg. Ongenþeów's bearn, *of his grandson*, 2388 ; nom. pl. ylda bearn, 70; gumena bearn, *children of men*, 879; häleða bearn, 1190; äðelinga bearn, 3172; acc. pl. ofer ylda bearn, 606; dat. pl. ylda bearnum, 150; gen. pl. niðða bearna, 1006. — Comp.: brôðor-, dryht-bearn.

bearn-gebyrdu, f., *birth, birth of a son :* gen. sg. þät hyre eald-metod êste wære bearn-gebyrdo, *has been gracious through the birth of such a son* (i.e. as Beówulf), 947.

bearu, st. m., (*the bearer*, hence properly only the *fruit-tree*, especially the oak and the beech), *tree*, collectively *forest:* nom. pl. hrinde bearwas, *rustling trees* (or *rustling forests*), 1364.

beácen, st. n., *sign, banner*, vexillum : nom. sg. beorht beácen godes, *of the sun*, 570 ; gen. pl. beácna beorhtost, 2778. See bēcn.

ge-beácnian, w. v., *to mark, to indicate:* pret. part. ge-beácnod, 140.

beág, st. m., *ring, ornament:* nom. sg. beáh (*neck-ring*), 1212; acc. sg. beáh (the collar of the murdered king of the Heaðobeardnas), 2042 ; bēg (collective for the acc. pl.), 3163 ; dat. sg. ewom Wealh-þeó forð gân under gyldnum beáge, *she walked along under a golden head-ring, wore a golden diadem*, 1164 ; gen. sg. beages (of a collar), 1217 ; acc. pl. beágas (rings in general), 80, 523, etc.; gen. pl. beága, 35, 352, 1488, 2285, etc.—Comp.: earm-, heals-beág.

beág-gyfa, w. m., *ring-giver*, designation of the prince: gen. sg. -gyfan, 1103.

beág-hroden, adj., *adorned with rings, ornamented with clasps:* nom. sg. beághroden, cwên, of Hróðgâr's consort, perhaps with reference to her diadem (cf. 1164), 624.

beáh-hord, st. m. n., *ring-hoard, treasure consisting of rings:* gen. sg. beáh-hordes, 895 ; dat. pl. beáh-hordum, 2827 ; gen. pl. beáh-horda weard, of King Hróðgâr, 922.

beáh-sele, st. m., *ring-hall, hall in which the rings were distributed:* nom. sg., of Heorot, 1178.

beáh-þegu, st. f., *the receiving of the ring:* dat. sg. æfter beáh-þege, 2177.

beáh-wriða, w. m *ring-band*, ring with prominence given to its having the form of a band : acc. sg. beáh-wriðan, 2019.

beám, st m., *tree*, only in the compounds fyrgen-, gleó-beám.

beátan, st. v., *thrust, strike:* pres. sg. mearh burhstede beáteð, *the steed beats the castle-ground* (place where the castle is built), i.e. with his hoofs, 2266 ; pret. part. swealt bille ge-beáten, *died, struck by the battle-axe*, 2360.

beorh, st. m.: 1) *mountain, rock:* dat. sg. beorge, 211 ; gen. sg. beorges, 2525, 2756 ; acc. pl. beorgas, 222. — 2) *grave-mound, tomb-hill:* acc. sg. biorh, 2808 ; beorh, 3098, 3165. A grave-mound serves the drake as a retreat (cf. 2277, 2412): nom. sg. beorh, 2242 ; gen. sg. beorges, 2323. — Comp. stân-beorh.

beorh, st. f., *veil, covering, cap;* only in the comp. heáford-beorh.

beorgan, st. v. (w. dat. of the interested person or thing), *to save, to shield:* inf. wolde feore beorgan, *place her life in safety*, 1294; here-byrne . . . seó þe bâncôfan beorgan cûðe, *which could protect his body*, 1446; pret. pl. ealdre burgan, 2600.

be-beorgan (w. dat. refl. of pers. and acc. of the thing), *to take care, to defend one's self from:* inf. him be-beorgan ne con wom, *cannot keep himself from stain* (fault), 1747; imp. bebeorh þe þone bealoniðð, 1759.

ge-beorgan (w. dat. of person or thing to be saved), *to save, to protect:* pret. sg. þæt gebearh feore, *protected the life*, 1549; scyld wel gebearg lîfe and lîce, 2571.

ymb-beorgan, *to surround pro-*

teetingly : pret. sg. hring ûtan ymb-bearh, 1504.

beorht, byrht, adj.: 1) *gleaming, shining, radiant, shimmering :* nom. sg. beorht, of the sun, 570, 1803; beorhta, of Heorot, 1178; þät beorhte bold, 998; acc. sg. beorhtne, of Beówulf's grave-mound, 2804; dat. sg. tô |ære byrhtan (here-byrhtan, MS.) byrig, 1200; acc. pl. beorhte frätwe, 214, 897; beorhte randas, 231; bord-wudu beorhtan, 1244; n. beorht hofu, 2314. Superl.: beácna beorh-tost, 2778. — 2) *excellent, remark-able :* gen. sg. beorhtre bôte, 158. — Comp.: sadol-, wlite-beorht.

beorhte, adv., *brilliantly, brightly, radiantly,* 1518.

beorhtian, w. v., *to sound clearly :* pret. sg. beorhtode benc-swèg, 1162.

beorn, st. m., *hero, warrior, noble man :* nom. sg. (Hrôðgâr), 1881, (Beówulf), 2434, etc.; acc. sg. (Beów.), 1025, (Äschere), 1300; dat. sg. beorne, 2261; nom. pl. beornas (Beówulf and his com-panions), 211, (Hrôðgâr's guests), 857; gen. pl. beorna (Beówulf's liege-men), 2405. — Comp.: folc-, gûð-beorn.

beornan, st. v., *to burn :* pres. part. byrnende (of the drake), 2273. — Comp. un-byrnende.

for-beornan, *to be consumed, to burn :* pret. sg. for-barn, 1617, 1668; for-born, 2673.

ge-beornan, *to be burned :* pret. gebarn, 2698.

beorn-cyning, st. m., *king of war-riors, king of heroes :* nom. sg. (as voc.), 2149.

beódan, st. v.: 1) *to announce, to inform, to make known :* inf. biô-dan, 2893. — 2) *to offer, to proffer* (as the notifying of a transaction in direct reference to the person concerned in it): pret. pl. him geþingo budon, *offered them an agreement,* 1086; pret. part. þâ wäs äht boden Sweona leodum, *then was pursuit offered the Swed-ish people,* 2958; inf. ic þâm gôdan sceal mâðmas beódan, *I shall offer the excellent man treasures,* 385.

â-beódan, *to present, to announce :* pret. word inne âbead, *made known the words within,* 390; *to offer, to tender, to wish :* pret. him hæl âbead, *wished him health* (greeted him), 654. Similarly, hælo âbeád, 2419; eoton weard âbead, *offered the giant a watcher,* 669.

be-beódan, *to command, to order :* pret. swâ him se hearda bebeád, *as the strong man commanded them,* 401. Similarly, swâ se rica be-beád, 1976.

ge-beódan: 1) *to command, to order :* inf. hêt þâ gebeódan byre Wihstânes häleða monegum, |ät hie . . ., *the son of Wihstan caused orders to be given to many of the men . . .,* 3111. — 2) *to offer :* him Hygd gebeád hord and rice, *of-fered him the treasure and the chief power,* 2370; inf. gûðe ge-beódan, *to offer battle,* 604.

beód-geneát, st. m., *table-compan-ion :* nom. and acc. pl. geneátas, 343, 1714.

beón, verb, *to be,* generally in the future sense, *will be :* pres. sg. I. gûðgeweorca ic beó gearo sôna, *I shall immediately be ready for warlike deeds,* 1826; sg. III. wâ bið þäm þe sceal . . ., *woe to him who . . .!* 183; so, 186; gifeðe bið is given, 299; ne bið þe wilna

gâd (*no wish will be denied thee*),
661; þær þe biðˀ manna þearf, *if*
thou shalt need the warriors, 1836;
ne biðˀ swylc cwênlic þeáw, *is not*
becoming, honorable to a woman,
1941; eft sôna biðˀ, *will happen*
directly, 1763; similarly, 1768, etc.;
pl. þonne bióðˀ brocene, *then are*
broken, 2064; feor cǫ̂ðˀðe beóðˀ
sêlran gesôhte þam þe . . ., " terrae
longinquae meliores sunt visitatu
ei qui . . ." (Grein), 1839; imp. beó
(bió) þu on ôfeste, *hasten!* 386,
2748; beó wiðˀ Geátas gläd, *be*
gracious to the Gedtas, 1174.

beór, st. n., *beer :* dat. sg. ät beóre,
at beer-drinking, 2042; instr. sg.
beóre druncen, 531; beóre druncne, 480.

beór-sceale, st. m., *keeper of the*
beer, cup-bearer : gen. pl. beór-
scealca sum (one of Hrôðˀgâr's followers, because they served the
Geátas at meals), 1241.

beór-sele, st. m., *beer-hall, hall in*
which beer is drunk : dat. sg. in
(on) beórsele, 482, 492, 1095;
biórsele, 2636.

beór-þegu, st. f., *beer-drinking,*
beer-banquet : dat. sg. äfter beór-
þege, 117; ät þære beórþege, 618.

beót, st. n., *promise, binding agree-*
ment to something that is to be
undertaken : acc. sg. he beót ne
âlêh, *did not break his pledge*, 80;
beót eal . . . gelæste, *performed all*
that he had pledged himself to, 523.

ge-beótian, w. v., *to pledge one's*
self to an undertaking, to bind
one's self : pret. gebeótedon, 480,
536.

beót-word, st. n., same as beót:
dat. pl. beót-wordum spräc, 2511.

biddan, st. v., *to beg, to ask, to pray :*
pres. sg. I. dôðˀswâ ic bidde! 1232;

inf. (w. acc. of the pers. and gen.
of the thing asked for) ic þe biddan wille ânre bêne, *beg thee for*
one, 427; pret. swâ he selfa bäd,
as *he himself had requested*, 29;
bäd hine bliðˀne (supply wesan) ät
þære beórþege, *begged him to be*
cheerful at the beer-banquet, 618;
ic þe lange bäd þät þu . . ., *begged*
you a long time that you, 1995;
frioðˀowære bäd hlâford sinne,
begged his lord for protection
(acc. of pers. and gen. of thing),
2283; bäd þät ge geworhton,
asked that you . . ., 3097; pl. wordum bædon þät . . ., 176.

on-biddan, w. v., *to await :* inf.
lætaðˀ hilde-bord her onbidan . . .
worda geþinges, *let the shields*
await here the result of the con-
ference (lay the shields aside here).
397.

bil, st. n. *sword :* nom. sg. bil, 1568;
bill, 2778; acc. sg. bil, 1558;
instr. sg. bille, 2360; gen. sg. billes,
2061, etc.; instr. pl. biilum, 40;
gen. pl. billa, 583, 1145.—Comp.:
gûðˀ-, hilde-, wig-bil.

bindan, st. v., *to bind, to tie :* pret.
part. acc. sg. wudu bundenne, *the*
bound wood, i.e. the built ship, 216;
bunden golde sword, *a sword bound*
with gold, i.e. either having its hilt
inlaid with gold, or having gold
chains upon the hilt (swords of
both kinds have been found),
1901 : nom. sg. heoru bunden,
1286, has probably a similar meaning.

ge-bindan, *to bind :* pret. sg. þær
ic fife geband, *where I had bound*
five(?), 420; pret. part. cyninges
þegn word ôðˀer fand sôðˀe gebunden, *the king's man found* (after
many had already praised Beówulf's

deed) *other words* (also referring to Beówulf, but in connection with Sigemund) *rightly bound together*, i.e. in good alliterative verses, as are becoming to a gid, 872; wundenmæl wrättum gebunden, *sword bound with ornaments*, i.e. inlaid, 1532; bisgum gebunden, *bound together by sorrow*, 1744; gomel gûðwiga eldo gebunden, *hoary hero bound by old age* (fettered, oppressed), 2112.

on-bindan, *to unbind, to untie, to loose:* pret. onband, 501.

ge-bind, st. n. coll., *that which binds, fetters:* in comp. is-gebind.

bite, st. m., *bite*, figuratively of the cut of the sword: acc. sg. bite irena, *the swords' bite*, 2260; dat. sg. äfter billes bite, 2061. — Comp. lâð-bite.

biter (primary meaning that of biting), adj.: 1) *sharp, cutting, cutting in:* acc. sg. biter (of a short sword), 2705; instr. sg. biteran strále, 1747; instr. pl. biteran bânum, *with sharp teeth*, 2693. — 2) *irritated, furious:* nom. pl. bitere, 1432.

bitre, adv., *bitterly* (in a moral sense), 2332.

bî, big (fuller form of the prep. be, which see), prep. w. dat.: 1) *near, at, on, about, by* (as under be, No. 1): bi sæm tweónum, *in the circuit of both seas*, 1957; ârâs bî ronde, *raised himself up by the shield*, 2539; bi wealle gesät, *sat by the wall*, 2718. With a freer position: him big stôdan bunan and orcas, *round about him*, 3048. — 2) *to, towards* (motion): hwearf þâ bi bence, *turned then towards the bench*, 1189; geóng bi sesse, *went to the seat*, 2757.

bid (see bîdan), st. n., *tarrying, hesitation:* þær wearð Ongenþió on bid wrecen, *forced to tarry*, 2963.

bîdan, st. v.: 1) *to delay, to stay, to remain, to wait:* inf. nô on wealle leng bidan wolde, *would not stay longer within the wall* (the drake), 2309; pret. in þýstrum bâd, *remained in darkness*, 87; flota stille bâd, *the craft lay still*, 301; receda ... on þäm se rica bâd, *where the mighty one dwell*, 310; þær se snottra bâd, *where the wise man* (Hrôðgâr) *waited*, 1314; he on searwum bâd, *he* (Beówulf) *stood there armed*, 2569; ic on earde bâd mælgesceafta, *lived upon the paternal ground the time appointed me by fate*, 2737; pret. pl. sume þær bidon, *some remained, waited there*, 400. — 2) *to await, to wait for*, with the gen. of that which is awaited: inf. bidan woldon Grendles gûðe, *wished to await the combat with Grendel, to undertake it*, 482; similarly, 528; wiges bidan, *await the combat*, 1269; n das andsware bidan wolde, *would await no answer*, 1495; pret. bâd beadwa geþinges, *awaited the event of the battle*, 710; sægenga bâd âgendfreán, *the sea-goer* (boat) *awaited its owner*, 1883; sele ... heaðowylma bâd, lâðan liges (the poet probably means to indicate by these words that the hall Heorot was destroyed later in a fight by fire; an occurrence, indeed, about which we know nothing, but which 1165 and 1166, and again 2068 ff. seem to indicate), 82.

â-bidan, *to await*, with the gen.: inf., 978.

ge-bidan: 1) *to tarry, to wait:*

imp. gebîde ge on beorge, *wait ye
on the mountain,* 2530; pret. part.
þeáh þe wintra lyt under burhlocan
gebiden häbbe Háreðes dôhtor,
*although H.'s daughter had dwelt
only a few years in the castle,*
1929. — 2) *to live through, to
experience, to expect* (w. **acc.**) :
inf. sceal endedäg mînne gebidan,
shall live my last day, 639; ne
wênde . . . bôte gebidan, *did not
hope . . . to live to see reparation,*
935; fela sceal gebîdan leófes and
láðes, *experience much good and
much affliction,* 1061; ende gebîdan, 1387, 2343; pret. he þäs frôfre
gebâd, *received consolation* (compensation) *therefor,* 7; gebâd wintra worn, *lived a great number of
years,* 264; in a similar construction, 816, 930, 1619, 2259, 3117.
With gen.: inf. tô gebîdanne ôðres
yrfeweardes, *to await another heir,*
2453. With depend. clause: inf.
tô gebîdanne þät his byre rîde on
galgan, *to live to see it, that his son
hang upon the gallows,* 2446; pret.
dreám-leás gebâd þät he . . ., *joyless he experienced it, that he . . .,*
1721; þäs þe ic on aldre gebâd þät
ic . . ., *for this, that I, in my old
age, lived to see that . . .,* 1780.
on-bîdan, *to wait, to await:* pret.
hordweard onbâd earfôðlice ôð þät
æfen cwom, *scarcely waited, could
scarcely delay till it was evening,*
2303.
bîtan, st. v., *to bite,* of the cutting of
swords: inf. bîtan, 1455, 1524;
pret. bât bânlocan, *bit into his body*
(Grendel), 743; bât unswîðor, *cut
with less force* (Beówulf's sword),
2579.
blanca, w. m., properly *that which
shines* here of the horse, not so

much of the white horse as the
dappled : dat. pl. on blancum, 857.
ge-bland, ge-blond, st. n., *mix-
ture, heaving mass, a turning.* —
Comp.: sund-, ðö-geblond, wind-
blond.
blanden-feax, blonden-feax, adj.,
mixed, i.e. having gray hair, *gray-
headed,* as epithet of an old man:
nom. sg. blondenfeax, 1792; blon-
denfexa, 2963; dat. sg. blonden-
feaxum, 1874; nom. pl. blonden-
feaxe, 1595.
blāc, adj., *dark, black:* nom. sg.
hrefn blaca, 1802.
blāc, adj.: 1) *gleaming, shining:*
acc. sg. blâcne leóman, *a brilliant
gleam,* 1518. — 2) of the white
death-color, *pale;* in comp. heoro-
blâc.
blæd, st. m.: 1) *strength, force, vigor:*
nom. sg. wäs hira blæd scacen (of
both tribes), *strength was gone,* i.e.
the bravest of both tribes lay slain,
1125; nu is þînes mägnes blæd
âne hwîle, *now the fulness of thy
strength lasts for a time,* 1762. —
2) *reputation, renown, knowledge*
(with stress upon the idea of filling
up, spreading out) : nom. sg. blæd,
18; (þin) blæd is âræred, *thy renown is spread abroad,* 1704.
blæd-âgend, pt., *having renown,
renowned:* nom. pl. blæd-âgende,
1014.
blæd-fäst, adj., *firm in renown, renowned, known afar:* acc. sg.
blædfästne beorn (of Äschere, with
reference to 1329), 1300.
bleát, adj., *miserable, helpless;* only
in comp. wäl-bleát.
bleáte, adv., *miserably, helplessly,*
2825.
blîcnn, st. v., *shine, gleam:* inf., 222.
blîðe, adj.: 1) *blithe, joyous, happy.*

acc. sg. blíðne, 618. — 2) *gracious, pleasing:* nom. sg. blíðe, 436. — Comp. un-bliðe.

blíð-heort, adj., *joyous in heart, happy:* nom. sg., 1803.

blôd, st. n., *blood:* nom. sg., 1122; acc. sg., 743; dat. sg. blôde, 848; äfter deórum men him langað beorn wið blôde, *the hero* (Hröðgâr) *longs for the beloved man contrary to blood,* i.e. he loves him although he is not related to him by blood, 1881; dat. as instr. blôde, 486, 935, 1595, etc.

blôd-fâg, adj., *spotted with blood, bloody,* 2061.

blôdig, adj., *bloody:* acc. sg. f. blôdge, 991; acc. sg. n. blôdig, 448; instr. sg. blôdigan gâre, 2441.

ge-blôdian, w. v., *to make bloody, to sprinkle with blood:* pret. part. ge-blôdegod, 2693.

blôdig-tôð, adj., *with bloody teeth:* nom. sg. bona blôdig-tôð (of Grendel, because he bites his victims to death), 2083.

blôd-reów, adj., *bloodthirsty, bloody-minded:* nom. sg. him on ferhðe greów breóst-hord blôd-reów, *in his bosom there grew a bloodthirsty feeling,* 1720.

be-bod, st. n., *command, order;* in comp. wundor-bebod.

bodian, w. v., *(to be a messenger), to announce, to make known:* pret. hrefn blaca heofones wynne blið-heort bodode, *the black raven announced joyfully heaven's delight* (the rising sun), 1803.

boga, w. m., *bow,* of the bended form; here of the dragon, in comp. hring-boga; as an instrument for shooting, in the comp. flân-, horn-boga; bow of the arch, in comp. stân-boga.

bolca, w. m., "forus navis" (Grein), *gangway;* here probably the planks which at landing are laid from the ship to the shore: acc. sg. ofer bolcan, 231.

bold, st. n., *building, house, edifice:* nom. sg. (Heorot), 998; (Hygelâc's residence), 1926; (Beówulf's residence), 2197, 2327. — Comp. fold-bold.

bold-âgend, pt., *house-owner, property-holder:* gen. pl. monegum boldâgendra, 3113.

bolgen-môd, adj., *angry at heart, angry,* 710, 1714.

bolster, st. m., *bolster, cushion, pillow:* dat. pl. (reced) geond-bræded wearð beddum and bolstrum, *was covered with beds and bolsters,* 1241. — Comp. hleór-bolster.

bon-. See ban-.

bora, w. m., *carrier, bringer, leader:* in the comp. mund-, ræd-,wæg-bora.

bord, st. n., *shield:* nom. sg., 2674; acc. sg., 2525; gen. pl. ofer borda gebräc, *over the crashing of the shields,* 2260. — Comp.: hilde-, wig-bord.

bord-häbbend, pt., *one having a shield, shield-bearer:* nom. pl. häbbende, 2896.

bord-hreóða, w. m., *shield-cover, shield* with particular reference to its cover (of hides or linden bark): dat. sg. -hreóðan, 2204.

bord-rand, st. m., *shield:* acc. sg., 2560.

bord-weall, st. m., *shield-wall, wall of shields:* acc. sg., 2981.

bord-wudu, st. m., *shield-wood, shield:* acc. pl. beorhtan beord-wudu, 1244.

botm, st. m., *bottom:* dat. sg. tô botme (here of the bottom of the fen-lake), 1507.

bôt (emendation, cf. bêtan), st. f. : 1)
relief, remedy: nom. sg., 281 ; acc.
sg. bôte, 935; dat. sg. bôte, 910. —
2) *a performance in expiation, a
giving satisfaction, tribute:* gen.
sg. bôte, 158.

braud, brond, st. m. : 1) *burning,
fire:* nom. sg. þâ sceal brond fretan (*the burning of the body*), 3015;
instr. sg. hy hine ne môston . . .
bronde forbärnan (*could not bestow upon him the solemn burning*),
2127; häfde landwara lige befangen, bæle and bronde, *with glow,
fire, and flame,* 2323. — 2) in the
passage, þät hine nô brond ne bea-
dumêcas bitan ne meahton, 1455,
b r o n d has been translated *sword,
brand* (after the O.N. brand-r).
The meaning *fire* may be justified
as well, if we consider that the old
helmets were generally made of
leather, and only the principal
parts were mounted with bronze.
The poet wishes here to emphasize
the fact that the helmet was made
entirely of metal, a thing which was
very unusual. — 3) in the passage,
forgeaf þâ Beówulfe brand Healfdenes segen gyldenne, 1021, our
text, with other editions, has emen-
dated, b e a r n, since b r a n d, if it
be intended as a designation of
Hrôðgâr (perhaps *son*), has not been
found in this
sense in A.-S.

brant, bront, adj., *raging, foaming,
going high,* of ships and of waves :
acc. sg. brontne, 238, 568.

brâd, adj. : 1) *extended, wide:* nom.
pl. brâde rîce, 2208. — 2) *broad:*
nom. sg. heáh and brâd (of Beówulf's grave-mound), 3159; acc.
sg. brâdne mêce, 2979; (seax)
brâd [and] brûnecg, *the broad,*

short sword with bronze edge, 1547.
— 3) *massive, in abundance:* acc.
sg. brâd gold, 3106.

ge-bräc, st. n., *noise, crash:* acc.
sg. borda gebräc, 2260.

geond-brædan, w. v., *to spread
over, to cover entirely:* pret. part.
geond-bræded, 1240.

brecan, st. v. : 1) *to break, to break
to pieces:* pret. bânhringas bräc,
(the sword) *broke the joints,* 1568.
In a moral sense : pret. subj. þät
þær ænig mon wære ne bræce, *that
no one should break the agreement,*
1101; pret. part. þonne bióð brocene . . . âð-sweord eorla, *then are
the oaths of the men broken,* 2064.
— 2) probably also simply *to break
in upon something, to press upon,*
w. acc. : pret. sg. sædeór monig
hildetuxum heresyrcan bräc, *many
a sea-animal pressed with his bat-
tle-teeth upon the shirt of mail* (did
not break it, for, according to 1549
f., 1553 f., it was still unharmed),
1512. — 3) *to break out, to spring
out:* inf. geseah . . . streám ût brecan of heorge, *saw a stream break
out from the rocks,* 2547; lêtðse
hearda Higelâces þegn brâdne
mêce . . . brecan ofer bordweal,
*caused the broadsword to spring out
over the wall of shields,* 2981. —
4) figuratively, *to vex, not to let
rest:* pret. hine fyrwyt bräc, *curiosity tormented* (N.H.G. brachte
die Neugier um), 232, 1986, 2785.

ge-b r e c a n, *to break to pieces:* pret.
bânhûs gebräc, *broke in pieces his
body* (Beówulf in combat with
Däghrefn), 2509.

tô-b r e c a n, *to break in pieces:* inf.,
781; pret. part. tô-brocen, 998.

þurh-brecan, *to break through:*
pret. wordes ord breósthord þurh•

brãc, *the word's point broke through his closed breast*, i.e. a word burst out from his breast, 2793.

breóð, st. f., *condition of being broken, breach :* nom. pl. môdes breeða (*sorrow of heart*), 171.

â-bredwian, w. v. w. acc., *to fell to the ground, to kill(?) :* pret. âbredwade, 2620.

bregdan, st. v., properly *to swing round*, hence : 1) *to swing :* inf. underseeadu bregdan, *swing among the shadows, to send into the realm of shadows*, 708; pret. brägd ealde lâfe, *swung the old weapon*, 796; brägd feorh-geniðlan, *swung his mortal enemy* (Grendel's mother), threw her down, 1541; pl. git eágorstreám ... mundum brugdon, *stirred the sea with your hands* (of the movement of the hands in swimming), 514; pret. part. broden (brogden) mæl, *the drawn sword*, 1617, 1668. — 2) *to knit, to knot, to plait :* inf., figuratively, inwitnet ôðrum bregdan, *to weave a way-laying net for another* (as we say in the same way, to lay a trap for another, to dig a pit for another), 2168; pret. part. beadohrägl broden, *a woven shirt of mail* (because it consisted of metal rings joined together), 522; similarly, 1549; brogdne beaduserecean, 2756.

â-bregdan, *to swing :* pret. hond up â-bräd, *swung, raised his hand*, 2576.

ge-bregdan : 1) *swing :* pret. hring-mæl gebrägd, *swung the ringed sword*, 1565; eald sweord eácen ... þät ic þý wæpne gebräd, *an old heavy sword that I swung as my weapon*, 1665; with interchanging instr. and acc. wälseaxe gebräd, biter and beadu-scearp, 2704; also,

to draw out of the sheath : sweord ær gebräd, *had drawn the sword before*, 2563. — 2) *to knit, to knot, to plait :* pret. part. here-byrne hondum gebroden, 1444. on-bregdan, *to tear open, to throw open :* pret. onbräd þâ recedes mûðan, *had then thrown open the entrance of the hall* (onbregdan is used because the opening door swings upon its hinges), 724.

brego, st. m., *prince, ruler :* nom. sg. 427, 610.

brego-róf, adj., *powerful, like a ruler, of heroic strength :* nom. sg. m., 1926.

brego-stól, st. m., *throne*, figuratively for *rule :* acc. sg. him gesealde seofon þûsendo, bold and brego-stól, *gave him seven thousand* (see under sceat), *a country-seat, and the dignity of a prince*, 2197; þær him Hygd gebeád ... brego-stól, *where H. offered him the chief power*, 2371; lêt þone bregostôl Beówulf healdan, *gave over to Beówulf the chief power* (did not prevent Beówulf from entering upon the government), 2390.

breme, adj., *known afar, renowned :* nom. sg., 18.

brenting (see **brant**), st. m., *ship, craft :* nom. pl. brentingas, 2808.

â-breótan, st. v., *to break, to break in pieces, to kill :* pret. âbreót brim-wisan, *killed the sea-king* (King Hæðcyn), 2931. See **breótan.**

breóst, st. n.: 1) *breast :* nom. sg., 2177; often used in the pl., so acc. þät mine breóst wereð, *which protects my breast*, 453; dat. pl. beadohrägl broden on breóstum läg, 552. — 2) *the inmost thoughts, the mind, the heart, the bosom :* nom.

sg. breóst innan weóll þeóstrum ge-
þoncum, *his breast heaved with
troubled thoughts,* 2332; dat. pl.
lêt þâ of breóstum word ût faran,
*ca.used the words to come out from
his bosom,* 2551.

breóst-gehygd, st. n. f., *breast-
thought, secret thought:* instr. pl.
-gehygdum, 2819.

breóst-gewædu, st. n. pl., *breast-
clothing, garment covering the
breast,* of the coat of mail: nom.,
1212; acc., 2163.

breóst-hord, st. m., *breast-hoard,
that which is locked in the breast,
heart, mind, thought, soul :* nom.
sg., 1720; acc. sg., 2793.

breóst-net, st. n., *breast-net, shirt
of chain-mail, coat of mail :* nom.
sg. breóst-net broden, 1549.

breóst-weorðung, st. f., *ornament
that is worn upon the breast :* acc.
sg. breóst-weorðunge, 2505: here
the collar is meant which Beówulf
receives from Wealhþeów (1196,
2174) as a present, and which B.,
according to 2173, presents to
Hygd, while, according to 1203, it
is in the possession of her husband
Hygelâc. In front the collar is
trimmed with ornaments (frätwe),
which hang down upon the breast,
hence the name breóst-weorðung.

breóst-wylm, st. m., *heaving of the
breast, emotion of the bosom :* acc.
sg., 1878.

breótan, st. v., *to break, to break in
pieces, to kill :* pret. breát beódge-
neátas, *killed his table-companions*
(courtiers), 1714.

â-breótan, same as above: pret.
þone þe heó on räste âbreát, *whom
she killed upon his couch,* 1299;
pret. part. þâ þät monige gewearð,
þät hine seó brimwylf âbroten häf-

de, *many believed that the sea-wolf*
(Grendel's mother) *had killed him,*
1600; hî hyne . . . âbroten häfdon,
had killed him (the dragon), 2708.

brim, st. n., *flood, the sea :* nom. sg.,
848, 1595; gen. sg. tô brimes faroðe, *to the sea,* 28; ät brimes nosan, *at the sea's promontory,* 2804;
nom. pl. brimu swaðredon, *the
waves subsided,* 570.

brim-clif, st. n., *sea-cliff, cliff washed
by the sea :* acc. pl. -clifu, 222.

brim-lâd, st. f., *flood-way, sea-way :*
acc. sg. þâra þe mid Beówulfe brim-
lâde teáh, *who had travelled the
sea-way with B.,* 1052.

brim-liðend, pt., *sea-farer, sailor :*
acc. pl. -liðende, 568.

brim-streám, st. m., *sea-stream, the
flood of the sea :* acc. pl. ofer brim-
streámas, 1911.

brim-wîsa, w. m., *sea-king :* acc. sg.
brimwisan, of Hæðcyn, king of the
Geátas, 2931.

brim-wylf, st. f., *sea-wolf* (designation of Grendel's mother): nom.
sg. seó brimwylf, 1507, 1600.

brim-wylm, st. m., *sea-wave :* nom.
sg., 1495.

bringan, anom. v., *to bring, to bear :*
prs. sg. I. ic þe þûsenda þegna
bringe tô helpe, *bring to your assist-
ance a thousand warriors,* 1830;
inf. sceal hringnaca ofer heáðu bringan lâc and luftâcen, *shall bring
gifts and love-tokens over the high
sea,* 1863; similarly, 2149, 2505;
pret. pl. we þâs sælâc . . . brôhton,
brought this sea-offering (Grendel's
head), 1654.

ge-bringan, *to bring:* pres. subj.
pl. þät we þone gebringan . . . on
âdfäre, *that we bring him upon the
funeral-pile,* 3010.

brosnian, w. v., *to crumble, to be-*

come rotten, to fall to pieces: prs. sg. III. herepâd ... brosnaꝺ æfter beorne, *the coat of mail falls to pieces after* (the death of) *the hero,* 2261.

brôꝺor, st. m., *brother:* nom. sg., 1325, 2441; dat. sg. brêꝺer, 1263; gen. sg. his brôꝺor bearn, 2620; dat. pl. brôꝺrum, 588, 1075. ge-brôꝺru, pl., *brethren, brothers:* dat. pl. sät be þæm gebrôꝺrum twæm, *sat by the two brothers,* 1192.

brôga, w. m., *terror, horror:* nom. sg., 1292, 2325, 2566; acc. sg. billa brôgan, 583. — Comp.: gryre-, here-brôga.

brûcan, st. v. w. gen., *to use, to make use of:* prs. sg. III. se þe longe her worolde brûceꝺ, *who here long makes use of the world,* i.e. lives long, 1063; imp. brûc manigra mêda, *make use of many rewards, give good rewards,* 1179; *to enjoy:* inf. Jät he beáhhordes brûcan môste, *could enjoy the ring-hoard,* 895; similarly, 2242, 3101; pret. breác lifgesceafta, *enjoyed the appointed life, lived the appointed time,* 1954. With the genitive to be supplied: breác þonne môste, 1488; imp. brûc þisses beáges, *enjoy this ring, take this ring,* 1217. Upon this meaning depends the form of the wish, wel brûcan (compare the German geniesze froh!): inf. hêt hine wel brûcan, 1046; hêt hine brûcan well, 2813; imp. brûc calles well, 2163.

brûn, adj., *having a metallic lustre, shining:* nom. sg. sióecg brûn, 2579.

brûn-ecg, adj., *having a gleaming blade:* acc. sg. n. (hyre seax) brâd [and] brûnecg, *her broad sword with gleaming blade,* 1547.

brûn-fâg, adj., *gleaming like metal:* acc. sg. brûnfâgne helm, 2616.

bryne-leôma, w. m., *light of a conflagration, gleam of fire:* nom. sg., 2314.

bryne-wylm, st. m., *wave of fire:* dat. pl. -wylmum, 2327.

brytnian (properly *to break in small pieces,* cf. breótan), w. v., *to bestow, to distribute:* pret. sinc brytnade, *distributed presents,* i.e. ruled (since the giving of gifts belongs especially to rulers), 2384.

brytta, w. m., *giver, distributer,* always designating the king: nom. sg. sinces brytta, 608, 1171, 2072; acc. sg. beága bryttan, 35, 352, 1488; sinces bryttan, 1923.

bryttian (*to be a dispenser*), w. v., *to distribute, to confer:* prs. sg. III. god manna cynne snyttru bryttaꝺ, *bestows wisdom upon the human race,* 1727.

brŷd, st. f.: 1) *wife, consort:* acc. sg. brŷd, 2931; brŷde, 2957, both times of the consort of Ongenþeów (?). — 2) *betrothed, bride:* nom. sg., of Hrôꝺgâr's daughter, Freáware, 2032.

brŷd-bûr, st. n., *woman's apartment:* dat. sg. eode ... cyning of brŷdbûre, *the king came out of the apartment of his wife* (into which, according to 666, he had gone), 992.

bunden-stefna, w. m., (*that which has a bound stem*), *the framed ship:* nom. sg., 1911.

bune, w. f., *can* or *cup, drinking-vessel:* nom. pl. bunan, 3048; acc. pl. bunan, 2776.

burh, burg, st. f., *castle, city, fortified house:* acc. sg. burh, 523; dat. sg. byrig, 1200; dat. pl. burgum, 53, 1969, 2434. — Comp.: freó-, freoꝺo-, heá-, hleó-, hord-, leód-, mæg-burg.

burh-locn, w. m., *castle-bars :* dat. sg. under burh-locan, *under the castle-bars,* i.e. in the castle (Hygelâc's), 1929.

burh-stede, st. m., *castle-place, place where the castle* or *city stands :* acc. sg. burhstede, 2266.

burh-wela, w. m., *riches, treasure of a castle* or *city :* gen. sg. þenden he burh-welan brûcan môste, 3101.

burne, w. f., *spring, fountain :* gen. þære burnan wälm, *the bubbling of the spring,* 2547.

bûnn, st. v.: 1) *to stay, to remain, to dwell :* inf. gif he wäccende weard onfunde on beorge, *if he had found the watchman watching on the mountain,* 2843. — 2) *to inhabit,* w. acc.: meduseld bûan, *to inhabit the mead-house,* 3066.

ge-bûan, w. acc., *to occupy a house, to take possession :* pret. part. heán hûses, hû hit Hring Dene äfter beórþege gebûn häfdon, *how the Danes, after their beer-carouse, had occupied it* (had made their beds in it), 117. — With the pres. part. bûend are the compounds ceaster-, fold-, grund-, lond-bûend.

bûgnn, st. v., *to bend, to bow, to sink; to turn, to flee :* prs. sg. III. bon-gâr bûgeð, *the fatal spear sinks,* i.e. its deadly point is turned down, it rests, 2032; inf. þät se byrnwiga bûgan sceolde, *that the armed hero had to sink down* (having received a deadly blow), 2919; similarly, 2975; pret. sg. beáh eft under eorðweall, *turned, fled again behind the earth-wall,* 2957; pret. pl. bugon tô bence, *turned to the bench,* 327, 1014; hy on holt bugon, *fled to the wood,* 2599.

â-bûgan, *to bend off, to curve away from :* pret. fram sylle âbeág me-

dubenc monig, *from the threshold curved away many a mead-bench,* 776.

be-bûgan, w. acc., *to surround, to encircle :* prs. swâ (*which*) wäter bebûgeð, 93; efne swâ side swâ sæ bebûgeð windige weallas, *as far as the sea encircles windy shores,* 1224.

ge-bûgan, *to bend, to bow, to sink :* a) intrans.: heó on flet gebeáh, *sank on the floor,* 1541; þâ gebeáh cyning, *then sank the king,* 2981; þâ se wyrm gebeáh snûde tôsomne (*when the drake at once coiled itself up*), 2568; gewât þâ gebogen scridan tô, *advanced with curved body* (the drake), 2570.—b) w. acc. of the thing to which one bends or sinks: pret. sclereste gebeáh, *sank upon the couch in the hall,* 691; similarly gebeág, 1242.

bûr, st. n., *apartment, room :* dat. sg. bûre, 1311, 2456; dat. pl. bûrum, 140. — Comp. brýd-bûr.

bûtan, bûton (from be and ûtan, hence in its meaning referring to what is without, excluded): 1) conj. with subjunctive following, *lest :* bûtan his lîc swîce, *lest his body escape,* 967. With ind. following, *but :* bûton hit wäs mâre þonne ænig mon ôðer tô beadulâce ätberan meahte, *but it* (the sword) *was greater than any other man could have carried to battle,* 1561. After a preceding negative verb, *except :* þâra þe gumena bearn gearwe ne wiston bûton Fitela mid hine, *which the children of men did not know at all, except Fitela, who was with him,* 880; ne nom he mâðm-æhta mâ bûton þone hafelan, etc., *he took no more of the rich treasure than*

the head alone, 1615. *::* prep.
with dat., *except :* bûton folescare,
73; bûton þe, 658; ealle bûton
ânum, 706.

byegan, w. v., *to buy, to pay :* inf.
ne wäs þät gewrixle til þät hie on
bâ healfa biegan scoldon freônda
feorum, *that was no good transaction, that they, on both sides (as
well to Grendel as to his mother),
had to pay with the lives of their
friends,* 1306.

be-byegan, *to sell :* pret. nu ic on
maðma hord mine bebohte frôde
feorhlege (*now I, for the treasure-
hoard, gave up my old life*), 2800.

ge-byegan, *to buy, to acquire : to
pay :* pret. w. acc. nô þær ænige
... frôfre gebohte, *obtained no sort
of help, consolation,* 974; hit (his,
MS.) ealdre gebohte, *paid it with
his life,* 2482; pret. part. sylfes
feore beágás [geboh]te, *bought
rings with his own life,* 3015.

byldan, w. v. (*to make* beald, which
see), *to excite, to encourage to brave
deeds :* inf. w. acc. swâ he Fresna
cyn on beórsele byldan wolde (by
distributing gifts), 1095.

ge-byrd, st. n., "fatum destinatum"
(Grein ?): acc. sg. hie on gebyrd
hruron gâre wunde, 1075.

ge-byrdu, st. f., *birth :* in compound, bearn-gebyrdu.

byrdu-scrûd, st. n., *shield-orna-
ment, design upon a shield(?):*
nom. sg., 2661.

byre, st. m., (*born*) *son :* nom. sg.,
2054, 2446, 2622, etc.; nom. pl.
byre, 1189. In a broader sense,
young man, youth : acc. pl. bæddæ
byre geonge, *encouraged the youths*
(at the banquet), 2019.

byrðen, st. f., *burden :* in comp.
mægen-byrðen.

byrele, st. m., *steward, waiter, cup-
bearer :* nom. pl. byrelas, 1162.

byrgan, w. v., *to feast, to eat :* inf.,
448.

ge-byrgea, w. m., *protector :* in
comp. leód-gebyrgea.

byrht. See beorht.

byrne, w. f., *shirt of mail, mail :*
nom. sg. byrne, 405, 1630, etc.;
hringed byrne, *ring-shirt,* consisting of interlaced rings, 1246; acc.
sg. byrnan, 1023, etc.; side byrnan, *large coat of mail,* 1292;
hringde byrnan, 2616; hâre byrnan, *gray coat of mail* (of iron),
2154; dat. sg. on byrnan, 2705;
gen. sg. byrnan hring, *the ring of
the shirt of mail* (i.e. the shirt of
mail), 2261; dat. pl. byrnum, 40,
238, etc.; beorhtum byrnum, *with
gleaming mail,* 3141. — Comp.:
gûð-, here-, heaðo-, iren-, isern-
byrne.

byrnend. See beornan.

byrn-wîga, w. m., *warrior dressed
in a coat of mail :* nom. sg.,
2919.

bysgu, bisigu, st. f., *trouble, difficulty, opposition :* nom. sg. bisigu,
281; dat. pl. bisgum, 1744, bysigum, 2581.

bysig, adj., *opposed, in need,* in the
compounds lif-bysig, syn-bysig.

bŷme, w. f., *a wind-instrument, a
trumpet, a trombone :* gen. sg.
bŷman gealdor, *the sound of the
trumpet,* 2944.

bŷwan, w. v., *to ornament, to prepare :* inf. þâ þe beado-grîman
bŷwan sceoldon, *who should prepare the helmets,* 2258.

C

cnmp, st. m., *combat, fight between two :* dat. sg. in campe (Beówulf's with Dāghrefn ; cempan, MS.), 2506.

candel, st. f., *light, candle :* nom. sg. rodores candel, of the sun, 1573. Comp. woruld-candel.

cempa, w. m., *fighter, warrior, hero :* nom. sg. ädele cempa, 1313; Geáta cempa, 1552 ; rêðe cempa, 1586 ; mære cempa (as voc.), 1762 ; gyrded cempa, 2079 ; dat. sg. geongum (geongan) cempan, 1040, 2045, 2627 ; Huga cempan, 2503 ; acc. pl. cempan, 206. — Comp. fêðe-cempa.

ceunan, w. v.: 1) *to bear*, w. acc.: efne swâ hwyle mäg a swâ bone magan cende, *who bore the son*, 944; pret. part. Jäm eafera wäs äfter cenned, *to him was a son born*, 12. — 2) reflexive, *to show one's self, to reveal one's self :* imp. cen þec mid crälte, *prove yourself by your strength*, 1220.

â-cennan, *to bear :* pret. part. nô hie fäder cunnon, hwäðer him ænig wäs ær âcenned dyrnra gâsta, *they* (the people of the country) *do not know his* (Grendel's) *father, nor whether any evil spirit has been before born to him* (whether he has begotten a son), 1357.

cênðu, st. f., *boldness :* acc. sg. cênðu, 2697.

cêne, adj., *keen, warlike, bold :* gen. pl. cênra gehwylcum, 769. Superl., acc. pl. cênoste, 206. — Comp.: dæd-, gâr-cêne.

ceald, adj., *cold :* acc. pl. cealde streámas, 1262 ; dat. pl. cealdum cearsiðum, *with cold, sad journeys*, 2397. Superl. nom. sg. wedera

cealdost, 546. — Comp. morgenceald.

cearlan, w. v., *to have care, to take care, to trouble one's self :* prs. sg. III. nâ ymb his lif cearað, *takes no care for his life*, 1537.

cearig, adj., *troubled, sad :* in comp. sorh-cearig.

cear-sîð, st. m., *sorrowful way, an undertaking that brings sorrow*, i.e. a warlike expedition : dat. pl. cearsiðum (of Beówulf's expeditions against Eádgils), 2397.

cearu, st. f., *care, sorrow, lamentation :* nom. sg., 1304 ; acc. sg. [ceare], 3173. — Comp.: ealdor-, gûð-, mæl-, môd-cearu.

cear-wälm, st. m., *care-agitation, waves of sorrow in the breast :* dat. pl. äfter cear-wälmum, 2067.

cear-wylm, st. m., *same as above :* nom. pl. þâ cear-wylmas, 282.

ceaster-bûend, pt., *inhabitant of a fortified place, inhabitant of a castle :* dat. pl. ceaster-bûendum, of those established in Hrôðgâr's castle, 769.

ceáp, st. m., *purchase, transaction :* figuratively, nom sg. näs Jät ýðe ceáp, *no easy transaction*, 2416 ; instr. sg. þeáh þe ôðer hit ealdre gebohte, heardan ceápe, *although the one paid it with his life, a dear purchase*, 2483.

ge-ceápian, w. v., *to purchase :* pret. part. gold unrime grimme geceápod, *gold without measure, bitterly purchased* (with Beówulf's life), 3013

be-ceorfan, st. v., *to separate, to cut off* (with acc. of the pers. and instr. of the thing) : pret. hine þâ heáflc becearf, *cut off his head*, 1592 ; similarly, 2139.

ceorl, st. m., *man :* nom. sg. snotor

ceorl monig, *many a wise man,*
909 ; dat. sg. gomelum ceorle, *the
old man* (of King Hrêðel), 2445;
so, ealdum ceorle, of King Ongenþeów, 2973 ; nom. pl. snotere ceorlas, *wise men,* 202, 416, 1592.
ceól, st. m., *keel,* figuratively for the
ship: nom. sg., 1913 ; acc. sg.
ceól, 38, 238 ; gen. sg. ceóles,
1807.
ceósan, st. v., *to choose,* hence, *to assume:* inf. þone cynedôm ciósan
wolde, *would assume the royal dignity,* 2377; *to seek:* pret. subj.ær he
bæl cure, *before he sought his funeral-pile* (before he died), 2819.
ge-ceósan, *to choose, to elect:*
gerund, tô geceósenne cyning
ænigne (sêlran), *to choose a better
king,* 1852; imp. þe þät sêlre geceós, *choose thee the better* (of two :
bealoniðand êce rædas), 1759;
pret. he usic on herge geceás tô
þyssum sîðfate, *selected us among
the soldiers for this undertaking,*
2639 ; geceás êcne ræd, *chose the
everlasting gain,* i.e. died, 1202 ;
similarly, godes leóht geceás, 2470;
pret. part. acc. pl. häfde ... cempan
gecorone, 206.
on-cirran, w. v., *to turn, to change :*
inf. ne meahte ... þäs wealdendas
[willan] wiht on-cirran, *could not
change the will of the Almighty,*
2858; pret. ufor oncirde, *turned
higher,* 2952; þyder oncirde, *turned
thither,* 2971.
â-cîgan, w. v., *to call hither :* pret.
âcîgde of corðre cyninges þegnas
syfone, *called from the retinue of
the king seven men,* 3122.
clam, clom, st. m., f. n.? *fetter,* figuratively of a strong gripe: dat. pl.
heardan clammum, 964; heardum
clammum, 1336; atolan clommum

(horrible claws of the mother of
Grendel), 1503.
clif, cleof, st. n., *cliff, promontory :*
acc. pl. Geáta clifu, 1912.—Comp.:
brim-, êg-, holm-, stân-clif.
ge-cnâwan, st. v., *to know, to recognize :* inf. meaht þu, mín wine,
mêce gecnâwan, *mayst thou, my
friend, recognize the sword,* 2048.
on-cnâwan, *to recognize, to distinguish :* hordweard oncniów mannes reorde, *distinguished the speech
of a man,* 2555.
cniht, st. m., *boy, youth :* dat. pl.
þyssum cnyhtum, *to these boys*
(Hrôðgâr's sons), 1220.
cniht-wesende, prs. part., *being a
boy* or *a youth :* acc. sg. ic hine cûðe
cniht-wesende, *knew him while
still a boy,* 372; nom. pl. wit þät
gecwædon cniht-wesende, *we both
as young men said that,* 535.
cnyssan, w. v., *to strike, to dash
against each other :* pret. pl. þonne
... eoferas cnysedan, *when the bold
warriors dashed against each other,*
stormed (in battle), 1329.
collen-ferhð, -ferð, adj., (properly,
of swollen mind), *of uncommon
thoughts, in his way of thinking,
standing higher than others, high-
minded :* nom. sg. cuma collen-
ferhð, of Beówulf, 1807 ; collen-
ferð, of Wiglâf, 2786.
corðer, st. n., *troop, division of an
army, retinue :* dat. sg. þä wäs ...
Fin slägen, cyning on corðre, *then
was Fin slain, the king in the
troop* (of warriors), 1154; of corðre cyninges, *out of the retinue of
the king,* 3122.
costian, w. v., *to try :* pret. (w. gen.)
he min costode, *tried me,* 2085.
côfa, w. m., *apartment, sleeping-
room, couch :* in comp. bân-côfa.

côl, adj., *cool :* compar. cearwylmas côlran wurðað, *the waves of sorrow become cooler*, i.e. the mind becomes quiet, 282; him wiflufan ... côlran weorðað, *his love for his wife cools*, 2067.

cräft, st. m., *the condition of being able*, hence : 1) *physical strength :* nom. sg. mägða cräft, 1284; acc. sg. mägenes cräft, 418; þurh ânes cräft, 700; cräft and cênðu, 2697; dat. (instr.) sg. cräfte, 983, 1220, 2182, 2361.— 2) *art, craft, skill :* dat. sg. as instr. dyrnum cräfte, *with secret* (magic) *art*, 2169; dyrnan cräfte, 2291; þeófes cräfte, *with thief's craft*, 2221; dat. pl. deófles cräftum, *by devil's art* (sorcery), 2089. — 3) *great quantity* (?) : acc. sg. wyrm-horda cräft, 2223. — Comp. : leoðo-, mägen-, nearo-, wig-cräft.

cräftig, adj.: 1) *strong, stout :* nom. sg. eafoðes cräftig, 1467; niða cräftig, 1963. Comp. wig-cräftig. — 2) *adroit, skilful :* in comp. lagu-cräftig. — 3) *rich* (of treasures); in comp. cácen-cräftig.

cringan, st. v., *to fall in combat, to fall with the writhing movement of those mortally wounded :* pret. subj. on wäl crunge, *would sink into death, would fall*, 636; pret. pl. for the pluperfect, sume on wäle crungon, 1114.

ge-cringan, same as above : pret. he under rande gecranc, *fell under his shield*, 1210; ät wîge gecrang, *fell in battle*, 1338; heó on flet gecrong, *fell to the ground*, 1569; in campe gecrong, *fell in single combat*, 2506.

cuma (*he who comes*), w. m., *newcomer, guest :* nom. sg. 1807. — Comp. : cwealm-, wil-cuma.

cuman, st. v., *to come :* pres. sg. II.

gyf þu on weg cymest, *if thou comest from there*, 1383; III. cymeð, 2059; pres. subj. sg. III. cume, 23; pl. þonne we ût cymen, *when we come out*, 3107; inf. cuman, 244, 281, 1870; pret. sg. com, 430, 569, 826, 1134, 1507, 1601, etc.; cwom, 419, 2915; pret. subj. sg. cwôme, 732; pret. part. cumen, 376; pl. cumene, 361. Often with the inf. of a verb of motion, as, com gongan, 711; com siðian, 721; com in gân, 1645; cwom gân, 1163; com scacan, 1803; cwômon lædan, 239; cwômon sêcean, 268; cwôman scriðan, 651, etc.

be-cuman, *to come, to approach, to arrive :* pret. syððan niht becom, *after the night had come*, 115; þe on þâ leóde becom, *that had come over the people*, 192; þâ he tô hâm becom, 2993. And with inf. following : stefn in becom ... hlynnan under hârne stân, 2553; lyt eft becwom ... hâmes niósan, 2366; ðâ þät ende becwom, 1255; similarly, 2117. With acc. of pers.: þâ hyne sió þrag becwom, *when this time of battle came over him*, 2884.

ofer-cuman, *to overcome, to compel :* pret. þŷ he þone feónd ofercwom, *thereby he overcame the foe*, 1274 : pl. hie feónd heora ... ofercômon, 700; pret. part. (w. gen.) niða ofercumen, *compelled by combats*, 846.

cumbol, cumbor, st. m., *banner :* gen. sg. cumbles hyrde, 2506. — Comp. hilte-cumbor.

cund, adj., *originating in, descended from :* in comp. feorran-cund.

cunnan, verb pret. pres.: 1) *to know, to be acquainted with* (w. acc. or depend. clause) : sg. pres. I. ic minne can glädne Hrôðulf þät he ... wile, *I know my gra-cious H., that he will ...*, 1181; II. eard git ne const, *thou knowest not yet the land*, 1378; III. he þät wyrse ne con, *knews no worse*, 1740. And reflexive : con him land geare, *knows the land well*, 2063; pl. men ne cunnon hwyder helrûnan scri-ðað, *men do not know whither ...*, 162; pret. sg. ic hine cûðe, *knew him*, 372; cûðe he duguð þeáwe, *knew the customs of the distin-guished courtiers*, 359; so with the acc., 2013; seolfa ne cûðe þurh hwät ..., *he himself did not know through what ...*, 3068; pl. sorge ne cûðon, 119; so with the acc., 180, 418, 1234. With both (acc. and depend. clause) : nô hie fäder cunnon (scil. nô hie cunnon) hwä-ðer him ænig wäs ær âcenned dyrnra gâsta, 1356. — 2) with inf. following, *can, to be able :* prs. sg. him bebeorgan ne con, *cannot de-fend himself*, 1747; prs. pl. men ne cunnon secgan, *cannot say*, 50; pret. sg. cûðe reccan, 90; beorgan cûðe, 1446; pret. pl. hêrian ne cûðon, *could not praise*, 182; pret. subj. healdan cûðe, 2373.

cunnian, w. v., *to inquire into, to try*, w. gen. or acc.: inf. sund cun-nian (figurative for *roam over the sea*), 1427, 1445; geongne cem-pan higes cunnian, *to try the young warrior's mind*, 2046; pret. eard cunnode, *tried the home*, i.e. came to it, 1501; pl. wada cunnedon, *tried the flood*, i.e. swam through the sea, 508.

cûð, adj.: 1) *known, well known ; manifest, certain :* nom. sg. un-dyrne cûð, 150, 410; wide cûð, 2924; acc. sg. fem. cûðe folme, 1304; cûðe stræte, 1635; nom. pl.

ecge cûðe, 1146; acc. pl. cûðe nässas, 1913. — 2) *renowned :* nom. sg. gûðum cûð, 2179; nom. pl. cystum cûðe, 868. — 3) also, *friend-ly, dear, good* (see **un-cûð**).— Comp.: un-, wîð-cûð.

cûð-lice, adv., *openly, publicly :* comp. nô her cûðlicor cuman on-gunnon lind-häbbende, *no shield-bearing men undertook more bold-ly to come hither* (the coast-watch-man means by this the secret land-ing of the Vikings), 244.

cwalu, st. f., *murder, fall :* in comp. deáð-cwalu.

cweccan (*to make alive,* see **cwic**), w. v., *to move, to swing :* pret. cwehte mägen-wudu, *swung the wood of strength* (= spear), 235.

cweðan, st. v., *to say, to speak :* a) ab-solutely : prs. sg. III. cwið ät beóre, *speaks at beer-drinking*, 2042. — b) w. acc. : pret. word äfter cwäð, 315; feá worda cwäð, 2247, 2663. — c) with þät following : pret. sg. cwäð, 92, 2159; pl. cwædon, 3182. — d) with þät omitted : pret. cwäð he gûð-cyning sêcean wolde, *said he would seek out the war-king*, 199; similarly, 1811, 2940.

â-cweðan, *to say, to speak*, w. acc.: prs. þät word âcwyð, *speaks the word*, 2047; pret. þät word âcwäð, 655.

ge-cweðan, *to say, to speak :* a) ab-solutely : pret. sg. II. swâ þu ge-cwæde, 2665.—b) w. acc.: pret. wel-hwylc gecwäð, *spoke everything*, 875; pl. wit þät gecwædon, 535.— c) w. þät following : pret. gecwäð, 858, 988.

cwellan, w. v., (*to make die*), *to kill, to murder :* pret. sg. II. þu Gren-del cwealdest, 1335.

â-cwellan, *to kill :* pret. sg. (he)

wyrm âcwealde, 887; þone þe Grendelær mâne âcwealde, *whom Grendel had bef re wickedly murdered,* 1056; beorn âcwealde, 2122.

cwên, st. f.: 1) *wife, consort* (of noble birth): nom. sg. cwên, 62; (Hrôðgâr's), 614, 924; (Finn's), 1154. — 2) particularly denoting the queen: nom. sg. beághroden cwên (Wealhþeów), 624; mæru cwên, 2017; fremu folces cwên (Þryðo), 1933; acc. sg. cwên (Wealhþeów), 666. — Comp. folc-cwên.

cwên-lîc, adj., *feminine, womanly:* nom. sg. ne bið swylc cwênlic þeáw (*such is not the custom of women, does not become a woman*), 1941.

cwealm, st. m., *violent death, murder, destruction:* acc. sg. þone cwealm gewräc, *avenged the death* (of Abel by Cain), 107; mændon mondrihtnes cwealm, *lamented the ruler's fall,* 3150. — Comp.: bealo-, deáð-, gâr-cwealm.

cwealm-bealu, st. n., *the evil of murder:* acc. sg., 1941.

cwealm-cuma, w. m., *one coming for murder, a new-comer who contemplates murder:* acc. sg. þone cwealm-cuman (of Grendel), 793.

cwic and **cwico,** adj., *quick, having life, alive:* acc. sg. cwicne, 793, 2786; gen. sg. âht cwices, *something living,* 2315; nom. pl. cwice, 98; cwico wäs þâ gena, *was still alive,* 3094.

cwide, st. m., *word, speech, saying:* in comp. gegn-, gilp-, hleó-, ðor-, word-cwide.

cwîðan, st. v., *to complain, to lament:* inf. w. acc. ongan . . . gioguðe cwîðan hilde-strengo, *began to lament the* (departed) *battle-strength of his youth,* 2113; [cearc] cwiðan, *lament their cares,* 3173.

cyme, st. m., *coming, arrival:* nom. pl. hwanan eówre cyme syndon, *whence your coming is,* i.e. whence ye are, 257. — Comp. eft-cyme.

cymlîce, adv., (convenienter), *splendidly, grandly:* comp. cymlicor, 38.

cyn, st. n., *race,* both in the general sense, and denoting noble lineage: nom. sg. Fresena cyn, 1094; Wedera (gara, MS.) cyn, 461; acc. sg. eotena cyn, 421; gîganta cyn, 1691; dat. sg. Caines cynne, 107; manna cynne, 811, 915, 1726; eówrum (of those who desert Beówulf in battle) cynne, 2886; gen. sg. manna (gumena) cynnes, 702, etc.; mæran cynnes, 1730; lâðan cynnes, 2009, 2355; ûsses cynnes Wægmundinga, 2814; gen. pl. cynna gehwylcum, 98. — Comp.: eormen-, feorh-, frum-, gum-, man-, wyrm-cyn.

cyn, st. n., *that which is suitable or proper:* gen. pl. cynna (of etiquette) gemyndig, 614.

ge-cynde, adj., *innate, peculiar, natural:* nom. sg., 2198, 2697.

cyne-dôm, st. m., *kingdom, royal dignity:* acc. sg., 2377.

cyning, st. m., *king:* nom. acc. sg. cyning, 11, 864, 921, etc.; kyning, 620, 3173; dat. sg. cyninge, 3094; gen. sg. cyninges, 868, 1211; gen. pl. kyning[a] wuldor, of God, 666. — Comp. beorn-, eorð-, folc-, gûð-, heáh-, leód-, sæ-, sôð-, þeód-, world-, wuldor-cyning.

cyning-beald, adj., "*nobly bold*" (Thorpe), *excellently brave* (?): nom. pl. cyning-balde men, 1635.

ge-cyssan, w. v., *to kiss:* pret. ge-cyste þâ cyning . . . þegen betstan, *kissed the best thane* (Beówulf), 1871.

cyst (*choosing*, see **ceósan**), st. f., *the select, the best of a thing, good quality, excellence:* nom. sg. irenna cyst, *of the swords*, 803, 1698; wæpna cyst, 1560; symbla cyst, *choice banquet*, 1233; acc. sg. irena cyst, 674; dat. pl. foldwegas . . . cystum cûðe, *known through excellent qualities*, 868; (cyning) cystum gecýðed, 924. — Comp. gum-, hilde-cyst.

cýð. See on-cýð.

cýðan (see **cûð**), w. v., *to make known, to manifest, to show:* imp. sg. mägen-ellen cýð, *show thy heroic strength*,660; inf. cwealmbealu cýðan, 1941; ellen cýðan, 2696.

ge-cýðan (*to make known*, hence): 1) *to give information, to announce:* inf. andsware gecýðan, *to give answer*, 354; gerund, tô gecýðanne hwanan cówre cyme syndon (*to show whence ye come*), 257; pret. part. sôð is gecýðed þät ...(*the truth has become known*, it has shown itself to be true), 701; Higeláce wäs sið Beówulfes snûde gecýðed, *the arrival of B. was quickly announced*, 1972; similarly, 2325.— 2) *to make celebrated*, in pret. part.: wäs min fäder folcum gecýðed (*my father was renowned in the world*), 262; wäs his môdsefa manegum gecýðed, 349; cystum gecýðed, 924.

cýððu (properly, *condition of being known*, hence *relationship*), st. f., *home, country, land:* in comp. feor-cýððu.

ge-cýpan, w. v., *to purchase:* inf. näs him ænig þearf þät he ... þurfe wyrsan wigfrecan weorðe gecýpan, *had need to buy with treasures no inferior warrior*, 2497.

D

daroð, st. m., *spear:* dat. pl. dareðum lâcan (*to fight*), 2849.

ge-dâl, st. n., *parting, separation:* nom. sg. his worulde gedâl, *his separation from the world* (his death), 3069.— Comp. ealdor-, lifgedâl.

däg, st. m., *day:* nom. sg. däg, 485, 732, 2647; acc. sg. däg, 2400; and-langne däg, *the whole day*, 2116; morgenlongne däg (*the whole morning*), 2895; ôð dômes däg, *till judgment-day*, 3070; dat. sg. on þäm däge þysses lifes (eo tempore, tunc), 197,791, 807; gen.sg. däges, 1601, 2321; hwil däges, *a day's time, a whole day*, 1496; däges and nihtes, *day and night*, 2270; däges, *by day*, 1936; dat. pl. on tyn dagum, *in ten days*, 3161. — Comp. ær-, deáð-, ende-, ealdor-, fyrn-, geâr-, læn-, lif-, swylt-, win-däg, andäges.

däg-hwîl, st. f., *day-time:* acc. pl. þät he däghwila gedrogen häfde eorðan wynne, *that he had enjoyed earth's pleasures during the days* (appointed to him), i.e. that his life was finished, 2727.— (After Grein.)

däg-rîm, st. n., *series of days, fixed number of days:* nom. sg. dôgera dägrim (*number of the days of his life*), 824.

dæd, st. f., *deed, action:* acc. sg. deórlîce dæd, 585; dômleásan dæd, 2891; frêcne dæde, 890; dæd, 941; acc. pl. Grendles dæda, 195; gen. pl. dæda, 181, 479, 2455, etc.; dat. pl.dædum, 1228, 2437, etc.—Comp. ellen-, fyren-, lof-dæd.

dæd-cêne, adj., *bold in deed:* nom. sg. dæd-cêne mon, 1646.

dæd-fruma, w. m., *doer of deeds,*
doer : nom. sg., of Grendel, 2091.

dæd-hata, w. m., *he who pursues*
with his deeds : nom. sg., of Grendel, 275.

dædla, w. m., *doer :* in comp. mân-
for-dædla.

dæl, st. m., *part, portion :* acc. sg.
dæl, 622, 2246, 3128; acc. pl. dælas, 1733. — Often dæl designates
the portion of a thing or of a quality which belongs in general to an
individual, as, ôð þät him on innan
oferhygda dæl weaxeð, *till in his*
bosom his portion of arrogance in-
creases : i.e. whatever arrogance he
has, his arrogance, 1741. Biówulfe wearð dryhtmâðma dæl deáðe, forgolden, *to Beówulf his part*
of the splendid treasures was paid
with death, i.e. whatever splendid
treasures were allotted to him,
whatever part of them he could
win in the fight with the dragon,
2844; similarly, 1151, 1753, 2029,
2069, 3128.

dælan, w. v., *to divide, to bestow, to*
share with, w. acc.: pres. sg. III.
mâdmas dæleð, 1757; pres. subj.
þät he wið aglæcean cofoðo dæle,
that he bestow his strength upon
(strive with) *the bringer of misery*
(the drake), 2535; inf. hringas
dælan, 1971; pret. beágas dælde,
80; sceattas dælde, 1687.

be-dælan, w. instr., (*to divide*), *to*
tear away from, to strip of : pret.
part. dreámum (dreáme) bedæled,
deprived of the heavenly joys (of
Grendel), 722, 1276.

ge-dælan: 1) *to distribue :* inf.
(w. acc. *of the thing distributed*);
þær on innan eall gedælan geongum and ealdum swylc him god
sealde, *distribute therein to young*

and old all that God had given him,
71. — 2) *to divide, to separate,* with
acc.: inf. sundur gedælan lif wið
lice, *separate life from the body,*
2423; so pret. subj. þät he gedælde
... ânra gehwylces lif wið lice, 732.

denn (cf. denu, dene, vallis), st. n.,
den, cave : acc. sg. þäs wyrmes
denn, 2761; gen. sg. (draca) gewât dennes niósian, 3046.

ge-dêfe, adj.: 1) (impersonal) *prop-*
er, appropriate : nom. sg. swâ hit
gedêfe wäs (bið), *as was appro-*
priate, proper, 561, 1671, 3176. —
2) *good, kind, friendly ;* nom sg.
beó þu suna mïnum dædum gedêfe,
be friendly to my son by deeds (support my son in deed, namely, when
he shall have attained to the government), 1228. — Comp. un-gedêfelice.

dêman (see dôm), w. v.: 1) *to*
judge, to award justly : pres. subj.
mærðo dême, 688. — 2) *to judge*
favorably, to praise, to glorify :
pret. pl. his ellenweorc duguðum
dêmdon, *praised his heroic deed*
with all their might, 3176.

dêmend, *judge :* dæda dêmend (of
God), 181.

deal, adj., "superbus, clarus, fretus"
(Grimm): nom. pl. þryðum dealle,
494.

deád, adj., *dead :* nom. sg. 467, 1324,
2373; acc. sg. deádne, 1310.

deáð, st. m., *death, dying :* nom. sg.
deáð, 441, 447, etc.; acc. sg. deáð,
2169; dat. sg. deáðe, 1389, 1590,
(as instr.) 2844, 3046; gen. sg.
deáðes wylm, 2270; deáðes nýd,
2455. — Comp. gûð-, wäl-, wundor-
deáð.

deáð-bed, st. n., *death-bed :* dat. sg.
deáð-bedde fäst, 2902.

deáð-cwalu, st. f., *violent death,*

ruin and death : dat. pl. tô deáŏ-cwalum, 1713.

deáŏ-cwealm, st. m., *violent death, murder :* nom. sg. 1671.

deáŏ-däg, st. m., *death-day, dying day :* dat. sg. äfter deáŏ-däge (*after his death*), 187, 886.

deáŏ-fæge, adj., *given over to death :* nom. sg. (Grendel) deáŏ-fæge deóg, *had hidden himself, being given over to death* (mortally wounded), 851.

deáŏ-scûa, w. m., *death bringing, ghostly being, demon of death :* nom. sg. deorc deáŏ-scûa (of Grendel), 160.

deáŏ-wêrig, adj., *weakened by death,* i.e. dead : acc. sg. deáŏ-wêrigne, 2126. See **wêrig.**

deáŏ-wîc, st. n. *death's house, home of death :* acc. sg. gewât deáŏwîc seón (*had died*), 1276.

deágan (O.H.G. pret. part. tougan, *hidden*), *to conceal one's self, to hide :* pret. (for pluperf.) deóg, 851. — I.co.

deorc, adj., *dark :* of the night, nom. sg. (nihthelm) deorc, 1791; dat. pl. deorcum nihtum, 275, 2212; of the terrible Grendel, nom. sg. deorc deáŏ-scûa, 160.

deófol, st. m. n., *devil :* gen. sg. deófles, 2089; gen. pl. deófla, of Grendel and his troop, 757, 1681.

deógol, dŷgol, adj., *concealed, hidden, inaccessible, beyond information, unknown :* nom. sg. deógol dædhatn (of Grendel), 275; acc. sg. dŷgel lond, *inaccessible land,* 1358.

deóp, st. n., *deep, abyss :* acc. sg., 2550.

deóp, adv., *deeply :* acc. sg. deóp wäter, 509, 1905.

diópe, adj., *deep :* hit ôŏ dômes däg diópe benemdon þeódnas mære, *the illustrious rulers had charmed*

it deeply till the judgment-day, had laid a solemn spell upon it, 3070.

deór, st. n., *animal, wild animal :* in comp. mere-, sæ-deór.

deór, adj.: 1) *wild, terrible :* nom. sg. diór dæd-fruma (of Grendel), 2091. — 2) *bold, brave :* nom. nænig . . . deór, 1934. — Comp. : heaŏu-, hilde-deór.

deóre, dŷre, adj.: 1) *dear, costly* (high in price) : acc. sg. dŷre íren, 2051; drincfät dŷre (deóre), 2307, 2255; instr. sg. deóran sweorde, 561; dat. sg. deórum mâŏme, 1529; nom. pl. dŷre swyrd, 3049; acc. pl. deóre (dŷre) mâŏmas, 2237, 3132. — 2) *dear, beloved, worthy :* nom. sg. f., äŏelum dióre, *worthy by reason of origin,* 1950; dat. sg. äfter deórum men, 1880; gen. sg. deórre duguŏe, 488; superl. acc. sg. aldorþegn þone deórestan, 1310.

deór-líc, adj., *bold, brave :* acc. sg. deórlice dæd, 585. See **deór.**

disc, st. m., *disc, plate, flat dish :* nom. acc. pl. discas, 2776, 3049.

ge-dígan. See **ge-dŷgan.**

dol-gilp, st. m., *promise of bold deeds, binding agreement to a bold undertaking :* dat. sg. for dolgilpe, 509.

dol-líc, adj., *audacious :* gen. pl. mæst . . . dæda dollicra, 2647.

dol-sceaŏa, w. m., *bold enemy :* acc. sg. þone dol-scaŏan (Grendel), 479.

dôgor, st. m. n., *day :* 1) day as a period of 24 hours : gen. sg. ymb ântid ôŏres dôgores, *at the same time of the next day,* 219; morgen-leóht ôŏres dôgores, *the morning-light of the second day,* 606. — 2) day in the usual sense : acc. sg. n. þys dôgor, *during this day,* 1396; instr. þ̣ŷ dôgore, 1798; forman dôgore, 2574; gen. pl. dôgora gehwam, 88; dôgra gehwylce, 1091; dôgera dägrim, *the number of his days* (the days of his life), 824. — 3) *day* in the wider sense of time: dat. pl. ufaran dôgrum, *in later days, times,* 2201, 2393. — Comp. ende-dôgor.

dôgor-gerîm, st. n., *series of days:* gen. sg. wäs eall sceacen dôgorgerimes, *the whole number of his days* (his life) *was past,* 2729.

dôhtor, st. f., *daughter:* nom. acc. sg. dôhtor, 375, 1077, 1930, 1982, etc.

dôm, st. m.: I., *condition, state in general;* in comp. cyne-, wis-dôm. — II., having reference to justice, hence: 1) *judgment, judicial opinion:* instr. sg. weotena dôme, *according to the judgment of the Witan,* 1099. 2) *custom:* äfter dôme, *according to custom,* 1721. 3) *court, tribunal:* gen. sg. miclan dômes, 979; ôð dômes däg, 3070, both times of the last judgment. — III., *condition of freedom* or *superiority,* hence: 4) *choice, free will:* acc. sg. on sinne sylfes dôm, *according to his own choice,* 2148; instr. sg. selfes dôme, 896, 2777. 5) *might, power:* nom. sg. dôm godes, 2859; acc. sg. Eofores ânne dôm, 2965; dat. sg. drihtnes dôme, 441. 6) *glory, honor, renown:* nom. sg. [dôm], 955; dôm unlytel, *not a little glory,* 886; þät wäs forma sîð deórum mâðme þät his dôm âlâg, *it was the first time to the dear treasure* (the sword Hrunting) *that its fame was not made good,* 1529; acc. sg. ic me dôm gewyrce, *make renown for myself,* 1492; þät þu ne âlæte dôm gedreósan, *that thou let not honor fall,* 2667; dat. instr. sg. þær he dôme forleás, *here he lost his repu-*tation, 1471; dôme gewurðad, *adorned with glory,* 1646; gen. sg. wyrce se þe môte dômes, *let him make himself reputation, whoever is able,* 1389. 7) *splendor* (in heaven): acc. sôð-fästra dôm, *the glory of the saints,* 2821.

dôm-leás, adj., *without reputation, inglorious:* acc. sg. f. dômleásan dæd, 2891.

dôn, red. v., *to do, to make, to treat:* 1) absolutely: imp. dôð swâ ic bidde, *do as I beg,* 1232. — 2) w. acc.: inf. hêt hire selfre sunu on bæl dôn, 1117; pret. þâ he him of dyde îsernbyrnan, *took off the iron corselet,* 672; (þonne) him Hûnlâfing, . . . billa sêlest, on bearm dyde, *when he made a present to him of Hûnlâfing, the best of swords,* 1145; dyde him of healse hring gyldenne, *took off the gold ring from his neck,* 2810; ne him þäs wyrmes wîg for wiht dyde, eafoð and ellen, *nor did he reckon as anything the drake's fighting, power, and strength,* 2349; pl. hi on beorg dydon bêg and siglu, *placed in the (grave-) mound rings and ornaments,* 3165. — 3) representing preceding verbs: inf. tô Geátum sprec mildum wordum! swâ sceal man dôn, *as one should do,* 1173; similarly, 1535, 2167; pres. metod eallum weóld, swâ he nu git dêð, *the creator ruled over all, as he still does,* 1059; similarly, 2471, 2860, and (sg. for pl.) 1135; pret. II. swâ þu ær dydest, 1677; III. swâ he nu gyt dyde, 957; similarly, 1382, 1892, 2522; pl. swâ hie oft ær dydon, 1239; similarly, 3071. With the case also which the preceding verb governs: wên' ic þät he wille . . . Geátena leóde etan unforhte, swâ he oft dyde

mägen Hrêðmanna, *I believe he
will wish to devour the Gєát people, the fearless, as he often did* (devoured) *the bloom of the Hrêðmen,*
444; gif ic þät gefriege ... þät þec
ymbsittend egesan þywað, swâ þec
hettende hwilum dydon, *that the
neighbors distress thee as once the
enemy did thee* (i.e. distressed),
1829; gif ic ôwihte mäg þinre môd-
lufan mâran tilian þonne ic gyt
dyde, *if I can with anything obtain
thy greater love than I have yet
done,* 1825; similarly, pl. þonne þâ
dydon, 44.

ge-dôn, *to do, to make,* with the acc.
and predicate adj.: prs. (god)
gedêð him swâ gewealdene worolde däelâs, *makes the parts of the
world* (i.e. the whole world) *so subject that ...,* 1733; inf. ne hyne
on medo-bence micles wyrðne
drihten wereda gedûn wolde, *nor
would the leader of the people much
honor him at the mead-banquet,*
2187. With adv.: he mec þær on
innan ... gedôn wolde, *wished to
place me in there,* 2091.

draca, w. m., *drake, dragon :* nom.
sg., 893, 2212; acc. sg. dracan,
2403, 3132; gen. sg., 2089, 2291,
2550.—Comp.: eorð-, fyr-, lêg-,
lig-, nið-draca.

on-drædan, st. v., w. acc. of the
thing and dat. of the pers., *to fear,
to be afraid of :* inf. þät þu him ondrædan ne þearft ... aldorbealu,
needest not fear death for them,
1675; pret. nô he him þâ säcce
ondrêd, *was not afraid of the combat,* 2348.

ge-dräg (from dragan, in the sense
se gerere), st. n., *demeanor, actions :*
acc. sg. sêcan deôlla gedräg, 757.

drepan, st. v., *to hit, to strike :* pret.

sg. sweorde drep ferhð-genîðlan,
2881; pret. part. bið on hreðre ...
drepen biteran stræle, *struck in the
breast with piercing arrow,* 1746;
wäs in feorh dropen (*fatally hit*),
2982.

drepe, st. m., *blow, stroke :* acc. sg.
drepe, 1590.

drêfan, ge-drêfan, w. v., *to move,
to agitate, to stir up :* inf. gewât
... drêfan deôp wäter (*to navi-
gate*), 1905; pret. part. wäter under
stôd dreôrig and gedrêfed, 1418.

dreám, st. m., *rejoicing, joyous actions, joy :* nom. sg. häleða dreám,
497; acc. sg. dreám hlûdne, 88;
þu ... dreám healdende, *thou who
livest in rejoicing* (at the drinking-
carouse), *who art joyous,* 1228;
dat. instr. sg. dreáme bedæled, 1276;
gen. pl. dreáma leás, 851; dat. pl.
dreámum (here adverbial) lifdon,
lived in rejoicing, joyously, 99;
dreámum bedæled, 722; the last
may refer also to heavenly joys.—
Comp. gleó-, gum-, man-, sele-
dreám.

dreám-leás, adj., *without rejoicing,
joyless :* nom. sg. of King Heremôd, 1721.

dreógan, st. v.: 1) *to lead a life, to
be in a certain condition :* pret.
dreáh äfter dôme, *lived in honor,
honorably,* 2180; pret. pl. fyren-
þearfe ongeat, þät hie ær drugon
aldorleáse lange hwîle, (*God*) *had
seen the great distress,* (*had seen*)
*that they had lived long without a
ruler*(?), 15.—2) *to experience, to
live through, to do, to make, to enjoy :* imp. dreóh symbelwynne, *pass
through the pleasure of the meal, to
enjoy the meal,* 1783; inf. driht-
scype dreógan (*do a heroic deed*),
1471; pret. sundnytte dreáh (*had*

the occupation of swimming, i.e.
swam through the sea), 2361; pret.
pl. hie gewin drugon (*fought*), 799;
hî sîð drugon, *made the war, went*,
1967. — 3) *to experience, to bear,
to suffer :* scealt werhðo dreógan,
shalt suffer damnation, 590; pret.
þegn-sorge dreáh, *bore sorrow for
his heroes*, 131; nearoþearfe dreáh,
422; pret. pl. inwidsorge þe hie ær
drugon, 832; similarly, 1859.
â-dreógan, *to suffer, to endure :* inf.
wræc âdreógan, 3079.
ge-dreógan, *to live through, to enjoy*,
pret. part. þät he ... gedrogen häfde
eorðan wynne, *that he had now enjoyed the pleasures of earth* (i.e.
that he was at his death), 2727.
dreór, st. m., *blood dropping or flowing from wounds :* instr. sg. dreóre,
447. — Comp. heoru-, sâwul-, wäl-
dreór.
dreór-fâh, adj., *colored with blood,
spotted with blood :* nom. sg. 485.
dreórig, adj., *bloody, bleeding :* nom.
sg. wäter stôd dreórig, 1418; acc.
sg. dryhten sinne driórigne fand,
2790. — Comp. heoru-dreórig.
ge-dreósan, st. v., *to fall down, to
sink :* pres. sg. III. lîc-homa læne
gedreóseð, *the body, belonging to
death, sinks down*, 1755; inf. þät
þâ ne âlæte dôm gedreósan, *honor
fall, sink*, 2667.
drincan, st. v., *to drink* (with and
without the acc.) : pres. part. nom.
pl. ealo drincende, 1946; pret.
blôd êdrum dranc, *drank the blood
in streams*(?), 743; þret. pl. druncon wîn weras, *the men drank wine*,
1234; þær guman drunc on, *where
the men drank*, 1649. The pret.
part., when it stands absolutely, has
an active sense: nom. pl. druncne
dryhtguman, *ye warriors who have*

drunk, are drinking, 1232; acc. pl.
nealles druncne slôg heorð-geneátas, *slew not his hearth-companions
who had drunk with him*, i.e. at the
banquet, 2180. With the instr. it
means *drunken :* nom. sg. beóre
(wîne) druncen, 531, 1468; nom.
pl. beóre druncne, 480.
drîfan, st. v., *to drive :* pres. pl. þâ
þe brentingas ofer flôda genipu
feoran drîfað, *who drive their ships
thither from afar over the darkness
of the sea*, 2809; inf. (w. acc.) þeáh
þe he [ne] meahte on mere drîfan
hringedstefnan, *although he could
not drive the ship on the sea*, 1131.
to-drîfan, *to drive apart, to dis-
perse :* pret. ôð þät une flôd tôdrâf,
545.
drohtoð, st. m., *mode of living* or
acting, calling, employment : nom.
sg. ne wäs his drohtoð þær swylce
he ær gemëtte, *there was no employment for him* (Grendel) *there
such as he had found formerly*, 757.
drusian, w. v. (cf. dreósan, properly, *to be ready to fall;* here of
water), *to stagnate, to be putrid .*
pret. lagu drusade (through the
blood of Grendel and his mother),
1631.
dryht, driht, st. f., *company, troop,
band of warriors ; noble band :* in
comp. mago-driht.
ge-dryht, ge-driht, st. f., *troop,
band of noble warriors :* nom sg.
mînra eorla gedryht, 431; acc. sg.
äðelinga gedriht, 118; mid his
eorla (häleða) gedriht (gedryht),
357, 663; similarly, 634, 1673. —
Comp. sibbe-gedriht.
dryht-bearn, st. n., *youth from a
noble warrior band, noble young
man :* nom. sg. dryhtbearn Dena,
2036.

dryhten, drihten, st. m., *commander, lord:* a) *temporal lord:* nom. sg. dryhten, 1485, 2001, etc.; drihten, 1051; dat. dryhtne, 2483, etc.; dryhten, 1832. — b) *God:* nom. drihten, 108, etc.; dryhten, 687, etc.; dat. sg. dryhtne, 1693, etc.; drihtne, 1399, etc.; gen. sg. dryhtnes, 441; drihtnes, 941. — Comp.: freáh-, freó-, gum-, man-, sige-, wine-dryhten.

dryht-guma, w. m., *one of a troop of warriors, noble warrior:* dat. sg. drihtguman, 1389; nom. pl. drihtguman, 99; dryhtguman, 1232; dat. pl. ofer dryhtgumum, 1791 (of Hróðgár's warriors).

dryht-lic, adj., *(that which befits a noble troop of warriors), noble, excellent:* dryhtlíc íren, *excellent sword,* 893; acc. sg. f. (with an acc. sg. n.) drihtlíce wíf (of Hildeburh), 1159.

dryht-máðum, st. m., *excellent jewel, splendid treasure:* gen. pl. dryhtmáðma, 2844.

dryht-scipe, st. m., *(warrior-ship), warlike virtue, bravery; heroic deed:* acc. sg. drihtscipe dreógan, *to do a heroic deed,* 1471.

dryht-sele, st. m., *excellent, splendid hall:* nom. sg. driht-sele, 485; dryhtsele, 768; acc. sg. dryhtsele, 2321.

dryht-sib, st. f., *peace or friendship between troops of noble warriors:* gen. sg. dryhtsibbe, 2069.

dryne, st. m., *drink:* in comp. heorudryne.

dryne-fät, st. n., *vessel for drink, to receive the drink:* acc. sg., 2255; drinc-fät, 2307.

drysmian, w. v., *to become obscure, gloomy* (through the falling rain): pres. sg. III. lyft drysmað, 1376.

drysne, adj. See on-drysne.

dugan, v., *to avail, to be capable, to be good:* pres. sg. III. húru se aldor deáh, *especially is the prince capable,* 369; ðonne his ellen deáh, *if his strength avails, is good,* 573; þe him selfa deáh, *who is capable of himself, who can rely on himself,* 1840; pres. subj. þeáh þín wit duge, *though, indeed, your understanding be good, avail,* 590; similarly, 1661, 2032; pret. sg. þu ûs wel dohtest, *you did us good, conducted yourself well towards us,* 1822; similarly, nu seó hand ligeð se þe eów welhwylera wilna dohte, *which was helpful to each one of your desires,* 1345; pret. subj. þeáh þu heaðoræsa gehwær dohte, *though thou wast everywhere strong in battle,* 526.

duguð *(state of being fit, capable),* st. f.: 1) *capability, strength:* dat. pl. for dugeðum, *in ability*(?), 2502; duguðum dêmdon, *praised with all their might*(?), 3176. — 2) *men capable of bearing arms, band of warriors,* esp., *noble warriors:* nom. sg. duguð unlytel, 498; duguð, 1791, 2255; dat. sg. for duguðe, *before the heroes,* 2021; nalles frätwe geaf ealdor duguðe, *gave the band of heroes no treasure* (more), 2921; leóda duguðe on lâst, *upon the track of the heroes of the people,* i.e. after them, 2946; gen. sg. cúðe he duguðe þeáw, *the custom of the noble warriors,* 359; deórre duguðe, 488; similarly, 2239, 2659; acc. pl. duguða, 2036. — 3) contrasted with geogoð, duguð designates the noted warriors of noble birth (as in the Middle Ages, knights in contrast with squires): so gen. sg. duguðe and geogoðe,

160; gehwylc…dugu♂e and iogo-
♂e, 1075; dugu♂e and geogu♂e
d.el æghwylene, 622.

durran, v. pret. and pres. *to dare;*
prs. sg. 11. þu dearst bîdan, *darest
to expect*, 527; III. he gesêcean
dear, 685; pres. subj. sêc gyf þu
dyrre, *seek* (Grendel's mother), *if
thou dare*, 1380 ; pret. dorste,
1463, 1469, etc.; pl. dorston, 2849.

duru, st. f., *door, gate, wicket:* nom.
sg., 722; acc. sg. [duru], 389.

ge-dûfan, st. v., *to dip in, to sink
into:* pret. þät sweord gedeáf (*the
sword sank into the drake*, of a
blow), 2701.

þurh-dûfan, *to dive through:* to
swim through, diving: pret. wäter
up þurh-deáf, *swam through the
water upwards* (because he was
before at the bottom), 1620.

dwellan, w. v., *to mislead, to hinder:*
prs. III. nô hine wiht dwele♂, ädl
ne yldo, *him nothing misleads,
neither sickness nor age*, 1736.

dyhtig, adj., *useful, good for:* nom.
sg. n. sweord … ecgum dyhtig,
1288.

dynnan, w. v., *to sound, to groan, to
roar:* pret. dryhtsele (healwudu,
hruse) dynede, 768, 1318, 2559.

dyrne, adj.: 1) *concealed, secret, re-
tired:* nom. sg. dyrne, 271; acc.
sg. dryhtsele dyrnne (of the drake's
cave-hall), 2321. — 2) *secret, malicious, hidden by sorcery:* dat. instr.
sg. dyrnan cräfte, *with secret magic
art*, 2291; dyrnum cräfte, 2169;
gen. pl. dyrnra gâsta, *of malicious
spirits* (of Grendel's kin), 1358. —
Comp. un-dyrne.

dyrne, adv., *in secret, secretly:* him
… äfter deórum men dyrne lan-
ga♂, *longs in secret for the dear
man*, 1880.

dyrstig, adj., *bold, daring:* þeáh
þe he dæda gehwäs dyrstig wære,
*although he had been courageous
for every deed*, 2839.

ge-dŷgan, ge-dîgan, w. v., *to endure, to overcome*, with the acc. of
the thing endured: pres. sg. II. gif
þu þät ellenweorc aldre gedigest,
*if thou survivest the heroic work
with thy life*, 662; III. þät þone
hilderæs hâl gedige♂, *that he sur-
vives the battle in safety*, 300; similarly, inf. unfæge gedigan weán
and wräcsi♂, 2293; hwä♂er sêl mæge wunde gedîgan, *which of the
two can stand the wounds better*
(come off with life), 2532; ne meahte unbyrnende deóp ged♂gan, *could
not endure the deep without burning* (could not hold out in the
deep), 2550; pret. sg. I. III. ge-
digde, 578, 1656, 2351, 2544.

dŷgol. See deógol.

dŷre. See deóre.

E

ecg, st. f., *edge of the sword, point:*
nom. sg. sweordes ecg, 1107; ecg,
1525, etc.; acc. sg. wi♂ ord and
wi♂ ecge ingang forstôd, *defended
the entrance against point and
edge* (i.e. against spear and swor.),
1550; mêces ecge, 1813; nom. pl.
ecge, 1146. — *Sword, battle-axe,
any cutting weapon:* nom. sg. ne
wäs ecg bona (*not the sword killed
him*), 2507; sió ecg brûn (Beówulf's sword Nägling), 2578; hyne
ecg fornam, *the sword snatched him
away*, 2773, etc.; nom. pl. ecga,
2829; dat. pl. âscum and ecgum,
1773; dat. pl. (but denoting only
one sword) eácnum ecgum, 2141;

gen. pl. ecga, 483, 806, 1169; — *blade:* ecg wäs íren, 1460. — Comp.: brûn-, heard-, stýl-ecg, adj.

ecg-bana, w. m., *murderer by the sword:* dat. sg. Cain wearð tô ecgbanan ângan brêðer, 1263.

ecg-hete, st. m., *sword-hate, enmity which the sword carries out:* nom. sg., 84, 1739.

ecg-þracu, st. f., *sword-storm* (of violent combat): acc. atole ecgþräce, 597.

ed-hwyrft, st. m., *return* (of a former condition): þa þær sôna wearð edhwyrft eorlum, siððan inne fealh Grendles môdor (i.e. after Grendel's mother had penetrated into the hall, the former perilous condition, of the time of the visits of Grendel, returned to the men), 1282.

ed-wendan, w. v., *to turn back, to yield, to leave off:* inf. gyf him edwendan æfre scolde bealuwa bisigu, *if for him the affliction of evil should ever cease,* 280.

ed-wenden, st. f., *turning, change:* nom. sg. edwenden, 1775; ed-wenden torna gehwylces (*reparation for former neglect*), 2189.

edwît-líf, st. n., *life in disgrace:* nom. sg., 2892.

efn, adj., *even, like,* with preceding on, and with depend. dat., *upon the same level, near:* him on efn ligeð ealdorgewinna, *lies near him,* 2904.

efnan (see üfnan) w. v., *to carry out, to perform, to accomplish:* pres. subj. eorlscype efne (*accomplish knightly deeds*), 2536; inf. eorlscipe efnan, 2623; sweorda gelác efnan (*to battle*), 1042; gerund. tô efnanne, 1942; pret. eorlscipe efnde, 2134, 3008.

efne, adv., *even, exactly, precisely, just,* united with swâ or swylc: efne swâ swiðe swâ, *just so much as,* 1093; efne swâ síde swâ, 1224; wäs se grvre lässa efne swâ micle swâ, *by so much the less as . . .,* 1284; leóht inne stôd efne swâ ... scineð, *a gleam stood therein* (in the sword) *just as when ... shines,* 1572; efne swâ hwylc mägða swâ þone magan cende (*a woman who has borne such a son*), 944; efne swâ hwylcum manna swâ him gemet þûhte, *to just such a man as seemed good to him,* 3058; efne swylce mæla swylce ... þearf gesælde, *just at the times at which necessity commanded it,* 1250.

eft, adv.: 1) *thereupon, afterwards:* 56, 1147, 2112, 3047, etc.; eft sôna bið, *then it happens immediately,* 1763; bôt eft cuman, *help come again,* 281. — 2) *again, on the other side:* þät hine on ylde eft gewunigen wilgesíðas, *that in old age again* (also on their side) *willing companions should be attached to him,* 22; — *anew, again:* 135, 604, 693, 1557, etc.; eft swâ ær, *again as formerly,* 643. — 3) *retro, rursus, back:* 123, 296, 854, etc.; þät hig äðelinges eft ne wêndon (*did not believe that he would come back*), 1597.

eft-cyme, st. m., *return:* gen. sg. eftcymes, 2897.

eft-sîð, st. m., *journey back, return:* acc. sg. 1892; gen. sg. eft-siðes georn, 2784; acc. pl. eftsíðas teáh, *went the road back,* i.e. returned, 1333.

egesa, egsa (*state of terror,* active or passive): 1) *frightfulness:* acc. sg. þurh egsan, 276; gen. egesan ne gýmeð, *cares for nothing ter-*

rible, is not troubled about future terrors(?), 1758. — 2) *terror, horror, fear:* nom. sg. egesa, 785; instr. sg. egesan, 1828, 2737. — Comp.: glêd-, lîg-, wäter-egesa.

eges-full, adj., *horrible (full of terribleness)*, 2930.

eges-lîc, adj., *terrible, bringing terror:* of Grendel's head, 1650; of the beginning of the fight with the drake, 2310; of the drake, 2826.

egle, adj., *causing aversion, hideous:* nom. pl. neut., or, more probably, perhaps, adverbial, egle (MS. egl), 988.

egsian (denominative from egesa), w. v., *to have terror, distress:* pret. (as pluperf.) egsode eorl(?), 6.

ehtian, w. v., *to esteem, to make prominent with praise:* III. pl. pres. þät þe ... weras ehtigað, *that the men esteem thee, praise thee,* 1223.

elde (*those who generate,* cf. O.N. al-a, generare), st. m. only in the pl., *men:* dat. pl. eldum, 2215; mid eldum, *among men,* 2612. — See ylde.

eldo, st. f., *age:* instr. sg. eldo gebunden, 2112.

el-land, st. n., *foreign land, exile:* acc. sg. sceall ... elland tredan, (*shall be banished*), 3020.

ellen, st. n., *strength, heroic strength, bravery:* nom. sg. ellen, 573; eafoð and ellen, 903; Geáta ... eafoð and ellen, 603; acc. sg. eafoð and ellen, 2350; ellen cyðan, *show bravery,* 2696; ellen fremedon, *exercised heroic strength, did heroic deeds,* 3; similarly, ic gefremman sceal eorlic ellen, 638; ferh ellen wräc, *life drove out the strength,* i.e. with the departing life (of the dragon) his strength left him, 2707;

dat. sg. on elne, 2507, 2817; as instr. þâ wäs ät þam geongum grim andswaru êðbegête þâm þe ær his elne forleás, *then it was easy for (every one of) those who before had lost his hero-courage, to obtain rough words from the young man* (Wîglâf), 2862; mid elne, 1494, 2536; elne, alone, in adverbial sense, *strongly, zealously,* and with the nearly related meaning, *hurriedly, transiently,* 894, 1098, 1968, 2677, 2918; gen. sg. elnes lät, 1530; þa him wäs elnes þearf, 2877. — Comp. mägen-ellen.

ellen-dæd, st. f., *heroic deed:* dat. pl. -dædum, 877, 901.

ellen-gæst, st. m., *strength-spirit, demon with heroic strength:* nom. sg. of Grendel, 86.

ellen-lîce, adv., *strongly, with heroic strength,* 2123.

ellen-mærðu, st. f., *renown of heroic strength,* dat. pl. -mærðum, 829, 1472.

ellen-rôf, adj., *renowned for strength:* nom. sg. 340, 358, 3064; dat. pl. -rôfum, 1788.

ellen-seóc, adj., *infirm in strength:* acc. sg. þeóden ellensiócne (*the mortally wounded king, Beówulf*), 2788.

ellen-weorc, st. n., (*strength-work*), *heroic deed, achievement in battle:* acc. sg. 662, 959, 1465, etc.; gen. pl. ellen-weorca, 2400.

elles, adv., *else, otherwise:* a (modal), *in another manner,* 2521. — b (local), elles hwær, *somewhere else,* 138; elles hwergen, 2591.

ellor, adv., *to some other place,* 55, 2255.

ellor-gâst, -gæst, st. m., *spirit living elsewhere* (standing outside of the community of mankind) : nom.

sg. se ellorgâst (Grendel), 808; (Grendel's mother), 1022; ellor-gest (Grendel's mother), 1018; acc. pl. ellorgestas, 1350.

ellor-siÐ, st. m., *departure, death:* nom. sg. 2452.

elra, adj. (comparative of a not existing form, ele, Goth. aljis, alius), *another:* dat. sg. on elran men, 753.

el-þeódig, adj., *of another people: foreign:* acc. pl. el-þeódige men, 336.

ende, st. m., *the extreme:* hence, 1) *end:* nom. sg. aldres (lîfes) ende, 823, 2845; ôÐ þät ende becwom (scil. unrihtes), 1255; acc. sg. ende lîfgesceafta (lîfes, len-daga), 3064, 1387, 2343; häfde corÐscrafa ende genyttod, *had used the end of the earth-caves* (had made use of the caves for the last time), 3047; dat. sg. caldres (lîfes) ät ende, 2791, 2824; eoletes ät ende, 224.— 2) *boundary:* acc. sg. sîde rîce þät he his selfa ne mäg ... ende ge-þencean, *the wide realm, so that he himself cannot comprehend its boundaries,* 1735.— 3) *summit, head:* dat. sg. eorlum on ende, *to the nobles at the end* (the highest cour-tiers), 2022.—Comp. woruld-ende.

ende-däg, st. m., *last day, day of death:* nom. sg. 3036; acc. sg. 638.

ende-dôgor, st. m., *last day, day of death:* gen. sg. bega on wênum endedôgores and efteymes leófes monnes (*hesitating between the be-lief in the death and in the return of the dear man*), 2897.

ende-lâf, st. f., *last remnant:* nom. sg. þu eart ende lâf ûsses cynnes, *art the last of our race,* 2814.

ende-leán, st. n., *final reparation:* acc. sg. 1693.

ende-sǽta, w. m., *he who sits on the border, boundary-guard:* nom. sg. (here of the strand-watchman), 241.

ende-stäf, st. m. (elementum finis), *end:* acc. sg. hit on endestäf eft gelimpeÐ, *then it draws near to the end,* 1754.

ge-endian, w. v., *to end:* pret. part. ge-endod, 2312.

enge, adj., *narrow:* acc. pl. enge ânpaÐas, *narrow paths,* 1411.

ent, st. m., *giant:* gen. pl. enta ær-geweorc (the sword-hilt out of the dwelling-place of Grendel), 1680; enta geweorc (the dragon's cave), 2718; eald-enta ær-geweorc (the costly things in the dragon's cave), 2775.

entisc, adj., *coming from giants:* acc. sg. entiscne helm, 2980.

etan, st. v., *to eat, to consume:* pres. sg. III. blôdig wäl ... eteÐ ân-genga, *he that goes alone* (Grendel) *will devour the bloody corpse,* 448; inf. Geátena leóde ... etan, 444.

þurh-etan, *to eat through:* pret. part. pl. nom. swyrd ... þurhetone, *swords eaten through* (by rust), 3050.

Ê

êe. See eáe.

êce, adj., *everlasting:* nom. êce drihten (God), 108; acc. sg. êce corÐreced, *the everlasting earth-hall* (the dragon's cave), 2720; geceás êene ræd, *chose the everlast-ing gain* (died), 1202; dat. sg. êcean dryhtne, 1693, 1780, 2331; acc. pl. geceós êce rædas, 1761.

êdre. See ædre.

êÐ-begête, adj., *easy to obtain, ready:* nom. sg. þâ wäs ät þam geongum grim andswaru êð-hegête, *th'n from the young man* (Wîglâf) *it was an easy thing to get a gruff answer,* 2862.

êðe. See eáðe.

êðel, st. m., *hereditary possessions, hereditary estate:* acc. sg. swǽsne êðel, 520; dat. sg. on êðle, 1731. — In royal families the hereditary possession is the whole realm: hence, acc. sg. êðel Scyldinga, *of the kingdom of the Scyldings,* 914; (Offa) wîsdôme heóld êðel sînne, *ruled with wisdom his inherited kingdom,* 1961.

êðel-riht, st. n., *hereditary privileges* (rights that belong to a hereditary estate) : nom. sg. eard êðelriht, *estate and inherited privileges,* 2199.

êðel-stôl, st m., *hereditary seat, inherited throne:* acc. pl. êðel-stôlas, 2372.

êðel-turf, st. f., *inherited ground, hereditary estate:* dat. sg. on mînre êðeltyrf, 410.

êðel-weard, st. m., *lord of the hereditary estate* (realm) : nom. sg. êðelweard (*king*), 1703, 2211; dat. sg. Eást-Dena êðel wearde (King Hrôðgâr), 617.

êðel-wyn, st. f., *joy in,* or *enjoyment of, hereditary possessions:* nom. sg. nu sceal ... eall êðelwyn eówrum cynne, lufen âlicgean, *now shall your race want all home-joy, and subsistence*(?) (your race shall be banished from its hereditary abode), 2886; acc. sg. he me lond forgeaf, eard êðelwyn, *presented me with land, abode, and the enjoyment of home,* 2494.

êð-gesýne, ðð-gesêne, adj., *easy to see, visible to all:* nom. sg. 1111, 1245.

êfstan, w.v., *to be in haste, to hasten:* inf. uton nu êfstan, *let us hurry now,* 3102; pret. êfste nid elne, *hastened with heroic strength,* 1494.

êg-clif, st. n., *sea-cliff:* acc. sg. ofer êg-clif (ecg-clif, MS.), 2894.

êg-streám, st. m., *sea-stream, sea-flood:* dat. sg. on êg-streámum, *in the sea-floods,* 577. See eágorstreám.

êhtan (M.H.G. æchten; cf. æht and ge-æhtla), w. v. w. gen., *to be a pursuer, to pursue:* pres. part. ágláca êhtende wäs duguðe and geogoðe, 159; pret. pl. êhton aglæcan, *they pursued the bringer of sorrow* (Beówulf)(?), 1513.

êst, st. m. f., *favor, grace, kindness:* acc. sg. he him êst geteáh meara and mâðma (*honored him with horses and jewels*), 2166; gearwor häfde âgendes êst ær gesceáwod, *would rather have seen the grace of the Lord* (of God) *sooner,* 3076. — dat. pl., adverbial, libenter : him on folce heóld, êstum mid âre, 2379; êstum gefwan (*to present*), 2150; him wäs ... wunden gold êstum geeáwed (*presented*), 1195; we þät ellenweorc êstum miclum fremedon, 959.

êste, adj., *gracious:* w. gen. êste bearn-gebyrdo, *gracious through the birth* (of such a son as Beówulf), 946.

EA

eafoð, st. n., *power, strength:* nom. sg. eafoð and ellen, 603, 903; acc. sg. eafoð and ellen, 2350; we frêcne geneðdon eafoð uncûðes, *we have boldly ventured against the strength of the enemy* (Grendel),

have withstood him, 961; gen. sg.
eafoðes cräftig, 1467; þät þec âdl
oððe ecg cafoðes getwæfed, *shall
rob of strength* 1764 ; acc. pl. eafeðo
(MS. earfeðo), 534; dat. pl. hine
mihtig god . . . eafeðum stêpte,
made him great through strength,
1718.

eafor, st. m., *boar ;* here the image
of the boar as banner: acc. sg.
eafor, 2153.

eafora (*offspring*), w. m.: 1) *son :*
nom. sg. eafera, 12, 898; eafora,
375; acc. sg. eaferan, 1548, 1848;
gen. sg. eafera, 19; nom. pl. eaferan, 2476; dat. pl. eaferum, 1069,
2471; uncran eaferan, 1186.—2) in
broader sense, *successor :* dat. pl.
caforum, 1711.

eahta, num., *eight :* acc. pl. eahta
mearas, 1036; eode eahta sum,
*went as one of eight, with seven
others,* 3124.

eahtian, w. v.: 1) *to consider, to
deliberate :* pret. pl. w. acc. ræd
eahtedon, *consulted about help,*
172; pret. sg. (for the plural) þone
sêlestan þâra þe mid Hrôðgâre
hâm eahtode, *the best one of those
who with Hrôðgâr deliberated
about their home* (ruled), 1408. —
2) *to speak with reflection of* (along
with the idea of praise): pret. pl.
eahtodan eorlscipe, *spoke of his
noble character,* 3175.

eal, eall, adj., *all, whole :* nom. sg.
werod eall, 652; eal bencþelu,
486; eall êðelwyn, 2886; eal worold, 1739, etc.; þät hit wearð eal
gearo, healärna mæst, 77; þät hit
(wîgbil) eal gemealt, 1609. And
with a following genitive : þær wäs
eal geador Grendles grâpe, *there
was all together Grendel's hand,
the whole hand of Grendel,* 836;

eall . . . lissa, *all favor,* 2150; wäs
eall sceacen dôgorgerîmes, 2728.
With apposition : þûhte him call
tô rûm, wongas and wîcstede, 2462;
acc. sg. beót eal, 523; similarly,
2018, 2081; oncyððe ealle, *all distress,* 831; heals ealne, 2692; hlæw
. . . calne ûtan-weardne, 2298; gif
he þät eal gemon, 1186, 2428; þät
eall geondsch, recedes geatwa,
3089; ealne wîde-ferhð, *through
the whole wide life, through all
time,* 1223; instr. sg. ealle mägene,
with all strength, 2668; dat. sg.
eallum . . . manna cynne, 914;
gen. sg. calles môncynnes, 1956.
Subst. ic þäs ealles mäg . . . gefeán
habban, 2740; brûc ealles well,
2163; freán ealles þanc secge, *give
thanks to the Lord of all,* 2795;
nom. pl. untydras ealle, 111; sceótend . . . ealle, 706; we ealle, 942;
acc. pl. feónd ealle, 700; similarly,
1081, 1797, 2815; subst. ofer ealle,
650; ealle hie deáð fornam, 2237;
lîg ealle forswealg þâra þe þær gûð
fornam, *all of those whom the war
had snatched away,* 1123; dat. pl.
callum ceaster-bûendum, 768; similarly, 824, 907, 1418; subst. âna wið
eallum, *one against all,* 145; with
gen. eallum gumena cynnes, 1058;
gen. pl. äðelinga bearn ealra twelfa,
the kinsmen of all twelve nobles
(twelve nobles hold the highest
positions of the court), 3172; subst.
he âh ealra geweald, *has power over
all,* 1728.

Uninflected : bil eal þurhwôd
flæschoman, *the battle-axe cleft the
body through and through,* 1568;
häfde . . . eal gefeormod fêt and
folma, *had devoured entirely feet
and hands,* 745; se þe eall geman
gâr-cwealm gumena, *who remem-*

bers thoroughly the death of the men by the spear, 2043, etc.

Adverbial: þeáh ic eal mæge, *although I am entirely able*, 681; hî on beorg dydon bêg and siglu eall swylce hyrsta, *they placed in the grave-mound rings, and ornaments, all such adornments*, 3165. —The gen. sg. ealles, adverbial in the sense of *entirely*, 1001, 1130.

eald, adj., *old:* a) of the age of living beings : nom.sg. eald, 357, 1703, 2211, etc.; dat. sg. ealdum, 2973; gen. sg. ealdes uhtflogan (*dragon*), 2761; dat. pl. ealdum, 1875; geongum and ealdum, 72.—b) of things and of institutions : nom. sg. helm monig eald and ômig, 2764. acc. sg. ealde lâfe (*sword*), 796, 1489; ealde wîsan, 1866; eald sweord, 1559, 1664, etc.; eald gewin, *old* (lasting years), *distress*, 1782; eald enta geweorc (*the precious things in the drake's cave*), 2775; acc. pl. calde mâðmas, 472; ofer ealde riht, *against the old laws* (namely, the Ten Commandments; Beówulf believes that God has sent him the drake as a punishment, because he has unconsciously, at some time, violated one of the commandments), 2331.

yldra, compar. *older:* mín yldra mæg, 468; yldra brôðor, 1325; ôð þät he (Heardrêd) yldra wearð, 2379.

yldesta, superl. *oldest*, in the usual sense; dat. sg. þam yldestan, 2436; in a moral sense, *the most respected:* nom. sg. se yldesta, 258; acc. sg. þone yldestan, 363, both times of Beówulf.

eald-fäder, st. m., *old-father, father who lived long ago:* nom. sg. 373.

eald-gesegen, st. f., *traditions from*

old times: gen. sg. eal-fela ealdgesegena, *very many of the old traditions*, 870.

eald-gesîð, st. m., *companion ever since old times, courtier for many years:* nom. pl. eald-gesiðas, 854.

eald-gestreón, st. n., *treasure out of the old times:* dat. pl. eald-gestreónum, 1382; gen. pl. -gestreóna, 1459.

eald-gewinna, w. m., *old-enemy, enemy for many years:* nom. sg. of Grendel, 1777.

eald-gewyrht, st. n., *merit on account of services rendered during many years:* nom. pl. þät næron eald-gewyrht, þät he âna scyle gnorn þrowian, *that has not been his desert ever since long ago, that he should bear the distress alone*, 2658.

eald-hláford, st. m., *lord through many years:* gen. sg. bill ealdhláfordes (of the old Beówulf(?)), 2779.

eald-metod, st. m., *God ruling ever since ancient times:* nom. sg. 946.

ealdor, aldor, st. m., *lord, chief* (king or powerful noble): nom. sg. ealdor, 1645, 1849, 2921; aldor, 56, 369, 392; acc. sg. aldor, 669; dat. sg. ealdre, 593; aldre, 346.

ealdor, aldor, st. n., *life:* acc. sg. aldor, 1372; dat. sg. aldre, 1448, 1525; ealdre, 2600; him on aldre stôd heresträl hearda (in vitalibus), 1435; nalles for ealdre mearn, *was not troubled about his life*, 1443; of ealdre gewât, *went out of life, died*, 2625; as instr. aldre, 662, 681, etc.; ealdre, 1656, 2134, etc.; gen. sg. aldres, 823; ealdres, 2791, 2444; aldres orwêna, *despairing of life*, 1003, 1566; ealdres scyldig, *having forfeited life*, 1339, 2062; dat.

pl. aldrum nĕꝺdon, 510, 538. — Phrases: on aldre (*in life*), *ever*, 1780; tô aldre (*for life*), *always*, 2006, 2499; âwa tô aldre, *for ever and ever*, 956.

ealdor-bealu, st. n., *life's evil:* acc. sg. Ju . . . ondrædan ne þearft . . . aldorbealu eorlum, *thou needest not fear death for the courtiers*, 1677.

ealdor-cearu, st. f., *trouble that endangers life, great trouble:* dat. sg. he his leódum wearꝺ . . . tô aldorceare, 907.

ealdor-dagas, st. m. pl., *days of one's life:* dat. pl. næfre on aldordagum (*never in his life*), 719; on ealder-dagum ær (*in former days*), 758.

ealdor-gedâl, st. n., *severing of life, death, end:* nom. sg. aldor-gedâl. 806.

ealdor-gewinna, w. m., *life-enemy, one who strives to take his enemy's life* (in N.H.G. the contrary conception, Tod-feind): nom. sg. caldorgewinna (*the dragon*), 2904.

ealdor-leás, adj., *without a ruler(?)*: nom. pl. aldor-leáse, 15.

ealdor-leás, adj., *lifeless, dead:* acc. sg. aldor-leásne, 1588; ealdor-leásne, 3004.

ealdor-þegn, st. m., *nobleman at the court, distinguished courtier:* acc. sg. aldor-þegn (Hróꝺgâr's confidential adviser, Æschere), 1309.

eal-fela, adj., *very much:* with following gen., eal-fela eald-gesegena, *very many old traditions*, 870; eal-fela eotena cynnes, 884.

ealgian, w. v., *to shield, to defend, to protect:* inf. w. acc. feorh ealgian, 797, 2656, 2669); pret. siꝺꝺan he (Hygelâc) under segne sine ealgode, wälreáf werede, *while under his banner he protected the treas-*

ures, *defended the spoil of battle* (i.e. while he was upon the Viking expeditions), 1205.

eal-gylden, adj., *all golden, entirely of gold:* nom. sg. swŷn ealgylden, 1112; acc.sg.segn eallgylden, 2768.

eal-îrenne, adj., *entirely of iron:* acc. sg. eall-irenne wigbord, *a wholly iron battle-shield*, 2339.

ealu, st. n., *ale, beer:* acc. sg. ealo drincende, 1946.

ealu-bene, st. f., *ale-bench, bench for those drinking ale:* dat. sg. in ealobence, 1030; on ealu-bence, 2868.

ealu-scerwen, st. f., *terror*, under the figure of a mishap at an ale-drinking, probably the sudden taking away of the ale: nom. sg. Denum eallum wearꝺ . . . caluscerwen, 770.

ealu-wæge, st. n., *ale-can, portable vessel out of which ale is poured into the cups:* acc. sg. 2022; hroden ealowæge, 495; dat. sg. ofer ealowæge (*at the ale-carouse*), 481.

eal-wealda, w.adj., *all ruling* God): nom. sg. fäder alwalda, 316; alwalda, 956, 1315; dat. sg. al-wealdan, 929.

eard, st. m., *cultivated ground, estate, hereditary estate:* in a broader sense, *ground in general, abode, place of sojourn:* nom. sg. him wäs bäm . . . lond gecynde, eard êꝺelriht, *the land was bequeathed to them both, the land and the privileges attached to it,* 2199; acc. sg. fifelcynnes eard, *the ground of the giant race, place of sojourn,* 104; similarly, älwihta eard, 1501; eard gemunde, *thought of his native ground, his home,* 1130; eard git ne const, *thou knowest not yet the place of sojourn,* 1378; eard and eorlscipe, *prædium et nobilitatem,* 1728; eard êꝺelwyn, *land and the enjoyment*

of home, 2494; dat. sg. ellor
hwearf of earde, *went elsewhere
from his place of abode*, i.e. died,
56; ðät we rondas beren eft tô
earde, *that we go again to our
homes*, 2655; on earde, 2737: acc.
pl. eácne eardas, *the broad ex-
panses* (in the fen-sea where Grendel's home was), 1622.

eardian, w. v.: 1) *to have a dwelling-
place, to live; to rest:* pret. pl. dŷre
swyrd swâ hie wið eorðan fäðm
þær eardodon, *costly swords, as they
had rested in the earth's bosom*, 3051.
—2) also transitively, *to inhabit:*
pret. sg. Heorot eardode, 166; inf.
wic eardian elles hwergen, *inhabit
a place elsewhere* (i.e. die), 2590.

eard-lufa, w. m., *the living upon
one's land, home-life:* acc. sg. eard-
lufan, 693.

earfoð-lîce, adv., *with trouble, with
difficulty*, 1637, 1658; *with vexation, angrily*, 86; *sorrowfully*,
2823; *with difficulty, scarcely*, 2304,
2935.

earfoð-þrag, st. f., *time full of troubles, sorrowful time:* acc. sg. -þrage,
283.

earh, adj., *cowardly:* gen. sg. ne bið
swylc earges sið (*no coward undertakes that*), 2542.

earm, st. m., *arm:* acc. sg. earm, 836,
973; wið earm gesät, *supported
himself with his arm*, 750; dat. pl.
earmum, 513.

earm, adj., *poor, miserable, unhappy:*
nom. sg. earm, 2369; earme ides,
the unhappy woman, 1118; dat. sg.
earmre teohhe, *the unhappy band*,
2939. —Comp. acc. sg. earmran
mannan, *a more wretched, more
forsaken man*, 577.

earm-beág, st. m., *arm-ring, bracelet:* gen. pl. earm-beága fela sear-

wum gesæled, *many arm-rings interlaced*, 2764.

earm-hreád, st. f., *arm-ornament:*
nom. pl. earm-hreáde twâ, 1195
(Grein's conjecture, MS. earm
reade).

earm-lîc, adj., *wretched, miserable:*
nom. sg. sceolde his ealdor-gedâl
earmlic wurðan, *his end should be
wretched*, 808.

earm-sceapen, pret. part. as adj.
(properly, *wretched by the decree
of fate*), *wretched:* nom. sg. 1352.

earn, st. m., *eagle:* dat. sg. earne, 3027.

eatol. See atol.

eaxl, st. f., *shoulder:* acc. sg. eaxle,
836, 973; dat. sg. on eaxle, 817,
1548; be eaxle, 1538; on eaxle ides
gnornode, *the woman sobbed on the
shoulder* (of her son, who has fallen
and is being burnt), 1118; dat. pl.
sät freán eaxlum neáh, *sat near the
shoulders of his lord* (Beówu'f lies
lifeless upon the earth, and Wîglâf
sits by his side, near his shoulder,
so as to sprinkle the face of his
dead lord), 2854; he for eaxlum
gestôd Deniga freán, *he stood before
the shoulders of the lord of the Danes*
(i.e. not directly before him, but
somewhat to the side, as etiquette
demanded), 358.

eaxl-gestealla, w. m., *he who has
his position at the shoulder* (sc. of
his lord), *trusty courtier, counsellor
of a prince:* nom. sg. 1327; acc. pl.
-gesteallan, 1715.

EÁ

eác, conj., *also:* 97, 388, 433, etc.;
êc, 3132.

eácen (pret. part. of a not existing
eácan, augere), adj., *wide-spread*,

large: acc. pl. eácne eordas, *broad plains,* 1622. — *great, h azy:* eald sweord eácen, 1664; dat. pl. eácnum ecgum, 2141, both times of the great sword in Grendel's habitation. — *great, mighty, powerful:* äðele and eácen, of Beówulf, 198.

eácen-eräftig, adj., *immense (of riches), enormously great:* acc. sg. hord-ärna sum eácen-cräftig, *that enormous treasure-house,* 2281; nom. sg. þät yrfe eácen-cräftig, iúmanna gold, 3052.

eádig, adj., *blessed with possessions, rich, happy by reason of property:* nom. sg. wes, þenden þu lifige, äðeling eádig, *be, as long as thou livest, a prince blessed with riches,* 1226; eádig mon, 2471. — Comp. sige-, sigor-, tir-eádig.

eádig-líce, adv., *in abundance, in joyous plenty:* dreámum lifdon eádiglíce, *lived in rejoicing and plenty,* 100.

eáðe, éðe, ýðe, adj., *easy, pleasant:* nom. pl. gode þancedon þäs þe him ýð-láde eáðe wurdon, *thanked God that the sea-ways* (the navigation) *had become easy to them,* 228; ne wäs þät éðe síð, *no pleasant way,* 2587; näs þät ýðe ceáp, *no easy purchase,* 2416; nô þät ýðe byð tô beflceónne, *not easy* (as milder expression for *in no way, not at all*), 1003.

eáðe, ýðe, adv., *easily:* eáðe, 478, 2292, 2705.

eáð-fynde, adj., *easy to find:* nom. sg. 138.

eáge, w. n., *eye:* dat. pl. him of eágum stôd leóht unfäger, *out of his eyes came a terrible gleam,* 727; þät ic ... eágum starige, *see with eyes, behold,* 1782; similarly, 1936; gen. pl. eágena bearhtm, 1767.

eágor-streám, st. m., *sea-stream, sea:* acc. sg. 513.

eá-land, st. n., *land with abundant water* (of the land of the Geátas): acc. sg. eá-lond, 2335.

eám, st. m., *uncle, mother's brother:* nom. sg. 882.

eástan, adv., *from the east,* 569.

eáwan, w. v., *to disclose, to show, to prove:* pres. sg. III. eáweð ... uncúðne níð, *shows evil enmity,* 276. See **cówan, ýwan.**

ge-eáwan, *to show, to offer:* pret. part. him wäs ... wunden gold êstum ge-eáwed, *was graciously presented,* 1195.

EO

eode. See **gangan.**

eodor, st. m., *fence, hedge, railing.* Among the old Germans, an estate was separated by a fence from the property of others. Inside of this fence the laws of peace and protection held good, as well as in the house itself. Hence **eodor** is sometimes used instead of *house:* acc. pl. bêht eahta mearas on flet teón, in under eoderas, *gave orders to lead eight steeds into the hall, into the house,* 1038. — 2) figuratively, *lord, prince,* as protector: nom. sg. eodor, 428, 1045; eodur, 664.

eofoð, st. n., *strength:* acc. pl. eofoðo, 2535. See **eafoð.**

eofer, st. m.: 1) *boar,* here of the metal boar-image upon the helmet: nom. sg. eofer Irenheard, 1113. — 2) figuratively, *bold hero, brave fighter* (O. N. iöfur): nom. pl. þonne ... eoferas cnysedan, *when the heroes rushed upon each other,* 1329, where **eoferas** and **fêðan**

stand in the same relation to each other as cnysedan and hniton.

eofor-líc, st. n. *boar-image* (on the helmet) : nom. pl. eofor-llc scionon, 303.

eofor-spreót, st. m., *b ar-spear :* dat. pl. mid eofer-spreótum heórohocyhtum, *with hunting-spears which were provided with sharp hooks,* 1438.

coguð, loguð. See geogoð.

eolet, st. m. n., *sea(?)* : gen. sg. eoletes, 224.

corelan-stân, st. m., *precious stone :* acc. pl. -stânas, 1209.

eorð-cyning, st. m., *king of the land :* gen. sg. eorð-cyninges (Finn), 1156.

eorð-draca, w. m., *earth-drake, dragon that lives in the earth :* nom. sg. 2713, 2826.

eorðe, w. f. : 1) *earth* (in contrast with heaven , *world :* acc. sg. álmihtiga eorðan worhte, 92; wlde geond eorðan, *far over the earth, through the wide world,* 266; dat. sg. ofer eorðan, 248, 803; on eorðan, 1823, 2856, 3139; gen. sg. eorðan, 753. — 2) *earth, ground :* acc. sg. he eorðan gefeóll, *fell to the ground,* 2835; forlèton corla gestreón eorðan healdan, *let the earth hold the nobles' treasure,* 3168; dat. sg. þät hit on eorðan läg, 1533; under eorðan, 2416; gen. sg. wið eorðan fäðm (*in the bos m of the earth*), 3050.

eorð-reced, st. n., *hall in the earth, rock-hall :* acc. sg. 2720.

eorð-scräf, st. n., *earth-cavern, cave :* dat. sg. eorð-[scräfe], 2233; gen. pl. eorð-scrafa, 3047.

eorð-sele, st. m., *hall in the earth, cave :* acc. sg. eorð-sele, 2411; dat. sg. of eorðsele, 2516.

eorð-weall, st. m., *earth-wall :* acc.

sg. (Ongenþeów) beáh eft under eorðweall, *fled again under the earth-wall* (into his fortified camp), 2958; þâ me wäs . . . sið âlýfed inn under eorðweall, *then the way in, under the earth-wall was opened to me* (into the dragon's cave), 3091.

eorð-weard, st. m., *land-property, estate :* acc. sg. 2335.

eorl, st. m., *noble born man, a man of the high nobility :* nom. sg. 762, 796, 1229, etc.; acc. sg. corl, 573, 628, 2696; gen. sg. eorles, 690, 983, 1758, etc.; acc. pl. eorlas, 2817; dat. pl. eorlum, 770, 1282, 1650, etc.; gen. pl. eorla, 248, 357, 369, etc. — Since the king himself is from the stock of the eorlas, he is also called eorl, 6, 2952.

eorl-gestreón, st. n., *wealth of the nobles :* gen. pl. eorl-gestreóna ... hardfyrdne dæl, 2245.

eorl-gewæde, st. n., *knightly dress, armor :* dat. pl. -gewædum, 1443.

eorlíc (i.e. eorl-llc), adj., *what it becomes a noble born man to do, chivalrous :* acc. sg. eorlic ellen, 638.

eorl-scipe, st. m., *condition of being noble born, chivalrous nature, nobility :* acc. sg. eorl-scipe, 1728, 3175; eorl-scipe efnan, *to do chivalrous deeds,* 2134, 2536, 2623, 3008.

eorl-weorod, st. n., *followers of nolles :* nom. sg. 2894.

eormen-cyn, st. n., *very extensive race, mankind :* gen. sg. eormencynnes, 1958.

eormen-grund, st. m., *immensely wide plains, the whole broad earth :* acc. sg. ofer eormen-grund, 860.

eormen-láf, st. f., *enormous legacy :* acc. sg. eormen-lâfe äðelan cynnes (*the treasures of the dragon's cave*), 2235.

corre, adj., *angry, enraged:* gen. sg. corres, 1448.

eoton, st. m.: 1) *giant:* nom. sg. eoten (Grendel), 762; dat. sg. uninflected, eoton (Grendel), 669; nom. pl. eotenas, 112. — 2) *harmful enemy*, in general(?) : gen. pl. eotena, 421, 884, (of the Danes) 1073, (of the Frisians) 1089, 1142; dat. pl. eotenum, 1146.

eotonisc, adj., *gigantic, coming from giants:* acc. sg. eald sweord eotenisc (eotonisc), 1559, 2980, (etonisc, MS.) 2617.

EÓ

eóred-geatwe, st. f. pl., *warlike adornments:* acc. pl., 2867.

eówan, w. v., *to show, to be seen:* pres. sg. III. ne gesacu ôhwær, ecghete eóweð, *nowhere shows itself strife, sword-hate*, 1739. See **eáwan, ȝwan.**

eówer: 1) gen. pl. pers. pron., vestrum : eówer sum, *that one of you* (namely, Beówulf), 248; fæhðe eówer leóde, *the enmity of the people of you* (of your people), 597; nis þæt eówer sið . . . nefne min ânes, 2533. — 2) poss. pron., *your*, 251, 257, 294, etc.

F

ge-fandian, -fondian, w. v., *to try, to search for, to find out, to experience:* w. gen. pret. part. þæt häfde gumena sum goldes gefandod, *that a man had discovered the gold*, 2302 ; þonne se ân hafað þurh deáðes nýd dæda gefondad, *now the one* (Herebeald) *has with death's pang experienced the deeds* (the unhappy bow-shot of Hæðcyn), 2455.

fara, w. m., *farer, traveller:* in comp. mere-fara.

faran, st. v., *to move from one place to another, to go, to wander:* inf. tô hâm faran, *to go home*, 124; lêton on geflit faran fealwe mearas, *let the fallow horses go in emulation*, 865; cwom faran flotherge on Fresna land, *had come to Friesland with a fleet*, 2916; com leóda dugoðe on lâst faran, *came to go upon the track of the heroes of his people*, i.e. to follow them, 2946; gerund wæron æðelingas eft tô leódum fûse tô farenne, *the nobles were ready to go again to their people*, 1806; pret. sg. gegnum fôr [þâ] ofer myrcan môr, *there had* (Grendel's mother) *gone away over the dark fen*, 1405; sægenga fôr, *the seafarer* (the ship) *drove along*, 1909; (wyrm) mid bæle fôr, (the dragon) *fled away with fire*, 2309; pret. pl. þæt . . . scawan scirhame tô scipe fôron, *that the visitors in glittering attire betook themselves to the ship*, 1896. ge faran, *to proceed, to act:* inf. hû se mânsceaða under færgripum gefaran wolde, *how he would act in his sudden attacks*, 739.

ût faran, *to go out:* w. acc. lêt of breóstum . . . word ût faran, *let words go out of his breast, uttered words*, 2552.

faroð, st. m., *stream, flood of the sea:* dat. sg. tô brimes faroðe, 28; äfter faroðe, *with the stream*, 580; ät faroðe, 1917.

faru, st. f., *way, passage, expedition:* in comp. âd-faru.

fâcen-stäf (elementum nequitiae), st. m., *wickedness, treachery, deceit:* acc. pl. fâcen-stafas, 1019.

fåh, fåg, adj., *many-colored, variegated, of varying color* (especially said of the color of gold, of bronze, and of blood, in which the beams of light are refracted): nom. sg. fåh (*covered with blood*), 420; blôde fåh, 935; återtånum fåh (sc. íren), 1460; sadol searwum fåh (*saddle artistically ornamented with gold*), 1039; sweord swåtefåh, 1287; brim blôdefåh,1595; wåldreórefåg,1632; (draca) fyrwylmum fåh (*because he spewed flame*), 2672; sweord fåh and fåted, 2702; blôde fåh, 2975; acc. sg. dreóre fåhne, 447; goldsele fåttum fåhne, 717; on fågne flôr treddode, *trod the shining floor* (of Heorot), 726; hrôf golde fåhne, *the roof shining with gold*, 928; nom. pl. euforlíc ... fåh and fyrheard. 305; acc. pl. þå hilt since fåge, 1616; dat. pl. fågum sweordum, 586. — Comp. bån-, blôd-, brûn-, dreór-, gold-, gryre-, searo-, sinc-, stån-, swåt-, wäl-, wyrm-fåh.

fåh, fåg, få, adj.: 1) *hostile:* nom. sg. fåh feónd-sceaða, 554; he wäs fåg wið god (Grendel), 812; acc. sg. fåne (*the dragon*), 2656; gen. pl. fåra, 578, 1464. — 2) *liable to pursuit, without peace, outlawed:* nom. sg. fåg, 1264; måne fåh, *outlawed through crime*, 979; fyrendædum fåg, 1002. — Comp. nearofåh.

fåmig-heals, adj., *with foaming neck:* nom. sg. flota fåmig-heals, 218, (sægenga) fåmig-heals, 1910.

fåc, st. n., *period of time:* acc. sg. lytel fåc, *during a short time*, 2241.

fåder, st. m., *father:* nom. sg. fåder, 55, 262, 459, 2609; of God, 1610; fåder alwalda, 316; acc. sg. fåder, 1356; dat. sg. fåder, 2430; gen. sg.

fåder, 21, 1480; of God, 188 — Comp.: ær-, eald-fåder.

fådera, w. m., *father's brother:* in comp. suhter-gefäderan.

fåder-åðelo, st. n. pl., *paternus principatus* (?): dat. pl. fåderåðelum, 912.

fåderen-mæg, st. m., *kinsman descended from the same father, codescendant:* dat. sg. fåderen-mæge, 1264.

fåðm, st. m.: 1) *the outspread, encircling arms:* instr. pl. feóndes fäð[mum], 2129. — 2) *embrace, encircling:* nom. sg. liges fäðm, 782; acc. sg. in fyres fäðm, 185. —3) *bosom, lap:* acc. sg. on foldan fäðm, 1394; wið eorðan fäðm, 3050; dat. pl. tô fäðer (God's) fäðmum, 188. — 4) *power, property:* acc. in Francna fäðm, 1211. — Cf. sîd-fäðmed, sîð-fäðme.

fåðmian, w. v., *to embrace, to take up into itself:* pres. subj. þät minne lîchaman ... glêd fäðmie, 2653; inf. lêton flôd fäðmian frätwa hyrde, 3134.

ge-fåg, adj., *agreeable, desirable* (Old Eng., fawe, *willingly*): comp. ge-fågra, 916.

fågen, adj., *glad, joyous:* nom. pl. ferhðum fägne, *the glad at heart*, 1634.

fåger, adj., *beautiful, lovely:* nom. sg. fäger fold-bold, 774; fäger foldan bearm, 1138; acc. sg. freoðoburh fägere, 522; nom. pl. þær him fold-wegas fägere þûhton, 867. — Comp. un-fåger.

fågere, fägre, adv., *beautifully, well, becomingly, according to etiquette:* fägere geþægon medoful manig, 1015; þå wäs flet-sittendun fägere gereorded, *becomingly the repast was served*, 1789; Higelåc ongan . . . fägre friegean, 1986; similarly, 2990.

fär, st. n., *craft, ship:* nom. sg., 33.

fäst, adj., *bound, fast:* nom. sg. biŏ se slæp tô fäst, 1743; acc. sg. freóndscipe fästne, 2070; fäste frioŏuware, 1097. — The prep. on stands to denote the where or wherein: wäs tô fäst on Jâm (sc. on fæhŏe and fyrene), 137; on ancre fäst, 303. Or, oftener, the dative: feónd-grâpum fäst, (*held*) *fast in his antagonist's clutch*, 637; fŷrbendum fäst, *fast in the forged hinges*, 723; handa fäst, 1291, etc.; hygebendum fäst (beorn him langaŏ), *fast (shut) in the bonds of his bosom, the man longs for* (i.e. in secret), 1879. — Comp.: âr-, blæd-, gin-, sôŏ-, tîr-, wîs-fäst.

fäste, adv., *fast:* 554, 761, 774, 789, 1296. — Comp. fästor, 143.

be-fästan, w. v., *to give over:* inf. hêt Hildeburh hire selfre sunu sweoloŏe befästan, *to give over to the flames her own son*, 1116.

fästen, st. n., *fortified place*, or *place difficult of access:* acc. sg. leóda fästen, *the fastness of the Ged'as* (with ref. to 2327), 2334; fästen (Ongenþeów's castle or fort), 2951; fästen (Grendel's house in the fensea), 104.

fäst-ræd, adj., *firmly resolved:* acc. sg. fäst-rædne geþoht, *firm determination*, 611.

fät, st. m., *way, journey:* in comp. stŏ-fät.

fät, st. n., *vessel:* vase, cup:* acc. pl. fyrn-manna fatu, *the (drinking-) vessels of men of old times*, 2762. — Comp.: bân-, drync-, mâŏŏum-, sinc-, wundor-fät.

fät, st. n. (?), *plate, sheet of metal*, especially *gold plate* (Dietrich Hpt.

Ztschr. XI. 420): dat. pl. gold-sele . . . fättum fâhne, *shining with gold plates* (the walls and the inner part of the roof were partly covered with gold), 717; sceal se hearda helm hyrsted golde fätum befeallen (sc. wesan), *the gold ornaments shall fall away from it*, 2257.

fäted, **fätt**, part., *ornamented with gold beaten into plate-form:* gen. sg. fättan goldes, 1094, 2247; instr. sg. fättan golde, 2103. Elsewhere, *covered, ornamented with gold plate:* nom. sg. sweord . . . fäted, 2702; acc. sg. fäted wæge, 2254, 2283; acc. pl. fätte scyldas, 333; fätte beágas, 1751.

fäted-hleór, adj., *phaleratus gena* (Dietr.): acc. pl. eahta mearas fäted-hleóre (*eight horses with bridles covered with plates of gold*), 1037.

fät-gold, st. n., *gold in sheets* or *plates:* acc. sg., 1922.

fæge, adj.: 1) *forfeited to death, allotted to death by fate:* nom. sg. fæge, 1756, 2142, 2976; fæge and ge-flŷmed, 847; fûs and fæge, 1242; acc. sg. fægne flæsc-homan, 1569; dat. sg. fægum, 2078; gen. sg. fæges, 1528. — 2) *dead:* dat. pl. ofer fægum (*over the warriors fallen in the battle*), 3026. — Comp.: deáŏ-, un-fæge.

fæhŏ (*state of hostility*, see **fâh**), st. f., *hostile act, feud, battle:* nom. sg. fæhŏ, 2404, 3062; acc. sg. fæhŏe, 153, 459, 470, 596, 1334, etc.; also of the unhappy bowshot of the Hrêŏling, Hæŏcyn, by which he killed his brother, 2466; dat. sg. fore fæhŏe and fyrene, 137; nalas for fæhŏe mearn (*did not recoil from the combat*), 1538;

gen. sg. ne gefeah he þære fæhðe,
109; gen. pl. fæhða gemyndig,
2690. — Comp. wäl-fæhð.

fæhðo, st. f., same as above: nom.
sg. sió fæhðo, 3000; acc. fæhðo,
2490.

fælsian, w. v., *to bring into a good
condition, to cleanse:* inf. þät ic
móte . . . Heorot fælsian (from the
plague of Grendel), 432; pret.
Hróðgáres . . . sele fælsode, 2353.
ge-fælsian, w. v., same as above:
pret. part. häfde gefælsod . . . sele
Hróðgáres, 826; Heorot is gefælsod, 1177; wæron ýð-gebland eal
gefælsod, 1621.

fæmne, w. f., *virgin, recens nupta:*
dat. sg. fæmnan, 2035; gen. sg.
fæmnan, 2060, both times of Hróðgár's daughter Freáware.

fær, st. m., *sudden, unexpected attack:* nom. sg. (attack upon Hnäf's
band by Finn's,, 1069.

fær-gripe, st. m., *sudden, treacher-
ous gripe, attack:* nom. sg. fær-
gripe flódes, 1517; dat. pl. under
færgripum, 739.

fær-gryre, st. m., *fright caused by a
sudden attack:* dat. pl. wið fær-
gryrum (against the inroads of
Grendel into Heorot), 174.

færinga, adv., *suddenly, unexpect-
edly*, 1415, 1989.

fær-nið, st. m., *hostility with sudden attacks:* gen. pl. hwät me
Grendel hafað . . . færniða gefremed, 476.

fäs, st. m. (?), 2231.

feðer-gearwe, st. f. pl. (*feather-
equipment*), *the feathers of the
shaft of the arrow:* dat. (instr.) pl.
sceft feðer-gearwum fús, 3120.

fel, st. n., *skin, hide:* dat. pl. glóf
. . . gegyrwed dracan fellum, *made
of the skins of dragons,* 2089.

fela, I., adj. indecl., *much, many:*
as subst.: acc. sg. fela friegende,
2107. With worn placed before:
hwät þu worn fela . . . ymb Brecan
spræce, *how very much you spoke
about Breca,* 530. — With gen. sg.:
acc. sg. fela fyrene, 810; wyrm-
cynnes fela, 1426; worna fela sorge, 2004; tó fela micles . . . Denigea
leóde, *too much of the race of the
Danes,* 695; uncúðes fela, 877;
fela láðes, 930; fela leófes and
láðes, 1061. — With gen. pl.: nom.
sg. fela máðma, 36; fela þæra wera
and wifa, 993, etc.; acc. sg. fela
missera, 153; fela fyrena, 164;
ofer landa fela, 311; maððum-
sigla fela (falo, MS.), 2758; ne
me swór fela áða on unriht, *swore
no false oaths,* 2739, etc.; worn
fela máðma, 1784; worna fela
gúða, 2543. — Comp. eal-fela.

II., adverbial, *very,* 1386, 2103,
2951.

fela-hrór, adj., valde agitatus, *very
active against the enemy, very warlike,* 27.

fela-módig, adj., *very courageous:*
gen. pl. -módigra, 1638, 1889.

fela-synnig, adj., *very criminal,
very guilty:* acc. sg. fela-sinnigne
secg (in MS., on account of the
alliteration, changed to simple sinnigne), 1380.

felgan, st. v., *to betake one's self
into a place, to conceal one's self:*
pret. siððan inne fealh Grendles
módor (in Heorot), 1282; þær
inne fealh secg syn-bysig (in the
dragon's cave), 2227. — *to come to
any place, to arrive:* searoníðas
fealh, 1201.

ät-felgan, w. dat., insistere, adhæ-
rere: pret. nó ic him þäs georne ätfealh (*did not hold him so fast*), 969.

fen, st. n., *fen, moor:* acc. sg. fen, 104; dat. sg. tô fenne, 1296; fenne, 2010.

fen-freoðo, st. f., *refuge in the fen:* dat. sg. in fen-freoðo, 852.

feng, st. m., *gripe, embrace:* nom. sg. fŷres feng, 1765; acc. sg. fâra feng (of the hostile sea-monsters), 578. — Comp. inwit-feng.

fengel (probably *he who takes possession*, cf. tô fôn, 1756, and fôn tô ríce, *to enter upon the government*), st. m., *lord, prince, king:* nom. sg. wîsa fengel, 1401; snottra fengel, 1476, 2157; hringa fengel, 2346.

fen-ge-lâd, st. n., *fen-paths, fen with paths:* acc. pl. frêcne fengelâd (*fens difficult of access*), 1360.

fen-hliþ, st. n., *marshy precipice:* acc. pl. under fen-hleoðu, 821.

fen-hôp, st. n., *refuge in the fen:* acc. pl. on fen-hôpu, 765.

ferh, st. m. n., *life;* see **feorh**.

ferh, st. m., *hog, boar*, here of the boar-image on the helmet: nom. sg., 305.

ferhð, st. m., *heart, soul:* dat. sg. on ferhðe, 755, 949, 1719; gehwylc hiora his ferhðe treówde, þät . . ., *each of them trusted to his* (Hûnferð's) *heart, that* . . ., 1167; gen. sg. ferhðes fore-þanc, 1061; dat. pl. (adverbial) ferhðum fägne, *happy at heart*, 1634; þät mon . . . ferhðum freóge, *that one . . . heartily love*, 3178. — Comp.: collen-, sârig-, swið-, wîde-ferhð.

ferhð-frec, adj., *having good courage, bold, brave:* acc. sg. ferhð-frecan Fin, 1147.

ferhð-genîðla, w. m., *mortal enemy:* acc. sg. ferhð-genîðlan, of the drake, 2882.

ferian, w. v. w. acc., *to bear, to bring, to conduct:* pres. II. pl. hwanon ferigeað fätte scyldas, 333; pret. pl. tô scypum feredon eal ingestealden eorðcyninges, 1155; similarly, feredon, 1159, 3114.

ät-ferian, *to carry away, to bear off:* pret. ic þät hilt þanon feóndum ätferede, 1670.

ge-ferian, *to bear, to bring, to lead:* pres. subj. I. pl. þonne (we) geferian freán ûserne, 3108; inf. geferian . . . Grendles heáfod, 1639; pret. þät hi ût geferedon dŷre mâðmas, 3131; pret. part. her syndon geferede feorran cumene . . . Geáta leóde, *men of the Geátas, come from afar, have been brought hither* (by ship), 361.

ôð-ferian, *to tear away, to take away:* pret. sg. I. unsôfte panon feorh ôð-ferede, 2142.

of-ferian, *to carry off, to take away, to tear away:* pret. ôðer swylc ût offerede, *took away another such* (sc. fifteen), 1584.

fetel-hilt, st. n., *sword-hilt*, with the gold chains fastened to it: acc. (sg. or pl.?), 1564. (See "Leitfaden f. nord. Altertumskunde," pp. 45, 46.)

fetian, w. v., *to bring near, bring:* pres. subj. nâh hwâ . . . fe[tige] fäted wæge, *bring the gold-chased tankard*, 2254; pret. part. hraðe wäs tô bûre Beówulf fetod, 1311.

ge-fetian, *to bring:* inf. hêt þâ eorla hleó in gefetian Hrêðles lâfe, *caused Hrêðel's sword to be brought*, 2191.

â-fêdan, w. v., *to nourish, to bring up:* pret. part. þær he âfêded wäs, 694.

fêða (O.H.G. fendo), w. m.: 1) *foot-soldiers:* nom. pl. fêðan, 1328, 2545. — 2) collective in sing., *band*

of foot-soldiers, troop of warriors :
nom. féﬃa eal gesät, 1425; dat. on
féﬃan, 2498, 2920. — Comp. gum-
feﬃa.

féﬃe, st. n., *gait, going, pace :* dat.
sg. wäs tô foremihtig feónd on
féﬃe, *the enemy was too strong in
going* (i.e. could ﬂee too fast), 971.

féﬃe-cempa, w. m., *foot-soldier :*
nom. sg., 1545, 2854.

féﬃe-gäst, st. m., *guest coming on
foot :* dat. pl. féﬃe-gestum, 1977.

féﬃe-läst, st. m., *signs of going, foot-
print :* dat. pl. férdon forﬃ þonon
féﬃe-lâstum, *went forth from there
upon their trail*, i.e. by the same
way that they had gone, 1633.

féﬃe-wîg, st. m., *battle on foot :* gen.
sg. nealles Hetware hrêmge þorf-
ton (sc. wesan) féﬃe-wîges, 2365.

fél (= feól), st. f., *file :* gen. pl. féla
lâfe, *what the ﬁles have left behind*
(that is, the swords), 1033.

féran, w. v., iter (A.S. fôr) facere,
to come, to go, to travel : pres. subj.
II. pl. ær ge . . . on land Dena
furﬃur féran, *ere you go farther
into the land of the Danes*, 254;
inf. féran on freán wäre (*to die*),
27; gewiton him þâ féran (*set out
upon their way*), 301; mæl is me tô
féran, 316; féran . . . gang sceáwigan, *go, so as to see the footprints*,
1391; wide féran, 2262; pret.
férdon folctogan . . . wundur sceáwian, *the princes came to see the
wonder*, 840; férdon forﬃ, 1633.

ge-féran : 1) adire, *to arrive at :*
pres. subj. þonne eorl ende gefére
lífgesceafta, *reach the end of life*,
3064; pret. part. häfde æghwäﬃer
ende geféred lænan lifes, *frail
life's end had both reached*, 2845.
— 2) *to reach, to accomplish, to
bring about :* pret. hafast þu gefé-

red þät . . ., 1222, 1856. — 3) *to
behave one's self, to conduct one's
self :* pret. frêcne geférdon, *had
shown themselves daring*, 1692.

feal, st. m., *fall :* in comp. wäl-feal.

feallan, st. v., *to fall, to fall head-
long :* inf. feallan, 1071; pret. sg.
þät he on hrusan ne feól, *that it*
(the hall) *did not fall to the ground*,
773; similarly, feóll on foldan,
2976; feóll on féﬃan (dat. sg.),
fell in the hand (of his warriors),
2920; pret. pl. þonne walu feóllon,
1043.

be-feallen, pret. part., w. dat. or
instr., *deprived of, robbed :* freóndum befeallen, *robbed of friends*,
1127; sceal se hearda helm . . .
fätum befeallen (sc. wesan), *be
robbed of its gold mountings* (the
gold mounting will fall away from
it moldering), 2257.

ge-feallan, *to fall, to sink down :*
pres. sg. III. þät se lic-homa . .
fæge gefealleﬃ, *that the body doomed
to die sinks down*, 1756. — Also,
with the acc. of the place whither :
pret. meregrund gefeóll, 2101; he
eorﬃan gefeóll, 2835.

fealu, adj., *fallow, dun-colored, taw-
ny :* acc. sg. ofer fealone ﬂôd (*over
the sea*), 1951; fealwe stræte (with
reference to 320), 917; acc. pl.
lêton on geﬂit faran fealwe mearas, 866. — Comp. äppel-fealo.

feax, st. n., *hair, hair of the head :*
dat. sg. wäs be feaxe on ﬂet boren
Grendles heáfod, *was carried by
the hair into the hall*, 1648; him
. . . swât . . . sprong forﬃ under
fexe, *the blood sprang out under the
hair of his head*, 2968. — Comp. :
blonden-, gamol , wunden-feax.

ge-feá, w. m., *joy :* acc. sg. þære
fylle gefeán, *joy at the abundant*

repast, 562; ic þäs ealles mäg ... gefeán habban (*can rejoice at all this*), 2741.

feá, adj., *free :* dat. pl. nemne feáum ânum, *except some few*, 1082; gen. pl. feára sum, *as one of a few, with a few*, 1413; feára sunne, *one of a few (some few)*, 3062. With gen. following : acc. pl. feá worda cwäð, *spoke few words*, 2063, 2247.

feá-sceaft, adj., *miserable, unhappy, helpless :* nom. sg. syððan ærest wearð feá-sceaft funden, 7 ; feá-sceaft guma (Grendel), 974; dat. sg. feásceaftum men, 2286; Eádgilse ... feásceaftum, 2394; nom. pl. feásceafte (the Geátas robbed of their king, Hygelác), 2374.

feoh, feó, st.n.,(properly *cattle, herd*), here, *possessions, property, treasure :* instr. sg. ne wolde ... feorhbealo feó þingian, *would not allay life's evil for treasure* (tribute), 156; similarly, þá feohðe feó þingode, 470; ic þe þá feohðe feó leánige, 1381.

ge-feohan, ge-feón, st. v., w. gen. and instr., *to enjoy one's self, to rejoice at something :* a) w. gen.: pret. sg. ne gefeah he þære feohðe, 109; hilde gefeh, beado-weorces, 2299; pl. fylle gefægon, *enjoyed themselves at the bounteous repast*, 1015; þeódnes gefégon, *rejoiced at* (the return of) *the ruler*, 1628. – b) w. instr.: niht-weorce gefeh, ellen-mærðum, 828; secg weorce gefeh, 1570; sælâce gefeah, mägenbyrðenne þâra þe he him mid häfde, *rejoiced at the gift of the sea, and at the great burden of that* (Grendel's head and the sword-hilt) *which he had with him*, 1625.

feoh-gift, -gyft, st. f., *bestowing of gifts or treasures :* gen. sg. þære

feoh-gyfte, 1026; dat. pl. ät feohgyftum, 1090; fromum feohgiftum, *with rich gifts,* 21.

feoh-leás, adj., *that cannot be atoned for through gifts :* nom. sg. þät wäs feoh-leás gefeoht, *a deed of arms that cannot be expiated* (the killing of his brother by Hæðcyn), 2442.

ge-feoht, st. n., *combat ; warlike deed :* nom. sg. (the killing of his brother by Hæðcyn), 2442; dat. sg. mêce þone þin fäder tô gefeohte bär, *the sword which thy father bore to the combat*, 2049.

ge-feohtan, st. v., *to fight :* inf. w. acc. ne mehte ... wig Hengeste wiht gefeohtan (*could by no means offer Hengest battle*), 1084.

feohte, w. f., *combat :* acc. sg. feohtan, 576, 960. See **were-fyhte.**

feor, adj., *far, remote :* nom. sg. nis þät feor heonon, 1362; näs him feor þanon tô gesêcanne sinces bryttan, 1922; acc. sg. feor eal (*all that is far, past*), 1702.

feor, adv., *far, far away :* a) of space, 42, 109, 809, 1806, 1917 ; feor and (oððe) neáh, *far and (or) near*, 1222, 2871; feorr, 2267.— b) of time : ge feor hafað feohðe gestæled (*has placed us under her enmity henceforth*), 1341.

Comparative, fyr, feorr, and feor: fyr and fästor, 143; fyr, 252; feorr, 1989; feor, 542.

feor-bûend, pl., *dwelling far away :* nom. pl. ge feor-bûend, 254.

feor-cyð, st. f., *home of those living far away, distant land :* nom. pl. feor-cyððe beóð sêlran gesôhte þäm þe him selfa deáh, *who trusts to his own ability, for him is it better that he seek foreign lands*, 1839.

feorh, ferh (Goth. fairhvu-s, *world*),

st. m. and n., *life, principle of life,
soul :* nom. sg. feorh, 2124; nô
þon lange wäs feorh äðelinges flæsce bewunden, *not for much longer
was the soul of the prince enveloped
in the body* (he was near death),
2425; ferh ellen wräc, *life ex-
pelled the strength* (i.e. with the
departing life the strength disap-
peared also), 2707; acc. sg. feorh
ealgian, 797, 2656, 2669; feorh
gehealdan, *preserve his life,* 2857;
feorh âlegde, *gave up his life,* 852;
similarly, ær he feorh seleð, 1371;
feorh oðferede, *tore away her life,*
2142; ôð þät hie forlæddan tô þam
lindplegan swæse gesiðas ond hyra
sylfra feorh, *till in an evil hour
they carried into battle their dear
companions and their lives* (i.e.
led them to their death), 2041;
gif þu þin feorh hafast, 1850; ymb
feorh sacan (*to fight for life*). 439;
wäs in feorh dropen, *was wounded
into his life,* i.e. mortally, 2982;
widan feorh, as temporal acc.,
through a wide life, i.e. always,
2015; dat. sg. feore, 1294, 1549;
tô widan feore, *for a wide life,* i.e.
at all times, 934; on swâ geongum
feore (*at a so youthful age*), 1844;
as instr., 578, 3014; gen. sg. feores,
1434, 1943; dat. pl. buton . . . feorum gumena, 73; freónda feorum,
1307. — Also, *body, corpse :* þâ wäs
heal hroden feónda feorum (*the
hall was covered with the slain of
the enemy*), 1153; gehwearf þâ in
Francna fäðm feorh cyninges, *then
the body of the king* (Hygelâc) *fell
into the power of the Franks,* 1211.
—Comp. geoguð-feorh.

feorh-bana, w. m., (*life-slayer*),
man-slayer, murderer : dat. sg.
feorh-bonan, 2466.

feorh-ben, st. f., *wound that takes
away life, mortal wound :* dat.
(instr.) pl. feorh-bennum seóc,
2741.

feorh-bealu, st. n., *evil destroying
life, violent death :* nom. sg., 2078,
2251, 2538; acc. sg., 156.

feorh-cyn, st. n., *race of the living,
mankind :* gen. pl. fela feorh-cynna, 2267.

feorh-geniðla, w. m., *he who seeks
life, life's enemy* (N.H.G. Tod-
feind), *mortal enemy :* acc. sg.
-geniðlan, 1541; dat. sg. -geni-
lan, 970; acc. pl. folgode feorh-
geniðlan, 970; acc. pl. folgode
feorh-geniðlan, (Ongenþeów) *pursued his mortal enemies,* 2934.

feorh-lagu, st. f., *the life allotted to
anyone, life determined by fate :*
acc. sg. on mâðma hord mine
(minne, MS.) bebohte fróde feorh-
lege, *for the treasure-hoard I sold
my old life,* 2801.

feorh-lâst, st. m., *trace of (vanish-
ing) life, sign of death :* acc. sg.
feorh-lâstas bär, 847.

feorh-seóc, adj., *mortally wounded :*
nom. sg., 821.

feorh-sweng, st. m., (*stroke robbing of life*), *fatal blow :* acc. sg.,
2490.

feorh-wund, st. f., *mortal wound,
fatal injury :* acc. sg. feorh-wunde
hleát. 2386.

feorm, st. f., *subsistence, entertainment :* acc. sg. nô þu ymb mînes
ne þearft lices feorme leng sorgian,
*thou needest no longer have care
for the sustenance of my body,* 451.
— 2) *banquet :* dat. on feorme (or
feorme, MS.), 2386.

feormend-leás, adj., *wanting the
cleanser :* acc. pl. geseah . . . fyrn-
manna fatu feormend-leáse, 2762.

feormian, w. v., *to clean, to cleanse, to polish :* pres. part. nom pl. feormiend swefað (feormynd, MS.), 2257.

ge-feormian, w. v., *to feast, to eat :* pret. part. sôna häfde unlyfigendes eal gefeormod fêt and folma, 745.

feorran, w. v., w. acc., *to remove :* inf. sibbe ne wolde wið manna hwone mägenes Deniga feorh-bealo feorran, feó þingian, (Grendel) *would not from friendship free any one of the race of the Danes of life's evil, nor allay it for tribute,* 156.

feorran, adv., *from afar :* a) of space, 361, 430, 826, 1371, 1820, etc.; siððan äðelingas feorran gefricgean fleám eówerne, *when noble men afar learn of your flight* (when the news of your flight reaches distant lands), 2890; fêrdon folctogan feorran and neán, *from far and from near,* 840; similarly, neán and feorran þu nu [friðu] hafast, 1175; wäs þäs wyrmes wig wíde gesýne . . . neán and feorran, *visible from afar, far and near,* 2318. — b) temporal: se þe cûðe frumsceaft fira feorran reccan (*since remote antiquity*), 91; similarly, feorran rehte, 2107.

feorran-cund, adj., *foreign-born :* dat. sg. feorran-cundum, 1796.

feor-weg, st. m., *far way :* dat. pl. mâdma fela of feorwegum, *many precious things from distant paths* (from foreign lands), 37.

ge-feón. See **feohan.**

feónd, st. m., *enemy :* nom. sg., 164, 726, 749; feónd on helle (Grendel), 101; acc. sg., 279, 1865, 2707; dat. sg. feónde, 143, 439; gen. sg. feóndes, 985, 2129, 2290; acc. pl. feónd, 699; dat. pl. feóndum, 420, 1670; gen. pl. feonda, 294, 809, 904.

feónd-grâp, st. f., *foe's clutch :* dat. (instr.) pl. feónd-grâpum fäst, 637.

feónd-sceaða, w. m., *one who is an enemy and a robber :* nom. sg. fâh feónd-scaða (*a gleaming sea-monster*), 554.

feónd-scipe, st. m., *hostility :* nom. sg., 3000.

feówer, num., *four :* nom. feówer bearn, 59; feówer mearas, 2164; feówer, as substantive, 1638; acc. feówer mâðmas, 1028.

feówer-tyne, num., *fourteen :* nom. with following gen. pl. feówertyne Geáta, 1642.

findan, st. v., *to find, to invent, to attain :* a) with simple object in acc.: inf. þâra þe he cênoste findan mihte, 207; swylce hie ät Finneshâm findan meahton sigla searogimma, 1157; similarly, 2871; mäg þær fela freónda findan, 1839; wolde guman findan, 2295; swâ hyt weorðlicost fore-snotre men findan mihton, *so splendidly as only very wise men could devise it,* 3164; pret. sg. healþegnas fand, 720; word ôðer fand, *found other words,* i.e. went on to another narrative, 871; grimne gryrelicne grundhyrde fond, 2137; þät ic gôdne funde beága bryttan, 1487; pret. part. syððan ärest wearð feásceaft funden (*discovered*), 7. — b) with acc. and pred. adj.: pret. sg. dryhten sinne driórigne fand, 2790. — c) with acc. and inf.: pret. fand þâ þær inne äðelinga gedriht swefan, 118; fand wäccendne wer wiges bidan, 1268; hord-wynne fond opene standan, 2271; ðð þät he fyrgen-beámas . . . hleonian funde, 1416; pret. pl. fundon þâ

sâwulleásne hlim - bed healdan, 3034. —d) with dependent clause : inf. nô þ·ŷ ær feásceafte findan meahton ât þam âʼelinge þät he Heardrêde hlâford wære (*could by no means obtain it from the prince*), 2374.

on - fin dan, *to be sensible of, to perceive, to notice :* a) w. acc.: pret. sg. landweard onfand eftsiðʼ eorla, *the coast-guard observed the return of the earls*, 1892; pret. part. þâ heó unfunden wäs(*was discovered*), 1294.—b) w. depend. clause : pret. sg. þâ se gist onfand þät se beadoleóma bitan nolde, *the stranger* (Beówulf) *perceived that the sword would not cut*, 1523; sôna þät onfunde, þât . . ., *immediately perceived that* . . ., 751; similarly, 810, 1498.

finger, st. m., *finger :* nom. pl. fingras, 761; acc. pl. fingras, 985; dat. (instr.) pl. fingrum, 1506; gen. pl. fingra, 765.

firas, fyras (O.H.G. firahl, i.e. *the living;* cf. feorh), st. m., only in pl., *men :* gen. pl. fira, 91, 2742; monegum fira, 2002; fyra gehwylcne leóda minra, 2251 ; fira fyrngeweorc, 2287.

firen, fyren, st. f., *cunning waylaying, insidious hostility, malice, outrage :* nom. sg. fyren, 916; acc. sg. fyrene and fæhðʼe, 153; fæhðʼe and fyrene, 830, 2481; firen' ondrysne, 1933; dat. sg. fore fæhðʼe and fyrene, 137; gen. pl. fyrena, 164, 629; and fyrene, 812; fyrena hyrde (of Grendel), 751. The dat. pl., fyrenum, is used adverbially in the sense of *maliciously*, 1745, or *fallaciously*, with reference to Hæðcyn's killing Herebeald, which was done unintentionally, 2442.

firen-dæd, st. f., *wicked deed :* acc. pl. fyren-dæda, 1670; instr. pl. fyren-dædum, 1002; both times of Grendel and his mother, with reference to their nocturnal inroads.

firen-þearf, st. f., *misery through the malignity of enemies :* acc. sg. fyren-þearfe, 14.

firgen-beám, st. m., *tree of a mountain-forest :* acc. pl. fyrgen-beámas, 1415.

firgen-holt, st. m., *mountain-wood, mountain-forest :* acc. sg. on fyrgen-holt, 1394.

firgen-streám, st. m., *mountain-stream :* nom. sg. fyrgen-streám, 1360; acc. sg. under fyrgen-streám (marks the place where the mountain-stream, according to 1360, empties into Grendel's sea), 2129.

fisc, st. m., *fish :* in comp. hron-, mere-fisc.

fíf, num., *five :* uninflect. gen. fíf nihta fyrst, 545; acc. fífe (? , 420.

fifel-cyn (O.N. fífl, stultus and gigas), st. n., *giant-race :* gen. sg. fifelcynnes eard, 104.

fíf-tene, fíf-tyne, num., *fifteen :* acc. fŷftyne, 1583; gen. fiftena sum, 207.

fíf-tig, num., *fifty :* 1) as substantive with gen. following ; acc. fíftig wintra, 2734 ; gen. se wäs fiftiges fôt-gemearces lang, 3043.— 2) as adjective : acc. fíftig wintru, 2210.

flân, st. m., *arrow :* dat. sg. flâne, 3120 ; as instr., 2439.

flân-boga, w. m., *bow which shoots the flân, bow :* dat. sg. of flânbogan, 1434, 1745.

flæsc, st. n., *flesh, body in contrast with soul :* instr. sg. nô þon lange wäs feorh âʼelinges flæsce bewunden, *not much longer was the soul* *of the prince contained in his body,* 2425.

flæsc-hama, w. m., *el thing of flesh,* i.e. the body : acc. sg. flæsc-homan, 1569.

flet, st. n.: 1) *ground, floor of a hall :* acc. sg. heó on flet gebeáh, *fell to the ground,* 1541; similarly, 1569. — 2) *hall, mansion :* nom. sg. 1977 : acc. sg. flet, 1037, 1648, 1950, 2018, etc. ; flett, 2035 ; Jæt hie him óðer flet eal gerýmdon, *that they should give up entirely to them another hall,* 1087 ; dat. sg. on flette, 1026.

flet-räst, st. f., *resting-place in the hall :* acc. sg. flet-rä-te gebeág, *reclined upon the couch in the hall,* 1242.

flet-sittend, pres. part., *sitting in the hall :* acc. pl. -sittende, 2023 ; dat. pl. -sittendum, 1789.

flet-werod, st. n., *troop from the hall :* nom. sg., 476.

fleám, st. m., *flight :* acc. sg. on fleám gewand, *had turned to flight,* 1002 : fleám cówerne, 2890.

fleógan, st. v., *to fly :* prs. sg. III. fleógeð, 2274.

fleón, st. v., *to flee :* inf. on heolster fleón, 756; fleón on fenhópu, 765; fleón under fen-hleoðu, 821 ; w. acc. hete-swengeas fleáh, 2226.

be-fleón, w. acc., *to avoid, to escape :* gerund nô Jæt ýðe byð tô befleónne, *that is not easy* (i.e. not at all) *to be avoided,* 1004.

ofer-fleón, w. acc., *to flee from one, to yield :* inf. nelle ic beorges weard oferfleón fótes trem, *will not yield to the warder of the mountain* (the drake) *a foot's breadth,* 2526.

fleótan, st. v., *to float upon the water, to swim :* inf. nô he wiht fram me flôd-ýðum feor fleótan meahte, hraðor on holme, *no whit, could he swim from me farther on the waves* (regarded as instrumental, so that the waves marked the distance), *more swiftly in the sea,* 542 ; pret. sægenga fleát fámigheals forð ofer ýðe, *floated away over the waves,* 1910.

fliht. See flyht.

flitme. See un-flitme.

flitan, st. v., *to exert one's self, to strive, to emulate :* pres. part. flitende fealwe stræte mearum mæton (*rode a race*), 917 ; pret. sg. II. eart þu se Beówulf, se þe wið Brecan . . . ymb sund flite, *art thou the Beówulf who once contended with Breca for the prize in swimming ?* 507.

ofer-flitan, *to surpass one in a contest, to conquer, to overcome :* pret. w. acc. he þe ät sunde oferflát (*overcome thee in a swimming-wager*), 517.

ge-flit, st. n., *emulation :* acc. sg. lêton on geflit faran fealwe mearas, *let the fallow horses go in emulation,* 866.

floga, w. m., *flyer :* in the compounds : gúð-, lyft-, uht-, wið-floga.

flota (see fleótan), w. m., *float, ship, boat :* nom. sg., 210, 218, 301 ; acc. sg. flotan cówerne, 294.— Comp. wæg-flota.

flot-here, st. m., *fleet :* instr. sg. cwóm faran flotherge on Fresna land, 2916.

flôd, st. m., *flood, stream, sea-current :* nom. sg., 545, 580, 1362, etc.; acc. sg. flôd, 3134; ofer fealone flôd, 1951; dat. sg. tô flôde, 1889; gen. pl. flôda begong, *the region of floods,* i.e. the sea, 1498, 1827 ; flôda genipu, 2809.

flôd-ẟẞ, st. f., *flood-wave*. instr. pl. flôd-ẟẟum, 542.

flôr, st. m., *floor, stone-floor:* acc. sg. on fágne flôr (the floor was probably a kind of mosaic, made of colored flags), 726; dat. sg. gang Já äfter flôre, *along the floor* (i.e along the hall), 1317.

flyht, fliht, st. m., *flight:* nom. sg. gáres fliht, *flight of the spear*, 1766.

ge-flẏman, w. v., *to put to flight:* pret. part. geflẏmed, 847, 1371.

folc, st. n., *troop, band of warriors; folk*, in the sense of the whole body of the fighting men of a nation: acc. sg. folc, 522, 694, 912; Súẟdene folc, 464; folc and rîce, 1180; dat. sg. folce, 14, 2596; folce Deninga, 465: as instr. folce gestepte ofer sæ side, *went with a band of warriors over the wide sea*, 2394; gen. sg. folces, 1125; folces Denigea, 1583. — The king is calle1 folces hyrde, 611, 1833, 2645, 2982; freáwine folces, 2358; or folces weard, 2514. The queen, folces cwên, 1933. — The pl., in the sense of *warriors, fightingmen:* nom. pl. folc, 1423, 2949; dat. pl. folcum, 55, 262, 1856; gen. pl. freó- (freá-) wine folca, *of the king*, 430, 2430; friẟu-sibb folca, *of the queen*, 2018. — Comp. sige-folc.

folc-ágend, pres. part., *leader of a band of warriors:* nom. pl. folc-ágende, 3114.

folc-beorn, st. m., *man of the multitude, a common man:* nom. sg. folc-beorn, 2222.

folc-cwên, st. f., *queen of a warlike host:* nom. sg., of Wealhþeów, 642.

folc-cyning, st. m., *king of a warlike host:* nom. sg., 2734, 2874.

folc-ræd, st. m., *what best serves a warlike host:* acc. sg., 3007.

folc-riht, st. n., *the rights of the fightingmen of a nation:* gen. pl. him ær forgeaf ... folcrihta gehwyle, swâ his fäder âhte, 2609.

folc-scearu, st. f., *part of a host of warriors, nation:* dat. sg. folc-scare, 73.

folc-stede, st. m., *position of a band of warriors, place where a band of warriors is quartered:* acc. sg. folcstede, of the hall, Heorot, 70; folcstede fâra (*the battle-field*), 1464.

folc-toga, w. m., *leader of a body of warriors, duke:* nom. pl., powerful liege-men of Hróẟgar are called folc-togan, 840.

fold-bold, st. n., *earth-house* (i.e. a house on earth in contrast with a dwelling in heaven): nom. sg. fäger fold-bold, of the hall, Heorot, 774.

fold-bûend, pres. part., *dweller on earth, man:* nom. pl. fold-bûend, 2275; fold-bûende, 1356: dat. pl. fold-bûendum, 309.

folde, w. f., *earth, ground:* acc. sg. under foldan, 1362; feóll on foldan, 2976; gen. sg. foldan bearm, *the bosom of the earth*, 1138; foldan sceátas, 96; foldan fäẟm, 1394. — Also, *earth, world:* dat. sg. on foldan, 1197.

fold-weg, st. m., *field-way, road through the country:* acc. sg. fold-weg, 1634; acc. pl. fold-wegas, 867.

folgian, w. v.: 1) *to perform vassal-duty, to serve, to follow:* pret. pl. þeáh hie hira beággyfan banan folgedon, *although they followed the murderer of their prince*, 1103. — 2) *to pursue, to follow after:* folgode feorh-geniẟlan (acc. pl.), 2934

folm, st. f., *hand:* acc. sg. folme, 971, 1304; dat. sg. mid folme, 749; acc. pl. fêt and folma, *feet and hands*, 746; dat. pl. tô banan folmum, 158; folmum (instr.), 723, 993.—Comp.: beado-, gearo-folm.

for, prep. w. dat., instr., and acc.: 1) w. dat. local, *before*, ante: þät he for eaxlum gestôd Deniga freán, 358; for hlâwe, 1121.—b) *before*, coram, in conspectu: nô he þære feohgyfte for sceótendum scamigan þorfte, *had no need to be ashamed of the gift before the warriors*, 1027; for þäm werede, 1216; for eorlum, 1650; for duguðe, *before the noble band of warriors*, 2021; for dugeðum, 2502.—Causal, a) to denote a subjective motive, *on account of, through, from:* for wlenco, *from bravery, through warlike courage*, 338, 1207; for wlence, 508; for his wonhydum, 434; for onmêdlan, 2927, etc.— b) objective, partly denoting a cause, *through, from, by reason of:* for metode, *for the creator, on account of the creator*, 169; for þreánŷdum, 833; for þreánêdlan, 2225; for dolgilpe, *on account of, in accordance with the promise of bold deeds* (because you claimed bold deeds for yourself), 509; him for hrôfsele hrinan ne mehte færgripe flôdes, *on account of the roofed hall the malicious grasp of the flood could not reach him*, 1516; ligegesan wäg for horde, *on account of* (the robbing of) *the treasure*, 2782; for mundgripe minum, *on account of, through the gripe of my hand*, 966; for þäs hildfruman handgeweorce, 2836; for swenge, *through the stroke*, 2967; ne meahte ... deóp gedŷgan for dracan

lêge, *could not hold out in the deep on account of the heat of the drake*, 2550. Here may be added such passages as ic þäm gôdan sceal for his môdþräce mâðmas beódan, *will offer him treasures on account of his boldness of character, for his high courage*, 385; ful-oft for lässan leán teohhode, *gave often reward for what was inferior*, 952; nalles for ealdre mearn, *was not uneasy about his life*, 1443; similarly, 1538. Also denoting purpose: for ârstafum, *to the assistance*, 382, 458.—2) w. instr. causal, *because of, for:* he hine feor forwräc for þŷ mâne, 110.—3) w. acc., *for, as, instead of:* for sunu freógan, *love as a son*, 948; for sunu habban, 1176; ne him þäs wyrmes wig for wiht dyde, *held the drake's fighting as nothing*, 2349.

foran, adv., *before, among the first, forward:* siðððan ... sceáwedon feóndes fingras, foran æghwylc (*each before himself*), 985; þät wäs ân foran ealdgestreóna, *that was one among the first of the old treasures*, i.e. a splendid old treasure, 1459; þe him foran ongeán linde bæron, *bore their shields forward against him* (went out to fight against him), 2365.

be-foran: 1) adv., local, *before:* he ... beforan gengde, *went before*, 1413; temporal, *before, earlier*, 2498.—2) prep. w. acc. *before*, in conspectu: mære mâððum-sweord manige gesâwon beforan beorn beran, 1025.

ford, st. m., *ford, water-way:* acc. sg. ymb brontne ford, 568.

forð: 1) local, *forth, hither, near:* forð neár ätstôp, *approached nearer*, 746; þâ cwom Wealhþeó forð gân,

1163; similarly, 613; him seleþegn
forð wlsade, *led him* (Beówulf)
forth (to the couch that had been
prepared for him in Heorot), 1796;
þát him swât sprong forð under
fexe, *forth under the hair of his
head*, 2968. *Forward, further:*
gewíttað forð beran wæpen and
gewædu, 291 ; he tô forð gestôp,
2290; freoðo-wong þone forð ofereodon, 2960. *Away, forth*, 45,
904: fyrst forð gewât, *the time* (of
the way to the ship) *was out*, i.e.
they had arrived at the ship, 210 ;
me . . . forð-gewitenum, *to me the
departed*, 1480 ; fèrdon forð, *went
forth* (from Grendel's sea), 1633;
þonne he forð scile, *when he must*
(*go*) *forth*, i.e. die, 3178; hine
mihtig god . . . ofer ealle men forð
gefremede, *carried him forth, over
all men*, 1719.— 2) temporal, *forth,
from now on:* heald forð tela niwe
sibbe, 949 ; ic sceal forð sprecan
gen ymbe Grendel, *shall from now
on speak again of Grendel*, 2070.
See **furðum** and **furðor**.

forð-gerímed, pres. part., *in un-
broken succession*, 59.

forð-gesceaft, st. f., *that which is
determined for farther on, future
destiny:* acc. sg. he þâ forð-gesceaft forgyteð and forgýmeð,1751.

forð-weg, st. m., *road that leads
away, journey:* he of ealdre gewât fród on forð-weg (*upon the
way to the next world*), 2626.

fore, prep. w. dat., local, *before,
coram, in conspectu:* heó fore
þám werede spræc, 1216. Causal,
through, for, because of: nô mearn
fore fæhðe and fyrene, 136 ; fore
fäder dædum, *because of the father's
deeds*, 2060. — Allied to this is the
meaning, *about*, de, super: þær

wäs sang and swêg samod ätgädere
fore Healfdenes hildewisan, *song
and music about Healfdene's general* (the song of Hnäf), 1065.

fore-mære, adj., *renowned beyond*
(*others*), præclarus: superl. þát
wäs fore-mærost foldbûendum receda under roderum, 309.

fore-mihtig, adj., *able beyond*
(*others*), præpotens: nom. sg. wäs
tô foremihtig feónd on fèðe, *the
enemy was too strong in going*
(could flee too rapidly), 970.

fore-snotor, adj., *wise beyond*
(*others*), sapientissimus: nom. pl.
foresnotre men, 3164.

fore-þanc, st. m., *forethought, con-
sideration, deliberation:* nom. sg.,
1061.

forht, adj., *fearful, cowardly:* nom.
sg. forht, 2968; he on môde wearð
forht on ferhðe, 755. — Comp. un-
forht.

forma, adj., *foremost, first:* nom.
sg. forma sið (*the first time*), 717,
1464, 1528, 2620; instr. sg. forman
siðe, 741, 2287 ; forman dôgore,
2574.

fyrmest, adv. superl., *first of all,
in the first place:* he fyrmest läg,
2078.

forst, st. m., *frost, cold:* gen. sg.
forstes bend, 1610.

for-þam, for-þan, for-þon, adv.
and conj., *therefore, on that account, then:* forþam, 149; forþan,
418, 680, 1060; forþon þe, *because*,
503.

fôn, st. v., *to catch, to grasp, to take
hold, to take:* prs. sg. III. fêhð
ôðer tô, *another lays hold* (takes
possession), 1756; inf. ic mid
grâpe sceal fôn wið feónde, 439 ;
pret. sg. him tôgeánes fêng, *caught
at him, grasped at him*, 1543; w.

dat. he þâm frätwum fêng, *received the rich adornments* (Ongenþeów's equipment), 2990.

be-fôn, *to surround, to ensnare, to encompass, to embrace:* pret. part. hyne sâr hafað ... nearwe befongen balwon bendum, 977; heó äðelinga ânne häfde fäste befangen (*had seized him firmly*), 1296; helm ... befongen freáwrâsnum (*encircled by an ornament like a diadem*), 1452; fenne bifongen, *surrounded by the fen*, 2010; (draca) fȳre befongen, *encircled by fire*, 2275, 2596; häfde landwara lige befangen, *encompassed by fire*, 2322.

ge-fôn, w. acc., *to seize, to grasp:* pres. he gefêng skæpendne rinc, 741; gûðrinc gefêng atolan clommum, 1502; gefêng þâ be eaxle ... Gûðgeáta leód Grendles môdor, 1538; gefêng þâ fetelhilt, 1564; hond rond gefêng, geolwe linde, 2610; ic on ôfoste gefêng micle mid mundum mägen-byrðenne, *hastily I seized with my hands the enormous burden*, 3091.

on-fôn, w. dat., *to receive, to accept, to take:* pres. imp. sg. onfôh þissum fulle, *accept this cup*, 1170; inf. þät þät þeódnes bearn ... scolde fäder-äðelum onfôn, *receive the paternal rank*, 912; pret. sg. hwâ þäm hläste onfêng, *who received the ship's lading*, 52; hleórbolster onfêng eorles andwlitan, *the pillow received the nobleman's face*, 689; similarly, 853, 1495; heal swêge onfêng, *the hall received the loud noise*, 1215; he onfêng hraðe inwit-þancum, *he* (Beówulf) *at once received him* (Grendel) *devising malice*, 749.

þurh-fôn, w. acc., *to break through*

with grasping, to destroy by grasping: inf. þät heó þone fyrd-hom þurh-fôn ne mihte, 1505.

wið-fôn, w. dat., (*to grasp at*), *to seize, to lay hold of:* pret. sg. him fäste wið-fêng, 761.

ymbe-fôn, w. acc., *to encircle:* pret. heals-ealne ymbefêng biteran bânum, *encircled his* (Beówulf's) *whole neck with sharp bones* (teeth), 2692.

fôt, st. m., *foot:* gen. sg. fôtes trem (*the measure of a foot, a foot broad*), 2526; acc. pl. fêt, 746; dat. pl. ät fôtum, *at the feet*, 500, 1167.

fôt-gemearc, st. n., *measure, determining by feet, number of feet:* gen. sg. se wäs fiftiges fôtgemearces long (*fifty feet long*), 3043.

fôt-lâst, st. m., *foot-print:* acc. sg. (draca) onfand feóndes fôt-lâst, 2290.

fracod, adj., *objectionable, useless:* nom. sg. näs seó ecg fracod hilderince, 1576.

fram, from, I. prep. w. dat. loc. *away from something:* þær fram sylle âbeág medubenc monig, 776, 1716; þanon-eft gewiton ealdgestðas ... fram mere, 856; cyning-balde men from þäm holmclife hafelan bæron, 1636; similarly, 541, 543, 2367. Standing after the dat.: he hine feor forwräc ... mancynne fram, 110; similarly, 1716. Also, *hither from something:* þâ ic cwom ... from feóndum, 420; æghwäðrum wäs ... brôga fram ôðrum, 2566. — Causal with verbs of saying and hearing, *of, about, concerning:* sägdest from his sîðe, 532; nô ic wiht fram þe swylcra scaro-niða secgan hȳrde, 581; þät he fram Sigemunde secgan hyrde, 876.

II. adv., *away, thence:* nô þỹ
ær fram meahte, 755; *forth, out:*
from ærest cwom oruð aglæcean
ût of stâne, *the breath of the
dragon came forth first from the
rock,* 2557.

fram, from, adj.: 1) *directed forwards,striving forwards:* in comp.
stð-fram.— 2) *excellent, splendid,*
of a man with reference to his warlike qualities: nom. sg. ic com on
môde from, 2528; nom. pl. frome
fyrd-hwate, 1642, 2477. Of things:
instr. pl. fromum feoh-giftum, 21.
—Comp. un-from; see freme,
forma.

ge-frägen. See frignan.

frätwe, st. f. pl., *ornament, anything costly,* originally *carved objects* (cf. Dietrich in Hpts. Ztschr.
X. 216 ff.), afterwards of any costly
and artistic work: acc. pl. frätwe,
2920; beorhte frätwe, 214; beorhte
frätwa, 897; frätwe . . . eorclan-
stânas, 1208; frätwe, . . . breóst-
weorðunge, 2504, both times of
Hygelâc's collar; frätwe and fät-
gold, 1922; frätwe (Eanmund's
sword and armor), 2621; dat. instr.
pl. þâm frätwum, 2164; on frätewum, 963; frätwum (Ileaðobeard
sword) hrêmig, 2055; frätwum, of
the drake's treasures, 2785; frätwum (Ongenþeów's armor), 2990;
gen. pl. fela . . . frätwa, 37; þâra
frätwa (drake's treasure), 2795;
frätwa hyrde (drake), 3134.

frätwan, w. v., *to supply with ornaments, to adorn:* inf. folc-stede
frätwan, 76.

ge-frätwian, w. v., *to adorn:* pret.
sg. gefrätwade foldan sceátas leomum and leáfum, 96; pret. part.
þâ wäs hâten Ileort innanweard
folmum gefrätwod, 993.

ge-fræge, adj., *known by reputation, renowned:* nom. sg. leód-
cyning . . . folcum gefræge, 55;
swâ hyt gefræge wäs, 2481.

ge-fræge, st. n., *information through
hearsay:* instr. sg. mine gefræge
(*as I learned through the narrative of others*), 777, 838, 1956, etc.

ge-frægnian, w. v., *to become known
through hearsay:* pret. part. fylle
gefrægnod (of Grendel's mother,
who had become known through
the carrying off of Aschere), 1334.

freca, w. m., properly *a wolf,* as one
that breaks in, robs; here a designation of heroes: nom. sg. freca
Scildinga, of Beówulf, 1564. —
Comp.: gûð-, hilde-, scyld-, sweord-,
wig-freca; ferhð-frec (adj.).

fremde, adj., properly *distant, foreign;* then *estranged, hostile:* nom.
sg. þät wäs fremde þeód êcean
dryhtne, of the giants, 1692.

freme, adj., *excellent, splendid:*
nom. sg. fem. fremu folces cwên,
of Þryðo, 1933(?).

fremman, w. v., *to press forward,
to further,* hence: 1) in general,
*to perform, to accomplish, to do, to
make:* pres. subj. without an object, fremme se þe wille, *let him do
(it) whoever will,* 1004. With acc.:
imp. pl. fremmað ge nu leóda
þearfe, 2801; inf. fyrene fremman,
101; säcce fremman, 2500; f.ehðe
. . . mærðum fremman, 2515, etc.;
pret. sg. folcræd fremede (*did what
was best for his men,* i.e. ruled
wisely), 3007; pl. hû jâ äðelingas
ellen fremedon, 3; feuhtan fremedon, 960; nalles fâceastafas . . .
þenden fremedon, 1020; pret. subj.
þät ic . . . mærðo fremede, 2135.
— 2) *to help on, to support:* inf.
þät he mec fremman wile wordum

and worcum (to an expedition),
1833.
ge-fremman, w. acc., *to do, to
make, to render:* inf. gefremman
eorlic ellen, 637; helpan gefremman, *to give help*, 2450; älter
weáspelle wyrpe gefremman, *to
work a change after sorrow* (to
give joy after sorrow), 1316; gerund, tô gefremmanne, 174, 2645;
pret. sg. gefremede, 135, 165, 551,
585, etc.;] eáh þe hine mihtig god
... ofer ealle men forð gefremede,
placed him away, above all men,
i.e. raised him, 1719; pret. pl. gefremedon, 1188, 2479; pret. subj.
gefremede, 177; pret. part. gefremed, 476 ; fem. nu sceale hafað
... dæd gefremede, 941 ; absolutely,]u]e self hafast dædum
gefremed,] ät . . ., *hast brought it
about by thy deeds that*, 955.
fretan, st. v., *to devour, to consume:*
inf.] â (the precious things) sceal
brond fretan, 3015; nu sceal glêd
fretan wigena strengel, 3115; pret.
sg. (Grendel) slæpende frät folces
Denigea fíftyne men, 1582.
frêcne, adj., *dangerous, bold:* nom.
sg. frêcne fýr-draca, 2690; feorh-
bealo frêcne, 2251, 2538; acc. sg.
frêcne dæde, 890; frêcne fengelâd,
1360; frêcne stôwe, 1379; instr.
sg. frêcnan spræce (*through pro-
voking words*), 1105.
frêcne, adv., *boldly, audaciously*,
960, 1033, 1692.
freá, w. m., *ruler, lord*, of a temporal ruler: nom. sg. freá, 2286; acc.
sg. freán, 351, 1320, 2538, 3003,
3108; gen. sg. freán, 359, 500, 1167,
1681; dat. sg. freán, 271, 291,
2663. Of a husband: dat. sg. eode
... tô hire freán sittan, 642. Of
God: dat. sg. freán ealles, *the Lord*

of all, 2795; gen. sg. freán, 27.—
Comp.: âgend-, líf-, sin-freá.
freá-dryhten, st. m., *lord, ruling
lord:* gen. sg. freá-drihtnes, 797.
freá-wine, st. m., *lord and friend,
friendly ruler:* nom. sg. freá-wine
folces (folca), 2358, 2430; acc. sg.
his freá-wine, 2439.
freá-wrâsn, st. f., *encircling ornament like a diadem:* instr. pl. helm
... befongen freáwrâsnum, 1452;
see wrâsn.
freoðu, friðu, f., *protection, asy-
lum, peace:* acc. sg. wel bið þäm
þe môt ... tô fäder fäðmum freoðo wilnian, *who may obtain an asy-
lum in God's arms*, 188; neán and
feorran þu nu [friðu] hafast, 1175.
—Comp. fen-freoðo.
freoðo-burh, st. f., *castle, city afford-
ing protection:* acc. sg. freoðoburh
fägere, 522.
freoðo-wong, st. m., *field of peace,
field of protection:* acc. sg., 2960;
seems to have been the proper
name of a field.
freoðo-wær, st. f., *peace-alliance,
security of peace:* acc. sg. þâ hie
getrûwedon on twâ healfa fäste
frioðu-wære, 1097; gen. sg. frioðo-
wære bäd hlâford sînne, *entreated
his lord for the protection of peace*
(i.e. full pardon for his delinquen-
cy), 2283.
freoðo-webbe, w. f., pacis textrix,
designation of the royal consort
(often one given in marriage as a
confirmation of a peace between
two nations): nom. sg., 1943.
freó-burh, st. f., = freá-burg (?),
ruler's castle (?) (according to
Grein, arx ingenua): acc. sg. freó-
burh, 694.
freód, st. f., *friendship:* acc. sg.
freóde ne woldon ofer heafo heal-

dan, 2477; gen. sg. näs þær mâra fyrst freóde tô friclan, *was no longer time to seek for friendship*, 2557; —*favor, acknowledgement:* acc. sg. ic þe sceal mine gelæstan freóde (*will show myself grateful*, with reference to 1381 ff.), 1708.

freó-dryhten (— freá-dryhten), st. m., *lord, rul. r;* according to Grein, dominus ingenuus vel nobilis: nom. sg. as voc. freó-drihten min! 1170; dat. sg. mid his freó-dryhtne, 2628.

freógan, w. v., *to love; to think of lovingly:* pres. subj. þät mon his wine-dryhten . . . ferhðum freóge, 3178; inf. nu ic þec . . . me for sunu wylle freógan on ferhðe, 949.

freó-lîc, adj., *free, free-born* (here of the lawful wife in contrast with the bond concubine): nom. sg. freólic wîf, 616; freólicu folc-cwên, 642.

freónd, st. m., *friend:* acc. sg. freónd, 1386, 1865; dat. pl. freóndum, 916, 1019, 1127; gen. pl. freónda, 1307, 1839.

freónd-laðu, st. f., *friendly invitation:* nom. sg. him wäs ful boren and freónd-laðu (*friendly invitation to drink*) wordum bewägned, 1193.

freónd-lâr, st. f., *friendly counsel:* dat. (instr.) pl. freónd-lârum, 2378.

freónd-lîce, adv., *in a friendly manner, kindly:* compar. freónd-lîcor, 1028.

freónd-scipe, st. m., *friendship:* acc. sg. freónd-scipe fästne, 2070.

freó-wine, st. m. (see freáwine, *lord and friend, friendly ruler;* according to Grein, amicus nobilis, princeps amicus: nom. sg. as voc. freó-wine folca! 430.

friegean, w. v., *to ask, to inquire into:* inf. ongan sinne geseldan

fägre friegean hwylce Sæ-Geáta sî as wæron, 1986; pres. part. gomela Scilding fela friegende feorran rehte, *the old Scilding, asking many questions* (having many things related to him), *told of old times* (the conversation was alternate), 2107.

ge-friegean, *to learn, to learn by inquiry:* pres. pl. syððan hie gefriegeað freán ûserne ealdorleásne, *when they learn that our lord is dead*, 3003; pres. subj. gif ic þät gefriege, þät . . ., 1827; pl. syððan äðelingas feorran gefriegean fleám eówerne, 2890.

friclan (see freca), w. v. w. gen., *to seek, to desire, to strive for:* inf. näs þær mâra fyrst freóde tô friclan, 2557.

friðu-sib, st. f., *kin for the confirming of peace*, designation of the queen (see freoðo-webbe), *peace-bringer:* nom. sg. friðu-sibb folca, 2018.

frignan, fringan, frinan, st. v., *to ask, to inquire:* imp. ne frin þu äfter sælum, *ask not after the well-being!* 1323; inf. ic þäs wine Deniga frinan wille . . . ymb þinne sîð, 351; pret. sg. frägn, 236, 332; frägn gif . . ., *asked whether* . . ., 1320.

ge-frignan, ge-fringan, ge-frinan, *to find out by inquiry, to learn by narration:* pret. sg. (w. acc.) þät fram hâm gefrägn Higelâces þegn Grendles dæda, 194; nô ic gefrägn heardran feohtan, 575; (w. acc. and inf.) þa ic wîde gefrägn weorc gebannan, 74; similarly, 2485, 2753, 2774; ne gefrägen ic þâ mægðe mâran weorode ymb hyra sinegyfan sêl gebæran, *I never heard that any people, richer in warriors, conducted itself better about its chief*, 1012; similarly, 1028; pret. pl. (w. acc.) we þeodcyninga þrym gefrunon, 2; (w. acc. and inf.) geongne gûð-cyning gôdne gefrunon hringas dælan, 1970; (parenthetical) swâ guman gefrungon, 667, (after þonne) medo-ärn micel (*greater*) ... þone yldo bearn æfre gefrunon, 70; pret. part. häfde Ilige-lâces hilde gefrunen, 2953; häfdon gefrunen þät ..., *had learned that* ..., 695; häfde gefrunen hwanan sió fæhð ârâs, 2404; healsbeága mæst þâra þe ic on foldan gefrägen häbbe, 1197.

from. See **fram.**

frôd, adj.: 1) ætate provectus, *old, gray:* nom. sg. frôd, 2626, 2951; frôd cyning, 1307, 2210; frôd folces weard, 2514; wintrum frôd, 1725, 2115, 2278; se frôda, 2929; acc. sg. frôde feorhlege (*the laying down of my old life*), 2801; dat. sg. frôdan fyrnwitan (may also, from its meaning, belong under No. 2), 2124. — 2) mente excellen-tior, *intelligent, experienced, wise:* nom. sg. frôd, 1367; frôd and gôd, 279; on môde frôd, 1845. — Comp.: in-, un-frôd.

frôfor, st. f., *consolation, compensation, help:* nom. sg. frôfor, 2942; acc. sg. frôfre, 7, 974; fyrena frô-fre, 629; frôfre and fultum, 1274; frôfor and fultum, 699; dat. sg. tô frôfre, 14, 1708; gen. sg. frôfre, 185.

fruma (see **forma**), w. m., *the fore-most,* hence: 1) *beginning:* nom. sg. wäs se fruma egeslic leódum on lande, swâ hyt lungre wearð on hyra sincgifan sâre geendod (*the be-ginning of the dragon-combat was terrible, its end distressing through*

the death of Beówulf), 2310. — 2) *he who stands first, prince:* in comp. dæd-, hild-, land-, leód-, ord-, wig-fruma.

frum-cyn, st. n., (genus primiti-vum), *descent, origin:* acc. sg. nu ic côwer sceal frumcyn witan, 252.

frum-gâr, st. m., primipilus, *duke, prince:* dat. sg. frumgâre (of Beó-wulf), 2857.

frum-sceaft, st. f., prima creatio, *beginning:* acc. sg. se þe cûðe frumsceaft fira feorran reccan, *who could tell of the beginning of man-kind in old times,* 91; dat. sg. frum-sceafte, *in the beginning,* i.e at his birth, 45.

fugol, st. m., *bird:* dat. sg. fugle gelîcost, 218; dat. pl. [fuglum] tô gamene, 2942.

ful, adj., *full, filled:* nom. sg. w. gen. pl. se wäs innan full wrätta and wîra, 2413. — Comp.: eges-, sorh-, weorð-ful.

ful, adv., plene, *very:* ful oft, 480, 952.

ful, st. n., *cup, beaker:* nom. sg., 1193; acc. sg. ful, 616, 629, 1026; ofer ðða ful, *over the cup of the waves* (the basin of the sea filled with waves), 1209; dat. sg. onfôh þissum fulle, 1170.—Comp.: medo-, sele-full.

fullæstian, w. v. w. dat., *to give help:* pres. sg. ic þe fullæstu, 2669.

fultum, st. m., *help, support, protec-tion:* acc. sg. frôfor (frôfre) and fultum, 699, 1274; mägenes ful-tum, 1836; on fultum, 2663. — Comp. mägen-fultum.

fundian, w. v., *to strive, to have in view:* pres. pl. we fundiað Ilige-lâc sêcan, 1820; pret. sg. fundode of geardum, 1138.

furðum, adv., primo, *just, exactly:*

then first : þa ic furðum weóld
folce Deninga, *then first governed
the people of the Danes* (had just
assumed the government), 465; þâ
hie tô sele furðum . . . gangan
cwômon, 323; ic þær furðum cwom
tô þam hringsele, 2010; — *before,
previously :* ic þe sceal mine gelæstan freóde, swâ wit furðum
spræcon, 1708.

furður, adv., *further, forward, more
distant,* 254, 762, 3007.

fûs, adj., *inclined to, favorable,
ready:* nom. sg. nu ic eom sîðes
fûs, 1476; leófra manna fûs, *prepared for the dear men,* i.e. expect-
ing them, 1917; sigel sûðan fûs,
the sun inclined from the south (midday sun), 1967; se wonna hrefn
fûs ofer fægum, *eager over the
slain,* 3026; sceft . . . feðer-gearwum fûs, 3120; nom. pl. wæron
. . . eft to leódum fûse tô farenne,
1806. — Sometimes fûs means
ready for death, moribundus : fûs
and fæge, 1242. — Comp.: hin-,
ût-fûs.

fûs-lic, adj., *prepared, ready:* acc.
sg. fûs-lic f[yrd]-leóð, 1425; fyrd-
searo fûs-lic, 2619; acc. pl. fyrd-
searu fûs-licu, 232.

fyl, st. m., *fall:* nom. sg. fyll cyninges, *the fall of the king* (in the
dragon-fight), 2913; dat. sg. þät
he on fylle wearð, *that he came to
a fall, fell,* 1545. — Comp. hrâ-fyl.

fylce (collective form from **folc** ,
st. n., *troop, band of warriors :* in
comp. äl-fylce.

ge-fyllan (see **feal**), w. v., *to fell,
to slay in battle:* inf. fâne gefyllan, *to slay the enemy,* 2656; pret.
pl. feónd gefyldan, *they had slain
the enemy,* 2707.

â-fyllan (see **ful**), w. v., *to fill :*

pret. part. Heorot innan wäs freóndum âfylled (*was filled with trusted
men*), 1019.

fyllo, st. f., *plenty, abundant meal :*
dat. (instr.) sg. fylle gefrægnod,
1334; gen. sg. näs hie þære fylle
gefeán häfdon, 562; fylle gefægon,
1015. — Comp.: wäl-, wist-fyllo.

fyl-werig, adj., *weary enough to
fall, faint to death,* moribundus :
acc. sg. fyl-wêrigne, 963.

fyr. See **feor.**

fyrian, w. v. w. acc. (= ferian), *to
bear, to bring, carry:* pret. pl. þâ
þe gif-sceattas Geáta fyredon þyder
tô þance, 378.

fyras. See **firas.**

fyren. See **firen.**

fyrde, adj., *movable, that can be
moved.*—Comp. hard-fyrde.—Leo.

fyrd-gesteallu, w. m., *comrade on
an expedition, companion in battle:* dat. pl. fyrd-gesteallum, 2874.

fyrd-ham, st. m., *war-dress, coat
of mail:* acc. sg. þone fyrd-hom,
1505.

fyrd-hrägl, st. n., *coat of mail,
war-dress:* acc. sg. fyrd-hrägl,
1528.

fyrd-hwät, adj., *sharp, good in
war, warlike:* nom. pl. frome
fyrd-hwate, 1642, 2477.

fyrd-leóð, st. n., *war-song, warlike
music:* acc. sg. horn stundum
song fûslic f[yrd]leoð, 1425.

fyrd-searu, st. n., *equipment for
an expedition :* acc. sg. fyrd-searu
fûslic, 2619; acc. pl. fyrd-searu
fûslicu, 232.

fyrd-wyrðe, adj., *of worth in war,
excellent in battle :* nom. sg. fyrd-
wyrðe man (Beówulf), 1317.

ge-fyrðran (see **forð**), w. v., *to
bring forward, to further :* pret.
part. âr wäs on ôfoste, eftsîðes

georn, fratwum gefyrðred, *he was hurried forward by the treasure* (i.e. after he had gathered up the treasure, he hasted to return, so as to be able to show it to the mortally-wounded Beówulf), 2785.

fyrmest. See forma.

fyrn-dagas, st. m. pl., *by-gone days:* dat. pl. fyrndagum (*in old times*), 1452.

fyrn-geweorc, st. n., *work, something done in old times:* acc. sg. fira fyrn-geweorc (the drinking-cup mentioned in 2283), 2287.

fyrn-gewin, st. n., *combat in ancient times:* gen. sg. ôr fyrn-gewinnes (*the origin of the battles of the giants*), 1690.

fyrn-man, st. m., *man of ancient times:* gen. pl. fyrn-manna fatu, 2762.

fyrn-wita, w. m., *counsellor ever since ancient times, adviser for many years:* dat. sg. frôdan fyrn-witan, of Äschere, 2124.

fyrst, st. m., *portion of time, definite time, time:* nom. sg. näs hit lengra fyrst, ac ymb âne niht . . ., 134; fyrst forð gewât, *the time* (of going to the harbor) *was past*, 210; näs þær mâra fyrst freóde tô friclan, 2556; acc. sg. niht-longne fyrst, 528; fíf nihta fyrst, 545; instr. sg. þý fyrste, 2574; dat. sg. him on fyrste gelomp . . ., *within the fixed time*, 76.

fyr-wit, -wet, -wyt, st. n., *prying spirit, curiosity:* nom. sg. fyrwyt, 232; fyrwet, 1986, 2785.

ge-fýsan (fûs), w. v., *to make ready, to prepare:* part. winde gefýsed flota, *the ship provided with wind* (for the voyage), 217; (wyrm) fýre gefýsed, *provided with fire*, 2310; þâ wäs hringbôgan (of

the drake) heorte gefýsed sæcce tô sêcanne, 2562; with gen., in answer to the question, for what? gûðe gefýsed, *ready for battle, determined to fight*, 631.

fýr, st. n., *fire:* nom. sg., 1367, 2702, 2882; dat. sg. fýre, 2220; as instr. fýre, 2275, 2596; gen. sg. fýres fâðm, 185; fýres feng, 1765. — Comp.: âd-, bæl-, heaðu-, wäl-fýr.

fýr-bend, st. m., *band forged in fire:* dat. pl. duru . . . fýr-bendum fäst, 723.

fýr-draca, w. m., *fire-drake, fire-spewing dragon:* nom. sg., 2690.

fýr-heard, adj., *hard through fire, hardened in fire:* nom. pl. (eofor-lic) fâh and fýr-heard, 305.

fýr-leóht, st. n., *fire-light:* acc. sg., 1517.

fýr-wylm, st. m., *wave of fire, flame-wave:* dat. pl. wyrm . . . fýrwyl-mum fâh, 2672.

G

galan, st. v., *to sing, to sound:* pres. sg. sorh-leóð gäleð, 2461; inf. gryre-leóð galan, 787; bearhtm ongeâton, gûðhorn galan, *heard the clang, the battle-trumpet sound*, 1433.

â-galan, *to sing, to sound:* pret. sg. þät hire on hafelan hringmæl âgôl grædig gûðleóð, *that the sword caused a greedy battle-song to sound upon her head*, 1522.

gamban, or, according to Bout., gambe, w. f., *tribute, interest:* acc. sg. gomban gyldan, 11.

gamen, st. n., *social pleasure, rejoicing, joyous doings:* nom. sg. gamen, 1161; gomen, 2460; gomen gleóbeámes, *the pleasure of the harp*, 2264; acc. sg. gamen and gleódreám, 3022; dat. sg. gamene, 2942; gomene, 1776.—Comp. heal-gamen.

gamen-wáð, st. f., *way offering social enjoyment, journey in joyous society:* dat. sg. of gomen-wáðe, 855.

gamen-wudu, st. m., *wood of social enjoyment,* i.e. harp: nom. sg. þær wäs ... gomenwudu gréted, 1066; acc. sg. gomenwudu grétte, 2109.

gamol, gomol, gomel, adj., *old;* of persons, *having lived many years, gray:* gamol, 58, 265; gomol, 3096; gomel, 2113, 2794; se go-mela, 1398; gamela (gomela) Scylding, 1793, 2106; gomela, 2932; acc. sg. þone gomelan, 2422; dat. sg. gamelum rince, 1678; gomelum ceorle, 2445; þam gomelan, 2818; nom. pl. blondenfeaxe gomele, 1596. — Also, *late, belonging to former time:* gen. pl. gomelra láfe (*legacy*, 2037. — Of things, *old, from old times:* nom. sg. sweord ... gomol, 2683; acc. sg. gomele láfe, 2564; gomel swyrd, 2611; g a m o l is a more respectful word than e a l d.

gamol-feax, adj., *with gray hair:* nom. sg., 609.

gang, st. m.: 1) *gait, way:* dat. sg. on gange, 1885; gen. sg. ic hine ne mihte ... ganges ge-twæman, *could not keep him from going,* 969. — 2) *step, foot-step:* nom. sg. gang (the foot-print of the mother of Grendel), 1405; acc. sg. uton hraðe féran Grendles mágan gang scea-wigan, 1392. — Comp. in-gang.

be-gang, bi-gang, st. m., (*so far as something goes*), *extent:* acc. sg. ofer geofenes begang, *over the ex-tent of the sea,* 362; ofer flóda be-gang, 1827; under swegles begong,

861, 1774; flóda begong, 1498; sio-leða higong, 2368.

gangan. See under gân.

ganot, st. m., *diver,* fulica marina: gen. sg. ofer ganotes bäð (i.e. the sea), 1862.

gâd, st. n., *lack:* nom. sg. ne bið þe wilna gâd (*thou shalt have no lack of desirable* [valuable] *things*), 661; similarly, 950.

gân, *expanded* = gangan, st. v., *to go:* pres. sg. III. gæð á Wyrd swa hió scel, 455; gæð eft ... tô medo, 605; þonne he ... on flett gæð, 2035; similarly, 2055; pres. subj. III. sg. gâ þær he wille, *let him go whither he will,* 1395; imp. sg. II. gâ nu tô setle, 1783; nu þu lungre geong, hord sceáwian, under hârne stân, 2744; inf. in gân, *to go in,* 386, 1645; forð gân, *to go forth, to go thither,* 1164; þät hie him tô mihton gegnum gangan, *to go towards, to go to,* 314; tô sele ... gangan cwômon, 324; in a similar construction, gongan, 1643; nu ge môton gangan ... Hróðgâr geseón, 395; þâ com of môre ... Grendel gongan, *there came Grendel (going) from the fen,* 712; ongeán gramum gangan, *to go to meet the enemy, to go to the war,* 1035; cwom ... tô hofe gongan, 1975; wutun gangan tô, *let us go thither,* 2649. — As preterite, serve, 1) geóng or giong: he tô healle geóng, 926; similarly, 2019; se þe on orde geóng, *who went at the head, went in front,* 3126; on innan gióng, *went in,* 2215; he ... gióng tô þâs þe he eorðsele ânne wisse, *went thither, where he knew of that earth-hall,* 2410; þâ se æðeling, gióng, þät he bî wealle gesät, *then went the prince* (Beówulf) *that he might sit down*

by the wall, 2716. — 2) gang: tô
healle gang Healfdenes sunu, 1010;
similarly, 1296; gang þâ äfter flore,
*went along the floor, along the
hall*, 1317. — 3) gengde (Goth.
gaggida): he ... beforan gengde
..., wong sceáwian, *went in front
to inspect the fields*, 1413; gengde,
also of riding, 1402. — 4) from
another stem, eode (Goth. iddja):
eode ellenrôf, þät he for eaxlum
gestôd Deniga freán, 358; similarly, 403; [wið duru healle Wulfgâr
eode], *went towards the door of the
hall*, 390; eode Wealhþeów forð,
went forth, 613; eode tô hire freán
sittan, 641; eode yrremôd, *went
with angry feeling*, 727; eode ...
tô sele, 919; similarly, 1233; eode
... þær se snottra bâd, 1313; eode
weorð Denum äðeling tô yppan,
the prince (Beówulf), *honored by
the Danes, went to the high seat*,
1815; eode ... under inwit-hrôf,
3124; pl. þær swiðferhðe sittan
eodon, 493; eodon him þâ tô-
geánes, *went to meet him*, 1627;
eodon under Earna näs, 3032.
â-gangan, *to go out, to go forth, to
befall :* pret. part. swâ hit âgangen
wearð eorla manegum (*as it befell
many a one of the earls*), 1235.
full-gangan, *to emulate, to follow
after :* pret. sg. þonne ... sceft
nytte heóld, feðer-gearwum fûs
flâne full-eode, *when the shaft had
employment, furnished with feathers it followed the arrow, did as
the arrow*, 3120.
ge-gân, ge-gangan: 1) *to go, to
approach :* inf. (w. acc.) his môdor
... gegân wolde sorhfulne sið,
1278; se þe gryre-siðas gegân
dorste, *who dared to go the ways of
terror* (to go into the combat),

1463; pret. sg. se maga geonga
under his mæges scyld elne geeode,
*went quickly under his kinsman's
shield*, 2677; pl. elne geeodon tô
þäs þe ..., *went quickly thither
where ...*, 1968; pret. part. syððan
hie tô-gädre gegân häfdon, *when
they* (Wiglaf and the drake) *had
come together*, 2631; þät his aldres
wäs ende gegongen, *that the end of
his life had come*, 823; þâ wäs ende-
däg gôdum gegongen, þät se gûð-
cyning ... sweealt, 3037. — 2) *to
obtain, to reach :* inf. (w. acc.)
þonne he ät gûðe gegân þenceð
longsumne lof, 1536; ic mid elne
sceall gold gegangan,2537; gerund,
näs þät sôe ceáp tô gegangenne
gumena ænigum, 2417; pret. pl.
elne geeodon ... þät se byrnwiga
bûgan sceolde, 2918; pret. part.
häfde ... gegongen þät, *had attained it, that ...*, 894; hord ys
gesceáwod, grimme gegongen,
3086. — 3) *to occur, to happen :*
pres. sg. III. gif þät gegangeð þät
..., *if that happen, that ...*, 1847;
pret. sg. þät geiode ufaran dôgrum
hilde-hlämmum, *it happened in
later times to the warriors* (the
Geátas), 2201; pret. part. þâ wäs
gegongen guman unfrôdum earfoðlíce þät, *then it had happened to
the young man in sorrowful wise
that ...*, 2822.
ôð-gangan, *to go thither :* pret. pl.
oð þät hi ôðeodon ... in Hrefnes-
holt, 2935.
ofer-gangan, w. acc., *to go over :*
pret. sg. ofereode þâ äðelinga bearn
steáp stân-hliðo, *went over steep,
rocky precipices*, 1409; pl. freoðo-
wong þone forð ofereodon, 2960.
ymb-gangan, w. acc., *to go around :*
pret. ymb-eode þâ ides Helminga

duguðe and geogoðe dæl æghwylcne, *went around in every
part, among the superior and the
inferior warriors*, 621.

gâr, st. m., *spear, javelin, missile :*
nom. sg., 1847, 3022 ; instr. sg.
gâre, 1076 ; blôdigan gâre, 2441 ;
gen. sg. gâres fliht, 1766; nom. pl.
gâras, 328; gen. pl., 161(?).—
Comp.: bon-, frum-gâr.

gâr-cêne, adj., *spear-bold :* nom. sg.,
1959.

gâr-cwealm, st. m., *murder, death
by the spear :* acc. sg. gâr-cwealm
gumena, 2044.

gâr-holt, st. n., *forest of spears*, i.e.
crowd of spears : acc. sg., 1835.

gâr-secg, st. m.(cf. Grimm, in Haupt
1.578), *sea, ocean :* acc. sg. on gâr-
secg, 49, 537 ; ofer gâr-secg, 515.

gâr-wîga, w. m., *one who fights with
the spear :* dat. sg. geongum gâr-
wîgan, of Wîglaf, 2675, 2812.

gâr-wîgend, pres. part., *fighting
with spear, spear-fighter :* acc. pl.
gâr-wîgend, 2642.

gâst, gærst, st. m., *ghost, demon :*
acc. sg. helle gâst (Grendel), 1275;
gen. sg. wergan gâstes (of Grendel),
133; (of the tempter), 1748 ; gen.
pl. dyrnra gâsta (Grendel's race),
1358; gæsta gîfrost (*flames con-
suming corpses*), 1124.—Comp.:
ellor-, geó-sceaf-gâst ; ellen-, wäl-
gæst.

gâst-bana, w. m., *slayer of the
spirit*, i.e. the devil : nom. sg. gâst-
bona, 177.

gädeling, st. m., *he who is connected
with another, relation, companion:*
gen. sg. gädelinges, 2618; dat. pl.
mid his gädelingum, 2950.

ät-gädere, adv., *together, united :*
321, 1165, 1191; samod ätgädere,
329, 387, 730, 1064.

tô-gädere, adv., *together*, 2631.

gäst, gîst, gyst, st. m., *stranger,
guest :* nom. sg. gäst, 1801; se gäst
(the drake), 2313; se grimma gäst
(Grendel), 102 ; gist, 1139, 1523;
acc. sg. gryre-lîcne gist (the nixy
slain by Beówulf), 1442 ; dat. sg.
gyste, 2229; nom. pl. gistas. 1603;
acc. pl. gäs[tas], 1894.—Comp.:
fède-, gryre-, inwit-, nîð-, sele-gäst
(-gyst).

gäst-sele, st. m., *hall in which the
guests spend their time, guest-hall :*
acc. sg., 995.

ge, conj., *and*, 1341 ; ge ... ge ...,
as well ... as ..., 1865; ge ... ge
..., ge ..., 1249 ; ge swylce, *and
likewise, and moreover*, 2259.

ge, pron., *ye, you*, plur. of þu, 237,
245, etc.

gegn-cwide, st. m., *reply :* gen. pl.
þinra gegn-cwida, 367.

gegnum, adv., *thither, towards,
away*, with the prep. tô, ofer,
giving the direction : þät hie him
tô mihton gegnum gangan (*that
they might go thither*), 314; gegnum fôr[þâ] ofer myrcan môr,
away over the dark moor, 1405.

gehðu, geohðu, st. f., *sorrow, care:*
instr. sg. giohðo mænde, 2268 ;
dat. sg. on gehðo, 3096; on giohðe,
2794.

gen (from gegn), adv., *yet, again :*
ne wäs hit lenge þâ gen, þät ..., *it
was not then long again that ...*,
83; ic sceal forð sprecan gen ymb
Grendel, *shall from now on speak
again of Grendel*, 2071; nô þý ær
ût þâ gen ... gongan wolde (*still
he would not yet go out*), 2082;
gen is eall ät þe lissa gelong (*yet
all my favor belongs to thee*),
2150; þâ gen, *then again*, 2678,
2703; swâ he nu gen deð, *as he*

still does, 2860 ; furður gen, *fur-ther still, besides*, 3007 ; nu gen, *now again*, 3169; ne gen, *no more*, *no farther :* ne wäs þät wyrd þâ gen, *that was no more fate* (fate no longer willed that), 735.

ge na, *still :* cwico wäs þâ gena, *was still living*, 3094.

genga, w. m., *goer ;* in comp. in-, säc-, sceadu-genga.

gengde. See gân (3).

genge. See ûð-genge.

genunga (from gegnunga), adv., *precisely, completely*, 2872.

gerwan, gyrwan, w. v.: 1) *to prepare, to make ready, to put in condition :* pret. pl. gestsele gyre-don, 995. — 2) *to equip, to arm for battle :* pret. sg. gyrede hine Beówulf eorl-gewædum (*dressed himself in the armor*), 1442.

ge-gyrwan: 1) *to make, to pre-pare :* pret. pl. him þâ gegiredan Geáta leóda âd . . . unwâclicne, 3138; pret. part. glôf . . . eall ge-gyrwed deófles cräftum and dracan fellum, 2088. — 2) *to fit out, to make ready :* inf. ceól gegyrwan hilde-wæpnum and heaðowædum, 38; hét him yðlidan gôdne gegyr-wan, *had (his) good ship fitted up for him*, 199. Also, *to provide warlike equipment :* pret. part. syð-ðan he hine tô gûðe gegyred häfde, 1473. — 3) *to endow, to provide, to adorn :* pret. part. nom. sg. bea-do-hrägl . . . golde gegyrwed, 553; acc. sg. lâfe . . . golde gegyrede, 2193; acc. pl. mâdmas . . . golde gegyrede, 1029.

getan, w. v., *to injure, to slay :* inf., 2941.

be-gête, adj., *to find, to attain ;* in comp. eð-begête.

geador, adv., *unitedly, together,*

jointly, 836 ; geadoı ätsomne, 491.

on-geador,adv., *unitedly, together*, 1596.

gealdor, st. n.: 1) *sound :* acc. sg. bŷman gealdor, 2944.— 2) *magic song, incantation, spell :* instr. sg. þonne wäs þät yrfe . . . galdre be-wunden (*placed under a spell*), 3053.

gealga, w. m., *gallows :* dat. sg. þät his byre ride giong on galgan, 2447.

gealg-môd, adj., *gloomy :* nom. sg. gifre and galgmôd, 1278.

gealg-treów, st. n., *gallows :* dat. pl. on galg-treówu[m], 2941.

geard, st. m , *residence :* in Beówulf corresponding to the house-com-plex of a prince's residence, used only in the plur.: acc. in geardas (*in Finn's castle*), 1135; dat. in geardum, 13, 2460; of geardum, 1139; ær he on weg hwurfe . . . of geardum, *before he went away from his dwelling-place*, i.e. died, 265. —Comp. middan-geard.

gearo, adj., properly, *made, pre-pared;* hence, *ready, finished, equipped :* nom. sg. þät hit wearð eal gearo, heal-ärna mæst, 77; wiht unhælo . . . gearo sôna wäs, *the demon of destruction was quickly ready, did not delay long*, 121; Here-Scyldinga betst beadorinca wäs on bæl gearu, *was ready for the funeral-pile* (for the solemn burning), 1110; þeód (is) eal gearo, *the warriors are altogether ready, always prepared*, 1231; hraðe wäs ät holme hýð-weard gearo (geara, MS.), 1915; gearo gûð-freca, 2415; sie sió bær gearo ädre ge-äfned, *let the bier be made ready at once*, 3106. With gen.: gearo gyrnwräce, *ready for revenge for harm done*, 2119; acc. sg. gearwe stôwe, 1007; nom. pl. beornas gearwe, 211; similarly, 1814.

gearwe, gearo, geare, adv., *completely, entirely:* ne ge ... gearwe ne wisson, *you do not know at all* ..., 246; similarly, 879; hine gearwe geman witena welhwylc (*remembers him very well*), 265; wisse he gearwe |ät ..., *he knew very well that* ..., 2340, 2726; |ät ic ... gearo sceáwige swegle searogimmas (*that I may see the treasures altogether, as many as they are*), 2749; ic wât geare |ät ..., 2657.—Comp. gearwor, *more readily, rather*, 3077.—Superl. gearwost, 716.

gearo-folm, adj., *with ready hand*, 2086.

gearwe, st. f., *equipment, dress;* in comp. feðer-gearwe.

geat, st. n., *opening, door;* in comp. ben-, hilde-geat.

geato-lîc, adj., *well prepared, handsome, splendid:* of sword and armor, 215, 1563, 2155; of Heorot, 308. Adv.: wisa fengel geatolic gengde, *passed on in a stately manner*, 1402.

geatwe, st. f. pl., *equipment, adornment:* acc. recedes geatwa, *the ornaments of the dragon's cave* (its treasures), 3089.—Comp.: eóred-, gryre-, gûð-, hilde-, wîg-geatwe.

geán (from gegn :, adv. in

on-geán, adv. and prep., *against, towards:* |ät he me ongeán sleá, 682; ræhte ongeán feónd mid folme, 748; foran ongeán, *forward towards*, 2365. With dat.: ongeán gramum, *against the enemy*, 1035.

tô-geánes, tô-gênes, prep, *against, towards:* Grendle tôgeánes, *towards Grendel, against Grendel*, 667;

grâp |â tôgeánes, *she grasped at* (Beówulf), 1502; similarly, him tôgeánes fêng, 1543; eodon him |â tôgeánes, *went towards him*, 1627; hêt |â gebeódan ... |ät hie bæl-wudu feorran feredon gôdum tôgênes, *had it ordered that they should bring the wood from far for the funeral-pyre towards the good man* (i.e. to the place where the dead Beówulf lay), 3115.

geáp, adj., *roomy, extensive, wide:* nom. sg. reced ... geáp, *the roomy hall*, 1801; acc. sg. under geápne hrôf, 837.—Comp.: horn-, sæ-geáp.

geâr, st. n., *year:* nom. sg., 1135; gen. pl. geâra, in adverbial sense, olim, *in former times*, 2665. See un-geâra.

geâr-dagas, st. m. pl., *former days:* dat. pl. in(on) geâr-dagum, 1, 1355.

geofe. See gifu.

geofon, gifen, gyfen (see Kuhn Zeitschr. I. 137), st. n., *sea, flood:* nom. sg. geofon, 515; gifen geótende, *the streaming flood*, 1691; gen. sg. geofenes begang, 362; gyfenes, 1395.

geoguð, st. f.: 1) *youth, time of youth:* dat. sg. on geoguðe, 409, 466, 2513; on gioguðe, 2427; gen. gioguðe, 2113.—2) contrasted with duguð, *the younger warriors of lower rank* (about as in the Middle Ages, the squires with the knights): nom. sg. geogoð, 66; giogoð, 1191; acc. sg. geogoðe, 1182; gen. duguðe and geogoðe, 160; duguðe and iogoðe (geoguðe), 1675, 622.

geoguð-feorh, st. n., *age of youth*, i.e. age in which one still belongs in the ranks of the geoguð: on geoguð-(geoguð-) feore, 537, 2665.

geohðo. See gehðo.

geolo, adj., *yellow:* acc. sg. geolwe linde (*the shield of yellow linden bark*), 2611.

geolo-rand, st. m., *yellow shield* (shield with a covering of interlaced yellow linden bark): acc. sg., 438.

geond, prep. w. acc., *through, throughout, along, over:* geond Jisne middangeard, *through the earth, over the earth,* 75; wide geond eorðan, 266, 3100; ferdon foletogan...geond wid-wegas, *went along the ways coming from afar,* 841; similarly, 1705; geond þät säld, *through the hall, through the extent of the hall,* 1281; similarly, 1982, 2265.

geong, adj., *young, youthful:* nom. sg., 13, 20, 855, etc.; giong, 2447; w. m. se maga geonga, 2676; acc. sg. geongne gûðcyning, 1970; dat. sg. geongum, 1949, 2045, 2675, etc.; on swā geongum feore, *at a so youthful age,* 1844; geongan cempan, 2627; acc. pl. geonge, 2019; dat. pl. geongum and ealdum, 72.—Superl. gingest, *the last:* nom. sg. w. f. gingeste word, 2818.

georn, adj., *striving, eager,* w. gen. of the thing striven for: eft stðes georn, 2784.—Comp. lof-georn.

georne, adv., *readily, willingly:* þät him wine-mâgas georne hŷrdon, 66; georne trûwode, 670. — *zealously, eagerly:* sôhte georne äfter grunde, *eagerly searched over the ground,* 2295. — *carefully, industriously:* nô ic him Jäs georne ätfealh (*did not hold him so fast*), 969. — *completely, exactly:* comp. wiste þê geornor, 822.

geó, iú, adv., *once, formerly, earlier,* 1477; gió, 2522; iú, 2460.

geóc, st. f., *help, support:* acc. sg.

geóce gefremman, 2675; þät him gást-bona geóce gefremede wið þeód-þreáum, 177; geóce gelŷfde, *believed in the help* (of Beówulf), 609; dat. sg. tô geóce, 1835.

geócor, adj., *ill, bad:* nom. sg., 766. —See Haupt's Zeitschrift 8, p. 7.

geó-man, iú-man, st. m., *man of former times:* gen. pl. iú-manna, 3053.

geó-meowle, w. f., (*formerly a virgin*), *wife:* acc. sg. ió-meowlan, 2932.

geómor, adj., *with depressed feelings, sad, troubled:* nom. sg. him wäs geómor sefa, 49, 2420, 2633, 2951; môdes geómor, 2101; fem. þät wäs geómuru ides, 1076.

geómore, adv., *sadly,* 151.

geómor-gid, st. n., *dirge:* acc. sg. giômor-gyd, 3151.

geómor-lîc, adj., *sad, painful:* swā bið geómorlic gomelum ceorle tô gebīdanne þät . . ., *it is painful to an old man to experience it, that* . . ., 2445.

geómor-môd, adj., *sad, sorrowful:* nom. sg., 2045, 3019; giômor-môd, 2268.

geómrian, w. v., *to complain, to lament:* pret. sg. geómrode giddum, 1119.

geó-sceaft, st. f., (*fixed in past times*), *fate:* acc. sg. geósceaft grimme, 1235.

geósceaft-gâst, st. m., *demon sent by fate:* gen. sg. fela geósceaft-gâsta, of Grendel and his race, 1267.

geótan, st. v. intrans., *to pour, to flow, to stream:* pres. part. gifen geótende, 1691.

gicel, st. m., *icicle:* in comp. hildegicel.

gid, gyd, st. n., *speech, solemn alli-*

krative song: nom. sg. þær wäs ... gid oft wrecan, 1066; leóð wäs åsungen, gleómannes gyd, *the song was :ung, the gleeman's lay,* 1161; þær wäs gidd and gleó, 2106; acc. sg. ic þis gid âwräc, 1724; gyd âwräc, 2109; gyd äfter wräc, 2155; þonne he gyd wrece, 2447; dat. pl. giddum, 151, 1119; gen. pl. gydda gemyndig, 869. — Comp.: geômor-, word-gid.

giddlan, w. v., *to speak, to speak in alliteration:* pret. gyddode, 631.

gif, conj.: 1) *if,* w. ind., 442, 447, 527, 662, etc.; gyf, 945, etc. With subj., 452, 594, 1482, etc.; gyf, 280, 1105, etc. — 2) *whether,* w. ind., 272; w. subj., 1141, 1320.

gifa, geofa, w. m., *giver;* in comp. gold-, sinc-, wil-gifa (-geofa).

gifan, st. v., *to g:ve:* inf. giofan, 2973; pret. sg. nallas beágas geaf Denum, 1720; he me [mâðmas] geaf, 2147; and similarly, 2174, 2432, 2624, etc.; pret. pl. geâfon (hyne on gârsecg, 49; pret. part. þâ wäs Hróðgâre here-spêd gyfen, 64; þâ wäs gylden hilt gamelum rince ... on hand gyfen, 1679; syððan ärest wearð gyfen ... geongum cempan (*given in marriage*), 1949.

â-gifan, *to give, to impart:* inf. andsware ... âgifan, *to give an ans er,* 355; pret. sg. sôna him se fróda fäder Ôhtheres ... ondslyht âgeaf (*gave him a counter-blow*), (*hand-blow?*), 2930.

for-gyfan, *to give, to grant:* pret. sg. him þäs lîf-freá ... worold-âre forgeaf, 17; þäm tô hâm forgeaf Hrêðel Geáta ângan dôhtor (*gave in marriage*), 374; similarly, 2998; he me lond forgeaf, *granted me*

land, 2493; similarly, 697, 1021, 2607, 2617; mägen-räs forgeaf hilde-bille, *he gave with his battle-sword a mighty blow,* i.e. he struck with full force, 1520.

of-gifan, (*to give up*), *to leave:* inf. þät se mæra maga Ecgþeówes grund-wong þone ofgyfan wolde (*was fated to leave the earth-plain*), 2589; pret. sg. þâs worold ofgeaf gromheort guma, 1682; similarly, gumdreám ofgeaf, 2470; Dena land ofgeaf, 1905; pret. pl. näs ofgeâfon hwate Scyldingas, *left the promontory,* 1601; þät þâ hildlatan holt ofgêfan, *that the cowards left the wood* (into which they had fled), 2847; sg. pret. for pl. þâra þe þis [lîf] ofgeaf, 2252.

gifeðe, adj., *given, granted:* Guð-fremmendra swylcum gifeðe bið þät ..., *to such a warrior is it granted that* ..., 299; similarly, 2682; swâ me gifeðe wäs, 2492; þær me gifeðe swâ ænig yð seweard äfter wurde, *if an h.ir,* (living) *after m·, had b.en gi· n me,* 2731. — Neut. as subst.: wäs þät gifeðe tô swîð, þe þone [þeóden] þyder ontyhte, *the fate wa: too harsh that has drawn hither the king,* 3086; gyfeðe, 555, 820. — Comp. un-gifeðe.

gif-heal, st. f., *hall in which fiefs were bestowed, throne-hall:* acc. sg. ymb þâ gifhealle, 839.

gif-sceat, st. m., *gift of value:* acc. pl. gif-sceattas, 378.

gif-stôl, st. m., *seat from which fiefs are granted, throne:* nom. sg., 2328; acc. sg., 168.

gift, st. f., *gift, present:* in comp. feoh-gift.

gifu, geofu, st. f., *gift, present, grant; fief:* nom. sg. gifu, 1885·

acc. sg. gimfäste gife þe him god
scalde, *the great gift that God had
granted him* (i.e. the enormous
strength), 1272; ginfästan gife þe
him god scalde, 2183; dat. pl. (as
instr.) geofum, 1959; gen. pl. gifa,
1931; geofena, 1174. — Comp.:
mâððum-, sinc-gifu.

gigant, st. m., *giant:* nom. pl. gigantas, 113; gen. pl. giganta, 1563,
1691.

gild, gyld, st. n., *reparation:* in
comp. wiðer-gyld (?).

gildan, gyldan, st. v., *to do something in return, to repay, to reward, to pay:* inf. gomban gyldan,
pay tribute, 11; he mid gôde gyldan wille uncran eaferan, 1185;
we him þâ gûðgeatwa gyldan woldon, 2637; pret. sg. heaðoræsas
geald mearum and mâðmum, *repaid the battles with horses and
treasures,* 1048; similarly, 2492;
geald þone gûðræs ... Jofore and
Wulfe mid ofermâðmum, *repaid
Eofor and Wulf the battle with exceedingly great treasures,* 2992.

an-gildan, *to pay for:* pret. sg.
sum sâre angeald æfenräste, *one
(Äschere) paid for the evening-
rest with death's pain,* 1252.

â-gildan, *to offer one's self:* pret.
sg. þâ me sæl âgeald, *when the favorable opportunity offered itself,*
1666; similarly, þâ him rûm âgeald,
2691.

for-gildan, *to repay, to do something in return, to reward:* pres.
subj. sg. III. alwalda þec gôde forgylde, *may the ruler of all reward
thee with good,* 957; inf. þone ænne
hêht golde forgyldan, *he ordered
that the one* (killed by Grendel) *be
paid for* (atoned for) *with gold,*
1055; he ... wolde Grendle for-

gyldan gûðræsa fela, *wished to pay
Grendel for many attacks,* 1578;
wolde se lâða lige forgyldan drinc-
fät dýre, *the enemy wished to repay
with fire the costly drinking vessel*
(the theft of it), 2306; pret. sg. he
him þäs leán forgeald, *he gave them
the reward therefor,* 114; similarly, 1542, 1585, 2095; forgeald
hraðe wyrsan wrixle wälhlem þone,
*repaid the murderous blow with a
worse exchange,* 2969.

gilp, gylp, st. m., *speech in which
one promises great things for himself in a coming combat, defiant
speech, boasting speech:* acc. sg.
häfde ... Geát-mecga leód gilp
gelæsted (*had fulfilled what he
had claimed for himself before the
battle*), 830; nallas on gylp seleð
fätte beágas, *gives no chased gold
rings for a boastful speech,* 1750;
þät ic wið þone gûðflogan gylp ofer-
sitte, *restrain myself from the
speech of defiance,* 2529; dat. sg.
gylpe wiðgripan (*fulfil my promise of battle*), 2522.—Comp. dol-
gilp.

gilpan, gylpan, st. v. w. gen., acc.,
and dat., *to make a defiant speech,
to boast, to exult insolently:* pres.
sg. I. nô ic þäs gilpe (after a break
in the text), 587; sg. III. morðres
gylpeð, *boasts of the murder,* 2056;
inf. swâ ne gylpan þearf Grendles
maga ænig ... uhthlem þone, 2007;
nealles folc-cyning fyrdgesteallum
gylpan þorfte, *had no need to boast
of his fellow-warriors,* 2875; pret.
sg. hreðsigora ne gealp goldwine
Geáta, *did not exult at the glorious
victory* (could not gain the victory
over the drake), 2584.

gilp-cwide, st. m., *speech in which
a man promises much for himself*

for a coming combat, speech of de-fiance: nom. sg., 641.

gilp-hläden, pret. part., *laden with boasts of defiance* (i.e. he who has made many such boasts, and consequently has been victorious in many combats), *covered with glory:* nom. sg. guma gilp-hläden, 869.

gilp-spræc, same as **gilp-cwide**, *speech of defiance, boastful speech:* dat. sg. on gylp-spræce, 982.

gilp-word, st. n., *defiant word before the coming combat, vaunting word:* gen. pl. gespräc ... gylp-worda sum, 676.

gim, st. m., *gem, precious stone, jewel:* nom. sg. heofones gim, *heaven's jewel,* i.e. the sun, 2073. Comp. searo-gim.

gimme-rice, adj., *rich in jewels:* acc. sg. gimme-rice hord-burh häleða, 466.

gin (according to Bout., **ginne**), adj., properly *gaping,* hence, *wide, extended:* acc. sg. gynne grund (*the bottom of the sea*), 1552.

gin-fast, adj., *extensive, rich:* acc. sg. gim-fäste gife (gim-, on account of the following *f*), 1272; in weak form, gin-fästan gife, 2183.

ginnan, st. v., original meaning, *to be open, ready;* in

on-ginnan, *to begin, to undertake:* pret. ðð þät ân ongan fyrene fremman feónd on helle, 100; secg eft ongan sið Beówulfes snyttrum styrian, 872; þâ þät sweord ongan ... wanian, *the sword began to diminish,* 1606; Higelâc ongan sînne geseldan ... fägre friegean, *began with propriety to question his companion,* 1984, etc.: ongon, 2791; pret. pl. nô her cûðlîcor cuman ongunnon lindhäbbende, *no shield-bear-*

ing men e'er undertook more openly to come hither, 245; pret. part. häbbe ic mærða fela ongunnen on geogoðe, *have in my youth undertaken many deeds of renown,* 409.

gist. See gäst.

gistran, adv., *yesterday:* gystran niht, *yesterday night,* 1335.

git, pron., *ye two,* dual of þu, 508, 512, 513, etc.

git, gyt, adv., *yet; then still,* 536, 1128, 1165, 2142; *hitherto,* 957; næfre git, *never yet,* 853; *still,* 945, 1059, 1135; *once more,* 2513; *moreover,* 47, 1051, 1867.

gitan (original meaning, *to take hold of, to seize, to attain*), in

be-gitan, w. acc., *to grasp, to seize, to reach:* pret. sg. begeat, 1147, 2231; þâ hine wîg beget, *when war seized him, came upon him,* 2873; similarly, begeat, 1069; pret. pl. hit ær on þe gôde be-geâton, *good men received it formerly from thee,* 2250; subj. sg. for pl. þät wäs Hrôðgâre hreówa tornost þâra þe leódfruman lange begeâte, *the bitterest of the troubles that for a long time had befallen the people's chief,* 2131.

for-gitan, w. acc., *to forget:* pres. sg. III. he þâ forðgesceaft forgyteð and forgýmeð, 1752.

an-gitan, on-gitan, w. acc.: 1) *to take hold of, to grasp:* imp. sg. gumcyste ongit, *lay hold of manly virtue, of what becomes the man,* 1724; pret. sg. þe hine se brôga angeat, *whom terror seized,* 1292.— 2 *to grasp intellectually, to comprehend, to perceive, to distinguish, to behold:* pres. subj. I. þät ic ærwelan ... ongite, *that I may behold the ancient wealth* (the treasures of the drake's cave), 2749; inf. säl

timbred . . . ongytan, 308, 1497;
Geáta clifu ongitan, 1912; pret. sg.
fyren-þearfe ongeat, *had perceived
their distress from hostile snares*,
14; ongeat . . . grund-wyrgenne,
beheld the she-wolf of the bottom,
1519; pret. pl. þearhtm ongeâton,
guðhorn galan, *perceived the noise*,
(heard) *the battle-trumpet sound*,
1432; syððan hie Higeláces horn
and býman gealdor ongeâton, 2944.

gîfre, adj., *greedy, eager :* nom. sg.
gífre and galgmôd, of Grendel's
mother, 1278. — Superl.: lîg . . .,
g.esta gifrost, 1124. — Comp. heoro-
gífre.

gîtsian, w. v., *to be greedy :* pres. sg.
III. gŷtsað, 1750.

gio-, glô-. See geo-, geó-.

gladian, w. v., *to gleam, to shimmer :*
pres. pl. III. on him gladiað gomelra lâfe, *upon him gleams the
legacy of the men of ancient times*
(armor), 2037.

glæd, adj., *gracious, friendly* (as a
form of address for princes) : nom.
sg. beó wið Geátas glæd, 1174; acc.
sg. glædne Hrôðgâr, 864; glædne
Hrôðulf, 1182; dat. sg. gladum
suna Frôdan, 2026.

glæde, adv., *in a gracious, friendly
way*, 58.

glædnian, w. v., *to rejoice :* inf. w.
gen., 367.

glæd-môd, adj., *joyous, glad*, 1786.

glêd, st. f., *fire, flame :* nom. sg.,
2653, 3115; dat. (instr.) pl. glêdum, 2313, 2336, 2678, 3042.

glêd-egesa, w. m., *terror on account
of fire, fire-terror :* nom. sg. glêd-
egesa grim (*the fire-spewing of the
drake*), 2651.

gleáw (Goth. glaggwu-s), adj., *con-
siderate, well-bred*, of social conduct; in comp. un-gleáw.

gleó, st. n., *social entertainment*,
(especially by music, play, and
jest) : nom. sg. þær wæs gidd and
gleó, 2106.

gleó-beám, st. m., (*tree of social
entertainment, of music*), *harp :*
gen. sg. gleó-beámes, 2264.

gleó-dreám, st. m., *joyous carrying-
on in social entertainment, mirth,
social gaiety :* acc. sg. gamen and
gleó-dreám, 3022.

gleó-man, m., (*gleeman, who enli-
vens the social entertainment, especially with music*), *harper :* gen.
sg. gleómannes gyd, 1161.

glitinian (O.H.G. glizinôn), w. v.,
to gleam, to light, to glitter : inf.
geseah þâ . . . gold glitinian, 2759.

glîdan, st. v., *to glide :* pret. sg. syððan heofones gim glâd ofer grun-
das, *after heaven's gem had glided
over the fields* (after the sun had
set), 2074; pret. pl. glidon ofer
gârsecg, *you glided over the ocean*
(swimming), 515.

tô-glîdan (*to glide asunder*), *to
separate, to fall asunder :* pret.
gûð-helm tô-glâd (*Ongenþeów's
helmet was split asunder by the
blow of Eofor*), 2488.

glôf, st. f., *glove :* nom. sg. glôf hangode, (on Grendel) *a glove hung*,
2086.

gneáð, adj., *niggardly :* nom. sg. f.
næs hió . . . tô gneáð gifa Geáta
leódum, *was not too niggardly with
gifts to the people of the Geátas*,
1931.

gnorn, st. m., *sorrow, sadness :* acc.
sg. gnorn þrowian, 2659.

gnornian, w. v., *to be sad, to complain :* pret. sg. earme . . . ides
gnornode, 1118.

be-gnornian, w. acc., *to bemoan,
to mourn for :* pret. pl. begnor-

nodon ... hlâfordes [hry]re, *be-moaned their lord's fall*, 3180.

god, st. m., *god:* nom. sg., 13, 72. 478, etc.; hâlig god, 381, 1554; witig god, 686; mihtig god, 702; acc. sg. god, 812; ne wiston hie drihten god, *did not know the Lord God*, 181; dat. sg. gode, 113, 227, 626, etc.; gen. sg. godes, 570, 712, 787, etc.

gold, st. n., *gold:* nom. sg., 3013, 3053: icge gold, 1108; wunden gold, *wound gold, gold in ring-form*, 1194, 3136; acc. sg. gold, 2537, 2759, 2794, 3169; hæðen gold, *heathen g ld* (that from the drake's cave), 2277; brâd gold, *massive gold*, 3106; dat. instr. sg. golde, 1055, 2932, 3019; fättan golde, *with chased gold, with gold in plate-form*, 2103: gehroden golde, *covered with gold, gild d*, 304; golde gegyrwed (gegyrede), *pro-vided with, ornamented with gold*, 553, 1029, 2193; golde geregnad, *adorned with gold*, 778; golde fâhne hrôf), *the roof shining with gold*, 928; bunden golde, *bound with gold* (see under **bindan**), 1901; hyrsted golde (helm , *the helmet ornamented with, mounted with gold*, 2256; gen. sg. goldes, 2302; fättan goldes, 1094, 2247; sciran goldes, *of pure gold*, 1695. — Comp. fät-gold.

gold-æht, st. f., *possessions in gold, treasure:* acc. sg., 2749.

gold-fâh, adj., *variegated with gold, shining with g ld:* nom. sg. reced ... goll-fâh, 1801; acc. sg. gold-fâhne helm, 2812; nom. pl. gold-fâg scinon web äfter wagum, *va-riegated with gold, the tapestry gleamed along the walls*, 995.

gold-gifa, w. m., *gold-giver*, desig-nation of the prince: acc. sg. mid minne goldgyfan, 2653.

gold-hroden, pret. part., (*covered with gold*), *ornamented with gold:* nom. sg., 615, 641, 1949, 2026; epithet of women of princely rank.

gold-hwät, adj., *striving after gold, greedy for gold:* näs he goldhwät, *he* (Beówulf) *was not greedy for gold* (he did not fight against the drake for his treasure, cf. 3067 ff.), 3075.

gold-mâðm, st. m., *jewel of gold:* acc. pl. gold-mâðmas (the treas-ures of the drake's cave), 2415.

gold-sele, st. m., *gold-hall*, i.e. the hall in which the gold was dis-tributed, ruler's hall: acc. sg., 716, 1254; dat. sg. gold-sele, 1640, 2084.

gold-weard, st. m., *gold-ward, de-funder of the gold:* acc. sg. (of the drake , 3082.

gold-wine, st. m., *friend who dis-tribute gold*, i.e. ruler, prince: nom. sg. (partly as voc.) goldwine gu-mena, 1172, 1477, 1603; goldwine Geáta, 2420, 2585.

gold-wlanc, adj., *proud of gold:* nom. sg. guðrinc goldwlanc (Beó-wulf rewarded with gold by Hrôð-gâr on account of his victory), 1882.

gomban, gomel, gomen. See gamban, gamal, gamen.

gong, gongan. See gang, gangan.

gôd, adj., *g d, fit*, of persons and things: nom. sg., 11, 195, 804, 2264, 2391, etc.; frôd and gôd, 279; w. dat. cyning äðelum gôd, *the king noble in birth*, 1871; gumcystum gôd, 2544; w. gen. wes þu ûs lârena gôd, *be good to us with teaching* (help us thereto through thy instruction), 269; in weak form, se gôda, 205, 355, 676, 1191, etc.; acc. sg. gôdne, 199, 347, 1596, 1970, etc.; gumcystum gôdne, 1487; neut. gôd, 1563; dat. sg. gôdum, 3037, 3115; Iäm gôdan, 384, 2328; nom. pl. gôdc, 2250; þâ gôdan, 1164; acc. pl. gôdc, 2642; dat. pl. gôdum dædum, 2179; gen. pl. gôdra gûðrinca, 2649. — Comp. ær-gôd.

gôd, st. n.: 1) *good that is done, benefit, gift* : instr. sg. gôde, 20, 957, 1185; gôde mære, *renowned on account of her gifts* (Fryðo), 1953; instr. pl. gôdum, 1962. — 2) *ability*, especially in fight: gen. pl. nât he þâra gôda, 682.

gram, adj., *hostile* : gen. sg. on grames grâpum, *in the gripe of the enemy* (Beówulf), 766; nom. pl. Iâ graman, 778; dat. pl. gramum, 424, 1035.

gram-heort, adj., *of a hostile heart, hostile* : nom. sg. grom-heort guma, 1683.

gram-hydig, adj., *with hostile feeling, maliciously inclined* : nom. sg. gromhydig, 1750.

grâp, st. f., *the hand ready to grasp, hand, claw* : dat. sg. mid grâpe, 438; on grâpe, 555; gen. sg. cal ... Grendles grâpe, *all of Grendel's claw, the whole claw*, 837; dat. pl. on grames grâpum, 766; (as instr.) grimman grâpum, *with grim claws*, 1543. — Comp.: feónd-, hilde-grâp.

grâpian, w. v., *to grasp, to lay hold of, to seize* : pret. sg. Iät hire wið halse heard grâpode, *that* (the sword) *griped hard at her neck*, 1567; he ... grâpode gearofolm, *he took hold with ready hand*, 2086.

grüs-molde, w. f., *grass-plot* : acc.

sg. gräsmoldan träd, *went over the grass-plot*, 1882.

grædig, adj., *greedy, hungry, voracious* : nom. sg. grim and grædig, 121, 1500; acc. sg. grædig gûðleóð, 1523.

græg, adj., *gray* : nom. pl. äsc-holt ufan græg, *the ashen wood, gray above* (the spears with iron points), 330; acc. pl. græge syrcan, *gray* (i.e. iron) *shirts of mail*, 334.

græg-mæl, adj., *having a gray color*, here = *iron* : nom. sg. sweord Beówulfes gomol and grægmæl, 2683.

græpe. See ät-græpe.

grêtan, w. v. w. acc.: 1) *to greet, to salute* : inf. hine swâ gôdne grêtan, 347; Hrôðgâr grêtan, 1647, 2011; eówic grêtan hêt (*bade me bring you his last greeting*), 3096; pret. sg. grêtte Geáta leód, 626; grêtte þâ guma ôðerne, 653; Hrôðgâr grêtte, 1817. — 2) *to come on, to come near, to seek out; to touch; to take hold of* : inf. gifstôl grêtan, *take possession of the throne, mount it as ruler*, 168; näs se folccyning ænig ... Ie mec gûðwinum grêtan dorste* (*attack with swords*), 2736; Wyrd ... se þone gomelan grêtan sceolde, 2422; þät þone sin-scaðan gûðbilla nân grêtan nolde, *that no sword would take hold upon the irreconcilable enemy*, 804; pret. sg. grêtte goldhroden guman on healle, *the gold-adorned* (queen) *greeted the men in the hall*, 615; nô he mid hearme . . . gästas grette, *did not approach the strangers with insults*, 1894; gomenwudu grêtte, *touched the wood of joy, played the harp*, 2109; pret. subj. II. sg. Iät þu þone walgæst wihte ne grêtte, *that thou shouldst by no means seek out the murderous spirit*

(Grendel), 1996; similarly, sg. III.
þät he ne grêtte goldweard þone,
3082; pret. part. þær wäs ... gomenwudu grêted, 1066.

ge-grêtan, w. acc.: 1) *to greet, to
salute, to address:* pret. sg. holdne
gegrêtte meaglum wordum, *greeted
the dear man with formal words,*
1981; gegrêtte þâ gumena gehwylcne ... hindeman siðe, *spoke
then the last time to each of the
men,* 2517. — 2) *to approach, to
come near, to seek out:* inf. sceal
... manig ôðerne gôdum gegrêtan
ofer ganotes bäð, *many a one will
seek another across the sea with
gifts,* 1862.

greót, st. m., *grit, sand, earth:* dat.
sg. on greóte, 3169.

greótan, st. v., *to weep, to mourn,
to lament:* pres. sg. III. se þe
äfter sincgyfan on sefan greóteð,
*who laments in his heart for the
treasure-giver,* 1343.

grim, adj., *grim, angry, wild, hostile:* nom. sg., 121, 555, 1500, etc.;
weak form, se grimma gäst, 102;
acc. sg. m. grimne, 1149, 2137;
fem. grimme, 1235; gen. sg. grimre gûðe, 527; instr. pl. grimman
grâpum, 1543. — Comp.: beado-,
heaðo-, heoro-, searo-grimm.

grimme, adv., *grimly, in a hostile
manner, bitterly,* 3013, 3086.

grim-lîc, adj., *grim, terrible:* nom.
sg. grimlic gry[re-gäst], 3042.

grimman, st. v., (properly *to snort*),
to go forward hastily, to hasten:
pret. pl. grummon, 306.

grindan, st. v., *to grind,* in

for-grindan, *to destroy, to ruin:*
pret. sg. w. dat. forgrand gramum,
destroyed the enemy, killed them(?),
424; pret. part. w. acc. häfde lîg-
draca leóda fästen ... glêdum for-

grunden, *had with flames destroyed
the people's feasts,* 2336; þâ his
âgen (scyld) wäs glêdum forgrunden, *since his own (shield) had
been destroyed by the fire,* 2678.

gripe, st. m., *gripe, attack:* nom. sg.
gripe mêces, 1766; acc. sg. grimne
gripe, 1149. — Comp.: fær-, mund-,
nið-gripe.

grîma, w. m., *mask, visor:* in comp.
beado-, here-grîma.

grîm-helm, st. m., *mask-helmet, helmet with visor:* acc. pl. grîm-hel-
mas, 334.

grîpan, st. v., *to gripe, to seize, to
grasp:* pret. sg. grâp | â tôgeánes,
then she caught at, 1502.

for-grîpan (*to gripe vehemently*),
*to gripe so as to kill, to kill by the
grasp,* w. dat.: pret. sg. ät gûðe
forgrâp Grendeles mægum, 2354.

wið-grîpan, w. dat., (*to seize at*),
to maintain, to hold erect: inf. hû
wið þam aglæcean elles meahte
gylpe wið-grîpan, *how else I might
maintain my boast of battle against
the monster,* 2522.

grôwan, st. v., *to grow, to sprout:*
pret. sg. him on ferhðe greów
breósthord blôdreów, 1719.

grund, st. m.: 1) *ground, plain,
fields* in contrast with highlands;
earth in contrast with heaven: dat.
sg. sôhte ... äfter grunde, *sought
along the ground,* 2295; acc. pl.
ofer grundas, 1405, 2074. — 2) *bottom, the lowest part:* acc. sg. grund
(of the sea of Grendel), 1368; on
gyfenes grund, 1395; under gynne
grund (*bottom of the sea*), 1552;
dat. sg. tô grunde (of the sea),
553; grunde (of the drake's cave)
getenge, 2759; so, on grunde,
2766. — Comp.: eormen-, mere-,
sæ-grund.

grund-búend, pres. part., *inhabitant of the earth :* gen. pl. grund-búendra, 1007.

grund-hyrde, st. m., *warder of the bottom* (of the sea): acc. sg. (of Grendel's mother), 2137.

grund-sele, st. m., *hall at the bottom* (of the sea): dat. sg. in þam [grund]sele, 2140.

grund-wang, st. m., *ground surface, lowest surface :* acc. sg. þone grund-wong (*bottom of the sea*), 1497; (bottom of the drake's cave), 2772, 2588.

grund-wyrgen, st. f., *she-wolf of the bottom* (of the sea): acc. sg. grund-wyrgenne (Grendel's mother), 1519.

gryn (cf. Gloss. Aldh. "retinaculum, rete gri n," Hpts. Ztschr. IX. 429), st. n., *net, noose, snare :* gen. pl. fela . . . grynna, 931. See **gyrn.**

gryre, st. m., *horror, terror, anything causing terror :* nom. sg., 1283; acc. sg. wið Grendles gryre, 384; hie Wyrd forsweóp on Grendles gryre, *snatched them away into the horror of Grendel, to the horrible Grendel,* 478; dat. pl. mid gryrum ecga, 483; gen. pl. swâ fela gryra, 592. — Comp.: fær-, wîg-gryre.

gryre-bróga, w. m., *terror and horror, amazement :* nom. sg. [gryre-]br[ó]g[a], 2229.

gryre-fáh, adj., *gleaming terribly :* acc. sg. gryre-fâhne (*the fire-spewing drake,* cf. also [draca] fyr-wylmum fáh, 2672), 2577.

gryre-gäst, st. m., *terror-guest, stranger causing terror :* nom. sg. grimlîc gry[regäst], 3042; dat. sg. wið þam gryregieste (the dragon), 2561.

gryre-geatwe, st. f. pl., *terror-armor, warlike equipment :* dat. pl. in hyra gryre-geatwum, 324.

gryre-leóð, st. n., *terror-song, fearful song :* acc. sg. gehŷrdon gryre-leóð galan godes andsacan (*heard Grendel's cry of agony*), 787.

gryre-lîc, adj., *terrible, horrible :* acc. sg. gryre-lîcne, 1442, 2137.

gryre-sið, st. m., *way of terror, way causing terror,* i.e. warlike expedition: acc. pl. se þe gryre-siðas gegân dorste, 1463.

guma, w. m., *man, human being :* nom. sg., 653, 869, etc.; acc. sg. guman, 1844, 2295; dat. sg. guman (gumum, MS.), 2822; nom. pl. guman, 215, 306, 667, etc.; acc. pl. guman, 615; dat. pl. gumum, 127, 321; gen. pl. gumena, 73, 328, 474, 716, etc. — Comp.: driht-, seld-guma.

gum-cyn, st. n., *race of men, people, nation :* gen. sg. we synt gum-cynnes Geáta leóde, *people from the nation of the Geátas,* 260; dat. pl. æfter gum-cynnum, *along the nations, among the nations,* 945.

gum-cyst, st. f., *man's excellence, man's virtue :* acc. sg. (or pl.) gumcyste, 1724; dat. pl. as adv., *excellently, preëminently :* gum-cystum gôdne beága bryttan, 1487; gumcystum gôd . . . hilde-hlemma (Beówulf), 2544.

gum-dreám, st. m., *joyous doings of men :* acc. sg. gum-dreám ofgeaf (died), 2470.

gum-dryhten, st. m., *lord of men :* nom. sg. 1643.

gum-féða, w. m., *troop of men going on foot :* nom. sg., 1402.

gum-man, st. m., *man :* gen. pl. gum-manna fela, 1029.

gum-stôl, st. m., *man's seat* kat'

ἕξοχήν, *ruler's seat, throne:* dat.
sg. in gumstôle, 1953.

gûð, st. f., *combat, battle:* nom. sg.,
1124, 1659, 2484, 2537; acc. sg.
gûðe, 604; instr. sg. gûðe, 1998;
dat. sg. tô (ät) gûðe, 438, 1473,
1536, 2354, etc.; gen. sg. gûðe, 483,
527,631, etc.; dat. pl. gûðum, 1959,
2179; gen. pl. gûða, 2513, 2544.

gûð-beorn, st. m., *warrior:* gen.
pl. gûð-beorna sum (*the strand-
guird on the Danish coast*), 314.

gûð-bil, st. n., *battle-bill:* nom. sg.
gûðbill, 2585; gen. pl. gûð-billa
nân, 804.

gûð-byrne, w. f., *battle-corselet:*
nom. sg., 321.

gûð-cearu, st. f., *sorrow which the
combat brings:* dat. sg. äfter gûð-
ceare, 1259.

gûð-cräft, st. m., *warlike strength,
power in battle:* nom. sg. Grendles
gûð-cräft, 127.

gûð-cyning, st. m., *king in battle,
king directing a battle:* nom. sg.,
199, 1970, 2336, etc.

gûð-deáð, st. m., *death in battle:*
nom. sg., 2250.

gûð-floga, w. m., *flying warrior:*
acc. sg. wið þone gûðflogan (the
drake), 2529.

gûð-freca, w. m., *hero in battle,
warrior* (see freca): nom. sg.
gearo gûð-freca, of the drake,
2415.

gûð-fremmend, pres. part., *fighting
a battle, warrior:* gen. pl. gûð-
fremmendra, 246; gûð- (gôd-,
MS.) fremmendra swylcum, *such a
warrior* (meaning Beówulf), 299.

gûð-gewæde, st. n., *battle-dress, armor:* nom. pl. gûð-gewædo, 227;
acc. pl. -gewædu, 2618, 2631(?),
2852,2872; gen. pl. -gewæda, 2624.

gûð-geweorc, st. n., *battle-work,*

warlike deed: gen. pl., -geweorca,
679, 982, 1826.

gûð-geatwe, st. f. pl., *equipment
for combat:* acc. }â gûð-geatwa
(-getawa, MS.), 2637; dat. in eówrum gûð-geatawum, 395.

gûð-helm, st. m., *battle-helmet:* nom.
sg., 2488.

gûð-horn, st. n., *battle-horn:* acc.
sg., 1433.

gûð-hréð, st. f., *battle-fame:* nom.
sg., 820.

gûð-leóð, st. n., *battle-song:* acc.
sg., 1523.

gûð-môd, adj., *disposed to battle,
having an inclination to battle:*
nom. pl. gûð-môde, 306.

gûð-ræs, st. m., *storm of battle, attack:* acc. sg., 2992; gen. pl. gûð-
ræsa, 1578, 2427.

gûð-reów, adj., *fierce in battle:*
nom. sg., 58.

gûð-rinc, st. m., *man of battle,
fighter, warrior:* nom. sg., 839,
1119, 1882; acc. sg., 1502; gen.
pl. gûð-rinca, 2649.

gûð-rôf, adj., *renowned in battle:*
nom. sg., 609.

gûð-sceaða, w. m., *battle-foe, enemy in combat:* nom. sg., of the
drake, 2319.

gûð-scearu, st. f., *decision of the battle:* dat. sg. äfter gûð-sceare, 1214.

gûð-sele, st. m., *battle-hall, hall in
which a battle takes place:* dat. sg.
in þäm gûðsele (in Heorot), 443.

gûð-searo, st. n. pl., *battle-equip-
ment, armor:* acc., 215, 328.

gûð-sweord, st. n., *battle-sword:*
acc. sg., 2155.

gûð-wêrig, adj., *wearied by battle,
dead:* acc. sg. gûð-wêrigne Grendel, 1587.

gûð-wine, st. m., *battle-friend, comrade in battle,* designation of the

sword : acc. sg., 1811; instr. pl. þe
mec gûð-winum grêtan dorste, *who
dared to attack me with his war-
friends*, 2736.

gûð-wiga, w. m., *fighter of battles,
warrior :* nom. sg., 2112.

gyd. See gid.

gyfan. See gifan.

gyldan. See gildan.

gylden, adj., *golden :* nom. sg. gylden hilt, 1678; acc. sg. segen gyldenne, 47, 1022; hring gyldenne,
2810; dat. sg. under gyldnum
beáge, 1164. — Comp. eal-gylden.

gylp. See gilp.

gyrdan, w. v., *to gird, to lace :* pret.
part. gyrded cempa, *the (sword-)
girt warrior*, 2079.

gyrn, st. n., *sorrow, harm :* nom.
sg., 1776.

gyrn-wracu, st. f., *revenge for
harm :* dat. sg. tô gyrn-wräce,
1139; gen. sg. þâ wäs eft hraðe
gearo gyrn-wräce Grendeles môdor,
*then was Grendel's mother in turn
immediately ready for revenge for
the injury*, 2119.

gyrwan. See gerwan.

gystran. See gistran.

gŷman, w. v. w. gen., *to take care
of, to be careful about :* pres. III.
gŷmeð, 1758, 2452; imp. sg. ofer-
hyda ne gŷm! *do not study arrogance* (despise it), 1761.

for-gŷman, w. acc., *to neglect, to
slight :* pres. sg. III. he þâ forð-
gesceaft forgyteð and forgŷmeð,
1752.

gŷtsian. See gîtsian.

H

habban, w. v., *to have :* 1) w. acc.:
pres. sg. 1. þäs ic wên häbbe (*as I
hope*), 383; þe ic geweald häbbe,

951; ic me on hafu bord and byrnan, *have on me shield and coat
of mail*, 2525; hafo, 3001; sg. II.
þu nu [friðu] hafast, 1175; pl. I.
habbað we ... micel ærende, 270;
pres. subj. sg. III. þät he þrittiges
manna mägencräft on his mund-
gripe häbbe, 381. Blended with
the negative : pl. III. þät þe Sæ-
Geátas sêlran näbben tô geceósenne cyning ænigne, *that the Sea-
Geátas will have no better king
than you to choose*, 1851; imp.
hafa nu and geheald hûsa sêlest,
659; inf. habban, 446, 462, 3018;
pret. sg. häfde, 79, 518, 554; pl.
häfdon, 539. — 2) used as an aux-
iliary with the pret. p. rt. : pres. sg.
I. häbbe ic ... ongunnen, 408;
häbbe ic ... geâhsod, 433; II. hafast, 954, 1856; III. hafað, 474,
596; pret. sg. häfde, 106, 220, 666,
2322, 2334, 2953, etc.; pl. häfdon,
117, 695, 884, 2382, etc. Pret.
part. inflected : nu sceale hafað
dæd gefremede, 940; häfde se gôda
... cempan gecorene, 205. With
the pres. part. are formed the compounds : bord-, rond-häbbend.

for-habban, *to hold back, to keep
one's self :* inf. ne mealite wäfre
môd forhabban in hreðre, *the expiring life could not hold itself
back in the breast*, 1152; ne mihte
þâ for-habban, *could not restrain
himself*, 2610.

wið-habban, *to resist, to offer resistance :* pret. þät se winsele wiðhäfde heaðo-deórum, *that the hall
resisted them furious in fight*, 773.

hafela, heafola, w. m., *head :* acc.
sg. hafelan, 1373, 1422, 1615, 1636,
1781; nâ þu mînne þearft hafalan
hŷdan, 446; þonne we on orlege
hafelan weredon, *protected our*

heads, defended ourselves, 1328 ; se hwîta helm hafelan werede, 1449; dat. sg. hafelan, 673, 1522; heafolan, 2680; gen. sg. heafolan, 2698; nom. pl. hafelan, 1121.— Comp. wîg-heafola.

hafenian, w. v., *to raise, to uplift :* pret. sg. wæpen hafenade heard be hiltum, *raised the weapon, the strong man, by the hilt,* 1575.

hafoc, st. m., *hawk.* nom. sg., 2264.

haga, w. m., *enclosed piece of ground, hedge, farm-enclosure :* dat. sg. tô hagan, 2893, 2961.

haga, w. m. See ân-haga.

hama, homa, w. m., *dress :* in the comp. flæsc-, fyrd-, lîc-hama, scîr-ham (adj.).

hamer, st. m., *hammer :* instr. sg. hamere, 1286 ; gen. pl. homera lâfe (swords), 2830.

hand, hond, st. f., *hand :* nom. sg. 2138 ; sió swîðre . . . hand, *the right hand,* 2100 ; hond, 1521, 2489, 2510; acc. sg. hand, 558, 984 ; hond, 657, 687, 835, 928, etc.; dat. sg. on handa, 495, 540; mid handa, 747, 2721 ; be honda, 815; dat. pl. (as instr.) hondum, 1444, 2841.

hand-bana, w. m., *murderer with the hand,* or *in hand-to-hand combat :* dat. sg. tô hand-bonan (-banan), 460, 1331.

hand-gemôt, st. n., *hand-to-hand conflict, battle :* gen. pl. (ecg) bo-lode ær fela hand-gemôta, 1527; nô þæt læsest wäs hond-gemôta, 2356.

hand-gesella, w. m., *hand-companion, man of the retinue :* dat. pl. hond-gesellum, 1482.

hand-gestealla, w. m., (*one whose position is near at hand*), *comrade,*

companion, attendant : dat. sg. hond-gesteallan, 2170; nom. pl. hand-gesteallan, 2597.

hand-geweorc, st. n., *work done with the hands,* i.e. achievement in battle : dat. sg. for | äs hild-fruman handgeweorce, 2836.

hand-gewriðen, pret. part., *hand-wreathed, bound with the hand :* acc. pl. wälbende . . . hand-gewriðene, 1938.

hand-locen, pret. part., *joined, united by hand :* nom. sg. (gûð-byrne, lîc-syrce) handlocen (because the shirts of mail consisted of interlaced rings), 322, 551.

hand-ræs, st. m., *hand-battle,* i.e. combat with the hands : nom. sg. hond-ræs, 2073.

hand-scalu, st. f., *hand-attendance, retinue :* dat. sg. mid his hand-scale (hond-scole), 1318, 1964.

hand-spere, st. n., *finger* (on Gren-del's hand), under the figure of a spear : nom. pl. hand-speru, 987.

hand-wundor, st. n., *wonder done by the hand, wonderful handwork :* gen. pl. hond-wundra mæst, 2769.

hangan. See hôn.

hangian, w. v., *to hang :* pres. sg. III. þonne his sunu hangað hrefne tô hrôðre, *when his son hangs, a joy to the ravens,* 2448; pl. III. ofer | äm (mere) hongiað hrînde bearwas, *over which rustling forests hang,* 1364 ; inf. hangian, 1663; pret. hangode, *hung down,* 2086.

hatian, w. v. w. acc., *to hate, to be an enemy to, to hurt :* inf. he þone heaðo-rinc hatian ne meahte lâðum dædum (*could not do him any harm*), 2467; pret. sg. hû se gûð-sceaða Geáta leóde hatode and hŷnde, 2320.

hâd, st. m., *form, condition, position, manner:* acc. sg. þurh hæstne hâd, *in a powerful manner,* 1336; on gesíðes hâd, *in the position of follower, as follower,* 1298 ; on sweordes hâd, *in the form of a sword,* 2194. See under on.

hâdor, st. m., *clearness, brightness:* acc. sg. under heofenes hâdor, 414.

hâdor, adj., *clear, fresh, loud:* nom. sg. scop hwilum sang hâdor on Heorote, 497.

hâdre, adv., *clearly, brightly,* 1572.

hâl, adj., *hale, whole, sound, unhurt:* nom. sg. hâl, 300. With gen. heaðo-lâces hâl, *safe from battle,* 1975. As form of salutation, wes . . . hâl, 407 ; dat. sg. hâlan lice, 1504.

hâlig, adj., *holy:* nom. sg. hâlig god, 381, 1554; hâlig dryhten, 687.

hâm, st. m., *home, residence, estate, land:* acc. sg. hâm, 1408; Hróð- gâres hâm, 718. Usually in adverbial sense: gewât him hâm, *betook himself home,* 1602; tô hâm, 124, 374, 2993; fram hâm, *from home,* 194; ät hâm, *at home,* 1249, 1924, 1157; gen. sg. hâmes, 2367; acc. pl. hâmas, 1128. — Comp. Finnes-hâm, 1157.

hâm-weorðung, st. f., *honor* or *ornament of home:* acc. sg. hâm- weorðunge (designation of the daughter of Hygelâc, given in marriage to Eofor), 2999.

hâr, adj., *gray:* nom. sg. hâr hilde- rinc, 1308, 3137; acc. sg. under (ofer) hârne stân, 888, 1416, 2554; hâre byrnan (i.e. iron shirt of mail), 2154; dat. sg. hârum hild- fruman, 1679; f. on heâre hæðe (on heaw . . . h . . . ðe, MS.), 2213; gen. sg. hâres, *of the old man,* 2989. — Comp. un-hâr.

hât, adj., *hot, glowing, flaming:* nom. sg., 1617, 2297, 2548, 2559, etc.; wyrm hât gemealt, *the drake hot* (of his own heat) *melted,* 898; acc. sg., 2282(?); inst. sg. hâtan heolfre, 850, 1424; g. sg. heaðu-fŷres hâtes, 2523; acc. pl. hâte heaðo-wylmas, 2820. — Sup.: hâtost heaðo-swâta, 1669.

hât, st. n., *heat, fire:* acc. sg. geseah his mondryhten . . . hât þrowian, *saw his lord endure the* (drake's) *heat,* 2606.

hata, w. m., *persecutor:* in comp. dæd-hata.

hâtan, st. v.: 1) *to bid, to order, to direct,* with acc. and inf., and acc. of the person : pres. sg. I. ic magu- þegnas mine hâte . . . flotan eôwer- ne ârum healdan, *I bid my thanes take good care of your craft,* 293; imp. sg. II. hât in gân . . . sibbe- gedriht, 386; pl. II. hâtað heaðo- nære hlæw gewyrcean, 2803; inf. þät healreced hâtan wolde . . . men gewyrcean, *that he wished to command men to build a hall-edi- fice,* 68. Pret. sg. hêht: hêht . . . eahta mearas . . . on flet teón, *gave command to bring eight horses into the hall,* 1036; þonne ænne hêht golde forgyldan, *commanded to make good that one with gold,* 1054; hêht þâ þät heaðo-weorc tô hagan biódan, *ordered the combat to be announced at the hedge*(?), 2893; swâ se snottra hêht, *as the wise* (Hróðgâr) *directed,* 1787; so, 1808, 1809. hêt : hêt him ŷðlidan gôdne gegyrwan, *ordered a good vessel to be prepared for him,* 198; so, hêt, 391, 1115, 3111. As the form of a wish: hêt hine wel brûcan, 1664; so, 2813; pret. part. þâ wäs hâten hraðe Heort innan-weard folmum gefrätwod, *forthwith was*

*ordered Heorot, adorned by hand on
the inside* i.e. that the edifice should
be adorned by hand on the inside,
992. — 2) *to name, to call:* pres.
subj. III pl. ʒät hit sǣ.'Vend . . .
hātan Biówu'fes biorh, *th it mari-
ners may call it Bēowulf's grave-
mound,* 2807; p.et. part. wǣs se
grimma gāst Grendel hā:en, 102;
so, 263, 373, 2003.
ge-hâtan, *to promise, to give one's
word, to vow, to threaten:* pres. sg.
I. ic hit þe gehâte, 1393; so, 1672;
pret. sg. he me mēde gehêt, *prom-
is'd me reward,* 2135; him fāgr-
gehêt leána ·gen. pl. ', *promised
them proper reward,* 2990; weán
oft gehêt earmre teohhe, *with woe
often threatened the unh ɪɣɣy band,*
2938; pret. pl. gehêton āt härg-
trafum wig-weorʃunga, *vowed of-
ferings at the shrines of the gods,*
175; þonne we gehêton ūssum
bʻɑʃ-rde þāt . . ., *when we prom-
ıs d our lord that . . .,* 2635; pret.
part. sɪó gehâtan ʼwǣ-] . . . gladum
suna Frʻɪdan, *b trothed to the glad
son of Froda,* 2025.
hâtor, st. m. n., *heat:* in comp.
anʻɪ-ɪ.ât·r.
hâft, adʻɪ., *held, bound, fettered·* nom.
sg., 2409 : acc. sg. heʻle hāftan,
hɪ ɪ fett.rıd'ɪ hell Grendel ,789.
hâft-mêce, st. m., *sword: ıth fett rs
or hɪɪɪɪ* cf. fetel-hllt : dat. sg.
þām hāʻ-mêce, 1458.
hûg-steald, st. m., *man, liegeman,
youth·* gen. pl. hāg-stealdra, 1890.
hâle, st. m., *man:* nom. sg., 1647,
1817, 3112; acc. sg. hāle, 720;
dat. pl. hælum hænum, MS. , 1984.
hâleʃ, st. m., *hero, fighter, warrior:
m ɪn:* nom. sg., 190, 331, 1070;
nom. pl. hāleʻ, 52, 2248, 2459,
3143; dat. pl. hāleʃum, 1710, 1962,

etc.; gen pl. hāleʃa, 467, 497,
612, 603, etc.
härg. See hearg.
hæʃ, st. f., *heath:* dat. sg. hæʃe,
2213.
hæʃen, adj., *heathenish:* acc. sg.
hæʃene sâwle, 853; dat. sg. hæʃ-
num horde, 2217; gen. sg. hæʻe-
nes, *of the heathen* (Grendel),987;
gen. pl. hæʃenra, 179.
hæʃ-stapa, w. m., *that which goes
a'out on the heath* (stag): nom.
sg., 1369
hæl, st. f.: 1 *health, welfare, luck:*
acc. sg. him hæl âbeád, 654; mid
hæle, 1218. — 2 *favorable sign,
favorable omen:* hæl sceáwedon,
o'erved favorable signs* (for Beó-
wulfʼs undertaking), 204.
hælo, st. f., *health, w lfare, luck:* acc.
sg. hælo âbeád heorʃ-geneátum,
2419. — Comp. un-hælo.
hæst (O.H.G. haisterâ hantl,
manu violenta; heist, ira; heis-
tig , iracunde , adj., *violent, vehe-
ment:* acc. sg. þurh hæstne hâd,
1336.
he, fem. heó, neut. hit, pers. pron.,
he, she, it; in the oblɪ jue caʂes
also reflexive, *himself, herself, itself:* acc. sg. hine, hi, hit; dat. sg.
him, hire, him; gen. sg. his, hire,
hit; plur. acc. nom. hl, hig, hie;
dat. lɪim; gen. hɪra, heora, hiera,
hi r·. — h e omitted before the
ver , 68, 300, 2309, 2345.
hebban, st. v., *to raɪʂ, to lift,* w.
acc.: inf. sɪʃʃan ic hond and rond
heʻɪ.n mihte, 657; pret. part. hafen, 1291; hâfen, 3024.
â-hebban, *to raise, to lift from, to
take away:* wǣs . . . icge gold âhafen of horde. *taken up from the
h ɑrd,* 1109; þâ wǣs . . . wôp up
âhafen, *a cry of distreʂs raiʂed,* 128.

ge-hegan (O.II.G. hagjan), w. v.,
to enclose, to fence : þing gehegan,
to mark off the court, hold court.
IIere figurative : inf. sceal ... âna
gehegan þing wið þyrse (*shall
alone decide the matter with Grendel*), 425.
hel, st. f., *hell :* nom. sg., 853; acc. sg.
helle, 179; dat. sg. helle, 101, 589;
(as instr.), 789; gen. sg. helle, 1275.
hel-bend, st. m. f., *bond of hell :* instr.
pl. hell-bendum fäst, 3073.
hel-rûna, w. m., *sorcerer :* nom. pl.
helrûnan, 163.
be-helan, st. v., *to conceal, to hide :*
pret. part. be-holen, 414.
helm, st. m.: 1) *protection in general, defence, covering that protects :*
acc. sg. on helm, 1393; under
helm, 1746. — 2) *helmet :* nom. sg.,
1630; acc. sg. helm, 673, 1023,
1527, 2988; (helo, MS.), 2724;
brûn-fâgne, gold-fâhne helm, 2616,
2812; dat. sg. under helme, 342,
404; gen. sg. helmes, 1031; acc.
pl. helmas, 240, 2639. — 3) *defence,
protector,* designation of the king:
nom. sg. helm Scyldinga (IIrôð-
gâr), 371, 456, 1322; acc. sg. heofena helm (*the defender of the
heavens* = God), 182; helm Scylfinga, 2382. — Comp.: grim-, gûð-,
heaðo-, niht-helm.
ofer-helmian, w. v. w. acc., *to cover over, to overhang :* pres. sg. III.
ofer-helmað, 1365.
helm-berend, pres. part., *helm-
wearing* (warrior) : acc. pl. helm-
berend, 2518, 2643.
helpan, st. v., *to help :* inf. þät him
holt-wudu helpan ne meahte, lind
wið lige, *that a wooden shield could
not help him, a linden shield
against flame,* 2341; þät him tren-
na ecge mihton helpan ät hilde,

2685; wutun gangan tô, helpan
hildfruman, *let us go thither to help
the battle-chief,* 2650; w. gen. ongan ... mæges helpan, *began to
help my kinsman,* 2880; so, pret.
g. þær he his mæges (MS. mägenes) healp, 2699.
help, helpe, f., *help, support :* in
strong form.: acc. sg. helpe, 551,
1553; dat. sg. tô helpe, 1831. In
weak form: acc. sg. helpan, 2449.
hende, adj., *-handed :* in comp. idel-
hende.
her, adv., *here,* 397, 1062, 1229,
1655, 1821, 2054, 2797, etc.; *hither,* 244, 361, 376.
here (Goth. harji-s), st. m., *army,
troops :* dat. sg. on herge, *in the
army, on a warlike expedition,*
1249; *in the army, among the
fighting men,* 2639; as instr. herge,
2348.—Comp.: flot-, scip-, sin-here.
here-brôga, w. m., *terror of the
army, fear of war :* dat. sg. for
here-brôgan, 462.
here-byrne, w. f., *battle-mail, coat
of mail :* nom. sg., 1444.
here-grîma, w. m., *battle-mask,* i.e.
helmet (with visor) : dat. sg. -gri-
man, 396, 2050, 2606,
here-net, st. n., *battle-net,* i.e. coat
of mail (of interlaced rings) : nom.
sg., 1554.
here-nið, st. m., *battle-enmity,* battle *of armies :* nom. sg., 2475.
here-pâd, st. f., *army-dress,* i.e. coat
of mail, armor : nom. sg., 2259.
here-rinc, st. m., *army-hero, hero
in battle, warrior :* acc. sg. here-
rinc (MS. here ric), 1177.
here-sceaft, st. m., *battle-shaft,* i.e.
spear : gen. pl. here-sceafta heáp,
335.
here-spêd, st. f., (*war-speed*), *luck
in war :* nom. sg., 64.

here-sträl, st. m., *war-arrow, missile:* nom. sg., 1436.

here-syrce, w. f., *battle-shirt, shirt of mail:* acc. sg. here-syrcan, 1512.

here-wǽd, st. f., *army-dress, coat of mail, armor:* dat. pl. (as instr.) here-wædum, 1898.

here-wǽsmu, w. m., *war-might, fierce strength in battle:* dat. pl. an here-wǽsmum, 678. — Leo.

here-wîsa, w. m., *leader of the army,* i.e. ruler, king: nom. sg., 3021.

herg, heurg, st. m., *image of a god, grove where a god was worshipped,* hence to the Christian a wicked place (?) : dat. pl. hergum ge-hea ˆerod, *confined in wicked places* (parallel with hell-bendum fäst), 3073.

herigean, w. v. w. dat. of pers., *to provide with an army, to support with an army:* pres. sg. I. ic þe wel herige, 1834. — Leo.

hete, st. m., *hate, enmity:* nom. sg. 142, 2555.—Comp.: ecg-, morðor-, wîg-hete.

hete-lic, adj., *hated:* nom. sg., 1268.

hetend, hettend, (pres. part. of hetan, see hatian), *enemy,* hostis: nom. pl. hetende, 1829 ; dat. pl. wið hettendum, 3005.

hete-nîð, st. m., *enmity full of hate:* acc. pl. hete-niðas, 152.

hete-sweng, st. m., *a blow from hate:* acc. pl. hete-swengeas, 2226.

hete-þanc, st. m., *hate-thought, a hostile design:* dat pl. mid his hete-þancum, 475.

hêdan, ge-hêdan, w. v. w. gen.: 1) *to protect:* pret. sg. ne hêdde he þäs heafolan, *did not protect his head,* 2698. — 2) *to obtain:* subj. pret. sg. III. gehêdde, 505.

hêrian, w. v. w. acc., *to praise, to commend;* with reference to God,

to adore: inf. heofena helm hêrian ne cûðon, *could not worship the defence of the heavens* (God), 182; ne hûru Hildeburh hêrian þorfte eotena treówe, *had no need to praise the fidelity of the Jutes,* 1072; pres. subj. þät mon his wine-dryhten wordum hêrge, 3177.

ge - heaðerian, w. v., *to force, to press in:* pret. part. ge-heaðerod, 3073.

heaðo-byrne, w. f., *battle-mail, shirt of mail:* nom. sg., 1553.

heaðo-deór, adj., *bold in battle, brave:* nom. sg., 689; dat. pl. heaðo-deórum, 773.

heaðo-fýr, st. n., *battle-fire, hostile fire:* gen. sg. heaðu-fýres, 2523; instr. pl. heaðo-fýrum, 2548, of the drake's fire-spewing.

heaðo-grim, adj., *grim in battle,* 548.

heaðo-helm, st. m., *battle-helmet, war-helmet:* nom. sg., 3157(?).

heaðo-lâc, st. n., *battle-play, battle:* dat. sg. ät heaðo-lâce, 584; gen. sg. heaðo-lâces hâl, 1975.

heaðo-mǽre, adj., *renowned in battle:* acc. pl. -mǽre, 2803.

heaðo-rǽs, st. m., *storm of battle, attack in battle, entrance by force:* nom. sg., 557; acc. pl. -rǽsas, 1048; gen. pl. -rǽsa, 526.

heaðo-reáf, st. n., *battle-dress, equipment for battle:* acc. sg. heaðo-reáf heóldon (*kept the equipments*), 401.

heaðo-rinc, st. m., *battle-hero, warrior:* acc. sg. þone heaðo-rinc (Hrêðel's son, Heðcyn), 2467; dat. pl. þǽm heaðo-rincum, 370.

heaðo-rôf, adj., *renowned in battle:* nom. sg., 381; nom. pl. heaðo-rôfe, 865.

heaðo-scearp, adj., *sharp in battle,*

bold: nom. pl. (-sccarde, MS.), 2830.

heaðo-seóc, adj., *battle-sick:* dat. sg. -siócum, 2755.

heaðo-steáp, adj., *high in battle, excelling in battle:* nom. sg. in weak form, heaðo-steápa, 1246; acc. sg. heaðo-steápne, 2154, both times of the helmet.

heaðo-swât, st. m., *blood of battle:* dat. sg. heaðo-swâte, 1607; as instr., 1461; gen. pl. hâtost heaðo-swâta, 1669.

heaðo-sweng, st. m., *battle-stroke* (blow of the sword): dat. sg. äfter heaðu-swenge, 2582.

heaðo-torht, adj., *loud, clear in battle:* nom. sg. stefn ... heaðo-torht, *the voice clear in battle,* 2554.

heaðo-wæd, st. f., *battle-dress, coat of mail, armor:* instr. pl. heaðo-wædum, 39.

heaðo-weorc, st. n., *battle-work, battle:* acc. sg., 2893.

heaðo-wylm, st. m., *hostile (flame-) wave:* acc. pl. hâte heaðo-wylmas, 2820; gen. pl. heaðo-wylma, 82.

heaf, st. n., *sea:* acc. pl. ofer heafo, 2478.

heafola. See hafela.

heal, st. f., *hall, main apartment, large building* (consisting of an assembly-hall and a banqueting-hall): nom. sg. heal, 1152, 1215; heall, 487; acc. sg. healle, 1088; dat. sg. healle, 89, 615, 643, 664, 926, 1010, 1027, etc.; gen. sg. [healle], 389.—Comp.: gif-, meodo-heal.

heal-ärn, st. n., *hall-building, hall-house:* gen. sg. heal-ärna, 78.

heal-gamen, st. n., *social enjoyment in the hall, hall-joy:* nom. sg., 1067.

heal-reced, st. n., *hall-building:* acc. sg., 68.

heal-sittend, pres. part., *sitting in the hall* (at the banquet): dat. pl. heal-sittendum, 2869; gen. pl. heal-sittendra, 2016.

heal-þegn, st. m., *hall-thane,* i.e. a warrior who holds the hall: gen. sg. heal-þegnes, of Grendel, 142; acc. pl. heal-þegnas, of Beówulf's band, 720.

heal-wudu, *hall-wood,* i.e. hall built of wood: nom. sg., 1318.

healdan, st. v. w. acc.: 1) *to hold, to hold fast; to support:* pret. pl. hû | â stânbogan ... êce corðreced innan heúldon (MS. healde), *how the arches of rock within held the everlasting earth-house,* 2720. Pret. sg., with a person as object: heóld hine tô fäste, *held him too fast,* 789; w. the dat. he hinr freóndlârum heóld, *supported him with friendly advice,* 2378. — 2) *to hold, to watch, to preserve, to keep;* reflexive, *to maintain one's self, to keep one's self:* pres. sg. II. eal þu hit gebyldum healdest, mägen mid môdes snyttrum, *all that preservest thou continuously, strength and wisdom of mind,* 1706; III. healdeð hige-mêðum heáfod-wearde, *holds for the dead the head-watch,* 2910; imp. sg. II. heald forð tela niwe sibbe, *keep well, from now on, the new relationship,* 949; heald (heold, MS.) þu nu hruse ... eorla æhte, *preserve thou now, Earth, the noble men's possessions,* 2248; inf. se þe holmclifu healdan scolde, *watch the sea-cliffs,* 230; so, 705; nacan ... ârum healdan, *to keep well your vessel,* 296; wearde healdan, 319; forlêton eorla gestreón eorðan healdan, 3108; pres. part. dreám heal-

dende, *holding rejoicing* (i.e. thou
who art rejoicing), 1228; pret. sg.
heóld hine syððan fyr and fástor,
*hept himself afterwards afar and
more secure*, 142; ægwearde heóld,
*I have (hitherto) kept watch on
the sea*, 241; so, 305; hióld heáh-
lufan wið hâleða brego, *preserved
high love*, 1955; ginfástan gife ...
heóld, 2184; gold-mâðmas heóld,
took care of the treasures of gold,
2415; heóld min tela, *protected well
mine own*, 2738; þonne ... sceft ...
nytte heóld, *had employment, was
employed*, 3119; heóld mec, *protected*, i.e. brought me up, 2431; pret.
pl. heaðo-reáf heóldon, *watched
over the armor*, 401; sg. for pl.
heáfodbeorge ... walan ûtan heóld,
*outwards, bosses kept guard over the
head*, 1032.—Related to the preceding meaning are the two following:
3) *to rule and protect the father-
land:* inf. gif þu healdan wylt maga
rîce, 1853; pret. heóld, 57, 2738.—
4) *to hold, to have, to possess, to inhabit:* inf. lêt þone brego-stôl Beówulf healdan, 2390; gerund. tô
healdanne hleóburh wera, 1732;
pret. sg. heóld, 103, 161, 466, 1749,
2752; lyftwynne heóld nihtes hwîlum, *at night-time had the enjoyment of the air*, 3044; pret. pl.
Geáta leóde hreâwîc heóldon, *the
Gedtas held the place of corpses*
(lay dead upon it), 1215; pret. sg.
þær heó ær mæste heóld worolde
wynne, *in which she formerly possessed the highest earthly joy*, 1080.
— 5) *to win, to receive:* pret. pl. I.
heóld on heáh gesceap, *we received
a heavy fate, heavy fate befell us*,
3085.

be-healdan, w. acc.: 1) *to take
care of, to attend to:* pret. sg. þegn

nytte beheóld, *a thane discharged
the office*, 494; so, 668.—2) *to hold:*
pret. sg. se þe flôda begong ...
beheóld, 1499. — 3) *to look at, to
behold:* þrýðswyð beheóld mæg
Higelâces hû ..., *great woe saw
II.'s kinsman, how ...*, 737.

for-healdan, w. acc., (*to hold bad-
ly*), *to fall away from, to rebel:*
pret. part. häfdon hy forhealden
helm Scylfinga, *had rebelled against
the defender of the Scylfings*, 2382.

ge-healdan: 1) *to hold, to receive,
to hold fast:* pres. sg. III. se þe
waldendes hyido gehealdeð, *who
receives the Lord's grace*, 2294;
pres. subj. fäder alwalda ... eówic
gehealde sîða gesunde, *keep you
sound on your journey*, 317; inf.
ne meahte he ... on þam frum-
gâre feorh gehealdan, *could not
hold back the life in his lord*,
2857. — 2) *to take care, to preserve, to watch over; to stop:* imp.
sg. hafa nu and geheald hûsa sêlest, 659; inf. gehealdan hêt bilde-
geatwe, 675; pret. sg. he frätwe
geheóld fela missera, 2621; þone
þe ær geheóld wið hettendum hord
and rîce, *him who before preserved
treasure and realm*, 3004. — 3) *to
rule:* inf. folc gehealdan, 912;
pret. sg. geheóld tela (brâde rîce),
2209.

healf, st. f., *half, side, part:* acc. sg.
on þâ healfe, *towards this side*,
1676; dat. sg. häleðum be healfe,
at the heroes' side, 2263; acc. pl.
on twâ healfa, *upon two sides, mutually*, 1096; on þâ healfa (healfe),
on both sides (to Grendel and his
mother), 1306; *on two sides, on
both sides*, 2064; gen. pl. on healfa
gehwone, *in half, through the
middle*, 801.

healf, adj., *half:* gen. sg. healfre, 1088.

heals, st. m., *neck:* acc. sg. heals, 2692; dat. sg. wið halse, 1567; be healse, 1873. — Comp.: the adjectives fānig-, wunden-heals.

heals-beáh, st. m., *neck-ring, collar:* acc. sg. þone heals-beáh, 2173; gen. pl. heals-beága, 1196.

heals-gebedda, w. m., *beloved bed-fellow, wife:* nom. sg. healsgebedda (MS. healsgebedda), 63.

healsian, w. v. w. acc., *to entreat earnestly, to implore:* pret. sg. þá se þeóden mec ... healsode hreóhmōd Iät ..., *entreated me sorrowful, that* ..., 2133.

heard, adj.: 1) of persons, *able, efficient in war, strong, brave:* nom. sg. heard, 342, 376, 404, 1575, 2540, etc.; in weak form, se hearda, 401, 1964; se hearda Jegn, 2978; þes hearda heáp, 432; nom. pl. hearde hilde-frecan, 2206; gen. pl. heardra, 989. Comparative: acc. sg. heardran häle, 720. With accompanying gen.: wíges heard, *strong in battle,* 887; dat. sg. niða heardum, 2171. — 2) of the implements of war, *good, firm, sharp, hard:* nom. sg. (gūð-byrne, lic-syrce) heard, 322, 551. In weak form: masc. here-strāl hearda, 1436; se hearda helm, 2256; neutr. here-net hearde, 1554; acc. sg. (swurd, wæpen), heard, 540, 2688, 2988; nom. pl. hearde ... homera láfe, 2830; heard and hring-mæl Heaðobeardna gestreón, 2038; acc. pl. heard sweord, 2639. Of other things, *hard, rough, harsh, hard to bear:* nom. sg. hreðer-bealo hearde, 1344; wrôht ... heard, 2915; here-nið hearda, 2475; acc. sg. heoro-sweng -heardne, 1591;

instr. sg. heardan ceápe, 2483; instr. pl. heardan, heardum clammum, 964, 1336; gen. pl. heardra hÿnða, 166. Compar.: acc. sg. heardran feohtan, 576. — Comp.: fŷr-, iren-, níð-, regen-, scûr-heard.

hearde, adv., *hard, very,* 1439.

heard-ecg, st. f., *sharp sword, sword good in battle:* nom. sg., 1289.

heard-fyrde, adj., *hard to take away, heavy:* acc. sg. hard-fyrdne, 2246. — Leo.

heard-hycgend, pres. part., *of a warlike disposition, brave:* nom. pl. -hicgende, 394, 800.

hearg-träf, st. n., *tent of the gods, temple:* dat. pl. ät härg-trafum (MS. hrærg trafum), 175.

hearm, st. m., *harm, injury, insult:* dat. sg. mid hearme, 1893.

hearm-sceaða, w. m., *enemy causing injury* or *grief:* nom. sg. hearm-scaða, 767.

hearpe, w. f., *harp:* gen. sg. hearpan swēg, 89, 3024; hearpan wynne (wyn), 2108, 2263.

heáðu, st. f., *sea, waves:* acc. sg. heáðu, 1863.

heáðu-liðend, pres. part., *sea-farer, sailor:* nom. pl. -liðende, 1799; dat. pl. -liðendum (designation of the Geátas), 2956.

heáfod, st. n., *head:* acc. sg., 48, 1640; dat. sg. heáfde, 1591, 2291, 2974; dat. pl. heáfdum, 1243.

heáfod-beorh, st. f., *head-defence, protection for the head:* acc. sg. heáfod-beorge, 1031.

heáfod-mæg, st. m., *head-kinsman, near blood-relative:* dat. pl. heáfod-mægum (*brothers*), 589; gen. pl. heáfod-mága, 2152.

heáfod-segn, st. n., *head-sign, banner:* acc. sg., 2153.

heáfod-weard, st. f., *head-watch:*

acc. sg. healdeð ... heáfod-wearde leófes and láðes, *for the friend and the foe* (Beówulf and the drake, who lie dead near each other), 2910.

heáh, heá, adj., *high, noble* (in composition, also primus): nom. sg. heáh Healfdene, 57; heá (Higelác), 1927; heáh (sele), 82; heáh hlæw, 2806, 3159; acc. sg. heáh (segn), 48, 2769; heáhne (MS. heánne) hróf, 984; dat. sg. in (tó) sele þam heáþ, 714, 920; gen. sg. heán húses, 116.—*high, heavy:* acc. heáh gesceap (*an unusual, heavy fate*), 3085.

heá-burh, st. f., *high city, first city of a country:* acc. sg., 1128.

heáh-cyning, st. m., *high king, mightiest of the kings:* gen. sg. -cyninges (of Hróðgár), 1040.

heáh-gestreón, st. n., *splendid treasure:* gen. pl. -gestreóna, 2303.

heáh-lufe, w. f., *high love:* acc. sg. heáh-lufan, 1955.

heáh-sele, st. m., *high hall, first hall in the land, hall of the ruler:* dat. sg. heáh-sele, 648.

heáh-setl, st. n., *high seat, throne:* acc. sg., 1088.

heáh-stede, st. m., *high place, ruler's place:* dat. sg. on heáh-stede, 285.

heán, adj., *depressed, low, despised, miserable:* nom. sg., 1275, 2100, 2184, 2409.

heáp, st. m., *heap, crowd, troop:* nom. sg. þegna heáp, 400; þes hearda heáp, *this brave band*, 432; acc. sg. here-sceafta heáp, *the crowd of spears*, 335; mago-rinca heáp, 731; dat. sg. on heápe, *in a compact body*, as many as there were of them, 2597.— Comp. wíg-heáp.

heáwan, st. v., *to hew, to cleave:* inf., 801.

ge-heáwan, *cleave:* pres. subj. ge-heáwe, 683.

heoðu, st. f., *the interior of a building:* dat. sg. þät he on heoðe gestód, *in the interior* (of the hall, Heorot), 404.

heofon, st. m., *heaven:* nom. sg., 3157; dat. sg. hefene, 1572; gen. sg. heofenes, 414, 576, 1802, etc.; gen. pl. heofena, 182; dat. pl. under heofenum, 52, 505.

heolfor, st. n., *putrid* or *festering blood:* dat. instr. sg. hátan heolfre, 850, 1424; heolfre, 2139; under heolfre, 1303.

heolster, st. n., *haunt, hiding-place:* acc. sg. on heolster, 756.

heonan, adv., *hence, from here:* heonan, 252; heonon, 1362.

heor, st. m., *door-hinge:* nom. pl. heorras, 1000.

heorde, adj. See wunden-heorde.

heorð-geneát, st. m., *hearth-companion*, i.e. a vassal of the king, in whose castle he receives his livelihood: nom. pl. heorð-geneátas, 261, 3181; acc. pl. heorð-geneátas, 1581, 2181; dat. pl. heorð-geneátum, 2419.

heorot, st. m., *stag:* nom. sg., 1370.

heorte, w. f., *heart:* nom. sg., 2562; dat. sg. ät heortan, 2271; gen. sg. heortan, 2464, 2508. — Comp.: the adjectives blíð-, grom-, rúm-, stare-heort.

heoru, st. m., *sword:* nom. sg. heoru bunden (cf. under bladun), 1286. In some of the following compounds heoro- seems to be confounded with here- (see here).

heoro-blác, adj., *pale through the sword, fatally wounded:* nom. sg. [heoro-]blác, 2489.

heoru-dreór, st. m., *sword-blood:* instr. sg. heoru-dreóre,487; heoro-dreore, 850.

heoro-dreórig, adj., *bloody through the sword:* nom. sg., 936; acc. sg. heoro-dreórigne, 1781, 2721.

heoro-dryne, st. m., *sword-drink,* i.e. blood shed by the sword: instr. pl. hioro-dryncum swealt, *died through sword-drink,* i.e. struck by the sword, 2359.

heoro-gifre, adj., *eager for hostile inroads:* nom. sg., 1499.

heoro-grim, adj., *sword-grim, fierce in battle:* nom. sg. m., 1565; fem. -grimme, 1848.

heoro-hócihte, adj., *provided with barbs, sharp like swords:* instr. pl. mid eofer-spreótum heoro-hócyh-tum, 1439.

heoro-seree, w. f., *shirt of mail:* acc. sg. hioro-sereean, 2540.

heoro-sweng, st. m., *sword-stroke:* acc. sg. 1591.

heoro-weallende, pres. part., *rolling around fighting,* of the drake, 2782. See **weallan.**

heoro-wearh, st. m., *he who is sword-cursed, who is destined to die by the sword:* nom. sg., 1268.

heófan, w. v., *to lament, to moan:* part. nom. pl. hiófende, 3143.

â-heóran, *to free* (?): w. acc. pret. sg. brýd âheórde, 2931.

heóre, adj., *pleasant, not haunted, secure:* nom. sg. fem. nis þät heóru stôw, *that is no secure place,* 1373. — Comp. un-heóre (-hýre).

hider, adv., *hither,* 240, 370, 394, 3093, etc.

ofer-higian, w. v. (according to the connection, probably), *to exceed,* 2767. (O.H.G. ubar-hugjan, *to be arrogant.*)

hild, st. f., *battle, combat:* nom. sg.,

452, 902, 1482, 2077; hild heoru-grimme, 1848; acc. sg. hilde, 648; instr. sg. hilde, *through the combat,* 2917; dat. sg. ät hilde, 1461.

hilde-bil, st. n., *battle-sword:* nom. sg., 1667; instr. dat. sg. hilde-bille, 557, 1521.

hilde-bord, st. n., *battle-shield:* acc. pl. hilde-bord, 397; instr. pl. -bordum, 3140.

hilde-cyst, st. f., *excellence in battle, bravery in battle:* instr. pl. -cystum, 2599.

hilde-deór, adj., *bold in battle, brave in battle:* nom. sg., 312, 835, 1647, 1817; hilde-diór, 3112; nom. pl. hilde-deóre, 3171.

hilde-freea, w. m., *hero in battle:* nom. pl. hilde-freean, 2206; dat. sg. hild-freean, 2367.

hilde-geatwe, st. f. pl., *equipment for battle, adornment for combat:* acc. hilde-geatwe, 675; gen. -geat-wa, 2363.

hilde-gicel, st. m., *battle-icicle,* i.e. the blood which hangs upon the sword-blades like icicles: instr. pl. hilde-gicelum, 1607.

hilde-gráp, st. f., *battle-gripe:* nom. sg., 1447, 2508.

hilde-hlemma, w. m., *one raging in battle, warrior, fighter:* nom. sg., 2352, 2545; dat. pl. eft þät ge-eode . . . hilde-hlämmum, *it happened to the warriors* (the Geátas), 2202.

hilde-leóma, w. m., *battle-light, gleam of battle,* hence: 1) the fire-spewing of the drake in the fight: nom. pl. -leóman, 2584. — 2) *the gleaming sword:* acc. sg. -leóman, 1144.

hilde-meeg, st. m., *man of battle, warrior:* nom. pl. hilde-meegas, 800.

hilde-mêce, st. m., *battle-sword:* nom. pl. -mêceas, 2203.

hilde-rand, st. m., *battle-shield:* acc. pl. -randas, 1243.

hilde-ræs, st. m., *storm of battle:* acc. sg., 300.

hilde-rinc, st. m., *man of battle, warrior, hero:* nom. sg., 1308, 3125, 3137; dat. sg. hilde-rince, 1496; gen. sg. hilde-rinces, 987.

hilde-säd, adj., *satiated with battle, not wishing to fight any more:* acc. sg. hilde-sädne, 2724.

hilde-secorp, st. n., *battle-dress, armor, coat of mail:* acc. sg., 2156.

hilde-setl, st. n., *battle-seat* (saddle): nom. sg., 1040.

hilde-strengo, st. f., *battle-strength, bravery in battle:* acc., 2114.

hilde-swât, st. m., *battle-sweat:* nom. sg. hât hilde-swât (the hot, damp breath of the drake as he rushes on), 2559.

hilde-tux, st. m., *battle-tooth:* instr. pl. hilde-tuxum, 1512.

hilde-wæpen, st. m., *battle-weapon:* instr. pl. -wæpnum, 39.

hilde-wîsa, w. m., *leader in battle, general:* dat. sg. fore Healfdenes hildewîsan, *of Healfdene's general* (Hnäf), 1065.

hild-freca. See hilde-freca.

hild-fruma, st. m., *battle-chief:* dat. sg. -fruma, 1679, 2650; gen. sg. þäs hild-fruman, 2836.

hild-lata, w. m., *he who is late in battle, coward:* nom. pl. þâ hild-latan, 2847.

hilt, st. n., *sword-hilt:* nom. sg. gylden hilt, 1678; acc. sg. þ ât hilt, 1669; hylt, 1668. Also used in the plural; acc. þâ hilt, 1615; dat. pl. be hiltum, 1575. — Comp.: fetel-, wreoðen-hilt.

hilte-cumbor, st. n., *banner with a staff:* acc. sg., 1023.

hilted, pret. part., *provided with a hilt* or *handle:* acc. sg. heard swyrd hilted, *sword with a (rich) hilt,* 2988.

hin-fûs, adj., *ready to die:* nom. sg. hyge wäs him hinfûs (i.e. he felt that he should not survive), 756.

hindema, adj. superl., *hindmost, last:* instr. sg. hindeman sîðe, *the last time, for the last time,* 2050, 2518.

hirde, hyrde, st. m., *(herd) keeper, guardian, possessor:* nom. sg. folces hyrde, 611, 1833, 2982; rîces hyrde, 2028; fyrena hyrde, *the guardian of mischief, wicked one,* 751, 2220; wuldres hyrde, *the king of glory,* God, 932; hringa hyrde, *the keeper of the rings,* 2246; cumbles hyrde, *the possessor of the banner, the bearer of the banner,* 2506; folces hyrde, 1850; frætwa hyrde, 3134; rîces hyrde, 3081; acc. pl. hûses hyrdas, 1667. — Comp.: grund-hyrde.

hît (O.N. hita), st. f.(?), *heat:* nom. sg. þenden hyt sŷ, 2650.

hladan, st. v.: 1) *to load, to lay:* inf. on bæl hladan leófne mannan, *lay the dear man on the funeral-pile,* 2127; him on bearm hladan bunan and discas, *laid cups and plates upon his bosom, loaded himself with them,* 2776; pret. part. þær wäs wunden gold on wæn hladen, *laid upon the wain,* 3135. — 2) *to load, to burden:* pret. part. þâ wäs ... sægeáp naca hladen herewædum, *loaded with armor,* 1898. — Comp. gilp-hläden.

ge-hladan, w. acc., *to load, to burden:* pret. sg. sæbât gehlôd (MS. gehleod), 896.

hláford, st. m., *lord, ruler:* nom. sg., 2376; acc. sg., 267; dat. sg. hláforde, 2635; gen. sg. hláfordes, 3181. — Comp. eald-hláford.

hláford-leás, adj., *without a lord:* nom. pl. hláford-leáse, 2936.

hláw, hlæw, st. m., *hill, grave-hill:* acc. sg. hlæw, 2803, 3159, 3171; dat. sg. for hláwe, 1121. Also, *grave-chamber* (the interior of the grave-hill), *cave:* acc. sg. hláw [under] hrusan, 2277; hlæw under hrusan, 2412; dat. sg. on hlæwe, 2774. The drake dwells in the rocky cavern which the former owner of his treasure had chosen as his burial-place, 2242–2271.

hläst, st. n., *burden, load:* dat. sg. hläste, 52.

hlem, st. m., *noise, din of battle, noisy attack:* in the compounds, uht-, wäl-hlem.

hlemma, w. m., *one raging, one who calls;* see hilde-hlemma.

â-hlehhan, st. v., *to laugh aloud, to shout, to exult:* pret. sg. his môd âhlôg, *his mood exulted,* 731.

hleahtor, st. m., *laughter:* nom. sg., 612; acc. sg., 3021.

hleápan, st. v., *to run, to trot, to spring:* inf. hleápan lêton . . . fealwe mearas, 865.

â-hleapan, *to spring up:* pret. âhleóp, 1398.

hleoðu. See hliðÞ.

hleonian, w. v., *to incline, to hang over:* inf. oð ðät he . . . fyrgenbeámas ofer hârne stân hleonian funde, *till he found mountain-trees hanging over the gray rocks,* 1416.

hleó, st. m., *shady, protected place; defence, shelter;* figurative designation of the king, or of powerful nobles: wîgendra hleó, of Hroðgâr, 429; of Sigemund, 900; of

Beówulf, 1973, 2338; eorla hleó, of Hroðgâr, 1036, 1867; of Beówulf, 792; of Hygelâc, 2191.

hleó-burh, st. f., *ruler's castle or city:* acc. sg., 913, 1732.

hleóðor-cwyde, st. m., *speech of solemn sound, ceremonious words,* 1980.

hleór, st. n., *cheek, jaw:* in comp. fäted-hleór (adj.).

hleór-bera, w. m., *cheek-bearer,* the part of the helmet that reaches down over the cheek and protects it: acc. pl. ofer hleór-beran (*visor?*), 304.

hleór-bolster, st. m., *cheek-bolster, pillow:* nom. sg., 689.

hleótan, st. v. w. acc., *to obtain by lot, to attain, to get:* pret. sg. feorhwunde hleát, 2386.

hlifian, w. v., *to rise, to be prominent:* inf. hlifian, 2806; pret. hlifade, 81, 1800, 1899.

hliðÞ, st. n., *cliff, precipice of a mountain:* dat. sg. on hliðe, 3159; gen. sg. hliðes, 1893; pl. hliðu in composition, stân-hliðu; hleoðu in the compounds fen-, mist-, näs-, wulf-hleoðu.

hlin-bed (Frisian hlen-bed, Richthofen 206²³, for which another text has cronk-bed), st. n., κλινίδιον, *bed for reclining, sick-bed:* acc. sg. hlin-bed, 3035.

tô-hlídan, st. v., *to spring apart, to burst:* pret. part. nom. pl. tô-hlidene, 1000.

hlûd, adj., *loud:* acc. sg. dreám . . . hlûdne, 89.

hlyn, st. m., *din, noise, clatter:* nom. sg., 612.

hlynnan, hlynian, w. v., *to sound, to resound:* inf. hlynnan (of the voice), 2554; of fire, *to crackle:* pret. sg. hlynode, 1121.

hlynslan, w. v., *to resound, to crash:* pret. sg. reced hlynsode, 771.

hlytm, st. m., *lot:* dat. sg. näs þâ on hlytme, hwâ þät hord strude, *it did not depend upon lot who should plunder the hoard,* i.e. its possession was decided, 3127.

hnâh, adj.: 1) *low, inferior:* comp. acc. sg. hnâgran, 678; dat. sg. hnâhran rince, *an inferior hero, one less brave,* 953. — 2) *familiarly intimate:* nom. sg. näs hió hnâh swâ þeáh, *was nevertheless not familiarly intimate* (with the Geátas, i.e. preserved her royal dignity towards them), (*niggardly?*), 1930.

huægan, w. v. w. acc., (for nægan), *to speak to, to greet:* pret. sg. þät he þone wîsan wordum hnægde freán Ingwina, 1319.

ge-huægan, w. acc., *to bend, to humiliate, to strike down, to fell:* pret. sg. ge-hnægde helle gâst, 1275; þær hyne Hetware hilde gehnægdon, 2917.

hnîtan, st. v., *to dash against, to encounter,* here of the collision of hostile bands: pret. pl. þonne hniton (hnitan) fêðan, 1328, 2545.

hoðma, w. m., *place of concealment, cave,* hence, *the grave:* dat. sg. in hoðman, 2459.

hof, st. n., *enclosed space, court-yard, estate, manor-house:* acc. sg. hof (Hrô gâr's residence), 312; dat. sg. tô hofe sînum (Grendel's home in the sea), 1508; tô hofe Hygelâc's residence), 1975; acc. pl. beorht hofu, 2314; dat. pl. tô hofum Geáta, 1837.

hogode. See **hycgan.**

hold, adj., *inclined to, attached to, gracious, dear, true:* nom. sg. w. dat. of the person, hold weorud

freán Scyldinga, *a band well disposed to the lord of the Scyldings,* 290; mandrihtne hold, 1230; Hygelâce wäs . . . nefa swýðe hold, *to H. was his nephew* (Beówulf) *very much attached,* 2171; acc. sg. þurh holdne hige, *from a kindly feeling, with honorable mind,* 267; holdne wine, 376; holdne, 1980; gen. pl. holdra, 487.

hold. See **healdan.**

holm, st. m., *deep sea:* nom. sg., 519, 1132, 2139; acc. sg., 48, 633; dat. sg. holme, 543, 1436, 1915; acc. pl. holmas, 240. — Comp. wæg-holm.

holm-clif, st. n., *sea-cliff:* dat. sg. on þam holm-clife, 1422; from þäm holmclife, 1636; acc. pl. holmclifu, 230.

holm-wylm, st. m., *the waves of the sea:* dat. sg. holm-wylme, 2412.

holt, st. n., *wood, thicket, forest:* acc. sg. on holt, 2599; holt, 2847. — Comp.: äsc-, fyrgen-, gâr-, Hrefnes-holt.

holt-wudu, st. m., *forest-wood:* 1) of the material: nom. sg., 2341. — 2) = *forest:* acc. sg., 1370.

hord, st. m. and n., *hoard, treasure:* nom. sg., 2284, 3085; beága hord, 2285; mâðma hord, 3012; acc. sg. hord, 913, 2213, 2320, 2510, 2745, 2774, 2956, 3057; sâwle hord, 2423; þät hord, 3127; dat. sg. of horde, 1109; for horde, *on account of* (the robbing of) *the hoard,* 2782; hæðnum horde, 2217; gen. sg. hordes, 888. — Comp.: beáh-, breóst-, word-, wyrmhord.

hord-ärn, st. n., *place in which a treasure is kept, treasure-room:* dat. hord-ärne, 2832; gen. pl. hordärna, 2280.

hord-burh, st. f., *city in which is*

the treasure (of the king's), *ruler's castle:* acc. sg., 467.

hord-gestreón, st. n., *hoard-treasure, precious treasure:* dat. pl. hord-gestreónum, 1900; gen. pl. mägen-byrðenne hord-gestreóna, *the great burden of rich treasures,* 3093.

hord-máððum, st. m., *treasure-jewel, precious jewel:* acc. sg. (-madmum, MS.), 1199.

hord-wela, w. m., *treasure-riches, abundance of treasures:* acc. sg. hord-welan, 2345.

hord-weard, st. m., *warder of the treasure, hoard-warden:* 1) of the king: nom. sg., 1048; acc. sg., 1853. — 2) of the drake: nom. sg., 2294, 2303, 2555, 2594.

hord-weorðung, st. f., *ornament out of the treasure, rich ornament:* acc. sg. -weorðunge, 953.

hord-wyn, st. f., *treasure-joy, joy-giving treasure:* acc. sg. hord-wynne, 2271.

horn, st. n., *horn:* 1) upon an animal: instr. pl. heorot hornum trum, 1370. — 2) wind-instrument: nom. sg., 1424; acc. sg., 2944.—Comp. gúð-horn.

horn-boga, w. m., *bow made of horn:* dat. sg. of horn-bogan, 2438.

horn-geáp, adj., of great extent between the (stag-)horns adorning the gables(?): nom. sg. sele ... heáh and horn-geáp, 82.

horn-reced, st. n., building whose two gables are crowned by the halves of a stag's antler(?): acc. sg., 705. Cf. Heyne's Treatise on the Hall, Heorot, p. 44.

hors, st. n., *horse:* nom. sg., 1400.

hóciht, adj., *provided with hooks, hooked:* in comp. heoro-hóciht.

be-**hófian**, w. v. w. gen., *to need, to want:* pres. sg. III. nu is se däg cumen þät úre man-dryhten mägenes behófað gódra gúðrinca, *now is the day come when our lord needs the might of strong warriors,* 2648.

on-**hóhsnian**, w. v., *to hinder:* pret. sg. þät onhóhsnode Heminges mäg (on hohsnod, MS.), 1945.

hólinga, adv., *in vain, without reason,* 1077.

be-**hón**, st. v., *to hang with:* pret. part. helmum behongen, 3140.

hóp, st. n., *protected place, place of refuge, place of concealment,* in the compounds fen-, mór-hóp.

hós (Goth. hansa), st. f., *accompanying troop, escort:* instr. sg. mägða hóse, *with an accompanying train of servingwomen,* 925.

hraðe, adv., *hastily, quickly, immediately,* 224, 741, 749, 1391, etc.; hräðe, 1438; hreðe, 992; compar. hraðor, 543.

hran-fix, st. m., *whale:* acc. pl. hron-fixas, 540.

hran-rád, st. f., *whale-road,* i.e. sea: dat. sg. ofer hron-ráde, 10.

hrá, st. n., *corpse:* nom. sg., 1589.

hrá-fyl, st. m., *fall of corpses, killing, slaughter:* acc. sg., 277.

hrädlíce, adv., *hasty, quick, immediate,* 356, 964.

hräfn, **hrefn**, st. m., *raven:* nom. sg. hrefn blaca, *black raven,* 1802; se wonna hrefn, *the dark raven,* 3025; dat. sg. hrefne, 2449.

hrägl, st. n., *dress, garment, armor:* nom. sg., 1196; gen. sg., hrägles, 1218; gen. pl. hrägla, 454. — Comp.: beado-, fyrd-, mere-hrägl.

hreðe. See **hraðe**.

hreðer, st. m., *breast, bosom* · nom. sg. hreðer inne weóll (*it surged in* *his breast*), 2114; hreðer æðme weóll, 2594; dat. sg. in hreðre, 1152; of hreðre, 2820. — *Breast as the seat of feeling, heart:* dat. sg. Jät wäs ... hreðre hygemêðe, *that was depressing to the heart* (of the slayer, Hæðcyn), 2443; on hreðre, 1879, 2329; gen. pl. þurh hreðra gehygd, 2046. — *Breast as seat of life:* instr. sg. hreðre, parallel with aldre, 1447.

hreðer-bealo, st. n., *evil that takes hold on the heart, evil severely felt:* acc. sg., 1344.

hrefn. See **hräfn.**

hrêð, st. f., *glory;* in composition, gûð-hrêð; *renown, assurance of victory,* in sige-hrêð.

hrêðe, adj., *renowned in battle:* nom. sg. hrêð (on account of the following ät, final *e* is elided, as wên ic for wêne ic, 442; frôfor and fultum' for frôfre and fultum, 699; firen ondrysne for firene ondr., 1933), 2576.

hrêð-sigor, st. m., *glorious victory:* dat. sg. hrêð-sigora, 2584.

hrêmig, adj., *boasting, exulting:* with instr. and gen. hûðe hrêmig, 124; since hrêmig, 1883; frätwum hrêmig, 2055 : nom. pl. nealles Hetware hrêmge þorfton (sc. wesan) fêðe-wîges, 2365.

on-hrêran, w. v., *to excite, to stir up:* pret. part. on-hrêred, 549, 2555.

hreâ-wîc, st. n., *place of corpses:* acc. sg. Geáta leóde hreâ-wîc heóldon, *held the place of corpses,* 1215.

hreâd, st. f., *ornament*(?), in comp. earm-hreâd. See **hreóðan.**

hreâm, st. m., *noise, alarm:* nom. sg., 1303.

hreóða, w. m., *cover,* in the compound bord-hreóða.

hreóðan, ge-hreóðan, st. v., *to cover, to clothe;* only in the pret. part. hroden, gehroden, *dressed, adorned:* hroden, 495, 1023; þâ wäs heal hroden feónda feorum, *then was the hall covered with the corpses of the enemy,* 1152; gehroden golde, *adorned with gold,* 304. — Comp.: beág-, gold-hroden.

hreóh, hreów, hreó, adj., *excited, stormy, wild, angry, raging; sad, troubled:* nom. sg. (Beówulf) hreóh and heoro-grim, 1565; Jät þam gôdan wäs hreów on hreðre, (*that came with violence upon him, pained his heart*), 2329; hreó wæron ýða, *the waves were angry, the sea stormy,* 548; näs him hreóh sefa, *his mind was not cruel,* 2181; dat. sg. on hreón môde, *of sad heart,* 1308; on hreóum môde, *angry at heart,* 2582.

hreóh-môd, adj., *of sad heart,* 2133; *angry at heart,* 2297.

hreósan, st. v., *to fall, to sink, to rush:* pret. hreás, 2489, 2832; pret. pl. hruron, 1075; hie on weg hruron, *they rushed away,* 1431; hruron him teáras, *tears burst from him,* 1873.

be-hreósan, *to fall from, to be divested of:* pret. part. acc. pl. fyrnmanna fatu ... hyrstum behrorene, *divested of ornaments* (from which the ornaments had fallen away), 2760.

hreów, st. f., *distress, sorrow:* gen. pl. þät wäs Hrôðgâre hreówa tornost, *that was to Hrôðgâr the bitterest of his sorrows,* 2130.

hring, st. m.: 1) *ring:* acc. sg. þone hring, 1203; hring gyldenne, 2810; acc. pl. hringas, 1196, 1971, 3035; gen. pl. l ringa, 1508, 2246. - 2) *shirt of mail* (of interlaced rings) : nom.

sg. hring, 1504; byrnan hring, 2261. — Comp. bân-hring.

hriugan, w. v., *to give forth a sound, to ring, to rattle :* pret. pl. byrnan hringdon, 327.

bring-boga, w. m., *one who bends himself into a ring:* gen. sg. hring-bogan (of the drake, bending himself into a circle), 2562.

hringed, pret. part., *made of rings :* nom. sg. hringed byrne, 1246; acc. sg. hringde byrnan, 2616.

hringed-stefna, w. m., *ship whose stem is provided with iron rings* (cramp-irons), especially of sea-going ships (cf. Friŏ-]iofs saga, 1 : þorsteinn âtti skip]at er Ellidi hêt, ... borŏit war spengt iarni) : nom. sg., 32, 1898 ; acc. sg. hringed-stefnan, 1132.

hring-îren, st. n., *sword ornamented with rings :* nom. sg., 322.

hring-mæl, adj., *marked with rings*, i.e. ornamented with rings, or marked with characters of ring-form : nom. acc. sg., of the sword, 1522, 1562(?); nom. pl. heard and hring-mæl Heaŏobeardna ge-streón (*rich armor*), 2038.

hring-naca, w. m., *ship with iron rings, sea-going ship :* nom. sg., 1863.

hring-net, st. n., *ring-net*, i.e. a shirt of interlaced rings : acc. sg., 2755; acc. pl. hring-net, 1890.

hring-sele, st. m., *ring-hall*, i.e. hall in which are rings, or in which rings are bestowed : acc. sg., 2841; dat. sg., 2011, 3054.

hring-weorŏnng, st. f., *ring-ornament :* acc. sg. -weorŏunge, 3018.

hrînan, st. v. w. dat.: 1) *to touch, lay hold of :* inf.]ät him heardra nân hrinan wolde iren ærgôd (*that*

no good sword of valiant men would make an impression on him), 989; him for hrôf-sele hrinan ne mehte færgripe flôdes (*the sudden grip of the flood might not touch him owing to the hall-roof*), 1516;]ät þam hring-sele hrinan ne môste gumena ænig (*so that none might touch the ringed-hall*), 3054; pret. sg. siŏŏan he hine folmum [hr]ân (*as soon as he touched it with his hands*), 723; ôŏ]ät deaŏes wylm hrân ät heortan (*seized his heart*), 2271. Pret. subj. þeáh]e him wund hrîne (*although he was wounded*), 2977. — 2) (O.N. hrîna, *sonare, clamare*), *to resound, rustle :* pres. part. nom. pl. hrînde bearwas (for hrînende), 1364.

hroden. See **hreôŏan**.

hron-fix. See **hran-fix**.

hrôŏor, st. m., *joy, beneficium :* dat. sg. hrefne tô hrôŏre, 2449; gen. pl. hrôŏra, 2172.

hrôf, st. m., *roof, ceiling of a house :* nom. sg., 1000; acc. sg. under Heorotes hrôf, 403; under geápne hrôf, 838; geseáh steápne hrôf (here *inner roof, ceiling*), 927; so, ofer heáhne hrôf, 984; ymb]äs helmes hrôf, 1031; under beorges hrôf, 2756. — Comp. inwit-hrôf.

hrôf-sele, st. m., *covered hall :* dat. sg. hrôf-sele, 1516.

hrôr, adj., *stirring, wide-awake, valorous :* dat. sg. of]äm hrôran, 1630. — Comp. fela-hrôr.

hruron. See **hreôsan**.

hruse, w. f., *earth, soil :* nom. sg., 2248, 2559; acc. sg. on hrusan, 773, 2832; dat. sg. under hrusan, 2412.

hrycg, st. m., *back :* acc. sg. ofer

wäteres hrycg (*over the water's back, surface*), 471.

hryre, st. m., *fall, destruction, ruin :* acc. sg., 3181 ; dat. sg., 1681, 3006. — Comp. : leód-, wíg-hryre.

hryslan, w. v., *to shake, be shaken, clatter :* pret. pl. syrcan hrysedon (*corslet ts rattled*, of men in motion), 226.

hund, st. m., *dog :* instr. pl. hundum, 1369.

hund, num., *hundred :* freó hund, 2279 ; w. gen. pl. hund missera, 1499 : hund fúsenda landes and locenra beága, 2995.

hú, adv., *how, quomodo*, 3, 116, 279, 738, 845, 2319, 2520, 2719, etc.

húð, st. f., *booty, plunder :* dat. (instr.) sg. húðe, 124.

húru, adv., *at least, certainly*, 369 ; *indeed, truly*, 182, 670, 1072, 1466, 1945, 2837 ; *yet, nevertheless*, 863 ; *now*, 3121.

hús, st. n., *house :* gen. sg. húses, 116 ; gen. pl. húsa sélest (Heorot), 146, 285, 659, 936.

hwan, adv., *whither :* tô hwan syððan wearð hondræs háleða (*what is ne the hand-to-hand fight of the heroes had*), 2072.

hwanan, hwanon, adv., *whence :* hwanan, 257, 2404 ; hwanon, 333.

hwá, interrog. and indef. pron., *who :* nom. sg. m. hwá, 52, 2253, 3127 ; neut. hwät, 173 ; änes hwät (*a part only*), 3011 ; hwät fâ men wæron (*who the men were*), 233, etc.; hwät syndon ge searo-häbhendra (*what armed men are ye ?* , 237; acc. sg. m. wið manna hwone *from*(?) *any man*), 155; neut. furh hwät, 3069; hwät wit geó spræcon, 1477; hwät ... hŷnðo (gen.), fær-níða (*what shame and sudden woes*), 474 ; so, hwät þu worn fela (*how very much*

thou\), 530; swylces hwät, 881 ; hwät ... Árna, 1187; dat. m. hwam, 1697. — Comp. æg-hwâ.

hwät, interj., *what! lo! indeea!* 1, 943, 2249.

ge-hwâ, w. part. gen., *each, each one :* acc. sg. m. wið feónda gehwine, 294; niða gehwane, 2398; mêca gehwane, 2686; gum-cynnes gehwone, 2766; fem. on healfa gehwone, 801 ; dat. sg. m. dôgora gehwam, 88 ; ät niða gehwam, 883; þegna gehwam, 2034; corla gehwäm, 1421 ; fem. in mægða gehwære, 25; nihta gehwäm, 1366; gen. sing. m. manna gehwäs, 2528; fem. dæda gehwäs, 2839.

hwâr. See hwær.

hwäder. See hwider.

hwäðer, pron., *which of two :* nom. sg. hwäðer ... uncer twega, 2531; swâ hwäðer, *utcreunque :* acc. sg. on swâ hwäðere hond swâ him gemet þince, 687. — Comp. æg-hwäðer.

ge-hwäðer, *each of two, either-o.her :* nom. sg. m. wäs gehwäðer ôðrum lifigende lâð, 815; wäs ... gehwäðer ôðrum hrôðra gemyndig, 2172; ne gehwäðer incer (*nor either of you tw*), 584; nom. sg. neut. gehwäðer þâra (*either of them*, i.e. ready for war or peace), 1249; dat. sg. hiora gehwäðrum, 2995; gen. sg. bega gehwäðres, 1044.

hwäðer, hwäðere, hwäðre, 1) adv., *yet, nevertheless :* hwäðre, 555, 891, 1271, 2099, 2299, 2378, etc. ; hwäðre swâ þeáh, *however, notwithstanding*, 2443; hwäðere, 574, 578, 971, 1719. — 2) conj., = *utrum, whether :* hwäðre, 1315; hwäðer, 1357, 2786.

hwät, adj., *sharp, bold, valiant :*

nom. sg. se secg hwata, 3029; dat.
sg. hwatum, 2162; nom. pl. hwate,
1002, 2053; acc. pl. hwate, 2643,
3036. — Comp.: fyrd-, gold-hwät.
hwät. See **hwä.**

hwær, adv., *where:* elles hwær,
elsewhere, 138; hwær, *somewhere,*
2030. In elliptical question: wun-
dar hwâr þonne..., *is it a wonder
when...?* 3063. — Comp. ô-hwær.

ge-hwær, *everywhere:* þeáh þu
heaðo-rœsa gehwær dohte (*everywhere good in battle*), 526.

hwele. See **hwyle.**

hwergen, adv., *anywhere:* elles
hwergen, *elsewhere,* 2591.

hwettan, w. v., *to encourage, urge:*
pres. subj. swâ þin sefa hwette (*as
thy mind urges, as thou likest*),
490; pret. pl. hwetton higeröfne
(*they whetted the brave one*), 204.

hwêne, adv., *a little, paululum,* 2700.

hwealf, st. f., *vault:* acc. sg. under
heofones hwealf, 576, 2016.

hweorfan, st. v., *to stride deliber-
ately, turn, depart, move, die:*
pres. pl. þâra þe cwice hwyrfað,
98; inf. hwilum he on lufan ke-
teð hworfan monnes môd-geþonc
(*sometimes on love (?) possessions (?) permits the thoughts of
man to turn*), 1729; londrihtes
môt ... monna æghwyle idel
hweorfan (*of rights of land each
one of men must be deprived*),
2889; pret. sg. fäder ellor hwearf
...of earde (*died*), 55; hwearf
þâ hrädliee þær Hrôðgâr sät, 356;
hwearf þâ bi bence (*turned then to
the bench*), 1189; so, hwearf þâ be
weaile, 1574; hwearf geond þät
reced, 1982; hläw oft ymbe hwearf
(*went oft round the cave*), 2297;
nalles äfter lyfte lâcende hwearf
(*not at all through the air did he

go springing), 2833; subj. pret. sg.
ær he on weg hwurfe ... of geardum (*died*), 264.

and-hweorfan, *to move against:*
pret. sg. ôð þät ... norðan wind
heaðo-grim and-hwearf (*till the
fierce north wind blew in our
faces*), 548.

ät-hweorfan, *to go to:* pret. sg.
hwilum he on beorh ät-hwearf (*at
times returned to the mountain*),
2300.

ge-hweorfan, *to go, come:* pret.
sg. gehwearf þâ in Francna fäðm
feorh cyninges, 1211; hit on æht
gehwearf ... Denigea freán, 1680;
so, 1685, 2209.

geond-hweorfan, *to go through
from end to end:* pres. sg. flet
eall geond-hwearf, 2018.

hwider, adv., *whither:* hwyder, 163;
hwäder (hwäðer, MS.), 1332.

hwîl, st. f., *time, space of time:* nom.
sg. wäs seo hwil micel (*it was a
long time*), 146; þâ wäs hwil däges
(*the space of a day*), 1496; acc. sg.
hwile, *for a time,* 2138: a *while,*
105, 152; lange (longe) hwile, *a
long while,* 16, 2781; âne hwîle,
a while, 1763; lytle hwîle, *brief
space,* 2031, 2098; ænige hwîle,
any while, 2549; lässan hwile, *a
lesser while,* 2572; dat. sg. ær däges hwîle, *before daybreak,* 2321;
dat. pl. nihtes hwilum, *sometimes
at night,* 3045. Adv., *sometimes,
often:* hwîlum, 175, 496, 917, 1729,
1829, 2017, 2112, etc.; hwilum ...
hwilum, 2108-9-10. — Comp.: däg-,
gescäp-, orleg-, sige-hwil.

hwît, adj., *brilliant, flashing:* nom.
sg. se hwita helm, 1449.

hworfan. See **hweorfan.**

hwôpan, st. v., *to cry, cry out,
mourn:* pret. sg. hweóp, 2269.

hwyder. See **hwider.**

hwyle, pron., *which, what, any:* 1) adj.: nom. sg. m. sceaða ic nât hwylc, 274; fem. hwylc orleghwtl, 2003; nom. pl. hwylce Sægeáta sîðas wæron, 1987.— 2) subst., w. gen. pl. nom. m.: Frisna hwylc, 1105; fem. efne swâ hwylc mägða swâ þone magan cende (*whatever woman brought forth this son*),944; neut. þonne his bearna hwylc (*than any one of his sons*), 2434; dat. sg. efne swâ hwylcum manna swâ him gemet þûhte, 3058.— Comp.: æg-, nât-, wel-hwylc.

ge-hwylc, ge-hwilc, ge-hwelc, w. gen. pl., *each:* nom. sg. m. ge-hwylc, 986, 1167, 1674; acc. sg. m. gehwylcne, 937, 2251, 2517; ge-hwelcne, 148; fem. gebwylce, 1706; neut. gehwylc, 2609; instr. sg. dôgra gehwylce, 1091; so, 2058, 2451; dat. sg. m. gehwylcum, 412, 769, 785, etc.; fem. ecga gehwylcre, 806; neut. cynna gehwylcum, 98; gen. sg. m. and neut. gehwylces, 733, 1397, 2095.

hwyrft, st. m., *circling movement, turn:* dat. pl. adv. hwyrftumscríðað (*wander, to and fro*), 163.—Comp. ed-hwyrft.

hycgan, w. v., *to think, resolve upon:* pret. sg. ic þ ât hogode þ ât . . . (*my intention was that . . .*), 633.—Comp. w. pres. part.: healo-, heard-, swíð-, þanc-, wis-hycgend.

for-hycgan, *to despise, scorn, reject with contempt:* pres. sg. I. ic þ ât þonne for-hicge, ât . . ., *reject with scorn the proposition that . . .*, 435.

ge-hycgan, *to think, determine upon:* pret. sg. þâ þu . . . feorr gehogodest sæcce sêcean, 1989.

ofer-hycgan, *to scorn:* pret. sg. ofer-hogode þâ hringa fengel þ ât he

þone wídflogan weorode gesôhte (*scorned to seek the wide-flier with a host*), 2346.

hydig (for **hygdig**), adj., *thinking, of a certain mind:* comp. ân-, bealo-, grom-, nið-, þrist-hydig.

ge-hygd, st. n., *thought, sentiment:* acc. sg. þurh hreðra gehygd, 2046.—Comp.: breóst-, môd-gehygd, won-hyd.

hyge, hige, st. m., *mind, heart, thought:* nom. sg. hyge, 756; hige, 594; acc. sg. þurh holdne hige, 267; gen. sg. higes, 2046; dat. pl. higum, 3149.

hyge-bend, st. m. f., *mind-fetter, heart-band:* instr. pl. hyge-bendum fäst, *fast in his mind's fetters, secretly,* 1879.

hyge-geômor, adj., *sad in mind:* nom. sg. hyge-giômor, 2409.

hyge-mêðe, adj.: 1) *sorrowful, soul-crushing:* nom. sg., 2443.— 2) *life-weary, dead:* dat. pl. hyge-mêðum (=maðum, MS.), 2910.

hyge-rôf, adj., *brave, valiant, vigorous-minded:* nom. sg. [hygerôf], 403; acc. sg. hige-rôfne, 204.

hyge-sorh, st. f., *heart-sorrow:* gen. pl. -sorga, 2329.

hyge-þyhtig, adj., *doughty, courageous:* acc. sg. hige-þihtigne (of Beówulf), 747. See þyhtig.

hyge-þrym, st. m., *animi majestas, high-mindedness:* dat. pl. for hige-þrymmum, 339.

hylt, st. m., *thought, pleasant thought, hope* (Dietrich): nom. sg., 179.

ge-hyld (see healdan), st. n., *support, protection:* nom. sg., 3057.— l.co.

hyldan, w. v., *to incline one's self, lie down to sleep:* pret. sg. hylde hine, *inclined himself, lay down,* 689.

hyldo, st. f., *inclination, friendli-*
ness, grace : acc. sg. hyldo, 2068,
2294; gen. sg. hyldo, 671, 2999.
â-hyrdan, w. v., *harden :* pret. part.
â-hyrded, 1461.
hyrde. See **hirde.**
hyrst, st. f., *accoutrements, orna-*
ment, armor : acc. sg. hyrste (Ongenþeów's *equipments and arms*),
2989; acc. pl. hyrsta, 3166; instr.
pl. hyrstum, 2763.
hyrstan, w. v., *to deck, adorn :* pret.
part. hyrsted sweord, 673; helm
[hyr]sted golde, 2256.
hyrtan, w. v., *to take heart, be em-*
boldened : pret. sg. hyrte hyne hord-
weard (*the drake took heart;* see
2566, 2568, 2570), 2594.
hyse, st. m., *youth, young man :* nom.
sg. as voc., 1218.
hyt. See **hit.**
hŷdan, w. v., *to hide, conceal, pro-*
tect, preserve : pres. subj. hŷde
[hine, *himself*] se þe wylle, 2767;
inf. w. acc. nô þu minne þearft hafalan hŷdan, 446; ær he in wille
hafelan [hŷdan] (*ere in it he* [the
stag] *will hide his head*), 1373.
ge-hŷdan, w. acc., *to conceal, pre-*
serve : pret. sg. gehŷdde, 2236,
3061.
hŷð, st. f., *haven :* dat. sg. ät hŷðe,
32.
hŷð-weard, st. m., *haven-warden :*
nom. sg., 1915.
hŷnan (see **heán**), w. v. w. acc., *to*
crush, afflict, injure : pret. sg.
hŷnde, 2320.
hŷnðu, st. f., *oppression, affliction,*
injury : acc. sg. hŷnðu, 277; gen.
sg. hwät . . . hŷnðo, 475; fela . . .
hŷnðo, 594; gen. pl. heardra hŷn-
ða, 166.
hŷran, w. v.: 1) *to hear, perceive,*
learn : a) w. inf. or acc. with inf. :

I. pret. sg. hŷrde ic, 38, 582, 1347,
1843, 2024; III. sg. þät he fram
Sigemunde secgan hŷrde, 876; I.
pl. swâ we sôðlice secgan hŷrdon,
273. b) w. acc.: nænigne ic . . .
sêlran hŷrde hordmâððum (*I heard*
of no better hoard-jewel), 1198.
c) w. dependent clause : I. sg. pret.
hŷrde ic | ät . . ., 62, 2164, 2173. —
2) w. dat. of person, *to obey :* inf.
ôð | ät him æghwilc þâra ymbsitten-
dra hŷran scolde, 10; hŷran heaðo-
siócum, 2755; pret. pl. þät him
winemâgas georne hŷrdon, 66.
ge-hŷran, *to hear, learn :* a) w.
acc.: II. pers. sg. pres. minne ge-
hŷrað ânfealdne geþôht, 255; III.
sg. pret. gehŷrde on Beówulfe fäst-
rædne geþôht, 610. b) w. acc. and
inf.: III. pl. pret. gehŷrdon, 786.
c) w. depend. clause : I. pres. sg.
ic þät gehŷre þät . . ., 290.

I

ic, pers. pron. *I :* acc. mec, dat. me,
gen. min; dual nom. wit, acc. uncit,
unc, dat. unc, gen. uncer; pl. nom.
we, acc. ûsic, ûs, dat. ûs, gen. ûser.
ic omitted before the verb, 470.
iege, *gold* (perhaps related to Sans-
krit iç, — dominare, imperare,
O.H.G. ôht, *wealth,* opes), *treas-*
ure?, sword (edge) ?, 1108. — KÖR-
NER.
ides, st. f., *woman, lady, queen :*
nom. sg., 621, 1076, 1118, 1169 ;
dat. sg. idese, 1650, 1942. Also
of Grendel's mother : nom. sg.,
1260; gen. sg. idese, 1352.
in. See **inn.**
in : I. prep. w. dat. and acc.: 1) w.
dat. (local, indicating rest), *in :* in
geardum, 13, 2460 ; in þäm gûð-
sele, 443; in beórsele, 2636; so,
89, 482, 589, 696, 729, 2140, 2233,

etc.; in mægða gehwære, 25 ; in
Þýstrum, 87; in Caines cynne, 107;
in hyra gryregeatwum (*in their accoutrements of terror, war-weeds*),
324; so, 395; in campe (*in battle*),
2506 ; hiora in ânum (*in one of
them*), 2600. Prep. postpositive:
Scedelandum in, 19. Also, *on,
upon*, like on : in eolo-bence,
1030; in gumstôle, 1953; in þam
wongstede (*on the grassy plain,
the battle-field*), 2787; in bælstede,
3098. Temporal: in geâr-dagum,
1. — 2) w. acc. (local, indicating
motion),*in, into:* in woruld, 60; in
fýres fäðm, 185; so, 1211 ; in
Hrefnesholt, 2936. Temporal, *in,
at, about, toward:* in Þâ tide (in
watide, MS.), 2228.
　II. adv., *in* (here or there), 386,
1038, 1372, 1503, 1645, 2153, 2191,
2228; inn, 3091.

inege, adj. (perhaps related to icge),
instr. sg. inege lâfe (*with the costly
sword? or with mighty sword?*),
2578. — [*Edge:* inege lâfe, *edge
of the sword.* — K. Körner?]

in-frôd, adj., *very aged:* nom. sg.,
2450; dat. pl. in-frôdum, 1875.

in-gang, st. m., *entrance, access to:*
acc. sg., 1550.

in-genga, w. m., *in-goer, visitor:*
nom. sg., of Grendel, 1777.

in-gesteald, st. m., *house-property,
possessions in the house:* acc. sg.,
1156.

inn, st. n., *apartment, house:* nom.
sg. in, 1301.

innan, adv., *within, inside*, 775,
1018, 2413, 2720; on innan (*in
the interior*), *within*, 1741, 2716;
þær on innan (*in there*), 71; burgum on innan (*within his city*),
1969. Also, *therein:* þær on innan, 2090, 2215, 2245.

innan-weard, adv., *inwards, inside, within*, 992, 1977 ; inne-
weard, 999.

inne, adv.: 1) *inside, within*, 643,
1282, 1571, 2114, 3060; word inne
abeád (*called, sent word, in,* i.e.
standing in the hall door), 390;
in it (i.e. the battle), 1142 ; þær
inne (*therein*), 118, 1618, 2116,
2227, 3088. — 2) — *insuper, still
further, besides*, 1867.

inwit, st. n., *evil, mischief, spite,
cunning hostility*, as in

inwit-feng, st. m., *malicious grasp,
grasp of a cunning foe:* nom. sg.,
1448.

inwit-gäst, st. m., *evil guest, hostile
stranger:* nom. sg., 2671.

inwit-hrôf, st. m., *hostile roof, hiding-place of a cunning foe:* acc. sg.
under inwit-hrôf, 3124.

inwit-net, st. n., *mischief-net, cunning snare:* acc. sg., 2168.

inwit-nið, st. n., *cunning hostility,
hostile contest:* nom. pl. inwit-
niðas (*hostility through secret attack*), 1859; gen. pl. inwit-niða,
1948.

inwit-scear, st. m., *massacre through
cunning, murderous attack:* acc.
sg. eatolne inwit-scear, 2479.

inwit-searo, st. n., *cunning, artful
intrigue:* acc. sg. þurh inwit-searo,
1102. See **searo**.

inwit-sorh, st. f., *grief, remorse,
mourning springing from hostile
cunning:* nom. sg., 1737; acc. sg.
inwid-sorge, 832.

inwit-þanc, adj., *ill-disposed, malicious:* dat. sg. he onfêng hraðe
inwit-þancum (*he quickly grasped
the cunning-in-mind* [Grendel]),
749.

irnan for rinnan), st. v., *to run;* so
be-irnan, *to run up to, occur:* pret.

sg. him on môd be-arn (*came into his mind*), 67.
on-irnan, *to open :* pret. sg. duru sôna onarn, 722.
irre-môd, adj. See yrre-môd.

Î

îdel, adj., *empty, bare ; deprived of :* nom. sg., 145, 413; w. gen. londrihtes þære mægburge •îdel (*deprived of his land-possessions among the people* [of the Geátas]), 2889.
îdel-hende, adj., *empty - handed,* 2082.
îren, st. n., *iron, sword :* nom. sg. drihtlíc íren (*the doughty, lordly sword*), 893; íren ær-gôd, 990; acc. sg. leóflíc íren, 1810; gen. pl. írena cyst (*choicest of swords*), 674; írenna cyst, 803; írenna ecge (*edges of swords*), 2684.
îren, adj., *of iron :* nom. sg. ecg wäs íren, 1460.
îren-bend, st. f., *iron band, bond, rivet :* instr. pl. íren-bendum fäst (bold), 775, 999.
îren-byrne, w. f., *iron corslet :* acc. sg. íren-byrnan, 2987. See îsern-byrne.
îren-heard, adj., *hard as iron :* nom. sg., 1113.
îrenne, adj., *of iron :* in comp. eall-írenne.
îren-þreát, st. m., *iron troop, armored band :* nom. sg., 330.
îs, st. n., *ice :* dat. sg. íse, 1609.
îsern-byrne, w. f., *iron corslet :* acc. sg. ísern-byrnan, 672. See îren-byrne.
îsern-scûr, st. f., *iron shower, shower of arrows :* gen. sg. þone þe oft gebâd ísern-scûre, 3117.
îs-gebind, st. n., *fetters of ice :* instr. sg. ís-gebinde, 1134.

îsig, adj., *shining, brilliant* (like brass) : nom. sg. îsig (said of a vessel covered with plates(?) of metal), 33.—Leo.

IO IU

îú. See geó.
îú-man. See geó-man.
îó-meówle. See geó-meówle.

L

laðu, st. f., *invitation.*—Comp.: freónd-, neód-laðu.
ge-laðian, w. v. w. acc. pers. and instr. of the thing, *to refresh, lave :* pret. sg. wine-dryhten his wätere gelafede, 2723.
lagu, st. m., *lake, sea :* nom. sg., 1631.
lagu-cräftig, adj., *acquainted with the sea :* nom. sg. lagu-cräftig mon (*pilot*), 209.
lagu-strǽt, st. f., *path over the sea :* acc. sg. ofer lagu-strǽte, 239.
lagu-streám, st. m., *sea-current, flood :* acc. pl. ofer lagu-streámas, 297.
land, st. n., *land :* nom. sg. lond, 2198; acc. sg. land, 221, 2063; lond, 2472, 2493; land Dena, 242, 253; lond Brondinga, 521; Finna land, 580; dat. sg. on lande (*in the land*), 2311, 2837; *at, near, land, shore,* 1914; tô lande (*to the land, ashore*), 1624; gen. sg. landes, 2996; gen. pl. ofer landa fela (*over much country, space; afar*), 311.—Comp.: el-, eá-land.
land-bûend, part. pres., terricola, *inhabitant of the land :* nom. pl. lond-bûend, 1346; dat. pl. land-bûendum, 95.
land-fruma, w. m., *ruler, prince of the country :* nom. sg., 31.

land-gemyrcu, st. n. pl., *frontier,*
land-mark: acc. pl., 209.

land-geweorc, st. n., *land-work,*
fortified place: acc. sg. leóda land-
geweorc, 939. See weorc, geweorc.

land-riht, st. n., *prerogatives based*
upon land-possessions, right to pos-
se.s land, hence *real estate* itself:
gen. sg. lond-rihtes idel, 2887.

land-warn, st. f., *inhabitants, popu-*
lation: acc. pl. land-wara, 2322.

land-weard, st. m., *guard, guar-*
dian of the frontier: nom. sg.,
1891.

lang, long, adj., *long:* 1) temporal:
nom. sg. tò lang, 2094; näs þâ
long (lang) tò þon (*not long after*),
2592, 2846; acc. sg. lange hwile
(*f r a long time*), 16, 2160, 2781;
longe (lange) þrage, 54, 114, 1258;
lange tid, 1916. Compar. nom.
sg. lengra fyrst, 134.—2) local,
nom. sg. se wäs fiftiges fòtge-
mearces lang, 3044.—Comp.: and-,
morgen-, niht-, up-lang.

lange, longe, adv., *long:* lange,
31, 1995, 2131, 2345, 2424; longe,
1062, 2752, 3109; tò lange (*too*
long, excessively long), 906, 1337,
1749. Compar. leng, 451, 1855,
2802, 3065; nô þ$ leng (*none*
the longer), 975. Superl. lengest
(*longest*), 2009, 2239.

ge-lang, adj., *extending, reaching*
to something or somebody, hence
ready, prepared: nû is red gelang
eft ät þe ânum (*now is help [coun-*
sel] at hand in thee alone), 1377;
gen is eall ät þe lissa gelong (*all*
of favor is still on thee dependent,
is thine), 2151. See ge-lenge.

lang-ge-streón, st. n., *long-lasting*
treasure: gen. pl. long-gestreóna,
2241.— Leo.

langian, w. v., reflex. w. dat., *to long,*
yearn: pres. sg. III. him ... äfter
deórum men dyrne langað beorn
(*the hero longeth secretly after the*
dear man), 1880.

lang-sum, adj., *long-lasting, con-*
tinuing: nom. sg. longsum, 134,
192, 1723 ; acc. sg. long-sumne,
1537.

lang-twidig, adj., *long-granted,*
assured: nom. sg., 1709.

lata, w. m., *a lazy, cowardly one;*
in comp. hild-lata.

lâ, interj., *yes! indeed!* 1701, 2865.

lâc, st. n.: 1) *measured movement,*
play: in comp. beadu-, heaðo-lâc.
—2) *gift, offering:* acc. pl. lâc,
1864; lâðlicu lâc (*loathly offer-*
ing, prey), 1585; dat. pl. lâcum,
43, 1869. — Comp. sæ-lâc.

ge-lâc, st. n., *sport, play:* acc. pl.
sweorda gelâc (*battle*), 1041; dat.
pl. ät ecga gelâcum, 1169.

lâcan, st. v., *to move in measured*
time, dancing, playing, fighting,
flying, etc.: inf. dare. um lâcan
(*fight*), 2849; part. pres. äfter lyfte
lâcende (*flying through the air*),
2833.

for-lâcan, *to deceive, betray:* part.
pret. he wearð on feónda geweald
forð forlâcen (*deceitfully betrayed*
into the enemy's hands), 904.

lâd, st. f., *street, way, journey:* dat.
sg. on lâde, 1988; gen. sg. lâde,
569. — Comp.: brim-, sæ-lâd.

ge-lâd, st. n., *way, path, road:* acc.
sg. uncûð gelâd, 1411.

lâð, adj., *loathly, evil, hateful, hos-*
tile: nom. sg. lâð, 816; lâð lyft-
floga, 2316; lâð (*enemy*), 440; ne
leóf ne lâð, 511; neut. lâð, 134,
192; in weak form, se lâða (*of the*
dragon), 2306; acc. sg. lâðne
(*wyrm*), 3041 ; dat. sg. lâðum,

440, 1258; gen. sg. láðes (of the enemy), 842; fela láðes (much evil), 930; so, 1062; láðan liges, 83; láðan cynnes, 2009, 2355; þäs láðan (of the enemy), 132; acc. pl. neut. láð gewiðru (hateful storms), 1376; dat. instr. pl. wið láðum, 550; láðum scuccum and scynnum, 939; láðum dædum (with evil deeds), 2468; láðan fingrum, 1506; gen. pl. láðra manna, spella, 2673, 3030; láðra (the enemy), 242. Compar. nom. sg. láðra ... beorn, 2433.

láð-bite, st. m., *hostile bite:* dat. sg. láð-bite lices (*the body's hostile bite* = the wound), 1123.

láð-geteóna, w. m., *evil-doer, injurer:* nom. sg., 975; nom. pl. láð-geteónan, 559.

láð-líc, adj., *loathly, hostile:* acc. pl. láð-licu, 1585.

láf, st. f.: 1) *what is left, relic; inheritance, heritage, legacy:* nom. sg. Hréðlan láf (Beówulf's corselet), 454; nom. pl. fèla láfe (*the leavings of files* = swords, Grein), 1033; so, homera láfe, 2830; on him gladiað gomelra láfe, heard and hringmæl Heaðobeardna gestreón (*on him gleams the forefather's bequest, hard and ring-decked, the Heaðobeardas' treasure,* i.e. the equipments taken from the slain king of the Heaðobeardas), 2037; acc. sg. sweorda láfe (*leavings of the sword,* i.e. those spared by the sword), 2937. — 2) *the sword as a specially precious heir-loom:* nom. sg., 2629; acc. sg. láfe, 796, 1489, 1689, 2192, 2564; instr. sg. incge láfe, 2578. — Comp.: ende-, eormen-, weá-, yrfe-, ðð-láf.

lár, st. f., *lore, instruction, prescription:* dat. sg. be fäder láre, 1951; gen. pl. lára, 1221; lárena, 269. — Comp. freónd-lár.

lást, st. m., *footstep, track:* acc. sg. lást, 132, 972, 2165; on lást (*on the traces of, behind*), 2946; nom. pl. lástas, 1403; acc. pl. lástas, 842. — Comp.: fèðe-, feorh-, fót-, wräc-lást.

läger. See leger.

läger-bed, st. n., *bed to lie on:* instr. sg. leger-bedde, 1008.

läs, adv., *less,* 1947; þý läs (*the less*), 487; quominus (*that not, lest*), 1919.

lässa, adj., *less, fewer:* nom. sg. lässa, 1283; acc. sg. m. lässan, 43; fem. lässan hwile, 2572; dat. sg. for lässan (*for less, smaller*), 952. Superl. nom. sg. nô þät läsest wäs hond-gemôt[a], 2355.

lät, adj., *negligent, neglectful;* w. gen.: nom. sg. elnes lät, 1530.

lædan, w. v. w. acc.: *to lead, guide, bring:* inf. lædan, 239; pret. pl. læddon, 1160.
for-lædan, *to mislead:* pret. pl. forlæddan, 2440(?).
ge-lædan, *to lead, bring:* part. pret. ge-læded, 37.

læfan, w. v.: 1), *to bequeathe, leave:* imper. sg. þinum magum læf folc and rice, 1179; pret. sg. eaferum læfde ... lond and leódbyrig, 2471. — 2) *spare, leave behind:* äht cwices læfan (*to spare aught living*), 2316.

læn-dagas, st. m. pl., *loan-days, transitory days* (of earthly existence as contrasted with the heavenly, unending): acc. pl. læn-dagas, 2592; gen. pl. læn-daga, 2342.

læne, adj., *inconstant, perishable, evanescent, given over to death or destruction:* nom. sg., 1755, 3179;

of rust-eaten treasures, 3130; acc.
sg. þâs kenan gesceaft (*this fleet-
ing life*), 1623; gen. sg. kenan
lifes, 2846.

læran, w. v., *to teach, instruct:* imper.
sg. þu þe lær be þon (*Learn this,
take this to heart*), 1723.

ge-læran, *to teach, instruct, give
instruction:* inf. ic þâs Hrôðgâr
mäg ... ræd gelæran (*I can give
H. good advice about this*), 278;
so, 3080; pret. pl. þâ me þät gelærdon leóde mine (*gave me the
advice*), 415.

læstan, w. v.: 1) *to follow, to sustain,
serve:* inf. þät him se lîc-homa
læstan nolde (*that his body would
not sustain him*), 813. — 2) *perform:* imper. læst eall tela (*do all
well*), 2664.

ge-læstan : 1) *to follow, serve:* pret.
sg. (sweord) þät mec ær and oft
gelæste, 2501. — 2) *to fulfil, grant:*
subj. pres. pl. þät ... wilgesîðas,
þonne wîg cume, leóde gelæstan
(*render war service*), 24; inf. ic
þe sceal mîne gelæstan freóde
(*shall grant thee my friendship,
be grateful*), 1707; pret. sg. beót
... gelæste (*fulfilled his boast*),
524; gelæste swâ (*kept his word*),
2991; pres. part. häfde Eást-Denum ... gilp gelæsted (*had fulfilled for the East Danes his boast*),
830.

lætan, st. v., *to let, allow,* w. acc.
and inf.: pres. sg. III. læteð,
1729; imper. pl. II. lætað, 397;
sg. II. læt, 1489; pret. sg. lêt, 2390,
2551,2978,3151(?); pret.pl.lêton,
48, 865, 3133: subj. pret. sg. II.
lête, 1997; sg. III. lête, 3083.

â-lætan: 1) *to let, allow:* subj. pres.
sg. II. þät þu ne âlæte ... dôm gedreósan, 2666. — 2) *to leave, lay*

aside: inf. âlætan læn-dagas (*die*),
2592; so, âlætan lîf and leódscipe,
2751.

for-lætan : 1) *to let, permit,* w. acc.
and inf. : pret. sg. for-lêt, 971; pret.
pl. for-lêton, 3168. Also with inf.
omitted : inf. nolde eorla hleó ...
þone cwealmcuman cwicne (i.e.
wesan) forlætan (*would not let
the murderous spirit go alive*),
793. — 2) *to leave behind, leave:*
pret. sg. in þam wong-stede ...
þær he hine ær forlêt (*where he
had previously left him*), 2788.

of-lætan, *to leave, lay aside:* pres.
sg. II. gyf þu ær þonne he worold
oflætest (*leavest the world, diest*),
1184; so pret. sg. oflêt lîf-dagas
and þâs kenan gesceaft, 1623.

on-lætan, *to release, liberate:* pres.
sg. III. þonne forstes bend fäder
on-læteð (*as soon as the Father
looseth the frost's fetters*), 1610.

â-lecgan, w. v.: 1) *to lay, lay down :*
pret. sg. syððan hilde-deór hond
â-legde ... under geápne hrôf,
835; þät he on Beówulfes bearm
â-legde (*this* [the sword] *he laid
in B.'s bosom, presented to him*),
2195; pret. pl. â-lêdon þâ leófne
þeóden ... on bearm scipes, 34;
â-legdon þâ tô middes mærne þeóden (*laid the mighty prince in the
midst* [of the pyre]), 3142. — 2) *to
lay aside, give up:* siððan ... in
fen-freoðo feorh â-legde (*laid
down his life, died*), 852; nu se
here-wîsa hleahtor â-legde, gamen
and gleó-dreám (*now the war-chief
has left laughter,* etc.), 3021.

leger, st. n., *couch, bed, lair :* dat.
sg. on legere, 3044.

lemian, w. v., *to lame, hinder, oppress:* pret. sg. (for pl.) hine sorh-
wylmas lemede tô lange, 906.

leng. See **lang.**

lenge, adj., *extending along* or *to, near* (of time) : nom. sg. neut. ne wäs hit lenge þâ gen (*nor was it yet long*), 83.

ge-lenge, adj., *extending, reaching to, belonging :* nom. sg. yrfe-weard ... lîce gelenge (*an heir belonging to one's body*), 2733.

let, st. m., *place of rest, sojourn :* in comp. eû-let (*voyage?*).

lettan, w. v., *to hinder :* pret. pl. (acc. pers. and gen. thing), þät syðdan nâ ... brim-lîðende lâde ne letton (*might no longer hinder seafarers from journeying*), 569.

â-lêdon. See **â-leegan.**

lêg, st. m., *flame, fire :* nom. sg. wonna lêg (*the lurid flame*), 3116; swôgende lêg, 3146; dat. sg. for dracan lêge, 2550. See **lîg.**

lêg-draca, w. m., *fire-drake, flaming dragon :* nom. sg., 3041.

leahan, leán, st. v. w. acc., *to scold, blame :* pres. sg. III. lyhð, 1049; pret. sg. lôg, 1812; pret. pl. lôgon, 203, 863.

be-leán, *to dissuade, prevent :* inf. ne inc ænig mon ... beleân mihte sorhfullne sîð (*no one might dissuade you twain from your difficult journey*), 511.

leahtre. See **or-leahtre.**

leáf, st. n., *leaf, foliage :* instr. pl. leáfum, 97.

leáfnes-word, st. n., *permission, leave :* acc. pl., 245.

leán. See **leahan.**

leán, st. n., *reward, compensation :* acc. sg., 114, 952, 1221, 1585, 2392; dat. sg. leáne, 1022. Often in the pl.: acc. þâ leán, 2996; dat. þâm leánum, 2146; gen. leána, 2991. — Comp.: and-, ende-leán.

leân (for læn, O.H.G. lêhan), st. n., *loan,* 1810.

leánian, w. v., *to reward, compensate :* pres. sg. I. ic þe þâ fæhðe feó leánige (*repay thee for the contest with old-time treasures*), 1381; pret. sg. me þone wäl-ræs wine Scyldinga fättan golde fela leánode (*the friend of the Scyldings rewarded me richly for the combat with plated gold*), 2103.

leás, adj., *false :* nom. pl. leáse, 253.

leás, adj., *deprived of, free from,* w. gen.: nom. sg. dreáma leás, 851; dat. sg. winigea leásum, 1665. — Comp.: dôm-, dreám-, ealdor-, feoh-, feormend-, hlâford-, sâwol-, sige-, sorh-, tîr-, þeóden-, wine-, wyn-leás.

leásig, adj., *concealing one's self;* in comp. sin-leásig(?).

leoðo-cräft, st. m., *the art of weaving* or *working in meshes, wire,* etc.: instr. pl. segn eall-gylden ... gelocen leoðo-cräftum (*a banner all hand-wrought of interlaced gold*), 2770.

leoðo-syrce, w. f., *shirt of mail* (*limb-sark*) : acc. sg. locene leoðo-syrcan (*locked linked sark*), 1506; acc. pl. locene leoðo-syrcan, 1891.

leomum. See **lim.**

leornian, w. v., *to learn, devise, plan :* pret. him þäs gûð-cyning ... wräce leornode (*the war-king planned vengeance therefor*), 2337.

leód, st. m., *prince :* nom. sg., 341, 348, 670, 830, 1433, 1493, 1613, 1654, etc.; acc. leód, 626.

leód, st. f., *people :* gen. sg. leóde, 597, 600, 697, 1214. In pl. indicates *individuals, people, kinsmen :* nom. pl. leóde, 362, 415, 1214 (gen. sg.?), 2126, etc.; gum-cynnes Geáta leóde (*people of the race of the Geátas*),

260; acc. pl. leóde, 24, 192, 443, 1337, 1346, etc.; dat. pl. leódum, 389, 521, 619, 698, 906, 1160, etc.; gen. pl. leóda, 205, 635, 794, 1674, 2034, etc.

leód-bealo, st. n., (*mischief, misfortune affecting an entire people*), *great, unheard-of calamity:* acc. sg., 1723; gen. pl. leód-bealewa, 1947.

leód-burh, st. f., *princely castle, stronghold of a ruler, chief city:* acc. pl. -byrig, 2472.

leód-cyning, st. m., *king of the people:* nom. sg., 54.

leód-fruma, w. m., *prince of the people, ruler:* acc. sg. leód-fruman, 2131.

leód-gebyrgea, w. m., *protector of the people, prince:* acc. sg. -gebyrgean, 269.

leód-hryre, st. m., *fall, overthrow, of the prince, ruler:* dat. sg. æfter leód-hryre (*after the fall of the king of the HeaÐobeardas,* Fróda, cf. 2051), 2031; gen. sg. þæs leód-hryres (of the fall of Heardred, cf. 2389), 2392.

leód-sceaða, w. m., *injurer of the people:* dat. sg. þam leód-sceaðan, 2094.

leód-scipe, st. m., *the whole nation, people:* acc. sg., 2752; dat. sg. on þam leód-scipe, 2198.

leóð, st. n., *song, lay:* nom. sg., 1160. — Comp.: fyrd-, gryre-, gûð-, sorh-leóð.

leóf, adj., *lief, dear:* nom. sg., 31, 54, 203, 511, 521, 1877, 2468; weak form m., leófa, 1217, 1484, 1855, 2664; acc. sg. m. leófne, 34, 297, 619, 1944, 2128, 3109, 3143; gen. sg. leófes (m.), 1995, 2081, 2898; (neut.), 1062, 2911; dat. pl. leófum, 1074; gen. pl. leófra,

1916. Compar. nom. sg. neut. leófre, 2652. Superl. nom. sg. m. leófost, 1297; acc. sg. þone leófestan, 2824.

leóflic, *dear, precious, valued:* nom. sg. m. leóflic lind-wiga, 2604; acc. sg. neut. leóflic íren, 1810.

leógan, st. v., *to lie, belie, deceive:* subj. pres. näfne him his wlite leóge (*unless his looks belie him*), 250; pret. sg. he ne leág fela wyrda ne worda, 3030.

â-leógan, *to deceive, leave unfulfilled:* pret. sg. he beót ne â-lêh (*he left not his promise unfulfilled*), 80.

ge-leógan, *to deceive, betray:* pret. sg. him seó wên geleáh (*hope deceived him*), 2324.

leóht, st. n., *light, brilliance:* nom. sg., 569, 728, 1751 (?) ; acc. sg. sunnan leóht, 649; godes leóht geceás (*chose God's light, died*), 2470; dat. sg. tô leóhte, 95. — Comp.: æfen-, fyr-, morgen-leóht.

leóht, adj., *luminous, bright:* instr. sg. leóhtan sweorde, 2493.

leóma, w. m.: 1) *light, splendor:* nom. sg., 311, 2770; acc. sg. leóman, 1518; sunnan and mónan leóman (*light of sun and moon*), 95. — 2) (as beadu- and hilde-leóma), *the glittering sword:* nom. sg. lixte se leóma (*the blade-gleam flashed*), 1571.

leósan, st. v., — amitti, in be-leósan, *to deprive, be deprived of:* pres. part. (heó) wearð beloren leófum bearnum and bróðrum (*was deprived of her dear children and brethren*), 1074.

for-leósan, with dat. instr., *to lose something:* pret. sg. þær he dóme for-leás, ellen-mærðum (*there lost he the glory, the repute, of his heroic deeds*), 1471: pret. sg. for pl. þâm þe ær his elne for-leás (*to him who, before, had lost his valor*), 2862; part. pret. nealles ic þâm leánum for-loren häfde (*not at all had I lost the rewards*), 2146.

libban, w. v., *to live, be, exist:* pres. sing. III. lifa∂, 3169; lyfa∂, 945; leofa∂, 975, 1367, 2009; subj. pres. sg. II. liſige, 1225; pres. part. liſigende, 816, 1954, 1974, 2063; dat. sg. be þe liſigendum (*in thy lifetime*), 2666; pret. sg. lifde, 57, 1258; lyfde, 2145; pret. pl. lifdon, 99. See **unliſigende**.

liegan, st. v.: 1) *to lie, lie down* or *low:* pres. sg. nu seó hand lige∂ (*now the hand lies low*), 1344; nu se wyrm lige∂, 2746, so 2904; inf. liegan, 3130; liegan, 967, 3083; pret. sg. läg, 40, 552, 2078; sy∂∂an Heardrêd läg (*after Heardrêd had fallen*), 2389; pret. pl. lâgon, 3049; legon, 566. — 2) *to lie prostrate, rest, fail:* pret. sg. næfre on ôre läg wid-cû∂es wig (*never failed the far-famed one's valor at the front*), 1042; sy∂∂an wi∂er-gyld läg (*after vengeance failed, or, when Withergyld lay dead, if W. is a proper name*), 2052.

â-liegan, *to succumb, fail, yield:* inf. 2887; pret. sg. þät his dôm â-läg (*that its power failed it*), 1529.

ge-liegan, *to rest, lie still:* pret. sg. wind-blond geläg, 3147.

lida, w. m., *boat, ship* (as in motion); in comp.: sund-, y∂-lida.

lid-man, st. m., *seafarer, sailor:* gen. pl. lid-manna, 1624.

lim, st. n., *limb, branch:* instr. pl. leomum, 97.

limpan, st. v., *to succeed, befall* (well or ill); impers. w. dat. pret. sg. hû

lomp eów on lâde (*how went it with you on the journey?*), 1988.

â-limpan, *to come about, offer itself:* pret. sg. ô∂ þät sæl â-lamp (*till the opportunity presented itself*), 623; pret. part. þâ him â-lumpen wäs wistfylle wên (*since a hope of a full meal had befallen him*), 734.

be-limpan, *to happen to, befall:* pret. sg. him sió sâr belamp, 2469.

ge-limpan, *to happen, occur, turn out:* pres. sg. III. hit eft gelimpe∂ þät..., 1754; subj. pres. þisse an-sŷne alwealdan þanc lungre gelimpe (*thanks to the Almighty forthwith for this sight!*), 930; pret. sg. him on fyrste gelamp þät..., 76; swâ him ful-oft gelamp (*as often happened to them*), 1253; þäs þe hire se willa gelamp þät... (*because her wish had been fulfilled*), 627; frôfor eft gelamp sârig-môdum, 2942; subj. pret. gif him þyslicu þearf gelumpe, 2638; pret. part. Denum eallum wear∂... willa gelumpen, 825.

lind, st. f. (properly *linden:* here, a a wooden shield covered with linden-bark or pith): nom. sg., 2342; acc. sg. geolwe linde, 2611; acc. pl. linde, 2366.

lind-gestealla, w. m., *shield-comrade, war-comrade:* nom. sg., 1974.

lind-häbbend, pres. part., *provided with a shield*, i.e. warrior: nom. pl. -häbbende, 245; gen. pl. häbbendra, 1403.

lind-plega, w. m., *shield-play*, i.e. battle: dat. sg. lind-plegan, 1074, 2040.

lind-wîga, w. m., *shield-fighter, warrior:* nom. sg., 2604.

linnan, st. v., *to depart, be deprived*

of· inf. aldre linnan (*dÿpart from life*), 1479; ealdres linnan, 2444.

lǐs, st. f., *favor, affection:* gen. pl. eall . . . lissa, 2151.

list, st. m., *art, skill, cleverness, cunning:* dat. pl. adverbial, listum (*cunningly*), 782.

lǐxan, w. v., *to shine, flash:* pret. sg. lixte, 311, 485, 1571.

lǐc, st. n.: 1) *body, corpse:* nom. sg., 967; acc. sg. lic, 2081; ðæt lic (*the body, corpse*), 2128; dat. sg. lǐce, 734, 1504, 2424, 2572, 2733, 2744; gen. sg. lǐces, 451, 1123. — 2) *form, figure:* in comp. eofor-, swin-lǐc.

ge-lǐc, adj., *like, similar:* nom. pl. m. ge-lǐce, 2165. Superl. ge-lǐcost, 218, 728, 986, 1009.

lǐc-hama, -homa, w. m. (*body-home, garment*), *body:* nom. sg. lǐc-homa, 813, 1008, 1755; acc. sg. lǐc-haman, 2652; dat. sg. lǐc-haman, 3179.

lǐcian, w. v., *to please, like* (impers.): pres. sg. III. me ðin môd-sefa lǐcað leng swâ wel, 1855; pret. pl. þam wife þâ word wel lǐcodon, 640.

lǐcnes. See **on-lǐcnes.**

lǐc-sâr, st. n., *bodily pain:* acc. sg. lǐc-sâr, 816.

lǐc-syrce, w. f., *body-sark, shirt of mail covering the body:* nom. sg., 550.

lǐðan, st. v., *to move, go:* pres. part. nom. pl. þâ lǐðende (*navigantes, sailors*, 221; þâ wäs sund liden (*the water was then traversed*), 223.—Comp.: heáðu-, mere-, wæg-lǐðend.

lǐðe (O.H.G. lindi), adj., *gentle, mild, friendly:* nom. sg. w. instr. gen. lâra lǐðe, 1221. Superl. nom. sg. lǐðost, 3184.

lǐð-wæge, st. n., *can in which ale*

(*a wine-like, foaming drink*) *is contained:* acc. sg., 1983.

lǐf, st. n., *life:* acc. sg. lǐf, 97, 734, 1537, 2424, 2744, 2752; dat. sg. life, 2572; tô life (*in one's life, ever*), 2433; gen. sg. lǐfes, 197, 791, 807, 2824, 2846; worolde lǐfes (*of the earthly life*), 1388, 2344.— Comp. edwît-lǐf.

lǐf-bysig, adj. (*striving for life or death*), *weary of life, in torment of death:* nom. sg., 967.

lǐf-dagas, st. m. pl., *lifetime:* acc. -dagas, 794, 1623.

lǐf-freá, w. m., *lord of life, God:* nom. sg., 16.

lǐf-gedâl, st. n., *separation from life:* nom. sg., 842.

lǐf-gesceaft, st. f., *fate, destiny:* gen. pl. -gesceafta, 1954, 3065.

lǐf-wraðu, st. f., *protection for one's life, safety:* acc. sg. lǐf-wraðe, 2878; dat. sg. tô lǐf-wraðe, 972.

lǐf-wyn, st. f., *pleasure, enjoyment, joy* (of life): gen. pl. lǐf-wynna, 2098.

lǐg, st. m., *flame, fire:* nom. sg., 1123; dat. instr. sg. lǐge, 728, 2306, 2322, 2342; gen. sg. lǐges, 83, 782. See **lêg.**

lǐg-draca, w. m., *fire-drake, flaming dragon:* nom. pl., 2334. See **lêg-draca.**

lǐg-egesa, w. m., *horror arising through fire, flaming terror:* acc. sg., 2781.

lǐge-torn, st. m., *false, pretended insult or injury, fierce anger* (?): dat. sg. äfter lǐge-torne (*on account of a pretended insult? or fierce anger?* cf. Bugge in Zacher's Zeits. 4, 208), 1944.

lǐg-ýð, st. m., *wave of fire:* instr. pl. lǐg-ýðum, 2673.

lǐhan, st. v., *to lend:* pret. sg. þät

him on þearfe lâh þyle Hröðgâres (*which H.'s spokesman lent him in need*), 1457.

on-lîhan, *to lend, grant as a loan*, with gen. of thing and dat. pers.: pret. sg. Iâ he Iäs wæpnes on-lâh sêlran sweord-frecan, 1468.

lôca, w. m., *bolt, lock:* in comp. bân-, burh-lôca.

locen. See lûcan.

lond, long. See land, lang.

lof, st. m., *praise, repute:* acc. sg. lof, 1537.

lof-dæd, st. f., *deed of praise:* instr. pl. lof-dædum, 24.

lof-georn, adj., *eager for praise, ambitious:* superl. nom. sg. lof-geornost, 3184.

loga, w. m., *liar;* in comp. treów-loga.

losian, w. v., *to escape, flee:* pres. sg. III. losað, 1393, 2063; pret. sg. he on weg losade (*fled away*), 2097.

lôcian, w. v., *to see, look at:* pres. sg. II. sæ-lâc . . . Ie þu her tô lô-cast (*booty of the sea that thou lookest on*), 1655.

ge-lôme, adv., *often, frequently,* 559.

lufe, w. f., *love:* in comp. heáh-, môd-, wîf-lufe.

lufa (cf. and-leofa, big-leofa, *nourishment*), w. m., *food, subsistence; property, real estate:* acc. sg. on lufan (*on possessions*), 1729. — Comp. card-lufa.

lufen, st. f. (cf. lufa), *subsistence, food; real estate, (enjoyment?):* nom. sg. lufen (parallel with êðel-wyn), 2887.

luf-tâcen, st. n., *love-token:* acc. pl. luf-tâcen, 1864.

lufian, w. v., *to love, serve affectionately:* pret. sg. III. lufode þâ leóde

(*was on affectionate terms with the people*), 1983.

lungre, adv.: 1) *hastily, quickly, forthwith,* 930, 1631, 2311, 2744. — 2) *quite, very, fully:* feówer mearas lungre gelîce (*four horses quite alike*), 2165.

lust, st. m., *pleasure, joy:* dat. pl. adv. lustum (*joyfully*), 1654; so, on lust, 619, cf. 600.

lûcan, st. v., *to twist, wind, lock, interweave:* pret. part. acc. sg. and pl. locene leoðo-syrcan (*shirt of mail wrought of meshes or rings interlocked*), 1506, 1891; gen. pl. locenra beága (*rings wrought of gold wire*), 2996.

be-lûcan: 1) *to shut, close in* or *around:* pret. sg. winter ýðe be-leác îs-gebinde (*winter locked the waves with icy bond*), 1133. — 2) *to shut in, off, preserve, protect:* pret. sg. I. hig wîge beleác manegum mægða (*I shut them in, protected them, from war arising from many a tribe*), 1771. Cf. me wîge belûc wrâðum feóndum (*protect me against mine enemies*), Ps. 34, 3.

ge-lûcan, *to unite, link together, make:* pret. part. gelocen, 2770.

on-lûcan, *to unlock, open:* pret. sg. word-hord on-leác (*opened the word-hoard, treasure of speech*), 259.

tô-lûcan, (*to twist, wrench, in two*), *to destroy:* inf., 782.

lyft, st. f. (m. n.?), *air:* nom. sg., 1376; dat. sg. äfter lyfte (*along, through, the air*), 2833.

lyft-floga, w. m., *air-flier:* nom. sg. (of the dragon), 2316.

lyft-geswenced, pret. part., *urged, hastened on, by the wind,* 1914.

lyft-wyn, st. f., *enjoyment of the air:* acc. sg. lyft-wynne, 3044.

lyh%. See leahan.

lystan, w. v., *to lust after, long for :*
pret. sg. Geát ungemetes wel ...
restan lyste (*the Gedt* [Beówulf]
longed sorely to rest), 1794.

lyt, adj. neut. (= parum), *little, very
little, few :* lyt eft becwom ...
hâmes niósan (*few escaped home-
ward*), 2366; lyt ænig (*none at
all*), 3130; usually with gen.: wintra lyt, 1928; lyt ... heáfod-mâga,
2151; wergendra tô lyt (*too few
defenders*), 2883; lyt swîgode
nîwra spella (*he kept to himself
little, none at all, of the new tidings*), 2898; dat. sg. lyt manna
(*too few of men*), 2837.

lytel, adj., *small, little :* nom. sg.
neut. tô lytel, 1749; acc. sg. f. lytle
hwile (*a little while*), 2031, 2098;
lif-wraðe lytle (*little protection for
his life*), 2878. — Comp. un-lytel.

lyt-hwon, adv., *little – not at all :*
lyt-hwon lôgon, 204.

lŷfe, st n., *leave, permission, (life?)* :
instr.sg. þine lŷfe (life, MS.), 2132.
— Leo. Cf. O.N. leyfi, n., *leave,
permission,* in Möbius' Glossary,
p. 266.

lŷfan, w. v., (fundamental meaning
to believe, trust) in

â-lŷfan, *to allow, grant, entrust :*
pret. sg. næfre ic ænegum men ær
âlŷfde ... þryð-ärn Dena (*never
before to any man have I entrusted
the palace of the Danes*), 656; pret.
part. (þâ me wäs) sið ... âlŷfed
inn under corð-weall (*the way in
under the wall of earth was allowed
me*), 3090.

ge-lŷfan, w. v., *to believe, trust :*
1) w. dat.: inf. þær gelŷfan sceal
dryhtnes dôme se þe hine deáð
nimeð (*whomever death carrieth
away, shall believe it to be the judg-*

ment of God, i.e. in the contest
between Beówulf and Grendel),
440. — 2) w. acc.: pret. sg. geóce
gelŷfde brego Beorht-Dena (*believed in, expected, help,* etc.), 609;
þät heó on ænigne eorl gelŷfde
fyrena frôfre (*that she at last should
expect from any earl comfort, help,
out of these troubles*), 628; se þe
him bealwa tô bôte gelŷfde (*who
trusted in him as a help out of
evils*), 910; him tô anwaldan âre
gelŷfde (*relied for himself on the
help of God*), 1273.

â-lŷsan, w. v., *to loose, liberate :*
pret. part. þâ wäs of þäm hrôran
helm and byrne lungre â-lŷsed
(*helm and corselet were straightway loosed from him*), 1631.

M

maðellan, w. v. (sermocinari), *to
speak, talk :* pret. sg. maðelode,
286, 348, 360, 371, 405, 456, 499,
etc.; maðelade, 2426.

maga, w. m., *son, male descendant,
young man :* nom. sg. maga Healfdenes (Hrôðgâr), 189, 1475, 2144;
maga Ecgþeówes (Beówulf), 2588;
maga (Grendel), 979 ; se maga
geonga (Wîglâf), 2676; Grendles
maga (*a descendant of Grendel*),
2007; acc. sg. þone magan, 944.

magan, v. with pret.-pres. form, *to
be able :* pres. sg. I. III. mäg, 277,
478, 931, 943, 1485, 1734, etc.; II.
meaht þu, 2048; subj. pres. mæge,
2531, 2750; þeáh ic eal mæge
(*even though I could*), 681; subj.
pl. we mægen, 2655 ; pret. sg.
meahte, 542, 755, 1131, 1660, 2465,
etc.; mihte, 190, 207, 462, 511, 571,
657, 1509, 2092, 2610; mehte, 1083,

1497, 1516, 1878; pl. meahton, 640, 942, 1455, 1912, 2374, 3080; mihton, 308, 313, 2684, 3164; subj. pret. sg. meahte, 243, 763, 2521; pres. sg. mäg, sometimes = licet, *may, can, will* (fut.), 1366, 1701, 1838, 2865.

mago (Goth. magu-s), st. m., *male, son:* nom. sg. mago Ecgláfes (Hunferð), 1466; mago Healfdenes (Hróðgár), 1868, 2012.

mago-dryht, st. f., *troop of young men, band of men:* nom. sg. magodriht, 67.

mago-rinc, st. m., *hero, man* (preeminently): gen. pl. mago-rinca, heáp, 731.

magu-þegn, mago-þegn, st. m., *vassal, war-thane:* nom. sg. 408, 2758; dat. sg. magu-þegne, 2080; acc. pl. magu-þegnas, 293; dat. pl. mago-þegnum, 1481; gen. pl. magoþegna . . . þone sêlestan (*the best of vassals*), 1406.

man, mon, st. m.: 1) *man, human being:* nom. sg. man, 25, 503, 534, 1049, 1354, 1399, 1535, 1877, etc.; mon, 209, 510, 1561, 1646, 2282, etc.; acc. sg. w. mannan, 297, 577, 1944, 2128, 2775; wid-cûðne man, 1490; dat. sg. men, 656, 753, 1880; menn, 2190; gen. sg. mannes, 1195 (?), 2081, 2534, 2542; monnes, 1730; nom. pl. men, 50, 162, 233, 1635, 3167; acc. pl. men, 69, 337, 1583, 1718; dat. pl. mannum, 3183; gen. pl. manna, 155, 201, 380, 702, 713, 736, etc.; monna, 1414, 2888. — 2) indef. pron. *- one, they, people* (Germ. *man*): man, 1173, 1176; mon, 2356, 3177. — Comp.: fyrn-, gleó-, gum-, iú-, lid-, sæ-, wæpnedman.

man. See **munan.**

man-cyn, st. n., *mankind:* dat. sg.

man-cynne, 110; gen. sg. mancynnes, 164, 2182; mon-cynnes, 196, 1956.

man-dreám, st. m., *human joy, mundi voluptus:* acc. sg. mandreám, 1265; dat. pl. mon-dreámum, 1716.

man-dryhten, st. m. (*lord of men*), *ruler of the people, prince, king:* nom. sg. man-dryhten, 1979, 2648; mon-drihten, 436; mon-dryhten, 2866; acc. sg. mon-dryhten, 2605; dat. sg. man-drihtne, 1230; mandryhtne, 1250, 2282; gen. sg. mandryhtnes, 2850; mon-dryhtnes, 3150.

ge-mang, st. m., *troop, company:* dat. sg. on gemonge (*in the troop* [of the fourteen Geátas that returned from the sea]), 1644.

munian, w. v., *to warn, admonish:* pres. sg. III. manað swâ and myndgað ... sârum wordum (*so warneth and remindeth he with bitter words*), 2058.

manig, monig, adj., *many, many a, much:* 1) adjectively: nom. sg. rinc manig, 399; geong manig (*many a young man*), 855; monig snellíc sæ-rinc, 690; medu-benc monig, 777; so 839, 909, 919, 1511, 2763, 3023, etc.; acc. sg. medo-ful manig, 1016; dat. sg. m. þegne monegum, 1342, 1420; dat. sg. f. manigre mægðe, 75; acc. pl. manige men, 337; dat. pl. manegum mâðmum, 2104; monegum mægðum, 5; gen. pl. manigra mêda, 1179. — 2) substantively: nom. sg. manig, 1861; monig, 858; dat. sg. manegum, 349, 1888; nom. pl. manige, 1024; monige, 2983; acc. pl. monige, 1599; gen. pl. manigra, 2092. — 3) with depend. gen. pl.: dat. manegum mægða, 1772; mone-

gum fíra, 2002; häleða monegum
bold-ágendra, 3112; acc. pl. rinca
manige, 729; (máðm)-æhta monige,
1614.

manig-oft, adv., *very often, frequently*, 171 [if manig and oft are
to be connected].

man-líce, adv., *man-like, manly*,
1047.

man-þwære, adj., *kind, gentle toward men, philanthropic:* nom.
sg. superl. mon-þwærust, 3183.

má, contracted compar., *more:*
with partitive gen., 504, 736, 1056.

máðum, máððum, st. m., *gift,
jewel, object of value:* acc. sg.
máððum, 169, 1053, 2056, 3017;
dat. instr. sg. máðme, 1529, 1903;
nom. pl. máðmas, 1861; acc. pl.
máðmas, 385, 472, 1028, 1483,
1757, 1868, etc.; dat. instr. pl.
máðmum, máðmum, 1049, 1899,
2104, 2789; gen. pl. máðma, 1785,
2144, 2167, etc.; máðma, 36, 41.
— Comp.: dryht-, gold-, hord-,
ofer-, sinc-, wundor-máðum.

máðm-æht, st. f., *treasure in jewels, costly objects:* gen. pl. máðm-
æhta, 1614, 2834.

máððum-fät, st. n., *treasure-casket*
or *cup, costly vessel:* nom. sg.,
2406.

máðm-gestreón, st. n., *precious
jewel:* gen. pl. máðm-gestreóna,
1932.

máðum-gifu, st. f., *gift of valuable
objects, largess of treasure:* dat. sg.
äfter máððum-gife, 1302.

máðum-sigl, st. n., *costly, sun-shaped
ornament, valuable decoration:*
gen. pl. máððum-sigla, 2758.

máðum-sweord, st. n., *costly sword*
(inlaid with gold and jewels): acc.
sg., 1024.

máðum-wela, w. m., *wealth of jew-*

els, *valuables:* dat. sg. äfter-máð-
ðum-welan (*after the sight of the
wealth of jewels*), 2751.

mágas. See mæg.

máge, w. f., *female relative:* gen.
sg. Grendles mágan (*mother*), 1392.

mán, st. n., *crime, misdeed:* instr.
sg. máne, 110, 979; adv., *crimi-
nally*, 1056.

mán-for-dædla, w. m., *evil-doer,
criminal:* nom. pl. mán-for-dæd-
lan, 563.

mán-sceaða, w. m., *mischievous,
hurtful foe, hostis nefastus:* nom.
sg. 713, 738, 1340; mán-sceaða,
2515.

mára (comp. of micel), adj., *greater,
stronger, mightier:* nom. sg. m.
mára, 1354, 2556; neut. máre,
1561; acc. sg. m. máran, 2017;
mund-gripe máran (*a mightier
hand-grip*), 754; with following
gen. pl. máran . . . eorla (*a more
powerful earl*), 247; fem. máran,
533, 1012; neut. máre, 518; with
gen. pl. morð-beala máre (*more,
greater, deeds of murder*), 136;
gen. sg. f. máran, 1824.

mæst (superl. of micel, mára), *great-
est, strongest:* nom. sg. neut. (with
partitive gen.), mæst, 78, 193; fem.
mæst, 2329; acc. sg. fem. fæhðe
mæste, 459; mæste . . . worolde
wynne (*the highest earthly pleasure*), 1080; neut. (with partitive
gen.) mæst marða, 2646; hond-
wundra mæst, 2769; bæl-fýra mæst,
3144; instr. sg. m. mæste cræfte,
2182.

mæg. See mæg.

mægð, st. f., *wife, maid, woman:*
nom. sg., 3017; gen. pl. mægða
hóse (*accompanied by her maids
of honor*), 925; mægða, 944, 1284.

mægen, st. n.: 1) *might, bodily*

strength, heroic power: acc. sg. mägen, 51S, 1707; instr. sg. mägene, 780(?), 2668; gen. sg. mägenes, 41S, 1271, 1535, 1717, etc.; mägnes, 671, 1762; mägenes strang, strengest (*great in strength*), 1845, 196; mägenes rôf (id., 2085. — 2) *prime, flower* (of a nation), *forces available in war:* acc. sg. swâ he oft (i.e. etan) dyde mägen Hrêðmanna (*the best of the Hrêð-men*), 445; gen. sg. wið manna hwone mägenes Deniga (*from*(?) *any of the forces of the Danes*), 155. — Comp. ofer-mägen.

mägen-âgend, pres. part., *having great strength, valiant:* gen. pl. -âgendra, 2838.

mägen-byrðen, st. f., *huge burthen:* acc. sg. mägen-byrðenne, 3092; dat. (instr.) sg., 1626.

mägen-eräft, st. m., *great, herolike, strength:* acc. sg., 380.

mägen-ellen, st. n. (the same), acc. sg., 660.

mägen-fultum, st. m., *material aid:* gen. pl. näs | ät | onne mätost mägen-fultuma (*that was not the least of strong helps*, i.e. the sword Hrunting), 1456.

mägen-ræs, st. m., *mighty attack, onslaught:* acc. sg., 1520.

mägen-strengo, st. f., *main strength, heroic power:* acc. sg., 2679.

mägen-wudu, st. m., *might-wood,* i.e. the spear, lance: acc. sg., 236.

mäst, st. m., *mast:* nom. sg., 1899; dat. sg. be mäste (*beside the mast*), 36; *to the mast,* 1906.

mæðum. See **mâðum, hyge-mâðum.**

mæg, st. m., *kinsman by blood:* nom. sg. mäg, 408, 738, 759, 814, 915, 1531, 1945, etc.; (*brother*), 468, 2605? acc. sg. mäg (*son*), 1340;

(*brother*), 2440, 2485, 2983; dat. sg. mäge, 1979; gen. sg. mäges, 2629, 2676, 2690, 2880; nom. pl. mâgas, 1016; acc. pl. mâgas, 2816; dat. pl. mâgum, 1179, 2615, 3066; (*to brothers*, 1168; mägum, 2354; gen. pl. mâga, 247, 1080, 1854, 2007, 2743. — Comp. : fäderen-, heâfod-, wine-mäg.

mæg-burh, st. f., *borough of blood-kinsmen, entire population united by ties of blood;* (in wider sense) *race, people, nation:* gen. sg. lond-rihtes... |äre mäg-burge (*of land possessions among the people,* i.e. of the Geátas), 2888.

mægð, st. f., *race, people:* acc. sg. mägðe, 1012; dat. sg. mägðe, 75; dat. pl. mägðum, 5; gen. pl. mägða, 25, 1772.

mæg-wine, st. m., *blood kinsman, friend,* 2480.

mæl, st. n.: 1) *time, point of time:* nom. sg. 316; | â wäs säl and mäl (*there was* [appropriate] *chance and time*), 1009; acc. sg. mäl, 2634; instr. pl. ärran mälum, 908, 2238, 3036; gen. pl. mäla, 1250; säla and mäla, 1612; mäla gehwylce (*each time, without intermission*), 2058. — 2) *sword, weapon:* nom. sg. broden (brogden) mäl (*the drawn sword*), 1617, 1668 (cf. Grimm, Andreas and Elene, p. 156). — 3) *mole, spot, mark.* — Comp.: gräg-, hring-, sceaðen-, wunden-mäl.

mæl-cearu, st. f., *long-continued sorrow, grief:* acc. sg. mäl-ceare, 189.

mæl-gesceaft, st. f., *fate, appointed time:* acc. pl. ic on earde bâd mäl-gesceafta (*awaited the time allotted for me by fate*), 2738.

mænan, w. v., with acc. in the sense

of (1) *to remember, mention, proclaim :* inf. mǣnan, ɟ06S; pret. part. þǣr wǣs Beówulfes mǣrðo mǣned, 85S. — 2) *to mention sorrowfully, mourn :* inf. 3173; pret. sg. giohðo mǣnde (*mourned sorrowfully*), 226S; pret. pl. mǣndun, 1150, 3150.

ge-mǣnan (see mǎn̄), w. v. with acc., *to injure maliciously, break :* subj. pret. pl. ge-mǣnden, 1102.

ge-mǣne, adj., *common, in common :* nom. sg. gemǣne, 2474; þǣr unc hwīle wǣs hand gemǣne (i.e. in battle), 213S; sceal ûrum þāt sweord and helm bâm gemǣne (i.e. wesan), 2661; nom. pl. gemǣne, 1S61; dat. pl. ɟāt þāṁ folcum sceal...sib gemǣnum (attraction for gemǣne, i.e. wesan), 1S5S; gen. pl. unc sceal (i.e. wesan) fela mâðma gemǣnra (*we two shall share many treasures together*), 17S5.

mǣrðu, st. f.: 1) *glory, a hero's fame :* nom. sg. 85S; acc. sg. mǣrðo, 600(?), 68S; acc. pl. mǣrða, 2997; instr. pl. mǣrðum (*gloriously*), 2515: gen. pl. mǣrða, 504, 1531. — 2) *deed of glory, heroism :* acc. sg. mǣrðo, 2135; gen. pl. mǣrða, 408, 2646. — Comp. ellen-mǣrðu.

mǣre, adj., *memorable; celebrated, noble; well known, notorious :* nom. sg. m. mǣre, 103, 129, 1716, 1762; se mǣra, 763, 2012, 25S8; also as vocative m. se mǣra, 1475; nom. fem. mǣru, 2017; mǣre, 1953; neut. mǣre, 2406; acc. sg. m. mǣrne, 36, 201, 353, 1599, 2385, 2722, 27S9, 3099; neut. mǣre, 1024; dat. sg. mǣrum, 345, 1302, 1993, 20S0, 2573; tô þām mǣran, 270; gen. sg. mǣres, 79S; mǣran, 1730; nom. pl.

mǣre, 3071; superl. mǣrost, 899. — Comp.: fore-, heaðo-mǣre.

mǣst. See mâra.

mǣte, adj., *moderate, small :* superl. nom. sg. mǣtost, 1456.

mecg, mǣcg, st.m., *son, youth, man :* in comp. hilde-, orct-mecg, wrǣc-mǣcg.

medla. See on-medla.

medu, st. m., *mead :* acc. sg. medu, 2634; dat. sg. tô medo, 605.

medo-ǣrn, st. n., *mead-hall :* acc. sg. medo-ärn (Heorot), 69.

medu-benc, st. f., *mead-bench, bench in the mead-hall :* nom. sg. medubenc, 777; dat. sg. medu-bence, 1053; medo-bence, 106S, 21S6; meodu-bence, 1903.

medu-dreám, st. m., *mead-joy, joyous carousing during mead-drinking :* acc. sg. 2017.

medo-ful, st. n., *mead-cup :* acc. sg. 625, 1016.

medo-heal, st. f., *mead-hall :* nom. sg., 4S4; dat. sg. meodu-healle, 639.

medu-scenc, st.m., *mead-can, vessel :* instr. pl. meodu-scencum, 19S1.

medu-seld, st. n., *mead-seat, mead-house :* acc. sg., 3066.

medo-setl, st. n., *mead-seat upon which one sits mead-drinking :* gen. pl. meodo-setla, 5.

medo-stig, st. f., *mead-road, road to the mead-hall :* acc. sg. medo-stig, 925.

medo-wang, st. m., *mead-field (where the mead-hall stood) :* acc. pl. medo-wongas, 1644.

meðel, st. n., *speech, conversation :* dat. sg. on meðle, 1S77.

meðel-stede, st. m., (properly *place of speech, judgment-seat*), here *meeting-place, battle-field* (so, also,

425, the battle is conceived under the figure of a parliament or convention) : dat. sg. on þäm meðelstede, 1083.

meðel-word, st. n., *words called forth at a discussion; address:* instr. pl. meðel-wordum, 236.

melda, w. m., *finder, informer, betrayer:* gen. sg. þäs meldan, 2406.

meltan, st. v. intrans., *to consume by fire, melt* or *waste away:* inf., 3012; pret. sg. mealt, 2327; pl. multon, 1121.

ge-meltan, the same: pret. sg. gemealt, 898, 1609, 1616; negemealt him se môd-sefa (*his courage did not desert him*), 2629.

men. See man.

mene, st. m., *neck ornament, necklace, collar:* acc. sg., 1200.

mengan, w. v., *to mingle, unite, with,* w. acc. of thing: inf. se þe meregrundas mengan scolde, 1450.

ge-mengan, *to mix with, commingle:* pret. part., 849, 1594.

menigeo, st. f., *multitude, many:* nom. and acc. sg. mâðma menigeo (*multitude of treasures, presents*), 2144; so, mänigo, 41.

mercels, st. m., *mark, aim:* gen. sg. mercelses, 2440.

mere, st. m., *sea, ocean:* nom. sg. se mere, 1363; acc. sg. on mere, 1131, 1604; on nicera mere, 846; dat. sg. fram mere, 856.

mere-deór, st. n., *sea-beast:* acc. sg., 558.

mere-fara, w. m., *seafarer:* gen. sg. mere-faran, 502.

mere-fix, st. m., *sea-fish:* gen. pl. mere-fixa (*the whale,* cf. 540), 549.

mere-grund, st. m., *sea-bottom:* acc. sg., 2101; acc. pl. mere-grundas, 1450.

mere-hrägl, st. n., *sea-garment,*

i.e., sail: gen. pl. mere-hrägla sum, 1906.

mere-liðend, pres. part., *moving on the sea, sailor:* nom. pl. mere-liðende, 255.

mere-stræt, st. f., *sea-street, way over the sea:* acc. pl. mere-stræta, 514.

mere-strengo, st. f., *sea-power, strength in the sea:* acc. sg., 533.

mere-wîf, st. n., *sea-woman, mer-woman:* acc. sg. (of Grendel's mother), 1520.

mergen. See morgen.

met, st. n., *thought, intention* (cf. metian = meditari): acc. pl. onsæl meoto, 489 (meaning doubtful; see Bugge, Journal 8, 292; Dietrich, Haupt's Zeits. 11, 411; Körner, Eng. Stud. 2, 251).

ge-met, st. n., *an apportioned share; might, power, ability:* nom. sg. nis þät . . . gemet mannes nefne mîn ânes (*nobody, myself excepted, can do that*), 2534; acc. sg. ofer mîn gemet (*beyond my power*), 2880; dat. sg. mid gemete, 780.

ge-met, adj., *well-measured, meet, good:* nom. sg. swâ him gemet þince (þûhte), (*as seemed meet to him*), 688, 3058. See un-gemete, adv.

metan, st. v., *to measure, pass over* or *along:* pret. pl. fealwe stræte mearum mæton (*measured the yellow road with their horses*), 918; so, 514, 1634.

ge-metan, the same: pret. sg. medu-stîg gemät (*measured, walked over, the road to the mead-hall*), 925.

metod, st. m. (the measuring, arranging) *Creator, God:* nom. sg., 110, 707, 968, 1058, 2528; scîr metod, 980; sôð metod, 1612; acc.

sg. metod, 180; dat. sg. metode, 169, 1779; gen. sg. metodes, 671. — Comp. cald-metod.

metod-sceaft, st. f.: 1) *the Creator's determination, divine purpose, fate:* acc. sg. -sceaft, 1078.— 2) *the Creator's glory:* acc. sg. metod-sceaft seón (i.e. die), 1181; dat. sg. tó metod-sceafte, 2816.

mêce, st. m., *sword:* nom. sg., 1939; acc. sg. mêce, 2048; brâdne mêce, 2979; gen. sg. mêces, 1766, 1813, 2615, 2940; dat. pl. instr. mêcum, 565; gen. pl. mêca, 2686.—Comp.: beado-, häft-, hilde-mêce.

mêd, st. f., *meed, reward:* acc. sg. mêde, 2135; dat. sg. mêde, 2147; gen. pl. mêda, 1179.

ge-mêde, st. n., *approval, permission* (Grein): acc. pl. ge-mêdu, 247.

mêðe, adj., *tired, exhausted, dejected:* in comp. hyge-, sæ-mêðe.

mêtan, w. v., *to meet, find, fall in with:* with acc., pret. pl. syððan Aescheres...hafelan mêtton,1422; subj. pret. sg.] ät he ne mêtte ... on elran man mundgripe mâran (*that he never met, in any other man, with a mightier hand-grip*), 752.

ge-mêtan, with acc., the same: pret. sg. gemêtte, 758, 2786; pl. näs]â long tó] on,] ät] â aglæcean hy eft gemêtton (*it was not long after that the warriors again met each other*), 2593.

ge-mêting, st. f., *meeting, hostile coming together:* nom. sg., 2002.

meagol, adj., *mighty, immense; formal, solemn:* instr. pl. meaglum wordum, 1981.

mearc, st. f., *frontier, limit, end:* dat. sg. tó mearce (*the end of life*), 2385.— Comp. Weder-mearc, 298.

ge-mearc, st. n., *measure, distance:* comp. fót-, mil-ge-mearc.

mearcian, w. v., *to mark, stain:* pres. ind. sg. mearcað mórhôpu (*will stain, mark, the moor with the blood of the corpse*), 450.

ge-mearcian, the same: pres. part. (Cain) morðre gemearcod (*murder-marked* [cf. 1 Book Mos. IV. 15]), 1265; swâ wäs on]æm scennum ...gemearcod ... hwam] ät sweord geworht wære (*engraved for whom the sword had been wrought*), 1696.

mearc-stapa, w. m., *march-strider, frontier-haunter* (applied to Grendel and his mother): nom. sg., 103; acc. pl. mearc-stapan, 1349.

mearh, st. m., *horse, steed:* nom. pl. mearas, 2164; acc. pl. mearas, 866, 1036; dat. pl. inst. mearum, 856, 918; mearum and mâðmum, 1049, 1899; gen. pl. meara and mâðma, 2167.

mearn. See murnan.

medu. See medu.

meoto. See met.

meotud. See metod.

meowle, w. f., *maiden:* comp. geó-meowle.

micel, adj., *great, huge, long* (of time): nom. sg. m., 129, 502; fem., 67, 146, 170; neut., 772; acc. sg. m. micelne, 3099; fem. micle, 1779, 3092; neut. micel, 270, 1168. The comp. mâre must be supplied before]one in: medu-ärn micel ... (mâre)]one yldo bearn æfre ge-frunon, 69; instr. sg. ge-trume micle, 923; micle (*by much, much*); micle leófre (*far dearer*), 2652; efne swâ micle (lässa), ([*l_ss] even by so much*), 1284; oftor micle (*much oftener*), 1580; dat. sg. weak form miclan, 2850; gen. sg.

miclan, 979. The gen. sg. micles is an adv. = *much, very:* micles wyrðne gedôn (*deem worthy of much*, i.e. honor very highly), 2186; tô fela micles (*far too much, many*), 695; acc. pl. micle, 1349. Compar., see **mâra.**

mid, I. prep. w. dat., instr., and acc., signifying preëminently *union, community, with,* hence: 1) w. dat.: a) *with, in company, community, with:* mid Finne, 1129; mid Hrôðgâre, 1593; mid scip-herge, 243; mid gesîðum (*with his comrades*), 1314; so, 1318, 1964, 2950, etc.; mid his freô-drihtne, 2628; mid þæm lâcum (*with the gifts*), 1869; so, 2789, 125; mid hæle (*with good luck!*), 1218; mid bæle fôr (*sped off amid fire*), 2309. The prep. postponed: him mid (*with him, in his company*), 41; *with him,* 1626; ne wäs him Fitela mid (*was not with him*), 890. b) *with, among:* mid Geátum (*among the Geátas*), 195, 2193, 2624; mid Scyldingum, 274; mid Eotenum, 903; mid yldum (eldum), 77, 2612; mid him (*with, among, one another*), 2949. In temporal sense: mid ær-däge (*at dawn*), 126. — 2) *with, with the help of, through,* w. dat.: mid âr-stafum (*through his grace*), 317; so, 2379; mid grâpe (*with the fist*), 438; so, 1462, 2721; mid his hete-þoncum (*through his hatred*), 475; mid sweorde, 574; so, 1660, 2877; mid gemete (*through, by, his power*), 780; so, 1220, 2536, 2918; mid gôde (*with benefits*), 1185; mid hearme (*with harm, insult*), 1893; mid þære sorge (*with [through?] this sorrow*), 2469; mid rihte (*by rights*), 2057. With

instr.: mid þý wîfe (*through [marriage with] the woman*), 2029. — 3) w. acc., *with, in community, company, with:* mid his eorla ge-driht, 357; so, 634, 663, 1673; mid hine, 880; mid mînne gold-gyfan, 2653. II. adv., mid, *thereamong, in the company,* 1643; *at the same time, likewise,* 1650.

middan-geard, st. m., *globe, earth:* acc. sg., 75, 1772; dat. sg. on mid-dan-gearde, 2997; gen. sg. middan-geardes, 504, 752.

midde, w. f., *middle = medius:* dat. sg. on middan (*through the middle, in two*), 2706; gen. sg. (adv.) tô-middes (*in the midst*), 3142.

middel-niht, st. f., *midnight:* dat. pl. middel-nihtum, 2783, 2834.

miht, st. f., *might, power, authority:* acc. sg.| urh drihtnes miht (*through the Lord's help, power*), 941; instr. pl. selfes mihtum, 701.

mihtig, adj.: 1) *physically strong, powerful:* nom. sg. mihtig mere-deôr, 558; mere-wif mihtig, 1520. — 2) *possessing authority, mighty:* nom. sg. mihtig god, 702, 1717, 1726; dat. sg. mihtigan drihtne, 1399. — Comp.: äl-, fore-mihtig.

milde, adj., *kind, gracious, generous:* nom. sg. môdes milde (*kind-hearted*), 1230; instr. pl. mildum wordum (*graciously*), 1173. Superl. nom. sg. worold-cyning mannum mildust (*a king most liberal to men*), 3183.

milts, st. f., *kindness, benevolence:* nom. sg., 2922.

missan, w. v. with gen., *to miss, err in:* pret. sg. miste mercelses (*missed the mark*), 2440.

missere, st. n., *space of a semester, half a year:* gen. pl. hund missera (*fifty winters*), 2734, 2210; generally, *a long period of time, season,* 1499, 1770; fela missera, 153, 2621.

mist-hliϑ, st. n., *misty cliff, cloud-capped slope:* dat. pl. under mist-hleoϑum, 711.

mistig, adj., *misty:* acc. pl. mistige móras, 162.

mil-gemearce, st. n., *measure by miles:* gen. sg. mil-gemearces, 1363.

min: 1) poss. pron., *my, mine,* 255, 345, etc.; Hygelâc mîn (*my lord,* or *king, II.*), 2435. — 2) gen. sg. of pers. pron. ic, *of me,* 2085, 2534, etc.

molde, w. f., *dust; earth, field:* in comp. grãs-molde.

mon. See **man.**

ge-mong. See **ge-mang.**

morϑ-bealu, st. n., *murder, deadly bale* or *deed of murder:* gen. pl. morϑ-beala, 136.

morϑor, st. n., *deed of violence, murder:* dat. instr. sg. morϑre, 893, 1265, 2783; gen. sg. morϑres, 2056; morϑres scyldig (*victim of a violent death*), 1684.

morϑor-bed, st. n., *bed of death, murder-bed:* acc. sg. wäs þam yldestan . . . morϑor-bed stred (*a bed of death was spread for the eldest,* i.e. through murder his death-bed was prepared), 2437.

morϑor-bealu, st. n., *death-bale, destruction by murder:* acc. sg. morϑor-bealo, 1080, 2743.

morϑor-hete, st. m., *murderous hate:* gen. sg. þäs morϑor-hetes, 1106

morgen, morn, mergen, st. m., *morning, forenoon:* also *morrow:* nom. sg. morgen, 1785, 2125; (*morrow*), 2104; acc. sg. on morgen (*in the morning*), 838; dat. sg. on morgne, 2485; on mergenne, 565, 2940; gen. pl. morna gehwylce (*every morning*), 2451.

morgen-ceald, adj., *morning-cold, dawn-cold:* nom. sg. gâr morgen-ceald (*spear chilled by the early air of morn*), 3023.

morgen-lang, adj., *lasting through the morning:* acc. sg. morgen-longne däg (*the whole forenoon*), 2895.

morgen-leóht, st. n., *morning-light:* nom. sg., 605, 918.

morgen-swêg, st. m., *morning-cry, cry at morn:* nom. sg., 129.

morgen-tîd, st. f., *morning-tide:* acc. sg. on morgen-tîde, 484, 818(?).

morn. See **morgen.**

môd, st. n.: 1) *heart, soul, spirit, mood, mind, manner of thinking:* nom. sg., 50, 731; wäfre môd (*the flickering spirit, the fading breath*), 1151; acc. sg. on môd (*into his mind*), 67; dat. instr. sg. môde geþungen *of mature, lofty spirit*), 625; on môde (*in heart, mind*), 754, 1845, 2282, 2528; on hreóum môde (*fierce of spirit*), 2582; gen. sg. môdes, 171, 811, 1707; môdes bliϑe (*gracious-minded, kindly disposed*), 436; so, môdes milde, 1230; môdes seóce (*depressed in mind*), 1604. — 2) *boldness, courage:* nom. and acc. sg., 1058, 1168. 3) *passion, fierceness:* nom. sg., 549. — Comp. form adj.: galg-, geômor-, gläd-, gûϑ-, hreóh-, irre-, sârig-, stîϑ-, swiϑ-, wêrig-môd.

môd-cearu, st. f., *grief of heart:* acc. sg. môd-ceare, 1993, 3150.

môd-gehygd, st. f., *thought of the heart; mind:* instr. pl. môd-ge-h gdum, 233

môd-ge-þanc, st. n., *mood-thought;*

meditation: acc. sg. môd-ge-þonc, 1730.

môd-giômor, adj., *grieved at heart, dejected:* nom. sg., 2895.

môdig, adj., *courageous:* nom. sg., 605, 1644, 1813, 2758; he þäs (Jäm, MS.) môdig wäs (*had the courage for it*), 1509; se môdega, 814; dat. sg. mid þam môdigan, 3012; gen. sg. môdges, 502; môdiges, 2699; Geáta leód georne trûwode môdgan mägnes (*trusted firmly in his bold strength*), 671; nom. pl. môdge, 856; môdige, 1877; gen. pl. môdigra, 312, 1889. — Comp. fela-môdig.

môdig-lîc, adj., *of bold appearance:* compar. acc. pl. môdiglicran, 337.

môd-lufe, w. f., *heart's affection, love:* gen. pl. þînre môd-lufan, 1824.

môd-sefa, w. m., *thought of the heart; brave, bold temper; courage:* nom. sg., 349, 1854, 2629; acc. sg. môd-sefan, 2013; dat. sg. môd-sefan, 180.

môd-þracu, st. f., *boldness, courage, strength of mind:* dat. sg. for his môd-þräce, 385.

môdor, f., *mother:* nom. sg., 1259, 1277, 1283, 1684, 2119; acc. sg. môdor, 1539, 2140, 2933.

môna, w. m., *moon:* gen. sg. mônan, 94.

môr, st. m., *moor, morass, swamp:* acc. sg. ofer myrcan môr, 1406; dat. sg. of môre, 711; acc. pl. môras, 103, 162, 1349.

môr-hôp, st. n., *place of refuge in the moor, hiding-place in the swamp:* acc. pl. môr-hôpu, 450.

ge-môt, st. n., *meeting:* in comp. hand-, torn-ge-môt.

môtan, pret.-pres. v.: 1) *power or permission to have something, to*

be permitted; may, can: pres. sg. I., III. môt, 186, 442, 604; II. môst, 1672; pl. môton, 347, 365, 395; pres. subj. ic môte, 431; III. se þe môte, 1388; pret. sg. môste, 168, 707, 736, 895, 1488, 1999, 2242, 2505, etc.; pl. môston, 1629, 1876, 2030, 2125, 2248; pres. subj. sg. II. þät þu hine selfne geseón môste (*mightest see*), 962. — 2) *shall, must, be obliged:* pres. sg. môt, 2887; pret. sg. môste, 1940; þær he þ9 fyrste forman dôgore wealdan môste, swâ him Wyrd ne gescrâf, hrêð ät hilde (*if he must for the first time that day be victorious, as Fate had denied him victory,* cf. 2681, 2683 sqq.), 2575.

ge-munan, pret.-pres. v., *to have in mind, be mindful; remember, think of,* w. acc.: pres. sg. hine gearwe geman witena wel-hwylc (*each of the knowing ones still remembers him well*), 265; ic þe þäs leán geman (*I shall not forget thy reward for this*), 1221; ic þät eall gemon (*I remember all that*), 2428; so, 1702, 2043; gif he þät eall gemon hwät . . . (*if he is mindful of all that which ...*), 1186; ic þät mæl gemon hwær . . . (*I remember the time when ...*), 2634; pret. sg. w. gemunde . . . æfen-spräce (*recalled his evening speech*), 759; so, 871, 1130, 1260, 1271, 1291, 2115, 2432, 2607, 2679; se þäs leód-hryres leán ge-munde (*was mindful of reward for the fall of the ruler*), 2392; þät he Eotena bearn inne gemunde (*that he in this should remember, take vengeance on, the children of the Jutes*), 1142; so, hond gemunde fæhðo genôge (*his hand remembered strife enough*), 2490; ne ge-

munde mago Ecgláfes þát ... (*remembered not that which* . . .),
1466; pret. pl. helle gemundon
in mód-sefan *their thoughts* [as
heathens] *fixed themselves on, remembered, hell* , 179.

on-munan, w. acc. pers. and gen.
of thing, *to admonish, exhort:*
pret. sg. onmunde úsic mæŕ a (*exhorted us to deeds of glory*), 2641.

mund, st. f., *hand:* instr. pl. mundum, mid mundum, 236, 514, 1462,
3023, 3092.

mund-bora, w. m., *protector, guardian, preserver:* nom sg., 1481, 2780.

mund-gripe, st. m., *hand-grip,
seizure:* acc. sg. mund-gripe, 754;
dat. sg. mund-gripe, 280(?), 1535;
áfter mund-gripe (*after having
seized the criminal*, 1939.

murnan, st. v., *to shrink from, be
afraid of, avoid:* pret. sg. nó
mearn fore fǽhðe and fyrene, 136;
so, 1538; nalles for ealdre mearn
(*was not apprehensive for his life*),
1443. — 2) *to mourn, grieve:* pres.
part. him wǽs ... murnende mód,
50; pres. subj., þonne he fela murne
(*than that he should mourn much*),
1386.

be-murnan, be-meornan, with
acc., *to mourn over:* pret. bemearn, 908, 1078.

murn-líce. See un-murn-líce.

múð-bana, w. m., *mouth-destroyer:*
dat. sg. tó múð-bonan (of Grendel
because he bit his victim to death),
2080.

múða, w. m., *mouth, entrance:* acc.
sg. recedes múðan (*mouth of the
house, door*), 725.

ge-mynd, st. f., *memory, memorial,
remembrance:* dat. pl. tó gemyndum, 2805, 3017. See weorð-mynd.

myndian, w. v., *to call to mind,
remember:* pres. sg. myndgað,
2058; pres. part. w. gen. gif þonne
Fresna hwylc ... þäs morðorhetes myndgiend wǽre (*were to
call to mind the bloody feud*), 1106.

ge-myndian, w. v. w. acc., *to remember:* hið gemyndgad ... eaforan ellor-síð (*is reminded of his
son's decease*), 2451.

ge-myndig, adj., *mindful:* nom.
sg. w. gen., 614, 869, 1174, 1531,
2083, etc.

myne, st. m.: 1) *mind, wish:* nom.
sg., 2573. — 2) *l v* (?): ne his
myne wisse (*whose [God's] love
he knew not*), 169.

ge-mynian, w. v. w. acc., *to be
mindful of:* imper. sg. gemyne
mǽrðu! 660.

myntan, w. v., *to intend, think of,
resolve:* pret. sg. mynte ... manna cynnes sumne besyrwan(*meant
to entrap all*(?) [see sum], *some
one of*(?), *the men*), 713; mynte
þát he gedǽlde ... (*thought to
sever*), 732; mynte se mǽra, þǽr
he meahte swá, widre gewindan
(*intended to flee* , 763.

myrce, adj., *murky, dark:* acc. sg.
ofer myrcan mór, 1406.

myrð, st. f., *joy, mirth:* dat. (instr.)
sg. módes myrðe, 811.

N

naca, w. m., *vessel, ship:* acc. sg.
nacan, 295; gen. sg. nacan, 214.
—Comp.: hring-, ýð-naca.

nacod, adj., *naked:* nom. and acc.
sg. swurd, gúð-bill nacod, 539,
2586; nacod níð-draca, 2274.

nallas, nales, nallas. See nealles.

nama, w. m., *name:* nom. sg. Beó-

wulf is mîn nama, 343; wäs þäm
häft-mêce Hrunting nama, 1458;
acc. sg. scôp him Heort naman
(*gave it the name Hart*), 78.
nâ (from ne-â), strength. negative,
never, not all, 445, 567, 1537.
nâh, from ne-âh. See âgan.
nân (from ne-ân), indef. pron., *none,
no:* with gen. pl. gûð-billa nân,
804; adjectively, nân ... îren ær-
gôd, 990.
nât, from ne-wât : *I know not* = *nescio.* See witan.
nât-hwyle (nescio quis, ne-wât-
hwyle, *know not who, which*, etc.),
indef. pron., *any, a certain one,
some or other:* 1) w. partitive gen. :
nom. sg. gumena nât-hwyle, 2234;
gen. sg. nât-hwylees (þâra banena),
2054; niða nât-hwylees(?), 2216;
nât-hwylees häleða bearna, 2225.
— 2) adjectively : dat. sg. in nið-
sele nât-hwylcum, 1514.
näbben, from ne-häbben (subj.
pres.). See habban.
näfne. See nefne.
nägel, st. m., *nail:* gen. pl. nägla
(of the finger-nails), 986.
nägled, part., *nailed?, nail-like?,
buckled?:* acc. sg. neut. nägled
(MS. gled) sinc, 2024.
näs, st. m., *naze, rock projecting
into the sea, cliff, promontory:* acc.
sg. näs, 1440, 1601, 2899; dat. sg.
nässe, 2244, 2418; acc. pl. windige
nässas, 1412; gen. pl. nässa, 1361.
näs, 'from ne-wäs (*was not*). See
wesan.
näs, neg. adv., *not, not at all*, 562,
2263.
näs-hlið, st. n., *declivity, slope of a
promontory that sinks downward
to the sea:* dat. pl. on näs-hleoðum,
1428.
næfre, adv., *never*, 247, 583, 592,

656, 719, 1042, 1049, etc.; also
strengthened by ne : næfre ne,
1461.
ge-nægan, w. v. w. acc. pers. and
gen. of thing, *to attack, press:*
pret. pl. niða genægdan nefan
Hererices (*in combats pressed hard
upon H.'s nephew*), 2207; pret.
part. wearð...niða genæged, 1440.
nænig (from ne-ænig), pron., *not
any, none, no:* 1) substantively w.
gen. pl.: nom. sg., 157, 242, 692;
dat. sg. nænegum, 599; gen. pl.
nænigra, 950. — 2) adjectively:
nom. sg. ôðer nænig, 860; nænig
wäter, 1515; nænig ... deór, 1934;
acc. sg. nænigne ... horð-mâðum,
1199.
nære, from ne-wære (*were not, would
not be*). See wesan.
ne, simple neg., *not*, 38, 50, 80, 83,
109, etc.; before imper. ne sorga !
1385; ne gŷm ! 1761, etc. Doubled
= *certainly not, not even that:* ne
ge ... gearwe ne wisson (*ye certainly have not known*, etc.), 245;
so, 863; ne ic ... wihte ne wêne
(*nor do I at all in the least expect*),
2923; so, 182. Strengthened by
other neg.: nôðer...ne, 2125; swâ
he ne mihte nô ... (*so that he absolutely could not*), 1509.
ne ... ne, *not ... and not, nor;
neither ... nor*, 154-157, 511,
1083-1085, etc. Another neg. may
supply the place of the first ne:
so, nô ... ne, 575-577, 1026-1028,
1393-1395, etc.; næfre ... ne, 583–
584; nalles ... ne, 3016-3017.
The neg. may be omitted the first
time: ær ne siððan (*neither before
nor after, before nor since*), 719;
sûð ne norð (*south nor north*),
859; âdl ne yldo (*neither illness
nor old age*), 1737; wordum ne

worcum (*neither by word nor deed*), 1101; wiston and ne wêndon (*knew not and weened not*), 1605.

nefa, w. m., *nephew, grandson:* nom. sg. nefa *(grandson)*, 1204; so, 1963; *(nephew)*, 2171; acc. sg. nefan (*nephew*), 2207; dat. sg. nefan (*nephew*), 882.

nefne, näfne, nemne (orig. from ni-iba-ni): 1) subj.: a) with depend. clause — *unless:* nefne him witig god wyrd forstôde (*if fate, the wise God, had not prevented him*), 1057; nefne god sylfa ... sealde (*unless God himself,* etc.), 3055; näfne him his wlite leóge (MS. næfne) (*unless his face belie him*), 250; näfne he wäs mâra (*except that he was huger*), 1354; nemne him heaðo-byrne helpe gefremede, 1553; so, 2655. — b) w. follow. substantive — *except, save, only:* nefne sin-freá (*except the husband*), 1935; ic lyt hafo heáfod-mâga nefne Hygelâc þec (*have no near kin but thee*), 2152; nis þät eówer (gen. pl.) stð ... nefne mîn ânes, 2534. — 2) Prep. with dat., *except:* nemne feáum ânum, 1082.

ge-nehost. See ge-neahhe.

nelle, from ne-wille (*I will not*). See willan.

nemnan, w. v. w. acc.: 1) *to name, call:* pres. pl. þone yldestan oretmecgas Beówulf nemnað (*the warriors call the most distinguished one Beówulf*), 364; so inf. nemnan, 2024; pret. pl. nemdon, 1355. — 2) *to address*, as in be-nemnan, *to pronounce solemnly, put under a spell:* pret. sg. Fin Hengeste ... âðum be-nemde þät (*asserted, promised under oath that*

...), 1098; pret. pl. swâ hit ôð dômes däg diópe benemdon þeódnas mære (*put under a curse*), 3070.

nemne. See nefne.

nerian, ge-nerian, w. v., *to save, rescue, liberate:* pres. sg. Wyrd oft nereð unfægne eorl, 573; pret. part. häfde ... sele Hrô gâres genered wið nîða (*saved from hostility*), 828.

ge-nesan, st. v.: 1) intrans., *to remain over, be preserved:* pret. sg. hrôf âna genäs ealles ansund (*the roof alone was quite sound*), 1000. — 2) w. acc., *to endure successfully, survive, escape from:* pret. sg. se þâ säcce ge-näs, 1978; fela ic ... gûð-ræsa ge-näs, 2427; pret. part. swâ he nîða gehwane genesen häfde, 2398.

net, st. n., *net:* in comp. breóst-, here-, hring-, inwit-, scaro-net.

nêdla, w. m., *dire necessity, distress:* in comp. þreá-nêdla.

nêðan (G. nanþjan), w. v., *to venture, undertake boldly:* pres. part. nearo nêðende (*encountering peril*), 2351; pret. pl. þær git ... on deóp wäter aldrum nêðdon (*where ye two risked your lives in the deep water*), 510; so, 538.

ge-nêðan, the same: inf. ne dorste under ýða gewin aldre ge-nêðan, 1470. With depend. clause: nænig þät dorste genêðan þät (*none durst undertake to ...*), 1934; pret. sg. he under hârne stân âna genêðde frêcne dæde (*he risked alone the bldeed, venturing under the grey rock*), 889; (ic) wige under wätere weorc genêðde earfoð-lice (*I with difficulty stood the work under the water in battle*, i.e. could hardly win the victory),

1657; ic geneðde fela gůða (ventured on, risked, many contests),
2512; pres. pl. (of majesty) we
... frêcne geneðdon eafoð uncûðes (we have boldly risked, dared,
the monster's power), 961.
nêh. See neáh.
ge-neahhe, adv., enough, sufficient-
ly, 784, 3153; superl. genehost
brägd eorl Beówulfes ealde lâfe
(many an earl of B.'s), 795.
nealles (from ne-ealles), adv., om-
nino non, not at all, by no means:
nealles, 2146, 2168, 2180, 2223,
2597, etc.; nallas, 1720, 1750;
nalles, 338, 1019, 1077, 1443, 2504,
etc.; nalas, 43, 1494, 1530, 1538;
nales, 1812.
nearo, st. n., strait, danger, distress:
acc. sg. nearo, 2351, 2595.
nearo, adj., narrow: acc. pl. f.
nearwe, 1410.
nearwe, adv., narrowly, 977.
nearo-cräft, st. m., art of rendering
difficult of access?, inaccessibility
(see 2214 seqq.): instr. pl. nearo-
cräftum, 2244.
nearo-fâh, m., foe that causes distress, war-foe: gen. sg. nearo-
fâges, 2318.
nearo-þearf, st. f., dire need, distress: acc. sg. nearo-þearfe, 422.
ge-nearwian, w. v., to drive into
a corner, press upon: pret. part.
genearwod, 1439.
neáh, nêh: 1) adj., near, nigh:
nom. sg. neáh, 1744, 2729. In
superl. also = last: instr. sg. nýhstan sîðe (for the last time), 1204;
niéhstan sîðe, 2512.
  2) adv., near: feor and (oððe)
neáh, 1222, 2871; w. dat. sæ-
grunde neáh, 564; so, 1925, 2243;
holm-wylme nêh, 2412. Compar.
neár, 746.

neán, adv., near by, (from) close
at hand, 528; (neon, MS.), 3105;
feorran and neán, 840; neán and
feorran, 1175, 2318.
ge-neát, st. m., comrade, companion:
in comp. beód-, heorð-geneát.
nioðor. See niðer.
neowol, adj., steep, precipitous:
acc. pl. neowle, 1412.
neód, st. f., polite intercourse regu-
lated by etiquette?, hall-joy? : acc.
sg. nióde, 2117.
neódu?, 2216.
neód-laðu, st. f., polite invitation;
wish : dat. sg. äfter neód-laðu (according to his wishes), 1321.
neósan, neósian, w. v. w. gen., to
seek out, look for; to attack: inf.
neósan, 125, 1787, 1792, 1807,
2075; niósan, 2389, 2672; neósian, 115, 1126; niósian, 3046;
pret. sg. niósade, 2487.
neótan, st. v., to take, accept, w.
gen.; to use, enjoy: imper. sg.
neót, 1218.
be-neótan, w. dat., to rob, deprive
of: inf. hine aldre be-neótan, 681;
pret. sg. cyning ealdre bi-neát (deprived the king of life), 2397.
nicor, st. m., sea-horse, walrus, sea-
monster (cf. Bugge in Zacher's
Journal, 4, 197): acc. pl. niceras,
422, 575; nicras, 1428; gen. pl.
nicera, 846.
nicor-hûs, st. n., house or den of sea-
monsters: gen. pl. nicor-hûsa, 1412.
nið, st. m., man, human being: gen.
pl. niðða, 1006; niða? (passage
corrupt), 2216.
niðer, nyðer, neoðor, adv., down,
downward: niðer, 1361; nioðor,
2700; nyðer, 3045.
nið-sele, st. m., hall, room, in the
deep (Grein): dat. sg. [in] nið-
sele nât-hwylcum, 1514.

nigen, num., *nine:* acc. sg. nigene,
575.

niht, st. f. *night:* nom. sg., 115,
547, 65o, 1321, 2117; acc. sg.
niht, 135, 737, 2939; g:strau niht
(*yester-night*), 1335; dat. sg. on
niht, 575, 634; on wanre niht, 703;
gen. sg. nihtes hwilum (*sometimes
at night, in t' · hours of the night*),
3045; as adv. · *of a nig ht, by night*,
G. nachts, 422, 2274; däges and
nihtes, 2270; acc. pl. seofon nil.t
(*se'nnight, seven days,* cf. Tac.
Germ. 11), 517; dat. pl. sweartum
nihtum, 167; deorcum nihtum, 275,
221; gen. pl. nihta, 545, 1360 –
Comp.: middel-, sin-niht.

niht-bealu, st. n., *night-bale, destruction by night:* gen. pl. niht-
bealwa, 193.

niht-helm, st. m., *veil* or *canopy of
night.* nom. sg., 1790.

niht-long, adj., *lasting through the
night:* acc. sg. m. niht-longne fyrst
(*space of a night*), 528.

niht-weorc, st. n., *night-work, deed
done at night:* instr. sg. niht-
weorce, 828.

niman, st. v. w. acc.: 1) *to take,
hold, seize, undertake:* pret. sg.
nam þä mid handa hige-þihtigne
rinc, 747; pret. pl. we . . . niôde
nâman, 2117. — 2) *to take, take
away, deprive of:* pres. sg. se þe
hine deâð nimeð (*he whom death
carrieth off*), 441; so, 447; nymeð, 1847; nymeð nyd-bâde, 599;
subj. pres. gif mec hild nime, 452,
1882; pret. sg. ind. nam on Ongenþió iren-byrnan, 2987; ne nom he
. . . mâ'm-æhta mâ (*he took no
more of the rich treasures*), 1613;
pret. part. þä wäs . . . seô cwên
numen (*the queen carried off*),
1154

be-niman, *to deprive of:* pret. sg.
ôð þät hine yldo benam mägenes
wynnum (*till age bereft him of j y
in his strength*), 1887.

for-niman, *to carry off:* pres. sg.
þe þä deâð for-nam (*whom death
arr..d of*), 488; so, 557, 696,
1081, 1124, 1206, 1437, etc. Also,
dat. f or acc.: pret. pl. him irenna
ecge fornâmon, 2829.

ge-niman: 1) *to take, seize:* pret.sg.
(hine) he healse ge-nam (*clasped
him around the neck, embraced
him*), 1873. — 2) *to take, take
away:* pret. on reste genam þritig
þegna, 122; heô under heolfre genam cûðe folme, 1303; segn eác
genom, 2777; þä mec sinca baldor . . . ät minum fäder genam
(*took me at my father's hands,
adopted me*), 2430; pret. part. genumen, 3167.

ge-nip, st. n., *darkness, mist, cloud:*
acc. pl. under nässa genipu, 1361;
ofer flôda genipu, 2809.

nis, from ne-is (*is not*) : see **wesan.**

niwe, niówe, adj., *new, novel; unheard-of:* nom. sg. swêg up â-stâg
niwe geneahhe (*a monstrous hub-
bub arose*), 784; beorh . . . niwe
(*a newly-raised(?) grave-mound*),
2244; acc. sg. niwe sibbe (*the new
kinship*), 950; instr. sg. niwan
stefne (properly, novâ voce; here
= de novo, iterum, *again*), 2595;
niówan stefne (*again*), 1790; gen.
pl. niwra spella (*new tidings*), 2899.

ge-niwian, w. v., *to renew:* pret
part. ge-niwod, 1304, 1323; geniwad, 2288.

niw-tyrwed, pret. part., *newly-
tarred:* acc. sg. niw-tyrwedne
(-tyrwydne, MS.) nacan, 295.

nîð, st. m., properly only *zeal, endeavor;* then *hostile endeavor, hos-*

tility, *battle, war :* nom. sg., 2318; acc. sg. nið, 184, 276; Wedera nið (*enmity against the W., the sorrows of the Weders*), 423; dat. sg. wið (ät) niðe, 828, 2586; instr. niðe, 2681; gen. pl. niða, 883, 2351, 2398, etc.; also instr. = *by*, *in, battle*, 846, 1440, 1963, 2171, 2207.— Comp.: bealo-, fær-, here-, hete-, inwit-, searo-, wäl-nið.

nið-draca, w. m., *battle-dragon :* nom. sg., 2274.

nið-gäst, st. m., *hostile alien, fell demon :* acc. sg. þone nið-gäst (*the dragon*), 2700.

nið-geweorc, st. n., *work of enmity, deed of evil :* gen. pl. -geweorca, 684.

nið-grim, adj., *furious in battle, savage :* nom. sg., 193.

nið-heard, adj., *valiant in war :* nom. sg., 2418.

nið-hydig, adj., *eager for battle, valorous :* nom. pl. nið-hydige men, 3167.

ge-nið́la, w. m., *foe, persecutor, waylayer :* in comp. ferhð-, feorh-genið́la.

nið-wundor, st. n., *hostile wonder, strange marvel of evil :* acc. sg., 1366.

nîpan, st. v., *to veil, cover over, obscure ;* pres. part. nipende niht, 547, 650.

nolde, from ne-wolde (*would not*); see **willan.**

norð, adv., *northward*, 859.

norðan, adv., *from the north*, 547.

nose, w. f., *projection, cliff, cape :* dat. sg. of hlîðes nosan, 1893; ät brimes nosan, 2804.

nô (strengthened neg.), *not, not at all, by no means*, 136, 244, 587, 755, 842, 969, 1736, etc.; strengthened by following ne, 459(?),

1509; nô ... nô (*neither ... nor*), 541-543; so, nô ... ne, 168. See **ne.**

nôðer (from nâ-hwäðer), neg., *and not, nor*, 2125.

ge-nôh, adj., *sufficient, enough :* acc. sg. fæhðo genôge, 2490; acc. pl. genôge ... beágas, 3105.

nôn, st. f., [Eng. *noon*], *ninth hour of the day, three o'clock in the afternoon of our reckoning* (the day was reckoned from six o'clock in the morning; cf. Bouterwek Screádunga, 24 *2 :* we hâtað ænne däg fram sunnan upgange ôð æfen): nom. sg. nôn, 1601.

nu, adv.: 1) *now, at present*, 251, 254, 375, 395, 424, 426, 489, etc.: nu gyt (*up to now, hitherto*), 957; nu gen (*now still, yet*), 2860; (*now yet, still*), 3169. — 2) conj., *since, inasmuch as :* nu þu lungre geong ... nu se wyrm ligeð (*go now quickly, since the dragon lieth dead*), 2746; so, 2248; þät þu me ne forwyrne ... nu ic þus feorran com (*that do not thou refuse me, since I am come so far*), 430; so, 1476; nu ic on mâðma hord mine bebohte frôde feorh-lege, fremmað ge nu (*as I now ..., so do ye*), 2800; so, 3021.

nymðe, conj. w. subj., *if not, unless*, 782; nymðe mec god scylde (*if God had not shielded me*), 1659.

nyt, st. f., *duty, service, office, employment :* acc. sg. þegn nytte beheóld (*did his duty*), 494; so, 3119. — Comp.: sund-, sundor-nyt.

nyt, adj., *useful :* acc. pl. m. nytte, 795; comp. un-nyt.

ge-nyttian, w. v., *to make use of, enjoy :* pret. part. häfde corð-scrafa ende ge-nyttod (*had enjoyed, made use of*), 3047.

nӯd, st. f., *force, necessity, need,* *pain :* acc. sg. þurh deáðes nӯd, 2455; instr. sg. nӯde, 1006. In comp. (like nӯd-maga, consanguineus, in Æthelred's Laws, VI. 12, Schmid, p. 228; néd-maga, in Cnut's Laws, I. 7, ibid., p. 258); also, *tie of blood.* — Comp. | reá-nӯd.

ge-nӯdan, w. v.: 1) *to force, compel :* pret. part. ní e ge-nӯded (*forced by hostile power*), 2681. — 2) *to force upon :* pret. part. acc.sg. f. nӯde genӯdde . . . gearwe stówe (*the inevitable place prepared for each,* i.e. the bed of death), 1006.

nӯd-bád, st. f., *forced pledge, pledge demanded by force :* acc. pl. nӯd-báde, 599.

nӯd-gestealla, w. m., *comrade in need* or *united by ties of blood :* nom. pl. nӯd-gesteallan, 883.

nӯd-gripe, st. m., *compelling grip :* dat. sg. in nӯd-gripe (mid-gripe, MS. , 977.

nӯd-wracu, st. f., *distressful persecution, great distress :* nom. sg., 193.

nӯhst. See neáh.

O

oððe, conj.: 1) *or ; otherwise,* 283, 437, 636, 638, 694, 1492, 1765, etc. — 2) *and(?), till(?),* 650, 2476 (*whilst ?*).

of, prep. w. dat., *from, off from :* 1) *from some point of view :* geseah of wealle (*from the wall*), 229; so, 786; of hefene scineð (*shineth from heaven*), 1572; of hliðes nosan gästas grětte (*from the cliff's projection*), 1893; of þam leóma stód (*from which light streamed*), 2770; þær wäs máðma fela of feorwegum . . . gelæded (*from distant lands*), 37; þá com of móre (*from the moor*), 711, 922. — 2) *forth from, out of :* hwearf of earde (*wandered from his home, died*), 56; so, 265, 855, 2472; þá ic of searwum com (*when I had escaped from the persecutions of the foe*), 419; þá him Hró gár gewât . . . ût of healle (*out of the hall*), 664; so, 2558, 2516; 1139, 2084, 2744; wudu-rêc â-stâh sweart of (ofer) swioðole (*black wood-reek ascended from the smoking fire*), 3145; (icge gold) â-häfen of horde (*lifted from the hoard*), 1109; lêt | â of breóstum . . . word ût faran (*from his breast*), 2551; dyde . . . helm of hafelan (*doffed his helmet*), 673; so, 1130; seal-don win of wunder-fatum (*presented wine from woudrous vessels*), 1163; siððan hyne Hæðcyn of horn-bogan . . . flâne geswencte (*with an arrow shot from the horned bow*), 2438; so, 1434. Prep. postponed : þá he him of dyde ï-sern-byrnan (*doffed his iron corselet*), 672.

ofer, prep. w. dat. and acc., *over, above :* 1) w. dat., *over* (rest, locality): Wiglâf siteð ofer Bió-wulfe, 2908; ofer äðelinge, 1245; ofer eorðan, 248, 803, 2008; ofer wer-þeóde (*over the earth, among mankind*), 900; ofer ӯðum, 1908; ofer hron-râde (*over the sea*), 10; so, 304, 1287, 1290, etc.; ofer ealo-wæge (*over the beer-cup, drinking*), 481. — 2) w. acc. of motion : a) *over* (local) : ofer ӯðe (*over the waves*), 46, 1910; ofer swan-râde (*over the swan-road, the sea*), 200; ofer wægholm, 217; ofer geofenes be-gang, 362; so, 239, 240, 297,

393, 464, 471, etc.; ofer bolcan
(*over the gangway*), 231; ofer
landa fela (*over many lands*), 311;
so, 1405, 1406; ofer heáhne hróf
(*along upon (under?) the high
roof*), 984; ofer cormen-grund
(*over the whole earth*), 860; ofer
ealle (*over all, on all sides*), 2900,
650; so, 1718; —606, 900, 1706;
ofer borda gebräc (*over, above, the
crashing of shields*), 2260; ofer
bord-(scild) weall, 2981, 3119.
Temporal: ofer þâ niht (*through
the night, by night*), 737. b) w.
verbs of saying, speaking, *about,
of, concerning:* he ofer benne
spräc, 2725. c) *beyond, over:* ofer
min ge-met (*beyond my power*),
2880; — hence, *against, contrary
to:* he ofer willan gióng (*went
against his will*), 2410; ofer ealde
riht (*against the ancient laws,* i.e.
the ten commandments), 2331;
— also, *without:* wig ofer wæpen
(*war sans, dispensing with, weapons*), 686; — temporal = *after:*
ofer eald-gewin (*after long, ancient, suffering*), 1782.

ofer-hygd, st. n., *arrogance, pride,
conceit:* gen. pl. ofer-hygda, 1741;
ofer-hyda, 1761.

ofer-máðum, st. m., *very rich treasure:* dat. pl. ofer-máðmum, 2994.

ofer-mägen, st. n., *over-might, superior numbers:* dat. sg. mid ofer-
mägene, 2918.

ofer þearf, st. f., *dire distress, need:*
dat. sg. [for ofer] þea[rfe], 2227.

oft, adv., *often,* 4, 165, 444, 572, 858,
908, 1066, 1239, etc.; oft [nô]
seldan, 2030; oft nalles æne, 3020;
so, 1248, 1888. Compar. oftor,
1580. Superl. oftost, 1664.

om-, on-. See am-, an-.

ombiht. See ambiht.

oncer. See ancer.

ond. See and.

onsyn. See ansyn.

on, prep. w. dat. and acc., signifying
primarily *touching on, contact with:*
I. local, w. dat.: a) *on, upon, in
at* (of exterior surface): on heáh-
stede (*in the high place*), 285; on
mínre éðel-tyrf (*in my native
place*), 410; on þäm meðel-stede,
1083; so, 2004; on þam holm-
clife, 1422; so, 1428; on foldan
(*on earth*), 1197; so, 1533, 2997;
on þære medu-bence (*on the mead-
bench*), 1053; beornas on blancum
(*the heroes on the dapple-greys*),
857, etc.; on räste (*in bed*), 1299;
on stapole (*at, near, the pillar*),
927; on wealle, 892; on wage (*on
the wall*), 1663; on þäm wäl-
stenge (*on the battle-lance*), 1639;
on eaxle (*on his shoulder*), 817,
1548; on bearme, 40; on breóstum, 552; on hafelan, 1522; on
handa (*in his hand*), 495, 540;
so, 555, 766; on him byrne scân
(*on him shone the corselet*), 405;
on ôre (*at the front*), 1042; on
corðre (*at the head of, among, his
troop*), 1154; scip on ancre (*the
ship at anchor*), 303; þät he on
heáðe ge-stôd (*until he stood in
the hall*), 404; on fäder stäle (*in
a father's place*), 1480; on yðum
(*on the waves, in the water*), 210,
421, 534, 1438; on holme, 543; on
êg-streámum, 577; on segl-râde,
1438, etc.; on flôde, 1367. The
prep. postponed: Freslondum on,
2358.—b) *in, inside of* (of inside
surface): secg on searwum (*a
champion in armor*), 249; so,
963; on wig-geatwum, 368; (reced) on þäm se rica bâd (*in which
the mighty one abode*), 310; on

Heorote (*in Heorot*), 475, 497,
594, 1303; on beór-sele, 492, 1095;
on healle, 615, 643; so, 639, 1017,
1026, etc.; on burgum (*in the
cities, boroughs*), 53; on helle,
101; on sefan minum (*in my
mind*), 473; on môde, 754; so,
755, 949, 1343, 1719, etc.; on aldre
(*in his vitals*), 1435; on middan
(in medio), 2706. — c) *among,
amid:* on searwum (*among the
arms*), 1558; on gemonge (*among
the troop*), 1044; on þam leód-
scipe (*among the people*), 2198;
nymðe líges fäðm swalge on swaðule (*unless the embracing flame
should swallow it in smoke*), 783;
— *in, with, touched by, possessing
something:* þâ wäs on sâlum sinces
brytta (*then was the dispenser of
treasure in joy*), 608; so, 644,
2015; wäs on hreón môde, 1308;
on sweofote (*in sleep*), 1582, 2296;
heó wäs on ôfste (*she was in haste*),
1293; so, 1736, 1870; þâ wäs on
blôde brim weallende (*there was
the flood billowing in, with, blood*),
848; (he) wäs on sunde (*was a-
swimming*), 1619; wäs tô fore-
mihtig feónd on feðe (*too powerful
in speed*), 971; þär wäs swigra
secg ... on gylpspräce (*there was
the champion more silent in his
boasting speech*), 982; — *in; full
of, representing, something:* on
weres wästmum (*in man's form*),
1353. — d) *attaching to*, hence *proceeding from; from something:*
ge-hýrde on Beówulfe fäst-rädne
ge-þoht (*heard in, from, B. the
fixed resolve*), 610; þät he ne mêtte ... on elran men mund-gripe
mâran, 753; — hence, with verbs
of taking: on räste genam (*took
from his bed*), 122; so, 748, 2987;

hit är on þe gôde be-geâton (*took
it before from thee*), 2249. — e)
with: swâ hit lungre wearð on
hyra sinc-gifan sâre ge-endod (*as
it, too, soon painfully came to an
end with the dispenser of treasure*),
2312. — f) *by:* mäg þonne on
þäm golde ongitan Geáta dryhten
(*the lord of the Geátas may perceive by the gold*), 1485. — g) *to,*
after weorðan: þät he on sylle
wearð (*that he came to a fall*), 1545.
With acc.: a) w. verbs of moving, doing, giving, seeing, etc., *up
to, on, upon, in:* â-lêdon þâ leófne
þeóden ... on bearm scipes, 35;
on stefn (on wang) stigon, 212,
225; þâ him mid scoldon on flôdes
äht feor ge-wîtan, 42; se þe wið
Brecan wunne on sidne sä (*who
strovest in a swimming-match with
B. on the broad sea*), 507, cf. 510;
þät ic on holma ge-þring eorlscipe
efnde (*that I should venture on
the sea to do valiant deeds*), 2133;
on feónda geweald slîðan, 809;
þâra þe on swylc staräð, 997; so,
1781; on lufan läteð hworfan
(*lets him turn his thoughts to love?,
to possessions?*), 1729; him on môd
bearn (*came into his mind, occurred to him*), 67; räsde on þone
rôfan (*rushed on the powerful one*),
2691; (ewom) on worðig (*came
into the palace*), 1973; so, 27, 242,
253, 512, 530, 580, 677, 726, etc.;
on weg (*away*), 764, 845, 1383,
1431, 2097. — b *against* (_ wið):
gôde gewyrcean ... on fäder wine
(pl.), 21. — c) aim or object, *to,
for the object, for, as, in, on:* on
þearfe (*in his need, in his strait*),
1457; so, on hyra man-dryhtnes
miclan þearfe, 2850; wrâðum on
andan (*as a terror to the foe*), 709;

Hróðgâr maðelode him on andsware (*said to him in reply*), 1841;
betst beado-rinca wäs on bæl gearu
(*on the pyre ready*), 1110; wig-
heafolan bär freán on fultum (*for
help*), 2663; wearð on bid wrecen
(*forced to wait*), 2963. — d) ground,
reason, *according to, in conformity
with:* rodera rædend hit on ryht
gesceód (*decided it in accordance
with right*), 1556; ne me swôr fela
âða on unriht (*swore no oaths unjustly, falsely*), 2740; on spêd (*skilfully*), 874; nallas on gylp seleð
fätte beágas(*giveth no gold-wrought
rings as he promised*), 1750; on
sinne selfes dôm (*boastingly, at his
own will*), 2148; him eal worold
wendeð on willen (*according to his
will*), 1740. — e) w. verbs of buy-
ing, *for, in exchange for:* me ic
on mâðma hord mine be-bohte
frôde feorh-lege (*for the hoard of
jewels*), 2800. — f) *of, as to:* ic
on Higelâce wât, Geáta dryhten
(*I know with respect to, as to, of,
H.*), 1831; so, 2651; þät heó on
ænigne eorl ge-lýfde fyrena frôfre
(*that she should rely on any earl
for help out of trouble*), 628; þâ
hie ge-trûwedon on twâ healfa (*on
both sides, mutually*), 1096; so,
2064; þät þu him ondrædan ne
þearft . . . on þâ healfe (*from, on
this side*), 1676. — g) after superlatives or virtual superlatives —
among: näs . . . sinc-mâðððum
sêlra (þät wäs sinc-mâðma sêlest)
on sweordes hâd (*there was no better jewel in sword's shape, i.e.
among all swords there was none
better*), 2194; se wäs Hróðgâre
häleða leófost on ge-siðes hâd
(*dearest of men as, in the character of, follower, etc.*), 1298.

II. Of time: a) w. dat., *in,
inside of, during, at:* on fyrste
(*in time, within the time appointed*), 76; on uhtan (*at dawn*),
126; on mergenne (*at morn, on
the morrow*), 565, 2940; on niht,
575; on wanre niht, 703; on tyn
dagum, 3161; so, 197, 719, 791,
1063, etc.; on geogoðe (*in youth*),
409, 466; on geogoð-feore, 537;
so, 1844; on orlege (*in, during,
battle*), 1327; hû lomp eów on lâde
(*on the way*), 1988; on gange (*in
going, en route*), 1885; on sweofote (*in sleep*), 1582. — b) w. acc.,
towards, about: on undern-mæl
(*in the morning, about midday*),
1429; on morgen-tid, 484, 518;
on morgen, 838; on ende-stäf
(*toward the end, at last*), 1754;
oftor micle þonne on ænne sið
(*far oftener than once*), 1580.

III. With particles: him on efn
(*beside, alongside of, him*), 2904;
on innan (*inside, within*), 71,1741,
1969, 2453, 2716; þær on innan
(*in there*), 2090, 2215, 2245. With
the relative þe often separated
from its case: þe ic her on starie
(*that I here look on, at*), 2797;
þe ge þær on standað (*that ye
there stand in*), 2867.

on-cýð (cf. Dietrich in Haupt's
Zeits. XI., 412), st. f., *pain, suffering:* nom. sg., 1421; acc. sg. or
pl. on-cýððe, 831.

on-drysne, adj., *frightful, terrible:*
acc. sg. firen on-drysne, 1933.

onettan (for anettan, from root
an-, Goth. inf. anan, *to breathe,
pant*), w. v., *to hasten:* pret. pl.
onetton, 306, 1804.

on-lícnes, st. f., *likeness, form, figure:* nom. sg., 1352.

on-mêdla, w. m., *pride, arrogance:*

dat. sg. for on-mêdlan, 2927. Cf.
Bugge in Zacher's Zeits. 4, 218
seqq.

on-sæge, adj., *tending to fall, fatal:*
nom. sg. þá wäs Hondsció (dat.)
hild on-sæge, 2077; Hæðcynne
wearð ... gûð on-sæge, 2484.

on-weald, st. m., *power, authority:*
acc. sg. (him) bega ge-hwäðres
... onweald ge-teáh (*gave him
power over, possession of, both*),
1044.

open, adj., *open:* acc. sg. hord-
wynne fund ... opene standan,
2272.

openian, w. v., *to open,* w. acc.: inf.
openian, 3057.

orc (O.S. orc, Goth. aúrkei-s), st. m.,
crock, vessel, can: nom. pl. orcas,
3048; acc. pl. orcas, 2761.

orenê, st. m., *sea-monster:* nom. pl.
orenêas, 112.

ord, st. n. *point:* nom. sg. ôð þät
wordes ord breóst-hord þurh-bräc
(*till the word-point broke through
his breast-hoard, came to utter-
ance*), 2792; acc. sg. ord (*sword-
point* , 1550; dat. instr. orde (id.),
556; on orde (*at the head of, in
front* [of a troop]), 2499, 3126.

ord-fruma, w. m., *head lord, high
prince:* nom. sg., 263.

oret-mecg, st. m., *champion, warrior, military retainer:* nom. pl.
oret-mecgas, 363, 481; acc. pl.
oret-mecgas, 332.

oretta, w. m., *champion, fighter,
hero:* nom. sg., 1533, 2539.

or-leg, st. n., *war, battle:* dat. sg.
on orlege, 1327; gen. sg. or-leges,
2408.

or-leg-hwîl, st. f., *time of battle,
war-time:* nom. sg. [or-leg]-hwîl,
2003; gen. sg. orleg-hwîle, 2912;
gen. pl. orleg-hwîla, 2428.

or-leahtre, adj., *blameless:* nom. sg.
1887.

or-þanc (cf. Gloss. Aldhelm. mid
or-þance = argumento in Haupt
XI., 436; orþancum = machina-
mentis, *ibid.* 477: or-þanc-scipe =
mechanica, 479), st. m., *mechani-
cal art, skill:* instr. pl. or-þoncum,
2088; smiðes or-þancum, 406.

or-wêna, adj. (weak form), *hopeless,
despairing,* w. gen.: aldres or-
wêna (*hopeless of life*), 1003, 1566.

or-wearde, adj., *unguarded, without watch or guard:* nom.sg., 3128.

oruð, st. n., *breath, snorting:* nom.
sg., 2558; dat. oreðe, 2840.

Ô

ôð (Goth. und, O.H.G. unt, unz):
1) prep. w. acc., *to, till, up to,* only
temporal: ôð þone ânne däg, 2400;
ôð dômes däg, 3070; ôð woruld-
ende, 3084. — 2) ôð þät, conj. w.
depend. indicative clause, *till, until,* 9, 56, 66, 100, 145, 219, 296,
307, etc.

ôðer (Goth. anþar), num. : 1) *one or
other of two, a second,* = alter : nom.
sg. subs. : se ôðer, 2062; ôðer (*one,*
i.e. of my blood-relations, Hæðcyn
and Hygelâc), 2482; ôðer ... ôðer
(*the one ... the other*), 1350–1352.
Adj.: ôðer ... mihtig mân-sceaða
(*the second mightly, fell foe,* referring to 1350), 1339; se ôðer ...
häle, 1816; fem. niht ôðer, 2118;
neut. ôðer geâr (*the next, second,
year*), 1134; acc. sg. m. ôðerne,
653, 1861, 2441, 2485; þenden
reáfode rinc ôðerne (*whilst one
warrior robbed the other,* i.e. Eofor
robbed Ongenþeów), 2986; neut.
ôðer swylc (*another such, an equal*

number), 1584; instr. sg. ôðre sîðe (*for the second time, again*), 2671, 3102; dat. sg. ôðrum, 815, 1030, 1166, 1229, 1472, 2168, 2172, etc.; gen. sg. m. ôðres dôgores, 219, 606; neut. ôðres, 1875.—2) *another, a different one*, = alius: nom. sg., subs. ôðer, 1756; ôðer nænig (*no other*), 860. Adj.: ænig ôðer man, 503, 534; so, 1561; ôðer in (*a different house or room*), 1301; acc. sg. ôðer flet, 1087; gen. sg. ôðres ... yrfe-weardes, 2452; nom. pl. calo drincende ôðer sædan (*ale drinkers said other things*), 1946; acc. pl. neut. word ôðer, 871.

Ôfer, st. m., *shore:* dat. sg. on ôfre, 1372.

Ôfost, st. f., *haste:* nom. sg. ôfost is sêlest tô gecýðanne (*haste is best to make known, best to say at once*), 256; so, 3008; dat. sg. beó þu on ôfeste (ôfoste) (*be in haste, hasten*), 386, 2748; on ôfste, 1293; on ôfoste, 2784, 3091.

Ô-hwær, adv., *anywhere*, 1738, 2871.

Ômig, adj., *rusty:* nom. sg., 2764; nom. pl. ômige, 3050.

Ôr, st. n., *beginning, origin; front:* nom. sg., 1689; acc. sg., 2408; dat. sg. on ôre, 1042.

Ô-wiht, *anything, aught:* instr. sg. ô-wihte (*in any way*), 1823, 2433.

P

pâd, st. f., *dress;* in comp. here-pâd.

pæð, st. m., *path, road, way;* in comp. ân-pâð.

plega, w. m., *play, emulous contest;* lind-plega, 1074.

R

raðe, adv., *quickly, immediately*, 725. Cf. **hraðe**.

rand, rond, st. m., *shield:* acc. sg. rand, 683; rond, 657, 2567, 2610; dat. ronde (rond, MS.), 2674; under rande, 1210; bî ronde, 2539; acc. pl. randas, 231; rondas, 326, 2654.— Comp.: bord-, hilde-, sîd-rand.

rand-häbbend, pres. part., *shield-bearer*, i.e. *man at arms, warrior:* gen. pl. rond-häbbendra, 862.

rand-wîga, w. m., *shield-warrior, shield-bearing warrior:* nom. sg., 1299; acc. sg. rand-wîgan, 1794.

râd, st. f., *road, street;* in comp. hran-, segl-, swan-râd.

ge-râd, adj., *clever, skilful, ready:* acc. pl. neut. ge-râde, 874.

râp, st. m., *rope, bond, fetter:* in comp. wäl-râp.

râsian, w. v., *to find, discover:* pres. part. þâ wäs hord râsod, 2284.

rûst. See rest.

ræcan, w. v., *to reach, reach after:* pret. sg. ræhte ongeán feónd mid folme (*reached out his hand toward the foe*), 748.

ge-ræcan, *to attain, strike, attack:* pret. sg. hyne ... wæpne ge-ræhte (*struck him with his sword*), 2966; so, 556.

ræd, st. m.: 1) *advice, counsel, resolution; good counsel, help:* nom. sg. nu is ræd gelong eft ät þe ânum (*now is help to be found with thee alone*), 1377; acc. sg. ræd, 172, 278, 3081.— 2) *advantage, gain, use:* acc. sg. þät ræd talað (*counts that a gain*), 2028; êcne ræd (*the eternal gain, everlasting life*), 1202; acc. pl. êce rædas, 1761.— Comp.: folc-ræd, and adj., ân-, fæst-ræd.

rǽdan, st. v., *to rule; reign; to possess:* pres. part. rodera rǽdend (*the ruler of the heavens*), 1556; inf. þone þe þu mid rihte rǽdan sceoldest (*that thou shouldst possess by rights*), 2057; wolde dôm godes dǽdum rǽdan gumena gehwylcum (*God's doom would rule over, dispose of, every man in deeds*), 2859. See sele-rǽdend.

rǽd-born, w. m. *counsel.or, adviser:* nom. sg., 1326.

rǽden, st. f., *order, arrangement, law:* acc. sg. rǽdenne(?), 51; comp. worold-rǽden.

â-rǽran, w. v.: 1) *to raise, lift up:* pret. pl. þâ wǽron monige þe his mǽg ... ricone â-rǽrdon (*there were many that lifted up his brother quickly* , 2984. — 2) figuratively, *to spread, disseminate:* pret. part. blǽd is â-rǽred (*thy renown is far-spread*), 1704.

rǽs, st. m., *on-rush, attack, storm:* acc. sg. gûðe rǽs (*the storm of battle, attack*), 2627; instr. pl. gûðe rǽsum,2357.—Comp.: gûð-, hand-, heaðo-, mägen-, wäl-rǽs.

rǽsan, w. v., *to rush (upon):* pret. sg. rǽsde on þone rôfan, 2691.

rǽswa, w. m., *prince, ruler:* dat. sg. weoroda rǽswan, 60.

reccan, w. v., *to explicate, recount, narrate:* inf. fruin-sceaft fira feorran reccan (*recount the origin of man from ancient times*), 91; gerund. tô lang is tô reccenne, hu ic ... (*too long to tell how I* ...), 2094; pret. sg. syllic spell rehte (*told a wondrous tale*), 2111; so intrans. feorran rehte (*told of olden times*), 2107.

reced, st. n., *building, house; hall* (complete in itself): nom. sg., 412, 771, 1800; acc. sg., 1238;

dat. sg. recede, 721, 729, 1573; gen. sg. recedes, 326, 725, 3089; gen. pl. receda, 310.— Comp.: eorð-, heal-, horn-, win-reced.

regn-heard, adj., *immensely strong, firm:* acc. pl. rondas regn-hearde, 326.

regnian, rênian, w. v., *to prepare, bring on* or *about:* inf. deáð rên[ian] hond-gesteallan (*prepare death for his comrade*), 2169.

ge-regnian, *to prepare, deck out, adorn:* pret. part. medu-benc monig ... golde ge-regnad, 778.

regn-, rên-weard, st. m., *mighty guardian:* nom. pl. rên-weardas (of Beówulf and Grendel contending for the possession of the hall), 771.

rest, rǽst, st. f.: 1) *bed, resting-place:* acc. sg. räste, 139; dat. sg. on räste (genam) (*from his resting-place*), 1299, 1586; tô räste (*to bed*), 1238. Comp.: flet-räst, sele-rest, wäl-rest.— 2) *repose, rest;* in comp. æfen-räst.

ge-reste (M.H.G. reste), f., *resting-place:* in comp. wind-gereste.

restan, w. v.: 1) *to rest:* inf. restan, 1794; pret. sg. reflex. reste hine þâ rûm-heort, 1800.— 2) *to rest, cease:* inf., 1858.

rêc (O.H.G. rouh), st. m., *reek, smoke:* instr. sg. rêce, 3157.— Comp.: wäl-, wudu-rêc.

rêcan (O.H.G. ruohjan), w. v. w. gen., *to reck, care about something, be anxious:* pres. sg. III. wǽpna ne rêceð (*recketh not for weapons, weapons cannot hurt him*), 434.

rêðe, adj., *wroth, furious:* nom. sg., 122, 1586; nom. pl. rêðe, 771. Also, of things, *wild, rough, fierce:* gen. sg. rêðes and-bâttres (*fierce, penetrating heat*), 2524.

reáf, st. n., *booty, plunder in war; clothing, garments* (as taken by the victor from the vanquished): in comp. heaðo-, wäl-reáf.

reáfian, w. v., *to plunder, rob,* w. acc.: inf. hord reáfian, 2774; pret. sg. þenden reáfode rinc ôðerne, 2986; wäl reáfode, 3028; pret. pl. wäl reáfedon, 1213.

be - reáfian, w. instr., *to bereave, rob of :* pret. part. since be-reáfod, 2747; golde be-reáfod, 3019.

reord, st. f., *speech, language; tone of voice :* acc. sg. on-cniów mannes reorde (*knew, heard, a human voice*), 2556.

reordian, w. v., *to speak, talk :* inf. fela reordian (*speak much*), 3026.

ge - reordian, *to entertain, to prepare for :* pret. part. þâ wäs eft swâ ær . . . flet-sittendum fägere ge-reorded (*again, as before, the guests were hospitably entertained*), 1789.

reot, st. m.?, f.?, *noise, tumult? (grave?)* : instr. sg. reote, 2458. Bugge, in Zacher's Zeits. 4, 215, takes reôte as dat. from reôt (*rest, repose*).

reóc, adj., *savage, furious :* nom. sg., 122.

be - reófan, st. v., *to rob of, bereave :* pret. part. w. instr. acc. sg. fem. golde berofene, 2932; acc. pl. n. reote berofene, 2458.

reón. See **rôwan.**

reótan, st. v., *to weep :* pres. pl. ôð þät . . . roderas reótað, 1377.

reów, adj., *excited, fierce, wild :* in comp. blôd-, gûð-, wäl-reów. See **hreów.**

ricone, *hastily, quickly, immediately*, 2984.

riht, st. n., *right* or *privilege; the* (abstract) *right :* acc. sg. on ryht

(*according to right*), 1556; sôð and riht (*truth and right*), 1701; dat. sg. wið rihte, 144; äfter rihte (*in accordance with right*), 1050; syllic spell rehte äfter rihte (*told a wondrous tale truthfully*), 2111; mid rihte, 2057; acc. pl. ealde riht (*the ten commandments*), 2331; — Comp. in êðel-, folc-, land-, un-, word-riht.

riht, adj., *straight, right :* in comp. up-riht.

rihte, adv., *rightly, correctly*, 1696. See **ät - rihte.**

rinc, st. m., *man, warrior, hero :* nom. sg., 399, 2986; also of Grendel, 721; acc. sg. rinc, 742, 748; dat. sg. rince, 953; of Hrôðgâr, 1678; gen. pl. rinca, 412, 729. — Comp. in beado-, gûð-, here-, heaðo-, hilde-, mago-, sæ-rinc.

ge - risne, **ge - rysne**, adj., *appropriate, proper :* nom. sg. n. ge-rysne, 2654.

ríce, st. n.: 1) *realm, land ruled over :* nom. sg., 2200, 2208; acc. sg. ríce, 913, 1734, 1854, 3005; gen. sg. ríces, 862, 1391, 1860, 2028, 3081. Comp. Swió-ríce. — 2) *council of chiefs, the king with his chosen advisers(?)* : nom. sg. oft gesät ríce tô rûne, 172.

ríce, adj., *mighty, powerful :* nom. sg. (of Hrôðgâr), 1238; (of Hygelâc), 1210; (of Äsc-here), 1299; weak form, se ríca (Hrôðgâr), 310; (Beówulf), 399; (Hygelâc), 1976. — Comp. gimme-ríce.

rícsian, **ríxian**, w. v. intrans., *to rule, reign :* inf. rícsian, 2212; pret. sg. rixode, 144.

rídan, st. v., *to ride :* subj. pres. þät his byre ríde giong on gealgan, 2446; pres. part. nom. pl. rídend, 2458; inf. wicge rídan, 234; mea-

rum rîdan, 856; pret. sg. sæ-genga
... se þe on ancre râd, 1884; him
tô-geánes râd (*rode to meet them*),
1894; pret. pl. ymbe hlæw riodan
(*rode round the grave-mound*),
3171.
ge-rîdan, w. acc., *to ride over :*
pret. sg. se þe näs ge-râd (*who rode
over the promontory*), 2899.
rîm, st. n., *series, number :* in comp.
däg-, un-rim.
ge-rîm, st. n., *series, number :* in
comp. dôgor-ge-rim.
ge-rîman, w. v., *to count together,
enumerate in all :* pret. part. in
comp. forð-gerimed.
â-rîsan, st. v., *to arise, rise :* imper.
sg. â-rîs, 1391; pret. sg. â-râs þâ
se rica, 399; so, 652, 1791, 3031;
â-râs þâ bî ronde (*arose by his
shield*), 2539; hwanan sió fæhð
â-râs (*whence the feud arose*), 2404.
rodor, st. m., *ether, firmament, sky*
(from *radius?*, Bugge): gen. sg.
rodores candel, 1573; nom. pl.
roderas, 1377; dat. pl. under roderum, 310; gen. pl. rodera, 1556.
rôf, adj., *fierce, of fierce, heroic,
strength, strong :* nom. sg., 1926,
2539; also w. gen. mägenes rôf
(*strong in might*), 2085; so, þeáh
þe he rôf sîe nîð-geweorca, 683;
acc. sg. rôfne, 1794; on þone rôfan,
2691. — Comp.: beadu-, brego-,
ellen-, heaðo-, hyge-, sige-rôf.
rôt, adj., *glad, joyous ;* in comp. un-
rôt.
rôwan, sf. v., *to row* (with the arms),
swim : pret. pl. reón (for reówon),
512, 539.
rûm, st. m., *space, room :* nom. sg.,
2691.
rûm, adj.: 1) *roomy, spacious :* nom.
sg. þûhte him eall tô rûm, wongas
and wîc-stede (*fields and dwelling*

seemed to him all too broad, i.e.
could not hide his shame at the
unavenged death of his murdered
son), 2462. — 2) in moral sense,
*great, magnanimous, noble-heart-
ed :* acc. sg. þurh rûmne sefan, 278.
rûm-heort, adj., *big-hearted, noble-
spirited :* nom. sg., 1800, 2111.
ge-rûm-lîce, adv., *commodiously,
comfortably :* compar. ge-rûm-lîcor,
139.
rûn, st. f., *secrecy, secret discussion,
deliberation or council :* dat. sg.
ge-sät rîce tô rûne, 172. — Comp.
beado-rûn.
rûn-stäf, st. m., *rune-stave, runic
letter :* acc. pl. þurh rûn-stafas, 1696.
rûn-wita, w. m., *rune-wit, privy
councillor, trusted adviser :* nom.
sg., 1326.
ge-rysne. See ge-risne.
ge-rŷman, w. v.: 1) *to make room
for, prepare, provide room :* pret.
pl. þät hie him ôðer flet eal ge-
rŷmdon, 1087; pret. part. þâ wäs
Geát-mäcgum ... benc gerŷmed,
492; so, 1976. — 2) *to allow, grant,
admit :* pret. part. þâ me ge-rŷmed
wäs (sîð) (*as access was permitted
me*), 3089; þâ him gerŷmed wearð,
þät hie wäl-stôwe wealdan môston,
2984.

S

ge-saca, w. m., *opponent, antagonist, foe :* acc. sg. ge-sacan, 1744.
sacan, st. v., *to strive, contend :* inf.
ymb feorh sacan, 439.
ge-sacan, *to attain, gain by contending* (Grein) : inf. gesacan sceal
sâwl-berendra ... gearwe stôwe
(*gain the place prepared*, i.e. the
death-bed), 1005.

on-sacan: 1) (originally in a law-suit), *to withdraw, take away, deprive of:* pres. subj. Jätte freoðuwebbe feores on-säce . . . leófne mannan, 1943. — 2) *to contest, dispute, withstand:* inf. Jät he sǽmannum on-sacan mihte (i.e. hord, bearn, and brýde), 2955.

sacu, st. f., *strife, hostility, feud:* nom. sg., 1858, 2473; acc. sg. säce, 154; säcce, 1978, 1990, 2348, 2500, 2563; dat. sg. ät (tô) säcce, 954, 1619, 1666, 2613, 2660, 2682, 2687; gen. sg. secce, 601; gen. pl. säcca, 2030.

ge-sacu, st. f., *strife, enmity:* nom. sg., 1738.

sadol, st. m., *saddle:* nom. sg., 1039.

sadol-beorht, adj., *with bright saddles(?):* acc. pl. sadol - beorht, 2176.

ge-saga. See secgan.

samne, somne, adv., *together, united;* in ät-somne, *together, united,* 307, 402, 491, 544, 2848.

tô-somne (*together*), 3123; þâ se wyrm ge-beáh snûde tô-somne (*when the dragon quickly coiled together*), 2569.

samod, somod: I. adv., *simultaneously, at the same time:* somod, 1212, 1615, 2175, 2988; samod, 2197; samod ät-gädere, 387, 730, 1064. — II. prep. w. dat., *with, at the same time with:* samod ær-däge (*with the break of day*), 1312; somod ær-däge, 2943.

sand, st. n., *sand, sandy shore:* dat. sg. on sande, 295, 1897, 3043(?); äfter sande (*along the shore*), 1965; wið sande, 213.

sang, st. m., *song, cry, noise:* nom. sg. sang, 1064; swutol sang scôpes, 90; acc. sg. sige-leasne sang (Grendel's cry of woe), 788; sâ-

rigne sang (Hrêðel's dirge for Hcrebeald), 2448.

sâl, st. m., *rope:* dat. sg. sâle, 1907; on sâle (sole, MS.), 302.

sâl. See sǽl.

sâr, st. n., *wound, pain* (physical or spiritual): nom. sg. sâr, 976; sió sâr, 2469; acc. sg. sâr, 788; sâre, 2296; dat. (instr.) sg. sâre, 1252, 2312, 2747. — Comp. lîc-sâr.

sâr, adj., *sore, painful:* instr. pl. sârum wordum, 2059.

sâre, adv., *sorely, heavily, ill,* graviter: se þe him [sâ]re gesceôd (*who injured him sorely*), 2224.

sârig, adj., *painful, woeful:* acc. sg. sârigne sang, 2448.

sârig-ferð, adj., *sore - hearted, grieved:* nom. sg. sârig-ferð (Wîglâf), 2864.

sârig-môd, adj., *sorrowful-minded, saddened:* dat. pl. sârig-môdum, 2943.

sâr-lîc, adj., *painful:* nom. sg., 843; acc. sg. neut., 2110.

sâwol, sâwl, st. f., *soul* (the immortal principle as contrasted with lif, the physical life): nom. sg. sâwol, 2821; acc. sg. sâwle, 184, 802; hæðene sâwle, 853; gen. sg. sâwele, 1743; sâwle, 1743.

sâwl-berend, pres. part., *endowed with a soul, human being:* gen. pl. sâwl-berendra, 1005.

sâwul-dreór, st. n., (blood gushing from the seat of the soul), *soulgore, heart's blood, life's blood:* instr. sg. sâwul-driôre, 2694.

sâwul-leás, adj., *soulless, lifeless:* acc. sg. sâwol-leásne, 1407; sâwul-leásne, 3034.

säce, säcce. See sacu.

säd, adj., *satiated, wearied:* in comp. hilde-säd.

säl, st. n., *habitable space, house,*

* *hall:* dat. sg. sel, 167; sāl, 307, 2076, 2265.

sāld, st. n., *hall, king's hall* or *palace:* acc. sg. geond þāt sāld (Heorot), 1281.

sæ, st. m. and f., *sea, ocean:* nom. sg., 579, 1224; acc. sg. on sîdne sæ, 507; ofer sæ, 2381; ofer sæ sîde, 2395; dat. sg. tô sæ, 318; on sæ, 544; dat. pl. be sæm tweonum, 859, 1298, 1686, 1957.

sæ-bât, st. m., *sea-boat:* acc. sg., 634, 896.

sæ-cyning, st. m., *sea-king, king ruling the sea:* gen. pl. sæ-cyninga, 2383.

sæ-deór, st. n., *sea-beast, sea-monster:* nom. sg., 1511.

sæ-draca, w. m., *sea-dragon:* acc. pl. sæ-dracan, 1427.

ge-sægan, w. v., *to fell, slay:* pret. part. häfdon eal-fela eotena cynnes sweordum ge-sæged (*felled with the sword*), 885.

sæge. See on-sæge.

sæ-genga, w. m., *sea-goer,* i.e. seagoing ship: nom. sg., 1883, 1909.

sæ-geáp, adj., *spacious* (broad enough for the sea): nom. sg. sægeáp naca, 1897.

sæ-grund, st. m., *sea-bottom, ocean-bottom:* dat. sg. sæ-grunde, 564.

sæl, sâl, sêl, st. f.: 1) *favorable opportunity, good* or *fit time:* nom. sg. sæl, 623, 1666, 2059; sæl and mæl, 1009; acc. sg. sêle, 1136; gen. pl. sæla and mæla, 1612. — 2) *Fate*(?): gen. sg. sêle rædenne, 51. — 3) *happiness, joy:* dat. pl. on sâlum, 608; sælum, 644, 1171, 1323. See sêl, adj.

ge-sælan, w. v., *t turn out favorably, succeed:* pret. sg. him ge-sælde þāt ... (*he was fortunate enough to,* etc.), 891; so, 574;

efne swylce mæla, swylce hira man-dryhtne þearf ge-sælde (*at such times as need disposed it for their lord*), 1251.

sælan (see sâl), w. v., *to tie, bind:* pret. sg. sælde ... si ð-fäðme scip, 1918; pl. sæ-wudu sældon, 226.

ge-sælan, *to bind together, weave, interweave:* pret. part. earm-beága fela searwum ge-sæled (*many curiously interwoven armlets,* i.e. made of metal wire: see Guide to Scandinavian Antiquities, p. 48), 2765.

on-sælan, with acc., *to unbind, unloose, open:* on-sæl meoto, sigehreð secgum (*disclose thy views to the men, thy victor's courage;* or, *thy presage of victory?*), 489.

sæ-lâc, st. n., *sea-gift, sea-booty:* instr. sg. sæ-lâce, 1625; acc. pl. þâs sæ-lâc, 1653.

sæ-lâd, st. f., *sea-way, sea-journey:* dat. sg. sæ-lâde, 1140, 1158.

sæ-liðend, pres. part., *seafarer:* nom. pl. sæ-liðend, 411, 1819, 2807; sæ-liðende, 377.

sæ-man, m., *sea-man, sea-warrior:* dat. pl. sæ-mannum, 2955; gen. pl. sæ-manna, 329 (both times said of the Geátas).

sæmra, weak adj. compar., *the worse, the weaker:* nom. sg. sæmra, 2881; dat. sg. sæmran, 954.

sæ-mêðe, adj., *sea-weary, exhausted by sea-travel:* nom. pl. sæ-mêðe, 325.

sæ-næs, st. m., *sea-promontory, cape, naze:* acc. pl. sæ-nässas, 223, 571.

sæne, adj., *careless, slow:* compar. sg. nom. he on holme wäs sundes þê sænra, þe hyne swylt fornam (*was the slower in swimming in the sea, whom death took away*), 1437.

sæ-rinc, st. m., *sea-warrior* or *hero :* nom. sg., 691.

sæ-sið, st. m., *sea-way, path, jour-ney :* dat. sg. äfter sæ-siðe, 1150.

sæ-wang, st. m., *sea-shore* or *beach :* acc. sg. sæ-wong, 1965.

sæ-weal, st. m., (*sea-wall*), *sea-shore :* dat. sg. sæ-wealle, 1925.

sæ-wudu, st. m., (*sea-wood*), *vessel, ship :* acc. sg. sæ-wudu, 226.

sæ-wylm, st. m., *sea-surf, billow :* acc. pl. ofer sæ-wylmas, 393.

seacan, sceacan, st. v., properly, *to shake one's self:* hence, *to go, glide, pass along* or *away :* pres. sg. þonne min sceaceð lif of lice, 2743; inf. þå com beorht [sunne] seacan [ofer grundas], (*the bright sun came gliding over the fields*), 1804; pret. sg. duguð eilor scôc (*the chiefs are gone elsewhither*, i.e. have died), 2255; þonne stræla storm . . . scôc ofer scild-weall (*when the storm of arrows leapt over the wall of shields*), 3119; pret. part. wäs hira blæd seacen (*their strength (breath?) had passed away*), 1125; þå wäs winter sca-cen (*the winter was past*), 1137; so, sceacen, 2307, 2728.

sceadu, sceadu, st. m., *shadow, con-cealing veil of night:* acc. sg. under sceadu bregdan (i.e. kill), 708.

sceadu-genga, w. m., *shadow-goer, twilight-stalker* (of Grendel): nom. sg. sceadu-genga, 704.

sceadu-helm, st. m., *shadow-helm, veil of darkness :* gen. pl. sceadu-helma ge-sceapu (*shapes of the shadow, evil spirits wandering by night*), 651.

scealu, st. f., *retinue, band* (part of an armed force); in comp. hand-scalu: mid his hand-scale (hond-scole), 1318, 1964.

scamian, w. v., *to be ashamed :* pres. part. nom. pl. scamiende, 2851; nô he þære feoh-gyfte . . . scami-gan þorfte (*needed not be ashamed of his treasure-giving*), 1027.

seawa (see sceáwian , w. m., *obser-ver, visitor :* nom. pl. seawan, 1896.

ge-scád, st. n., *difference, distinc-tion :* acc. sg. æg-hwäðres gescåd, worda and worca (*difference be-tween, of, both words and deeds*), 288.

ge-scádan, st. v., *to decide, adjudge:* pret. sg. rodera rædend hit on ryht gesceôd (*decided it in accordance with right*), 1556.

scånan, redupl. verb?, *to shine :* pret. pl. sciônon, 303. Cf. O.S. pret. an-skian, from an-skênan (Heliand, 5800).

ge-sceáp-hwîle, st. f., *fated hour, hour of death (appointed rest?) :* dat. sg. tô gesceáp-hwîle (*at the fated hour*), 26.

sceððan, w. v., *to scathe, injure :* inf. w. dat. pers., 1034; aldre sceð-ðan (*hurt her life*), 1525; lät on land Dena låðra nænig mid scip-herge sceððan ne meahte (*injure through robber incursions*), 243; pret. sg. lär him nænig wäter wihte ne sceðede, 1515.

ge-sceððan, the same : inf. lät him . . . ne mihte corres inwit-feng aldre gesceððan, 1448.

scene, st. m., *vessel, can :* in comp. medu-scene.

scencan, w. v., *to hand drink, pour out :* pret. sg. scencte scîr wered, 496 (cf. skinker = cup-bearer).

scenne, w. f.?, *sword-guard?:* dat. pl. on þæm sceunnum scîran goldes, 1695.

sceran, st. v., *to shear off, cleave, hew to pieces :* pres. sg. þonne heoru bunden . . . swîn ofer helme andveard scireð (*hews off the boar-head on the helm*), 1288.

ge-sceran, *to divid.*, *hew in two:* pret. sg. helm oft ge-scär (*often clove the helm in two*), 1527; so, gescer, 2974.

scerwen, st. f.?, in comp. ealu-scerwen (*ale-scare* or *panic?*), 770.

scêt. See sceótan.

scendu. See sendu.

sceaða, w. m.: 1) *scather, foe:* gen. pl. sceaðena, 4. — 2) *fighter, warrior:* nom. pl. scaðan, 1804. — Comp.: âttor-, dol-, feónd-, gûð-, hearm-, leód-, mân-, sin-, ʃeód-, uht-sceaða.

sceaðan, st. v. w. dat., *to scathe, injure, crush:* pret. sg. se ʃe oft manegum scôd (*which has oft oppress d many*), 1888.

ge-sceaðan, w. dat., the same: pret. sg. swâ him ær gescôd hild ät Heorote, 1588; se ʃe him sâre gesceôd (*i ho injured him sorely*), 2224; nô ʃỹ ær in gescôd hâlan lîce, 1503; bill ær gescôd eald-hlâfordes ʃam ʃâra mâðma mundbora wäs (*the weapon of the ancient chieftain had before laid low the dragon, the guardian of the treasure*), 2778 (or, *sheathed in brass?*, if ær and gescôd form compound).

sceaðen-mæl, st. n., *deadly weapon, hostile sword:* nom. sg., 1940.

sceaft, st. m., *shaft, spear, missile:* nom. sg. sceft, 3119. — Comp.: here-, wäl-sceaft.

ge-sceaft, st. f.: 1) *creation, earth, earthly existence:* acc. sg. ʃâs læ-nan ge-sceaft, 1623. — 2) *fate, destiny:* in comp. forð-, lîf-, mæl-gesceaft.

sceale, st. m., *servant, military retainer:* nom. sg., 919; (of Beówulf), 940. — Comp. beór-scealc.

ge-sceap, st. n.: 1) *shape, creature:* nom. pl. scadu-helma ge-sceapu, 651. — 2) *fate, providence:* acc. sg. heáh ge-sceap (*heavy fate*), 3085.

sceapan, sceppan, scyppan, st. v., *to shape, create, order, arrange, establish:* pres. part. scyppend (*the Creator*), 106; pret. sg. scôp him Heort naman (*shaped, gave, it the name Heorot*), 78; pres. part. wäs sió wrôht scepen heard wið Hugas, syðð̃an Hygelâc cwom (*the contest with the Hugas became sharp after H. had come*), 2915.

ge-sceapan, *to shape, create:* pret. sg. ïlf ge-sceôp cynna gehwylcum, 97.

scear, st. m., *massacre:* in comp. gûð-, inwit-scear, 2429, etc.

scearp, adj., *sharp, able, brave:* nom. sg. scearp scyld-wîga, 288. — Comp.: beadu-, heaðo-scearp.

scearu, st. f., *division, body, troop:* in comp. folc-scearu; *that is decided or determined*, in gûð-scearu (*overthrow?*), 1214.

sceat, st. m., *money;* also *unit of value in appraising* (cf. Rieger in Zacher's Zeits. 3, 415): acc. pl. sceattas, 1687. When numbers are given, sceat appears to be left out, cf. 2196, 2995 (see ʃûsend). — Comp. gif-sceat.

sceát, st. m., *region, field:* acc. pl. gefrätwade foldan sceátas leomum and leáfum, 96; — *top, surface, part:* gen. pl. eorðan sceáta, 753.

sceáwere, st. m., *observer, spy:* nom. pl. sceáweras, 253.

sceáwian, w. v. w. acc., *to see, look at, observe:* inf. sceáwian, 841, 1414, 2403, 2745, 3009, 3033; sceáwigan, 1392; pres. sg. II. ʃät ge genôge neán sceáwiað beágas

and brâd gold, 3105; subj. pres.
Jät ic ... sceáwige swegle searo-
gimmas, 2749; pret. sg. sceáwode, 1688, 2286, 2794; sg. for
pl., 844; pret. pl. sceáwedon, 132,
204, 984, 1441.
ge-sceáwian, *to see, behold, observe:*
pret. part. ge-sceáwod, 3076, 3085.
sceorp, st. n., *garment:* in comp.
hilde-sceorp.
sceótan, st. v., *to shoot, hurl missiles:*
pres. sg. se |c of flân-bogan fyre-
num sceóteð, 1745; pres. part.
nom. pl. sceótend (*the warriors,
bowmen*), 704, 1155; dat. pl. for
sceótendum (MS.scotenum), 1027.
ge-sceótan, w. acc., *to shoot off,
hurry:* pret. sg. herd eft gesceát
(*the dragon darted again back to
the treasure*), 2320.
of-sceótan, *to kill by shooting:* pret.
sg. his mæg of-scét ... blôdigan
gâre (*killed his brother with bloody
dart*), 2440.
scild, scyld, st. m., *shield:* nom.
sg. scyld, 2571; acc. sg. scyld, 437,
2676;acc.pl.scyldas,325,333,2851.
scildan, scyldan, w. v., *to shield,
protect:* pret. subj. nymðe mec god
scylde (*if God had not shielded
me*), 1659.
scild-freca, w. m., *shield-warrior*
(warrior armed with a shield):
nom. sg. scyld-freca, 1034.
scild-weall, st. m., *wall of shields:*
acc. sg. scild-weall, 3119.
scild-wîga, w. m., *shield-warrior:*
nom. sg. scyld-wîga, 288.
scinna, w. m., *apparition, evil spirit:*
dat. pl. scynnum, 940.
scip, st. n., *vessel, ship:* nom. sg.,
302; acc. sg., 1918; dat. sg. tô
scipe, 1896; gen. sg. scipes, 35,
897; dat. pl. tô scypum (scypon,
MS.), 1155.

scip-here, st. m., (exercitus navalis),
armada, fleet: dat. sg. mid scip-
herge, 243.
ge-scîfe (for ge-scýfe), adj., *ad-
vancing* (of the dragon's movement), 2571.
scînan, st. v., *to shine, flash:* pres.
sg. sunne ... sûðan scîneð, 607;
so, 1572; inf. gesceah blâcne leóman beorhte scînan, 1518; pret.
sg. (gûð - byrne, woruld - candel)
scân, 321, 1966; on him byrne
scân,405; pret. pl. gold-fâg scînon
web äfter wagum, 995; scionon,
303; cf. scînan.
scîr, adj., *sheer, pure, shining:* nom.
sg. hring-îren scîr, 322; scîr metod, 980; acc. sg. n. scîr wered,
496; gen. sg. scîran goldes, 1695.
scîr-ham, adj., *bright-armored, clad
in bright mail:* nom. pl. scîr-hame,
1896.
scoten. See sceóten.
ge-scôd, pret. part.,*shod* (calceatus),
covered: in comp. ær-ge-scôd(?).
See ge-sceaðan.
scôp, st. m., *singer, shaper, poet:*
nom. sg., 496, 1067; gen. sg. scôpes, 90.
scräf, st. n., *hole in the earth, cavern:* in comp. eorð-scräf.
scriðan, st. v., *to stride, go:* pres.
pl. scriðað, 163; inf. scriðan, 651;
704; scriðan tô, 2570.
scrîfan, st. v., *to prescribe, impose*
(punishment): inf. hû him (Grendel) scîr metod scrîfan wille, 980.
for-scrîfan, w. dat. pers., *to pro-
scribe, condemn:* pret. part. siððan him scyppend for-scrifen häfde, 106.
ge-scrîfan, *to permit, prescribe:*
pret. sg. swâ him Wyrd ne ge-scrâf
(*as Weird did not permit him*),
2575.

scrûd, st. m., *clothing, covering; ornament:* in comp. beadu-, byrdu-scrûd.

scucca, w. m., *shadowy sprite, demon:* dat. pl. scuccum, 940.

sculan, aux. v. w. inf.: 1) *shall, must* (obligation): pres. sg. I., III. sceal, 20, 24, 183, 251, 271, 287, 440, 978, 1005, 1173, 1387, 1535, etc.; scel, 455, 2805, 3011; II. scealt, 589, 2667; subj. pres. scyle, 2658; scile, 3178; pret. ind. sg. I., III. scolde, 10, 806, 820, 966, 1071, 1444, 1450, etc.; sceolde, 2342, 2409, 2443, 2590, 2964; II. sceoldest, 2057; pl. scoldon, 41, 833, 1306, 1638; subj. pret. scolde, 1329, 1478; sceolde, 2709. — 2) w. inf. following it expresses futurity, = *shall, will:* pres. sg. I., III. sceal beódan (*shall offer*, 384; so, 424, 438, 602, 637, 1061, 1707, 1856, 1863, 2070; sceall, 2499, 2509, etc.; II. scealt, 1708; pl. wit sculon, 684; subj. pret. scolde, 280, 692, 911; sceolde, 3089. 3) sculan sometimes forms a periphrastic phrase or circumlocution for a simple tense, usually with a slight feeling of obligation or necessity: pres. sg. he ge-wunian sceall (*he inhabits; is said to inhabit?*, 2276; pret. sg. se) e wäter-egesan wunian scolde, 1261; wäcnan scolde (*was to awake*), 85; se þone gomelan grêtan sceolde (*was to, should, approach*, 2422; Jât se byrn-wîga bûgan sceolde (*the corseleted warrior ha l to bow, fell*), 2919; pl. Jâ þe beado-grîman býwan sceoldon (*they that had to p lish or deck the battlemasks*), 2258; so, 230, 705, 1068. — 4) w. omitted inf., such as wesan, gangan: unc sceal worn

fela mâ᾿ma ge-mænra (i.e. wesan), 1784; so, 2660; sceal se hearda helm . . . fätum befeallen (i.e. wesan), 2256; ic him äfter sceal (i.e. gangan), 2817; subj. Jonne Ju forð scyle (i.e. gangan), 1180. A verb or inf. expressed in an antecedent clause is not again expressed with a subsequent sceal: gað â Wyrd swâ hió scel (*Weird goeth ever as it shall* [go]), 455; gûð-bill ge-swâc swâ hit nô sceolde (i.e. ge-swîcan), 2586.

scûa, w. m., *shadowy demon:* in comp. deáð-scûa.

scûfan, st. v.: 1) intrans., *to move forward, hasten:* pret. part. Jâ wäs morgen-leóht scofen and scynded, 919. — 2) w. acc., *to shove, push:* pret. pl. guman ût scufon . . . wudu bundenne (*pushed the vessel from the land*), 215; dracan scufun . . . ofer weall-clif (*pushed the dragon over the wall-like cliff*), 3132. See wîd-scûfen.

be-scûfan, w. acc., *to pu h, thrus! down, in:* inf. wâ biðJään) e sceal . . . sâwle be-scûfan in fýres fä m (*woe to him that shall thrust his soul into fire's embrace*, 184.

scûr, st. m., *shower, battle-shower:* in comp. îsern-scûr.

scûr-heard, adj., *fight-hardened? (file-hardened?):* nom. pl. scûr-heard, 1034.

scyld, scyldan. See scild, scildan.

scyldig, adj., *under obligations or bound for; guilty of,* w. gen. and instr.: ealdres (mor res) scyldig, 1339, 1684, 2062; synnum scyldig (*guilty of evil deeds*), 3072.

scyndan, w. v., *to hasten:* inf. scyndan, 2571; pret. part. scynded, 919.

scynna. See scinna.

scyppend. See sceapau.

scyran, w. v., *to arrange, decide:* inf. þät hit scea∂en-mæl scyran móste (*that the sword must decide it*), 1940. O.N. skora, *to score, decide.*

scŷne, adj., *sheen, well-formed, beautiful:* nom. sg. mägð scŷne, 3017.

se, pron. dem. and article, *the:* m. nom., 79, 84, 86, 87, 90, 92, 102, etc.; fem. seó, 66, 146, etc.; neut. þät; — relative: se (*who*), 1611, 2866; se þe (*he who*), 2293; seó þe (*she who*), 1446; se þe (for seó þe), 1345, 1888, 2686; cf. 1261, 1498; (Grendel's mother, as a wild, demonic creature, is conceived now as man, now as woman: woman, as having borne a son; man, as the incarnation of savage cunning and power); se for seó, 2422; dat. sg. þam (for þam þe), 2780.

secce. See sacu.

secg, st. m., *man, warrior, hero, spokesman* (secgan?): nom. sg., 208, 872, 2228, 2407, etc.; (Beówulf), 249, 948, 1312, 1570, 1760, etc.; (Wulfgâr), 402; (Hûnferð), 981; (Wîglâf), 2864; acc. sg. synnigne secg (Grendel's mother, cf. se), 1380; dat. sg. secge, 2020; nom. pl. secgas, 213, 2531, 3129; dat. pl. secgum, 490; gen. pl. secga, 634, 843, 997, 1673.

secg, st. f., *sword* (sedge?): acc. sg. secge, 685.

secgan, w. v., *to say, speak:* 1) w. acc.: pres. sg. gode ic þanc secge, 1998; so, 2796; pres. part. swâ se secg hwata secgende wäs lâðra spella (partitive gen.), 3029; inf. secgan, 582, 876, 881, 1050; pret. sg. sägde him þäs leánes þanc, 1810; pret. sg. II. hwät þu worn fela . . . sägdest from his sîðc, 532.

— 2) without acc.: inf. swâ we sôðlîce secgan hŷrdon, 273; pret. sg. sägde, 2633, 2900. — 3) w. depend. clause: pres. sg. ic secge, 591; pl. III. secgað, 411; inf. secgan, 51, 391, 943, 1347, 1701, 1819, 2865, 3027; gerund. tô secganne, 473, 1725; pret. sg. sägde, 90, 1176; pl. sägdon, 377, 2188; sædan, 1946.

â-secgan (edicere), *to say out, deliver:* inf. wille ic â-secgan suna Healfdenes . . . mîn ærende, 344.

ge-secgan, *to say, relate:* imper. sg. II. ge-saga, 388; þät ic his [ôr] ærest þe eft ge-sägde (*that I should first tell thee its origin*), 2158; pret. part. gesägd, 141; gesæd, 1697.

sefa, w. m., *heart, mind, soul, spirit:* nom. sg., 49, 490, 595, 2044, 2181, 2420, 2601, 2633; acc. sg. sefan, 278, 1727, 1843; dat. sg. sefan, 473, 1343, 1738.—Comp. môd-sefa.

ge-segen, st. f., *legend, tale:* in comp. eald-ge-segen.

segl, st. n., *sail:* nom. sg., 1907.

segl-râd, st. f., *sail-road,* i.e. sea: dat. sg. on segl-râde, 1430.

segn, st. n., *banner,* vexillum: nom. sg., 2768, 2959; acc. sg. segen, 47, 1022; segn, 2777, 2959; dat. sg. under segne, 1205. — Comp. heáfod-segn.

sel, st. n., *hall, palace.* See säl.

seld, st. n., *dwelling, house:* in comp. medu-seld.

ge-selda, w. m., contubernalis, *companion:* acc. sg. geseldan, 1985.

seldan, adv., *seldom:* oft [nô] seldan, 2030.

seld-guma, w. m., *house-man, home-stayer*(?); *common man?, house-carl?:* nom. sg., 249.

sele, st. m. and n., *building consist-*

ing of one apartment; apartment, room : nom. sg., 81, 411; acc. sg. sele, 827, 2353; dat. sg. tô sele, 323, 1641; in (on, tô) sele þam heán, 714, 920, 1017, 1985: on sele (*in the den of the dragon*), 3129.—Comp.: beáh-, beór-, dryht-, eorð-, gest-, gold-, grund-, gûð-, heáh-, hring-, hróf-, nið-, win-sele.

sele-dreám, st. m., *hall-glee, joy in the hall :* acc. sg.] âra]e] is lîf ofgeaf, gesâwon sele-dreám (referring to the joy of heaven?), 2253.

sele-ful, st. n., *hall-goblet :* acc. sg., 620.

sele-gyst, st. m., *hall-guest, stranger in hall or house :* acc. sg. þone selegyst, 1546.

sele-rædend, pres. part., *hall-ruler, guardian or possessor of the hall :* acc. leóde mîne sele-rædende, 1347.

sele-rest, st. f., *bed in the hall :* acc. sg. sele-reste, 691.

sele-þegn, st. m., *retainer, hall-thane, chamberlain :* nom. sg., 1795.

sele-weard, st. m., *hall-ward, guardian of the hall :* acc. sg., 668.

self, sylf, pron., *self :* nom. sg. strong form, self, 1314, 1925 (? selfa);]u self, 595;]u]e self, 954; self cyning (*the king himself, the king too*), 921, 1011; sylf, 1965; in weak form, selfa, 1469; he selfa, 29, 1734;]âm]e him selfa deáh (*that can rely upon, trust to, himself*), 1840; seolfa, 3068; he sylfa, 505; god sylfa, 3055; acc. sg. m. selfne, 1606; hine selfne (*himself*), 962; hyne selfne *himself,* reflex.), 2876; wið sylfne (*opposite*), 1978; gen. sg. m. selfes, 701, 896; his selfes, 1148; on sînne sylfes dôm (*at his own will*), 2148; sylfes, 2224, 2361, 2640, 2711, 2777, 3014; his sylfes, 2014, 2326;

fem. hire selfre, 1116; nom. pl. selfe, 19(?); Sûð-Dene sylfe, 1997. ge-sella, w. m., *house-companion, comrade :* in comp. hand-gesella.

sellan, syllan, w. v.: 1) w. acc. of thing, dat. of pers., *to give, deliver; permit, grant, present :* pres. sg. III. seleð him on êðle corðan wynne, 1731; inf. syllan, 2161, 2730; pret. sg. sealde, 72, 673, 1272, 1694, 1752, 2025, 2156, 2183, 2491, 2995; nefne god sylfa sealde]am]e he wolde hord openian (*unless God himself gave to whom he would to open the hoard*), 3056; pret. sg. II. sealdest, 1483. — 2) *to give, give up* (only w. acc. of thing): ær he feorh seleð (*he prefers to give up his life*), 1371; nallas on gylp seleð fätte beágas (*giveth out gold-wrought rings, etc.*), 1750; pret. sg. sinc-fato sealde, 623; pl. byrelas sealdon wîn of wunder-fatum, 1162.

ge-sellan, w. acc. and dat. of pers., *to give, deliver; grant, present :* inf. ge-sellan, 1030; pret. sg. ge-sealde, 616, 1053, 1807, 1902, 2143, etc.

sel-lîc, syl-lîc (from seld-lîc), adj., *strange, wondrous :* nom. sg. glôf ... syllîc, 2087; acc. sg. n. syllîc spell, 2110; acc. pl. sellîce sæ-dracan, 1427. Compar. acc. sg. syllîcran wiht (the dragon), 3039.

semninga, adv., *straightway, at once,* 645, 1641, 1768.

sendan, w. v. w. acc. of thing and dat. of pers., *to send :* pret. sg. þone god sende folce tô frôfre (*whom God sent as a comfort to the people*), 13; so, 471, 1843.

for-sendan, *to send away, drive off :* pret. part. he wearð on feónda geweald ... snûde for-sended, 905.

on-sendan, *to send forth, away*, w. acc. of thing and dat. of pers.: imper. sg. on-send, 452, 1484; pret. sg. on-sende, 382; pl. þe hine ... forð on-sendon ænne ofer ýðe (*who sent him forth alone over the sea*), 45; pret. part. bealo-cwealm hafað fela feorh-cynna feorr on-sended, 2267.

sendan (cf. Gl. Aldhelm, sanda = ferculorum, epularum, in Haupt IX. 444), w. v., *to feast, banquet:* pres. sg. III. sendeð, 601. — Leo.

serce, syrce, w. f., *sark, shirt of mail:* nom. sg. syrce, 1112; nom. pl. syrcan, 226; acc. pl. græge syrcan, 334. — Comp.: beadu-, heoro-serce; here-, leoðo-, lic-syrce.

sess, st. m., *seat, place for sitting:* dat. sg. sesse, 2718; Jâ he bî sesse geóng (*by the seat*, i.e. before the dragon's lair), 2757.

setl, st. n., *seat, settle:* acc. sg., 2014; dat. sg. setle, 1233, 1783, 2020; gen. sg. setles, 1787; dat. pl. set-lum, 1290. — Comp.: heáh-, hilde-, meodu-setl.

settan, w. v., *to set:* pret. sg. setton sæ-meðe side scyldas ... wið þâs recedes weall (*the sea-wearied ones set their broad shields against the wall of the hall*), 325; so, 1243.

â-settan, *to set, place, appoint:* pret. pl. hie him â-setton segen [gyl]-denne heáh ofer heáfod, 47; pret. part. hâfde kyninga wulder Grendle tô-geánes...sele-weardâ-seted,668.

be-settan, *to set with, surround:* pret. sg. (helm) besette swîn-lîcum (*set the helm with swine-bodies*), 1454.

ge-settan: 1) *to set, set down:* pret. part. swâ wâs ... þurh rûn-stafas rihte ge-mearcod, ge-seted and ge-sæd (*thus was ... in rune-*

staves rightly marked, set down and said), 1697. — 2) *to set, ordain, create:* pret. sg. ge-sette ... sunnan and mônan leóman tô leóhte land-bûendum, 94. — 3) = componere, *to lay aside, smooth over, appease:* pret. sg. Jât he mid Ið wîfe wäl-fæhða ... dæl ... ge-sette, 2030.

sêcan, w. v., *to follow after*, hence: 1) *to seek, strive for*, w. acc.: pret. sg. sinc-fät sôhte (*sought the costly cup*), 2301; ne sôhte searo-niðas, 2739; so, 3068. Without acc.: þonne his myne sôhte (*than his wish demanded*), 2573; hord-weard sôhte georne äfter grunde (*the hoard-warden sought eagerly along the ground*), 2294. — 2) *to look for, come* or *go some whither, attain something*, w. acc.: pres. sg. III. se þe ... biorgas sêceð, 2273; subj. Jeáh þe hæð-stapa holt-wudu sêce, 1370; imper. sêc gif þu dyrre (*look for her*, i.e. Grendel's mother, *if thou dare*), 1380; inf. sêcean, 200, 268, 646, 1598, 1870, 1990, 2514(?), 3103, etc.; sêcan, 665, 1451; drihten sêcean (*seek, go to, the Lord*), 187; sêcean wyn-leás wîc (*Grendel was to seek a joyless place*, i.e. Hell), 822; so, sêcan deófla gedräg, 757; sâwle sêcan (*seek the life, kill*), 802; so, sêcean sâwle hord, 2423; gerund. sæcce tô sêceanne, 2563; pret. sg. I., III. sôhte, 139, 208, 376, 417, 2224; II. sôhtest, 458; pl. sôhton, 339. — 3) *to seek, attack:* þe ûs sêceað tô Sweóna leóde, 3002; pret. pl. hine wräc-mæcgas ofer sæ sôhtan, 2381.

ge-sêcan: 1) *to seek*, w. acc.: inf. gif he gesêcean dear wîg ofer wæpen, 685. — 2) *to look for, come* or *go to* *attain*, w. acc.: inf. ge-sêcean, 693; gerund. tô ge-sêcanne, 1923; pret. sg. ge-sôhte, 463, 520, 718, 1952; pret. part. acc. pl. feor-cyðñe beóð sêlran ge-sôhte | am |e hine selfa deâh, 1840. — 3) *to seek with hostile intent, to attack :* pres. sg. ge-sêceð 2516; pret. sg. ge-sôhte, 2347; pl. ge-sôhton, 2927; ge-sôhtan, 2205.

ofer-sêcan, w. acc., *to surpass, outdo* (in an attack): pres. sg. wäs sió hond tô strong, se |e mêca gehwane ... swenge ofer-sôhte, |onne he tô sæcce bär wæpen wundrum heard (*too strong was the hand, that surpassed every sword in stroke, when he* [Beówulf] *bore the wondrous weapon to battl*, i.e. the hand was too strong for any sword; its strength made it useless in battle), 2687.

sêl, st. f. See sa•l.

sêl, sa•l, adj., *good, excellent, fit,* only in compar.: nom. sg. m. sêlra, 861, 2194; |æm |ær sêlra wäs (*to the one that was the better,* i.e. Hygelâc), 2200; deáð bið sêlla |onne edwît-lîf, 2891; neut. sêlre, 1385; acc. sg. m. sêlran |e (*a better than thee*), 1851; sêlran, 1198; neut. |ät sêlre, 1760; dat. sg. m. sêlran sweord-frecan, 1469; acc. pl. fem. sêlran, 1840. Superl., strong form: nom. sg. neut. sêlest, 173, 1060; hûsa sêlest, 146, 285, 936; ôfost is sêlest, 256; bolda sêlest, 2327; acc. sg. neut. hrägla sêlest, 454; hûsa sêlest, 659; billa sêlest, 1145: — weak form: nom. sg. m. reced sêlesta, 412; acc. sg. m. |one sêlestan, 1407, 2383; (|äs, MS.), 1957; dat. sg. m. |äm sêlestan, 1686; nom. pl. sêlestan, 416; acc. pl. | â sêlestan, 3123.

sêl, compar. adv., *better, fitter, more excellent,* 1013, 2531; ne byð him wihte | ê sêl (*he shall be nought the better for it*), 2278; so, 2688.

sealma (Frisian selma, in bed-selma), w. m., *bed-chamber, sleeping-place :* acc. sg. on sealman, 2461.

sealt, adj., *salty :* acc. sg. neut. ofer sealt wäter (*the sea*), 1990.

searo (G. sarwa, pl.), st. n.: 1) *armor, accoutrements, war-gear :* nom. pl. sæ-manna searo, 329; dat. pl. secg on searwum (*a man, warrior, in panoply*), 249, 2701; in (on) searwum, 323, 1558; 2531, 2569; instr. pl. searwum, 1814. — 2) *insidiae, ambuscade, waylaying, deception, battle :* | â ic of searwum cwom, fâh from feóndum, 419. — 3) *cunning, art, skill :* instr. pl. sadol searwum fâh (*saddle cunningly ornamented*), 1039; earm-beága fela, searwum ge-sæled (*many cunningly-linked armlets*), 2765. — Comp. fyrd-, gûð-, inwit-searo.

searo-bend, st. f., *band, bond, of curious workmanship :* instr. pl. searo-bendum fäst, 2087.

searo-fâh, adj., *cunningly inlaid, ornamented, with gold :* nom. sg. here-byrne hondum ge-broden, sid and searo-fâh, 1445.

searo-ge-|ræc, st. n., *heap of treasure-objects :* acc. sg., 3103.

searo-gim, st. m., *cunningly set gem, rich jewel :* acc. pl. searo-gimmas, 2750; gen. pl. searo-gimma, 1158.

searo-grim, adj., *cunning and fierce :* nom. sg., 595.

searo-häbbend, pres. part. as subst., *arms-bearing, warrior with his trappings :* gen. pl. searo-häbbendra, 237.

searo-net, st. n., *armor-net, shirt of mail, corselet:* nom. sg., 406.

searo-nîð, st. m.: 1) *cunning hostility, plot, wiles:* acc. pl. searo-nîðas, 1201, 2739. — 2) also, only *hostility, feud, contest:* acc. pl. searo-nîðas, 3068; gen. pl. searo-nîða, 582.

searo-þanc, st. m., *ingenuity:* instr. pl. searo-þoncum, 776.

searo-wundor, st. n., *rare wonder:* acc. sg., 921.

seax, st. n., *shortsword, hip-knife; dagger:* instr. sg. seaxe, 1546. — Comp. wäl-seax.

seax - ben, st. f., *dagger-wound:* instr. pl. siex-bennum, 2905.

seofon, num., *seven*, 517; seofan, 2196; decl. acc. syfone, 3123.

seomian, w. v.: 1) intrans., *to be tied; lie at rest:* inf. siomian, 2768; pret. sg. seomode, 302. — 2) w. acc., *to put in bonds, entrap, catch:* pret. sg. duguðe and geogoðe seomade (cf. 2086–2092), 161.

seonu, st. f., *sinew:* nom. pl. seonowe, 818.

seóc, adj., *feeble, weak; fatally ill:* nom. sg. feorh-bennum seóc (of Beówulf, *sick unto death*), 2741; siex-bennum seóc (of the dead dragon), 2905; nom. pl. môdes seóce(*sick of soul*), 1604.—Comp.: ellen-, feorh-, heaðo-seóc.

seóðan, st. v. w. acc., *to seethe, boil;* figuratively, *be excited over, brood:* pret. sg. ic þäs môd-ceare sorh-wylmum seáð (*I pined in heart-grief for that*), 1994; so, 190.

seóloð, st. m.?, *bight, bay* (cf. Dietrich in Haupt XI. 416): gen. pl. sióleða bi-gong (*the realm of bights* = the [surface of the] sea?), 2368.

seón, sŷn, st. f., *aspect, sight:* in comp. wlite-, wundor-seón, an-sŷn.

seón, st. v., *to see:* a) w. acc.: inf. searo-wunder seón, 921; so, 387, 1181, 1276, 3103; þær mäg nihta ge-hwæm nîð-wundor seón (*there may every night be seen a repulsive marvel*), 1366; pret. sg. ne seah ic . . . heal-sittendra medudreám mâran, 2015. — b) w. acc. and predicate adj.: ne seah ic elleódige þus manige men môdiglîcran, 336. — c) w. prep. or adv.: pret. sg. seah on enta ge-weorc, 2718; seah on un-leófe, 2864; pl. folc tô sægon (*looked on*), 1423.

ge-seón, *to see, behold:* a) w. acc.: pres. sg. III. se þe beáh ge-syhð, 2042; inf. ge-seón, 396, 571, 649, 962, 1079, etc.; pret. sg. geseah, 247, 927, 1558, 1614; pl. ge-sâwon, 1606, 2253. — b) w. acc. and predicate adj., pres. sg. III. ge-syhð . . . on his suna bûre win-sele wêstne (*sees in his son's house the wine-hall empty;* or, *hall of friends?*), 2456. — c) w. inf.: pret. sg. ge-seah . . . beran ofer bolcan beorhte randas (*saw shining shields borne over the gang-plank*), 229; pret. pl. mære mâðððum-sweord monige ge-sâwon beforan beorn beran, 1024. — d) w. acc. and inf.: pret. sg. ge-seah, 729, 1517, 1586, 1663, 2543, 2605, etc.; pl. ge-sâwon, 221, 1348, 1426; ge-sêgan, 3039; ge-sêgon, 3129. — e) w. depend. clause: inf. mäg þonne . . . gesćón sunu Hrêðles, þät ic (*may the son of H. see that I . . .*), 1486; pret. pl. ge-sâwon, 1592.

geond-seón, *to see, look through, over*, w. acc.: pret. sg. (ic) þät eall geond-seh, 3088.

ofer-seón, *to see clearly, plainly:* pret. pl. ofer-sâwon, 419.

on-seón, *to look on, at,* w. acc.: pret. pl. on-sâwon, 1651.

seówlan, w. v., *to sew, put together, link:* pret. part. searo-net seówed smiðes or-þancum (*the corselet woven by the smith's craft*), 406.

sib, st. f., *peace, friendship, relationship:* nom. sg., 1165, 1858; sibb, 2601; acc. sibbe, 950, 2432, 2923; instr. sg. sibbe (*in peace?*), 154. — Comp.: dryht-, friðu-sib.

sib-æðeling, st. m., *nobilis consanguineus, kindred prince or nobleman* nom. pl. -æðelingas, 2709.

sibbe-gedryht, st. f., *body of allied or related warriors:* acc. sg. sibbe-gedriht (the Danes), 387; (the Geátas), 730.

siððan, syððan: 1) adv.: a) *since, after, from now on, further,* 142, 149, 283, 567, 1903, 2052, 2065, 2176, 2703, 2807, 2921; seoððan, 1876. — b) *then, thereupon, after,* 470, 686, 1454, 1557, 1690, 2208; seoððan, 1938; ær ne siððan (*neither before nor after*), 719.

2) Conj.: a) w. ind. pres., *as soon as, when,* 413, 605, 1785, 2889, 2912. — b) w. ind. pret., *when, whilst,* 835, 851, 1205, 1207, 1421, 1590, 2357, 2961, 2971, 3128; seoð-ðan, 1776; — *since,* 649, 657, 983, 1199, 1254, 1309, 2202; — *after,* either with pluperf.: siððan him scyppend forscrifen hæfde (*after the Creator had proscribed him*), 106; so, 1473; or with pret. = pluperf.: syððan niht becom (*after night had come on*), 115; so, 6, 132, 723, 887, 902, 1078, 1149, 1236, 1262, 1282, 1979, 2013, 2125; or pret. and pluperf. together, 2104–2105.

siex. See seax.

sige-dryhten, st. m., *lord of vic-* *tory, victorious lord:* nom. sg. sige-drihten, 391.

sige-eádig, adj., *blest with victory, victorious:* acc. sg. neut. sige-eádig bil, 1558.

sige-folc, st. n., *victorious people, troop:* gen. pl. sige-folca, 645.

sige-hreð, st. f., *confidence of victory(?):* acc. sg., 490.

sige-hreðig, adj., *victorious:* nom. sg., 94, 1598, 2757.

sige-hwîl, st. f., *hour or day of victory:* gen. sg. sige-hwîle, 2711.

sige-leás, adj., *devoid of victory, defeated:* acc. sg. sige-leásne sang, 788.

sige-rôf, adj., *victorious:* nom. sg., 620.

sige-þeód, st. f., *victorious warrior troop:* dat. sg. on sige-þeóde, 2205.

sige-wæpen, st. n., *victor-weapon, sword:* dat. pl. sige-wæpnum, 805.

sigl, st. n.: 1) *sun:* nom. sg. sigel, 1967. — 2) *sun-shaped ornament:* acc. pl. siglu, 3165; sigle (bracteates of a necklace), 1201; gen. pl. sigla, 1158. — Comp. mâðð̄um-sigl.

sigor, st. m., *victory:* gen. sg. sigores, 1022; gen. pl. sigora, 2876, 3056. — Comp.: hreð-, wîg-sigor.

sigor-eádig, adj., *victorious:* nom. sg. sigor-eádig secg (of Beówulf), 1312, 2353.

sin. See syn.

sinc, st n., *treasure, jewel, property:* nom. sg., 2765; acc. sg. sinc, 81, 1205, 1486, 2384, 2432; instr. sg. since, 1039, 1451, 1616, 1883, 2218, 2747; gen. sg. sinces, 608, 1171, 1923, 2072; gen. pl. sinca, 2429.

sinc-fâh, adj., *treasure-decked:* acc. sg. neut. weak form, sinc-fâge sel, 167.

sinc-fât, st. n., *costly vessel:* acc. sg., 2232, 2301; — *a costly object:* acc.

sg., 1201 (i.e. mene); acc. pl. sinc-fato, 623.

sinc-ge-streón, st. n., *precious treasure, jewel of value:* instr. pl. -ge-streónum, 1093; gen. pl. -gestreóna, 1227.

sinc-gifu, w. m., *jewel-giver, treasure-giver* = *prince, ruler:* acc. sg. sinc-gyfan, 1013; dat. sg. sinc-gifan (of Beówulf), 2312; (of Aschere), 1343.

sinc-mâððum, st. m., *treasure:* nom. sg., 2194.

sinc-þego, f., *acceptance, taking, of jewels:* nom. sg., 2885.

sin-dolh, st. n., *perpetual,* i.e. incurable, *wound:* nom. sg. syn-dolh, 818.

sin-freá, w. m., *wedded lord, husband:* nom. sg., 1935.

sin-gal, adj., *continual, lasting:* acc. sg. fem. sin-gale säce, 154.

sin-gales, adv. gen. sg., *continually, ever,* 1778; syngales, 1136.

singala, adv. gen. pl., the same, 190.

singan, st. v., *to sound, ring, sing:* pret. sg. hring-iren scir song in searwum (*the ringed iron rang in the armor*), 323; horn stundum song fûs-lîc f[yrd]-leóð (*at times the horn rang forth a ready battle-song*), 1424; scôp hwîlum sang (*the singer sang at whiles*), 496.

â-singan, *to sing out, sing to an end:* pret. part. leóð wäs â-sungen, 1160.

sin-here, st. m., (*army without end?*), *strong army, host:* instr. sg. sin-herge, 2937.

sin-niht, st. f., *perpetual night, night after night:* acc. pl. sin-nihte (*night after night*), 161.

sin-sceaða, w. m., *irreconcilible foe:* nom. sg. syn-sceaða, 708; acc. sg. syn-sceaðan, 802.

sin-snæd, st. f., (*continuous biting*), *bite after bite:* dat. pl. syn-snædum swealh (*swallowed bite after bite, in great bites*), 744.

sittan, st. v.: 1) *to sit:* pres. sg. Wiglâf siteð ofer Biówulfe, 2907; imper. sg. site nu tô symle, 489; inf.)ær swîð-ferhðe sittan eodon (*whither the strong-minded went and sat*), 493; eode...tô hire freán sittan (*went to sit by her lord*), 642; pret. sg. on wicge sät (*sat on the horse*), 286; ät fôtum sät (*sat at the feet*), 500, 1167; þær Hrôð-gâr sät (*where H. sat*), 356; so, 1191, 2895; he gewêrgad sät... freán eaxlum neáh, 2854; pret. pl. sæton, 1165; gistas sêtan (MS. sêcan)... and on mere staredon (*the strangers sat and stared on the sea*), 1603.—2) *to be in a certain state* or *condition* (*quasi* copula): pret. sg. mære þeóden... unbliðe sät, 130.—Comp.: flet-, heal-sittend.

be-sittan, obsidere, *to surround, besiege,* w. acc.: besät þâ sin-herge sweorda lâfe wundum wêrge (*then besieged he with a host the leavings of the sword, wound-weary*), 2937.

for-sittan, obstrui, *to pass away, fail:* pres. sg. eágena bearhtm for-siteð (*the light of the eyes passeth away*), 1768.

ge-sittan: 1) *to sit, sit together:* pret. sg. monig-oft ge-sät rice to rûne (*very often sat the king deliberating with his council* (see rîce)), 171; wið earm ge-sät (*supported himself upon his arm, sat on his arm?*), 750; fêða eal ge-sät (*the whole troop sat down*), 1425; ge-sät þâ wið sylfne (*sat there beside, opposite?, him,* i.e. Hygelâc), 1978;

ge-sǣt þá on nǣsse, 2418; so, 2718;
pret. part. (syððan) . . . we tô
symble ge-seten háfdon, 2105. —
2) w. acc., *to seat one's self upon*
or *in something, to board:* pret.
sg. þá ic . . . sæ-bât ge-sǣt, 634.
of-sittan, w. acc., *to sit over* or
upon: pret. sg. of-sǣt þâ þone sele-
gyst, 1546.
ofer-sittan, w. acc., *to dispense
with, refrain from* (cf. ofer, 2
[c]): pres. sg. I. þät ic wið þone
gúð-flogan gylp ofer-sitte, 2529;
inf. secge ofer-sittan, 685.
on-sittan (O.H.G. int-sizzan, *to
start from one's seat, to be startled*),
w. acc., *to fear:* inf. þâ fæhðe,
eatole ecg-þrǣce eówer leóde swiðe
onsittan (*to dread the hostility, the
fierce contest, of your people*), 598.
ymb-sittan, *to sit around,* w. acc.:
pret. pl. (þát hie) . . . symbel ymb-
sǣton (*sat round the feast*), 564.
See ymb-sittend.
sîd, adj.: 1) *wide, broad, spacious,
large:* nom. sg. (here-byrne, glôf)
sîd, 1445, 2087; acc. sg. m. sidne
scyld, 437; on sidne sǣ, 507; fem.
byrnan side (of a corselet extending over the legs), 1292; ofer sǣ
sîde, 2395; neut. sîde rice, 1734,
2200; instr. sg. sîdan herge, 2348;
acc. pl. sîde sǣ-nässas, 223; sîde
scyldas, 325; gen. pl. sîdra sorga
(*of great sorrows*), 149. — 2) in
moral sense, *great, noble:* acc. sg.
þurh sîdne sefan, 1727.
sîde, adv., *far and wide, afar,* 1224.
sîd-fäðme, adj., *broad-bosomed:* acc.
sg. sîd-fäðme scif, 1918.
sîd-fäðmed, *quasi* pret. part., the
same: nom. sg. sîd-fäðmed scip,
302.
sîd-rand, st. m., *broad shield:* nom.
sg., 1290.

sîð (G. seiþu-s), adj., *late:* superl.
nom. sg. sîðast sige-hwîle (*the last
hour, day, of victory*), 2711; dat.
sg. ät sîðestan (*in the end, at last*),
3014.
sîð, adv. compar., *later:* ǣr and
sîð (*sooner and later, early and
late*), 2501.
sîð (G. sinþ-s), st. m.: 1) *road, way,
journey, expedition;* esp., *road to
battle:* nom. sg., 501, 3059, 3090;
nǣs þät éðe sîð (*that was no easy
road, task*), 2587; so, þät wǣs geócor sîð, 766; acc. sg. sîð, 353, 512,
909, 1279, 1430, 1967; instr. dat.
sîðe, 532, 1952, 1994; gen. sg.
sîðes, 579, 1476, 1795, 1909. Also,
return: nom. sg., 1972. — 2) *undertaking, enterprise;* esp., *battle-
work:* nom. sg. nis þät eówer sîð,
2533; ne bið swylc earges sîð
(*such is no coward's enterprise*),
2542; acc. sg. sîð, 873. In pl. -
adventures: nom. sîðas, 1987;
acc. sîðas, 878; gen. sîða, 318. —
3) time (as iterative): nom. sg. nǣs
þät forma sîð (*that was not the first
time*), 717, 1464; so, 1528, 2626;
acc. sg. ofter micle þonne on ǣnne
sîð, 1580; instr. sg. (forman, ôðre,
þriddan) sîðe, 741, 1204, 2050,
2287, 2512, 2518, 2671, 2689, 3102.
— Comp.: cear-, eft-, ellor-, gryre-,
sǣ-, wil-, wrǣc-sîð.
ge-sîð, st. m., *comrade, follower:*
gen. sg. ge-sîðes, 1298; nom. pl.
ge-sîðas, 29; acc. pl. ge-sîðas,
2041, 2519; dat. pl. ge-sîðum,
1314, 1925, 2633; gen. pl. ge-sîða,
1935. — Comp.: eald-, wil-gesîð.
sîð-fät, st. m., *way, journey:* acc.
sg. þone sîð-fät, 202; dat. sg. sîð-
fate, 2640.
sîð-fram, -from, adj., *ready for the
journey:* nom. pl. sîð-frome, 1814.

sîðian, w. v., *to journey, march :* inf., 721, 809; pret. sg. sîðode, 2120.

for-sîðian, *iter fatale inire* (Grein): pret. sg. häfde þâ for-sîðod sunu Ecg-þeówes under gynne grund *(would have found his death,* etc.), 1551.

sie, sŷ. See **wesan.**

sîgan, st. v., *to descend, sink, incline:* pret. pl. sigon ät-somne *(descended together),* 307; sigon þâ tô skepe *(they sank to sleep),* 1252.

ge-sîgan, *to sink, fall:* inf. ge-sîgan ätsäcce *(fall in battle),* 2600.

sin, poss. pron., *his:* acc. sg. m. sînne, 1001, 1985, 2284, 2790; dat. sg. sînum, 1508.

slæp, st. m., *sleep:* nom. sg., 1743; dat. sg. tô slæp :, 1252.

slæpan, st. v., *to sleep:* pres. part. nom. sg. slæpende, 2220; acc. sg. he gefêng...slæpendne rinc *(seized a sleeping warrior),* 742; acc. pl. slæpende frät folces Denigea fîf-tyne men *(devoured, sleeping, fif-teen of the people of the Danes),* 1582.

sleac, adj., *slack, lazy:* nom. sg., 2188.

sleahan, sleán : 1) *to strike, strike at :* a) intrans.: pres. subj. sg. þät he me ongeán sleá *(that he should strike at me),* 682; pret. sg. yrrin-ga slôh *(struck angrily),* 1566; so, slôh hilde-bille, 2680. b) trans.: pret. sg. þät he þone nîð-gäst nio-ðor hwêne slôh *(that he struck the dragon somewhat lower,* etc.), 2700. — 2) w. acc.: *to slay, kill:* pret. sg. þäs þe he Abel slôg *(be-cause he slew A.),* 108; so, slôg, 421, 2180; slôh, 1582, 2356; pl. slôgon, 2051; pret. part. þâ wäs Fin slägen, 1153.

ge-sleán, w. acc.: 1) *to fight a bat-*

tle : pret. sg. ge-slôh þîn fäder fæhðe mæste, 459. — 2) *to gain by fighting:* syððan hie þâ mærða ge-slôgan, 2997.

of-sleán, *to ofslay, kill,* w. acc.: pret. sg. of-slôh, 574, 1666, 3061.

slîðe (G. sleiþ-s), adj., *savage, fierce, dangerous:* acc. sg. þurh slîðne nîð, 184; gen. pl. slîðra ge-slyhta, 2399.

slîðen, adj., *furious, savage, deadly:* nom. sg. sweord-bealo slîðen, 1148.

slîtan, st. v., *to slit, tear to pieces,* w. acc.: pret. sg. slât (slæpendne rinc), 742.

slyht, st. m., *blow:* in comp. and-slyht.

ge-slyht, st. n. (collective), *battle, conflict:* gen. pl. slîðra ge-slyhta, 2399.

smið, st. m., *smith, armorer:* nom. sg. wæpna smið, 1453; gen. sg. smiðes, 406. · Comp. wundor-smið.

be-smiðian, w. v., *to surround with iron-work, bands,* etc.: pret. part. he (the hall Heorot) þäs fäste wäs innan and ûtan îren-bendum searo-þoncum besmiðod (i.e. the beams out of which the hall was built were held together skilfully, within and without, by iron clamps), 776.

snell, adj., *fresh, vigorous, lively; of martial temper:* nom. sg. se snella, 2972.

snellîc, adj., the same: nom. sg., 691.

snotor, snottor, adj., *clever, wise, intelligent:* nom. sg. snotor, 190, 827, 909, 1385; in weak form, (se) snottra, 1314, 1476, 1787; sno-tra, 2157, 3121; nom. pl. snotere, 202, 416; snottre, 1592. — Comp. fore-snotor.

snotor-lîce, adv., *intelligently, wise-ly:* compar. snotor-lîcor, 1483.

snûde, adv., *hastily, quickly, soon,* 905, 1870, 1972, 2326, 2569, 2753.

be - snyðian, w. v., *to rob, deprive of :* pret. sg.]ätte Ongenþió caldre be-snyðede Hæðcyn, 2925.

snyrian, w. v, *to hasten, hurry :* pret. pl. snyredon ät-somne (*hurried forward together*), 402.

snyttru, f., *intelligence, wisdom :* acc. sg. snyttru, 1727; dat. pl. mid módes snyttrum, 1707;]e we ealle ær ne meahton snyttrum be-syrwan (*a deed which all of us together could not accomplish before with all our wisdom*), 943. Adv., *wisely,* 873.

somne. See samne.

sorgian, w. v.: 1) *to be grieved, sorrow :* imper. sg. II. ne sorga! 1385. — 2) *to care for, trouble one's self about :* inf. nô þu ymb mînes ne]earft lîces feorme leng sorgian (*thou needst not care longer about my life's [body's] sustenance*), 451.

sorh, st. f., *grief, pain, sorrow :* nom. sg., 1323; sorh is me tô secganne (*pains me to say*), 473; acc. sg. sorge, 119, 2464; dat. instr. sg. mid]ære sorge, 2469; sorge (*in sorrow, grieved*), 1150; gen. sg. worna fela . . . sorge, 2005; dat. pl. sorgum, 2601; gen. pl. sorga, 149. —Comp.: hyge-, in-wit-,]egn-sorh.

sorh-cearig, adj., *curis sollicitus, heart-broken :* nom. sg., 2456.

sorh-ful, adj., *sorrowful, troublesome, difficult :* nom. sg., 2120; acc. sg. sorh-fullne (sorh-fulne) sîð, 512, 1279, 1430.

sorh-leás, adj., *free from sorrow or grief :* nom. sg., 1673.

sorh-leóð, st. n., *dirge, song of sorrow :* acc. sg., 2461.

sorh-wylm, st. m., *wave of sorrow :* nom. pl. sorh-wylmas, 905.

sôcn, st. f., *persecution, hostile pursuit or attack* (see sêcan): dat. (instr.) bære sôcne (by reason of Grendel's persecution), 1778.

sôð, st. n., *sooth, truth :* acc. sg. sôð, 532, 701, 1050, 1701, 2865; dat. sg. tô sôðe (*in truth*), 51, 591, 2326.

sôð, adj., *true, genuine :* nom. sg.]ät is sôð metod, 1612; acc. sg. n. gyd âwräc sôð and sâr-lîc, 2110.

sôðe, adv., *truly, correctly, accurately,* 524; sôðe gebunden (of alliterative verse : *accurately put together*), 872.

sôð-cyning, st. m., *true king :* nom. sg. sigora sôð-cyning (*God*), 3056.

sôð-fäst, adj., *soothfast, established in truth, orthodox* (here used of the Christian martyrs): gen. pl. sôð-fästra dôm (*glory, realm, of the saints*), 2821.

sôð-lîce, adv., *in truth, truly, truthfully,* 141, 273, 2900.

sôfte, adv., *gently, softly :* compar. þý sêft (*the more easily*), 2750. — Comp. un-sôfte.

sôna, adv., *soon, immediately,* 121, 722, 744, 751, 1281, 1498, 1592, 1619, 1763, etc.

on - spannan, st. v., *to un-span, unloose :* pret. sg. his helm onspeón (*loosed his helm*), 2724.

spel, st. n., *narrative, speech :* acc. sg. spell, 2110; acc. pl. spel, 874; gen. pl. spella, 2899, 3030.—Comp. weá-spel.

spêd, st. f.: 1) *luck, success :* in comp. here-, wîg-spêd. — 2) *skill, facility :* acc. sg. on spêd (*skilfully*), 874.

spîwan, st. v., *to spit, spew,* w. instr.: inf. glêdum spîwan (*spit fire*), 2313.

spor, st. n., *spur:* in comp. hand-spor.

spôwan, st. v., *to speed well, help, avail:* pret. sg. him wiht ne speów (*availed him naught*), 2855; hû him ät æte speów (*how he sped in the eating*), 3027.

spræc, st. f., *speech, language:* instr. sg. frécnan spræce (*through bold, challenging, discourse*), 1105. — Comp. : æfen-, gylp-spræc.

sprecan, st. v., *to speak:* inf. ic sceal forð sprecan gen ymbe Grendel (*I shall go on speaking about G.*), 2070; w. acc. se ǀe wyle sôð sprecan (*he who will speak the truth*), 2865; imper. tô Geátum sprec (spræc, MS.), 1172; pret. sg. III. spräc, 1169, 1699, 2511, 2725; word äfter spräc, 341; nô ymbe ǀâ fæhðe spräc, 2619; II. hwät ǀu worn fela ... ymb Brecan spræce (*how much thou hast spoken of Breca!*), 531; pl. hwät wit geó spræcon (*what we two spoke of before*), 1477; gomele ymb gôdne on-geador spræcon, ǀät hig ... (*the graybeards spoke together about the valiant one, that they ...*), 1596; swâ wit furðum spræcon (*as we two spoke, engaged, before*), 1708; pret. part. ǀâ wäs ... þryð-word sprecen, 644.

ge-sprecan, w. acc., *to speak:* pret. sg. ge-spräc, 676, 1399, 1467, 3095.

spreót, st. m., *pole; spear, pike:* in comp. eofor-spreót.

springan, st. v., *to jump, leap; flash:* pret. sg. brâ wîde sprong (*the body bounded far*), 1589; swât ædrum sprong forð under fexe (*the blood burst out in streams from under his hair*), 2967; pl. wîde sprungon hilde - leóman (*flashed*

afar), 2583. Also figuratively: blæd wîde sprang (*his repute spread afar*), 18.

ät-springan, *to spring forth:* pret. sg. swâ ǀät blôd ge-sprang (*as the blood burst forth*), 1668. Figuratively, *to arise, originate:* pret. sg. Sigemunde gesprong äfter deáð-däge dôm un-lytel, 885.

on-springan, *to burst in two, spring asunder:* pret. pl. seonowe onsprungon, burston bânlocan 818.

standan, st. v.: 1) absolutely or with prep., *to stand:* pres. III. pl. córed-geatwe þe ge ǀær on standað (*the warlike accoutrements wherein ye there stand*), 2867; inf. ge-seah ... orcas stondan (*saw vessels standing*), 2761; pret. sg. ät hýðe stôd hringed-stefna (*in the harbor stood the curved-prowed?, metal-covered?, ship*), 32; stôd on stapole (*stood near the [middle] column*), 927; so, 1914, 2546; ǀät him on aldre stôd here-sträl hearda (*that the sharp war-arrow stood in his vitals*), 1435; so, 2680; pl. gâras stôdon ... samod ät-gädere (*the spears stood together*), 328; him big stôdan bunan and orcas (*by him stood cans and pots*), 3048. Also of still water: pres. sg. III. nis ǀät feor heonon ... ǀät se mere standeð, 1363. — 2) with predicate adj., *to stand, continue in a certain state:* subj. pres. ǀät þes sele stande ... rinca ge-hwylcum îdel and unnyt (*that this hall stands empty and useless for every warrior*), 411; inf. hord-wynne fand eald uht-sceaða opene standan, 2272; pret. sg. ôð ǀät îdel stôd hûsa sêlest, 145; so, 936; wäter under stôd dreórig and ge-dréfed, 1418.

— 3) *to belong* or *attach to ; issue :*
pret. sg. Norð-Denum stôd atelîc
egesa (*great terror clung to, over-
came, the North Danes*), 784; |âra
ânum stôd sadol searwum fâh (*on
one of the steeds lay an ingeniously-
inlaid saddle*), 1038; byrne-leóma
eldum on andan (*burning light
stood forth, a horror to men*), 2314;
leóht inne stôd (*a light stood in it*,
i.e. the sword), 1571; him of eágum stôd . . . leóht unfâger (*an
uncanny light issued from his eyes*,
727; so, |ät [fram] þam gyste
[gyre-] bróga stôd, 2229.
â-standan, *to stand up, arise :*
pret. sg. â-stôd, 760, 1557, 2093.
ät-standan, *to stand at, near,* or
in : pret. sg. |ät hit (i.e. þät swurd)
on wealle ät-stôd, 892.
for-standan, *to stand against* or
before, hence : 1) *to hinder, prevent:*
pret. sg. |breóst-net) wið erd and
wið ecge in-gang for-stôd (*the shirt
of mail prevented point or edge
from entering*), 1550; subj. nefne
him witig god wyrdfor-stóde (*if the
wise God had not warded off such
a fate from them*, i.e. the men
threatened by Grendel), 1057. —
2) *defend,* w. dat. of person against
whom : inf. |ät he . . . mihte heáðo-
lîðendum hord for-standan, bearn
and brýde (*that he might protect
his treasure, his children, and his
spouse from the sea - farers*),
2956.
ge-standan, intrans., *to stand :*
pret. sg. ge-stôd, 358, 404, 2567;
pl. nealles him on heápe hand-gesteallan . . . ymbe gestôdon (*not
at all did his boon-companions
stand serried around him*), 2597.
stapa, w. m., *stepper, strider :* in
comp. hæð-, mearc-stapa.

stapan, st. v., *to step, stride, go forward :* pret. sg. eorl furðor stôp,
762; gum-fêða stôp lind-häbbendra (*the troop of shield-warriors
strode on*), 1402.
ät-stapan, *to stride up* or *to :* pret.
sg. fcrð neár ät-stôp (*strode up
near r*), 746.
ge-stapan, *to walk, stride :* pret.
sg. he tô forð gestôp dyrnan cräfte,
dracan heáfde neáh (*he,* i.e. the
man that robbed the dragon of
the vessel, *had through hidden
craft come too near the dragon's
head*), 2290.
stapol, st. m., (= βάσις), *trunk of a
tree ;* hence, *support, pillar, column :* dat. sg. stôd on stapole
(*stood by* or *near the wooden middle column of Heorot*), 927; instr.
pl. |â stân-bogan stapuluin fäste
(*the arches of stone upheld by pil-
lars*), 2719.
starian, w. v., *to stare, look intently
at :* pres. sg. I. |ät ic on þone ha-
felan . . . eágum starige (*that I see
the head with my eyes*, 1782; |âra
frätwa . . . þe ic her on starie (*for
the treasures . . . that I here look
upon*), 2797; III. þonne he on |ät
sinc staraðs, 1486: sg. for pl. |âra
þe on swylc staraðs, 997; pret. sg.
þai (sin-freá) hire an däges eágum
starede, 1936; pl. on mere staredon, 1604.
stân, st. m.: 1) *stone :* in comp.
eorclan-stân. — 2) *rock :* acc. sg.
under (ofer) hârne stân, 888, 1416,
2554, 2745; dat. sg. stâne, 2289,
2558.
stân-beorh, st. m., *rocky elevation,
stony mountain :* acc. sg. stân-
beorh steápne, 2214.
stân-boga, w. m., *stone arch, arch
hewn out of the rock :* dat. sg. stân-

hogan, 2546; nom. pl. stân-hogan, 2719.

stân-clif, st. n., *rocky cliff :* acc. pl. stân-cleofu, 2541.

stân-fâh, adj., *stone-laid, paved with stones of different colors :* nom. sg. stræt wäs stân-fâh *the street was of different colored stones*, 320.

stân-hliđ, st. n., *rocky slope :* acc. pl. stân-hliđo, 1410.

stäf, st. m.: 1) *staff :* in comp. rûn-stäf. — 2) *elementum :* in comp. âr-, ende-, fâcen-stäf.

stäl, st. m., *place, stead :* dat. sg. þät þu me â wære forđ-gewitenum on fäder stäle (*that thou, if I died, wouldst represent a father's place to me*), 1480.

stælan, w. v., *to place; allure or instigate :* inf. þâ ic on morgne ge-frägn mæg ôđerne billes ecgum on bonan stælan (*then I learned that on the morrow one brother instigated the other to murder with the sword's edge :* or, *one avenged the other on the murderer?*, cf. 2962 seqq.), 2486.

ge-stælan, *to place, impose, institute :* pret. part. ge feor hafađ fæhđe ge-stæled (*Grendel's mother has further begun hostilities against us*), 1341.

stede, st. m., *place, -stead :* in comp. bæl-, burh-, folc-, heáh-, međel-, wang-, wîc-stede.

stefn, st. f., *voice :* nom. sg., 2553; instr. sg. niwan (niówan) stefne (properly novâ voce) = denuo, *anew, again*, 2595, 1790.

stefn, st. m., *prow of a ship :* acc. sg., 213; see bunden-, hringed-, wunden-stefna.

on-stellan, w. v., *constituere, to cause, bring about :* pret. sg. se þäs or-leges ôr on-stealde, 2408.

steng, st. m., *pole, pike :* in comp. wäl-steng.

ge-steppan, w. v., *to stride, go :* pret. sg. folce ge-stepte ofer sæ sîde sunu Ohtheres (*O.'s son*, i.e. Eádgils, *went with warriors over the broad sea*), 2394.

stêde (O.H.G. stâti, M.H.G. stæte), adj., *firm, steady :* nom. sg. wäs stêde nägla ge-hwylc stŷle ge-lîcost (*each nail-place was firm as steel*), 986.

stêpan, w. v. w. acc., *to exalt, honor :* pret. sg. þeáh þe hine mihtig god . . . eafeđum stêpte, 1718.

ge-steald, st. n., *possessions, property :* in comp. in-gesteald, 1156.

ge-stealla, w. m., (contubernalis), *companion, comrade :* in comp. eaxl-, fyrd-, hand-, lind-, nŷd-ge-stealla.

steare-heort, adj., (fortis animo), *stout-hearted, courageous :* nom. sg. (of the dragon), 2289; (of Beówulf), 2553.

steáp, adj., *steep, projecting, towering :* acc. sg. steápne hróf, 927; stân-beorh steápne, 2214; wiđ steápne rond, 2567; acc. pl. m. beorgas steápe, 222; neut. steáp stân-hliđo, 1410. — Comp. heađo-steáp.

stille, adj., *still, quiet :* nom. sg. wîd-floga wundum stille, 2831.

stille, adv., *quietly*, 301.

stincan, st. v., *to smell; snuff :* pret. sg. stonc þâ äfter stâne (*snuffed along the stone*), 2289.

stîđ, adj., *hard, stiff :* nom. sg. wunden-mæl (sword) . . . stîđ and stŷl-ecg, 1534.

stîđ-môd, adj., *stout-hearted, unflinching :* nom. sg., 2567.

stîg, st. m., *way, path :* nom. sg., 320, 2214; acc. pl. stîge nearwe, 1410. — Comp. medu-stîg.

stîgan, st. v., *to go up, ascend:* pret. sg. Þâ he tô holme [st]âg (*when he plunged forward into the sea*), 2363; pl. beornas ... on stefn stigon, 212; Wedera leóde on wang stigon, 225; subj. pret. ær he on bed stige, 677.

â-stîgan, *to ascend:* pres. sg. Þonon ÿð-geblond up â-stigeð won tô wolcnum, 1374; gûð-rinc â-stâh (*the fierce hero ascended*, i.e. was laid on the pyre? or, *the fierce smoke* [rêc] *ascended?*), 1119; gamen eft â-stâh *joy again went up, resounded*), 1161; wudu-rêc â-stâh sweart of swioðole, 3145; swêg up â-stâg, 783.

ge-stîgan, *to ascend, go up:* pret. sg. Þâ ic on holme ge-stâh, 633.

storm, st. m., *storm:* nom. sg. stræla storm (*storm of missiles*), 3118; instr. sg. holm storme weól (*the sea billowed stormily*), 1132.

stôl, st. m., *chair, throne, seat:* in comp. brego-, êðel-, gif-, gum-stôl.

stôw, st. f., *place, -stow:* nom. sg. nis Þät heóru stôw (*a haunted spot*), 1373; acc. sg. frêcne stôwe, 1379: grund-bûendra gearwe stôwe (*the place prepared for men*, i.e. death-bed; see **gesnean** and **genÿdan**), 1007: comp. wäl-stow.

strang, strong, adj., *strong; valiant; mighty:* nom. sg. wäs Þät ge-win tô strang (*that sorrow was too great*), 133; Þu eart mägenes strang (*strong of body*), 1845; wäs sió hond tô strong (*the hand was too powerful*), 2685; superl. wigena strengest (*strongest of warriors*), 1544; mägenes strengest (*strongest in might*, 196; mägene strengest, 790.

strâdan (cf. stræde = passus, gressus), *to tread*, (be)-*stride, stride*

over (Grein): subj. pres. se Þone wong strâde, 3074.

stræl, st. m., *arrow, missile:* instr. sg. biteran stræle, 1747; gen. pl. stræla storm, 3118.

stræt, st. f., *street, highway:* nom. sg., 320; acc. sg. stræte, 1635; fealwe stræte, 917. — Comp.: lagu-, mere-stræt.

strengel, st. m., (*endowed with strength*), *ruler, chief:* acc. sg. wigena strengel, 3116.

strengo, st. m., *strength, power, violence:* acc. sg. mägenes strenge, 1271; dat. sg. strenge, 1534; strengo, 2541; — dat. pl. strengum = *violently, powerfully* [*loosed from the strings?*], 3118: in comp. hilde-, mägen-, mere-strengo.

strêgan (O. S. strôwian), w. v., *to strew, spread:* pret. part. wäs Þäm yldestan ... morðorbed strêd (*the death-bed was spread for the eldest one*), 2437.

streám, st. m., *stream, flood, sea:* acc. sg. streám, 2546; nom. pl. streámas, 212; acc. pl. streámas, 1262: comp. brim-, eágor-, firgen-, lagu-streám.

ge-streón (cf. **streón** – robur, vis), st. n., *property, po sessions;* hence, *valuables, treasure, jewels:* nom. pl. Heaðo-beardna ge-streón (*the costly treasure of the Heaðobeardas*, i.e. the accoutrements belonging to the slain H.), 2038; acc. pl. äÿelinga, eorla ge-streón, 1921, 3168. — Comp.: ær-, eald-, eorl-, heáh-, hord-, long-, mâðm-, sinc-, Þeód-ge-streón.

strûdan, st. v., *to plunder, carry off:* subj. pres. näs Þâ on hlytme hwâ Þät hord strude, 3127.

ge-strÿnan, w. v. w. acc., *to acquire, gain:* inf. Þäs Þe (*because*) ic môste mĭnum leódum ... swylc ge-strŷnan, 2799.

stund, st. f., *time, space of time, while :* adv. dat. pl. stundum (*at times*), 1424.

styrian, w. v. w. acc.: 1) *to arrange, put in order, tell :* inf. secg eft on-gan sĭð Beówulfes snyttrum styrian (*the poet then began to tell B.'s feat skilfully*, i.e. put in poetic form), 873. — 2) *to rouse, stir up :* pres. sg. III. þonne wind stỹreð láð ge-wiðru (*when the wind stirreth up the loathly weather*), 1375. — 3) *to move against, attack, disturb :* subj. pres. þät he ... hring-sele hondum styrede (*that he should attack the ring-hall with his hands*), 2841.

styrman, w. v., *to rage, cry out :* pret. sg. styrmde, 2553.

stỹle, st. n., *steel :* dat. sg. stỹle, 986.

stỹl-ecg, adj., *steel-edged :* nom. sg., 1534.

be-stỹman, w. v., *to inundate, wet, flood :* pret. part. (wäron) eal benc-þelu blôde be-stỹmed, 486.

suhtor-ge-fäderan (collective), w. m. pl., *uncle and nephew, father's brother and brother's son :* nom. pl., 1165.

sum, pron.: 1) indef., *one, a, any, a certain ;* neut. *something :* a) without part. gen.: nom. sg. sum, 1252; hilde-rinc sum, 3125; neut. ne sceal þær dyrne sum wesan (*naught there shall be hidden*), 271; acc. sg. m. sumne, 1433; instr. sg. sume worde (*by a word, expressly*), 2157; nom. pl. sume, 400, 1114; acc. pl. sume, 2941. b) with part. gen.: nom. sg. gumena sum (*one of men, a man*), 1500, 2302; mere-hrägla sum, 1906; þät wäs wundra sum, 1608; acc. sg. gylp-worda

sum, 676. c) with gen. of cardinals or notions of multitude : nom. sg. fîftena sum (*one of fifteen, with fourteen companions*), 207; so, eahta sum, 3124; feára sum (*one of few, with a few*), 1413; acc. sg. manigra sumne (*one of many, with many*), 2092; manna cynnes sumne (*one of the men*, i.e. one of the watchmen in Heorot), 714; feára sumne (*some few, one of few ;* or, *one of the foes?*), 3062. — 2) with part. gen. sum sometimes = *this, that, the afore-mentioned :* nom. sg. eówer sum (*a certain one, that one, of you*, i.e. Beówulf), 248; gûð-beorna sum (*the afore-mentioned warrior*, i.e. who had shown the way to Hróðgâr's palace), 314; eorla sum (*the said knight*, i.e. Beówulf), 1313; acc. sg. hord-ärna sum (*a certain hoard-hall*), 2280.

sund, st. m.: 1) *swimming :* acc sg. ymb sund, 507; dat. sg. ät sunde (*in swimming*), 517; on sunde (*a-swimming*), 1619; gen. sg. sundes, 1437. — 2) *sea, ocean, sound :* nom. sg., 223; acc. sg. sund, 213, 512, 539, 1427, 1445.

ge-sund, adj., *sound, healthy, unimpaired :* acc. sg. m. ge-sundne, 1629, 1999; nom. pl. ge-sunde, 2076; acc. pl. w. gen. fäder al-walda ... eówic ge-healde sîða ge-sunde (*the almighty Father keep you safe and sound on your journey!*), 318. — Comp. an-sund.

sund-ge-bland, st. n., (*the commingled sea*), *sea-surge, sea-wave :* acc. sg., 1451.

sund-nyt, st. f., *swimming-power* or *employment, swimming :* acc. sg. sund-nytte dreáh (*swam through the sea*), 2361.

sundur, sundor, adv., *asunder, in*

twain : sundur gedælan (*to separate, sunder*), 2423.

sundor-nyt, st. f., *special service* (service in a special case): acc. sg. sundor-nytte, 668.

sund-wudu, st. m., (*sea-wood*), *ship :* nom. acc. sg. sund-wudu, 208, 1907.

sunne, w. f., *sun :* nom. sg., 607; gen. sg. sunnan, 94, 649.

sunu, st. m., *son :* nom. sg., 524, 591, 646, 981, 1090, 1486, etc.; acc. sg. sunu, 268, 948, 1116, 1176, 1809, 2014, 2120; dat. sg. suna, 344, 1227, 2026, 2161, 2730; gen. sg. suna, 2456, 2613, (1279) ; nom. pl. suna, 2381.

sûð, adv., *south, southward,* 859.

sûðan, adv., *from the south,* 607; sigel sûðan fûs (*the sun inclined from the south*), 1967.

swaðrian, w. v., *to sink to rest, grow calm :* brimu swaðredon (*the waves became calm*), 570. See **sweðrian.**

swaðu, st. f., *trace, track, pathway :* acc. sg. swaðe, 2099. — Comp. : swât-, wald-swaðu.

swaðul, st. m.? n.?, *smoke, mist* (Dietrich in Haupt V. 215): dat. sg. on swaðule, 783. See **sweoðol.**

swancor, adj., *slender, trim :* acc. pl. þrió wicg swancor, 2176.

swan-râd, st. f., *swan-road, sea :* acc. sg. ofer swan-râde, 200.

and-swarian, w. v., *to answer :* pret. sg. him se yldesta and-swarode, 258; so, 340.

swâ : 1) demons. adv., *so, in such a manner, thus :* swâ sceal man dôn, 1173, 1535; swâ þâ driht-guman dreámum lifdon, 99; þæt ge-æfndon swâ (*that we thus accomplished*), 538; þær hie meahton (i.e. feorh

ealgian), 798; so, 20, 144, 189, 559, 763, 1104, 1472, 1770, 2058, 2145, 2178, 2991; swâ manlîce (*so like a man*), 1047; swâ fela (*so many*), 164, 592; swâ deórlîce dæd (*so valiant a deed*), 585; hine swâ gôdne (*him so good*), 347; on swâ geongum feore (*in so youthful age*), 1844; ge-deð him swâ ge-wealdene worolde dælas þæt ... (*makes parts of the world so subject to him that ...*), 1733. In comparisons = *ever, the* (adv.) : me þîn môd-sefa lîcað leng swâ wel (*thy mind pleases me ever so well, the longer the better*), 1855. As an asseverative = *so :* swâ me Higelâc sie ... môdes blîðe (*so be Higelac gracious-minded to me!*), 435; swâ þeáh (*nevertheless, however*), 973, 1930, 2879; swâ þêh, 2968; hwæðre swâ þeáh (*yet however*), 2443.—2): a) conj., *as, so as :* ôð þæt his byre mihte eorlscipe efnan swâ his ærfäder (*until his son might do noble deeds, as his old father did*), 2623; eft swâ ær (*again as before*), 643; — with indic.: swâ he selfa bäd (*as he himself requested*), 29; swâ he oft dyde (*as he often did*), 444; gæð â Wyrd swâ hió sceal, 455; swâ guman gefrungon, 667; so, 273, 352, 401, 561, 1049, 1056, 1059, 1135, 1232, 1235, 1239, 1253, 1382, etc.; — with subj. : swâ þîn sefa hwette (*as pleases thy mind,* i.e. anyway thou pleasest), 490. b) *as, as then, how,* 1143; swâ hie â wæron ... nŷd-gesteallan (*as they were ever comrades in need*), 882; swâ hit diópe ... be-nemdon þeódnas mære (*as, [how?] the mighty princes had deeply cursed it*), 3070; swâ he manna wäs wîgend weorðfullost (*as he of men the worthiest warrior was*), 3099. c) *just as, the moment when :* swâ Jät blôd gesprang, 1668. d) *so that :* swâ he ne mihte nô (*so that he might not . . .*), 1509; so, 2185, 2007. — 3) – qui, quae, quod, German so : worhte wlite-beorhtne wang swâ wäter bebûgeð (*wrought the beauteous plain which* (acc.) *water surrounds*), 93. — 4) swâ . . . swâ = so . . . as, 595, 687-8, 3170; efne swâ . . . swâ (*even so . . . as*), 1093-4, 1224, 1284; efne swâ hwylc mägða swâ (*such a woman as, whatsoever woman*), 944; efne swâ hwylcum manna swâ (*even so to each man as*), 3058.

for-swâfan, st. v., *to carry away, sweep off :* pret. sg. ealle Wyrd forsweóf mîne mâgas tô metod-sceafte, 2815.

for-swâpan, st. v., *to sweep off, force :* pret. sg. hie Wyrd forsweóp on Grendles gryre, 477.

swât, st. m., (*sweat*), *wound-blood :* nom. sg., 2694, 2967; instr. sg. swâte, 1287.— Comp. heaðo-, hilde-swât.

swât-fâh, adj., *blood-stained :* nom. sg., 1112.

swâtig, adj., *gory :* nom. sg., 1570.

swât-swaðu, st. f., *blood-trace :* nom. sg., 2947.

be-swælan, w. v., *to scorch :* pret. part. wäs se lêg-draca . . . glêdum beswæled, 3042.

swæs, adj., *intimate, special, dear :* acc. sg. swæsne êðel, 520; nom. pl. swæse ge-sîðas, 29; acc. pl. leóde swæse, 1869; swæse ge-sîðas, 2041, 2519; gen. pl. swæsra ge-sîða, 1935.

swæs-lîce, adv., *pleasantly, in a friendly manner*, 3090.

swebban, w. v., (*to put to sleep*), *to kill :* inf. ic hine sweorde swebban nelle, 680; pres. sg. III. (absolutely) swefeð, 601.

â-swebban, *to kill, slay :* pret. part. nom. pl. sweordum â-swefede, 567.

sweðrian, w. v., *to lessen, diminish :* inf. Jät Jät fyr ongan sweðrian, 2703; pret. siððan Heremôdes hild sweðrode, 902.

swefan, st. v.: 1) *to sleep :* pres. sg. III. swefeð, 1742; inf. swefan, 119, 730, 1673; pret. sg. swäf, 1801; pl. swæfon, 704; swæfun, 1281. — 2) *to sleep the death-sleep, die :* pres. sg. III. swefeð, 1009, 2061, 2747; pl. swefað, 2257, 2458.

swegel, st. n., *ether, clear sky :* dat. sg. under swegle, 1079, 1198; gen. sg. under swegles begong, 861, 1774.

swegle, adj., *bright, etherlike, clear :* acc. pl. swegle searo-gimmas, 2750.

swegel-wered, *quasi* pret. part., *ether-clad :* nom. sg. sunne sweglwered, 607.

swelgan, st. v., *to swallow :* pret. sg. w. instr. syn-snædum swealh (*swallowed in great bites*), 744; object omitted, subj. pres. nymðe lîges fäðm swulge on swaðule, 783.

for-swelgan, w. acc., *to swallow, consume :* pret. sg. for-swealg, 1123, 2081.

swellan, st. v., *to swell :* inf. Jâ sió wund on-gan . . . swêlan and swellan, 2714.

sweltan, st. v., *to die, perish :* pret. sg. swealt, 1618, 2475; draca morðre swealt (*died a violent death*), 893, 2783; wundor-deáðe swealt, 3038; hioro-dryncum swealt, 2359.

swencan, w. v., *to swink, oppress, strike :* pret. sg. hine wundra þäs

fela swencte (MS. swecte) on sunde, 1511.

ge-swencan, *to oppress, strike, injure:* pret. sg. sy Ŏŏan hine Hæðcyn ... flâne geswencte, 2439;
pret. part. synnum ge-swenced, 976;
hæðstapa hundum ge-swenced,
1369. — Comp. lyft-ge-swenced.

sweng, st. m., *blow, stroke:* dat.
sg. swenge, 1521, 2967; swenge
(*with its stroke*), 2687; instr. pl.
sweordes swengum, 2387.—Comp.:
feorh-, hete-, heaðu-, heoro-sweng.

swerian, st. v., *to swear:* pret. w.
acc. I. ne me swôr fela âŏa on
unriht (*swore no false oaths*), 2739;
he me âŏas swôr, 472.

for-swerian, w. instr., *to forswear,
renounce (protect with magic for-
mula?)*: pret. part. he sige-wæpnum for-sworen häfde, 805.

swêg, st. m., *sound, noise, uprear:*
nom. sg. swêg, 783: hearpan swêg,
89, 2459, 3024; sige-folca swêg,
645; sang and swêg, 1064; dat.
sg. swêge, 1215.—Comp.: benc-,
morgen-swêg.

swêlan, w. v., *to burn* (here of
wounds): inf. swêlan, 2714. See
swælan.

sweart, adj., *swart, black, dark:*
nom. sg. wudu-rêc sweart, 3146;
dat. pl. sweartum nihtum, 167.

sweoðol (cf. O.H.G. suedan, sue-
than = cremare; M.H.G. swadem
= vapor; and Dietrich in Haupt
V., 215), st. m.? n.?, *vapor, smoke,
smoking flame:* dat. sg. ofer swioðole (MS. swic ðole), 3146. See
swaðul.

sweofot, st. m., *sleep:* dat. sg. on
sweofote, 1582, 2296.

sweoloð, st. m., *heat, fire, flame:*
dat. sg. sweoloðe, 1116. Cf. O.H.G.
suilizo, suilizunga = ardor, cauma.

sweorcan, st. v., *to trouble, darken:*
pres. sg. III. ne him inwit-sorh on
sefan sweorceð (*darkens his soul*),
1738.

for-sweorcan, *to grow dark* or
dim: pres. sg. III. eágena bearhtm
for-siteð and for-sworceð, 1768.

ge-sweorcan (intrans.), *to darken:* pret. sg. niht-helm ge-swearc,
1790.

sweord, swurd, swyrd, st. n.,
sword: nom. sg. sweord, 1287,
1290, 1570, 1606, 1616, 1697;
swurd, 891; acc. sg. sweord, 437,
673, 1559, 1664, 1809, 2253, 2500,
etc.; swurd, 539, 1902; swyrd,
2611, 2988; instr. sg. sweorde,
561, 574, 680, 2493, 2881; gen. sg.
sweordes, 1107, 2194, 2387; acc.
pl. sweord, 2639; swyrd, 3049; instr.
pl. sweordum, 567, 586, 885; gen.
pl. sweorda, 1041, 2937, 2962.—
Comp.: gûð-, maððum-, wæg-
sweord.

sweord, st. f., *oath:* in comp. âð-
sweord (*sword-oath?*), 2065.

sweord-bealo, st. n., *sword-bale,
death by the sword:* nom. sg., 1148.

sweord-freca, w. m., *sword-war-
rior:* dat. sg. sweord-frecan, 1469.

sweord-gifu, st. f., *sword-gift, giving of swords:* nom. sg. swyrd-gifu,
2885.

sweotol, swutol, adj.: 1) *clear,
bright:* nom. sg. swutol sang scôpes, 90. — 2) *plain, manifest:*
nom. sg. syndolh sweotol, 818;
tâcen sweotol, 834; instr. sg. sweotolan tâcne, 141.

sweóf, sweóp. See swâfan, swâ-
pan.

swið, st. n.? (O.N. swiði), *burning
pain:* in comp. bryð-swið(?).

swift, adj., *swift:* nom. sg. se swifta
mearh, 2265.

swimman, swymman, st. v., *to*
swim : inf. swymman, 1625.
ofer-swimman, w. acc., *to swim*
over or *through :* pret. sg. oferswam sioleða bigong (*swam over*
the sea), 2368.
swincan, st. v., *to struggle, labor,*
contend : pret. pl. git on wäteres
æht seofon niht swuncon, 517.
ge-swing, st. n., *surge, eddy :* nom.
sg. atol ýða geswing, 849.
swingan, st. v., *to swing one's self,*
fly : pres. sg. III. ne gôd hafoc
geond säl swingeð, 2265.
swican, st. v.: 1) *to deceive, leave*
in the lurch, abandon : pret. sg.
næfre hit (*the sword*) ät hilde ne
swâc manna ængum, 1461. — 2) *to*
escape : subj. pres. bûtan his lic
swice, 967.
ge-swican, *to deceive, leave in the*
lurch : pret. sg. gûð-bill ge-swâc
nacod ät niðe, 2585, 2682; w. dat.
seó ecg ge-swâc ļeodne ät ļearfe
(*the sword failed the prince in*
need), 1525.
swið, swýð (Goth. swinþ-s), adj.,
strong, mighty : nom. sg. wäs þät
ge-win tô swýð, 191. — Comp. nom.
sg. sió swiðre hand (*the right*
hand), 2099.
swiðe, adv., *strongly, very, much,*
508, 998, 1093, 1744, 1927; swýðe,
2171, 2188. Compar. swiðor, *more,*
rather, more strongly, 961, 1140,
1875, 2199. — Comp. un-swiðe.
ofer-swiðian, w. v., *to overcome,*
vanquish, w. acc. of person : pres.
sg. III. oferswýðeð, 279, 1769.
swið-ferhð, adj., (*fortis animo*),
strong-minded, bold, brave : nom.
sg. swýð-ferhð, 827; gen. sg. swið-
ferhðes, 909; nom. pl. swið-ferhðe,
493; dat. pl. swið-ferhðum, 173.
swið-hycgend, pres. part. (*strenue*

cogitans), *bold-minded, brave in*
spirit : nom. sg. swið-hycgende,
920; nom. pl. swið-hycgende, 1017.
swið-môd, adj., *strong-minded :*
nom. sg., 1625.
on-swifan, st. v. w. acc., *to swing,*
turn, at or *against, elevate :* pret.
sg. biorn (Beówulf) bord-rand onswâf wið ļam gryre-gieste, 2560.
swigian, w. v., *to be silent, keep*
silent : pret. sg. lyt swigode niwra
spella (*kept little of the new tidings*
silent), 2898; pl. swigedon ealle,
1700.
swigor, adj., *silent, taciturn :* nom.
sg. weak, þâ wäs swigra secg . . .
on gylp-sprä́ce gûð-ge-weorca,
981.
swin, swýn, st. n., *swine, boar*
(image on the helm) : nom. sg.
swýn, 1112; acc. sg. swin, 1287.
swin-lic, st. n., *swine-image* or *body :*
instr. pl. swin-licum, 1454.
swôgan, st. v., *to whistle, roar :*
pres. part. swôgende lêg, 1346.
swutol. See sweotol.
swyle, swile (Goth. swa-leik-s),
demons. adj. = *talis, such, such a ;*
relative = *qualis, as, which :* nom.
sg. swyle, 178, 1941, 2542, 2709;
swyle . . . swyle = talis . . . qualis,
1329; acc. sg. swyle, 2799; eall
. . . swyle (*all . . . which, as*), 72;
ôðer swyle (*such another,* i.e.
hand), 1584; on swyle (*on such*
things), 997; dat. sg. gûð-fremmendra swylcum (*to such a battle-*
worker, i.e. Beówulf), 299; gen.
sg. swylces hwät (*some such*), 881;
acc. pl. swylce, 2870; eall swylce
. . . swylce, 3166; swylce twegen
(*two such*), 1348; ealle þearfe
swylce (*all needs that*), 1798;
swylce hic . . . findan meahton
sigla searo-gimma (*such as they*

might find of jewels and cunning gems), 1157; efne swylce mæla swylce (at just such times as), 1250; gen. pl. swylcra searo-niða, 582; swylcra fela ... ær-gestreóna, 2232.

s w y l c e , adv., as, as also, likewise, similarly, 113, 293, 758, 831, 855, 908, 921, 1147, 1166, 1428, 1483, 2460, 2825; ge swylce (and likewise), 2259; swilce, 1153.

swylt, st. m., death : nom. sg., 1256, 1437.

swylt-dāg, st. m., death-day : dat. sg. ær swylt-däge, 2799.

swynslan, w. v., to sound : pret. sg. hlyn swynsode, 612.

swyrd. See sweord.

swyð. See swið.

swyn. See swin.

syððan (seðian, Gen. 1525), w. v., to punish, avenge, w. acc.: inf. þonne hit sweordes ecg syððan scolde (then the edge of the sword should avenge it), 1107.

syððan. See slððan.

syfan-wintre, adj., seven-winters-old : nom. sg., 2429.

syhð. See seón.

syl (O.H.G. swella), st. f., sill, bench-support : dat. sg. fram sylle, 776.

sylfa. See selfa.

syllan. See sellan.

syllic. See sellic.

symbel, syml, st. n., banquet, entertainment : acc. sg. symbel, 620, 1011; geaf me sinc and symbl (gave me treasure and feasting, i.e. made me his friend and table-companion), 2432; þät hie ... symbel ymbsæton (that they might sit round their banquet), 564; dat. sg. symle, 81, 489, 1009; symble, 119, 2105; gen. pl. symbla, 1233.

symble, symle, adv., continually, ever : symble, 2451; symle, 2498; symle wäs | 9 sæmra (he was ever the worse, the weaker, i.e. the dragon), 2881.

symbel-wyn, st. f., banqueting-pleasure, joy at feasting : acc. sg. symbel-wynne dreóh, 1783.

syn, st. f., sin, crime : nom. synn and sacu, 2473; dat. instr. pl. synnum, 976, 1256, 3072.

syn. See sin.

syn-bysig, adj., (culpa laborans), persecuted on account of guilt? (Rieger), guilt-haunted? : nom. sg. secg syn-[by]sig, 2228.

ge-syngian, w. v., to sin, commit a crime : pret. part. þät wäs feohleás ge-feoht, fyrenum ge-syngad, 2442.

synnig, adj., sin-laden, sinful : acc. sg. m. sinnigne secg, 1380. — Comp.: fela-, un-synnig.

ge-synto, f., health : dat. pl. on gesyntum, 1870.

syrce. See serce.

syrwan, w. v. w. acc., to entrap, catch unawares : pret. sg. duguðe and geogoðe seomade and syrede, 161.

be-syrwan : 1) to compass or accomplish by finesse ; effect : inf. dæd þe we ealle ær ne meahton snyttrum be-syrwan (a deed that all of us could not accomplish before with all our wisdom), 943. — 2) to entrap by guile and destroy : inf. mynte se mânscaða manna cynnes sumne be-syrwan (the fell foe thought to entrap some one (all?, see sum) of the men), 714.

sŷn, f., seeing, sight, scene : comp. an-sŷn.

ge-sŷne, adj., visible, to be seen : nom. sg. 1256, 1404, 2948, 3059, 3160. — Comp.: eð-ge-sŷne, yð-ge-sêne.

T

taligean, w. v.: 1) *to count, reckon, number ; esteem, think :* pres. sg. I. nô ic me ... hnâgran gûð-geweorca þonne Grendel hine (*count myself no worse than G. in battle-works*), 678; wên ic talige ... þät (*I count on the hope ... that*), 1846; telge, 2068; sg. III. þät ræd talað þät (*counts it gain that*), 2028. — 2) *to tell, relate :* sôð ic talige (*I tell facts*), 532; swâ þu self talast (*as thou thyself sayst*), 595.

tâcen, st. n., *token, sign, evidence :* nom. sg. tâcen sweotol, 834; dat. instr. sg. sweotolan tâcne, 141; tîres tô tâcne, 1655. — Comp. luftâcen.

tân, st. m., *twig :* in comp. âter-tân.

ge-tæcan, w. v., *to show, point out :* pret. sg. him þâ hilde-deór hof môdigra torht ge-tæhte (*the warrior pointed out to them the bright dwelling of the bold ones*, i.e. Danes), 313. Hence, *to indicate, assign :* pret. sôna me se mæra mago Healfdenes ... wið his sylfes sunu setl getæhte (*assigned me a seat by his own son*), 2014.

tæle, adj., *blameworthy :* in comp. un-tæle.

ge-tæse, adj., *quiet, still :* nom. sg. gif him wære ... niht ge-tæse (*whether he had a pleasant, quiet, night*), 1321.

tela, adv., *fittingly, well,* 949, 1219, 1226, 1821, 2209, 2738.

telge. See **talian.**

tellan, w. v., *to tell, consider, deem :* pret. sg. ne his lîf-dagas gumena ænigum nytte tealde (*nor did he count his life useful to any man*), 795; þät ic me ænigne under swe-gles begong ge-sacan ne tealde (*I believed not that I had any foe under heaven*), 1774; cwäð he þone gûð-wine gôdne tealde (*said he counted the war-friend good*), 1811; he ûsic gâr-wîgend gôde tealde (*deemed us good spear-warriors*), 2642; pl. swâ (*so that*) hine Geáta bearn gôdne ne tealdon, 2185. — 2) *to ascribe, count against, impose :* pret. sg. (þryðo) him wälbende weotode tealde handgewriðene, 1937.

ge-tenge, adj., *attached to, lying on :* w. dat. gold ... grunde getenge, 2759.

teár, st. m., *tear :* nom. pl. teáras, 1873.

teoh, st. f., *troop, band :* dat. sg. earmre teohhe, 2939.

(ge?)-teohhian, w. v., *to fix, determine, assign :* pret. sg. ic for lässan leán teohhode ... hnâhran rince, 952; pres. part. wäs ôðer in ær geteohhod (*assigned*) ... mærum Geáte, 1301.

teón, st. v., *to draw, lead :* inf. hêht ... eahta mearas ... on flet teón (*bade eight horses be led into the hall*), 1037; pret. sg. me tô grunde teáh fâh feónd-sceaða (*the many-hued fiend-foe drew me to the bottom*), 553; eft-sîðas teáh (*withdrew, returned*), 1333; sg. for pl. æg-hwylcum ... þâra þe mid Beówulfe brim-lâde teáh (*to each of those that crossed the sea with B.*), 1052; pret. part. þâ wäs ... heard-ecg togen (*then was the hard edge drawn*), 1289; wearð ... on näs togen (*was drawn to the promontory*), 1440.

â-teón, *to wander, go,* intrans.: pret. sg. tô Heorute â-teáh (*di ro to Heorot*), 767.

ge-teón: 1) *to draw:* pret. sg. gomel swyrd ge-teáh, 2611; w. instr. and acc. hire seaxe ge-teáh, brâd brûn-ecg, 1546. — 2) *to grant, give, lend:* imp. nô þu him wearne geteóh þînra gegn-cwida glädnian (*refuse not to gladden them with thy answer*), 366; pret. sg. and þâ Beówulfe hega gehwäᶜres eodor Ingwina onweald ge-teáh (*and the prince of the Ingwins gave B. power over both*), 1045; so, he him êst geteáh (*gave possession of*), 2166.

of-teón, *to deprive, withdraw*, w. gen. of thing and dat. pers.: pret. sg. Scyld Scêfing . . . monegum mægᵹum meodo-setla of-teáh, 5; w. acc. of thing, hond . . . feorh-sweng ne of-teáh, 2490; w. dat. hond (herd, MS.) swenge ne of-teáh, 1521.

þurh-teón, *to effect:* inf. gif he torn-gemôt þurh-teón mihte, 1141.

teón (cf. teóh, *materia*, O.H.G. ziuc), w. v. w. acc., *to make, work:* pret. sg. teóde, 1453; — *to furnish out, deck:* pret. pl. naläs hi hine lässan lâcum teodan (*provided him with no less gifts*), 43.

ge-teón, *to provide, do, bring on:* pres. sg. unc sceal weorᵹan . . . swâ unc Wyrd ge-teóᵹ, 2527; pret. sg. þe him . . . sâre ge-teóde (*who had done him this harm*), 2296.

ge-teóna, w. m., *injurer, harmer:* in comp. lâᵹ-ge-teóna.

til, adj., *good, apt, fit:* nom. sg. m. Hâlga til, 61; þegn ungemete till (of Wîglâf), 2722; fem. wäs seó þeód tilu, 1251; neut. ne wäs þät ge-wrixle til, 1305.

tilian, w. v. w. gen., *to gain, win:* inf. gif ic . . . ôwihte mäg þînre

môd-lufan mâran tilian (*if I . . . gain*), 1824.

timbrian, w. v., *to build:* pres. part. acc. sg. säl timbred (*the well-built hall*), 307.

be-timbrian, (construere), *to finish building, complete:* pret. pl. betiml redon on tyn dagum beadu-rôfes bêcn, 3161.

tîd, st. f., *-tide, time:* acc. sg. twelf wintra tîd, 147; lange tîd, 1916; in þâ tîde, 2228. — Comp.: ân-, morgen-tîd.

ge-tîᵹian (from tigᵹian), w. v., *to grant:* pret. part. impers. wâs . . . bêne (gen.) ge-tîᵹad feáscenftum men, 2285.

tîr, st. m., *glory, repute in war:* gen. sg. tîres, 1655.

tîr-eádig, adj., *glorious, famous:* dat. sg. tîr-eádigum menn (of Beówulf), 2190.

tîr-fäst, adj., *famous, rich in glory:* nom. sg. (of Hrôᵹgâr), 923.

tîr-leás, adj., *without glory, infamous:* gen. sg. (of Grendel), 844.

toga, w. m., *leader:* in comp. folc-toga.

torht, adj., *bright, brilliant:* acc. sg. neut. hof . . . torht, 313. — Comp.: wuldor-torht, heaᵹo-torht (*loud in battle*).

torn, st. n. : 1) *wrath, insult, distress:* acc. sg. torn, 147, 834; gen. pl. torna, 2190. — 2) *anger:* instr. sg. torne ge-bolgen, 2402. — Comp. lîge-torn.

torn, adj., *bitter, cruel:* nom. sg. hreówa tornost, 2130.

torn-ge-môt, st. n., (*wrathful meeting*), *angry engagement, battle:* acc. sg., 1141.

tô, I. prep. w. dat. indicating direction or tending to, hence : 1) local = whither after verbs of motion,

to, up to, at : com tô recede (*to the
hall*), 721; eode tô sele, 920; eode
tô hire freán sittan, 642; gæð eft
...tô medo (*goeth again to mead*),
605; wand tô wolcnum (*wound
to the welkin*), 1120; sigor tô slæpe
(*sank to sleep*), 1252; 28, 158, 234,
438, 553, 926, 1010, 1014, 1155,
1159, 1233, etc.; lîð-wæge bär
hälum tô handa (*bore the ale-cup
to the hands of the men? at hand?*),
1984; ôð þät niht becom ôðer tô
yldum, 2118; him tô bearme cwom
mâððum-fät mære (*came to his
hands, into his possession*), 2405;
sælde tô sande sîd-fäðme scip
(*fastened the broad-bosomed ship
to the shore*), 1918; þät se harm-
scaða tô Heorute â-teáh (*went
forth to Heorot*), 767. After verb
sittan : sitte nu tô symble (*sit now
to the meal*), 489; siððan ...we
tô symble geseten häfdon, 2105;
tô hâm (*home, at home*), 124, 374,
2993. With verbs of speaking :
maðelode tô his wine-drihtne (*spake
to his friendly lord*), 360; tô Geátum sprec, 1172; so, hêht þät heaðo-weorc tô hagan biódan (*bade
the battle-work be told at the hedge*),
2893. — 2) with verbs of bringing
and taking (cf. under on, I., d) :
hraðe wäs tô bûre Beówulf fetod
(*B. was hastily brought to the hall*),
1311; siððan Hâma ät-wäg tô
þære byrhtan byrig Brôsinga mene
(*since H. carried the Brosing-
necklace off to(?) the bright city*),
1200; weán âhsode. fæhðo tô Frysum (*suffered woe, feud as to, from,
the Frisians*), 1208. — 3) = end
of motion, hence : a) *to, for, as,
in :* þone god sende folce tô frôfre
(*for, as, a help to the folk*), 14;
gesette ...sunnan and mônan

leóman tô leóhte (*as a light*), 95;
ge-sät ...tô rûne (*sat in counsel*),
172; wearð he Heaðo-lâfe tô
hand-bonan, 460; bringe ...tô
helpe (*bring to, for, help*), 1831;
Eofore forgeaf ângan dôhtor ...
hyldo tô wedde (*as a pledge of his
favor*), 2999; so, 508(?), 666,
907, 972, 1022, 1187, 1263, 1331,
1708, 1712, 2080, etc.; secgan
tô sôðe (*to say in sooth*), 51;
so, 591, 2326. b) with verbs of
thinking, hoping, etc., *on, for, at,
against :* he tô gyrn-wräce swîðor
þôhte þonne tô sæ-lâde (*thought
more on vengeance than on the sea-
voyage*), 1139; säcce ne wêneð tô
Gâr-Denum (*nor weeneth of conflict with the Spear-Danes*), 602;
þonne wêne ic tô þe wyrsan geþinges (*then I expect for thee a
worse result*), 525; ne ic tô Sweó-
þeóde sibbe oððe treówe wihte ne
wêne (*nor expect at all of, from,
the Swedes ...*), 2923; wiste þäm
ahlæcan tô þäm heáh-sele hilde
ge-þinged (*battle prepared for the
monster in the high hall*), 648;
wel bið þäm þe môt tô fäder fäðmum freoðo wilnian (*well for him
that can find peace in the Father's
arms*), 188; þâra þe he ge-worhte
tô West-Denum (*of those that he
wrought against the West-Danes*),
1579. — 4) with the gerund. inf. :
tô gefremmanne (*to do*), 174; tô
ge-cýðanne (*to make known*), 257;
tô secganne (*to say*), 473; tô befleónne (*to avoid, escape*), 1004;
so, 1420, 1725, 1732, 1806, 1852,
1923, 1942, etc. With inf. : tô
fêran, 316; tô friclan, 2557. —
5) temporal : gewât him tô gescäp-hwîle (*went at(?) the hour
of fate ; or, to his fated rest?*), 26;

tô wîdan feore (*ever, in their
lives*), 934; âwa tô aldre (*for life,
forever*), 956; so, tô aldre, 2006,
2499; tô lîfe (*during life, ever*),
2433.— 6) with particles: wôd
under wolcnum tô | äs | e ... (*went
under the welkin to the point
where* ...); 715; so, elne ge-eodon
tô | äs | e, 1968: so, 2411; he him
þäs leán for-geald ... tô | äs | e he
on reste geseah Grendel licgan (*he
paid him for that to the point that
he saw G. lying dead*), 1586; wäs
þät blôd tô | äs hât (*the blood was
hot to that degree*), 1617; näs | â
long tô þon þät ('*twas not long
till*), 2592, 2846; wäs him se man
tô þon leóf þät (*the man was dear
to him to that degree*), 1877; tô
hwan siðdan weard hond-ræs häleða (*up to what point, how, the
hand-contest turned out*), 2072; tô
middes (*in the midst*), 3142.

II. Adverbial modifier, *quasi*
preposition [better explained in
many cases as prep. postponed] :
1) *to, towards, up to, at :* geóng
sôna tô, 1786; so, 2649; fchð ðer
tô, 1756; sæ-lâc ... | e þu her tô
lôcast (*upon which thou here lookest*), 1655; folc tô sægon (*the folk
looked on*), 1423; þät hî him tô
mihton gegnum gangan (*might
proceed thereto*), 313; se | e him
bealwa tô bôte gelŷfde (*who believed in help out of evils from him*,
i.e. Beówulf), 910; him tô anwaldan âre ge-lŷfde (*trusted for himself to the Almighty's help*), 1273;
þe ûs sêceað tô Sweóna leóde
(*that the Swedes will come against
us*), 3002.— 2) before adj. and
adv., *too :* tô strang (*too mighty*),
133; tô fäst, 137; tô swŷð, 191;
so, 789, 970, 1337, 1743, 1749, etc.;

tô fela micles (*far too much*), 695;
he tô furð ge-stôp (*he had gone
too far*), 2290.
tôð (G. tunþu-s), st. m., *tooth :* in
comp. blôdig-tôð (adj.).
tredan, st. v. w. acc., *to tread :* inf.
sæ-wong tredan, 1965; el-land tredan, 3020; pret. sg. wräc-lâstas
träd, 1353; medo-wongas träd,
1644; gräs-moldan träd, 1882.
treddian, tryddian (see trod),
w. v., *to stride, tread, go :* pret. sg.
treddode, 726; tryddode getrume
micle (*strode about with a strong
troop*), 923.
trem, st. n., *piece, part :* acc. sg. ne
... fôtes trem (*not a foot's
breadth*), 2526.
treów, st. f., *fidelity, good faith :*
acc. sg. treówe, 1073; sibbe oððe
treówe, 2923.
treów, st. n , *tree :* in comp. galg-
treów.
treówian. See trûwian.
treów-loga, w. m., *troth-breaker,
pledge-breaker :* nom. pl. treów-
logan, 2848.
trodu, st. f., *track, step :* acc. sg. or
pl. trode, 844.
ge - trum, st. n., *troop, band :* instr.
sg. ge-trume micle, 923.
trum, adj., *strong, endowed with :*
nom. sg. heorot hornum trum, 1370.
ge - trûwan, w. v. w. acc., *to con-
firm, pledge solemnly :* pret. sg. þâ
hie getrûwedon on twâ healfe fäste
frioðu-wäre, 1096.
trûwian, treówan, w. v., *to trust
in, rely on, believe in :* 1) w. dat.:
pret. sg. siðe ne trûwode leófes
mannes (*I trusted not in the dear
man's enterprise*), 1994; bearne
ne trûwode þät he ... (*she trusted
not the child that ...*), 2371; ge-
hwylc hiora his ferhðe treówde

þät he ... (*each trusted his heart that* ...), 1167. — 2) w. gen.: pret. sg. Geáta leód georne trûwode môdgan mägnes, 670; wiðres ne trûwode, 2954.

ge-trûwian, *to rely on, trust in*, w. dat.: pret. sg. strenge ge-trûwode, mund-gripe mägenes, 1534; — w. gen. pret. sg. beorges getrûwode, wîges and wealles, 2323; strenge ge-trûwode ânes mannes, 2541.

tryddian. See treddian.

trŷwe, adj., *true, faithful:* nom. sg. þâ gyt wäs ... æghwylc ôðrum trŷwe, 1166.

ge-trŷwe, adj., *faithful:* nom. sg. her is æghwylc eorl ôðrum getrŷwe, 1229.

turf, st. f., *sod, soil, seat:* in comp. êðel-turf.

tux, st. m., *tooth, tusk:* in comp. hilde-tux.

ge-twæfan, w. v. w. acc. of person and gen. thing, *to separate, divide, deprive of, hinder:* pres. sg. III. þät þee âdl ôððe ecg eafoðes getwæfeð (*robs of strength*), 1764; inf. god eáðe mäg þone dol-scaðan dæda ge-twæfan (*God may easily restrain the fierce foe from his deeds*), 479; pret. sg. sumne Geáta leód ... feores getwæfde (*cut him off from life*), 1434; nô þær wæg-flotan wind ofer ŷðum sîðes ge-twæfde (*the wind hindered not the wave-floater in her course over the water*), 1909; pret. part. ätrihte wäs gûð ge-twæfed (*almost had the struggle been ended*), 1659.

ge-twæman, w. v. acc. pers. and gen. thing, *to hinder, render incapable of, restrain:* inf. ic hine ne mihte ... ganges getwæman, 969.

twegen, f. neut. twâ, num., *twain,*

twô: nom. m. twegen, 1164; acc. m. twegen, 1348; dat. twæm, 1192; gen. twega, 2533; acc. f. twâ, 1096, 1195.

twelf, num., *twelve:* gen. twelfa, 3172.

tweone (Frisian twine), num. = *bini, two:* dat. pl. be sæm tweonum, 859, 1298; 1686.

twidig, adj., in comp. lang-twidig (*long-assured*), 1709.

tyder, st. m., *race, descendant:* in comp. un-tyder, 111.

tydre (Frisian teddre), adj., *weak, unwarlike, cowardly:* nom. pl. tydre, 2848.

tyn, num., *ten:* uninflect. dat. on tyn dagum, 3161; inflect. nom. tyne, 2848.

tyrwian, w. v., *to tar:* pret. part. tyrwed in comp.: niw-tyrwed.

on-tyhtan, w. v., *to urge on, incite, entice:* pret. sg. on-tyhte, 3087.

þ

þafian, w. v. w. acc., *to submit to, endure:* inf. þät se þeód-cyning þafian sceolde Eofores âne dôm, 2964.

þanc, st. m.: 1) *thought:* in comp. fore-, hete-, or-, searo-þanc; inwit-þanc (adj.). — 2) *thanks* (w. gen. of thing): nom. sg., 929, 1779; acc. sg. þanc, 1998, 2795. — 3) *content, favor, pleasure:* dat. sg. þâ þe gif-sceattas Geáta fyredon þyder tô þance (*those that tribute for the Geátas carried thither for favor*), 379.

ge-þanc, st. m., *thought:* instr. pl. þeóstrum ge-þoncum, 2333. — Comp. môd-ge-þanc.

þanc-hycgende, pres. part., *thoughtful,* 2236.

þancian, w. v., *to thank:* pret. sg.
gode þancode ... þäs þe hire se
willa ge-lamp (*thanked God that
her wish was granted*), 626; so,
1398; pl. þancedon, 627(?).

þanon, þonon, þonan, adv.,*thence:*
1) local: þanon eft gewât (*he went
thence back*), 123; þanon up ...
stigon (*went up thence*), 224; so,
þanon, 463, 692, 764, 845, 854,
1293; þanan, 1881; þonon, 520,
1374, 2409; þonan, 820, 2360,
2957.— 2) personal: þanon un-
tydras ealle on-wôcon (*from him,*
i.e. Cain, etc.), 111; so, þanan,
1266; þonon, 1961; unsôfte þonon
feorh ôð-ferede (i.e. from Grendel's mother), 2141.

þâ, adv.: 1) *there, then,* 3, 26, 28,
34, 47, 53, etc. With þær: þâ þær,
331. With nu: nu þâ (*now then*),
658.— 2) conjunction, *when, as,
since,* w. indic., 461, 539, 633, etc.;
— *because, whilst, during, since,*
402, 465, 724, 2551, etc.

þät, I. demons. pron. acc. neut. of
se: demons. nom. þät (*that*), 735,
766, etc.; instr. sg. þý, 1798, 2029;
þät ic þý wæpne ge-bräd (*that I
brandished as(?) a weapon; that
I brandished the weapon?*), 1665;
þý weorðra (*the more honored*),
1903; þý sêft (*the more easily*),
2750; þý läs hym ðôc þrym wudu
wynsuman for-wrecan meahte (*lest
the force of the waves the winsome
boat might carry away*), 1919; nô
þý ær (*not sooner*), 755, 1503,
· 2082, 2374, 2467; nô þý leng (*no
longer, none the longer*), 975. þý
=adv.,*therefore, hence,*1274, 2068;
þê ... þê = *on this account; for
this reason ... that, because,* 2639–
2642; wiste þê geornor (*knew but
too well*), 822; he ... wäs sundes

þê sænra þe hine swylt fornam (*he
was the slower in swimming as
[whom?] death carried him off*),
1437; näs him wihte þê sêl (*it was
none the better for him*), 2688; so,
2278. Gen. sg. þäs = adv., *for
this reason, therefore,* 7, 16, 114,
350, 589, 901, 1993, 2027, 2033,
etc. þäs þe, especially after verbs
of thanking, = *because,* 108, 228,
627, 1780, 2798; — also = secun-
dum quod: þäs þe hie gewislîcost
ge-witan meahton, 1351; — *therefore, accordingly,* 1342, 3001; tô
þäs (*to that point; to that degree*),
715, 1586, 1617, 1968, 2411; þäs
georne (*so firmly*), 969; ac he þäs
fäste wäs ... besmiðod (*it was too
firmly set*), 774; nô þäs frôd leofað gumena bearna þät þone grund
wite (*none liveth among men so
wise that he should know its bottom*), 1368; he þäs (þäm, MS.)
môdig wäs (*had the courage for
it*), 1509.

II. conj. (relative), *that, so that,*
15, 62, 84, 221, 347, 358, 392, 571,
etc.; ôð þät (*up to that, until*);
see ôð.

þätte (from þät þe, see þe), *that,*
151, 859, 1257, 2925, etc.; þät þe
(*that*), 1847.

þær: 1) demons. adv., *there (where),*
32, 36, 89, 400, 757, etc.; morðor-
bealo mâga, þær heô ær mæste
heôld worolde wynne (*the death-
bale of kinsmen where before she
had most worldly joy*), 1080. With
þâ: þâ þær, 331; þær on innan
(*therein*), 71. Almost like Eng.
expletive *there,* 271, 550, 978, etc.;
— *then, at that time,* 440; —
thither: þær swîð-ferhðe sittan
eodon (*thither went the bold ones
to sit,* i.e. to the bench), 493, etc.

— 2) relative, *where*, 356, 420, 508, 513, 522, 694, 867, etc.; eode ... þær se snotera bâd (*went where the wise one tarried*), 1314; so, 1816; — *if*, 763, 798, 1008, 1836, 2731, etc.; — *whither:* gâ þær he wille, 1395.

þe, I. relative particle, indecl., partly standing alone, partly associated with se, seó, þät: Hunferð maðelode, þe ät fôtum sät (*II., who sat at his feet, spake*), 500; so, 138, etc.; wäs þät gewin tô swýð þe on þâ leóde be-com (*the misery that had come on the people was too great*), 192, etc.; ic wille ... þe þâ and-sware ädre ge-cýðan þe me se gôda â-gifan þenceð (*I will straightway tell thee the answer that the good one shall give*), 355; ôð þone ânne däg þe he ... (*till that very day that he ...*), 2401; heó þâ fæhðe wräc þe þu ... Grendel cwealdest (*the fight in which thou slewest G.*), 1335; mid þære sorge þe him sió sâr belamp (*with the sorrow wherewith the pain had visited him*), 2469; pl. þonne þâ dydon þe ... (*than they did that ...*), 45; so, 378, 1136; þâ mâðmas þe he me sealde (*the treasures that he gave me*), 2491; so, gimfästan gife þe him god sealde (*the great gifts that God had given him*), 2183. After þâra þe (*of those that*), the depend. verb often takes sg. instead of pl. (Dietrich, Haupt XI., 444 seqq.): wundor-siôna fela secga ge-hwylcum þâra þe on swylc staraðð (*to each of those that look on such*), 997; so, 844, 1462, 2384, 2736. Strengthened by se, seó, þät: sägde se þe cûðe (*said he that knew*), 90; wäs se grimma gäst Grendel hâten, se þe môras

heóld (*the grim stranger hight Grendel, he that held the moors*), 103; here-byrne ... seó þe bân-cofan beorgan cûðe (*the corselet that could protect the body*), 1446, etc.; þær ge-lýfan sceal dryhtnes dôme se þe hine deáð nimeð (*he shall believe in God's judgment whom death carrieth off*), 441; so, 1437, 1292 (cf. Heliand l., 1308).

þäs þe. See þät.

þeáh þe. See þeáh.

for þam þe. See for-þam.

þý, þê, *the, by that*, instr. of se: âhte ic holdra þý läs ... þe deáð fornam (*I had the less friends whom death snatched away*), 488; so, 1437.

þeccan, w. v., *to cover* (thatch), *cover over:* inf. þâ sceal brond fretan, äled þeccean (*fire shall eat, flame shall cover, the treasures*), 3016; pret. pl. þær git eágor-streám earmum þehton (*in swimming*), 513.

þegn, st. m., *thane, liegeman, king's higher vassal; knight:* nom. sg., 235, 494, 868, 2060, 2710; (Beówulf), 194; (Wîglâf), 2722; acc. sg. þegen (Beówulf, MS. þegn), 1872; dat. sg. þegne, 1342, 1420; (Hengest), 1086; (Wîglâf), 2811; gen. sg. þegnes, 1798; nom. pl. þegnas, 1231; acc. pl. þegnas, 1082, 3122; dat. pl. þegnum, 2870; gen. pl. þegna, 123, 400, 1628, 1674, 1830, 2034, etc.—Comp.: ambiht-, ealdor-, heal-, magu-, sele-þegn.

þegnian, þênian, w. v., *to serve, do liege service:* pret. sg. ic him þênode deóran sweorde (*I served them with my good sword*, i.e. slew them with it), 560.

þegn-sorh, st. f., *thane-sorrow, grief for a liegeman:* acc. sg. þegn-sorge, 131.

þegu, st. f., *taking:* in comp.: beáh-, beór-, sinc-þegu.

þel, st. n., *deal-board, board for benches:* in comp. benc-þel, 486, 1240.

þencan, w. v.: 1) *to think* · absolutely: pres. sg. III. se þe wel þenceð, 289; so, 2602. With depend. clause: pres. sg. nænig heora þóhte þät he ... (*none of them thought that he*), 692. — 2) w. inf., *to intend:* pres. sg. III. þä and-sware ... þe me se góda â-gifan þenceð (*the answer that the good one intendeth to give me*), 355; (blódig wäl) byrgean þenceð, 448; þonne he ... gegân þenceð longsumne lof (*if he will win eternal fame*), 1536; pret. sg. ne þät aglæca yldan þóhte *the monster did not mean to delay that*), 740; pret. pl. wit unc wið hronfixas werian þóhton, 541; (hine) on healfa ge-hwone heáwan þóhton, 801.

â-þencan, *to intend, think out:* pret. sg. (he) þis ellen weorc âna â-þóhte tó ge-fremmanne, 2644.

ge-þencan, w. acc.: 1) *to think of:* þät he his selfa ne mäg ... ende ge-þencean (*so that he himself may not think of, know, its limit*), 1735. — 2) *to be mindful:* imper. sg. ge-þenc nu ... hwät wit geó spræcon, 1475.

þenden: 1) adv., *at this time, then, whilst:* nalles fácen-stafas þeód-Scyldingas þenden fremedon (*not at all at this time had the Scyldings done foul deeds*), 1020 (referring to 1165: cf. Wîdsîð, 45 seqq.); þenden reáfode rinc óðerne (*whilst one warrior robbed*

another, i.e. Eofor robbed Ongen-þeów), 2986. — 2) conj., *so long as, whilst,* 30, 57, 284, 1860, 2039, 2500, 3028; — *whilst,* 2419. With subj., *whilst, as long as:* þenden þu môte, 1178; þenden þu litige, 1255; þenden hit sý (*whilst the heat lasts*), 2650.

þengel, st. m., *prince, lord, ruler:* acc. sg. hringa þengel (Beówulf), 1508.

þes (m.), þeós (f.), þis (n.), demons. pron., *this:* nom. sg. 411, 432, 1703; f., 484; nom. acc. neut., 2156, 2252, 2644; þys, 1396; acc. sg. m. þisne, 75; f. þâs, 1682; dat. sg. neut. þissum, 1170; þyssum, 2640; f. þisse, 639; gen. m. þisses, 1217; f. þisse, 929; neut. þysses, 791, 807; nom. pl. and acc. þâs, 1623, 1653, 2636, 2641; dat. þyssum, 1063, 1220.

þê. See þät.

þêh. See þeáh.

þearf, st. f., *need:* nom. sg. þearf, 1251, 2494, 2638; þâ him wäs manna þearf (*as he was in need of men*), 201; acc. sg. þearfe, 1457, 2580, 2850; fremmað ge nu leóda þearfe (*do ye now what is needful for the folk*), 2801; dat. sg. ät þearfe, 1478, 1526, 2695, 2710; acc. pl. se for andrysnum ealle beweotede þegnes þearfe (*who would supply in courtesy all the thane's needs*), 1798 (cf. sele-þegn, 1795). —Comp.: firen-, nearo-, ofer-þearf.

þearf. See þurfan.

ge-þearfian, w. v., = *necessitatem imponere:* pret. part. þâ him swâ ge-þearfod wäs (*since so they found it necessary*, 1104.

þearle, adv., *very, exceedingly,* 560.

þeáh, þêh, conj., *though, even though* or *if:* 1) with subj. þeáh, 203,

526, 588, 590, 1168, 1661, 2032, 2162. Strengthened by þe: þeáh þe, 683, 1369, 1832, 1928, 1942, 2345, 2620; þeáh ... eal (*although*), 681.— 2) with indic.: þeáh, 1103; þêh, 1614.— 3) doubtful: þeáh he úðe wel, 2856; swâ þeáh (*nevertheless*), 2879; nô ... swâ þeáh (*not then however*), 973; näs þe forht swâ þêh (*he was not, though, afraid*), 2968; hwäðre swâ þeáh (*yet however*), 2443.

þeáw, st. m., *custom, usage:* nom. sg., 178, 1247; acc. sg. þeáw, 359; instr. pl. þeáwum (*in accordance with custom*), 2145.

þeód, st. f.: 1) *war-troop, retainers:* nom. sg., 644, 1231, 1251.— 2) *nation, folk:* nom. sg., 1692; gen. pl. þeóda, 1706.— Comp.: sige-, wer-þeód.

þeód-cyning, st. m., (= folc-cyning), *warrior-king, king of the people:* nom. sg. (Hróðgár), 2145; (Ongenþeów), 2964, 2971; þiódcyning (Beówulf), 2580; acc. sg. þeód-cyning (Beówulf), 3009; gen. sg. þeód-cyninges (Beówulf), 2695; gen. pl. þeód-cyninga, 2.

þeóden, st. m., *lord of a troop, warchief, king; ruler:* nom. sg., 129, 365, 417, 1047, 1210, 1676, etc.; þióden, 2337, 2811; acc. sg. þeóden, 34, 201, 353, 1599, 2385, 2722, 2884, 3080; þióden, 2789; dat. sg. þeódne, 345, 1526, 1993, 2573, 2710, etc.; þeóden, 2033; gen. sg. þeódnes, 798, 911, 1086, 1628, 1838, 2175; þiódnes, 2657; nom. pl. þeódnas, 3071.

þeóden-leás, adj., *without chief or king:* nom. pl. þeóden-leáse, 1104.

þeód-gestreón, st. n., *people's-jewel, precious treasure:* instr. pl.

þeód-ge-streónum, 44; gen. pl. þeód-ge-streóna, 1219.

þeódig, adj., *appertaining to a þeód:* in comp. el-þeódig.

þeód-sceaða, w. m., *foe of the people, general foe:* nom. sg. þeód-sceaða (*the dragon*), 2279, 2689.

þeód-þreá, st. f., *popular misery, general distress:* dat. pl. wið þeód-þreáum, 178.

þeóf, st. m., *thief:* gen. sg. þeófes cräfte, 2221.

þeón (for þíhan), st. v.: 1) *to grow, ripen, thrive:* pret. sg. weorðmyndum þâh (*grew in glory*), 8.— 2) *to thrive in, succeed:* pret. sg. hûru þät on lande lyt manna þâh (*that throve to few*), 2837.
ge-þeón, *to grow, thrive; increase in power and influence:* imper. ge-þeóh tela, 1219; inf. lof-dædum sceal ... man geþeón, 25; þät þät þeódnes bearn ge-þeón sculde, 911.
on-þeón, *to begin, undertake,* w. gen.: pret. he þäs ær onþâh, 901 (O.H.G. inthîhan, w. gen., Otfrid I, 1, 31).

þeón (for þeówan), w. v., *to oppress, restrain:* inf. näs se folccyning ymb-sittendra ænig þâra þe mec ... dorste egesan þeón (*that durst oppress me with terror*), 2737.

þeóstor, adj., *dark, gloomy:* instr. pl. þeóstrum ge-þoncum, 2333.

þicgan, st. v. w. acc., *to seize, attain, eat, appropriate:* inf. þät he (Grendel) mâ môste manna cynnes þicgean ofer þâ niht, 737; symbel þicgan (*take the meal, enjoy the feast*), 1011; pret. pl. þät hie me þêgon, 563; þær we medu þêgun, 2634.
ge-þicgan, w. acc., *to grasp, take:* pret. sg. (symbel and sele-ful, ful) ge-þeah, 619, 629; Beówulf ge-

þah ful on flette, 1025 ; pret. pl.
(medo-ful manig) ge-þægon, 1015.
þider, þyder, adv., *thither :* þyder,
3087, 370, 2971.
þihtig, þyhtig, adj., *doughty, vigorous, firm :* acc. sg. neut. sweord
... ecgum þyhtig, 1559. — Comp.
hyge-þihtig.
þincan. See þyncan.
þing, st. n.: 1) *thing :* gen. pl. ænige
þinga (*ullo modo*), 792, 2375, 2906.
— 2) *affair, contest, controversy :*
nom. sg. me wearð Grendles þing
... undyrne cûð (*Grendel's doings
became known to me*), 409. — 3)
*judgment, issue, judicial assem-
bly* (?) : acc. sg. sceal ... âna ge-
hegan þing wið þyrse (*shall bring
the matter alone to an issue against
the giant :* see hegan), 426.
ge-þing, st. n.: 1) *terms, covenant :*
acc. pl. ge-þingo, 1086. — 2) *fate,
providence, issue :* gen. sg. geþinges, 398, 710; (ge-þingea, MS.),
525.
ge-þingan, st. v., *to grow, mature,
thrive* (Dietrich, Haupt IX., 430) :
pret. part. cwên môde ge-þungen
(*mature - minded, high - spirited,
queen*), 625. See wel-þungen.
ge-þingan (see ge-þing, w. v.:
1) *to conclude a treaty :* w. refl.
dat., *enter into a treaty :* pres. sg.
III. gif him þonne Hrêðric tô
hofum Geáta ge-þingeð (*if H. enters into a treaty* (seeks aid at ?)
with the court of the Geátas, referring to the old German custom of
princes entering the service or suite
of a foreign king), 1838. Leo. —
2) *to prepare, appoint :* pret. part.
wiste [ät] þäm ahlæcan ... hilde
ge-þinged, 648; hraðe wäs ...
mêce ge-þinged, 1939.
þinglan, w. v.: 1) *to speak in an*

assembly, make an address :* inf.
ne hýrde ic snotor-licor on swâ
geongum feore guman þingian (*I
never heard a man so young speak
so wisely*), 1844. — 2) *to compound,
settle, lay aside :* inf. ne wolde feorh-
bealo ... feó þingian (*would not
compound the life-bale for money*),
156; so, pret. sg. þâ fæhðe feó
þingode, 470.
þihau. See þeón.
þin, possess. pron., *thy, thine*, 267,
346, 353, 367, 459, etc.
ge-þôht, st. m., *thought, plan :* acc.
sg. ân-fealdne ge-þôht, 256; fäst-
rædne ge-þôht, 611.
þolian, w. v. w. acc.: 1) *to endure,
bear :* inf. (inwid-sorge) þolian,
833; pres. sg. III. þreá-nýd þolað,
284; pret. sg. þolode þryðswyð,
131. — 2) *to hold out, stand, survive :* pres. sg. (intrans.) þenden
þis sweord þolað (*as long as this
sword holds out*), 2500; pret. sg.
(seó ecg) þolode ær fela hand-gemôta, 1526.
ge-þolian: 1) *to suffer, bear, endure :* gerund. tô ge-þolianne, 1420;
pret. sg. earfoð-lice þrage ge-þolode
..., þât he ... dreám gehýrde
(*bore ill that he heard the sound
of joy*), 87; torn ge-þolode (*bore
the misery*), 147. — 2) *to have patience, wait :* inf. þær he lunge
sceal on þäs waldendes wære ge-
þolian, 3110.
þon (Goth. þan) = *tum, then, now*,
504; äfter þon (*after that*), 725;
ær þon däg cwôme (*ere day came*),
732 ; nô þon lange (*it was not
long till then*), 2424; näs þâ long
tô þon (*it was not long till then*),
2592, 2846; wäs him se man tô
þon leóf þät ... (*the man was to that
degree dear to him that ...*), 1877.

Þonne: 1) adv., *there, then, now,*
377, 435, 525, 1105, 1456, 1485,
1672, 1823, 3052, 3098(?). — 2)
conj., *if, when, while :* a) w. indic.,
573, 881, 935, 1034, 1041, 1043,
1144, 1286, 1327, 1328, 1375, etc.;
þät ic gum-cystum gôdne funde
beága bryttan, breác þonne môste
(*that I found a good ring-giver
and enjoyed him whilst I could*),
1488. b) w. subj., 23, 1180, 3065;
þonne . . . þonne (*then . . . when*),
484-85, 2447-48 ; gif þonne . . .
þonne (*if then . . . then*), 1105-
1107. c) *than* after comparatives,
44, 248, 469, 505, 534, 679, 1140,
1183, etc.; a comparative must be
supplied, l. 70, before þone : þät he
. . . hâtan wolde medo-ärn micel
men ge-wyrcean þone yldo bearn
æfre ge-frunon (*a great mead-
house* (greater) *than men had ever
known*).

Þracu, st. f., *strength, boldness :* in
comp. môd-þracu ; = impetus in
ecg-þracu.

Þrag, st. f., *period of time, time :*
nom. sg. þâ hine sió þrag be-cwom
(*when the* [battle]*-hour befell him*),
2884; acc. sg. þrage (*for a time*),
87; longe (lange) þrage, 54, 114.
— Comp. earfoð-þrag.

ge-þräc, st. n., *multitude, crowd :*
in comp. searo-ge-þräc.

Þrec-wudu, st. m., (*might-wood*),
spear (cf. mägen-wudu) : acc. sg.,
1247.

Þreá, st. f., *misery, distress :* in
comp. þeód-þreá, þreá-nêdla, -nŷd.

Þreá-nêdla, w. m., *crushing distress, misery :* dat. sg. for þreánêdlan, 2225.

Þreá-nŷd, st. f., *oppression, distress :*
acc. sg. þreá-nŷd, 284; dat. pl.
þreá-nŷdum, 833.

Þreát, st. m., *troop, band :* dat. sg.
on þam þreáte, 2407 ; dat. pl.
sceaðena þreátum, 4.—Comp. iren-
þreát.

Þreátian, w. v. w. acc., *to press, oppress :* pret. pl. mec . . . þreátedon,
560.

Þreot-teoða, num. adj. w. m., *thir-
teenth :* nom. sg. þreot-teoða secg,
2407.

Þreó, num. (neut.), *three :* acc. þrió
wicg, 2175 ; þreó hund wintra,
2279.

Þridda, num. adj. w. m., *third :* instr.
þriddan siðe, 2689.

ge-þring, st. n., *eddy, whirlpool,
crush :* acc. on holma ge-þring, 2133.

Þringan, st. v., *to press :* pret. sg.
wergendra tô lyt þrong ymbe þeóden (*too few defenders pressed
round the prince*), 2884; pret. pl.
syððan Hreðlingas tô hagan þrun-
gon (*after the Hrethlingas had
pressed into the hedge*), 2961.

for-þringan, *to press out; rescue,
protect :* inf. þät he ne mehte . . . þâ
weá-lâfe wige for-þringan þeódnes
þegne (*that he could not rescue the
wretched remnant from the king's
thane by war*), 1085.

ge-þringan, *to press :* pret. sg. ceól
up ge þrang (*the ship shot up,* i.e.
on the shore in landing), 1913.

Þritig, num., *thirty* (neut. subst.) :
acc. sg. w. partitive gen. : þritig þegna, 123; gen. þrittiges (XXXtiges,
MS.) manna, 379.

Þrist-hydig, adj., *bold-minded, valorous :* nom. sg. þióden þrist-hydig
(Beówulf), 2811.

Þrowian, w. v. w. acc., *to suffer,
endure :* inf. (hât, gnorn) þrowian,
2606, 2659 ; pret. sg. þrowade,
1590, 1722; þrowode, 2595.

Þrýðu, st. f., *abundance, multitude,*

excellence, power : instr. pl. þrýðum
(*excellently, extremely ; excellent
in strength?*), 494.

þrýð-ærn, st. n., *excellent house,
royal hall:* acc. sg. (of Heorot), 658.

þrýðlic, adj., *excellent, chosen :*
nom. sg. þrýð-lic þegna heáp, 400,
1628; superl. acc. pl. þrýð-licost,
2870.

þrýð-swýð, st. n.?, *great pain(?)* :
acc., 131, 737 [? adj., *very powerful, exceeding strong*].

þrýð-word, st. n., *bold speech, choice
discourse:* nom. sg., 644. (Great
store was set by good table-talk :
cf. Lachmann's Nibelunge, 1612;
Rigsmâl, 29, 7, in Möbius, p. 79 b,
22.)

þrym, st. m. : 1) *power, might, force :*
nom. sg. ýða þrym, 1919; instr. pl.
= adv. þrymmum (*powerfully*),
235. — 2) *glory, renown :* acc. sg.
þrym, 2. — Comp. hyge-þrym.

þrym-lic, adj., *powerful, mighty :*
nom. sg. þrec-wudu þrym-lic (*the
mighty spear*), 1247.

þu, pron., *thou,* 366, 407, 445, etc.;
acc. sg. þec (poetic), 948, 2152,
etc.; þe, 417, 426, 517, etc.; after
compar. sælran þe (*a better one
than thee*), 1851. See ge, eów.

þunca, w. m. See áf-þunca.

ge-þungen. See þingan.

þurfan, pret.-pres. v., *to need :* pres.
sg. II. nô þu ne þearft . . . sorgian
(*needest not care*), 450; so, 445,
1675; III. ne þearf . . . ôhsittan
(*need not fear*), 596; so, 2007,
2742; pres. subj. þät he . . . sêcean
þurfe, 2496; pret. sg. þorfte, 157,
1027, 1072, 2875, 2996; pl. nealles
Iletware hrêmge þorfton (i.e. wesan) fêðe-wîges (*needed not boast
of their foot-fight*), 2365.

ge-þuren. See þweran.

þurh, prep. w. acc. signifying motion through, hence : I. local,
through, throughout : wôd | â þurh
þone wäl-rêc (*went then through
the battle-reek*), 2662.—II. causal :
1) *on account of, for the sake of,
owing to :* þurh slîðne nîð (*through
fierce hostility, heathenism*), 184;
þurh holdne hige (*from friendli-
ness*), 267; so, þurh rûmne sefan,
278; þurh sîdne sefan, 1727; có-
weð þurh egsan uncûðne nîð
(*shows unheard-of hostility by the
terror he causes*), 276; so, 1102,
1336, 2046. 2) *by means of,
through :* heaðo-ræs for-nam mihtig
mere-deór þurh mîne hand, 558;
þurh ânes cräft, 700; so, 941,
1694, 1696, 1980, 2406, 3069.

þus, adv., *so, thus,* 238, 337, 430.

þunian, w. v., *to din, sound forth :*
pret. sg. sund-wudu þunede, 1907.

þûsend, num., *thousand :* 1) fem.
acc. ic þe þûsenda þegna bringe tô
helpe, 1830.— 2) neut. with measure of value (sceat) omitted : acc.
seófon þûsendo, 2196; gen. hund-
þûsenda landes and locenra beága
(*100,000 sceattas' worth of land and
rings*), 2995.—3) uninflected : acc.
þûsend wintra, 3051.

þwære, adj., *affable, mild :* in comp.
man-þwære.

ge-þwære, adj., *gentle, mild :* nom.
pl. ge-þwære, 1231.

ge-þwêran, st. v., *to forge, strike :*
pret. part. heoru . . . hamere ge-
þuren (for ge-þworen) (*hammer-
forged sword*), 1286.

þylitig. See þlitig.

ge-þyld (see þollan), st. f. : 1)
patience, endurance : acc. sg.
ge-þyld, 1396. — 2) *steadfastness :*
instr. pl. = adv. : ge-þyldum (*stead-
fastly, patiently*), 1706.

þyle, st. m., *spokesman, leader of the conversation at court:* nom. sg., 1166, 1457.

þyncan, þincean, w. v. w. dat. of pers., *to seem, appear:* pres. sg. III. þinceð him tô lytel (*it seems to him too little*), 1749; ne þynceð me gerysne, þät we (*it seemeth to me not fit that we* ...), 2654; pres. pl. hy ... wyrðe þinceað eorla geæhtlan (*they seem worthy contenders with(?) earls; or, worthy warriors*), 368; pres. subj. swâ him ge-met þince, 688; inf. þincean, 1342; pret. sg. þûhte, 2462, 3058; nô his lîf-gedâl sâr-lîc þûhte secga ænigum (*his death seemed painful to none of men*), 843; pret. pl. þær him fold-wegas fägere þûhton, 867.

of-þincan, *to displease, offend:* inf. mäg þäs þonne of-þyncan þeóden (dat.) Heaðo-beardna and þegna gehwam þâra leóda, 2033.

þyrs, st. m., *giant:* dat. sg. wið þyrse (Grendel), 426.

þys-lîc, adj., *such, of such a nature:* nom. sg. fem. þys-lîcu þearf, 2638.

þŷ. See þät.

þŷwan (M.H.G. diuhen, O.H.G. dûhan), w. v., *to crush, oppress:* inf. gif þec ymb-sittend egesan þŷwað (*if thy neighbors oppress thee with dread*), 1828.

þŷstru, st. f., *darkness:* dat. pl. in þŷstrum, 87.

ge-þŷwe, adj., *customary, usual:* nom. sg. swâ him ge-þŷwe ne wäs (*as was not his custom*), 2333.

U

ufan, adv., *from above*, 1501; *above*, 330.

ufera (prop. *higher*), adj., *later:* dat. pl. ufaran dôgrum, 2201.

ufor, adv., *higher*, 2952.

uhte, w. f., *twilight* or *dawn:* dat. or acc. on uhtan, 126.

uht-floga, w. m., *twilight-flier, dawn-flier* (epithet of the dragon) : gen. sg. uht-flogan, 2761.

uht-hlem, st. m., *twilight-cry, dawn-cry:* acc. sg., 2008.

uht-sceaða, w. m., *twilight-* or *dawn-foe:* nom. sg., 2272.

umbor, st. n., *child, infant:* nom. sg., 46, 1188.

un-blîðe, adv.(?), *unblithely, sorrowfully*, 130, 2269; (adj., nom. pl.?), 3032.

un-byrnende, pres. part., *unburning, without burning*, 2549.

unc, dat. and acc. of the dual wit, *us two, to us two*, 1784, 2138, 2527; gen. hwäðer ... uncer twega (*which of us two*), 2533; uncer Grendles (*of us two, G. and me*), 2003.

uncer, poss. pron., *of us two:* nom. sg. [uncer], 2002(?); dat. pl. uncran eaferan, 1186.

un-cûð, adj.: 1) *unknown:* nom. sg. stîg ... eldum uncûð, 2215; acc. sg. neut. uncûð ge-lâd (*unknown ways*), 1411. — 2) *unheard-of, barbarous, evil:* acc. sg. uncûðne nîð, 276; gen. sg. un-cûðes (*of the foe*, Grendel), 961.

under, I. prep. w. dat. and acc.: 1) w. dat., answering question where? = *under* (of rest), contrasted with *over:* þät (wäs) under beorge, 211; þâ cwom Wealhþeó forð gân under gyldnum beáge (*IV. walked forth under a golden circlet*, i.e. decked with), 1164; siððan he under segne sinc ealgode (*under his banner*), 1205; he under rande ge-cranc (*sank under his shield*),

1210; under wolcnum, 8, 1632;
under heofenum, 52, 505; under
roderum, 310; under helme, 342,
404 ; under here - grîman, 396,
2050, 2606; so, 711, 1198, 1303,
1929, 2204, 2416, 3061, 3104.—
2) w. acc.: a) answering question
whither? = *under* (of motion) : þâ
secg wîsode under Heorotes hrôf,
403; siððan æfen-leóht under heofenes hâdor be-holen weorðeð,
414; under sceadu bregdan, 708;
león under fen-hleoðu, 821 ; hond
âlegde . . . under geápne hrôf,
837; teón in under coderas, 1038;
so, 1361, 1746, 2129, 2541, 2554,
2676, 2745; so, häfde þâ for-sîðod
sunu Ecg-þeówes under gynne
grund, 1552 (for-sîðian requires
acc.). b) after verbs of venturing
and fighting, with acc. of object
had in view : he under hârne stân
. . . âna ge-nêðde frêcne dæde, 888;
ne dorste under ýða ge-win aldre
ge - nêðan, 1470. c) indicating
extent, with acc. after expressions
of limit, etc.: under swegles begong (*as far as the sky extends*),
861, 1774; under heofenes hwealf
(*as far as heaven's vault reaches*),
2016.
II. Adv., *beneath, below :* stîg
under läg (*a path lay beneath,* i.e.
the rock), 2214.

undern-mæl, st. n., *midday :* acc.
sg., 1429.

un-dyrne, un-derne, adj., *without
concealment, plain, clear :* nom.
sg., 127, 2001 ; un-derne, 2912.

un-dyrne, adv., *plainly, evidently :*
un-dyrne cûð, 150, 410.

un-fäger, adj., *unlovely, hideous :*
nom. sg. leóht un-fäger, 728.

un-fræcne, adj., *without malice, sin-
cere :* nom. sg., 2069.

un-fæge, adj., *not death-doomed* or
"*fey*" : nom. sg., 2292; acc. sg.
un-fægne eorl, 573.

un-flitme, adv., *solemnly, incontest-
ably :* Finn Hengeste elne unflitme
âðum benemde (*F. swore solemnly
to H. with oaths*) [if an adj., elne
un-f. = *unconquerable in valor*],
1098.

un-forht, adj., *fearless, bold :* nom.
sg., 287; acc. pl. unforhte (adv.?),
444.

un-from, adj., *unfit, unwarlike :*
nom. sg., 2189.

un-frôd, adj., *not aged, young :* dat.
sg. guman un-frôdum, 2822.

un-gedêfelice, adv., *unjustly, contrary to right and custom,* 2436.

un-gemete, adv., *immeasurably,
exceedingly,* 2421, 2722, 2729.

un-gemetes, adv. gen. sg., the
same, 1793.

un-geâra, adv., (*not old*), *recently,
lately,* 933; *soon,* 603.

un-gifeðe, adj., *not to be granted;
refused :* nom. sg., 2922.

un-gleáw, adj., *regardless, reckless :*
acc. sg. sweord . . . ecgum un-
gleáw (of a sharp-edged sword),
2565.

un-hâr, adj., *very gray :* nom. sg.,
357.

un-hælo, st. f., *mischief, destruction :*
gen. sg. wiht un-hælo (*the demon
of destruction,* Grendel), 120.

un-heóre, un-hýre, adj., *monstrous,
horrible :* nom. sg. m., weard un-
hióre (the dragon), 2414; neut.
wîf un-hýre (Grendel's mother),
2121; nom. pl. neut. hand-speru
. . . unheóru (of Grendel's claws),
988.

un-hlytme, un-hlitme, adv. (cf.
A.S. hlytm = *lot;* O.N. hluti = *part,
division*), *undivided, unseparated,*

united, 1130 [unless = un-flitme, 1098].

un-leóf, adj., *hated:* acc. pl. scah on un-leófe, 2864.

un-lifigende, pres. part., *unliving, lifeless:* nom. sg. un-lifigende, 468; acc. sg. un-lyfigendne, 1309; dat. sg. un-lifgendum, 1390; gen. sg. un-lyfigendes, 745.

un-lytel, adj., *not little, very large:* nom. sg. duguð un-lytel (*a great band of warriors?* or *great joy?*), 498; dôm un-lytel (*no little glory*), 886; acc. sg. torn un-lytel (*very great shame, misery*), 834.

un-murnlîce, adv., *unpityingly, without sorrowing*, 449, 1757.

unnan, pret.-pres. v., *to grant, give; wish, will:* pret.-pres. sg. I. ic þe an tela sinc-gestreóna, 1226; weak pret. sg. I. ûðe ic swîðor þät þu hine selfne ge-scón môste, 961; III. he ne ûðe þät ... (*he granted not that ...*), 503; him god ûðe þät ... he hyne sylfne ge-wräc (*God granted to him that he avenged himself*), 2875; þeáh he ûðe wel (*though he well would*), 2856.

ge-unnan, *to grant, permit:* inf. gif he ûs ge-unnan wile þät we hine ... grêtan môton, 346; me ge-ûðe ylda waldend, þät ic ... ge-seah hangian (*the Ruler of men permitted me to see hanging ...*), 1662.

un-nyt, adj., *useless:* nom. sg., 413, 3170.

un-riht, st. n., *unright, injustice, wrong:* acc. sg. unriht, 1255, 2740; instr. sg. un-rihte (*unjustly, wrongly*), 3060.

un-rîm, st. n., *immense number:* nom. sg., 1239, 3136; acc. sg., 2625.

un-rîme, adj., *countless, measureless:* nom. sg. gold un-rîme, 3013.

un-rôt, adj., *sorrowing:* nom. pl. un-rôte, 3149.

un-snyttru, f., *lack of wisdom:* dat. pl. for his un-snyttrum (*for his unwisdom*), 1735.

un-softe, adv., *unsoftly, with violence (hardly ?)*, 2141; *scarcely*, 1656.

un-swŷðe, adv., *not strongly* or *powerfully:* compar. (ecg) bât unswîðor þonne his þiód-cyning þearfe häfde (*the sword bit less sharply than the prince of the people needed*), 2579; fŷr unswîðor weóll, 2882.

un-synnig, adj., *guiltless, sinless:* acc. sg. un-synnigne, 2090.

un-synnum, adv. instr. pl., *guiltlessly*, 1073.

un-tæle, adj., *blameless:* acc. pl. un-tæle, 1866.

un-tyder, st. m., *evil race, monster:* nom. pl. un-tydras, 111. [Cf. Ger. un-mensch.]

un-wâclîe, adj., *that cannot be shaken; firm, strong:* acc. sg. âd ... un-wâclîene, 3139.

un-wearnum, adv. instr. pl., *unawares, suddenly; (unresistingly?)*, 742.

un-wrecen, pret. part., *unavenged*, 2444.

up, adv., *up, upward*, 224, 519, 1374, 1620, 1913, 1921, 2894; (of the voice), þâ wäs ... wôp up âhafen, 128; so, 783.

up-lang, adj., *upright, erect:* nom. sg., 760.

uppe (adj., ûfe, ûffe), adv., *above*, 566.

up-riht, adj., *upright, erect:* nom. sg., 2093.

uton. See wuton.

Û

ûð-genge, adj., *transitory, evanescent, ready to depart,* (*fled?*) : þær wäs Asc-here ... feorh ûð-genge, 2124.

ûs, pers. pron. dat. and acc. of we ('see **we**), *us, to us,* 1822, 2636, 2643, 2921, 3002, 3079 ; acc. (poetic), ûsic, 2639, 2641, 2642 ; — gen. ûre : ûre æg-hwilc (*each of us*), 1387; ûser, 2075.

ûser, possess. pron.: nom. sg. ûre man-drihten, 2648; dat. sg. ûssum hláforde, 2635; gen. sg. neut. ûsses cynnes, 2814 ; dat. pl. ûrum ... bâm (*to us both, two*) (for unc bâm), 2660.

ût, adv., *out,* 215, 537, 664, 1293, 1584, 2082, 2558, 3131.

ûtan, adv., *from without, without,* 775, 1032, 1504, 2335.

ût-fûs, adj., *ready to go:* nom. sg. hringed-stefna îsig and ût-fûs, 33.

ût-weard, adj., *outward, outside, free:* nom. sg. eoten (Grendel) wäs ût-weard, 762.

ûtan-weard, adj., *without, outward, from without:* acc. sg. blæw ... ealne ûtan-weardne, 2298.

W

wacan, st. v., *to awake, arise, originate:* pret. sg. þanon (from Cain) wôc fela geó-sceaft-gâsta, 1266 ; so, 1961; pl. þâm feówer bearn ... in worold wôcon, 60.

on-wacan: 1) *to awake* (intrans.): pret. sg. þâ se wyrm on-wôc (*when the drake awoke*), 2288. — 2) *to be born:* pret. sg. him on-wôc heáh Healfdene, 56; pl. on-wôcon, 111.

wacian, w. v., *to watch:* imper. sg. waca wið wrâðum! 661.

wadan, st. v., (cf. wade, waddle), *to traverse: stride, go:* pret. sg. wôd þurh þone wäl-rêc, 2662; wôd under wolcnum (*stalked beneath the clouds*), 715.

ge-wadan, *to attain by moving, come to, reach:* pret. part. ôð þät ... wunden-stefna ge-waden häfde, þät þâ liðende land ge-sâwon (*till the ship had gone so far that the sailors saw land*), 220.

on-wadan, w. acc., *to invade, befall:* pret. sg. hine fyren on-wôd(?), 916.

þurh-wadan, *to penetrate, pierce:* pret. sg. þät swurd þurh-wôd wrätlîcne wyrm, 891 : so, 1568.

wag, st. m., *wall:* dat. sg. on wage, 1663; dat. pl. äfter wagum (*along the walls*), 996.

wala, w. m., *boss:* nom. pl. walan, 1032 (cf. Bouterwek in Haupt XI., 85 seqq.).

walda, w. m., *wielder, ruler:* in comp. an-, eal-walda.

wald-swaðu, st. f., *forest-path:* dat. pl. äfter wald-swaðum (*along the wood-paths*), 1404.

wam, wom, st. m., *spot, blot, sin:* acc. sg. him be-beorgan ne con wom (*cannot protect himself from evil* or *from the evil strange orders,* etc.; wom -: wogum? – *crooked?*), 1748; instr. pl. wommum, 3074.

wan, won, adj., *wan, luria dark:* nom. sg, ðð-geblond ... won (*the dark waves*), 1375; se wonna hrefn (*the black raven*), 3025; wonna lêg (*lurid flame*), 3116; dat. sg. f. on wanre niht, 703; nom. pl. neut. scadu-helma ge-sceapu ... wan, 652.

wang, st. m., *mead, field; place:* acc. sg. wang, 93, 225; wong, 1414, 2410, 3074; dat. sg. wange, 2004;

wonge, 2243, 3040; acc. pl. wongas, 2463. — Comp.: freoðo-, grund-, medo-, sæ-wang.

wang-stede, st. m., (locus campestris), *spot, place*: dat. sg. wongstede, 2787.

wan-hŷd (for hygd), st. f., *heedlessness, recklessness*: dat. pl. for his won-hŷdum, 434.

wanian, w. v.: 1) intrans., *to decrease, wane*: inf. þá þæt sweord ongan . . . wanian, 1608. — 2) w. acc., *to cause to wane* or *lessen*: pret. sg. he tô lange leóde mîne wanode, 1338.

ge-wanian, *to decrease, diminish*: pret. part. is mîn flet-werod . . . ge-wanod, 477.

wan-sælig, adj., *unhappy, wretched*: nom. sg. won-sælig wer (Grendel), 105.

wan-sceaft, st. f., *misery, want*: acc. sg. won-sceaft, 120.

warian, w. v. w. acc., *to occupy, guard, possess*: pres. sg. III. þær he heáðen gold waraÐ (*where he guards heathen gold*), 2278; pl. III. hie (Grendel and his mother) dŷgel land warigeaÐ, 1359; pret. sg. (Grendel) goldsele warode, 1254; (Cain) wêsten warode, 1266.

waroÐ, st. m., *shore*: dat. sg. tô waroÐe, 234; acc. pl. wîde waroÐas, 1966.

waru, st. f., *inhabitants*, (collective) *population*: in comp. land-waru.

wâ, interj., *woe*! wâ biÐ þâm þe . . . (*woe to him that* . . .), 183.

wâÐu, st. f., *way, journey*: in comp. gamen-waÐu.

wânian, w. v., *to weep, whine, howl*, w. acc.: inf. gehŷrdon . . . sâr wânigean helle häftan (*they heard the hell-fastened one lamenting his*

pain), 788; pret. sg. [wânode], 3152(?).

wât. See witan.

wäccan, w. v., *to watch*: pret. part. wäccende, 709, 2842; acc. sg. m. wäccendne wer, 1269. See wacian.

wäcnan, w. v., *to be awake, come forth*: inf., 85.

wäd, st. n., (the moving) *sea, ocean*: acc. wado weallende, 546; wadu weallendu, 581; gen. pl. wada, 508.

wäfre, adj., *wavering* (like flame), *ghostlike, without distinct bodily form*: nom. sg. wäl-gæst wäfre (of Grendel's mother), 1332; — *flickering, expiring*: nom. sg. wäfre môd, 1151; him wäs geômor sefa, wäfre and wäl-fús, 2421.

be-wägnan, w. v., *to offer*: pret. part. him wäs . . . freónd-laÐu wordum be-wägned, 1194.

wäl, st. n., *battle, slaughter, the slain in battle*: acc. sg. wäl, 1213, 3028; blôdig wäl, 448; oÐÐe on wäl crunge (*or in battle, among the slain, fall*), 636; dat. sg. sume on wäle crungon (*some fell in the slaughter*), 1114; dat. sg. in Ir . . . es wäle (proper name in MS. destroyed), 1071; nom. pl. walu, 1043.

wäl-bed, st. n., *slaughter-bed, death-bed*: dat. sg. on wäl-bedde, 965.

wäl-bend, st. f., *death-bond*: acc. sg. or pl. wäl-bende . . . hand-ge-wriÐene, 1937.

wäl-bleát, adj., *deadly, deadly-pale*(?): acc. sg. wunde wäl-bleáte, 2726.

wäl-deáÐ, st. m., *death in battle*: nom. sg., 696.

wäl-dreór, st. m., *battle-gore*: instr. sg. wäl-dreóre, 1632.

wäl-fäh, adj., *slaughter - stained, blood-stained:* acc. sg. wäl-fägne winter, 1129.

wül-fæhð, st. f., *deadly feud:* gen. pl. wäl-fæhða, 2029.

wäl-feall, st. m., (*fall of the slain), death, destruction:* dat. sg. tô wälfealle, 1712.

wül-fûs, adj., *ready for death, foreboding death:* nom. sg., 2421.

wäl-fyllo, st. f., *fill of slaughter:* dat. sg. mid þære wäl-fulle (i.e. the thirty men nightly slaughtered at Heorot by Grendel), 125; wälfylla? 3155.

wäl-fyr, st. n.: 1) *deadly fire:* instr. sg. wäl-fyre (of the fire-spewing dragon), 2583. — 2) *corpse-consuming fire, funeral pyre:* gen. pl. wäl-fyra mæst, 1120.

wäl-gæst, st. m., *deadly sprite* (of Grendel and his mother): nom. sg. wäl-gæst, 1332; acc. sg. þone wäl-gæst, 1996.

wäl-hlem, st. m., *death-stroke:* acc. sg. wäl-hlem þone, 1996.

wülm, st. m., *flood, whelming water:* nom. sg. þære burnan wälm, 2547; gen. sg. þäs wälmes (*of the surf*), 2136. — Comp. cear-wälm.

wül-nið, st. m., *deadly hostility:* nom. sg., 3001; dat. sg. äfter wälníðe, 85; nom. pl. wäl-níðas, 2066.

wäl-ráp, st. m., *flood-fetter,* i.e. *ice:* acc. pl. wäl-rápas, 1611; (cf. wäll, wel, wyll — *well, flood:* leax sceal on wäle mid sceôte scríðan, Gnom. Cott. 39).

wäl-ríes, st. m., *deadly onslaught:* nom. sg., 2948; dat. sg. wäl-ræse, 825, 2532.

wül-rest, st. f., *death-bed:* acc. sg. wäl-reste, 2903.

wäl-rêc, st. m., *deadly reek* or *smoke:* acc. sg. wôd þâ þurh þone wäl-rêc, 2662.

wül-reáf, st, n., *booty of the slain, battle-plunder:* acc. sg., 1206.

wül-reów, adj., *bold in battle:* nom. sg., 630.

wül-sceaft, st. m., *deadly shaft, spear:* acc. pl. wäl-sceaftas, 398.

wül-seax, st. n., *deadly knife, war-knife:* instr. sg. wäll-seaxe, 2704.

wäl-stenge, st. m., *battle-spear:* dat. sg. on þäm wäl-stenge, 1639.

wül-stów, st. f., *battle-field:* dat. sg. wäl-stôwe, 2052, 2985.

wästm, st. m., *growth, form, figure:* dat. sg. on weres wästmum (*in man's form*), 1353.

wüter, st. n., *water:* nom. sg., 93, 1417, 1515, 1632; acc. sg. wäter, 1365, 1620; deóp wäter (*the deep*), 509, 1905; ofer wíd wäter (*over the high sea*), 2474; dat. sg. äfter wätere (*along the Grendel-sea*), 1426; under wätere (*at the bottom of the sea*), 1657; instr. wätere, 2723; wätre, 2855; gen. sg. ofer wäteres hrycg (*over the surface of the sea*), 471; on wäteres æht, 516; þurh wäteres wylm (*through the sea-wave*), 1694; gen. – instr. wäteres weorpan (*to sprinkle with water*), 2792.

wäter-egesa, st. m., *water-terror,* i.e. *the fearful sea:* acc. sg., 1261.

wüter-yð, st. f., *water-wave, billow:* dat. pl. wäter-yðum, 2243.

wied, st. f., (*weeds*), *garment:* in comp. here-, hilde-wæd.

ge - wæde, st. n., *clothing,* especially *battle - equipments:* acc. pl. gewædu, 292. — Comp. corl-gewæde.

wæg, st. m., *wave:* acc. sg. wæg, 3133.

wæg - born, w. m., *wave-bearer, swimmer* (bearing or propelling the waves before him) : nom. sg. wundorlîc wæg-bora (of a sea-monster), 1441.

wæg-flota, w. m., *sea-sailer, ship :* acc. sg. wêg-flotan, 1908.

wæg-holm, st. m., *the wave-filled sea :* acc. sg. ofer wæg-holm, 217.

wæge, st. n., *cup, can :* acc. sg. fäted wæge, 2254, 2283.—Comp. : ealo-, lîð-wæge.

wæg-lîðend, pres. part., *sea-farer :* dat. pl. wæg-lîðendum (et lîðendum, MS.), 3160.

wæg-sweord, st. n., *heavy sword :* acc. sg., 1490.

wæn, st. m., *wain, wagon :* acc. sg. on wæn, 3135.

wæpen, st. n., *weapon ; sword :* nom. sg., 1661 ; acc. sg. wæpen, 686, 1574, 2520, 2688 ; instr. wæpne, 1665, 2966 ; gen. wæpnes, 1468 ; acc. pl. wæpen, 292 ; dat. pl. wæpnum, 250, 331, 2039, 2396. — Comp. : hilde-, sige-wæpen.

wæpned-man, st. m., *warrior, man :* dat. sg. wæpned-men, 1285.

wær, st. f., *covenant, treaty :* acc. sg. wære, 1101 ;— *protection, care :* dat. sg. on freán (on þäs waldendes) wære (*into God's protection*), 27, 3110. — Comp. : frioðo-wær.

wæsma, w. m., *fierce strength, war-strength :* in comp. here-wæsma, 678.

we, pers. pron., *we*, 942, 959, 1327, 1653, 1819, 1820, etc.

web, st. n., *woven work, tapestry :* nom. pl. web, 996.

webbe, w. f., *webster, female weaver :* in comp. freoðu-webbe.

weccan, weccean, w. v. w. acc., *to wake, rouse ; recall :* inf. wîg-bealu weccan (*to stir up strife*), 2047 ; nalles hearpan swêg (sceal) wîgend weccean (*the sound of the harp*

shall not wake up the warriors), 3025 ; ongunnon þâ ... bæl-fýra mæst wîgend weccan (*the warriors then began to start the mightiest of funeral pyres*), 3145 ; pret. sg. wehte hine wätre (*roused him with water*, i.e. Wîglâf recalled Beówulf to consciousness), 2855.

tô-weccan, *to stir up, rouse :* pret. pl. hû þâ folc mid him (*with one another*), fahðe tô-wehton, 2949.

wed, st. n., (cf. wed-ding), *pledge :* dat. sg. hyldo tô wedde (*as a pledge of his favor*), 2999.

weder, st. n., *weather :* nom. pl. wuldor-torhtan weder, 1137; gen. pl. wedera cealdost, 546.

ge-wef, st. n., *woof, weaving :* acc. pl. wîg-spêda ge-wiofu (*the woof of war-speed :* the battle-woof woven for weal or woe by the Walkyries; cf. Njals-saga, 158), 698.

weg, st. m., *way :* acc. sg. on weg (*away, off*), 264, 764, 845, 1431, 2097; gyf þu on weg cymest (*if thou comest off safe*, i.e. from the battle with Grendel's mother), 1383. — Comp. : feor-, fold-, forð-, wîd-weg.

wegan, st. v. w. acc., *to bear, wear, bring, possess :* subj. pres. nâh hwâ sweord wege (*I have none that may bear the sword*), 2253; inf. nalles (sceal) eorl wegan mâððum tô ge-myndum (*no earl shall wear a memorial jewel*), 3016; pret. ind. he þâ frätwe wäg ... ofer ýða ful (*bore the jewels over the goblet of the waves*), 1208; wäl-seaxe ... þät he on byrnan wäg, 2705; heortan sorge wäg (*bore heart's sorrow*); so, 152, 1778, 1932, 2781.

ät-wegan = *auferre, to carry off :* syððan Hâma ät-wäg tô þære byrhtan byrig Brosinga mene *(since ll. bore from (to?) the bright city the Brosing-collar)*, 1199.

ge-wegan (O.N. wega), *to fight :* inf. þe he wið þam wyrme ge-wegan sceolde, 2401.

wel, adv.: 1) *well :* wel bið þäm þe ... (*well for him that* ...!), 186; se þe wel þenceð (*he that well thinketh, judgeth*), 289 ; so, 640, 1046, 1822, 1834, 1952, 2602 ; well, 2163, 2813. — 2) *very, very much :* Geát ungemetes wel . . . restan lyste (*the Geat longed sorely to rest*), 1793. — 3) *indeed, to be sure,* 2571, 2856.

wela, w. m., *wealth, goods, possessions :* in comp. ær-, burg-, hord-, mäððum-wela.

wel-hwlc, indef. pron., = quivis, *any you please, any* (each, all): gen. pl. wel-hwylcra wilna, 1345; w. partitive gen.: nom. sg. witena wel-hwylc, 266; — substantively: acc. neut. wel-hwylc, 875.

wellg, adj., *wealthy, rich :* acc. sg. wíc-stede weligne Wægmundinga, 2608.

wel þungen, pres. part., *well-thriven* (in mind), *mature, high-minded :* nom. sg. llygd (wäs) swiðe geong, wís, wel-þungen, 1928.

wenlan, w. v., *to accustom, attract, honor :* subj. pret. þät ... Folcwaldan sunu ... llengestes heáp hringum wenede (*honored*), 1092. **be-(bi-)wenian,** *to entertain, care for, attend :* pret. sg. mäg þäs þonne of-þyncan þeóden Heaðo-beardna ... þonne he mid fæmnan on flet gæð, dryht-bearn Dena duguða bi-wenede (*may well displease the prince of the H. ... when he with the woman goes into the hall, that a noble scion of the Danes should entertain, bear wine to, the knights,*

cf. 494 seqq.; or, *a noble scion of the Danes should attend on her?*), 2036; pret. part. nom. pl. wæron her tela willum be-wenede, 1822.

wendan, w. v., *to turn :* pres. sg. III. him eal worold wendeð on willan (*all the world turns at his will*), 1740.

ge-wendan, w. acc.: 1) *to turn, turn round :* pret. sg. wicg gewende (*turned his horse*), 315. — 2) *to turn* (intrans.), *change :* inf. wä bið þäm þe sceal ... frófre ne wénan, wihte ge-wendan (*woe to him that shall have no hope, shall not change at all*), 186.

on-wendan, *to avert, set aside :* 1) w. acc.: inf. ne mihte snotor häleð weán on-wendan, 191. — 2) intrans.: sibb æfre ne mäg wiht on-wendan þam þe wel þenceð (*in, to, him that is well thinking friendship can not be set aside*), 2602.

wer, st. m., *man, hero :* nom. sg. (Grendel), 105; acc. sg. wer (Beówulf), 1269. 3174 ; gen. sg. on weres wästmum (*in man's form*), 1353 ; nom. pl. weras, 216, 1223, 1234, 1441, 1651; dat. pl. werum, 1257; gen. pl. wera, 120, 994, 1732, 3001; (MS. weora), 2948.

wered, st. n., (as adj. = *sweet*), *a sort of beer* (probably without hops or such ingredients): acc. sg. scír wered, 496.

were-feohte, f., *defensive fight, fight in self-defence :* dat. pl. for werefyhtum (fere fyhtum, MS.), 457.

werhðo, st. f., *curse, outlawry, condemnation :* acc. sg. þu in helle scealt werhðo dreógan, 590.

werlan, *to defend, protect :* w. acc., pres. sg. III. beaduscrúd ... þät míne breóst wered, 453; inf. wit unc wið hron-fixas werian þóhton,

541 ; pres. part. w. gen. pl. wer-gendra tô lyt (*too few defenders*), 2883 ; pret. ind. wäl-reáf werede (*guarded the battle-spoil*), 1206; se hwîta helm hafelan werede (*the shining helm protected his head*), 1449; pl. hafeian weredon, 1328; pret. part. nom. pl. ge ... byrnum werede (*ye ... corselet-clad*), 238, 2530.

be-werian, *to protect, defend:* pret. pl. þät hie ... leóda land-geweorc láðum be-weredon scuccum and scynnum (*that they the people's land-work from foes, from monsters and demons, might defend*), 939.

werlg, adj., *accursed, outlawed:* gen. sg. wergan gâstes (Grendel), 133; (of the devil), 1748.

werod, weorod, st. n., *band of men, warrior-troop:* nom. sg. werod, 652; weorod, 290, 2015, 3031; acc. sg. werod, 319; dat. instr. sg. weorode, 1012, 2347; werede, 1216; gen. sg. werodes, 259; gen. pl. wereda, 2187; weoroda, 60.—Comp.: eorl-, flet-werod.

wer-þeód, st. f., *people, humanity:* dat. sg. ofer wer-þeóde, 900.

wesan, v., *to be:* pres. sg. I. ic eom, 335, 407; II. þu eart, 352, 506; III. is, 256, 272, 316, 343, 375, 473, etc.; nu is þínes mägenes blæd âne hwîle (*the prime* [*fame?*] *of thy powers lasteth now for a while*), 1762; ys, 2911, 3000, 3085; pl. I. we synt, 260, 342; II. syndon, 237, 393; III. syndon, 257, 361, 1231; synt, 364; sint, 388; subj. pres. sîe, 435, 683, etc.; sŷ, 1832, etc. ; sig, 1779, etc. ; imper. sg. II. wes, 269 (cf. was-sail, wes hæl), 407, 1171, 1220, 1225, etc.; inf. wesan, 272, 1329,

1860, 2709, etc. The inf. wesan must sometimes be supplied : nalles Hetware hrêmge þorfton (i.e. we-san) feðe-wîges, 2364 ; so, 2498, 2660, 618, 1858; pres. part. we-sende, 46 ; dat. sg. wesendum, 1188; pret. sg. I., III. wäs, 11, 12, 18, 36, 49, 53, etc.; wäs on sunde (*was a-swimming*), 1619; so, 848, 850(?), 970, 981, 1293; progres-sive, wäs seegende (for sæde), 3029; II. wære, 1479, etc.; pl. wæron, 233, 536, 544, etc. ; wæran (w. reflex. him), 2476 ; pret. subj. wære, 173, 203, 594, 946, etc.; progressive, myndgiend wære (for myndgie), 1106.—Contracted neg. forms : nis = ne + is, 249, 1373, etc.; näs = ne + wäs, 134, 1300, 1922, 2193, etc. (cf. uncontracted: ne wäs, 890, 1472); næron = ne + wæron, 2658; nære = ne + wære, 861, 1168. See eniht-wesende.

wêg. See wæg.

wên, st. f., *expectation, hope:* nom. sg., 735, 1874, 2324; nu is leódum wên orlêg-hwîle (gen.) (*now the people have weening of a time of strife*), 2911; acc. sg. þäs ic wên häbbe (*as I hope, expect*), 383; so, þäs þe ic [wên] hafo, 3001; wên ic talige, 1846; dat. pl. bega on wênum (*in expectation of both*, i.e. the death and the return of Beówulf), 2896. See ôr-wena.

wênan, w. v., *to ween, expect, hope:* 1) absolutely: pres. sg. I. þäs ic wêne (*as I hope*), 272; swâ ic þe wêne tô (*as I hope thou wilt:* Beó-wulf hopes Hrôðgâr will now suffer no more pain), 1397.— 2) w. gen. or acc. pres. sg. I. þonne wêne ic tô þe wyrsan ge-þinges, 525 ; ic þær heaðu-fŷres hâtes wêne, 2523; III. säcce ne wêneð tô Gâr-

Denum (*weeneth not of contest with the Gar-Danes*), 601 ; inf. (beorhtre bôte) wēnan (*to expect, count on, a brilliant* [? *a lighter penalty*] *atonement*), 157; pret. pl. þās ne wēndon ær witan Scyldinga, þāt . . . (*the wise men of the Scyldings weened not of this before, that* . . .), 779; þāt hig þās äðelinges eft ne wēndon þāt he . . . sēcean cwôme (*that they looked not for the atheling again that he . . . would come to seek* . . .), 1597. — 3) w. acc. and inf.: pret. sg. wēnde, 934. — 4) w. depend. clause : pres. sg. I. wēne ic þāt . . ., 1185; wēn' ic þāt . . ., 338, 442; pret. sg. wēnde, 2330; pl. wēndon, 938, 1605.

wēpan, st. v., *to weep:* pret. sg. [weóp], 3152(?).

wērig, adj., *weary, exhausted,* w. gen. : nom. sg. sîðes wêrig (*weary from the journey, way-weary*), 579; dat. sg. sîðes wêrgum, 1795; — w. instr.: acc. pl. wundum wêrge (*wound-weary*), 2938. — Comp.: deáð-, fyl-, gûð-wêrig.

ge-wērigean, w. v., *to weary, exhaust:* pret. part. ge-wêrgad, 2853.

wērig-môd, adj., *weary-minded* (*animo defessus*) : nom. sg., 845, 1544.

wēste, adj., *waste, uninhabited:* acc. sg. win-sele wêstne, 2457.

wēsten, st. n., *waste, wilderness:* acc. sg. wêsten, 1266.

wēsten, st. f., *waste, wilderness:* dat. sg. on þære wêstenne, 2299.

weal, st. m.: 1) *wall, rampart:* dat. instr. sg. wealle, 786, 892, 3163; gen. sg. wealles, 2308. — 2) *elevated sea-shore:* dat. sg. of wealle, 229; acc. pl. windige weallas, 572, 1225. — 3) *wall of a building:* acc. sg. wið þās recedes weal,

326; dat. sg. be wealle, 1574; hence, the inner and outer rock-walls of the dragon's lair (cf. Heyne's essay : Halle Heorot, p. 59) : dat. sg., 2308, 2527, 2717, 2760, 3061, 3104; gen. sg. wealles, 2324. — Comp.: bord-, corð-, sæ-, scyld-weal.

ge-wealc, st. n., *rolling:* acc. sg. ofer ýða ge-wealc, 464.

ge-weald, st. n., *power, might:* acc. sg. on fcónda ge-weald (*into the power of his foes*), 809, 904; so, 1685 ; geweald âgan, häbban, â-beódan (w. gen. of object = *to present*) = *to have power over,* 79, 655, 765, 951, 1088, 1611, 1728. See on-weald.

wealdan, st. v., *to wield, govern, rule over, prevail:* 1) absolutely or with depend. clause: inf. gif he wealdan môt (*if he may prevail*), 442; þær he . . . wealdan môste swâ him Wyrd ne ge-scrâf (*if* [*where?*] *he was to prevail, as Weird had not destined for him*), 2575; pres. part. waldend (*God*), 1694; dat. wealdende, 2330; gen. waldendes, 2293, 2858, 3110. — 2) with instr. or dat.: inf. þâm wæpnum wealdan (*to wield, prevail with, the weapons*), 2039; Geátum wealdan (*to rule the Gedtas*), 2391; beáh-hordum wealdan (*to rule over, control, the treasure of rings*), 2828; wäl-stôwe wealdan (*to hold the field of battle*), 2985; pret. sg. weóld, 465, 1058, 2380, 2596; þenden wordum weóld wine Scyldinga (*while the friend of the S. ruled the G.*), 30; pl. weóldon, 2052. — 3) with gen.: pres. sg. I. þenden ic wealde widan rîces, 1860; pres. part. wuldres wealdend (waldend), 17, 183, 1753;

ylda waldend, 1662; waldend fira,
2742; sigora waldend, 2876 (des-
ignations of God) ; pret. sg. weóld,
703, 1771.

ge-wealdan, *to wield, have power
over, arrange:* 1) w. acc.: pret.
sg. hálig god ge-weóld wíg-sigor,
1555. — 2) w. dat.: pret. cyning
ge-weóld his ge-witte (*the king
possessed his senses*), 2704. — 3) w.
gen.: inf. he ne mihte nó . . .
wǽpna ge-wealdan, 1510.

ge-wealden, pret. part., *subject,
subjected:* acc. pl. gedéð him swâ
gewealdene worolde dǽlas, 1733.

weallan, st. v.: 1) *to toss, be agitated* (of the sea) : pres. part. nom.
pl. wadu weallende (weallendu),
546, 581; nom. sg. brim weallende,
848; pret. ind. weól, 515, 850,
1132; weóll, 2139. — 2) figuratively (of emotions), *to be agitated:*
pres. pl. III. syððan Ingelde weallað wäl-níðas (*deadly hate thus
agitates Ingeld*), 2066; pres. part.
weallende, 2465; pret. sg. hreðer
inne weóll (*his heart was mov'd
within him*), 2114; hreðer ǽðme
weóll (*his breast* [the dragon's]
swelled from breathing, snorting),
2594; breóst innan weóll þeóstrum
ge-þoncum, 2332; so, weóll, 2600,
2715, 2883.

weall-clif, st. n., *sea-cliff:* acc. sg.
ofer weall-clif, 3133.

weallian, w. v., *to wander, rove
about:* pres. part. in comp. heoro-
weallende, 2782.

weard, st. m., *warden, guardian;
owner:* nom. sg. weard Scyldinga
(*the Scyldings' warden of the
march*), 229: weard, 286, 2240;
se weard, sâwele hyrde, 1742; the
king is called beáh-horda weard,
922; ríces weard, 1391; folces

weard, 2514; the *dragon* is called
weard, 3061; weard un-hióre, 2414;
beorges weard, 2581; acc. sg.
weard, 669; (dragon), 2842; beorges weard (dragon), 2525, 3067.
— Comp.: bât-, éðel-, gold-, heá-
fod-, hord-, hýð-, land-, rên-, sele-,
yrfe-weard.

weard, st. m., *possession* (Dietrich
in Haupt XI., 415) : in comp. eorð-
weard, 2335.

weard, st. f., *watch, ward:* acc. sg.
wearde healdan, 319; wearde heóld,
305. — Comp. ǽg-weard.

weard, adj., -*ward:* in comp. and-,
innan-, ût-weard, 1288, etc.

weardian, w. v. w. acc.: 1) *to watch,
guard, keep:* inf. he his folme for-
lêt tô líf-wraðe, lâst weardian
(*Grendel left his hand behind as a
life-support, to guard his track*
[Kemble]), 972; pret. sg. him sió
swíðre swaðe weardade hand on
Hiorte (*his right hand kept guard
for him in H.*, i.e. showed that he
had been there), 2099; sg. for pl.
hýrde ic þät þâm frätwum feówer
mearas lungre gelîce lâst weardode
(*I heard that four horses, quite
alike, followed in the traces of the
armor*), 2165. — 2) *to hold, possess,
inhabit:* pret. sg. fîfel-cynnes eard
. . . weardode (*dwelt in the abode
of the sea-fiends*), 105; reced weardode un-rîm eorla (*an immense
number of earls held the hall*),
1238; pl. þær we gesunde sǽl weardodon, 2076.

wearh, st. m., *the accursed one;
wolf:* in comp. heoro-wearg, 1268.

wearn, st. f.: 1) *resistance, refusal,*
366. — 2) *warning?, resistance?.*
See un-wearnum, 742.

weaxan, st. v., *to wax, grow:* pres.
sg. III. óð þät him on innan ofer-

hygda dæl weaxeð (*till within him pride waxeth*), 1742; inf. weaxan, 3116; pret. sg. weôx, S.

ge-weaxan, *to grow up:* pret. sg. ôð þät seó geogoð ge-weôx, 66.

ge-weaxan to, *to grow to* or *for something.* pret. sg. ne ge-weôx he him tô willan (*grew not for their benefit*), 1712.

weá, w. m., *woe, evil, misfortune:* nom. sg., 937; acc. sg. weán, 191, 423, 1207, 1992, 2293, 2938; gen. pl. weána, 148, 934, 1151, 1397.

weá-láf, st. f., *wretched remnant:* acc. pl. þâ weá-láfe (*the wretched remnant*, i.e. Finn's almost annihilated band), 1085, 1099.

weá-spel, st. n., *woe-spell, evil tidings:* dat. sg. weá-spelle, 1316.

ge-weoldum. See ge-wild.

weorc, st. n.: 1) *work, labor, deed:* acc. sg., 74; (*war-deed*), 1657; instr. sg. weorce, 1570; dat. pl. weorcum, 2097; wordum ne (and) worcum, 1101, 1834; gen. pl. worda and worca, 289. — 2) *work, trouble, suffering:* acc. sg. þäs ge-winnes weorc (*misery on account of this strife*), 1722; dat. pl. adv. weorcum (*with labor*), 1639. — Comp.: beado-, ellen-, heaðo-, niht-weorc.

ge-weorc, st. n.: 1) *work, deed, labor:* nom. acc. sg., 455, 1563, 1682, 2718, 2775; gen. sg. ge-weorces, 2712. Comp.: ær-, fyrn-, gúð-, hond-, nîð-ge-weorc. — 2) *fortification, rampart:* in comp. land-geweorc, 939.

weorce, adj., *painful, bitter:* nom. sg., 1419.

weorð, st. n., *precious object, valuable:* dat. sg. weorðe, 2497.

weorð, adj., *dear, precious:* nom. sg. weorð Denum äðeling (*the*

atheling dear to the Danes, Beówulf), 1815; compar. nom. sg. þät he syððan wäs . . . máðme þý weorðra (*more honored from the jewel*), 1903; cf. wyrðe.

weorðan, st. v.: 1) *to become:* pres. sg. III. beholen weorðeð (*is concealed*), 414; underne weorðeð (*becomes known*), 2914; so, pl. III. weorðað, 2067; wurðað, 282; inf. weorðan, 3179; wurðan, 808; pret. sg. I., III. wearð, 6, 77, 149, 409, 555, 754, 768, 819, 824, etc.; pl. wurdon, 228; subj. pret. wurde, 2732. — 2) inf. tô frôfre weorðan (*to become a help*, 1708; pret. sg. wearð he Heaðoláfe tô hand-bonan, 460; so, wearð, 906, 1262; ne wearð Heremôd swâ i.e. tô frôfre) eaforum Ecgwelan, 1710; pl. wurdon, 2204; subj. pret. sg. II. wurde, 588. — 3) pret. sg. þät he on fylle wearð (*that he came to a fall*, 1545. — 4) *to happen, befall:* inf. unc sceal weorðan . . . swâ unc Wyrd ge-teôð (*it shall befall us two as Fate decrees*), 2527; þurh hwät his worulde gedâl weorðan sceolde, 3069; pret. sg. þâ þær sôna wearð ed-hwyrft eorlum (*there was soon a renewal to the earls*, i.e. of the former perils), 1281.

ge-weorðan: 1) *to become:* pret. sg. ge-wearð, 3062; pret. part. cearu wäs geniwod ge-worden (*care was renewed*), 1305; swâ ûs ge-worden is, 3079. — 2) *to finish; complete?:* inf. þät þu . . . lête Sûð-Dene sylfe ge-weorðan gûðe wið Grendel (*that thou wouldst let the S. D. put an end to their war with Grendel*, 1997. — 3) impersonally with acc., *to seem, appear:* pret. sg. þâ þäs monige ge-wearð þät . . . (*since it seemed to many that . . .*),

1599; pret. part. hafað þäs ge-
worden wine Scyldinga, rîces hyrde, and þät ræd talað þät he ...
(*therefore hath it so appeared?*,
happened?, *to the friend of the S.*,
*the guardian of the realm, and he
counts it again that* ...), 2027.

weorð-ful, adj., *glorious, full of
worth :* nom. sg. weorð-fullost,
3100.

weorðian, w. v., *to honor, adorn :*
pret. sg. þær ic ... þine leóde weorðode weorcum (*there honored I
thy people by my deeds*), 2097; subj.
pret. (þät he) ät feoh-gyftum ...
Dene weorðode (*that he would
honor the Danes at, by, treasure-
giving*), 1091.

ge-weorðian, **ge-wurðian**, *to
deck, ornament :* pret. part. hire
syððan wäs äfter beáh-þege breóst
ge-weorðod, 2177; wæpnum ge-
weorðad, 250; since ge-weorðad,
1451; so, ge-wurðad, 331, 1039,
1646; wîde ge-weorðad (*known,
honored, afar*), 1960.

weorð-lîce, adv., *worthily, nobly :*
superl. weorð-licost, 3163.

weorð-mynd, st. f., *dignity, honor,
glory :* nom. sg., 65; acc. sg. geseah þâ eald sweord ..., wigena
weorðmynd (*saw an ancient sword
there, the glory of warriors*), 1560;
dat. instr. pl. weorð-myndum, 8;
tô worð-myndum, 1187; gen. pl.
weorð-mynda dæl, 1753.

weorðung, st. f., *ornament :* in
comp. breóst-, hâm-, heorð-, hring-,
wig-weorðung.

weorod. See **werod.**

weorpan, st. v.: 1) *to throw, cast
away*, w. acc.: pret. sg. wearp þâ
wunden-mæl wrättum gebunden
yrre oretta, þät hit on eorðan läg
(*the wrathful warrior threw the

*ornamented sword, that it lay on
the earth*), 1532.— 2) *to throw
around* or *about*, w. instr.: pret. sg.
beorges weard ... wearp wäl-fýre
(*threw death-fire around*), 2583.
— 3) *to throw upon :* inf. he hine
eft ongan wäteres (instr. gen.)
weorpan (*began to cast water upon
him again*), 2792.

for-weorpan, w. acc., *to cast away,
squander :* subj. pret. þät he genunga gûð-gewædu wrâðe for-
wurpe (*that he squandered useless-
ly the battle-weeds*, i.e. gave them
to the unworthy), 2873.

ofer-weorpan, *to stumble :* pret.
sg. ofer-wearp þâ ... wigena
strengest, 1544.

weotian, w. v., *to provide with, ad-
just(?):* pret. part. acc. pl. wäl-
bende weotode, 1937.

be-weotian, **be-witian**, w. v. w.
acc., *to regard, observe, care for :*
pres. pl. III. be-witiað, 1136; pret.
sg. þegn ... se þe ... ealle beweotede þegnes þearfe (*who would
attend to all the needs of a thane*),
1797; draca se þe ... hord beweotode (*the drake that guarded a
treasure*), 2213; — *to carry out,
undertake :* pres. pl. III. þâ ... oft
bewitigað sorh-fulne sîð on segl-
râde, 1429.

wicg, st. n., *steed, riding-horse :*
nom. sg., 1401; acc. sg. wicg, 315;
dat. instr. sg. wicge, 234; on wicge,
286; acc. pl. wicg, 2175; gen. pl.
wicga, 1046.

ge-widor, st. n., *storm, tempest :*
acc. pl. lâð ge-widru (*loathly
weather*), 1376.

wið, prep. w. dat. and acc., *with
fundamental meanings of division
and opposition :* 1) w. dat., *against,
with*(in hostile sense), *from :* þâ wið

gode wunnon, 113; âna (wan) wið
eallum, 145; ymb feorh sacan, lâð
wið lâðum, 440; so, 426, 439, 550,
2372, 2521, 2522, 2561, 2840, 3005;
þät him holt-wudu ... helpan ne
meahte, lind wið lige, 2342; hwät
... sêlest wære wið fær-gryrum tô
ge-fremmanne, 174; þät him gâst-
bona geóce gefremede wið þeód-
þreáum, 178; wið rihte wan (*strove
against right*), 144; häfde ... sele
Hróðgâres ge-nered wið niðe (*had
saved H.'s hall from strife*), 828;
(him dyrne langað...) beorn wið
blôde (*the hero longeth secretly
contrary to his blood*, i.e. H. feels
a secret longing for the non-re-
lated Beówulf), 1881; sundur gedælan lîf wið lice (*to sunder soul
from body*), 2424; streámas wundon sund wið sande (*the currents
rolled the sea against the sand*),
213; lîg-ýðum forborn bord wið
ronde (rond, MS.) (*with waves of
flame burnt the shield against, as
far as, the rim*), 2674; holm
storme weól, won wið winde (*the
sea surged, wrestled with the wind*),
1133; so, hiora in ânum weóll sefa
wið sorgum (*in one of them surged
the soul with sorrow* [*against*?,
Heyne]), 2601; þät hire wið
healse heard grâpode (*that the
sharp sword bit against her neck*),
1567. — 2) w. acc.: a) *against,
towards:* wan wið Hróðgâr (*fought
against H.*), 152; wið feónda gehwone, 294; wið wrâð werod, 319;
so, 540, 1998, 2535; hine hâlig
god ûs on-sende wið Grendles
gryre, 384; þät ic wið þone gûðflogan gylp ofer-sitte (*that I refrain from boastful speech against
the battle-flier*), 2529; ne wolde
wið manna ge-hwone ... feorh-

bealo feorran (*would not cease his
life-plotting against any of the
men;* or, *withdraw life-bale from,*
etc.? or, *peace would not have with
any man ..., mortal bale withdraw?,* Kemble), 155; ic þâ leóde
wât ge wið feónd ge wið freónd
fäste geworhte (*towards foe and
friend*), 1865; heóld heáh-lufan
wið häleða brego (*cherished high
love towards the prince of heroes*),
1955; wið ord and wið ecge in-
gang forstôd (*prevented entrance
to spear-point and sword-edge*),
1550. b) *against, on, upon, in:*
setton side scyldas ... wið þäs recedes weal (*against the wall of
the hall*), 326; wið eorðan fäðm
(eardodon) (*in the bosom of the
earth*), 3050; wið earm ge-sät (*sat
on, against, his arm*), 750; so,
stîð-môd ge-stôd wið steápne rond,
2567; [wið duru healle eode]
(*went to the door of the hall*), 389;
wið Hrefna-wudu (*over against,
near, H.*), 2926; wið his sylfes
sunu setl ge-tæhte (*showed me to
a seat with, near, beside, his own
son*), 2014. c) *towards, with* (of
contracting parties): þät hie healfre
ge-weald wið eotena bearn âgan
môston (*that they power over half
the hall with the enemies'* (Jutes?)
sons were to possess), 1089; þenden he wið wulf wäl reáfode
(*whilst with the wolf he was robbing the slain*), 3028. — 3) Alter-
nately with dat. and acc., *against:*
nu wið Grendel sceal, wið þam
aglæcan, âna gehegan þing wið
þyrse, 424–426; — *with, beside:*
ge-sät þâ wið sylfne ..., mæg wið
mæge, 1978–79.

wiðer-gyld, st. n., *compensation:*
nom. sg., 2052, [proper name?].

wiðer-rähtes, adv., *opposite, in front of*, 3040.

wiðre, st. n., *resistance:* gen. sg. wiðres ne trûwode, 2954.

wig-weorðung, st. f., *idol-worship, idolatry, sacrifice to idols:* acc. pl. -weorðunga, 176.

wiht, st. f.: 1) *wight, creature, demon:* nom. sg. wiht unhælo (*the demon of destruction,* Grendel), 120; acc. sg. syllîcran wiht (the dragon), 3039. — 2) *thing, something, aught:* nom. sg. w. negative, ne hine wiht dweleð (*nor does aught check him*), 1736; him wiht ne speów (*it helped him naught*), 2855; acc. sg. ne him ðæs wyrmes wig for wiht dyde (*nor did he count the worm's warring for aught*), 2349; ne meahte ic ... wiht gewyrcean (*I could not do aught ...*), 1661; — w. partitive gen.: nô ... wiht swylcra searoniða, 581; — the acc. sg. – adv. like Germ. *nicht:* ne hie hûru wine-drihten wiht ne lôgon (*did not blame their friendly lord aught*), 863; so, ne wiht – *naught, in no wise,* 1084, 2602, 2858; nô wiht, 541; instr. sg. wihte (*in aught, in any way*), 1992; ne ... wihte (*by no means*), 186, 2278, 2688; wihte ne, 1515, 1990, 2465, 2924. — Comp.: â-wiht (âht = *aught*), äl-wiht, ô-wiht.

wil-cuma, w. m., *one welcome* (qui gratus advenit): nom. pl. wil-cuman Denigea leódum (*welcome to the people of the Danes*), 388; so, him (the lord of the Danes) wil-cuman, 394; wil-cuman Wedera leódum (*welcome to the Geátas*), 1895.

ge-wild, st. f., *free-will?* dat. pl. nealles mid ge-weoldum (*sponte, voluntarily,* Bugge), 2223.

wil-deór (for wild-deór), st. n., *wild beast:* acc. pl. wil-deór, 1431.

wil-gesîð, st. m., *chosen* or *willing companion:* nom. pl. -ge-sîðas, 23.

wil-geofa, w. m., *ready giver* (= voti largitor: princely designation), *joy-giver?*: nom. sg. wil-geofa Wedra leóda, 2901.

willa, w. m.: 1) *will, wish, desire, sake:* nom. sg. 627, 825; acc. sg. willan, 636, 1740, 2308, 2410; instr. sg. ânes willan (*for the sake of one*), 3078; so, 2590; dat. sg. tô willan, 1187, 1712; instr. pl. willum (*according to wish*), 1822; sylfes wyllum, 2224, 2640; gen. pl. wilna, 1345. — 2) *desirable thing, valuable:* gen. pl. wilna, 661, 951.

willan, aux. v., *will:* in pres. also *shall* (when the future action is depend. on one's free will): pres. sg. I. wille ic â-secgan (*I will set forth, tell out*), 344; so, 351, 427; ic tô sæ wille (*I will to sea*), 318; wylle, 948, 2149, 2513; sg. II. þu wylt, 1853; sg. III. he wile, 346, 446, 1050, 1182, 1833; wyle, 2865; wille, 442, 1004, 1185, 1395; ær he in wille (*ere he will in,* i.e. go or flee into the fearful sea), 1372; wylle, 2767; pl. I. we ... wyllað, 1819; pret. sg. I., III. wolde, 68, 154, 200, 646, 665, 739, 756, 797, 881, etc.; nô ic fram him wolde (i.e. fleótan), 543; so, swâ he hira mâ wolde (i.e. â-cwellan), 1056; pret. pl. woldon, 482, 2637, 3173; subj. pret., 2730. — Forms contracted w. negative: pres. sg. I. nelle (= ne + wille, *I will not,* nolo), 680, 2525(?); pret. sg. III. nolde (= ne + wolde), 792, 804, 813, 1524; w. omitted inf. þâ metod. nolde, 707, 968; pret. subj. nolde, 2519.

wilnian, w. v., *to long for, beseech:* inf. wel biðð þám þe mót ... tô fáðer fáðmum freoðo wilnian (*well for him that may beseech protection in the Father's arms*), 188.

wil-sîð, st. m., *chosen journey:* acc. sg. wil-sîð, 216.

ge-win, st. n.: 1) *strife, struggle, enmity, conflict:* acc. sg., 878; þâ hie ge-win drugon (*endured strife*), 799; under ðða ge-win (*under the tumult of the waves*), 1470; gen. sg. þäs ge-winnes weorc (*misery for this strife*), 1722.— 2) *suffering, oppression:* nom. sg., 133, 191; acc. sg. eald ge-win, 1782.—Comp.: fyrn-, ðð-ge-win.

win-ärn, st. n., *hall of hospitality, hall (wine-hall?):* gen. sg. win-ärnes, 655.

wind, st. m., *wind, storm:* nom. sg., 547, 1375, 1908; dat. instr. sg. winde, 217; wið winde, 1133.

windan, st. v.: 1) intrans., *to wind, whirl:* pret. sg. wand tô wolcnum wäl-fŷra mæst, 1120.— 2) w. acc., *to twist, wind, curl:* pret. pl. streámas wundon sund wið sande, 212; pret. part. wunden gold (*twisted, spirally-twined, gold*), 1194, 3135; instr. pl. wundnum (wundum, MS.) golde, 1383.

ät-windan, *to wrest one's self from, escape:* pret. sg. se þám feónde ät-wand, 143.

be-windan, *to wind with or round, clasp, surround, envelop* (involvere): pret. sg. þe hit (the sword) mundum be-wand, 1462; pret. part. wîrum be-wunden (*wound with wires*), 1032; feorh ... flæsce be-wunden (*flesh-enclosed*), 2425; gâr ... mundum be-wunden (*a spear grasped with the hand*), 3023; iú-manna gold galdre be-

wunden (*spell-encircled gold*), 3053; (âstâh ...) lêg wôpe be-wunden (*uprose the flame mingled with a lament*), 3147.

ge-windan, *to writhe, get loose, escape.* inf. wîdre ge-windan (*to flee further*), 764; pret. sg. on fleám ge-wand, 1002.

on-windan, *to unwind, loosen:* pres. sg. (þonne fäder) on-windeð wäl-râpas, 1611.

win-däg, st. m., *day of struggle or suffering:* dat. pl. on þyssum win-dagum (*in these days of sorrow,* i.e. of earthly existence), 1063.

wind-bland (blond), st. n., *wind-roar:* nom. sg., 3147.

wind-gereste, f., *resting-place of the winds:* acc. sg., 2457.

windig, adj., *windy:* acc. pl. windige (weallas, nässas), 572, 1359; windige weallas (wind geard weallas, MS.), 1225.

wine, st. m., *friend, protector,* especially the *beloved ruler:* nom. sg. wine Scyldinga, leóf land-fruma (Scyld), 30; wine Scyldinga (Hrôðgâr), 148, 1184. As vocative: mîn wine, 2048; wine mîn, Beówulf (Hunferð), 457, 530, 1705; acc. sg. holdne wine (Hrôðgâr), 376; wine Deniga, Scyldinga, 350, 2027; dat. sg. wine Scyldinga, 170; gen. sg. wines (Beówulf), 3097; acc. pl. wine, 21; dat. pl. Denum eallum, winum Scyldinga, 1419; gen. pl. winigea leásum, 1665; winia bealdor, 2568.— Comp.: freá-, freó-, gold-, gûð-, mæg-wine.

wine-dryhten, st. m., (dominus amicus), *friendly lord, lord and friend:* acc. sg. wine-drihten, 863, 1605; wine-dryhten, 2723, 3177; dat. sg. wine-drihtne, 360.

wine-geómor, adj., *friend-mourn-ing:* nom. sg., 2240.

wine-leás, adj., *friendless:* dat. sg. wine-leásum, 2614.

wine-mæg, st. m., *dear kinsman:* nom. pl. wine-mágas, 65.

ge-winna, w. m., *striver, struggler, foe:* comp. cald-, caldor-gewinna.

winnan, st. v., *to struggle, fight:* pret. sg. III. wan âna wið eallum, 144; Grendel wan ... wið Hróð-gâr, 151 ; holm ... won wið winde (*the sea fought with the wind:* cf. wan wind endi water, Heliand, 2244), 1133; II. eart þu se Beó-wulf, se þe wið Brecan wunne, 506; pl. wið gode wunnon, 113; þær þâ graman wunnon (*where the foes fought*), 778.

win-reced, st. n., *friend-hall, guest-hall, house for entertaining guests* (*wine-hall?*) : acc. sg., 715, 994.

win-sele, st. n., the same (*wine-hall?*) : nom. sg., 772; acc. sg. win-sele, 696 (cf. Heliand Glossary, 369 [364]).

winter, st. m.: 1) *winter:* nom. sg., 1133, 1137; acc. sg. winter, 1129; gen. sg. wintres, 516. — 2) *year* (counted by winters): acc. pl. fîftig wintru (neut.), 2210; instr. pl. wintrum, 1725, 2115, 2278; gen. pl. wintra, 147, 264, 1928, 2279, 2734, 3051.

wintre, adj., *so many winters* (old) : in comp. syfan-wintre.

ge-wislîce, adv., *certainly, un-doubtedly:* superl. gewislîcost, 1351.

wist, st. f., fundamental meaning = *existentia*, hence : 1) *good condi-tion, happiness, abundance:* dat. sg. wunað he on wiste, 1736. — 2) *food, subsistence, booty:* dat. sg. þâ wäs äfter wiste wôp up â-hafen (*a cry was then uplifted after the*

meal, i.e. Grendel's meal of thirty men), 128.

wist-fyllo, st. f., *fulness* or *fill of food, rich meal:* gen. sg. wist-fylle, 735.

wit, st. n., (wit), *understanding:* nom. sg., 590. — Comp.: fyr-, in-wit.

ge-wit, st. n.: 1) *consciousness:* dat. sg. ge-weóld his ge-witte, 2704. — 2) *heart, breast:* dat. sg. fŷr unswîðor weóll (*the fire surged less strongly from the dragon's breast*), 2883.

wit, pers. pron. dual of we, *we two,* 535, 537, 539, 540, 544, 1187, etc. See une, uncer.

wita, weota, w. m., *counsellor, royal adviser:* pl., *the king's coun-cil of nobles:* nom. pl. witan, 779; gen. pl. witena, 157, 266, 937 ; weotena, 1099. — Comp.: fyrn-, rûn-wita.

witan, pret.-pres. v., *to wot, know:* 1) w. depend. clause : pres. sg. I., III. wât, 1332, 2657; ic on Hige-lâce wât þät he ... (*I know as to II., that he ...*), 1831; so, god wât on mec þät ... (*God knows of me, that ...*), 2651; sg. II. þu wâst, 272; weak pret. sg. I., III. wiste, 822; wisse, 2340, 2726; pl. wiston, 799, 1605 ; subj. pres. I. gif ic wiste, 2520. — 2) w. acc. and inf.: pres. sg. I. ic wât, 1864. — 3) w. object, predicative part. or adj.: pret. sg. III. tô þäs he win-reced ... gearwost wisse, fättum fâhne, 716; so, 1310; wiste þäm ahlæcan hilde ge-þinged, 647. — 4) w. acc., *to know:* inf. witan, 252, 288 ; pret. sg. wisse, 169 ; wiste his fingra ge-weald on grames grâpum, 765; pl. II. wisson, 246; wiston, 181.

nât = ne + wât, *I know not :* 1) elliptically with hwilc, indef. pronoun = *some or other :* sceaða ic nât hwilc. — 2) w. gen. and depend. clause: nât he þâra gôda, þät he me on-geán sleá, 682.

ge-witan, *to know, perceive :* inf. þäs þe hie gewis-lîcost ge-witan meahton, 1351.

be-witlan. See be-weotian.

witig, adj., *wise, sagacious :* nom. sg. witig god, 686, 1057 ; witig drihten (God),1555; wittig drihten, 1842.

ge-wittig, adj., *conscious :* nom. sg. 3095.

ge-wltnian, w. v., *to chastise, punish :* wommum gewitnad (*punished with plagues*), 3074.

wîc, st. n., *dwelling, house :* acc. sg. wîc, 822, 2590; —often in pl. because houses of nobles were complex : dat. wîcum, 1305, 1613, 3084; gen. wîca, 125, 1126.

ge-wîcan, st. v., *to soften, give way, yield* (here chiefly of swords): pret. sg. ge-wâc, 2578, 2630.

wîc-stede, st. m., *dwelling-place :* nom. sg. 2463; acc. sg. wîc-stede, 2608.

wîd, adj., *wide, extended :* 1) space : acc. sg. neut. ofer wîd wäter, 2474; gen. sg. wîdan rîces, 1860; acc. pl. wîde sîðas, waroðas, 878, 1966. — 2) temporal : acc. sg. wîdan feorh (acc. of time), 2015; dat. sg. tô wîdan feore, 934.

wîde, adv., *widely, afar,* 18, 74, 79, 266, 1404, 1589, 1900, etc.; wîde cûð (*widely, universally, known*), 2136, 2924 ; so, underne wîde, 2914; wîde geond eorðan (*over the whole earth, widely*), 3100 ; — modifier of superl.: wreccena wîde mærost (*the most famous of wan-*

derers, *exiles*), 899. — Compar. wîdre, 764.

wîd-cûð, adj., *widely known, very celebrated :* nom. sg. neut., 1257; acc. sg. m. wîd-cûðne man (Beówulf), 1490 ; wîd-cûðne weán, 1992; wîd-cûðes (Hrôðgâr), 1043.

wîde-ferhð, st. m., (*long life*), *great length of time :* acc. sg. as acc. of time : wîde-ferhð (*down to distant times, always*), 703, 938 ; ealne wîde-ferhð, 1223.

wîd-floga, w. m., *wide-flier* (of the dragon) : nom. sg., 2831; acc. sg. wîd-flogan, 2347.

wîd-scofen, pret. part., *wide-spread? causing fear far and wide ?* 937.

wîd-weg, st. m., *wide way, long journey :* acc. pl. wîd-wegas, 841, 1705.

wîf, st. n., *woman, lady, wife :* nom. sg. freó-lîc wîf (Queen Wealhþeów), 616 ; wîf un-hŷre (Grendel's mother), 2121; acc. sg. drihtlice wif (Finn's wife), 1159; instr. sg. mid þŷ wîfe (Hrôðgâr's daughter, Freáware), 2029; dat. sg. þam wîfe (Wealhþeów), 640; gen. sg. wîfes (as opposed to *man*), 1285; gen. pl. wera and wîfa, 994. — Comp. : aglæc-, mere-wîf.

wîf-lufe, w. f., *wife-love, love for a wife, woman's love :* nom. pl. wîf-lufan, 2066.

wîg, st. m.: 1) *war, battle :* nom. sg., 23, 1081, 2317, 2873; acc. sg., 686, 1084, 1248 ; dat. sg. wîge, 1338, 2630; as instr.,1085: (wigge, MS.), 1657, 1771 ; gen. sg. wîges, 65, 887, 1269. — 2) *valor, warlike prowess :* nom. sg. wäs his môd-sefa manegum ge-cŷðed, wîg and wîsdôm, 350; wîg, 1043; wîg . . . eafoð and ellen, 2349: gen. sg. wîges, 2324. — Comp. fêðe-wîg.

wîga, w. m., *warrior, fighter :* nom. sg., 630; dat. pl. wigum, 2396; gen. pl. wigena, 1544, 1560, 3116. — Comp.: äsc-, byrn-, gâr-, gûð-, lind-, rand-, scyld-wiga.

wîgan, st. v., *to fight :* pres. sg. III. wigeð, 600; inf., 2510.

wîgend, pres. part., *fighter, warrior :* nom. sg., 3100 ; nom. pl. wigend, 1126, 1815, 3145; acc. pl. wigend, 3025; gen. pl. wigendra, 429, 900, 1973, 2338.— Comp. gâr-wigend.

wîg-bealu, st. n., *war-bale, evil contest :* acc. sg., 2047.

wîg-bil, st. n., *war-bill, battle-sword:* nom. sg., 1608.

wîg-bord, st. n., *war-board* or *shield :* acc. sg., 2340.

wîg-cräft, st. m., *war-power :* acc. sg., 2954.

wîg-eräftig, adj., *vigorous in fight, strong in war :* acc. sg. wig-cräftigne (of the sword Hrunting), 1812.

wîg-freca, w. m., *war-wolf, war-hero :* acc. sg. wig-frecan, 2497; nom. pl. wig-frecan, 1213.

wîg-fruma, w. m., *war-chief* or *king :* nom. sg., 665; acc. sg. wig-fruman, 2262.

wîg-geatwe, st. f. pl., *war-ornaments, war-gear :* dat. pl. on wig-geatwum (-getawum, MS.), 368.

wîg-ge-weorðad, pret. part., *war-honored, distinguished in war,* 1784.

wîg-gryre, st. m., *war-horror* or *terror :* nom. sg., 1285.

wîg-hete, st. m., *war-hate, hostility :* nom. sg., 2121.

wîg-heafola, w. m., *war head-piece, helmet :* acc. sg. wig-heafolan, 2662. — Leo.

wîg-heáp, st. m., *war-band :* nom. sg., 447.

wîg-hryre, st. m., *war-ruin, slaughter, carnage :* acc. sg., 1620.

wîg-sigor, st. m., *war-victory :* acc. sg., 1555.

wîg-sped, st. f.?, *war-speed, success in war :* gen. pl. wig-spêda, 698.

wîn, st. n., *wine :* acc. sg., 1163, 1234; instr. wine, 1468.

wîr, st. n., *wire, spiral ornament of wire :* instr. pl. wirum, 1032; gen. pl. wira, 2414.

wîs, adj., *wise, experienced, discreet :* nom. sg. m. wis (*in his mind, conscious*), 3095; f. wis, 1928; in w. form, se wisa, 1401, 1699, 2330; acc. sg. þone wisan, 1319; gen. pl. wisra, 1414; w. gen. nom. sg. wis wordcwida (*wise of speech*), 1846.

wîsa, w. m., *guide, leader :* nom. sg. werodes wisa, 259.—Comp.: brim-, here-, hilde-wisa.

wîsete. See wŷscan.

wîs-dôm, st. m., *wisdom, experience :* nom. sg., 350; instr. sg. wisdôme, 1960.

wîse, w. f., *fashion, wise, custom :* acc. sg. (instr.) ealde wisan (*after ancient custom*), 1866.

wîs-fäst, adj., *wise, sagacious* (sapientiâ firmus) : nom. sg. f., 627.

wîs-hycgende, pres. part., *wise-thinking, wise,* 2717.

wîsian, w. v., *to guide* or *lead to, direct, point out :* 1) w. acc.: inf. heán wong wisian, 2410; pret. sg. secg wisade land-gemyrcu, 208. — 2) w. dat.: pres. sg. I. ic eów wisige (*I shall guide you*), 292, 3104; pret. sg. se þæm heaðorincum hider wisade, 370; sôna him sele-þegn ... forð wisade (*the hall-thane led him thither forthwith,* i.e. to his couch), 1796; stig

wîsode gumum ät-gädere, 320; so,
1664. — 3) w. prep.?: pret. sg. þâ
secg wîsode under Heorotes hrôf
(*when the warrior showed them
the way under Heorot's ro f*, [but
under II.'s hrôf depends rather on
snyredon âtsomne]', 402.

wîtan, st. v., properly *to look at; to
look at with censure, to blame, re-
proach, accuse*, w. dat. of pers. and
acc. of thing: inf. for-þam me
wîtan ne þearf waldend fira morðor-bealo mâga, 2742.

ät-wîtan, *to blame, censure* (cf.
'twit), w. acc. of thing: pret. pl.
ät-witon weána dæl, 1151.

ge-wîtan, properly *spectáre ali-
quo; to go* (most general verb of
motion): 1) with inf. after verbs
of motion: pret. sg. þanon eft gewât ... tô hâm faran, 123; so,
2570; pl. þanon eft gewiton ...
mearum rîdan, 854. Sometimes
with reflex. dat.: pres. sg. him þâ
Scyld ge-wât ... fêran on freán
wäre, 26; gewât him ... rîdan,
234; so, 1964; pl. ge-witon, 301.
— 2 associated with general infin-
itives of motion and aim: imper. pl.
ge-wîtað forð beran wæpen and
gewædu, 291; pret. sg. ge-wât þâ
neósian heán hûses, 115; he þâ
fâg ge-wât ... man-dreám fleón,
1264; nyðer eft gewât dennes niósian, 3045; so, 1275, 2402, 2820.
So, with reflex. dat.: him eft gewât ... hâmes niósan, 2388; so,
2950; pl.ge-witon.1126.— 3) without inf. and with prep. or adv.:
pres. sg. III. þær firgen-streám
under nässa genipu niðer ge-wîteð,
1361; ge-wîteð on sealman, 2461;
inf. on flôdes æht feor ge-wîtan,
42; pret. sg. ge-wât, 217; him gewât, 1237, 1904; of lîfe, ealdre

ge-wât (*died*), 2472, 2625; fyrst
forð ge-wât (*time went on*), 210;
him ge-wât ût of healle, 663; gewât him hâm, 1602; pret. part. dat.
sg. me forð ge-witenum (*me de-
functo, I dead*), 1480.

ôð-wîtan, *to blame, censure, re-
proach:* inf. ne þorfte him þâ leán
ôð-wîtan man on middan-gearde,
2996.

wlanc, wlonc, adj., *proud, exulting:* nom. sg. wlanc, 341; w. instr.
æse wlanc (*proud of, exulting in,
her prey, meal*), 1333; wlonc,
331; w. gen. mâðm-æhta wlonc
(*proud of the treasures*), 2834;
gen. sg. wlonces, 2954. — Comp.
guld-wlanc.

wlâtian, w. v., *to look* or *gaze out,
forth:* pret. sg. se þe ær ... feor
wlâtode, 1917.

wlenco, st. f., *pride, heroism:* dat.
sg. wlenco, 338, 1207; wlence, 508.

wlite, st. m., *form, noble form, look,
beauty:* nom. sg., 250.

wlite-beorht, adj., *beauteous, brilliant in aspect:* acc. sg. wlite-
beorhtne wang, 93.

wlite-seón, st. n., *sight, spectacle:*
acc. sg., 1651.

wlitig, adj., *beautiful, glorious, fair
in form:* acc. sg. wlitig (sweord),
1663.

wlîtan, st. v., *to see, look, gaze:* pret.
sg. he äfter recede wlât (*looked
along the hall*), 1573; pret. pl.
on holm wliton (*looked on the sea*),
1593; wlitan on Wîglâf, 2853.

geond-wlîtan, w. acc., *to examine, look through, scan:* inf. wräte
giond-wlîtan, 2772.

woh-bogen, þret. part., (*bent
crooked*), *crooked, twisted:* nom.
sg. wyrm woh-bogen, 2828.

wolcen, st. n., *cloud* (cf. welkin):

dat. pl. under wolcnum (*under the clouds, on earth*), 8, 052, 715, 1771; tô wolcnum, 1120, 1375.

wollen-teár, adj., *tear-flowing, with flowing tears:* nom. pl. wollen-teáre, 3033.

wom. See **wam.**

won. See **wan.**

wore. See **weore.**

word, st. n.: 1) *word, speech :* nom. sg., 2818; acc. sg. þät word, 655, 2047; word, 315, 341, 390, 871, 2552; instr. sg. worde, 2157; gen. sg. wordes, 2792; nom. pl. þâ word, 640; word, 613; acc. pl. word (of an alliterative song), 871; instr. pl. wordum, 176, 366, 627, 875, 1101, 1173, 1194, 1319, 1812, etc.; ge-saga him wordum (*tell them in words, expressly*), 388. The instr. wordum accompanies biddan, þancian, be-wäg-nan, secgan, hêrgan, to empha-size the verb, 176, 627, 1194, 2796, 3177; gen. pl. worda, 289, 398, 2247, 2263(?), 3031. — 2) *command, order ·* gen. sg. his wordes geweald habban (*to rule, reign*), 79; so, instr. pl. wordum weóld, 30. — Comp.: beót-, gylp-, meðel-, þryð-word.

word-cwide, st. m., (*word-utter-ance·, speech:* acc. pl. word-cwy-das, 1842; dat. pl. word-cwydum, 2754; gen. pl. word-cwida, 1846.

word-gid, st. m., *speech, saying:* acc. sg. word-gyd, 3174.

word-hord, st. n., *word-hoard, treasury of speech, mouth :* acc. sg. word-hord on-leác (*unlocked his word-hoard*, opened his mouth, spoke), 259.

word-riht, st. n., *right speech, suit-able word:* gen. pl. Wîglâf maðe-lode word-rihta fela, 2632.

worð-mynd. See **weorð-mynd.**

worðig (for **weorðig**), st. m., *pal-ace, estate, court:* acc. sg. on wor-ðig (*into the palace*), 1973.

worn, st. n., *multitude, number:* acc. sg. worn eall (*very many*), 3095; wintra worn (*many years*), 264; þonne he wintrum frôd worn ge-munde (*when he old in years thought of their number*), 2115. Used with fela to strengthen the meaning: nom. acc. sg. worn fela, 1784; hwät þu worn fela...spræce (*how very much thou hast spoken!*), 530; so, eal-fela eald-gesegena worn, 871; gen. pl. worna fela, 2004, 2543.

woruld, worold, st. f., *humanity, world, earth :* nom. sg. eal worold, 1739; acc. sg. in werold (wacan) (*to be born, come into the world*), 60; worold oflætan, of-gifan (*die*), 1184, 1682; gen. sg. worolde, 951, 1081, 1388, 1733; worulde, 2344; his worulde ge-dâl (*his separation from the world, death*), 3069; worolde brûcan (*to enjoy life, live*), 1063; worlde, 2712.

woruld-âr, st. f., *worldly honor or dignity:* acc. sg. worold-âre, 17.

woruld-candel, st. f., *world-candle, sun :* nom. sg., 1966.

worold-cyning, st. m., *world-king, mighty king:* nom. sg., 3182; gen. pl. worold-cyninga, 1685.

woruld-ende, st. m., *world's end:* acc. sg., 3084.

worold-ræden, st. f., *usual course, fate of the world, customary fate:* dat. sg. worold-rædenne, 1143.

wôp, st. m., (*whoop*), *cry of grief, lament:* nom. sg., 128; acc. sg. wôp, 786; instr. sg. wôpe, 3147.

wracu, st. f., *persecution, vengeance, revenge:* nom. sg. wracu (MS.

uncertain), 2614; acc. sg. wräce, 2337. — Comp.: gyrn-, nýd-wracu.

wraðu, st. f., *protection, safety:* in comp. lîf-wraðu.

wrâð, adj., *wroth, furious, hostile:* acc. sg. neut. wrâð, 319; dat. sg. wrâðum, 661, 709; gen. pl. wrâðra, 1620.

wrâðe, adv., *contemptibly, disgracefully,* 2873.

wrâð-lîce, adv., *wrathfully, hostilely* (in battle), 3063.

wrâsn, st. f., *circlet of gold for the head, diadem, crown:* in comp. freâ-wrâsn.

wräc-lâst, st. m., *exile-step, exile, banishment:* acc. sg. wräc-lâstas träd (*trod exile-steps, wandered in exile*), 1353.

wräc-mäcg, st. m., *exile, outcast:* nom. pl. wräc-mäcgas, 2380.

wräc-sîð, st. m., *exile-journey, banishment, exile, persecution:* acc. sg., 2293; dat. sg. -sîðum, 338.

wrät, st. f., *ornament, jewel:* acc. pl. wräte (wräce, MS.), 2772, 3061; instr. pl. wrättum, 1532; gen. pl. wrätta, 2414.

wrät-lîc, adj.: 1) *artistic, ornamental; valuable:* acc. sg. wrätlîcne wundor - mâððum, 2174; wrät-lîc wäg-sweord, 1490; wîgbord wrät-lîc, 2340. — 2 *wondrous, strange:* acc. sg. wrät-lîcne wyrm [from its rings or spots?], 892; wlite-seón wrät-lîc, 1651.

wräc, st. f., *persecution:* hence, *wretchedness, misery:* nom. sg., 170; acc. sg. wrec, 3079.

wrecan, st. v. w. acc.: 1 *to press, force:* pret. part. þær wäs Ongenþeó . . . on bîd wrecen, 2963. — 2) *to drive out, expel:* pret. sg. ferh el'en wräc, 2707. — 3 *to wreak or utter:* gid, spel wrecan

(*to utter words or songs*); subj. pres. sg. III. he gyd wrece, 2447; inf. wrecan spel ge-râde, 874; wordgyd wrecan, 3174; pret. sg. gyd âfter wräc, 2155; pres. part. þâ wäs . . . gid wrecen, 1066. — 4) *to avenge, punish:* subj. pres. þät he his freónd wrece, 1386; inf. wolde hire mäg wrecan, 1340; so, 1279, 1547; pres. part. wrecend (*an avenger*), 1257; pret. sg. wräc Wedera nîð, 423; so, 1334, 1670.

â-wrecan, *to tell, recount:* pret. sg. ic þis gid he þe â-wräc (*I have told this tale for thee*), 1725; so, 2109.

for-wrecan, w. acc., *to drive away, expel: carry away:* inf. þý läs him ýða þrym wudu wyn-suman for-wrecan meahte (*lest the force of the waves might carry away the winsome ship*), 1920; pret. sg. he hine feor for-wräc . . . man-cynne fram, 109.

ge-wrecan, w. acc., *to avenge, wreak vengeance upon, punish:* pret. sg. ge-wräc, 107, 2006; he ge-wräc (i.e. hit, *this*) cealdum cear-sîðum, 2396; he hine sylfne ge-wräc (*avenged himself*), 2876; pl. ge-wräcan, 2480; pret. part. ge-wrecen, 3063.

wreccen, w. m., (*wretch*), *exile, adventurer, wandering soldier, hero:* nom. sg. wrecca Hengest, 1138; gen. pl. wreccena wîde märost (Sigemund), 899.

wreoðen-hilt, adj., *wreathen-hilted, with twisted hilt:* nom. sg., 1699.

wrîdian, w. v., *to flourish, spring up:* pret. sg. III. wridað, 1742.

wrîðu, w. m., *band:* in comp. beâg-wriða (*bracelet,*), 2019.

wrixl, st. n., *exchange, change:* instr. sg. wyrsan wrixle (*in a worse

way, with a worse exchange),
2970.

ge-wrixle, st. n., *exchange, ar-rangement, bargain :* nom. sg. ne
wäs þät ge-wrixle til (*it was not a good arrangement, trade*), 1305.

wrixlan, w. v., *to exchange :* inf.
wordum wrixlan (*to exchange words, converse*), 366; 875 (*tell*).

wríðan, st. v. w. acc.: 1) *to bind, fasten, wreathe together :* inf. ic
hine (him, MS.) . . . on wäl-bedde
wríðan þôhte, 965. — 2) *to bind up*
(a wounded person, a wound):
pret. pl. þâ wæron monige þe his
mæg wriðon, 2983. See hand-
▼ gewriðen.

wrîtan, st. v., *to incise, engrave :*
pret. part. on þäm (hilte) wäs ôr
writen fyrn-gewinnes (*on which was engraved the origin of an ancient struggle*), 1689.

for-wrîtan, *to cut to pieces* or *in two :* pret. sg. for-wrât Wedra helm
wyrm on middan, 2706.

wrôht, st. f., *blame, accusation, crime;* here *strife, contest, hostility :*
nom. sg., 2288, 2474, 2914.

wudu, st. m., *wood :* 1) *material, timber :* nom. pl. wudu, 1365;
hence, *the wooden spear :* acc. pl.
wudu, 398. — 2) *forest, wood :* acc.
sg. wudu, 1417. — 3) *wooden ship :*
nom. sg. 298; acc. sg. wudu, 216,
1920. — Comp.: bäl-, bord-, gamen-,
heal-, holt-, mägen-, sæ-, sund-,
þrec-wudu.

wudu-rêc, st. m., *wood-reek* or
smoke : nom. sg., 3145.

wuldor, st. n., *glory :* nom. sg.
kyninga wuldor (*God*), 666; gen.
sg. wuldres wealdend, 17, 183,
1753; wuldres hyrde, 932, (desig-
nations of God).

wuldor-cyning, st. m., *king of glory,*

God : dat. sg. wuldur-cyninge, 2796.

wuldor-torht, adj., *glory-bright, brilliant, clear :* nom. pl. wuldor-
torhtan weder, 1137.

wulf, st. m., *wolf :* acc. sg., 3028.

wulf-hlíð, st. n., *wolf-slope, wolf's retreat, slope whereunder wolves house :* acc. pl. wulf-hleoðu, 1359.

wund, st. f., *wound :* nom. sg., 2712,
2977; acc. sg. wunde, 2532, 2907;
dat. sg. wunde, 2726; instr. pl.
wundum, 1114, 2831, 2938. —
Comp. feorh-wund.

wund, adj., *wounded, sore :* nom.
sg., 2747; dat. sg. wundum, 2754;
nom. pl. wunde, 565, 1076.

wunden-feax, adj., *curly-haired*
(of a horse's mane): nom. sg., 1401.

wunden-heals, adj., *with twisted*
or *curved neck* or *prow :* nom. sg.
wudu wunden-hals (*the ship*), 298.

wunden-heorde?, *curly-haired?* :
nom. sg. f., 3153.

wunden-mæl, adj., *damascened, etched, with wavy ornaments*(?) :
nom. sg. neut., 1532 (of a sword).

wunden-stefna, w. m., *curved prow, ship :* nom. sg., 220.

wundor, st. n.: 1) *wonder, wonder-work :* nom. sg., 772,1725; wundur,
3063: acc. sg. wundor, 841; wun-
der, 932; wundur, 2760, 3083(?),
3104; dat. sg. wundre, 932; instr.
pl. wundrum (*wondrously*), 1453,
2688; gen. pl. wundra, 1608. —
2) *portent, monster :* gen. pl. wundra, 1510. — Comp.: hand-, níð-,
searo-wundor.

wundor-bebod, st. n., *wondrous command, strange order :* instr.
pl. -bebodum, 1748.

wundor-deáð, st. m., *wonder-death, strange death :* instr. sg. wundor
deáðe, 3038.

wundor-fät, st. n., *wonder-vat,*

strange vessel: dat. pl. of wundor-fatum (*from wondrous vessels*), 1163.

wundor-lîc, adj., *wonderlike, remarkable:* nom. sg., 1441.

wundor-mâðð̄um, st. m., *wonder-jewel, wonderful treasure:* acc. sg., 2174.

wundor-smið, st. m., *wonder-smith, skilled smith, worker of marvellous things:* gen. pl. wundor-smiða geweorc (the ancient giant's sword), 1682.

wundor - seón, st. f., *wondrous sight:* gen. pl. wunder-sióna, 996.

wunian, w. v.: 1) *to stand, exist, remain:* pres. sg. III. þenden þær wunað on heáh-stede hûsa sêlest (*as long as the best of houses stands there on the high place*), 284; wunað he on wiste (*lives in plenty*), 1736; inf. on sele wunian (*to remain in the hall*), 3129; pret. sg. wunode mid Finne (*remained with F.*), 1129. — 2) w. acc. or dat., *to dwell in, to inhabit, to possess:* pres. sg. III. wunað wäl-reste (*holds his death-bed*), 2903; inf. wäter-egesan wunian, cealde streámas, 1261; wîcum wunian, 3084; w. prep.: pres. sg. Higelâc þær ät hâm wunað, 1924.

ge-wunian, w. acc.: 1) *to inhabit:* inf. ge-[wunian], 2276. — 2) *to remain with, stand by:* subj. pres. þät hine on ylde eft ge-wunigen wil-ge-sîðas, 22.

wurðan. See weorðan.

wuton, v. from wîtan, used as interj., *let us go! up!* w. inf.: wutun gangan tô (*let us go to him!*), 2649; uton hraðe fêran! 1391; uton nu êfstan, 3102.

wylf, st. f., *she-wolf:* in comp. brim-wylf.

wylm, st. m., *surge, surf, billow:* nom. sg. flôdes wylm, 1765; dat. wintres wylme (*with winter's flood*), 516; acc. sg. þurh wäteres wylm, 1694; acc. pl. heortan wylmas, 2508.—Comp.: breóst-, brim-, byrne-, cear-, fŷr-, heaðo-, holm-, sæ-, sorh-wylm. See wälm.

wyn, st. f., *pleasantness, pleasure, joy, enjoyment:* acc. sg. mäste ... worolde wynne (*the highest earthly joy*), 1081; eorðan wynne (*earth-joy, the delightful earth*), 1731; heofenes wynne (*heaven's joy,* the rising sun), 1802; hearpan wynne (*harp-joy, the pleasant harp*), 2108; þät he ... ge-drogen häfde eorðan wynne (*that he had had his earthly joy*), 2728; dat. sg. weorod wäs on wynne, 2015; instr. pl. mägenes wynnum (*in joy of strength*), 1717; so, 1888.—Comp.: êðel-, hord-, lîf-, lyft-, symbel-wyn.

wyn-leás, adj., *joyless:* acc. sg. wyn-leásne wudu, 1417; wyn-leás wîc, 822.

wyn-sum, adj., *winsome, pleasant:* acc. sg. wudu wyn-suman (*the ship*), 1920; nom. pl. word wäron wyn-sume, 613.

wyrcan, v. irreg.: 1) *to do, effect,* w. acc.: inf. (wundor) wyrcan, 931. — 2) *to make, create,* w. acc.: pret. sg. þät se äl-mihtiga eorðan worh[te], 92; swâ hine (*the helmet*) worhte wäpna smið, 1453.— 3) *to gain, win, acquire,* w. gen.: subj. pres. wyrce, se þe môte, dômes ær deaðe, 1388.

be-wyrcan, *to gird, surround:* pret. pl. bronda betost wealle be-worhton, 3163.

ge-wyrcan: 1) intrans., *to act, behave:* inf. swâ sceal geong guma gôde gewyrcean ... on fäder wine, þät ... (*a young man shall so act with benefits towards his father's friends that* ...), 20. — 2) w. acc., *to do, make, effect, perform :* inf. ne meahte ic ät hilde mid Hruntinge wiht ge - wyrcan, 1661 ; sweorde ne meahte on þam aglæcan ... wunde ge-wyrcean, 2907 ; pret. sg. ge-worhte, 636, 1579, 2713; pret. part. acc. ic þâ leóde wât ... fäste ge-worhte. 1865. — 3) *to make, construct :* inf. (medoärn) ge-wyrcean, 69; (wîg-bord) ge-wyrcean, 2338 ; (hlæw) ge-wyrcean, 2803; pret. pl. II. ge-worhton, 3097; III. ge-worhton, 3158; pret. part. ge-worht, 1697. — 4) *to win, acquire :* pres. sg. ic me mid Hruntinge dôm ge-wyrce, 1492.

Wyrd, st. f., *Weird* (one of the Norns, guide of human destiny: mostly weakened down = *fate, providence*) : nom. sg., 455, 477, 572, 735, 1206, 2421, 2527, 2575, 2815; acc. sg. wyrd, 1057, 1234; gen. pl. wyrda, 3031. (Cf. *Weird Sisters of Macbeth*.)

wyrdan, w. v., *to ruin, kill, destroy :* pret. sg. he tô lange leóde mine wanode and wyrde, 1338.

â - wyrdan, w. v., *to destroy, kill :* pret. part. : äðeling monig wundum â-wyrded, 1114.

wyrðe, adj., *noble; worthy, honored, valued :* acc. sg. m. wyrðne (gedôn) (*to esteem worthy*), 2186 ; nom. pl. wyrðe, 368; compar. nom. sg. rîces wyrðra (*worthier of rule*), 862. — Comp. fyrd-wyrðe. See **weorð.**

wyrgen, st. f., *throttler* [cf. sphinx], *she-wolf :* in comp. grund-wyrgen.

ge - wyrht, st. n., *work; desert :* in comp. eald-gewyrht, 2658.

wyrm, st. m., *worm, dragon, drake :* nom. sg., 898, 2288, 2344, 2568, 2630, 2670, 2746, 2828; acc. sg. wyrm, 887, 892, 2706, 3040, 3133; dat. sg. wyrme, 2308, 2520; gen. wyrmes, 2317, 2349, 2760, 2772, 2903; acc. pl. wyrmas, 1431.

wyrm-cyn, st. m., *worm-kin, race of reptiles, dragons :* gen. sg. wyrmcynnes fela, 1426.

wyrm-fâh, adj., *dragon-ornamented, snake - adorned* (ornamented with figures of dragons, snakes, etc.: cf. Dietrich in Germania X., 278) : nom. sg. sweord ... wreoðen-hilt and wyrm-fâh, 1699.

wyrm-hord, st. n., *dragon-hoard :* gen. pl. wyrm-horda, 2223.

for-wyrnan, w. v., *to refuse, reject :* subj. pres. II. þät þu me nô for-wyrne, þät ... (*that thou refuse me not that* ...), 429; pret. sg. he ne for-wyrnde worold-rædenne, 1143.

ge - wyrpan, w. v. reflex., *to raise one's self, spring up :* pret. sg. he hyne ge-wyrpte, 2977.

wyrpe, st. m., *change :* acc. sg. äfter weá-spelle wyrpe ge-fremman (*after the woe-spell to bring about a change of things*), 1316.

wyrsa, compar. adj., *worse :* acc. sg. neut. þät wyrse, 1740; instr. sg. wyrsan wrixle, 2970; gen. sg. wyrsan geþinges, 525; nom. acc. pl. wyrsan wîg-frecan, 1213, 2497.

wyrt, st. f., [*-wort*], *root :* instr. pl. wudu wyrtum fäst, 1365.

wŷscan, w. v., *to wish, desire :* pret. sg. wîscte (rihde, MS.) þäs yldan (*wished to delay that* or *for this reason*), 2240.

Y

yfel, st. n., *evil :* gen. pl. yfla, 2095.

yldan, w. v., *to delay, put off :* inf. ne þæt se aglæca yldan þôhte, 740; weard wine-geômor wîscte þäs yldan, þät he lytel fäc long-gestreóna brûcan môste, 2240.

ylde, st. m. pl., *men :* dat. pl. yldum, 77, 706, 2118; gen. pl. ylda, 150, 606, 1062. See **elde**.

yldest. See **eald.**

yldo, st. f., *age (senectus), old age :* nom. sg., 1737, 1887; atol yldo, 1767; dat. sg. on ylde, 22. — 2) *age (aetas), time, era :* gen. sg. yldo bearn, 70. See **eldo.**

yldra. See **eald.**

ylf, st. f., *elf (incubus, alp)* : nom. pl. ylfe, 112.

ymb, prep. w. acc.: 1) local, *around, about, at, up n :* ymb hine (*around, with, him*), 399. With prep. postponed : hine ymb, 690; ymb brontne ford (*around the seas, on the high sea* . 568; ymb þâ gif-healle (*around the gift-hall, throne-hall*), 839; vmb þäs helmes hrôf (*around the helm's ro f, crown*), 1031. — 2) temporal, *about, after :* ymb ânuîd ôþres dôgores (*about the same time the next day*), 219; ymb âne niht (*after a night*), 135. — 3) causal, *about, on account of, for, owing to :* (frînan) ymb þinne sîð (*on account of, concerning?, thy journey* , 353; hwät þu ... ymb Brecan spræce (*hast spoken about B.*), 531; so, 1596, 3174; nâ ymb his lîf ceараð (*careth not f.r his life*), 1537; so, 450; ymb feorh sacan, 439; sundor-nytte beheóld ymb aldor Dena, 669; ymb sund (*about the swimming, the prize for swimming*), 507.

ymbe, I. prep. w. acc. — ymb: 1) local, 2884, 3171; hlæw oft ymbe hwearf (prep. postponed), 2297. 2) causal, 2071, 2619. — II. adv., *around :* him ... ymbe, 2598.

ymb-sittend, pres. part., *neighbor :* gen. pl. ymb-sittendra, 9.

ymbe-sittend, the same : nom. pl. ymbe-sittend, 1828; gen. pl. ymbe-sittendra, 2735.

yppe, w. f., *high seat, dais, throne :* dat. sg. eode ... tô yppan, 1816.

yrfe, st. n., *bequest, legacy :* nom. sg., 3052.

yrfe-lâf, st. f., *sword left as a bequest :* acc. sg. yrfe-lâfe, 1054; instr. sg. yrfe-lâfe, 1904.

yrfe-weard, st. m., *heir, son :* nom. sg., 2732; gen. sg. yrfe-weardes, 2454.

yrmðo, st. f., *misery, shame, wretchedness :* acc. sg. yrmðe, 1260, 2006.

yrre, st. n., *anger, ire, excitement :* acc. sg. godes yrre, 712; dat. sg. on yrre, 2093.

yrre, adj., *angry, irate, furious :* nom. sg. yrre oretta (Beówulf), 1533; þegn yrre (the same), 1576; gäst yrre (Grendel), 2074; nom. pl. yrre, 770. See **eorre.**

yrringa, adv., *angrily, fiercely*, 1566, 2965.

yrre-môd, adj., *wrathful-minded, wild :* nom. sg., 727.

ys, *he is.* See **wesan.**

Ŷ

ŷð (O.H.G. unda), st. f., *wave; sea :* nom. pl. ŷða, 548; acc. pl. ŷðe, 46, 1133, 1910; dat. pl. ŷðum, 210, 421, 534, 1438, 1908; ŷðum weallan (*to surge with waves*), 515, 2694; gen. pl. ŷða, 464, 849, 1209,

1470, 1919.—Comp: flôd-, lîg-, wäter-ýð.

ýðan, w. v., *to ravage, devastate, destroy:* pret. sg. ýðde eotena cyn, 421 (cf. iðende = *depopulating,* Bosworth, from Ælfric's Glossary; pret. ýðde, Wanderer, 85).

ýðe. See eáðe.

ýðe-lîce, adv., *easily:* ýðe-lîce he eft â-stôd (*he easily arose afterwards*), 1557.

ýð-gebland, st. n., *mingling or surging waters, water - tumult:* nom. sg. -geblond, 1374, 1594; nom. pl. -gebland, 1621.

ýð-gewin, st. n., *strife with the sea, wave-struggle, rushing of water:* dat. sg. ýð-gewinne, 2413; gen. sg. -gewinnes, 1435.

ýð-lâd, st. f., *water-journey, sea-voyage:* nom. pl. ýð-lâde, 228.

ýð-lâf, st. f., *water-leaving, what is left by the water (undarum reliquiae), shore:* dat. sg. be ýð-lâfe, 566.

ýð-lida, w. m., *wave-traverser, ship:* acc. sg. ýð-lidan, 198.

ýð-naca, w. m., *sea-boat:* acc. sg. [ýð-]nacan, 1904.

ýð-gesêne. See êð-gesŷne.

ŷwan, w. v. w. acc., *to show:* pret. sg. an-sŷn ŷwde (*showed itself, appeared*), 2835. See eáwan, eó-wan.

ge-ŷwan, w. acc. of thing, dat. of pers., *to lay before, offer:* inf., 2150.

GLOSSARY TO FINNSBURH.

âbrecan, st. v., *to shatter:* part. his byrne âbrocen wære (*his byrnie was shattered*).

ânyman, st. v., *to take, take away.*

bân-helm, st. m., *bone-helmet; skull,* [heald, Bosw.].

buruh-þelu, st. f., *castle-floor.*

cêlod, part. (adj.?), *keeled,* i.e. boat-shaped or hollow.

dagian, w. v., *to dawn:* ne þis ne dagiað eástan (*this is not dawning from the east*).

deór-môd, adj., *brave in mood:* deór-môd hæleð.

driht-gesîð, st. m., *companion, associate.*

eástan, adv., *from the east.*

eorð-bûend, st. m., *earth-dweller, man.*

fêr, st. m., *fear, terror.*

fŷren, adj., *flaming, afire:* nom. f. swylce eal Finns - buruh fŷrenu wære (*as if all Finnsburh were afire*).

gehlyn, st. n., *noise, tumult.*

gellan, st. v., *to sing* (i.e. ring or resound): pres. sg. gylleð græg-hama (*the gray garment* [byrnie] *rings*).

genesan, st. v., *to survive, recover from:* pret. pl. þâ wîgend hyra wunda genæson (*the warriors were recovering from their wounds*).

gold-hladen, adj., *laden with gold* (wearing heavy gold ornaments).

græg-hama, w. m., *gray garment, mail-coat.*

gûð-wudu, st. m., *war-wood, spear.*

hāg-steald, st. m., *one who lives in his lord's house, a house-carl.*

heaðo-geong, adj., *young in war.*

here-sceorp, st. n., *war-dress, coat of mail.*

hleoðrian, w. v., *to speak, exclaim :* pret. sg. hleoðrode . . . cyning (*the prince exclaimed*).

hræw, st. n., *corpse.*

hrŏr, adj., *strong :* here-sceorpum hrŏr (*strong* [though it was] *as armor,* Bosw.).

lac (laŏ?)?.

oneweðan, st. v., *to answer :* pres. sg. scyld scefte oncwyŏ (*the shield answers the spear*).

onwaenian, w. v., *to awake, arouse one's self :* imper. pl. onwacnigeaŏ . . ., wîgend mîne (*awake, my warriors !*).

sceft (sceaft), st. m., *spear, shaft.*

sealo-brûn, adj., *dusky-brown.*

sige-beorn, st. m., *victorious hero, valiant warrior.*

swäðer (swâ hwâðer), pron., *which of two, which.*

swûn, st. m., *swain, youth ; warrior.*

sweart, adj., *swart, black.*

swêt, adj., *sweet :* acc. m. swêtne medo . . . forgyldan (*requite the sweet mead,* i.e. repay, by prowess in battle, the bounty of their chief).

swurd-leóma, w. m., *sword-flame, flashing of swords.*

þyrl, adj., *pierced, cloven.*

undearninga, adv., *without concealment, openly.*

wandrian, w. v., *to fly about, hover :* pret. sg. hräfn wandrode (*the raven hovered*).

waðol, st. m., *the full moon* [Grein]; [adj., *wandering,* Bosw.].

wäl-sliht (-sleaht), st. m., *combat, deadly struggle :* gen. pl. wälslihta gehlyn (*the din of combats*).

weâ-dæd, st. f., *deed of woe :* nom. pl. ârisaŏ weâ-dæda.

witian (weotian), w. v., *to appoint, determine :* part. þe is . . . witod.

wurðlice (weorðlice), adv., *worthily, gallantly :* compar. wurŏ-lîcor.

CORRECTIONS AND ADDITIONS.

LIST OF NAMES.

Eeg-þeów, end, for *arranges the strife*, read *terminates the strife*.

Heaðo-ræmas, for *reaches Breca*, read *reached by Breca*.

GLOSSARY.

UNDER

aglæca read æglæca for äglæca, and eikileihhi for egileihhi; insert (?) after *trouble*.

an-drisno, omit parenthesis (fr. rîsan, etc.).

aglæc-wif, read *demon in the form of woman* for *demoniacal*, etc.

an-sund, add anforht (after and-wlita) adj., *timid:* acc. pl., 444. —Kluge (see "List of Recent Readings").

an-wealda, add = *sole ruler?*

an-wealda, add anwîg-gearn (after an-walda): adj., *ready for single combat*, nom. pl., 1248 (see "List of Recent Readings").

ædre, read ædre; äled, read æled, and put O.N. for O.H.G.; same under äl-fylce.

äppel-fealu, for *dappled*, etc., read *apple-fallow*, or *apple-yellow:* *apple-yellow steeds*, 2166.

ge-æhtan, ge-æhtla read ge-æhtan, etc.

ærest, ... 2) *history, origin:* omit parenthesis, and read *that I its history should tell thee*, 2158.

bædan and bæl, for O.H.G. read O.N.

ge-bæran, in first citation, for *troop bore itself* read *people bore themselves*, 1013.

ät-beran, add, at the end, *to bear away*, 2128.

ge-beran, at the end, for *better born* read *born of the better*, 1704.

brand, broud, translate second citation *could not burn him with fire*, 2127.

bregdan, l. 1617, broden-mæl is now regarded as a comp'd noun = *inlaid or damasceened sword.*— Wülker, Holder, etc.

breme, read brême.

bringan, in first citation, for *thousand* read *thousands of.*

broðor, insert broden-mæl: st. n., *inlaid or damasceened sword:* nom. sg., 1617.

brûn, add *brown.*

brûn-ecg, add *brown-edged.*

brûn-fâg, add *brown-hued.*

bûan, insert bûan after onfunde in first citation.

bunden-stefna, for *stern* read *prow.*

burh-loca, add *city-lock.*

cuman and its comp'ds read côm, cwôm, etc., in pret.

däg-hwîl, for *day-time* read *day's time;* "days," lifetime.

dæd-hâta, add *instigator;* dæd-hwata. — Kluge.

deâð-scûn, for *death bringing, ghostly being,* read *death shadow, deadly being.*

deúgan, add *to dye.* — Thorpe (see " List," etc.).

dol-gilp, omit second definition, and read *idle boasting.*

dôn, add "reduplicated v."

drincan, druncne dryhtguman, "*joyous from, elate with, wine.*" — Sievers.

ge-drûg, add *tumult.*

dreógan, second citation (15), read "*For God had seen the dire need which the rulerless ones before endured.*" — Sievers.

dryht-lic, omit parenthesis, and read *lordly.*

dryht-scipe, for *warrior-ship* read *lord-ship.*

dugan, pret pres. v.

durran, in first citation, for *expect* read *await.*

eges-full, for *terribleness* read *fear.*

egslan, add *to terrify.*

eald-fäder, for *father who lived long ago* read *ancestor.*

eâ-land, add *island.*

eolet, add *voyage*(?), *hasty journey*(?). — Groschopp. — Grein.

faroð, add *shore.*

fäs, for(?), read *terror, dread.*

fäder-âðelo, add *father's honors.*

fâted, etc., read fæted, etc.

fäs, omit (?), and read *horror, dread.*

felgan, at the end, for *to come to any place, to arrive,* read *to fall into.* — Cosijn reads feulh fleah.

feor-cýð, at the end, instead of *for him is it better,* etc., read *for him are far countries better* (when) *sought.*

flâ, add *barb.*

findan, add = **impetrare.** — Cosijn.

folc-riht, add *folk-right.*

folc-scearu, add *folk-share.*

freme, read fremu = frêcnu. — Cosijn.

freene, add 1933.

freoðo-webbe, add *peace-weaver.*

frignan and its compounds mark û in pret.

fûs, add *furnished with.*

â-fyllan should stand before. **ge-fyllan.**

full-gangan, at the end, for *followed the arrow, did as the arrow,* read *followed the barb*(?).

gâr-holt, omit *forest of spears,* etc., read *spear-shaft.*

gâst, gist, gyst, for *stranger* read *demon.*

gê, pron., for ge, etc. ⎫ to be placed
gên, ⎬ after getuu.
gêna, ⎭

geato-lic, add *ready, agile.*

be-gête, for *to find, to attain,* read *attainable.*

ät-gifan (after â-gifan), *to render, to afford:* inf., 2879.

gold-mâðm, for *jewel* read *treasure.*

gryn, add *sorrow.*

hand-sper, read hand-sporu = *claw, hand-spur.*

hâta, for *persecutor* read *ruler.*

häft-mêce, for *sword with fetters* read *sword with hilt.*

hêrian, read herian, and place after herg.

he read hê, and place after hete-þanc.

heard-ecg, add acc. sg., 1491.

ge-hegan, read ge-hêgan, and place after hêdan; omit O.H.G. hagjan.

heaf, add (haef, Sievers), heafu, 1863 (Kluge).

heard-ecg, for *sharp sword* read *hard-edged,* and for st. f. read adj.: acc. sg., 1491.

healfor, for *putrid or festering blood* read *gore, blood.*

hild, in citation 2917, for *through* read *in.*

heals-beah, add dat. (?), 1215. — Cosijn.

heals-gebedde, read -a, w. m. f.

heáðu, Kluge reads **heafu** (pl. of **heaf,** *sea*); **hæf.** — Sievers.

hóp, read **hop;** so in compounds of hop.

hrädlíce, for *hasty, quick, imme-date,* read *hastily, quickly, imme-diately.*

hreðer, read **hreðer,** and add in third line from top of p. 213, on hréðre, 1746.

hring-íren, add *ring-mail!*

hruse, read **hrûse.**

ge-lafian, read *cheer* for *lave.*

lässa, read **læssa.**

let(?), insert (?) after *sojourn.* Groschopp omits **let** as a separate word.

leoðo-cräft, add *skill.*

leód (*people*), put 24 before 362, and omit 24 before 192 (acc.).

for-leósan, add *destroy.*

limpan, read *happen* for *succeed.*

lig, add n.

lóca, read **loca.**

lof, add n.

lufa, add (?); and after card-lufa(?).

lyft-wyn, add after *of, or in,* etc.

lyt-hwon, read **lyt-hwôn** (neut.).

má, omit adv.

mæst, add (7th line) subs.

medu, add **meodu.**

medu-scene, read *mead-pourer* for *mead-can,* etc.

medo-setl, read *mead-hall* for *mead-seat,* etc.

meðel, read *council, assembly,* for *speech,* etc.

môd-ge-þanc, add m.

môr-hóp, read **môr-hop.**

myndian, ge-myndian, read **myndgian,** etc.

myrð, read *sorrow* for *joy,* etc.

naca, add nom. sg, 1897.

nefne, read ne-gif-ne for (ni-iba-ni).

ge-nearwian, add adj. = infensus?

neáh : 2), add, after 2871, prep.

neód, add *zeal, desire.*

neód-laðu, add 1321 = **neádlaðu[m]** = *deadly hostility?* — Cosijn.

nið-wundor, read **nið-,** and add *wonder of the sea.*

nose, read **nôse.**

rand, add *edge of shield.*

ræden, add 51(?) (see "List").

reced, add m.

ge-rûm-líce, read *abundantly, far, afar,* for *commodiously,* etc.

sæl, read **sêle-rædende** = *hall-pos-sessors.* — Sievers.

on-sælan, read sige-hreðsecgum = *loose the restraints of etiquette,* before *disclose thy views to, the vic-torious heroes.* — Kluge.

scadu, for m. read f.? n. pl.?

seawa, read *spy* for *observer;* scaða? — Cosijn.

scenc, read *cup-bearer* for *vessel,* etc.

scerwen, read part. of scerwan, *to waste, squander.*

scóp, read **scop.**

se, read **sê** (þæm, etc.).

segn, add m.

sele-rædend, omit *guardian* or.

sele-rest, add *rest.*

sendan, read *to despatch* (a meal). — Bright.

sige-hrêð, read sige-hrêðsecg(?), *victorious hero.* — Kluge.

sið, real *arrival* for *journey;* (?) after 501 and 353.

snotor-lice, add *-ly.*

springan, add ät-springan, *to spring forth, arise:* pret sg ät-spranc, 1122.

ät-springan, the references belong to ge-springan.

stän fäh, add (?) after *colors* and *tines.*

stigan, omit *up,* and read *walk* for *ascend,* and *walked* for *plunged.*

strädan, read stridan(?), stride(?), 3074. — Sievers; and omit stræde, etc.

strengo, add st. m.; and (?) before strengum.

twegen, add m.

tweone should be treated under be as a separable prep.

þeód-þreá, add m.

þinglan, add *intercede for, ask pardon for.*

þollan, 4th line, read pret. for instr.

þrag, read þrâg (also in comp'ds).

þreá, add m.

þritig, read þritig.

þryð-swyð, read þrÿð-swÿð(?).

þryð-word, read nom. for acc.

þu, read þû, þê.

un-forht, un-forht *timid,* 444. — Kluge.

un-hâr, read *bald.*

un-hlytme, add for un-flitme = *with whom none can contend.*

un-snytiru, add st.

un-wearnum, read *irresistibly* for *unresistingly.*

up, read ûp.

wag, read wâg.

wurian, 1206, read fârode, *to ravage?* — Wülker. hergode?

wäd, read nom. pl. for acc.

wäl-fyllo, add st.

we, read wê

werian, add w. v.

werig, read wêrig.

wêsten, add st.

weaxan, add *to eat* (= vescor? — Cosijn)? 3116.

weorð-mynd, add n.

wîg-weorðung, read acc. pl. for nom.

winter, add n.

witan, omit 1605.

wîde-ferð, add n.

wîg-ge-weorðad, read wigge-[ge-]weorðad. — Cosijn.

wlite-seón, add f.

wolcen, add m.

wreccon, 5th line, read e[a]llne for ellen. — Kluge.

wróht, add m.

ge-wyrpan, read *to recover, get well,* for *to raise,* etc.

wÿscan, add 1605. — Cosijn.

TEXT.

---—◆—---

SOME RECENT READINGS AND SUGGESTIONS.

l.l⸱⸱

15, þâ (acc. f.) for þät. — (Bouterwek) Sievers.

31, læn-dagas for lange. — Kluge.

51, sele-rædende. — Kemble and Cosijn.

106, destroy period, and read in Caines, etc., with þonne .. drihten in parenthesis. — Sievers.

120, wera[s]. — Sievers. unfælo. — Rieger.

146, destroy period after sêlest, put wäs . . . micel in parenthesis, and insert colon after tîd. — Sievers.

159, ac se for atol. — Rieger.

240, supply hringed-stefnan for helmas bæron. — Wülker.

254, supply comma after feorbûend. — Sievers.

259, supply comma after wîsa. — Sievers.

280, edwenden for edwendan. — Bugge.

322, comma after seîr. — Sievers.

443, gold- for gûð-sele. — Bugge.

444, anforhte (timid) for un-. — Kluge.

447, colon after nimeð. — Sievers.

489, destroy comma after meoto, and read sige-hrêðseegum. — Kluge.

499, [H]unferð. — Rieger (on account of alliteration).

516, wylmum. — Kluge.

524, Breáhstânes. — Bugge.

525, geþinges. — Rieger.

574, swâ þær for hwäðere. — Bugge.

586, supply gefllites before þäs, and blend the two broken lines. — Kluge.

648, supply period after geþinged. — Kluge.

695, read hiera after þät. — Kluge.

723, [ge]hrân. — Zupitza.

759, modega for gôda. — Rieger (alliteration).

851, destroy semicolon after weól, and read deóp for deóg. — Sievers.

898, hâte. — Scherer.

901, âron = ârum þâh. — Cosijn.

992, hroden for hâten. — Kluge.

1005, supply gehwâ after s. . . . b. — Kluge.

1084, wið for wiht. — Rieger.

1117, destroy period after dôn, and insert semicolon after eaxle. — Kluge.

1152, [h⸱]roden (= redden). — Sievers.

1201, semicolon after sinc-fät; fealh = fleah. — Cosijn.

1213, insert næfre before wäl. — Holtzmann.

1215, hræ-wîc. — Kluge; heals-bēge. — Cosijn.

1229, sî. — Kluge.

1231, sŷn[don]. — Kluge.

1235, gea-sceaft. — Kluge.

1248, unwig-gearwe (*ready for single combat*). — Cosijn.

1254, fārode (*ravaged*). — Wülker, Kölbing, etc., hergode?

1301, hlm . . . æru. — Cosijn.

1321, neád-lāðum (*crushing hostility*). — Cosijn.

1364, hrîmde (*frosty*). — Cosijn; hrîmige. Sweet and Morris.

1460, âter-teárum. — Cosijn.

1490, wül-. — Kluge.

1538, feaxe. — Rieger.

1542, [h]and-leán. — Holder.

1546, seax[e]. — Sweet, etc.

1556, destroy comma after gesêêd, and insert one after ſðelîce. — Sweet and Sievers.

1605, wiston : wiseton(_wished). — Cosijn.

1748, wô[u]m. — Kluge.

1784, wigge-[ge-]weorðad. — Cosijn.

1810, liènes. — Müllenhoff.

1832, dryhtne. — Kluge.

1858, gemæne. — Sievers.

1863, heafu (= *seas*) — Kluge.

1896, scaðan. — Cosijn.

1904, -naen. — Rieger.

1914, insert þät he before on lande. — Sievers.

1924, wunade. — Wülker, Holder, etc.

1927, on heán. — Kluge.

1933, frêenu. — Cosijn.

1936, and-êges. — Bugge.

1943, onsêce. — Rieger.

2025, is for wäs. — Kluge.

2030, insert semicolon after gesette, destroy nô, and read Lytle, etc. - Holder and Kluge.

2030, wære for hwær. — Kluge.

2036, -beorn. — Kluge.

2153, ealdor. -- Kluge.

2158, wrist. — Rieger.

2232, senh. — Wülker.

2233, earð-hûse. — Zupitza.

2276, supply instead of wide, etc., swŷðe ondrædnð. — Zupitza; gesêcean for gewunian. — Holder.

2277, read hord on hrûsan. — Zupitza (Kemble).

2285, read sum for hord. — Cosijn.

2386, read [f']or feorme. — Möller.

2494, êðel-wynne. — Sievers.

2601, bŷwdu. — Bugge.

2702, read þâ þät. — Sievers.

2707, read gefylde. — Sievers (Thorpe); e[a]llue. — Kluge.

2767, read gehwone on same line with cynnes; gum-cynnes for gumena. — Holder; insert hord before ofer-higian. — Grein.

2776, hladon. — Ettmüller.

2871, ôwêr. - Sievers and Wülker.

2873, Sievers divides: wrâðe for-wurpe, þû, etc.

2919, hige-mêðe. — Sievers.

2959, read sæce for segn.— Sievers; Ilgelâces. — Thorpe.

3039, insert þær before gesêgan. — Wülker and Holder.

3042, gryre-fâh. — ...

3057, gehyht mannu.—Grundtvig and Kluge.

3063, þonne belongs to next line. — Wülker and Holder.

3074, strhle. — Sievers.

3075, gold-hwætes. — Sievers.

Press of
Berwick & Smith,
Boston.